THE
TIMELINE
WARS

Other Books by John Barnes

The Man Who Pulled Down the Sky
Sin of Origin
Orbital Resonance
A Million Open Doors
Mother of Storms
Kaleidoscope Century
One for the Morning Glory

By Buzz Aldrin and John Barnes

Encounter with Tiber

The Timeline Wars

Patton's Spaceship

Washington's Dirigible

Caesar's Bicycle

John Barnes

GUILDAMERICA BOOKS

PATTON'S SPACESHIP Copyright © 1997 by John Barnes
WASHINGTON'S DIRIGIBLE Copyright © 1997
by John Barnes
CAESAR'S BICYCLE Copyright © 1997 by John Barnes

THE TIMELINE WARS Copyright © 1997 by John Barnes

Published by arrangement with:
HarperCollins*Publishers*
10 East 53rd Street
New York, NY 10022-5299

ISBN 1-56865-461-8

Printed in the United States of America

Contents

Patton's Spaceship

This one's for David Wintersteen

·1·

"I get bored really easy," I explained to the kid. "Easily, I mean."

"And this isn't boring?" She was a nice kid, as kids go, sitting at the kitchen table in the little temp suite I'd gotten us as a safe house. I liked the fact that she didn't make any noise or run around much—it's a pain to have to guard something that runs and zigzags unexpectedly.

"No, this is dull, but it's not boring." Anything but; I'd been up all night while ten-year-old Porter Brunreich, who wanted to know if it was boring, and her mother were sleeping their first safe sleep in several days. I'd been sitting here, at this cheap wood-grain table in an anonymous apartment building, a .45 in my shoulder holster, a little auto button on my cellular phone that would dial 911 and tell the cops where to come, waiting for her crazed father to turn up and try to break in.

In books they always say a kid looks "solemn," when all they really mean is "serious" or "not giggling." Porter just looked like she was thinking about something very important. "So it's dull because there's not much to do, but it's not boring because there's danger."

"Something like that," I said. Actually, not boring because there was a good chance of getting into a brawl, and just possibly of having to beat up her father. But that didn't seem like a nice thing to tell her.

Porter looked pretty much like any other skinny blonde ten-year-old. In a few years she might be sort of handsome or elegant in a horsey kind of way, like her mother. Or rather like her mother usually looked—right now Mrs. Brunreich had two black eyes, some nasty abrasions on her face and neck, and her nose under a piece of steel that was being held on with a complicated bandage. Things Mr. Brunreich had done to her two days before; reasons why she had hired a bodyguard.

"You're carrying a gun," Porter said. "Are you going to have to shoot Dad?"

Mrs. Brunreich stirred at that, and I let her have the chance to answer, but she just took an extra-deep drag on her cigarette and continued to stare at the wall. So I had to answer. "I don't shoot people, usually," I said. "I carry the gun so I can protect you and your mother, because since I have it, they can't get rid of me by waving a gun in *my* face. That's why I carry such a big, ugly-looking one—to help keep them thinking straight about that."

It's a Colt Model 1911A1, the "Army .45" you've seen in a million war movies and private-eye movies, and people recognize it instantly; it says "Blows big holes in people." Saying it is nicer than doing it, I guess, and if you say it loud enough, you don't have to do it as much.

She didn't look successfully diverted by the comment, so I added, "I hope I won't have to use it, ever. And I don't want to use it on your dad. I guess if he came after you or your mother with a gun, I might have to. But only if it was your lives at stake, Porter."

"But you do shoot people."

"I've never had to. I've never fired this thing at a person."

Mrs. Brunreich stubbed out her cigarette and said, "Porter, don't ask so many questions."

The kid nodded and gulped the last of her milk. It seemed unfair—she was just worried about her dad—but considering all the marks he'd given Mrs. Brunreich to remember him by, I could see where the lady might prefer the subject was dropped.

On the other hand, Porter wasn't the kind of kid who'd ever been subjected to much discipline that she'd had to pay any attention to. "If you've never shot anybody, how good a bodyguard are you?"

"*Porter!*"

"It's all right, ma'am, it's a fair question." I was keeping an eye out the window for the van we were using for this job. Robbie and Paula were complete pros, and they wouldn't be one minute off either way from the set time of 8:37 A.M., still nine minutes away, but we were running the pizza routine, and that has to be done quickly. "I haven't shot anyone because there hasn't been any reason to. Shooting people is not my job; keeping people safe is. And the people I guard are *safe*."

The kid nodded.

"If anyone even *thinks* they need the bathroom," I added, "go right now. It might be a while before there is another chance."

Porter got up and went down the hall to the pot; she did it just as I'd told her always to do it, with her little bag (two changes of clothes, two books, one very old teddy bear) with her.

As soon as the bathroom door closed, Mrs. Brunreich said, "You can shoot the son of a bitch for all I care."

It came out "sunuffafish" because of the way her mouth was swollen from where he'd beaten on her face with his fists.

I nodded to indicate I'd heard her. I didn't say anything because I didn't want to encourage her. No matter what one of them's like, I hate it when one parent bad-mouths another in front of the kids.

She lit another cigarette, and said something I had to ask her to repeat. "You're a quiet man, Mr. Strang." She blew out smoke in a way they all learn to do from movies—I guess it's supposed to look sophisticated, and maybe she needed that considering what she looked like just then. "Is that because it's more professional?"

"I'm just quiet." I kept my eye out the window, on the street. Robbie and Paula had just a couple of minutes to go.

I just had to hope that *Mr.* Brunreich, if he was watching or even still in the state, didn't figure there was something weird about a pizza delivery at this hour of the morning.

It wasn't the cover we'd have used if we'd had a choice. But Robbie and Paula had had to do surveillance the night before from the parking lot, and the only company that I had a standing cover arrangement with was Berto's Pizza.

This was the second apartment Mrs. Brunreich had been in within the past three days; the other one had been one of the secure houses for Steel Curtain, a big bodyguard company here in the city. The trouble with a big agency is that there are a lot of people around who know them, and lawyers especially tend to know them—that was how Brunreich had found out where it was, or so everyone guessed.

Brunreich, besides being a lawyer, was a big, dangerous, crazy bastard with quite a bit of martial arts training—the kind of training you can buy if you're lucky enough to inherit the money, which also gives you time to train a lot when you're young. I knew—I had the same kind of training, and, in fact, I'd sparred with him a few times.

I wasn't looking forward to doing it for real. Hal Payton, who ran Steel Curtain, had been escorting Mrs. Brunreich on a quick trip around the block—supposedly his men had swept it first—when Brunreich had just popped up from behind a yew bush, slammed poor old Payton in the face with one hard fast one that put him out for the count, and started whaling away on Mrs. Brunreich. Payton's backup had jumped right in, but that still gave Brunreich time to land four or five savage blows on his soon-to-be-ex, and from the look of things she would have to be lucky to avoid seeing a plastic surgeon before it was over.

Hal Payton's assistant was a burly guy, my height but with a lot more muscle, and he'd given Brunreich a good hard one upside the head with a police flashlight. He said it seemed to startle him more than hurt him—"at least Brunreich didn't run off like a man who was hurt."

I couldn't exactly remember which of us had won when we'd sparred. I think I had a slight edge in speed, and I know he had a big one in strength.

I like to pretend it's all just a job, and I don't worry more about one guy than another, but the fact was the job before this one had been chasing off a 130-pound computer nerd who was pestering an underage girl for a date, and I had liked that job a *lot* better.

Mrs. Brunreich's lawyer hadn't liked me much, either, but when she insisted on taking Payton off the case (bad move—Steel Curtain was a good outfit and anyone could have rotten luck, and her lawyer knew this but couldn't win an argument with his client just then), he'd asked Payton whom to hire instead, and Payton had said me. One more thing I owed the old fart, along with my training, my experience, my life, and the lives of my sister and father. I buy him a beer now and then.

Her lawyer had not asked the "ever shot anyone?" question. I wondered if he would have hired me if he had. Especially if he'd found out that although I'd been in business five years, this was really just a temporary job, while I was taking a little time out from doing a doctorate in art history, just a little time to get my head a little more together . . .

The toilet flushed. Porter came back, still carrying her bag, balanced and ready. I glanced at her and gave her a little smile, hoping it looked encouraging—I mean, I don't know anything about kids, except it's hard to keep the parent that doesn't have custody from grabbing them—but there was something about the way she was behaving . . . more adult than most adults I had guarded, certainly more adult than her mother—

She nodded at me but didn't smile herself. Maybe she had nothing to smile about, or was just very serious. You never really know unless you've known them for a while.

Lately I hadn't known anyone for more than a few weeks.

I was getting extremely morbid in my thinking. Bad before going into action, I reminded myself, and Hal Payton could tell me that this was likely to be bad action. I scanned the street again; nothing but six-block flats and row houses, high stoops and barred windows, like any other Pittsburgh street. It was a cloudy spring day, so the street seemed to be almost in black-and-white. They film a lot of horror movies in this town—the mood is right.

The big van marked "Berto's Pizza" came around the corner and parked at the curb; I'd have known it in any paint job, and it had had plenty, because Robbie and Paula supplied what I thought was the best secure-vehicle service in the city, and I always used them when I could. You couldn't have put a shot into that van at point-blank range, or into its engine, and various other things were set up in it to make it a bit tougher to stop than a light tank.

Paula got out with the red box; red meant she'd seen nobody but wasn't perfectly sure the area was secure.

She's a big young woman, halfway between "Rubens" and "East German Swim Champ," and though she can look pretty good when she wants to (she only wants to on a job), right now she looked thoroughly up-all-night bored and tired, which was just what you would have expected.

Through the tinted windows you couldn't see Robbie sliding into the driver's seat, but I knew she was, the way I knew the .45 in my shoulder holster already had a round chambered. Paula had left the engine running; if we could get to it, we had the ride for the getaway.

I motioned Mrs. Brunreich and Porter to follow me downstairs, with their bags, and they obeyed instructions, not turning out any lights. Paula rang the doorbell behind us, an obnoxious buzz designed to be heard on the street and make things look convincing.

When Mrs. Brunreich and Porter were directly behind me, I opened the door. Paula dropped the empty pizza box and stepped to the hinge side of the door, facing outward; I moved to the lock side, my back toward Paula. As we'd rehearsed, Mrs. Brunreich and Porter came through the door, and Paula and I closed up ranks with them between us.

I really had to give credit to Porter—she stuck right by Paula's right side, where she was supposed to be. (I was grateful for the millionth time that Paula is a lefty.) I was on the other side because the main threat was supposed to be to Mrs. Brunreich.

We were almost down the long flight of concrete steps to the cab when he came charging out from between the buildings behind us. He must have stood there with his gut sucked in all night—the space between the row houses was barely a foot—and maybe that was why he stumbled a little, and it made some noise.

I got a glimpse of him and whirled to get up on the step behind Mrs. Brunreich; Paula got another glimpse and reached out to hurry the mother and daughter down the steps to the van. Robbie kicked the automatic open on the van, the door slid open, and behind me I could feel Paula practically lift both of them up by the scruffs of their necks and *heave* them across the sidewalk and into the van.

Brunreich was ignoring me and heading straight for the open door of the van, right down the grassy slope.

My job is always to be between the client and trouble. I grabbed the old pipe railing, vaulted onto the dew-wet grass, braced myself hard, and aimed a shoulder into Brunreich's chest.

I had just an instant to think that tripping him would be more effective, and another to realize that if I had missed the trip, he'd have gotten right through me, before he hit my shoulder hard enough to knock the air out of me.

He was a big guy, as I've said, and he was running full tilt downhill, so the impact was quite a shock. But in my favor, I had the better position—to control himself coming down, he'd had to let his feet get a little in front of him to steady him, and I was leaning forward, with my feet well back of me. We compromised; I was driven down the slope but remained on my feet, and he flopped backwards and slid, legs sprawled and ass first, right into me.

He was reaching for me as he came, and I grabbed for a counterstrangle; as a result I fell on top of him, with each of us clutching the other by the collar, neither with quite the grip to squeeze a windpipe or close a carotid.

Brunreich's momentum was more than enough for both of us. With me on top, he went careering down that grassy, wet slope on his back.

The push-and-pull grip I had—basically pulling his lapel down with my left and trying to force his collar over his windpipe with my right—wasn't tight enough to put him out, but it at least let me keep both hands on him. I can recommend it highly if you ever go mud-tobogganing on top of a lawyer. And give some credit to L.L. Bean as well—his shirt never tore in the process.

But I really can't recommend the experience.

As we hit bottom I was thinking I'd just disengage and run for it, get enough space to use my tube of Mace or even the can of NoBear I keep in my car, when I realized that there was a lot more yelling than just me and Brunreich, and the van hadn't left yet.

I didn't have time to assess what the matter was, but it meant I had to keep fighting.

I got my feet planted before he did and kicked myself upright, but I didn't quite break his grip—he caught one lapel of my jacket with both hands and started the quick climb hand over hand that ends with an elbow whip and a brutal headlock, if not a broken neck. It forced my head back down toward him, and his feet moved in around mine to get better balance.

In self-defense class the students always ask why you can't just kick a man in the testicles when he does that. If you're wondering, put a chair in front of your refrigerator. Bend over the chair and pick up the refrigerator.

Now do it standing on one leg.

Luckily he was a bit out of it; maybe a rock or two had clipped the back of his head on the way down. I turned outward, and he "forgot to let go"—not an uncommon mistake, which is why the trick is old—and as his arm straightened, I braced the elbow with one hand, grasped his wrist with the other, pinned the knife edge of his hand to my body, and turned against his shoulder joint.

His free hand flew around wildly trying to slap me off him, but couldn't reach far enough to do any damage. As I increased the pressure he flipped over onto his side, and I drove his arm up into a hammerlock, taking a grip on the back of his head by the hair and arching his back to prevent him getting any traction.

Something hit me hard from behind.

It was well above the kidneys, so it stung like hell but didn't do any other damage. Then I was being flailed at, not effectively, by long thin arms and soft hands, but for all its weakness the attack was still fierce.

Whatever was slapping me got pulled away from my back. In the confusion Brunreich had gotten his free hand most of the way under him, so I said, "Put that arm out in front of you," and when he didn't obey instantly I started cranking on the hammerlocked elbow. That made him move.

I had some breathing time, finally. I got my grip well set and looked around.

Mrs. Brunreich was sitting in the open door of the pizza van, sobbing. Paula had an arm around her and was saying soothing things.

Robbie, a thin woman with dark crew-cut hair, dressed in backward Pirates' cap, baggy sweatshirt, and parachute pants, was off to my side, Taser in hand, as she was supposed to be.

Brunreich's breathing was loud and labored; he sounded like he'd just run a few miles. I realized I was holding his head up by the hair, arching his back at a painful angle, and that I might not be able to keep that up forever.

I figured I'd enjoy it while I could.

"Where's Porter?" I asked.

"Here in the van," she said. "You said to stay in here no matter what."

I was really beginning to like that kid. She followed instructions, and she was the only member of her family who hadn't hit me yet this morning.

"Well, you can come out," I said. "But I'm afraid I'm going to have to be mean to your dad. And Brunreich, I'd rather not have to do anything uglier to you than I've already done, in front of your daughter. But you know I will."

"Yeah, I know." He sounded sad and tired.

"Right then. You're covered by a Taser. At the moment you're under a citizen's arrest. When I let go of you I'm going to step back and get my Mace out; you can't possibly turn around fast enough to get to me before I'm ready to put that into your face.

"Now, I can keep you in this hold, which I'm sure is extremely painful, or I can let you up. If you say you will behave, I will let you up. Clear?"

"Clear. I'll behave."

"You know that if you *don't* behave once I release you, you get cut no slack? You'll get the Taser and the Mace right then?"

"I understand. I'll behave."

I let go of him and took a long step back. He brought himself around to where he was half-leaning, half-lying on the grassy bank in the streak of mud he'd made coming down it.

He wasn't looking his best. The front of his shirt and pants were smeared with grass and mud, there were huge dark circles under his eyes, he'd gotten a slight bloody nose somewhere in the process, he was a few days behind in his shaving, and somewhere in the fight with me, or maybe the fight the day before with Payton, he'd torn out one knee of what used to be expensive trousers. He was breathing more easily, but his mouth was still open and gasping like a carp's, and his eyes seemed to wander from thing to thing—Robbie and her Taser, me and the Mace, his sobbing soon-to-be-ex-wife, and then just off into space.

Finally he spoke. "What happens now?"

"Cops happen," I said. "Lots and lots of cops happen. Once the trouble started Robbie called nine-one-one on the cellular. You'd really better just sit tight. If you like, Paula can call your lawyer for you."

"Thank you very much." He gave us the number, and Paula called; at least Brunreich had a guy who did some criminal practice, and knew about getting it together for the client in a hurry, even at a strange time.

It wasn't nine o'clock yet—it had only been five minutes since we'd come out the door—but I was good and tired from the events of the morning so far.

I was a bit worried about the flight time, but the cops got right there and the handover was very smooth. I showed my license, and they agreed that I was indeed a licensed bodyguard in Pennsylva-

nia, as was Robbie, as was Paula. We all three agreed that Mr.
Brunreich had assaulted me, and I would be pressing charges, and
they agreed that I could come to the station to swear out the complaint later.

At least Mrs. Brunreich was willing to corroborate it. Sometimes in these divorce things they'll suddenly start lying to protect
the bastard.

It didn't take more than another ten minutes for them to book
Brunreich and take him away. We still had a little slack at the airport, and Paula had phoned ahead anyway and been assured it
would all be okay. I was a tiny bit nervous about the lack of security—I thought Brunreich was paying too much attention to the
flight number—but I wasn't much worried in that when they released him on bail he'd be restricted to Pittsburgh until his trial,
and I figured a lawyer would know enough not to jump bail.

"All right," I said, when the cops said we could go and started
to hustle Brunreich into the police cruiser, "you all still have a
flight to catch, and my contract's not complete till you're on it. Let's
roll."

Everyone piled into the van; I sat in the back with Porter, Paula
in the middle seat with Mrs. Brunreich, Robbie driving. Mrs.
Brunreich was still sniffling, and Paula was talking to her in a low,
soft way that I call her Sensitive Feminist Grandma Voice, which
seems to be able to hypnotize even the most spineless or co-depen-
dent people into doing something sensible.

Porter leaned against me, her face on my left sleeve. And said,
"Thank you for not shooting him."

"Aw, heck, Porter, it was never even close. Really."

She nodded and kept leaning on my arm. "How do you get to
be a bodyguard? Do you go to a special school or something?"

"Well," I said, "it's not the greatest job in the world." The kid
seemed to need a hug, so I sort of let her slide under my arm and
found myself being held on to like a teddy bear. "But I guess if you
really want to, you should start martial arts soon, and maybe learn
pistol in a couple of years—that's all competitive sports anyway,
and it's fun—and, oh, I don't know, play a lot of sports so you're
strong and agile and used to thinking fast on your feet. And it
wouldn't hurt to go to college and take some psych and some police
science. So you need to make good grades."

At least I didn't know anyone in any field who was actually

harmed by good grades, and besides, if I was going to be stuck as a role model, it was the kind of things role models said.

"Should I enlist in the Army?"

"Some do, some don't. I didn't, but Robbie did. But don't worry about it too much. You have a lot of time to decide what you're going to be." I was starting to realize, as the adrenaline from the fight wore off, that I was pretty tired, and on top of that I was beginning to sound like Mr. Rogers.

"Yeah, I know," she said, "but how often do I get to talk to a real bodyguard?"

The way she said "real bodyguard" made me feel about ten feet taller, which I suppose is a natural reaction to a cute blonde woman who thinks you're wonderful. Even if she's ten.

"You want to be a bodyguard like me?"

"Well, yeah, but more like Robbie. She's *awesome*."

I suppose I deserved that. The rest of the drive out to the airport we talked about names for dogs, the *Hardy Boys* and why real-life crime wasn't much like that, and the riding lessons she was supposed to start soon.

Part of the back of my brain kept figuring that Brunreich was really well-and-truly crazy, and if his lawyer got right over to municipal court, and there was no line in front of him—and on this kind of weekday morning there might not be—

We had at least a forty-minute head start, which should be good enough.

At the airport, I just handed my automatic, holster and all, to Paula (much easier than getting it cleared through security), and Robbie and I took them through. We'd phoned ahead so we could have them preboard during cleaning; it's a routine little trick, since it makes it all but impossible for the client to be physically attacked.

As we walked up the corridor, Porter asked, "Do you believe in ESP?"

"Not me," I said. "But I wouldn't mind having it, in this line of work."

"Me either," Robbie said. "I'm strictly a materialist."

"You ask too many questions," Mrs. Brunreich said.

Porter ignored that last and said, "Uh, I just had like a . . . like a dream but I was awake, this flash of the future, like . . . I'm *always* going to be walking between bodyguards."

That got to Robbie. "Aw, *honey*," she said, "it's not like that.

This kind of thing could happen to anybody. It's not necessarily going to happen to you forever."

"It didn't seem like a *bad* dream," Porter said, "just like that was the way it was going to be."

Naturally, at the gate, the airline flunkies had decided they'd never heard of the arrangement, and that we would have to stand around in plain sight while they phoned the universe.

Mrs. Brunreich seemed just as happy, since it let her get another couple of cigarettes in (and with the way her nerves must be by now that was probably a plus). "And could I possibly get in a trip to the ladies' room?"

It didn't seem like there was much danger, even with the annoyance of having to wait around, so Robbie peeled off to escort Mrs. Brunreich in there, and I stuck around with Porter, doing my best to keep us standing where we wouldn't be too visible, behind a couple of outsized plants near a column.

"You're probably just getting those pictures because you want all this to be over," I said to Porter. "When life sucks you think it'll stay that way forever; but it doesn't."

She sighed. It was not a good kind of sound to hear out of a tiny little girl on a bright, sunny spring morning. "Mom's sending me to camp in another few days, as soon as she finds a new camp since she doesn't want to send me anywhere Dad knows about. So it won't be my regular place, and I'll have to get used to all new bunkmates."

"That's rough," I said. "It would be nice to have the friends you're used to."

"Yeah." She said it with a hopeless little shrug. "Anyhow when I'm twelve I get shipped to boarding school, and then I won't be home much after that. So it won't last forever."

All I could think of to say was, "You're a nice kid, and anyone would like to have you around. Your parents have huge problems, but there's *nothing* wrong with you."

She nodded, but I doubted that she believed me.

There was a commotion down the corridor from us, and some instinct made me move Porter in among the plants, whisper "Stay put," and step out to see what it was.

Brunreich burst out of the crowd. He was carrying a ball bat. His eyes looked utterly mad; I suppose whatever grip he'd had on himself, he had none now.

I strode out to face him, doing my best to draw his attention; the corner of my eye showed me Robbie taking a pop glance out of the women's room and jumping right back in.

I walked straight toward him, kept my voice level, and said, "Put down the bat and go away. You're in enough trouble already."

Every now and then some lunatic will really listen to you. Usually not. This time it was the usual thing.

His training might have been good, but it was pretty well gone from his mind by now—he just swung the bat at me, one-handed and overhand, down toward my head, like he was driving a huge nail.

Time slowed down. I was a step out to the side, so I reached up with my right arm—up, up, as if I were swimming in Karo syrup . . . my right hand got there, just barely, just to the left of the bat. It scraped down over all my knuckles and the bulge of my wrist, slapping my arm into a hard flop against my head, skipping the elbow to slam the outer muscles on the upper arm—

Time sped up again. My right arm slammed like a half-full sandbag against my head, and from wrist to armpit I felt the force of the blow.

I planted the ball of my right foot, pivoted, picked up my left in a tight coil, and snap-kicked him in the solar plexus with everything I had. He bent over, clutching his gut, and the bat went bouncing off on its own—he couldn't have held on to it one-handed after hitting the unyielding floor that hard.

Sounds came back then—along with more pain—the bat ringing on the cold, hard floor, people screaming, the crash and bang of people dropping their things and scattering to get away.

I let him have another snap-kick, this time across the face, and when he didn't rear up but didn't go down, I stepped into him. He tried to swing at me, a funny groping little punch like he was doing a Barney the Dinosaur impression, and I slipped inside that and rabbit-punched him.

He hit the floor hard—was probably out before he landed. I backed away.

The airport cops showed up. They knew they were looking for Brunreich, so they didn't have any trouble hauling him off; they let Porter and Mrs. Brunreich get on their flight, but the last hug I got from Porter was a bit strained since they had me in handcuffs.

By the time Robbie and Porter got that one talked out (at least

Norm, my lawyer, didn't have to get involved, and I didn't end up
with another arrest on my record), I had been up twenty straight
hours. My right hand was swelling up into an interesting purple
blob, which was going to be a hassle since I don't do much of
anything very effective left-handed.

"Relax," Robbie said. "You've never shot anybody, anyway."

"Unless that's the hand you use—well, never mind," Paula said.
She was driving.

"Where are we going?" I asked, as we came around onto the
Parkway, headed back into Pittsburgh.

"You're going to a doctor and then home to bed, or else home
to bed and then to a doctor. No other choices on the menu," Paula
said. "In fact why don't you just try to fall asleep back there? We'll
get you home."

I started to argue I wasn't sleepy, and we could go someplace to
get breakfast, but suddenly the pent-up sleep hit me, and I didn't
have the energy. I'd just close my eyes for a few minutes and then
maybe I'd wake up before we got back to my place—

For some reason that silly kid's face invaded my dreams. She
seemed to be asking, again, *How do you get to be a bodyguard? Do you
go to a special school or something?*

As I slid into uneasy dreams, part of me answered that kid:
"Yeah, sure. Special school. Shadyside Academy then Yale for un-
dergrad and grad." And I was back into the dream . . . the dream
that I always wanted to be interrupted from, where in the middle
of things I would wake up and nothing would have gone any farther than that . . . .

·2·

Used to be that I spent many long hours unable to sleep, sitting in Ritter's or the Eat'n'Park, drinking coffee without end, and while I was doing it I would think: people get it all wrong about the trouble with being lucky in your childhood. They have this idea that if there's money and parents who love you, and you've got a lot of natural talent, you get spoiled and weak.

Wrong.

Trouble is you grow up so healthy and strong that when things go really, horribly wrong, you're too stubborn and too strong to just collapse and give up, wind up in a mental hospital or a casket the way sensible people would.

I won't bore you, and a really great childhood is boring to hear about. The worst you could say about it was that Dad pushed us kids pretty hard to do well at everything, and the twins—Jerry and Carrie, two years younger than I—and I did pretty well at things naturally.

My father was at the Center for Studies in Islamic Politics at Carnegie-Mellon, and Mom taught part-time and got grants and edited the *Journal of Formalist Method in Philosophy*, not one page of which I've ever understood. All us kids (except Carrie, the math whiz) really had a handle on was that Mom worked at home, and you weren't supposed to interrupt her, but that every so often she'd just take a day off and we'd all go do something together, like climb a mountain or go down into a cave or all sorts of things the other kids envied us.

Grade school faded into high school, where I was a valedictorian, as was Carrie (poor Jerry got a B in Driver's Ed, leading to a standing joke that he was the "family dunce" and god knows how many times we told him we wouldn't let him drive). Between the three of us we lettered in everything.

Girls were a pretty simple matter to me; not every one I asked said yes, but if the one I asked out didn't, there was sort of a bench waiting, and if I do say so myself, the team had depth in those years.

It stayed the same way at Yale. The first girl I ever really fell hard for was Marie, whom I met because she and Carrie roomed together on gymnastics team road trips, and after that there wasn't anyone else; I married her a month after I graduated, when she had a year to go, and I was going right back into Yale to get a doctorate in art history.

By the time I was twenty-six I was about to start a dissertation and had already had a job offer or two; I had settled into a rhythm of teaching and writing during the school year and going to archaeological digs (taking Marie along) during the summers.

I never really appreciated my wife, I suppose. She was beautiful and highly intelligent, and I appreciated that; she supported everything I did, but having only my parents' very happy marriage to judge by, I didn't realize it wasn't always that way. And I think I didn't pay enough attention in those years, because to this day I wish I remembered more of the things she used to say that made me laugh. Or more moments when the light hit her just right, and I thought what one painter or another might have made out of her . . . or the way she could be on a long day on a dig, the patience with which she would clean one little artifact, the neat way she noted down every one of the tiny facts . . .

No, I never appreciated any of them enough.

I don't know exactly when I figured out there was anything at all dangerous about what Dad did for a living. Not much before I was in junior high, I guess. When he came back from every trip he had a lot of fascinating stories, most of which were about how he got to meet the "real people involved" and get the "real story behind it."

It took me a long time to realize that Dad's specialties were political violence and terror, and that that meant those people he was talking to were top security people, both Communist and Free World, and the people who trained terrorists (East, West, freelance, anybody)—and the terrorists themselves.

I remember realizing that when he described a secret PLO/ Mossad prisoner swap, he was talking about going there with the PLO and leaving with the Mossad, not as a prisoner but to get both sides of the story. I have a vague recollection, one night at the dinner table before I went off to a movie with some interchangeable cheerleader, of abruptly realizing that to talk about what he was talking about, he must have spent time inside a ChiCom terror and subversion school, must have interviewed the instructors after observing the classes.

It still didn't really register with me. I suppose everyone with good luck as a kid thinks their family leads a charmed life. Dad went everywhere, alone and unarmed, to talk to everyone; Mom ran the house and had the occasional phone call from a Nobel laureate; I won judo tournaments, Jerry won shotokan tournaments, Carrie competed in women's rifle and gymnastics, and we all excelled at Scrabble. So what?

Marie fit right in—bright, athletic, beautiful, from the same kind of family.

By tradition Dad always got us all together on the Fourth of July. He said he was an old-fashioned patriot and besides, he needed an excuse for homemade ice cream. Usually—a law student like Jerry, a physics grad student like Carrie, and young marrieds like Marie and I didn't have much spare cash—he'd end up springing for the plane tickets, not to mention flying himself back from wherever. It was one of the few predictable things Dad did, and one of the most predictable—every Fourth of July we'd all be there in the big house overlooking Frick Park.

That particular year, the Fourth fell on a Saturday, and we all got there on Friday night in one big laughing and giggling gaggle at the airport. Marie and I had to be back at the dig in Tuscany Tuesday morning, but it was great to be back for these couple of days.

The Fourth itself, we all slept late, and then got up to just walk around the old neighborhood after a pleasant brunch. Jerry leaned close to me at one point, while Marie and Carrie were talking about whoever or whatever Carrie's latest flame was, and said, "Did Dad seem a little strange to you?"

"Yeah, a little. Could be jet lag—he's not saying officially, but you can tell he just came from Teheran—"

"We've seen jet lag on him before, Mark, and all that does is make him sleepy." Jerry stuck his hands in his pockets and looked down at the ground. "This is different. Something's eating him."

"Could be," I admitted. "Figure he'll tell us about it?"

"If he thinks we need to know. Or if he thinks it's not dangerous for us to know . . . and if he thinks we won't worry. But *he's* worried. Do you think we should tackle him about it?"

I watched a couple of kids rolling in somersaults down Sled Hill. "Think we should have Sis and Marie run over and teach those kids to do it right?"

"You're evading the question."

"I'm not on your witness stand, counselor." We walked on a ways; I admired the way the white dress and white pumps showed off the tan Marie had gotten on the dig, and the way the breeze pushed it against her. The Fourth, this year, wasn't hot, but there was no hint of rain. I think, maybe, then, I felt just a little of how lucky my life had been.

After a while I answered, "I think he's old enough to decide for himself, and let's respect that. What he wants to tell us he can tell us."

"Lots of common sense in that, big brother. Wanna see if we can get these debutantes to be seen with us getting a beer someplace?"

"You're on." And that was all we said about it, then.

That evening the problem with Dad was a little more noticeable, but not enough to spoil anything. Mom's homemade ice-cream cake came off as always, but still Dad seemed sort of abstracted and not quite there, and Mom was working pretty hard to keep us all convinced that she didn't notice, that there was nothing to notice.

The oddest part was that Dad had no stories at all to tell. Tonight—when he wasn't staring at the wall—he wanted to hear about the Etruscan pottery we'd found and what it implied about the connections to the Greeks, about Jerry's candidacy for being a clerk to a Supreme Court justice, and about Carrie's "summer job" at Battelle—it sounded like she was working on Star Wars to us, but she was being a good girl and not dropping hints, not even when Jerry tried to surprise her . . . "So, Sis, would you like another slice of cake, and some more coffee, and are you really building a disintegrator ray?"

"Yes, yes, and I can neither confirm nor deny that."

"Better go into corporate law," I advised Jerry, "or hang around with dumber criminals."

In that sense it was a very strange Fourth—usually Dad dominated dinner table conversations. And why not? It was pretty hard to top a guy whose stories began with, "Yasser Arafat once told me—" or "In Tunis, there's a tiny little bar, hardly more than a hole in the wall divided by a board, with a one-eyed bartender who serves only German beer in bottles from iced coolers, and a lot of old SS men gather there—"

As the light faded into soft grays outside, and the first fireflies were dancing over the wide lawn, we went out on the second-floor back porch to watch the fireworks over the park. I remember the silky tube top Marie was wearing and her soft, deeply tanned skin pressing back against my arm as we sat on the bench next to each other and watched the bursts of flame and listened to the distant roar of explosions.

"The bombs bursting in air," Marie said softly, musing aloud.

Dad glanced over at her. "What I was thinking, too. Phrase from a dangerous time . . . within days of those lines being written the White House was set on fire by a foreign army . . ." He leaned back and stared off into space. There was a long sputtering burst of those very bright, white, loud ones. The light flickered on Dad's face as he looked up at them, and a long second later the distant booms echoed across our house; we could hear the "ooohs" and "aaahs" coming from the park beyond us. "It's not a bad country, really, and most amazing is that it's such a *safe* country."

The finale came then, a whole big string of things blowing up and scattering streams of bright colors into the air.

As we went inside, Mom asked Marie for some help on kitchen cleanup, and the two of them headed down that way, just as Dad asked us three to come into his study "for a nightcap." It had a suspiciously planned feel to it, and after the odd way Dad had been acting all day, Jerry and I glanced at each other; I knew we were both figuring we'd finally find out what was up.

We'd always said our parents' studies were like them; Mom's

was obsessively neat and orderly, ringed with blackboards from which she copied her work into lined and numbered bound notebooks; Dad's was a huge untidy heap of books, papers, offprints, journals, videotapes, audiotapes, and crazy-quilt bulletin boards. He heaved a pile of papers off each of three leather chairs onto the floor, then moved his own briefcase off the big old swivel chair next to the mountain of paper that was his desk.

Lifting a crumpled map from the top of the pile on one shelf, he uncovered a bottle of brandy, some little French label I'd never seen before, and a set of snifters beside it. He put a splash in all four glasses, handed them round, took his own glass, and raised it in a toast, "Another year." We drank to that, and then he sat down in the desk chair and added, "The USA—peace, safety, and prosperity." That was good for another sip from all of us.

The light in his study was gold-colored from the warm yellow lampshades and the brass fixtures it reflected from. There were many crevices and cracks, dark corners and crumpled papers, forming patterns of warm yellow light and deep shadow. Not for the first time, I reflected that it would have been a perfect place for one of the Old Masters to paint.

Carrie sat so still that she looked like a painted angel in the warm glow from the lamp; Jerry's face shone with light coming down from above like a martyr's; and Dad was backlit like an old burgher in a crowd scene, or like the way Death was often depicted, with deep, distorting shadows masking most of his appearance.

"It's not easy to admit I may have done something dangerous and stupid," Dad said. "I don't know yet what the consequences of the dangerous, stupid thing I've done will be, or if perhaps I've acted quickly enough to avoid them." He sighed.

Jerry stirred a little, as if to ask a question, and Dad held up a finger for silence. "Let me explain a little. Some years ago I became aware that there was some new force at work in Mideastern terrorism. You all know, I think, that I am not an alarmist. Indeed, with both students and the press, I have always tried to make it clear that there is rarely or never such a thing as 'mindless terrorism.' If you think it's that way, you'll never be able to combat it—"

For the moment he was talking as if he were lecturing his seminar, and just for that long he was his old self, the way he'd always been before. "Terrorism, at least in the planning stages, is the work of men who go about their business as sensibly, deliberately, and rationally as any banker.

"I know you've all heard this before, but bear with me.

"All the same, after all those years of preaching that terrorism happens in a situation where terrorism works, and where there is something to be gained by it—that people do it because it pays off in something they want—all the same, having preached that all these years, I was finding myself confronting the evidence of a terror movement that seemed not to have read that particular book. Moreover, this new group was more shadowy, kept its secrets better . . . and was also better financed, better organized, better equipped—in fact they were so well equipped that I spent months chasing the red herring of superpower involvement, for some of the small amount of captured equipment seemed to be so sophisticated that the source almost had to be an American, European, Soviet, or Japanese laboratory—no one else could do that kind of work on that kind of scale and get the weapon operational."

Carrie caught my eye and winked. I don't think it reassured either of us. She looked too frightened.

Dad coughed and went on. "I could find no rationale for this new group's activities—*none*. Much as I have always stressed that terrorists do things for rational if deplorable reasons—though perhaps not the ones they announce—I had to admit that here was a group whose interest was in outrages, and not merely outrages but huge outrages that were difficult to pull off, and ones with no point at all. When Palestinians attack Israeli settlers, it makes a certain sense, for once that land is settled by Israelis the government of Israel cannot give it back—machine-gunning schoolchildren is evil and disgusting, but *one understands why they do it*. It makes sense for a Shiite fundamentalist to shoot a garrison commander who is Sunni, if uprisings will happen later that year, and the officer next in line is a coward, a sympathizer, or corrupt. It even makes sense to set off bombs in Europe and invite American and European retaliation by aerial bombing, for the population's reaction to the bombing can be used to shore up a leader—nothing makes a man more popular than to have him denounce the Americans and pledge he won't knuckle under to them when the night before American bombers were blasting away at his city.

"All these things are horrible and involve gross harm to innocents, but they can be understood. And I long ago learned that I, at least, could look evil straight in the face as long as I knew *why* it was. But this group—" Dad sighed, almost groaned, and the hand that stuck, pale white like a claw, out of the deep shadow in which he sat, tightened on the brandy snifter. "They call themselves Blade of the Most Merciful. They have staged actions on every continent except Antarctica—and they're so fierce and so fond of outrage that I wouldn't be surprised if they blew up an airliner full of tourists making the trip across the Pole. They have accounted for perhaps five thousand deaths and a billion dollars' worth of property in less than three years. The IRA, Red Army Faction, and PFLP combined have never even come close to such a record.

"And yet because they operate in secret most of the time and in conjunction with other groups—and because they never issue public statements—Blade of the Most Merciful have received very little publicity.

"Their level of activity and the ease with which they have evaded capture suggests Blade must have close to fifteen hundred fighters and a covert logistical tail at least as large, and so far as I can tell none of them ever has to do anything for money, so that the usual tracing through the employment of low-level, part-time members has proved impossible.

"In short they are the kind of organization that cannot have been created or financed by its members. They must surely have been set up by some large, significant power for some large, significant purpose. Yet their purpose does not even seem to be to consistently cause chaos.

"In one African nation they assassinated the dictator, *plus* every significant opposition leader, in or out of the country, in a single night. That same night they blew up the radio station, phone central, national bank, and Ministry of Defense. All this triggered weeks of rioting and something far too chaotic to be called civil war, while the country writhed like a beheaded snake, not even able to find a bad or an incompetent leader. And then the Blade did *nothing* to take advantage of the chaos; anyone could have done anything, and yet they did nothing.

"In Colombia they staged a dozen bank robberies, murdered four judges, had the government teetering—and then suddenly the Blade slaughtered the leadership of the drug cartel they were supposed to be working for and shipped so much solid evidence to the government that it may be a decade before they can even get all the criminal charges filed.

"And in both of these cases, they seemed to be functioning much more like a mercenary army than like an Islamic covert terror group. Yet at the same time, they were competing fiercely for turf in the Mideast. The more established groups seemed to learn quickly to get out of their way.

"Which wasn't always possible." He lifted the rest of the brandy to his lips—it was good stuff—and swallowed it as if it had been cough medicine. "The Blade often literally forced themselves onto other groups. They would demand that the 'host' group they had pinned down act as 'sponsor' and claim responsibility for some Blade crime, sometimes insisting that the group supply arms and men for what amounted to suicide missions. They were thus able to keep every little group on every side in the Mideast hating and distrusting each other . . . not that that ever requires anything like the effort the Blade put into it.

"A senior Mossad official—yes, the Israeli Secret Service itself—told me that their refusal to cooperate with a Blade demand that they butcher one whole refugee camp led to a Blade attack on a secret Mossad safe house in Germany and cost them the lives of six agents. They lost eight more hitting back at a Blade base deep inside Libya—"

I whistled. "Fourteen Mossad agents—"

Dad shook his head. "For what comfort it may be, they aren't supermen. Mossad killed almost fifty of them, between shooting back in Germany and the Libyan raid. One reason they were able to make the Libyan raid is that Qaddafi saw a chance to get rid of Blade and offered Mossad the chance to 'sneak past his radar unseen.' Hell, he even gave them topo maps; the Blade apparently offends Qaddafi."

"Has Blade of the Most Merciful announced any goals at all?" Carrie asked. Her face was drawn and tight, and so was Jerry's; mine must have been, too. Dad had already told us that he had done something he considered dangerous and stupid, and this didn't sound like a group to do that kind of thing around.

Dad shook his head. "None at all. No goals. No purpose. If I had to deduce them from the evidence, I'd say they like to see either complete anarchy or iron-fisted autocracy."

"Maybe they're nihilists," Jerry suggested, "like the old anticzarist terror movement."

Dad shook his head. "Those people were out to create chaos, but only so that the revolution could happen once authority collapsed, and to make sure the revolution was complete. Blade has no such strategy; they don't follow up on it when they create chaos, and they sometimes turn the other way and help repressive regimes. They seem to just want violence to happen."

There was a long silence. Dad stirred slightly in his chair, as if about to speak, but said nothing. Maybe because I was oldest and had usually been first to speak up, I finally said, "And why did you take us aside to tell us all this? Do you think they're after you?"

Dad pulled his single, exposed, white hand in from the light; now only his bony white knees, exposed by his Bermuda shorts, and the shining bald top of his head, were in the light. He might have been a skeleton. "I don't think so. Not anymore. I spent the past three years, you see, trying to get to meet some of them, and working on a book about them. After all, studying terrorism and writing books about it is what I do. And strange as it might seem, it has never seemed very dangerous to me, before now, because most of these groups, you know, have a message to get out, and so they are not going to shoot a potential messenger.

"So long as I took no sides and reported honestly and carefully, I was much more useful alive than dead. To normal terror and antiterror organizations, that is. But Blade is not normal . . .

"Just how not normal took me a long time to realize. For two years I tried to meet anyone, anyone at all, connected with Blade of the Most Merciful. First I tried for the leaders, then for just any spokesman, finally just anyone—couriers, former members, anyone.

"I had no luck. I had to assemble the book from tertiary sources and circumstantial evidence. As sheer detective work it was brilliant. I assembled a very complete picture of the size, scope, resources, activities, and *modi operandi* of Blade—of everything about them—except for one little detail: why they did what they did. On that, there was nothing, nothing, nothing at all. And despite every plea I sent by third parties, I heard nothing back—until this spring.

"The man who came to see me was short and dark, with large muscles under his baggy sweater. He said to call him 'George.' He had a long irregular scar across his nose, and he stepped into my office on the campus as if he had just materialized there.

"He sat down and said he was from Blade of the Most Merciful. To prove that he rattled off sufficient details of every major attempt I had made to contact them. Then he said—I quote him in his entirety—'Do not publish your book. Cancel it with your publisher. We are speaking to them as well. They will understand.' And he left.

"I darted out into the hall to expostulate with the man, and he was as gone as if he had never existed.

"Well, of course I went back into my office a very puzzled man. I had no idea what to do. It almost might have all been a hallucination, but if so it had been the first of my life. I knew they meant what they said, and time was short to cancel—my publisher was bound to be angry. Indeed for all I knew the copies were already printed and sitting in a warehouse somewhere.

"The phone rang. It was my publisher. The presses had been bombed, with a man killed, hours before the print run of my book was to start. Blade of the Most Merciful had paid a call on the publisher as well."

His sigh was deep and heavy, and he seemed to sink far into his chair, as if he might recede right through the black hole of darkness in which he sat and vanish completely. "And there you have it. The publisher is the feisty sort and wanted to make a public stink about it and defy them. But I have a family and a quiet life. Perhaps back when I started in all this . . . or even if it were just me and your mother . . . or if anything assured me that the Blade would concentrate its vengeance so that only I would be struck . . . well, then I would have the courage to defy them. Perhaps. I cannot deny there is a deeply romantic part of me that wants to tell them to go to hell.

"But for all your sakes, and your mother's—and because I have *seen* men blown to bits and don't want to end up the same way—I withdrew publication of the book. The only copy is in safe hands, and I have given instructions such that whether I am alive or not, it will not be released to the publisher if there is even the slightest danger to anyone in my family. As a practical matter that probably means that no one will see it within our lifetimes."

He sat perfectly still, and by now the room seemed very dim. It was all but impossible for me to connect the things Dad was saying with my own life. Bombs and irrational vengeance, and for that matter the suppression of a book, seemed like something in the movies. What was real was Marie's white dresses, and our little apartment in Italy, and the nice academic friends we had in New Haven, and the little parties where we drank too much and got profound about art and solved the world's problems. Terrorism was on some other planet entirely.

Finally, as the whole room seemed to be receding into unreality, I said, "Well, I don't see anything wrong in what you did. It won't hurt your career at this point if it's a long time before your next book, and it isn't like you're the only person who knows about the Blade. They sound more like a job for the CIA or the big news organizations anyway."

Jerry mumbled something, Carrie said "yeah," and Dad asked him to repeat it.

Looking down at the floor, the light from the table lamp glowing off the back of his head, Jerry said, "It seems to me like . . . well, I can't criticize your choice but . . . I wish you hadn't made that choice. It's um, well . . . Dad, it's just now how you raised us, and that's all there is to it. And I . . . well, it's water under the bridge anyway, I guess, since you've already done it."

Dad shrugged. "I can finish your opening speech for you, Mr. Prosecutor. It's nothing I haven't said to myself many times at night. The real problem now is that it will be known that I can be threatened. Blade of the Most Merciful will make sure enough of that. And once it is known that I can be threatened, whatever small security I once had is gone. Anyone who wants to slant my scholarly writing can now do so, just by threatening me.

"The fact is that I'm now afraid to go out in the field again. I could not return to Teheran, Islamabad, Baghdad, or Beirut. I would only wonder who would first say to me, 'Don't write this, or thus-and-so will happen.' And from there it's a very short step to 'You must write this, and sign your name to it, and swear publicly that it is so—or thus-and-so will happen.'

"They've broken me already, you see. I am going to take early retirement. Then perhaps I will devote myself to a little study of mine on arms smuggling in the Persian Gulf before World War I. I don't think Fiscus has said the last word on the subject. Perhaps I'll also translate some modern Arabic literature that I think hasn't yet received a fair hearing in the West. But my career as you and I have known it is over."

Carrie shook her head. "Dad, this isn't right. This is America, and a bunch of rag-headed—"

"Carrie, I still do not tolerate racist—"

"When they threaten my father, they're rag-heads." Her eyes were burning with anger; she'd have made a great model for a Joan of Arc right now. "And when he gives in to them, he's a coward. Excuse me. I meant to say a fucking coward." She got up and stormed out. There was a very long awkward silence.

Jerry stood. "She got all the temper, you know, and most of the brains, but . . . she's right, Dad. I'm not mad, but I'm very disappointed. I guess you can't help it, and we're still family and all that, but I'm real disappointed."

He went out with no sound at all.

That left me. After a bit Dad said, "And you think I did right?"

"Well, I'm married, too. And this might not be the time to mention it—I was saving it for breakfast tomorrow so don't let on—but maybe my feelings will be made clearer if I mention—" Deep breath here; how do you tell them these things? "Marie is pregnant—you're going to be a grandfather."

He jumped to his feet and surprised hell out of me by hugging me. "Yes, I guess you do understand."

I don't know what Mom told Marie or said to her about why all of us were off with Dad. Probably just kept her distracted—Mom could babble up a storm of small talk when she needed it—but when I came up to bed Marie asked nothing about what had been up.

We made love slowly and without any noise, with the lights on—she was so beautiful I always preferred it that way—and it took a long, long time. I don't think we knew what was coming; I think we just knew that in a few months we would not be able to do this for a while. It was very gentle and felt wonderful, both during it and after. I remember her whispering, "Mark, Mark, Mark" in my ear at the end as her slim fingers danced along my back and her long, thin thighs held me close.

The next morning our announcement seemed to break the ice at the breakfast table—there was a lot of cheering and whooping, and Jerry and Carrie started an immediate argument about whether a child is better off with a favorite aunt or a favorite uncle.

But Marie and I, knowing the family, had planned this one out carefully—there wasn't much time until we were to take the twins back to the airport, since both of them were flying out that day.

Dad was always a rotten driver—he thought about too many things besides the road—so as always, Mom was to drive the van. She got into the driver's seat, and Marie got in behind her. Jerry, saying something silly about adjusting the child-restraint seat, climbed in next, and then Carrie reached out for the doorframe and stepped onto the running board.

The van exploded.

The bomb under it had been wired to the ignition—Mom must have turned the key, but I never saw that—and was big enough to flip the van over and roll it down the lawn, slamming most of the frame and floor up into the ceiling.

Carrie was flung back against me like a sandbag. I didn't so much catch her as cushion her impact. It was only all those years of training that kept my head up as I hit the pavement on my back, with Carrie on top of me.

Dad, who was farther away than we were, grabbing some last-minute thing, saw more than Carrie or I did. I've always been sorry for that.

As I pushed Carrie to the side and slid out from under her, my ears and nose running with blood from the force of the blast, the first thing I saw was that the stumps where her legs had been were squirting blood like paint from a sprayer running out of pressure.

It was pure instinct—in a case like that you don't think about how much of the limb you can save. I had my belt off in an instant, wrapping it around one of Carrie's legs and passing it through the buckle, hauling it tight with all my strength.

Praise god Sis had skinny legs. There was enough slack left in the belt to reloop around the other stump and come back through the buckle again. It was messy work—her blood was everywhere on me and the pavement, and I was afraid my hands would slip on the makeshift tourniquet, but I had kept it dry enough; I hauled, tugged, used my other hand to straighten things and make the rough figure-eight tourniquet bite deep into her flesh, then tied the anchor knot to keep the free end from going back through the buckle.

The stench of blood was everywhere and when I unconsciously wiped my face I got more of it there. I didn't really realize that until days later, when I was looking at a *Post-Gazette* and there was a "scene of the tragedy" picture. I looked like hell—though I wasn't much hurt. Physically I mean.

I was just telling myself I should have used Carrie's belt to make a second tourniquet when I finally looked up far enough to see that her left arm was also gone, shredded bits of meat and bone hanging from eight inches or so of upper arm. I undid her belt, yanked it through, whipped it around the stump up close to the armpit where the pressure points tend to be—I vaguely remember the next day a doctor bawled me out because if I'd put the tourniquet down lower, or used the pressure points, they might have given her a bigger stump to tie a prosthetic arm to.

The evil spurting and the sickening spat-spat-spat of blood on the flagstone pavement stopped at once.

She was still breathing, and a quick check showed no more wounds and nothing that looked like a hole in her. For all I knew she was hemorrhaging internally, but there was nothing I could do about that.

At last I looked up. Maybe it would be more accurate to say that I had run out of things I could do for Carrie and couldn't stop myself from looking up. It had been maybe twenty seconds since the bomb had gone off. (I was just realizing it must have been a bomb.) A lot had changed in those twenty seconds.

Dad had run by me, moving terribly fast for such a heavy old guy. I turned to get up and follow him, and that was when I fell—looking back I discovered, quite suddenly, that my ankle was broken. That can happen, I guess, with enough adrenaline pumping into the system. But though it could keep me from feeling the pain, it couldn't make me stand up on something that would no longer support me.

So I could do little, as I pushed myself up off the blood-slick pavement with my hands, except to look toward the van.

It wasn't there, because the blast had flipped it and rolled it down the lawn, but it was easy enough to follow the track. It had rolled several times, smashing a hole through the yew hedge, crushing roses into the soft damp mulch of their beds, tearing deep gouges in the dew-wet sod. There were long strips where the black mud showed through, as if the yard had been raked by giant fingernails.

Now the van lay on its side, flame and smoke pouring from it.

The underside was toward me, and I could see how it had been slammed upward, bending into the body everywhere it wasn't tied down, broken at the top of the crude dome it formed.

Dad, forced back by the heat, was dancing around it like an overmatched boxer, trying to find a way to the still-open side door now on the top of the van. From where I lay, I could see it was hopeless—the frame had been bent and jammed up into that space, and even without the fire he couldn't have gotten anything out through there.

He said he saw something or someone moving in there in the long second between when he got there and when the gas tank blew. The coroner said, though, that to judge from the shattering of the bones that remained afterward, there was nothing alive in there at the time; he thought Dad was probably hallucinating, or perhaps had seen a body sliding down a seat or falling over on its side.

Anyway, if the coroner was right, Mom was probably crushed against the ceiling instantly; the brains that people all over the world wanted to talk to were smashed like a pumpkin in the wreck of her skull. Jerry was impaled on a piece of chassis that—again, to judge from where they found him and it—must have ripped up through the seat, moving at bullet velocity, entered his body somewhere near the rectum and exited by way of breaking the collarbone. His whole body cavity must have been torn to jam before the first time the truck rolled, and the sudden pressure loss would have meant he was unconscious before he knew what happened.

The coroner spent quite a bit of time on the question of what had happened to Marie. The skeleton—what was left of it after it burned—was in a horribly distorted, coiled form, and his best guess was that the whole seat had been hurled against the ceiling, fracturing her skull (but the cracks could have been caused by the fire, and people sometimes survive fractured skulls), breaking vertebrae in all three dimensions (I would have tended her for fifty years if she'd been a quadriplegic) and ripping both shattered femurs out through her leg muscles. There were undoubtedly many internal injuries that mere bones could not document . . . the coroner figured the pressures involved must have ruptured many of her internal organs. He assured me, repeatedly, that there wasn't any way at all that she could have been conscious by the time Dad got to the van. Chances were she was dead before the first time the van rolled, dead while it had not yet crushed the roses let alone rolled down the lawn.

Chances were.

She probably never knew.

But Dad saw something moving in there, just before the gas tank blew, and if Mom and Jerry had both received unquestionably instantly fatal wounds . . .

It could have been a hallucination. Dad doesn't hallucinate, but anyone might in the circumstances. Anyway, the door was blocked. Anyway, it could have been a body falling. Anyway, moving someone with a fractured skull and spine would kill the person immediately. Anyway, a severed spinal cord wouldn't transmit pain, not even if the body were on fire.

Anyway anyway anyway.

Dad said he saw something moving in the van. But the van burned all but completely before the fire trucks even got there, burned while he danced around it trying to get in and see and maybe pull something out, burned while I crawled miserably down the lawn, my clothes still drenched in Carrie's blood.

· 3 ·

There had been a lot of weeks afterward when they just gave me pills, and a lot of mornings when I would wake up and try to pretend that at some point or other it had all become a dream. Sometimes I pretended that Marie was going to be there next to me when I rolled over, and we would be back in our house with our new IKEA furniture and the walls covered with Pre-Raphaelite prints. Sometimes instead I pretended that I was waking up in my dorm bed my freshman year, and that I had dreamed Marie, that Jerry and Carrie were still in high school and nothing had really changed my life yet, but there were all sorts of adventures in front of me. And sometimes I pretended that I was about ten, that the whole dream of being an adult was just a nightmare, and I was really still going to grow up to be an astronaut. Mom and the twins and I were going to go for a day hike up in the Laurel Caverns area.

I pretended pretty hard, so it wasn't for lack of effort that I always opened my eyes on the bleak world I had closed them on.

I stayed that way for months. I rarely was awake for ten hours in a day, and when I was I sat around in a bathrobe, looking at old pictures or just staring out at the yard where the burned and torn scars on the grass were healing, watching as leaves fell and snow began to blow.

Dad, meanwhile, got better. The Center went out and got donors like crazy, and they funded a full set of bodyguards for him. Then he went ahead and published his book about Blade of the Most Merciful, after a revision to make it more readable by laymen—a thing called *Solely for the Kill.*

It was the kind of smart, effective revenge you might expect. The news stories plus Dad's book did the job. Any normal terror outfit tries never to hit in the USA because they know how crazy the public goes and how completely it unleashes the President, who is suddenly trying to look as tough and mean as possible to the voters. Most of the time Americans are merely annoyed by terrorism as "something weird that foreigners do, over there." But let it get "over here," and the sky falls in on whoever brought it. Look at what happened to Libya a few years ago . . .

Blade of the Most Merciful went from something whispered about to front-page news, instantly. Moreover, they were too hot for anyone to touch—they had nowhere to hide and everybody was glad to turn them in. There were strikes by the American Delta Force, by Seals and Green Berets; SAS, Mossad, the West Germans, Egypt, all got into the act. I followed it in a half-interested kind of way, on the news and in things like *Time* and *USA Today.* It seemed like one more branch of the sports news . . . something else to read in my bathrobe as I ate cold cereal up in Dad's spare bedroom, and fell asleep, and woke up again and again hoping it hadn't happened.

Once what had happened to our family—plus Dad's book—made it clear to everyone that this was a mad-dog outfit, it was cleaned out in a hurry. *Newsweek* did a front-page profile of Dad, and they used the word "courage" about every other paragraph, which made him furious.

They ignored me—one look and I suppose they decided that was the kindest thing—but they just loved Carrie. In just a few weeks she was getting around on her powered wheelchair and doing her physics grad work mostly over computer modem; it seemed to take her only a day or so to master the one-handed keyboard. She began to move very quickly toward her Ph.D.—she said it was a matter of not having sports to distract her anymore.

There were two Blade of the Most Merciful assaults on the house, finally; they came when the organization was on the ropes and desperate and, I suppose, wanted to show that it had any fight left at all.

The first was the night before Christmas. I'd done no shopping
and barely knew what day it was; I suppose in my strange, mud-
dled state I was hoping that Santa would bring me a new life or
take back all the bad things that had happened, or some such. I was
asleep, in the usual restless dreams, when the delivery van leaped
the curb from the alley, crashed through the wire fence at the back
of the yard, and headed straight for the house.

The men from Steel Curtain Guards were on the stick. By the
time my feet were hitting the floor after the crash of the fence, the
Steel Curtain guy watching the back had flipped on his infrared
spotting scope, seen the crude armoring of the engine on the oncoming van (strips of Kevlar stretched across it), put his laser designator spot on the biggest gap, and started pumping rounds in.
Those nifty little .22s were designed for SWAT teams, and they
have practically no kick and a very high rate of fire—once they're
sighted in they'll chew whatever is in front of them to hamburger.
In an instant he'd cut a hole through the radiator, and he could see
a scattering of hot little lights, like crazed fireflies, streaking and
pinging around in there.

I was still reaching for my robe when the SCG "utility in-
fielder" on the second floor got to a window, sized up the situation,
brought his AK to his shoulder, and started blasting down into the
roof of the oncoming van.

The angle was lousy. He might have gotten the driver, but it's
hard to say. At least he was able to rake the unarmored roof twice,
and if he didn't do any damage, he surely made the driver's last
moments a little more nervous.

More likely if the driver was hit it was by something coming
through the fire wall from the first sharpshooter. In any case both
the riflemen guarding our house agreed that the driver never tried
to get out, the door handle never moved, when the van slid to a
halt in the good old Pittsburgh mud, thirty yards short of the
house, its engine dead—by that point the engine had absorbed
most of a magazine, and no doubt plenty of wires, belts, and hoses
were severed, or maybe the alternator had gotten zapped. Anyway,
the van sat there for three long seconds—meanwhile I was in my
robe and running out into the hallway—and then the forty or so
pounds of C4 in it, probably placed under a barrel of kerosene,
blew up with a deafening roar.

I was running down the stairs screaming like a madman, which

I suppose I was at the time. One of the nice strong woman guards from Steel Curtain—their specialist in mental patients—grabbed me and pinned me down just after the bomb went off. Other people were charging upstairs to get Carrie and Dad, and they quickly swept us into the "secure room"—the old laundry room that they'd fortified as a kind of bomb shelter in the middle of the house.

By the time they let us out, the Steel Curtain guys had put out three minor fires on the roof and one blazing curtain inside the house, a repair crew was on its way to board up and reglaze the broken windows, and the house and yard were crawling with cops, FBI, and various guys who never exactly said who they worked for but looked like they were more used to wearing uniforms than the new suits they were in.

It was Christmas morning. I got up, wandered through the house that smelled strangely of smoke, and went to my untouched bedroom. I shrugged off the robe, got out the razor, changed the blade, and carefully shaved, then took a shower. I needed a haircut but I had no idea where I'd find a barber today.

My clothes fit really loose, and I realized that several months of not eating or exercising much had taken a lot off me. Well, the old weight set was down in the basement, and maybe the Steel Curtain people had an idea where I could get a little roadwork in on a track. And certainly I ought to be safe enough at my old dojo— being surrounded by friendly martial artists, with armed guards outside . . .

I went down and asked the cook Dad had hired (the book was rapidly making him rich, which was a good thing considering how much Carrie needed) to fix me a huge breakfast. Carrie stared at me for a long moment, then pulled her wheelchair around next to me to eat her own bagel and coffee.

"What are you going to do today?" she asked.

"I'll start by apologizing," I said. "I'm afraid I haven't gotten a thing for either you or Dad."

Dad came in then, and he said, "Seeing you like this is a pretty good gift as is. We didn't exactly know what you'd like, Mark, so we took some guesses. Want to come and see how we did?"

"Sure." I pushed the now-empty plate away, grabbing a last piece of toast to tuck into my jaws—I needed my strength back quickly—and went out with them to discover that I had gained a few sweaters, a pair of running shoes, and several large collections of prints. I was careful to praise all of them thoroughly.

I spent most of the rest of that day talking to the Steel Curtain people, and then on the phone to the extremely annoying shrink Dad had hired to pester me. Something about giving guns to mental patients bothered the guy, even when the mental patient could explain perfectly coherently that a gun was exactly what he needed.

It was simple. When that bomb went off—even before, when I knew something was happening—I wanted a gun in my hand and a chance to shoot back. I'd never fired a shot at anything but a paper target, nor hit anybody since I was a kid other than in the dojo, but that didn't matter. I'd found a purpose in life—hitting back.

It wasn't exactly the kind of thing a shrink approves of, but Dad and Carrie backed me up, and eventually Doctor Svetlana went for it as well. I think they figured it was just a phase, but a better one than watching me slowly fade away to a ghost. Anyway, it took about three days, and then all of a sudden everyone caved in, and I had the clearance to start getting myself qualified as a bodyguard.

If the shrink wasn't crazy about it, Hal Payton, the head of Steel Curtain, was about as unenthusiastic as you can get. Having the client decide to join the bodyguards was not at all in his recipe for how things ought to work. Once again, though, I wore him down; the fact was that if I'd been an applicant off the street, with my skills, he'd have hired me in an instant. Moreover, he had the testimony of half a dozen people, plus his own eyesight, to tell him that I had found something that I could really take an interest in, and that, irregular as it was, it was making me better.

I passed his qualifiers on pistol and martial arts with no hassle at all, even showing one of his guys a thing or two about the pugil stick. It didn't take long for me to get through the bonding process—there was practically nothing to investigate and it was all out in the open. And the exam for a Pennsylvania PI's license could be passed by a young chimp. By the new year I was a licensed bodyguard, working as a freelance contractor, nominally hired by Dad (for the minimum wage—I could hardly ask him to pay me a "real" salary for something as crazy as this) to work with Steel Curtain.

The other bodyguards seemed a little bemused by it all, but when they found they could rib me about it and that I'd tease back in a friendly way, they accepted me pretty quickly. I realized early on that I would have done better to have a little military experience—you live closer to weapons for a longer time that way—and that maybe I should think about studying for the police exams; a surprising number of rent-a-cops are guys who found the test too tough, but I figured the police exam couldn't be any tougher than the Ph.D. comprehensive exam I had been preparing for.

I especially liked sitting up at night; maybe that was because I figured that was when it would happen. Maybe because the bomb had gone off in bright daylight. I didn't care—one perk that my strange position carried was that I could pick my own hours, and I was certainly going to exercise that.

The family had always gone to church on Epiphany, January 6, the celebration of the coming of the Wise Men, and although Reverend Hamlin took a little persuading—he thought armed men sitting around in Ninth Presbyterian might disturb the parishioners a bit—he came around after Dad made a big donation to the building fund.

This was partly Dad's idea and partly Doctor Svetlana's—"reestablishing family rituals" was what he called it, meaning it was better to get used to doing things without Jerry, Marie, and Mom than to have the empty time there to prey on our minds.

Epiphany evening service is not one of the biggies among even the most devoted churchgoers, but Reverend Hamlin gave a pretty good sermon, told the old familiar story pretty well, and had just gotten to the point of announcing that we would be taking communion next when the doors at the side of the sanctuary flew open.

The Steel Curtain guy on the other side of Dad pounced on him and brought him down to the floor; the one next to Carrie would have rolled her from her wheelchair to the floor except that she'd already gotten down there herself. Most of the congregation just gaped and gasped, but Reverend Hamlin did a very creditable job of taking cover under the communion table, knocking grape juice and little chunks of Wonder Bread everywhere.

Payton should have tackled me, but he was busy reaching for his sidearm, so I lunged, cleared the pew in front of me, dropped between pews, and had my Colt up and leveled before I was even aware that the top of the pew to my left had suddenly splintered. I saw the men bursting through the door to the right and fired twice, not really aiming so much as just getting shots off to make them keep their heads down, slow them up, and spoil their aim. From around the church, wherever a Steel Curtain guard could get a clear line of fire, pistol shots were cracking out, and the first two Blades to make it through the door made it only a step or two before they were cut down.

If they'd come with a bomb or a grenade, they might have pulled it off, but even then it would have been close. There was a clatter of gunfire outside, and the terrorists bursting into the sanctuary whirled to run back out. Steel Curtain men shot them in the back—I was shooting myself, but later it turned out that the bodies had only .38 slugs and one .357 Magnum in them, and all my shots were found in places like the doorframe or the side of the choir loft. Payton later told me it was buck fever.

Thirty seconds after the attack began, the Blades were all dead or dying on the floor. The firing outside turned out to be the city cops, who had been closing in and had caught the getaway vehicle.

But it took us a while to find that out. First everyone had to get up from behind pews and look around nervously, and the Steel Curtain people made Dad and Carrie stay down and quiet for a long time. There were a few holes in the stained-glass windows—I noted that the Lamb of God seemed to have taken one right between the eyes—and a lot of the older parishioners weren't going to be exactly the same for a while, but the only innocent bystander hit was the Sunday School director, a kind-of cute young thing who had all sorts of "very serious and important raps" with kids; some plaster chips had gotten blown into her thigh, and the blood ruined a good blue wool dress.

Aside from the dress, Dad ended up paying for new carpets by the sanctuary doors (bloodstains don't come out easily), new paneling and woodwork in various places where rounds had hit, plastering to cover pockmarks in the walls, and a new surplice and stole for Reverend Hamlin, his having been ruined in a rain of grape juice. (He looked pretty grim getting up from under the communion table, but I could see where his sense of humor might have gone to hell about that point.)

And though I hadn't hit a thing, I was confirmed in my choice of profession. Three months later the FBI said they were pretty sure Blade of the Most Merciful was out of business, and Dad and Carrie started traveling with just a guard or two each. I opened Mark Strang Bodyguards.

———

Since then I'd been hit several times, and hit people back, and I found that it was what I lived for. Five years had gone by, and Carrie was Dr. Strang now and doing all sorts of hush-hush stuff for Uncle Sam, Dad had two more books out and was on the talk shows a lot to explain the Mideast—and I was still living over my storefront office.

But hey, with the exception of getting thumped on by nuts like Brunreich, it wasn't such a bad life, and it wasn't like I'd be doing anything else. And I still had two years left on my leave of absence before I would actually have to tell them I was never coming back to settle into the quiet life of art history.

My whole life wasn't exactly flashing by me as I rode in the back of Robbie and Paula's van, but that was the gist of it. The dreams kept returning to two things . . . the last glimpses I had had of Marie, alive, and the moment when I found out how good it felt to hit people.

Not necessarily to hit them back, either. They didn't have to have done anything to me. What it was, I think, was simply that a part of me had figured out that the whole world was just too damned violent, and people hurt each other much too often. And one way to get people out of the habit of hurting other people was to hit the aggressor with whatever force was to hand.

It was simplistic and dumb. And I believed in it down to the very core of my being.

My face was a little damp from my own slobber when Robbie gently shook me awake; Robbie's a small woman, and it was some effort for her and Paula to get me inside my apartment and dump me on my bed. They knew where the spare key was—they'd done house-sitting for me a time or two—so they just locked the place up behind them. (I was dimly aware of this as I considered whether or not I wanted to get undressed and get under the covers rather than just stay where I was.)

After a while, I slept, and when I woke up, the world looked very slightly better. It was late in the afternoon, and the answering machine downstairs showed that the phone had not rung at all during the day, which made it a typical day. The mail was the phone bill and Ed McMahon; I considered referring them to each other. I was loaded, between Marie's life insurance and the allowance Dad had settled on me, and it was a good thing too, because the business needed infusions of cash pretty regularly.

My right hand was aching where the tip of Brunreich's bat had grazed me, and though I could flex all the fingers, I suspected I was bruised pretty deeply. This was going to cut into my ability to do anything effective for a while; I'm not much good on the left side in karate, judo, or hapkido, and I don't shoot left at all. Probably I should practice all of that, but I never seem to get around to it.

I wandered back upstairs, fixed myself macaroni and cheese, took off my clothes, and got into a hot tub, with the plate of food on the toilet lid beside me. The warm water and the cold beer seemed to do my hand some good, and the meal helped, too; pretty soon I was quietly drifting, thinking of any old thing. That poor kid Porter had a tough row to hoe . . . she was just about the first client I'd ever cared about much, other than as a source of income and the "prisoner's base" I was supposed to guard in this elaborate game that gave a grown-up man an excuse for violence, or for threatening violence, on public streets.

The other agencies in town didn't like me much. They liked to work by intimidation. I liked to work by preemptive strike. I wondered what Porter might eventually hear about me, and I wondered even more why I cared.

Maybe it was getting time to date somebody again, though that seemed a waste of time and effort, too. I had a couple of alternatives, as it were—I could always get Robbie and Paula, who were always broke, to go to dinner and the movies, with no risk that either of them was going to want a good-night kiss, let alone to get into bed with me. And there was a former client, Melissa, whose ex-pimp I'd roughed up, who didn't mind occasionally giving me some in-kind payment on the bill she still owed me, if I just wanted physical contact.

She was a nice enough girl in her way . . . what if I actually took her out? She said she wasn't a working girl anymore, except for what she was doing for me (she didn't seem to keep books, so I never told her whether she was anywhere near paying off the debt. The truth was, I didn't see any reason to let her stop, and I didn't care enough if she just decided to).

That was kind of an odd thought. Dinner with Melissa. Not a great idea—might lead to conversation. She knew my story well enough, and I knew all about hers, but that didn't mean conversation was safe. I wasn't quite ready to have opinions about anything.

So what did I want next year to be like? Maybe I just wanted to have an opinion about something, living versus dying, say, or liking some client or other.

Well, I had liked Porter. There. Smart quiet ten-year-olds were nicer than their crazy parents. I had an opinion about something. And heck, by the time I was thinking about dating anybody again, Porter would probably be looking for her second husband, the way things work these days.

Having an opinion didn't seem to require any action, which was fine with me. I finished off the mac and cheese, looked at my hand—it was still swelling a little further, but I was sure now it was just bruised—and opened another beer for dessert.

I had just about finished beer number two and once again reached the conclusion that I wasn't going to change anything about my life right away when the buzzer from downstairs went off. I jumped out of the tub, spilling the last of the beer into the gray suds, wrapped a towel around myself, went into the single large room that's the rest of my apartment, and flipped on the video camera for the peephole.

He was a big, square-built guy, standing there patiently in the late-afternoon spring sunshine, and at first glance I would have figured he had a job lifting boxes somewhere, but the way he moved, sort of leading with his head as he looked around the street, suggested that he did some kind of brain work, might even be a scholar, and just happened to keep himself in shape. His hair was salt-and-pepper gray, thick, and overdue for a haircut; his nose spread across his face like someone had used a chisel to reshape it into a triangle. If he had students, they probably thought he looked like Fred Flintstone.

I pushed down the talk button on the intercom. "Can I help you?"

"I need to engage your services—or someone's—as soon as possible." His voice had that "educated American" accent that my dad's does, the one that professors cultivate.

"Are you being followed right now?" I asked.

"It's entirely possible."

"Then come inside. I'll be down to let you into the office part in a couple of minutes." I pushed the door release button, and the buzzer went off; he turned the doorknob and came into the front room of my office, quickly closing the door behind himself. I flipped the video camera control over so that I could keep an eye on him there, though there wasn't much to worry about—the desk, file cabinets, and safe were all behind a dead-bolted solid-core door in the inner office. I suppose he could have torn up the old copies of *Architecture Today*, *Reader's Digest*, and *Art Collector* that I keep there, or stolen one of the plastic chairs.

This made it a little more intriguing. He had two cases with him, one about big enough for a few changes of clothes and maybe some books and papers, the other about the size for an outsized briefcase. Usually if someone is being followed when they come to my office, it's a woman with a crazy husband or boyfriend, or a couple of times it's been a woman who was being stalked by one of those strange characters who decide they're in love with a pretty face on the street.

Well, maybe he was in a love triangle or something.

I threw clothes on and hurried downstairs. When I opened the door from the inner office, he had set his cases down but he was keeping his hands close to the handles, not making a big thing of it but obviously ready to grab and run if he had to.

I said, "Come on in and have a seat." He did, and I dead-bolted the door again behind us, then took my own seat behind my desk.

The first thing he did was lift the smaller case up, thump it down on the desk on its side, and open it. He took out a small bound stack of bills, the kind you get from the bank, and handed it to me; it was a set of fifty one-hundred-dollar bills.

I looked at it and said, "I don't work for the mob, religious cults, or governments-in-exile."

"Neither do I," he said. "You may find this hard to believe, but I'm just a plain old professor of sociology at Pitt; the cash is from my savings. My name is Harry Skena. I'm only hiring a bodyguard because I can't get the police or FBI to believe me."

I nodded. "Who's after you, and what do they want?"

"What they want is easy enough to explain. They want to kill me in order to silence me. As for who they are—well, that's where I'm getting into trouble, getting the police and FBI to take me seriously. Have you read—"

He happened to glance up at the wooden plaque Robbie had

made for me, over the desk, the one that said "Mark Strang, Licensed Professional Bodyguard." His eyes got wide, and he said, "You are not, by any chance, related to *Gus* Strang?"

This made me believe him a little more; his academic colleagues all call him Gus, family and old friends call him Augie. "He's my father."

There was a long silence, while he licked his lips and seemed to think. "Well, then you're either going to think this is a strange practical joke, or you're the best man for the job.

"Let me start at the beginning. As a scholar, I'm afraid I am not in your father's league; I'm not an original theorist and I don't do anything very groundbreaking. My area of study is the formation of organized crime in immigrant communities. It's not really a hot area because there haven't been many new ideas in it for a long time, and my research isn't exactly hot either, because I end up confirming what everyone knows already, but it's the sort of thing that has to be done, making sure that what 'everyone knows' has some correspondence to the truth.

"What I do is hang around with an immigrant group for a while, talk with them, get to know them, establish trust so they'll tell me things, and then find out what I can about organized crime, if any, among them. And normally what I find is that if the job ladder is blocked for them, their businesses aren't succeeding in reaching a wider market than their own community, and they're frozen out of city politics, there's an organized crime syndicate pretty soon. If the doors are open to them, for whatever reason, usually there's not. And if they're the kind of ethnic group that makes a big deal about family loyalty, then it will tend to be a bigger and more systematic crime syndicate, because the hoods have more brothers and cousins to go into business with.

"None of that's very new, and it really just confirms what everyone knows. And I've been doing that kind of study for fifteen years." He raised both his hands and made a funny little flipping gesture, as if shooing away his work, showing how unimportant it was.

"It's dull and it's routine and I do it because it's my job. As soon as the crooks find out I'm not a reporter or a cop, they don't really care about what I'm doing, so it's not even dangerous.

"Or it wasn't till just recently. About three months ago, I got interested in a new organized crime mob that seemed to be show-

ing up everywhere across the country all at once, and that seemed
to target practically all Islamic American communities. Now, that
was strange enough—there are many different kinds of Islamic im-
migrants and, for that matter, many different kinds of Islam in the
United States, and they don't have a lot in common with each
other. Some of them don't even like each other much.

"And this mob was a really bad-ass outfit, too. They seemed to
prefer threats and extortion—often they didn't really give the first
people in a community that they threatened time enough to give
in, they just did something to scare hell out of everyone else. The
kind of mob that kills just to prove they'll do it, like some of the
really nasty crack mobs, or the bad old days of the Colombian cow-
boys, or going back farther, like the early days of the Capone mob
or the Bronx Irish gangs.

"And most of the Islamic groups have been very resistant to
organized crime anyway; too many successful businessmen and kids
going to college in the first generation for them to get interested in
crime.

"Sociologically speaking, this new mob was the wrong kind of
criminal in the wrong kind of community at the wrong time. It
made no sense for them to be there according to all the orthodox
theory. So naturally they got my attention." He sighed and stared
into space a moment. "After all, if you're not brilliant, but you're
pretty good at documenting things, your best ticket is to find something interesting to document.

"Anyway, in no time at all, in the Turkish, Pakistani, Algerian,
Syrian, and Iranian neighborhoods around the country, there was
just plain *terror* of these guys, and small wonder."

I felt my throat tightening, and I wasn't sure whether I was
hoping for or frightened of what I might hear, so I made myself
ask, "And who are they?"

He looked down at the floor. "I think they're the remnants of
Blade of the Most Merciful."

·4·

There was a long silence, and when I didn't laugh or throw him out, he went on. "The leadership of Blade of the Most Merciful was never caught, you must know, and only about half of them are accounted for by the raids that put it out of business. And the only ones in prison were the few whose lives were saved medically—did you know about those?"

"Yeah," I said, my mouth completely dry. "Yeah, I know. Nine captured, wounded members. Four died in the hospitals they were in, a couple of them probably with help. The rest died in prison within a year of going in, all of them ruled suicide, though I think a couple of them also had help. Not one of them ever said a thing, not even the simplest political statement to the world."

Harry Skena nodded, tugged at his ear gently. "In the other case I have the evidence I could show you that these are Blade people."

"If they are—why are they doing it? And what's a terror organization doing turning into organized crime?"

He shrugged. "Maybe they're broke and they need the money, and they've got a lot of practice at violence. The Soviet Union recently went out of business, and though I don't think they were behind Blade, maybe Blade was getting money from them for contract jobs. Or maybe they were never really a terrorist outfit—maybe they were always just a plain old criminal enterprise, that found a way to make cash in the terrorist biz. Or maybe what they really are is something totally different, and organized crime and political terrorism are both means to the same end, which is something different from either politics or profit. I have no idea. The trouble is, I have good reason to think that at about the same time that I was figuring out who they had to be, they were also noticing me, and figuring out what I knew.

"They aren't the type of outfit that gives warnings, but I didn't want to run until I had to. So I got kind of a habit of not being at home, keeping irregular hours, making myself unpredictable. Not hard to do, I'm a bachelor, and I've lived by myself for years. This afternoon I came by my apartment to get a change of clothes for after handball. My side of my building—the Park Plaza, up on Craig Street—was caved in. Cops and fire trucks were running in all directions. I called the newsline and learned that it had been a bomb blast—there were a bunch of people hurt in Duranti's, but luckily very few tenants were home. Best guess was that a maintenance man had accidentally set off the bomb.

"Maintenance was coming to my place to set mousetraps this afternoon. They left me a note to that effect.

"I walked back to Pitt—just a few blocks to my office in Forbes Quad—picked up these two cases, which I already had packed, and took a cab here. One car stayed with us four blocks, so I asked the driver to do some evading. He thought he had lost them."

I nodded. "Mind if I make a phone call?"

"I'd *expect* you to."

I picked up the phone. I had a secure line—they're a necessity in my line of business—and so did Dad, because with the ever-present danger he'd decided he had to have one, too. We'd never used them to talk about anything other than where to meet for lunch (and come to think of it we usually met at Duranti's—that would have to change). The phone rang twice, then Dad picked it up and said hello.

I told him what was up, in a few short sentences.

"Well, yes, I know Harry Skena slightly," Dad said. "Tallish, big, square-shouldered, graying hair, clean-shaven . . . looks sort of like—maybe I shouldn't say this, but one of my grad students is a former student of Harry's and always said Harry looked like Fred Flintstone."

"That's the guy," I said. "Is what he's saying plausible?"

Dad sighed. "Well, Blade has to have gone somewhere. I suppose organized crime might suit them as well as anything. They really had nowhere to run once the world started hunting them down, so there's nothing too wildly implausible about that part of the story. As for why—well, Harry's absolutely right. You remember that's what baffled me about it—why on Earth they were doing the strange, pointless violence they were doing. So in a way the parts that don't make any sense are exactly the parts that are really consistent with their known character."

"Okay, but then why haven't the FBI and the cops believed him?" I glanced up from the phone and saw that he was sitting there, his hands folded in his lap, listening patiently. If what Harry Skena was telling me was true, then he was sitting there watching me decide whether or not to help, which might be literally life and death for him, but he looked no more alarmed than he would waiting for a dog license or for a restaurant to approve his credit card. I liked that about him at once, so I wanted him to be telling me the truth.

Dad sighed. "Well, you and I both got to know them—and I was a consultant while they were hunting down Blade. Mark, we both know the official cops are good, but they're also file-closers by nature. They like to have things officially over with and they don't like to reopen investigations. So somebody you've barely heard of— a nothing-special professor at a second-rate university—comes to you with a story like that . . . and you can either reopen the file and trigger all kinds of hard work for yourself . . . or you can pat him on his head, note him down as a nut, and most likely it will turn out fine. And if it doesn't—well, Harry Skena may be dead, but then they'll really *know*, won't they? As long as the evidence isn't ironclad, and it's not their neck on the line, it's awfully easy to leave that file closed, and pretty hard to decide to open it. That's what I would say is going on."

"It makes sense," I admitted. "Uh, in present circumstances I'm going to have to get Harry to a safe house somewhere and do it right away. If you like, once I have him somewhere safe with a secure phone line, I'll fax you his evidence."

"I'd appreciate that. If Blade is back, I've got another book to write. Besides, maybe I can get some official action on this—I think the FBI would listen to me, especially after this bombing attack.

Give them a call, too, once you're dug in somewhere. Tell Harry hi from me. And Mark?"

"Yeah."

"Be careful. I wish like hell you'd get out of that stupid line of work and start using that good brain of yours again, but if you're going to do it, at least stay sharp and tough. And if you do find you're shooting at Blade bastards . . . shoot me a couple too, okay?"

"Deal, Dad. Love to Carrie. You guys get careful, too. Might be worth having Payton put more guards on for a few days."

"I'd already thought of it."

We said "bye" and hung up. I nodded to Skena. "You check out okay. So we're leaving right away—my car's in a secure area a block away, and we need to get walking before anyone turns up. We'll head out of town and work out where we're going as we go— if we take 79 North we can go either way on the pike or just keep heading north, or backtrack and bypass the town. It's about the fastest way there is to make our tracks hard to follow."

"Fine," he said. "Er—on the matter of payment and expenses—"

"What you've given me is good for a while," I said, "and if it really is Blade that's after you, for purely personal reasons I'd be willing to do this as a *pro bono* case."

"Good, then. I shall pay you every cent I'm able, but I'm afraid my case still won't be much of a moneymaker for you."

He stood up and extended his hand; we shook on the deal.

Then there was a terrifying roar as the front door of the storefront was blown down with a small shaped charge. Skena grabbed his cases; I yanked a drawer open and grabbed the .45 in there, leaped over the desk, ran to the office door. I could hear the heavy footsteps and the rush of deep breathing, and then the doorknob turned uselessly as they tried it before blowing this door as well.

I put a shot straight through the door—it was solid-core, but at point-blank range a .45 slug will get through the wood, and even if the slug itself doesn't have the energy left to kill, the spray of splinters into the guy's chest and face ought to distract him a moment. There was a howl of pain and, as I stepped aside, two answering rounds punched holes in the door, spraying splinters all over the back wall.

"This way," I said to Skena, keeping my voice a lot calmer than

I felt. One thing I had learned from Payton was to have a back way out; you never knew when you might have to move a client through undercover. Mine was a steel fire door behind a fake bookcase; I opened it and gestured him through. A shot rang off the dead-bolt, but the office door held; as I closed the bookcase door it was still holding. "Down," I said. "This takes us to the place next door's basement."

The place next door was Berto's pizza joint. Jim Berto, the owner, was an old beer buddy. I paid him a retainer every month for these occasions. I'd only had to use this twice before, in five years of business, and it was worth every penny.

The basement was his garage, and I had keys to every delivery car. I had Skena get down in the backseat of one, jumped into the driver's seat, and we were off through the back alley. From my office I could hear shouting and running, and there was a swarthy type standing by my back Dumpster, but he didn't look at the pizza car departing—or not right away.

As we were just turning the corner out of the alley, I saw men run out of Berto's garage, and the Dumpster leaner suddenly looked a lot more excited. Damn—if I'd had a few seconds more they'd have had no idea where we were headed. I couldn't make an effective run for it in the pizza car—aside from being bright red and white and easy to spot anywhere, it also had less than a quarter tank of gas. And if they knew I was rolling, they'd be headed for my private garage as fast as they could.

If you're given the choice between impossible and difficult, take difficult. I laid rubber right through the alley stop sign, scaring the hell out of one of Berto's real pizza drivers, and roared right up Beacon Street toward my office, with its plume of smoke pouring from its shattered door and front window. A crowd was already starting to gather to see what was going on, and I decided more diversion would be a good idea.

I held down the horn and sped up. Sure enough, that had to be their car pulled up on the sidewalk—I guess terrorists don't worry much about parking tickets—so I took a chance, pushed the electric window down button, pulled my .45 from its shoulder holster, slowed just a little, and leaned over to the passenger side, putting a round into one rear tire and one front tire on their van, and then one into the startled driver. I had just an instant of seeing his shocked face and the hole torn in his neck before I had to get control of the car again and floor it up the steep, winding street.

I'd finally shot someone, and it was a Blade terrorist. My life was made—from here on out anything good that happened was going to be pure profit.

A shot screamed off a phone pole on one side of me, and the back window of a car shattered—whoever was shooting wasn't being very effective just yet—then we were around the corner and headed down Murray Avenue. With luck they might split up forces and lose me, trying to cover the parking garage and both directions on the parkway all at once. "You okay back there, Dr. Skena?"

"Fine so far. Should I stay down?"

"Might as well. Do you have a gun?"

"Yes, but it hasn't been fired in twenty years, and it's been longer than that for me—"

It figured, somehow. "Okay, then just stay down and let me do the shooting."

I whipped the pizza wagon into the entry of the parking garage I use without signaling or slowing down; it fishtailed pretty badly, knocking a traffic post a little, but it minimized the time to react in case anyone was following or watching. At least there was no line, so I rolled up to the ticket booth, grabbed the ticket, and the pizza car was through the gate before it was entirely raised.

You're really not supposed to drive up the down ramps in a parking garage at forty miles per hour, but it was still a bit before rush hour, and I figured the more chaos I created the better, at the moment. What I hoped for happened; two exiting cars pulled over to get away from me and ended up in fender-bender situations on the ramp. One ramp partially blocked, and I knew which one . . .

The high-security area was on the top floor of the parking garage; I had the electronic key in my hand as we pulled up to it, and the Mercedes 510 SL "woke up" for me in its stall, the engine running smoothly and the lights coming on, before I had fully stopped the now-battered Berto's pizza wagon. It occurred to me that if I'd seen the way I was driving, and not known who I was, I'd have ordered all my pizzas from Berto's from then on—it sure looked like the most determined delivery driver I'd ever seen.

I yanked the car to a stop just short of the gate. "Out, and bring your cases," I said to Skena, and jumped to push my combination into the gate lock's buttons. The gate opened smoothly, and

Skena and I ran to the Mercedes; another press of the electronic key opened my trunk, and we heaved his cases next to the packed suitcase, spare pistol case, and spare ammo I always keep in there. Then we were inside the car, and I pulled it sharply out and headed outward.

"You've blocked yourself in with that—" Skena was saying, but before he could get out "pizza car," I had slowed briefly, bumped it hard, and, since I had left it in neutral, rolled the pizza car backward onto the down ramp, its doors still hanging open. It gathered speed and headed downward to jam someplace or other, making one more barrier, but I was already on my way—down the up ramp, this time, to balance out the way I had come in.

We damned near made it. Would have made it, too, except for a vanload of Little Leaguers coming up the other way, and Mom who insisted on straddling the center of the ramp instead of moving to the side. It only took about thirty seconds for me to pull out of her way and let her through, but that was enough.

The Mercedes was just zooming out of the last turn when the first shot made a dent in the bulletproof windshield. I yanked it hard in the basic 180 maneuver—wrapping and unwrapping my arms to make it jump briefly sideways—and that got us past them with just two more hits on the glass and armor, one of which broke a back window—

But then luck really ran out. They had an old pickup and they backed it straight into the path of the Mercedes as I tried to go through the apparent hole. We must have been doing thirty-five when we hit the truck, hard enough to knock it sideways against the concrete retaining wall.

It was up too high for bumpers to meet, and the truck slid up the hood, its weight crushing downward, the undercarriage peeling away metal from my hood like a can opener. Something or other got the engine, and, anyway, I could hardly have backed out and run away with a truck jammed halfway onto my hood.

They tossed a grenade in the open back window; I saw it for just the instant before Skena flipped it back out, and it blew only a few feet from us, making my car echo like the inside of the bass drum in a hard-rock band. They had all dived clear of it; they were back in an instant, pumping rounds into the Mercedes's armor and glass.

"Bulletproof" doesn't mean it stops every round forever; it just means it doesn't shatter easily, and it takes a lot of punishment. In a second or so the back window had taken twenty rounds, and it was starting to crumble. I was down behind the seat, glad I'd put a Kevlar sheet into the back of each seat, gladder still I'd been belted in when we hit because right now I needed all the coordination I had—

I grabbed for the .45, and a funny thing happened. My hand wouldn't close around it.

I looked down to see that my hand was an amusing shade of deepest purple. It figured; I'd had that bad injury from the ball bat this morning, and then I'd used that hand twice in a few minutes to fire a .45. Normally no problem—my arm and hand muscles are well developed—but with the injury I'd probably started a major hemorrhage in the muscles, and while I'd been driving here it had been enough to put my right hand out of commission.

All this flashed into my head in one moment of awareness, along with two other facts:

I am, and have always been, a lousy shot left-handed.

And anyway, I didn't dare roll down a window to get a clear shot, and when the back window caved in as it was going to do any second, it would be too late to do much shooting back.

Through the maze of cracks, holes, and shattered glass, I dimly saw a figure running for the car, and realized we were probably about to get a satchel charge tossed underneath us. I had just time to realize we couldn't do a thing about it, and to remember Blade's tendency to overdo it with explosives.

I figured it was going to be quick.

Then suddenly there were bright lights everywhere, and the refraction in the shredded window made things invisible for every practical purpose. Some kind of gun I'd never heard before was firing; it made a sort of whoosh noise, like the miniguns on helicopters, those little high-speed Gatling guns, but it was deeper in pitch and loud enough to make the Mercedes vibrate. It fired three bursts; then there was a huge, booming explosion that echoed throughout the parking garage. The rear window gave way and flew into the compartment in a thousand pieces; bits of it rattled off the windshield and sprayed my back, stinging me but not penetrating my heavy shirt.

I popped up, the automatic in my left hand, and saw that there was nobody shooting back at me anymore; every Blader was scattered on the ground. As I reared a little higher, I saw there was something odd about them—and then I realized they all looked like their heads had been blown up from the inside.

In training films I'd seen what slugs do to human flesh—the way a modern pistol round goes in through a hole you could cover with your thumb, but takes out a chunk of flesh bigger than your fist on its way out. This was a lot worse than that; it was more as if their heads had simply ceased to be, turning into the thin red jam that was smeared all over the parking-lot walls, leaving them with stringy flesh sticking up from the abrupt ends of their necks.

The bomb blast had raked over the already fallen bodies, and dust, dirt, and smoke were stuck on the bloody walls, but nothing obscured the strange way they'd been killed.

I climbed a little higher in the seat, looked around a little more. Still there was no sound.

I looked down at Skena; he had a strange grin. "There's a fire in the past of most things," he said, very loudly. I was about to hush him since I had no idea who or what might be around, when the who or what answered.

A soft, low-pitched female voice—one I liked immediately—said, "And where there's fire, there's light, and where there's light, truth."

Harry Skena sat up abruptly; obviously he felt perfectly safe. "There's something you haven't been telling me," I said, partly because I really was irritated and partly because I was doing my best to hide my shock.

"We're taking the whole vehicle," the voice outside said, "so brace yourselves."

The whole vehicle? Brace—?

It got very dark. The world fell away the way it does in a plane that has suddenly gone into a dive to let gravity have its way. There was a silence that was like being struck deaf, and another part of me noted how like a dream it all was, how I didn't exactly seem to be in touch with my body, and I wasn't precisely where I seemed to be.

Then a kind of gray light came through, and a low humming that was about an octave lower than the sixty-cycle hum you sometimes hear on stereo systems, and the world started to take shape again.

I was pretty sure I was not in a parking garage in Squirrel Hill anymore. First of all, the land around me seemed to stretch out for quite a ways, and though there was a wall in the distance, it wasn't nearly as close as the one in the parking garage had been. Then after a bit I realized that there was no wall at all, we were in something like a great big parking lot, with no other cars on it, and the pavement seemed to be metal.

I sat up farther, tried using the power switch to lower the windows; it didn't work, so I cranked mine down. The metal parking lot, in very bright sunshine, stretched out in all directions, and then more of the gray fog lifted, and sound came back, and I suddenly realized that the metal parking lot was trough-shaped, with the car at the bottom of the trough.

Hesitantly, I opened the door and stepped out. Far to either side of me, immense buildings, like giant high-rises or apartment complexes, rose up into the sky; we seemed to be right between two rows of them, and they looked to be about a mile apart.

I looked on up the side of one of the huge buildings, and it just kept going up—it seemed to be bigger than the World Trade Center is when you're standing on the sidewalk in front of it—and then . . .

I saw the sky. You can't have grown up a kid in America and not recognize that sky.

The Earth hung overhead, a little to the side of the building tops, eighty times wider than the full moon. And cutting across it was a wide dark line that swung around across the sky and converged with the building tops over my head.

I was on some huge, ring-shaped space station, the kind of thing you ran into when you were a kid reading science fiction.

The bright sunlight, I realized, was coming from thousands of overhead lights; as I watched, the Earth "set" over one end of the "street" in which I stood, and the Sun and Moon rolled by. A couple of spaceships—at least that seemed like what flying assemblages of metal like that had to be—whizzed right into the ring, and, strangely enough, a silvery airplane, not much different from the old DC-3 "Gooney Birds," flew by overhead.

I could do nothing but stand and gape; while I was doing that, very dimly a part of my consciousness was aware that some kind of conversation was happening beside me, and that Skena was answering a lot of questions.

The Earth rolled back into the sky. It had been less than ten minutes, I figured, so this space station must be spinning pretty fast. I figured it probably had to since the gravity under my feet felt normal.

The most likely explanation was that I was dying on the pavement back in the parking garage, and this was a hallucination borrowed from my childhood reading. The second most likely thing was that I was already clinically dead, and this was the last hallucination before the lights went out. Then after that there came that I'd had a breakdown earlier in the day—say maybe Brunreich really got me with that bat—and had hallucinated everything since, including Harry Skena.

There was also the extremely unlikely possibility that this was really happening. I did my best to dismiss that thought, but the metal deck under my feet seemed disturbingly real.

I looked back at the Mercedes—it was a thorough mess. The armoring I'd had put in was all internal, so the body had a bunch of nasty-looking holes all over it. The rear window, of course, was gone pretty completely. There were still bits of the underside of the pickup truck jammed onto and through its hood, and a mix of engine fluids was dripping underneath it.

"Naturally we'll fully restore it," Harry Skena said. "Good as new, or actually, given the relative state of technology, better than new. Better grab our things from the trunk—the pickup will be here in a minute or so."

My feet started moving, probably because whatever was left of my mind had just heard a program of action, and even if it didn't make any sense, at least it was something to do.

I unlocked the trunk—had to use my left hand, as my right would not now close to grip the keys—and raised it. The armoring had kept bullets out of any of our stuff, and I sort of mechanically unloaded everything to a few steps away from the car, not sure what a "pickup" was—I doubted he meant a pickup truck—and therefore not knowing how much room it might require.

As I moved the last of the cases and laid the spare pistol and supplies on top, it got sort of dark. I looked up to see something huge and round descending, and decided that as hallucinations go, this one was pretty amazing, and, moreover, that I had a lot more of an imagination than I ever had thought I did.

It was a strange angle, but I finally decided that, yes, it really was a big, silvery blimp coming down over us.

The soft, female voice from before spoke. "The airship will take us around to the other side of the station, where you can get medical treatment, and then it will drop your vehicle off for repair."

I looked around to see that she was standing there next to Harry Skena, and saw what she looked like for the first time. She was tall—I'm six-two and she was just about exactly my height— and built like a female bodybuilder. (I'm not sure whether I'd have bet on her or on Paula in an arm-wrestling contest.) Her face wasn't so much pretty as handsome—her features were very strong, cheekbones high but thick, jaw a little square—and her eyes were a cold, piercing blue. Her hair was jet black and very thick and wavy.

She was wearing a set of coveralls that looked more like clothing for fixing a car or painting an apartment than anything else, and under that some kind of thin clingy stuff. It looked sort of college-girl dress-down cute, except for the wide brown belt, from which hung a weird-looking polished metal thing that resembled nothing so much as one of those high-powered squirt guns—but which pretty clearly was the gun she'd used in settling the Bladers before she brought us here.

Wherever here was.

If there was any such place, I reminded myself.

"Where . . . am . . . I?" I asked very slowly. It felt very much as if I were in some kind of dream.

"You're at Hyper Athens," she said. "Specifically you're at the Crux Operations Rescue Landing Field here; we're taking you around to another part of Crux Ops in a few minutes. Meanwhile, you'll get to look over the city a little."

"Hyper Athens . . ." I said. "Athens . . . Georgia? Athens, Ohio?"

"Athens," she said. "In this history there's only one."

The Earth rolled back overhead as the huge space station continued to turn.

Harry Skena came forward to steady me a little.

"My name is Ariadne Lao," the woman said, gently, "and I'm a Crux Op. None of this is familiar to you, and you shouldn't expect it to be for a while."

Her eyes were very kind; her features, I realized, were sort of Eurasian.

I groped for a question to ask and came up with a stupid one. "Your last name is . . . Chinese?"

"Of course. The Chinese have been Athenian in this history for

. . . oh, a thousand years or so, give or take." She smiled at me very warmly. "We don't really look different from any other Athenians."

Well, that cleared that up. I shook my head to clear it, and she gestured to the long tube which had descended from the blimp. "This is a . . ." she seemed to think for a moment ". . . your word might be 'lift' or 'dumbwaiter'—"

"An elevator?" I suggested. I've always been good at crosswords.

She nodded briskly. "Thank you, yes, that's the English word I was looking for. For some silly reason they gave me East Atlantic English instead of West Atlantic English in the translator, and only updated to about fifty years before your time. It will all become clearer once we get onto the airship and get you to a physician."

Pretty clearly this bizarre dream was not going to go away, so I let her and Skena herd me into the small, soft, baggy thing that hung at the end of a translucent hose from the blimp. As soon as we were inside, it hugged us all close—very gently, and it didn't feel frightening—and we shot up into the belly of the dirigible, coming out in what looked for all the world like an Art Deco cocktail lounge overlooking the area. I looked down through one glass-bottomed port in the floor to see what looked like a lot of spiderwebs wrapping up my car, then the car was on its way up to the bowels of the blimp. I was about to say "our bags" when a door in the wall opened, and there they were.

Ariadne was already at the bar, and she said, "I'm afraid this is a history that's never learned to like distilled liquor much, or tobacco, but I can offer you strong wine, beer, coffee, tea, hemp, or chocolate. I'm afraid we're rather prudes about opium and cocaine."

"Um, it's okay, so am I," I said. "Coffee would be great, I guess."

With everything picked up from the landing field, the blimp rose quickly into the air, and as it did I felt my weight dropping down toward nothing. By the time she floated over to me, extending a little squeeze bulb of strong coffee, we had cleared the tops of the buildings, and I could see that the whole space station formed one giant ring, with its open ends roofed over in glass or some such; we were flying through the weightless middle of it, and all around us dozens of other blimps and airplanes were doing the same. Through the spidery steel girderwork and the occasional reflections from the transparent windows far below, I could see the stars, the moon, and the shining edge of the Earth. Overhead was more of the city-in-a-ring that was Hyper Athens, and as I watched the city below me fell away and the city above me grew.

In a moment the blimp rolled slowly over, while we were completely weightless. We had passed through the center of the station, and now we were slowly descending toward the other side of the ring.

"You haven't tried your coffee," Ariadne said.

"Sorry, uh, Ariadne? Miss Lao?"

"Citizen Lao would be customary here."

"Thank you, Citizen Lao." I took a swallow of the coffee; here it was served with honey, clove, and cardamom, as far as I could tell. My hallucination was being very clever about what the differences were going to be, I decided.

"Er, if I may ask . . . *when* am I? I must be somewhere in the future?" Weight was returning rapidly, and I made my way to a sofa to sit. It was quite comfortable, but I still felt pretty weird.

"Well," she said, very gently (she really did seem like a very kind person and I was glad I had made her up that way) "er, Citizen Skena, you know, um . . ."

"Mark Strang," I said. "I'm a citizen of the USA, but I bet that doesn't count."

"Mister Strang, I think we'll call you," she said. "Citizen Skena, you know Mister Strang's world far better than I do. Perhaps you'll know how to answer his question."

"The truth will do," I said. I felt a little grouchy at being handled like a kid, and, besides, my hand was beginning to really hurt me.

"It's more a question of telling you the truth in a way that lets you believe it," Skena explained. "Er, let me think—it takes me a moment to convert. Locally we would say the year is 3157. But that actually corresponds to your year of 2726."

"I'm . . . eight hundred years in the future?" I began to feel a little weak and woozy, and I slid down the couch cushions a bit.

"Not in *your* future," Skena said.

Things rolled around once more and beneath the vast city street stretching through space and arcing up around us, I saw the great sphere of the Earth, the Horn of Africa plain as day to my right, the edge of South America far off to my left. Another silver Gooney Bird flew by, and as I watched a complex trusswork of metal beams—some kind of spaceship I supposed that never came down into the atmosphere—passed by the glass far below us. "Not in *my* future?" I think I asked—just before I fainted.

·5·

The first thought I had as I woke up was that the game I had been playing with myself since the bomb killed Jerry, Marie, and Mom had somehow finally worked, because I knew I wasn't in my own bed in my apartment, nor in my old bed at home.

Then I started to wonder about what I remembered. I still had not opened my eyes, and it didn't quite seem like I should yet. The bed had that kind of comfortable feel that your own bed doesn't, but it was somehow—too clean? too impersonal? Like it was designed to really fit my body, but my body hadn't quite worn it into shape.

All right. The Brunreich case. Porter Brunreich had talked to me quite a bit. Mrs. Brunreich jumping me while I was fighting her crazy husband the first time. Another fight with Brunreich in the airport, and getting my hand hurt. Robbie and Paula getting me home to bed. Yep, all there. So now I should be waking up and deciding to get a shower and some chow and a beer—

Wrong. Then the buzzer would go off and Harry Skena would be standing outside my office door.

Unfortunately all the memories I had connected with Harry Skena were every bit as vivid as the ones I had connected with the goofy Brunreich family. Right down to the call to Dad. No, if I was having a hallucination, I couldn't find the point where I had slipped over into it. So chances were that when I opened my eyes I'd be somewhere I'd never seen before.

I was right. The room was a pleasant soft blue color, very clean, obsessively cheerful, and bare. I knew I was in a hospital right away.

I sat up in bed and looked at my right hand. It was perfectly fine, though the nails were kind of long—which is odd in a guy who bites his nails as much as I do. Then I checked the other hand, and those nails were pretty much as always.

Getting out of bed to look for a toilet, I decided if this was the future, it was amazing that they still hadn't invented hospital gowns that fastened in the back. I also noted that there wasn't the funny twinge a cold floor always gave me in the ankle that got broken in the bomb attack, five years back; in fact the long white scar where the surgeons had gone in to fix it was gone, too.

"If you need a toilet," a pleasant, friendly voice from nowhere said, "put your hand on the black bar on the wall to the right."

I looked, saw what looked like a strip of black duct tape sticking to the blue wallpaper, and put my hand on it. A door slid open, and there was a small, comfortable-looking seat, very low to the ground. "Push the red button to dilate the seat," the voice said. It didn't seem to be in my ears; more like in my head.

I pushed the button and a hole formed in the seat; I used the thing more or less the way I would at home, and a voice said, "Push the blue button for a wash," so I did and what happened was startling but not unpleasant, and no different really from a bidet . . . when I stood up the hole in the toilet closed, and I heard a gurgling noise that I assumed was the flush. Well, clearly, in this part of the future no one was ever going to complain about men leaving the seat up.

The voice told me that if I pushed another black strip, I'd find temporary clothing "while yours is being repaired," so I did, and sure enough there was a soft unitard-like thing that the voice assured me was underwear (it turned out to have a built-in jock), a comfortable coverall to put on over it, and a pair of perfectly fitting slippers that were shaped a bit like high-top sneakers and automatically contracted to grasp my feet and ankles when I put them on. It told me to go back to the bathroom and push the red button for the toilet again; I put the hospital gown in there, and it closed up and gurgled.

I had a question, and experimentally I tried just thinking it. Who was this voice?

"I am a module installed in your brain temporarily, to allow you to understand our language and to explain customs and situations to you as they come up. I am physically located in a small socket just below your right ear. If you pluck me out, you will stop hearing me, but the local language will become unintelligible."

It made a certain amount of sense—enough for the moment anyway—and I wondered what I was supposed to do now. It turned out that the chip in my head didn't know either, so probably someone was coming to tell me. Or us. I wasn't sure I knew what to make of this "passenger," though as a way of acquiring a language it beat the hell out of memorizing verb conjugations.

There was a knock at the door, and I said, "Come in," realizing my mouth was forming some other words entirely. A door opened where there had just been blank wall, and Harry Skena came in, which confirmed one part of my memories, followed by Ariadne Lao, which confirmed another part. "The hospital said you were up and getting dressed, Mister Strang," Ariadne explained. I noticed I really wanted to be invited to call her by first name, but the voice in my head said that even in the best of circumstances that was going to take a long time—this was a polite society.

The chip also told me it wasn't anywhere near time to ask her to call me by my first name. "I seem to be a lot better," I said. "And, um—my hand, I thought, was—"

"That was the major thing we had you in here for. You're young, healthy, and resilient enough to be able to deal with a slightly unbelievable situation—or rather with one you've never had to believe before. We injected you with nanos, Mr. Strang— that's a word your culture has just coined, and you won't actually have the thing the name goes with for a while yet, but what they are is tiny machines that can duplicate the work of cells in your body. In this particular case they swam around in your hand marking the damaged tissue to be destroyed and causing the healthy tissue to grow in to replace it. They also have a tendency to get loose in the body and fix anything else that looks like damage, so if you've lost any old scars or badly healed injuries, it's with our compliments, but if you've lost any tattoos, piercing, or scars you were proud of, do let us know, and we can restore them."

"Oh, I'm pretty happy with the quality of work," I said.

She smiled slightly. "You'd be surprised how many people are upset when they find their pierced ears and noses have been completely healed—or that a tattoo that took months has vanished overnight." Then she turned to Skena. "You're the one who knows both cultures, Citizen Skena. What do you suggest?"

Skena chuckled a little. "Well, let me think a bit . . . it's been a long cultural leap for me, too. But if you didn't find the view of space too disorienting, Mr. Strang, then perhaps we could go out on one of the terraces, have something to drink, and have a long talk. First question—do you accept, for the moment, that this place is real, and you are really here?"

The question took me a bit aback because I had been doing my best to ignore it for quite a while. There was the remarkable fact that everything stayed consistent—in my dreams, places and people usually flowed into each other. And how often do you meet strangers in a dream? And also, although this place was obviously a century or so advanced beyond my own time, it was *consistently* advanced and in ways I believed. It made sense that when a space station got big enough, since you'd only have "artificial gravity" at the rim, you'd use airplanes and blimps to get around inside. The little translator voice was like something out of the *Time* magazine article about cyberpunk. And maybe the most convincing thing of all was that toilet, which seemed like something you might find in a Neiman-Marcus catalog in ten years or so. And the fact was too that my experience was continuous—I fell asleep and I woke up, but that was the only interruption, and even that was normal, right down to the normal-for-me waking up wishing that I were somewhere else at some other time.

I could go on thinking of this as a hallucination if I tried, but I couldn't make myself *feel* that it was a hallucination. I suppose I could have thought Pittsburgh to be a hallucination, too, but the reality of the concrete and brick, wind and rain, traffic noise and strangers would have convinced me pretty fast.

"I think this place is real," I said, "and I think that I'm not crazy. Or at least not crazy in seeing this place; I reserve the right to be crazy independently."

Ariadne Lao snickered, and said, "Good enough." A smile from her was worth a lot at that point. Harry Skena opened the door—I noticed that now that it had been opened from the outside, it had somehow grown one of those black "door-open buttons"—and we walked out onto a pleasant, rambling gallery that overlooked a big, parklike commons a few stories below.

"This is a beautiful place," I said.

"Oh, yeah," Harry Skena hadn't lost his Pittsburgh accent yet. "I'm always glad to get back. Unfortunately they don't rotate us very often." We walked along the long gallery, looking out over the parklike malls and terraces below. Many people seemed to be out just enjoying the day.

"Is this all a hospital?" I asked.

Ariadne made a strange face. I realized the word "hospital" had not passed through the automatic processor, or had been left alone, so that it came out in English. It had somehow felt funny in my mouth, after some hours of speaking—what did they say? Attic?

The little gadget embedded in my skull explained that there was no such word in Attic.

Harry Skena shook his head. "We don't exactly have hospitals." I could hear the gadget in my ear hesitate before deciding not to translate; it was a pretty smart little box but didn't have much of a memory. "Since medicine is all done by nanos and robots, we just have spare rooms here and there in every city. If you get sick or hurt, they put you in the nearest room available—usually a private home."

"How do people feel about having strangers in their houses?"

"For us, having a guest is an honor. Not to mention we get a large tax break for it, since most of us feel it's an absolute duty to take good care of one's guests, and the state has no right to tax money you need for such a sacred purpose." Skena was explaining it very slowly, really, as if to a small kid, and then I realized this was something so basic that if I was to get around at all in this culture, I would have to know it. "Those who can't afford or don't want a guest room pay a tax that goes to cover medical equipment."

"So whose guest was I? And is some form of thanks due to the host?"

"You were ATN's guest," Harry explained. "The people we work for. ATN stands for Allied Timelines for Nondeterminism . . . and that will get a lot clearer over lunch."

Just as he said "lunch," we came around the bend to a place where the gallery widened into something that looked like a street-corner café. "And here *is* lunch," Skena said. "To give you advance warning, our custom is that there's one dinner served at any given place, and you eat what that is. So if you don't like lamb, speak up, because that's what there is today."

"Suits me fine," I said, and we sat.

We started out with a mixture of fruit and vegetables that didn't taste very much like anything else I'd ever had; the thin syrup poured over it wasn't exactly salad dressing but wasn't exactly not salad dressing either. I was all set to find out what was actually happening, but Ariadne said the place was secure and we could stay as long as we wanted, and that I might as well enjoy the meal before we got down to business.

I still had not exactly figured out just which of them was the other's boss; maybe they were both colleagues?

The not-exactly-a-salad was followed by plain boiled noodles in butter; copying my hosts, I didn't eat much of them. It seemed to be some kind of ritual. Then the roast lamb came out, and it was pretty much like spicy roast lamb anywhere—that got my undivided attention. At first I figured I was just hungry after missing some meals, but Skena mentioned that the nanos got power directly from blood sugar, so I had a lot of replacing to do anyway.

That was followed by some more plain boiled noodles with butter, and a little dish of honey and vanilla; following their leads, I sprinkled that on my noodles, too, and ate more of them this time.

As I ate, I found myself deciding I was going to have to believe in pretty nearly everything they told me, at least at first; it was clear we were in some culture I'd never heard of, from a dozen things. The seasonings on the food were peculiar but consistently peculiar, the way you'd expect; dinner was eaten with spoons, chopsticks, and a little set of tongs; that odd little bit with the noodles, too, was the kind of thing that a society develops naturally without thinking.

When we'd eaten, I finally swallowed hard and said, "So . . . um, from what I understand of what you said yesterday before I went to sleep—I would guess that this must be a society descended from Periklean Athens?"

They glanced at each other, and Skena said, "Well, I told you the data we had indicated he was sharp."

"Sort of," she said, answering my question. "Perikles existed in our timeline, but there were a couple of important figures who actually took over from him in . . . er—"

"What you'd call the 430s B.C.," Skena finished for her. "Look,

in your timeline, who won the Peloponnesian War, and how long
did it last?"

Anybody in any branch of history at least knows that. "Sparta.
And it lasted about thirty years."

"Well, in this timeline Athens won, very early in the war, and all
but bloodlessly. And then a couple of people you didn't have in
your timeline—Thukydides the Younger and Kleophrastes were
the important ones—created a new Athenian Empire, with a very
generous citizenship policy, structured as a sort of federation. That
federation went on to win control of the Mediterranean, and then
to conquer Asia east to Burma, all of Europe to the Urals, and all of
Africa. A couple of thousand years later, they fought a long war
with China over control of the New World—and at the end of that,
Athens ruled the Earth, which meant one generation later, everyone was Athenian."

"Everyone male was Athenian," Ariadne corrected him.

Skena blushed a little; I realized this society was obviously just
about where mine was in terms of equality of women—not terrible
but not yet perfect. At least it was something that I would be able to
relate to.

"And you found a way to visit other timelines?" I asked.

They both made a funny chopping motion with their hands;
then Skena laughed, and said, "Uh, that's the same thing as shaking our heads. No, definitely not. What happened is that about a
hundred years ago—in fact, just when there was a lot of discussion
of ending the five years required military service for everyone, on
grounds that we hadn't actually had anyone to fight in centuries—
we were hit with a Closer invasion. It was a very near thing, but we
beat it back by the skin of our teeth—"

"The first timeline ever to do that—" Ariadne added, and there
was so much pride in her voice I swallowed my questions for a
moment.

"And we got their technology for crossing timelines. So ever
since, we've been locked in a war between the Closer timelines and
ourselves, and our many allies, of course."

"Uh, this is still a bit fast for me," I said. "The Closers are . . .
I don't know, a bunch of antinudists?"

Harry Skena laughed, and Ariadne Lao scratched at her ear
where the translator must be. "The gadgets don't deal well with
puns," he said. "No, Closers, like 'one who closes.' That's not what

they call themselves. They call themselves Masters. We call them Closers because they close off all but one possibility for every time-line—you could call them very aggressive imperialists; what they try to establish in every timeline is totalitarian rule. Then one small family of Closers moves in and rules the Earth, or the solar system, or sometimes even the solar system plus some of the nearer stars, as the hereditary top of the hierarchy. As near as I can tell every Closer we ever deal with is the slave of some other Closer; presumably somewhere back in their home timeline there's just one Closer that owns everyone."

"And, uh, your side—you said ATN—"

"It's a translated expression—the abbreviation for Allied Time-lines for Nondeterminism. We're everybody that is trying to fight off the Closers, ganged up for mutual defense. We have members of all sorts—there's a couple in which humans never left the Stone Age, there's one that has starships. The only general principle is that we want to go our own way in our own timelines—though we don't have many slave societies, or global police states. Those tend to join up with the other side."

"I see. So, uh . . . what were you doing back in my timeline?"

"Oh, strangely enough, just what I said I was doing. Investigating Blade of the Most Merciful."

"Investigating them for what? Are they going to be more important in the future of my timeline?"

"Not if we can help it," Skena said, and his voice was grim. "They're a Closer front. Part of their usual strategy. They destroy all the alternatives between police state and anarchy—because most people will pick the police state—and then take over the police state. They get you to destroy your own freedom and then they just knock over the local masters and take over the operation them-selves."

I nodded slowly. "So what were you supposed to do to them?"

Skena shrugged. "Timelines are sticky. They tend to fall back into each other one way or another. If you shoot somebody in one, the world where he exists and the world where he doesn't will tend to drift back together and merge. That's part of why there's so much contradictory data in history, you know. You said you were in art history at Yale—"

"I didn't," I said. "But obviously you knew it anyway. So you had looked up things about me before coming to my office? What are you up to?"

Ariadne seemed to be fighting down a smile. "I do believe you said he was sharp."

Skena seemed to have the beginnings of a blush forming, but then he shrugged and said, "Well, it's like this, then. You were on my list of people to look up eventually, and I'd been keeping a tab or two on you for some years. Then when it turned out that your family was targeted by Blade . . . well, it was the kind of thing that sometimes falls into place."

"How did I get on your list?"

He shrugged. "In timelines who join the Alliance, sometimes we find records of our agents. You've turned up in several. That means we must have recruited you at one time or another, or that you got involved in this. Always assuming that you are the Mark Strang—it's always possible that some other version of yourself is the one who ends up working for us."

"So if you offer me a job—"

"Well, that's just it," Skena said. "I was playing a hunch when I came to your office. I had just gotten a threatening visit from Blade of the Most Merciful. I decided I had better run for it while the running was good. And since you were on my list for eventual investigation and contact, and you work as a bodyguard—"

"I see." I took a sip of their strangely flavored coffee and decided that I might just get to like it. "Am I the only person in my timeline you're tracking?"

"Oh, no," he said. "There are eight others. Six of them were with Blade of the Most Merciful—they're the ones I think are ringers from another timeline—and the other's in Pittsburgh, but you wouldn't have any reason to know her, at least not yet."

"All right, and what happened after we got rescued?"

Ariadne Lao smiled, and that's very impressive and pleasant. "Well, Mr. Strang, it so happens that we were able to fix things up pretty well. Your vehicle was repaired while you were asleep, and I've taken the liberty of returning it to its locked parking space—a few seconds after you left it. I moved the damaged delivery vehicle down to where yours had been, so now the witnesses will be in hopeless contradiction . . . moreover, when you're feeling ready for it, I'm going to have you visit the police station on some small matter of business at just the right time to give yourself a complete set of alibis."

I thought about that for a bit and shuddered. "So I'm going to be within a few miles of myself . . ."

She looked very sympathetic. "It takes getting used to. Yes."

"And—er, about my being an agent for you—"

"Well, that's the odd part," Skena said. "We aren't supposed to recruit agents from a timeline until at least the leadership knows about us . . . and you don't even have a unified leadership, you know. So clearly you're supposed to come to us irregularly . . ."

"Can't you just *look?*" I asked.

They explained a lot more to me that day; in later years I was to realize just how much I hated briefings, which are never brief. They couldn't just look because timelines are braided and twisted through the past, and different ones are close to different others at different times. And although it's cheap to jump crosstime, it's terribly expensive to jump back in time along one of those lines. So to find a critical incident would require an agent leaping back to about when it should have happened, staying in the field long enough to find out if it had yet or not, and if it hadn't, jumping forward till it had . . . and then once the incident was finally found (kind of like running down a runner between bases), observing it. By that point, apparently, they'd have expended enough juice, or whatever it is that time machines run on, to power a small planet for several days.

What Harry Skena was doing was nudging our timeline toward the ATN path. That meant in general he was working for personal freedom and against dictatorships, but other than that he had very little in the way of a program; mostly he just tracked the people he was supposed to track and kept an eye on things. I got a distinct feeling our timeline was a backwater, but Ariadne said no, several important timelines were descended from it, and if it had really been a backwater, they wouldn't have had an agent on station.

That was Skena's title, Special Agent. A Special Agent was "our man in that timeline" and in charge of either keeping it headed for the ATN or turning it that way. "I had an assignment when I was younger in a timeline that was headed the Closer way," he said. "One where Stalin got the nuclear bomb way ahead of everyone else, and then lived clear till 1975. The Closers hadn't found that timeline yet . . . and the job was to get it loosened up before they

found it. Scary job, and I had to do a lot of things I'm not very
proud of. That's why I got sent to your timeline—because it was an
important one, headed our way, that the Closers didn't know
about."

"But they do," I said. "Didn't you say Blade—"

"Oh, yeah," Skena said. "They do now. And worse than that,
they're better equipped than we are in that time—because they've
got a crosstime gate installed in a world they control. That's why
they can hide so effectively and have so many resources—because
their bases are in a world where Hitler won World War II. At least a
lot of their gear looks like souped-up descendants of German
stuff . . ."

"Can't you do anything about it?"

"All kinds of things, if we could find the timeline they're coming out of," Harry said.

"You just said it was the one where Hitler won World War II."

Ariadne coughed. "It takes some getting used to, Mr. Strang.
There are just over eight hundred timelines in which Hitler won."

I whistled. "That seems like a lot."

"It's not, relatively speaking. There are about eighty thousand
in which he lost. And then there are just over a million where he
never existed or never amounted to anything."

I thought about that for a little bit . . . and then for a little bit
more. It seemed like a huge number . . . that was all I seemed to
be able to think about. "And that's how many timelines there are?"

"That's how many we know about. The Closers probably know
about more, since they've been at it longer. They don't talk to us,
exactly, they just send people over to demand that we surrender."

"I'm familiar with the style," I said.

"Our best guess is there might be around a billion timelines
with human beings in them. And then of course there's all the
lifeless ones, all the ones with no intelligent life, all the ones with
alternate intelligent life . . . but it's the ones near you that are
easiest to find, and so we've only made a couple of sampling probes
and small expeditions. Despite the comforts of this place, Mr.
Strang, we *are* at war. The first attack of the Closers leveled the
Acropolis; one way you can spot our agents in any timeline, I'm
afraid, is we always find an excuse to go see the Parthenon."

"Ours is damaged," I said, I guess to have something to say, but Harry Skena sighed and nodded significantly. "I've still been there four times," he said.

Ariadne made a face. "Wretched security practice. I would bet that the Closers set up somebody to watch the Acropolis within half an hour of arriving in a new timeline."

"Have you ever gotten to see it?" I asked.

"No, and I'd crawl through fire to. But seeing the Acropolis is not likely to come up—unless the next time Citizen Skena gets into trouble he has the good taste to do it in Greece somewhere."

I looked back and forth between them. "Uh, I'd figured you must be his supervisor?"

Harry Skena shook his head. "She's my Den Mother."

She looked as puzzled as I felt, so I figured the translator had not picked that one up either.

"I'm a Crux Op," she said. "Crux Operations Recovery Specialist. A 'crux' is one of those places where events are being manipulated to form a new timeline; manipulating the events is called 'special operations.' Every so often we stop getting messages from a Special Agent like Citizen Skena, or we get a distress call like the one he sent us. We know our agents well enough to know they don't cry wolf—so if we get such a call, a Crux Op jumps in to get the agent out, and if possible to make sure the original mission gets accomplished."

"Search and Rescue," I said.

"Exactly. Now, as far as I can tell, I've straightened it out; while you were asleep I raided every Blade HQ Citizen Skena had identified, and staged a bunch of very nice massacres if I do say so myself—leaving evidence pointing to other Blade groups. Your FBI and CIA, at the least, will be all over them during the few weeks after you return—they'll think an internal war broke out in the outfit. So if I return you and Citizen Skena, I'm probably done—unless I've missed a loose end somewhere."

"I don't think you have," Skena said. "And as much as you've stirred them up, maybe there's a better chance now of finding their crosstime gate. Especially since I've now got a much better native guide." He looked at me significantly. "Could you stand to have a secret client for a few months, one who pays you a lot, in cash?"

"With a big risk of getting killed," Ariadne Lao pointed out.

"And a good shot at Blade of the Most Merciful? Maybe even tracking them back to where they came from?" I grinned at them.

"Not to mention my ankle feels better than it has in years. Oh, yeah, I'm in. Just try to keep me out."

From the way they laughed—and the glint I saw in both their eyes—I knew I had finally found my own kind of people.

·6·

It didn't take long for me to get reequipped; they'd cleaned and pressed my clothes and in fact repaired some spots that I'd been careless about. I suspected nanos had had a hand in that, and knew it for sure when I noticed that all the bills in my wallet had become crisp and new.

Going back wasn't quite so dramatic; I knew what was happening. It got dark, and quiet, and then gray, and then sound and sight came back. Harry Skena and I were standing by Panther Hollow Lake, a scum-covered pond in Schenley Park that hardly anyone goes to, especially in the middle of a warm day. We had half an hour to go establish my alibi. Right now I was opening my second beer in the tub . . . but that was a week ago to me.

Time travel won't be popular till it's reasonably easy to find your way around, I decided.

Skena was just going to lay low in some hideout or other for a few hours, someplace where he knew Blade wouldn't find him; if he just didn't poke his head up where they saw it until tomorrow, things should be fine—they'd be on the run, not him.

I had a perfectly great excuse to go down to the police station—I had to swear out a complaint against Brunreich, as I explained to Skena.

He got a very strange expression. "Brunreich."

"Yeah, Roland Brunreich."

"You were guarding—"

"His wife Angelica Brunreich. And their daughter Porter. If you get an offer of a double date, pick Angela for sex and Porter for conversation."

"I'll bear that in mind." He grinned at me. "By the way, now that we're in this timeline, I would consider it normal for you to call me Harry—I noticed you were having to remember to address us as 'Citizen.' "

"Just not used to it. And you know how we Americans are. Every damned receptionist and car rental guy and mechanic addresses you by your first name. So I didn't want to give offense—"

"Not wanting to give offense is one of the more charming characteristics your people have," Skena said, "along with apologizing for what in fact is generally fairly polite behavior and a lot of willingness to learn other people's customs. You should see what the Frenchmen are like in the timelines where Napoleon's heirs went on to rule the world."

I had the odd thought, climbing up the path to the bridge that would take me out of the park, that he'd made me just a bit proud to be an American. It seemed only fair; he was certainly proud to be Athenian . . .

Visited the Acropolis four times. And just glowed when I mentioned it.

It was the same nice spring day it had been, but now I was rested and my hand was healed. It occurred to me that I wasn't going to have much of a civil case for medical expenses, but I didn't let that bother me much.

I figured I'd just walk across the Pitt campus and catch a bus downtown. The area right around the library and the Cathedral of Learning is sort of nice, except they tore down Forbes Field, where the Pirates belong, and the last place in which Babe Ruth ever played professional ball, to build a butt-ugly classroom building that looks like something Albert Speer rejected for one of his Nazi-era city centers. I always take a moment to spit on it as I go by.

Another thought that occurred to me, crossing the street, was that there were a lot of short skirts and bare midriffs around. Either I needed to give Melissa a call, or . . . well, hell, who would I ask?

"Mark! Hey, Mark!" It was Robbie—she's in some kind of part-time program at Pitt, one that seems set up so that you can get your law degree just before you die.

"Hi! How are you doing?" Aside from the fact that she's a friend, and I'm always glad to see her, there was also the strength to be added to the alibi.

"I didn't expect to see you awake quite this early. How's your hand? Did you have a doctor look at it? I know it's too much to hope that you'd have a natural healer look into it—"

"Whoa. Yeah, the doctor checked it out, and it's fine—here, look, see? Moves in every direction it's supposed to. Good as new. So I don't need anybody to wave a feather rattle over it—"

"You're incorrigible. Got time for coffee or something?"

"Well, unfortunately, I'm supposed to be heading downtown to swear out the complaint against Brunreich. Assault, battery, being a weenie . . ."

"At least twenty counts of being a weenie. I can give you a ride if you like—"

"Deal."

Her van was parked nearby, and traffic was fairly light with rush hour not yet started. Mostly we talked about old jobs, scrapes we'd been through together, that sort of thing.

In five years there can get to be a lot to talk about, especially because old friends have a way of sharing stuff. "You know," she mentioned, "there are some detective agencies that won't hire us because me and Paula are, um, together?"

"Their loss," I said. "Are you not getting enough business?"

"It's tight. Real tight."

"I've got a new heavy client that just came aboard this afternoon," I said, "and I can throw you some business I'm sure. Maybe not before next week. And I'll pay you as soon as the Brunreich check clears."

"That's what I was hinting around about," she said, smiling a little. "Stupid business, eh, boss-man, where we have to get paid in cash and all? Takes the fun out of being a paladin."

I grinned back at her. "You see yourself as a paladin? When there really were knights-errant and all that, you'd have been flat on your back under some fat drunken lord, getting pumped full of babies."

"Boss-man talks nasty. Kids would be okay. I'd just have to talk His Obesity into taking off on a crusade . . . and staff the castle with some buxom serving wenches. So what about you? I know either of us could get a better job than this; hell, you could be Professor Strang someplace in no time. Why do you stick with a moron job?"

"It's not a moron job," I said, a little defensively. "It's just not a book-smart kind of job. And you know how I—"

"I know how you got in. I've heard Hal Payton tell that story many times. But why the hell do you stay in? I mean, for your own good, Mark, this is a business where you mostly get bashed up when you aren't being bored."

I shrugged and told her the truth. "Well, in the first place, I like to beat people up. But in the second place, the client I'm going to be covering is . . . um, well, dealing with outside terrorists coming into the USA, let's say. I don't think he'd want me to tell you his business. But suffice it to say what I'm going to be beating up, or shooting, is people a lot like the ones who killed my family. So for this job, anyway, I know exactly why I'm doing it. Okay?"

Robbie made the turn by the back of the City County Building and said, "Well, sorry if Aunt Robbie has been tough on you. And it sounds like your new client is going to be interesting."

Inside it was the usual routine; fill out forms, talk with cops, get papers in order. Norman, my lawyer, has a "kit" for all this that I use—sort of a checklist to make sure I'm giving the prosecutor enough to work with in the unlikely event it ever comes to trial. The purpose of pressing charges isn't usually to put these guys in jail—most of the people clients are afraid of are their "loved ones," and they don't want them imprisoned—it's to have a bargaining chip so they can't sue *me*, and in the case of a few very dangerous aggressors, to give the prosecutor something to crack them open with, make them confess to the more serious crimes that would otherwise be merely their word against the client's.

About an hour into the process, I felt a hand on my shoulder, and a voice behind me said, "I think I've got bad news for you."

I turned around and found myself facing Lieutenant DeJohn Johnston, a guy who looks more like an all-pro linebacker than anything else. I should say I was facing his chest.

DeJohn's an old friend, so I looked up to make sure this wasn't a joke, and saw right away it wasn't—he was making the kind of "sorry to tell you about this" face that meant bad news.

My first thought was that Blade was on the loose again, and

"You got it. Say, did your client get through the Seattle airport okay this morning? That is where they were headed, isn't it?"

"Yeah—what do you mean, get through okay—"

"Well, you put 'em on the plane early in the morning, and it's about a six-hour flight, so I was just thinking that when the hostage situation developed there it must have been about when your client was landing."

"*Hostage situation?!* I haven't had the radio on all day. When was this—"

"Middle of this afternoon—still morning their time," DeJohn said. His face got sort of soft and concerned, and I realized I must look pretty bad.

"Who's doing it?"

He blew out his breath like a man who has just realized he has to do something tough. "Ah, shit. Mark, buddy, I really shouldn't have mentioned it. It's the old enemy, Blade of the Most Merciful. Looks like they're back, and some kind of gang warfare seems to have erupted around them—they've been running the crime in the Islamic communities in a dozen cities around here. In fact a CMU prof was working on documenting that, and now he's disappeared, guy name of Harry Skena, and—"

"Damn, damn, damn," I said, more to shut him up so I could get away than anything else. "Skena was supposed to be my client starting tomorrow! He's turned up missing?"

"Didn't show up for class, and the dean's office at Pitt got a call—"

I knew Harry was okay, of course—this was leftover information from earlier—but it was a good way to get DeJohn out of the way while I ran to see what was up about Seattle. I didn't exactly know what powers an ATN Special Agent had, but maybe he was kind of like a US Marshal in the Old West, or a freelance superhero, and if I could get him to hit Blade I wanted to watch him do it. I hadn't forgotten how effective that little silvery gadget Ariadne had used to waste a dozen Bladers had been.

"We had a private hideout for something like this—sorry but I'll have to grab a cab and go there. I'll call you if he's okay, all right, DeJohn? And save a few strikes for me."

"Will do, buddy, and 'preciate it."

He went back toward his desk, the bag of McDonald's lunch still under his arm, and I bolted out the door and down the steps.

they'd attacked Dad or Carrie—I have nightmares about then ting Sis at home alone, Payton's guards drawn off or knocked with her trapped in her wheelchair and with just the little 9 mm keeps strapped beside her to fight back with.

DeJohn said, "I think your car has been stolen and used in major felony. At least the garage where you park it is where ther was some kind of shoot-out, and we have a description from a Mrs. Goldfarb and her four children that matches your Mercedes, so—"

I wanted to laugh with relief, not to mention the thought that Mrs. Goldfarb was going to look pretty stupid when they found the Mercedes where it belonged and a Berto's pizza wagon shot up in its place. But I still had adrenaline pumping from when I had thought it was my family, so I was able to let my jaw drop, and say, "Somebody stole a car out of the locked area? And a big obvious red 510SL, instead of something that would blend into traffic?"

"Unhhunh. Sounds like. I'm real sorry to tell you about it, buddy."

"Shit." I did my best to look disgusted.

"I'll drop an unofficial request to the squad car at the scene so that they'll check it out, but it sure sounds like yours. Wish I had better news for you . . . you going to make the softball game this year?"

It's a standing joke; every spring there's an "ops versus cops" game at South Park, a bunch of private investigators and body-guards from around town playing ball with a bunch of policemen. It has to be one of the greatest places ever developed for picking up rumors.

"If I'm in town, you know I won't miss it."

"Well, try not to hit so many straight into the ground by third base this year. My arm gets tired."

I did a big mock wince; it was true, unfortunately, that some-thing about my not-quite-healed right ankle had always made me hit just a little funny, right toward DeJohn. Of course he's tall enough to play third and second at the same time . . .

"Oh, I'm in better shape these days. Might surprise you. Any-way, I have to run—meeting a client soon—but thanks for letting me know about the car. I'll call the garage in an hour or so and see if they can tell me anything. If they can't, I imagine I'll need your help again."

I was just dashing out to look for a cab—in Pittsburgh hailing a cab is nearly impossible, but I didn't want to run all the way to the next cab stand—when a hand caught my elbow. "You heard the news from Seattle?"

It was Skena. "Yeah, I heard," I said.

"Come on with me," Skena said. "I've already notified base, and we will be expected there—they'll have weapon packs for both of us. We just need to get down to my van in the garage, here."

We got on the elevator, and it dropped quickly. "I might have a former client on the site."

Skena grunted. "Of course you do. That's why I was so surprised earlier. She's the one I thought you couldn't possibly know, that I'm keeping an eye on in this timeline."

"Mrs. Brunreich?"

"The daughter, Porter."

I gaped at him. "She's just a ten-year-old kid—"

"Yeah? Well in more than fifty timelines descended from this one, she gets a *lot* more important, pal. So far we don't think any of those timelines have been found by the Closers, but maybe one has, or one in which she's important has, whether we know about it or not. Doesn't matter much; the point is, it's quite possible their whole reason for coming here, aside from capturing this timeline, was to find her and kill her." The elevator door opened and Skena ran through, pretty fast for such a big guy.

He unlocked the back of his van, and, just as he opened the door, a window shattered. I turned, saw the man with the pistol, and had my .45 out instantly, giving him a couple of rounds to pin him down.

"Inside!" Skena shouted. I wasn't sure why it was urgent, but I could tell it was, so I jumped in—

It got dark, and silent, then gray, then vision returned, then sound returned. I was getting used to this.

We were standing in a little white room with two of those silvery "super squirt guns" on holster belts lying on a table. He put one on and handed me the other. "Sorry to rush, but we're in real time, Mark. It's only the big machines up at ATN that can go forward and backward. These little gadgets just take us short distances crosstime. But it's still the fastest way to SeaTac."

"Well, if we're in real time, then let's go," I said, buckling mine on. "How do I use this gadget?"

"It's called a SHAKK. Seeking Hypersonic Ammunition Kinetic Kill. Point it and squeeze the trigger. It hits whatever is in its sights at the time you pull the trigger, out to about six miles, so be sure you aim—hip shots are a real bad idea. Don't lead anything—it homes in on what it's pointed at, and anyway at Mach 10, you don't need much of a lead. You have two thousand rounds in the magazine. Move the switch back, here, for semiauto. Middle position is six-round bursts that hit in a hex pattern about a meter on a side. Far position is full auto, about 400 rpm, and you'd use it against a whole army—won't need it this time. Better stick to semiauto. Got that?"

"How much recoil?"

"Zip. Ammo is self-propelling, like a rocket. Any other questions?"

"Nope. Let's go grease some Bladers."

He grinned at me. "Knew I could count on you for a fun time. All right, god knows what we're going to find. I'm bouncing us right into one of the airline frequent flyer clubs, which with a little luck won't have anyone in it at the time. Use your common sense. Radio traffic that the artificial intelligence is analyzing says there's no good guys inside—just the hostages, us, and Blade. Remember the goal is wipe out the Bladers, then get back out—soon as we've got 'em all we've got to run back to the club. I don't want to have to shoot my way through your local police just to avoid having to explain these gadgets."

"With you all the way," I said. I made sure my SHAKK was set for semiauto, and Skena said, "Delivery system, attention, activate please destination specified *now*."

When he said "now" it got dark, silent, gray—

Luck was not with us, or maybe it was. We popped into the clubroom that Blade of the Most Merciful was obviously using as a headquarters. There were about ten of them standing around, and when something went poof in their midst, being the sort of guys they were, they were pointing guns before they knew what it was.

Moreover, at that HQ level, figure a few of them had seen Closers pop in and out, and had a good idea what was going on. The only thing that saved us, I think, was that they didn't know the Closers had enemies with the same technology.

I saw nothing but men with guns in front of me, so I brought my SHAKK to bear, squeezed the trigger, popped it from man to man doing that. They were grabbing for their guns, but I'd gotten most of them before one of them did get an AK swung around—

There was a deep whirring noise beside me and the rest of the enemy fell over. "Wha—?"

"Never say never. I used full auto. Your authorities are really going to wonder about all the little holes in the walls, but the ammo has already self-destructed in there. Let's go."

When we came out the door, there was a Blade guy coming in the other way. I popped him, and that was the first time I had time to see what the SHAKK actually did. A long time later it was explained to me that when you point a SHAKK at a human being, the round not only homes in on him, it finds his head and then, after penetrating his brain pan, "slows down" by spiraling through his head. Since it starts out at Mach 10, by the time it comes to a stop it's pretty much converted the head to puree.

What I saw was that I squeezed the trigger and his head bulged for an instant, there was a sort of pink spray from his ears, nose, and mouth, and then his head fell inward like a deflating water balloon, which in a sense was what it was. I took a moment to heave, but I ran after Skena all the same; next time I wouldn't be freaked out, but this first one was a surprise.

We were suddenly out in the common area, and the Blade guys were everywhere, standing with their AK's over the hundred or so hostages lying prone on the floor. They'd tied their hands and made them lie down close together so that when the time came to kill them they need only spray the floor with full auto, and I found out later that when we burst in on them, the hostages had been in that position, with no bathroom breaks, for seven hours. Quite a few of them had ended up pissing themselves, and one diabetic had gone into a coma and quietly died during that time . . . but I don't suppose any of that bothered Blade of the Most Merciful.

Skena belly-flopped onto the hard concourse floor, and I followed his lead, flipping my own SHAKK to full auto. From the angle I was at, anything live and standing was a Blader, so I swung the SHAKK back and forth twice, holding the trigger down. It made that deep bass whoosh that I realized must be the sonic booms of its tiny ammunition. (Later, again, I learned a SHAKK round was about a third the volume of a BB shot and almost entirely propulsion and guidance system. It was the sheer energy of impact that did all the damage with those things.)

Skena had been spraying, too. As soon as we'd hit every target we could see, we leaped up again. A shot rang off a pillar, giving away the Blader just coming out of the men's room—a lesson in taking the time to aim. I sent a shot after him, and it nailed him as he turned to run.

Skena pointed his SHAKK at a hand slowly reaching up over a sofa and fired a shot at the hand (a little crack! noise like popcorn popping hard); an instant later we saw the pink spray from behind the couch. "Neat gadget, hunh?" he whispered to me.

I didn't answer—I'd seen a flicker of movement near the women's room, and I was running toward it while I tried to think what it might be. Maybe just a female Blader deciding to hide in the toilet—

I charged in anyway. As I rounded the corner a shot bounced off the tile beside me, spraying me with the fine gravel of the wall, and the boom of the pistol echoed through the bathroom. I dove in in a headfirst slide, the SHAKK in front of me, had just an instant to see three men and Porter, pointed at the first man and squeezed the trigger—

The second man leveled a pistol at me, the third jammed his gun into Porter's neck, lifting her head, and as time slowed down I saw his finger start to move down onto the trigger.

I was already squeezing the trigger on the SHAKK, and I brought it to bear on the gun thrust into Porter's throat. There was no time to think of aiming, I just hoped I was pointed right—or did I even have time to think that? Remembering it now, anyway, I always hope it was pointed right—

It was. The SHAKK round recognized explosives at the bottom of metal tubes as dangerous, so first it looped around, smashing the inside of the barrel into a thick mess of metal fragments, blocking it, then it smashed the bullet backward. The gun blew through at the hammer end. I imagine it would have hurt like hell, since it tore most of his hand into pieces and sprayed them up his sleeve, but I was squeezing off my second round, and this one went right into him; his head did the inflate/deflate routine.

A round had screamed off the floor in my face, and I brought the SHAKK around, got it pointed at the surviving Blader's foot, squeezed the trigger, and made his head do that funny pulse, too.

Then it was quiet with a ring. I was about three-quarters deaf from the effect of all those shots in a bathroom, and so it took me a moment to realize I was hearing something besides the high-pitched scream of my own tortured ears.

It was Porter, and she was starting to sob. I stepped forward and scooped her up into my arms—

"Mr. Strang?"

"Yeah, kid, it's me. Never mind how I happen to be here. And listen, you've got to *not* tell anyone it was me, you got that?"

She pulled back and nodded solemnly. "Are you—you must be working for some very important organization or something. Like the CIA or something?"

"Like that, yeah."

"That gun is some kind of special equipment, isn't it?"

"You bet," I said. "Just trust me, I'm working for the good guys, okay? Where's your mother?"

Porter's face folded up like it was being sucked inward, and I knew before she gasped it out. "They, they, they . . . they said they were going to show us what they'd do and they . . . they said they'd show us . . . they—"

"Oh, Porter." I held her tight; I knew, god I knew, from the way I'd lost Mom and Jerry and Marie to the same bunch, but what consolation could that be to her?

Later when I got the full story, it was what I would have expected if I'd been thinking at all. They "decided" to kill someone right off to "let the other hostages know they were serious." (Of course it was really what they were there to do right along.) They announced they were going to kill Porter Brunreich, who they pretended was just a random name from a passenger manifest. So Harry Skena had their number right.

But they hadn't bet on Angelica Brunreich. She might have been crazy as hell, and sometimes she was pretty unpleasant, but she was more of a hero than I'll ever be; she switched tickets with her daughter and volunteered herself to spare everyone else's life. Poor Porter had been so stunned she had no idea what was happening until it was too late—a big Blader just grabbed her mother by the hair, slapped her, shouted "open your mouth," and when she did, jammed a short pistol on full auto between her jaws, hard enough to break her front teeth, deep enough to gag her, and pulled the trigger, emptying the clip.

She probably died too fast to feel much pain. That's what I've always told Porter since.

They forced a couple of people to clean up the hideous mess;
Porter sat and watched them drag her mother's bloody body away.
Then, somehow, she thought after they got a phone call of some
kind, all of a sudden they had figured out that perhaps they hadn't
executed who they had meant to. It gave their game away, of
course, to admit that "Porter Brunreich" wasn't a random name
but in fact their real target—but by then they must have been desperate, for the FBI was within an hour of storming the place (a
process that was to scare the living daylights out of most of the
hostages, who were still lying tied on the floor, unable to get up).

So they had just grabbed all the kids between about eight and
twelve—clearly they had some idea of what age person they were
looking for—and started interrogating them. "Porter" could be a
name for either sex, and anyway most kids carry no ID, so it took
them a while.

They had just grabbed Porter and figured out that the ticket
they had seen her trying to throw away must be her mother's.
Blade of the Most Merciful were about to execute her when they
heard Harry Skena and me making our fast, rude entrance and
decided that she might be more useful to them alive, as a hostage;
they had just reached that decision when I burst in.

She couldn't tell me any of that—I learned all of it later. All she
could do at the time was sob into my shoulder, and all I could do
was hold her. I wanted to tell her it was okay, it was going to be all
right, but I remembered my own experience. It wasn't okay, and it
was never going to be all right again.

"I'll take care of you," I whispered. "I promise. I'll make sure
you're taken care of." It was all I could think of.

As I carried her out of that blood-spattered public toilet, Harry
Skena came in. "All secured, and—oh, god, then you know."

"Yeah," I said. "What can we do—?"

"I've got someone coming over from HQ, one timeline over, to
take care of things. She'll be all right—or as all right as you can be,
I guess—and we'll make sure she's taken care of. You and I have
something else we have to do right now. We've got a chance to get
at the Closers themselves if we rush."

I hesitated. Porter was hanging on to me like she'd never let go,
and I couldn't bear to pry the poor kid off me.

"She really will be well taken care of—my word of honor on
that," Harry Skena said, "and what we've got is a chance to shut

down the Closer bridge into your world. That means possibly years of peace before you have to fight them again—"

"Go do it," Porter whispered into my neck.

"Do what, honey?"

"Your friend says you can go beat the bad guys and make them go away for good, right?"

"Pretty much, yeah."

"So do whatever you have to do. If he's sending someone to take care of me, I'll be okay. But you *have* to shut down the bad guys. It's *important*."

She pushed away from me just a little and looked me in the eye. Her blue eyes were red-rimmed from crying, and there was a dribble of snot at the end of her nose, but I have never seen a more serious or dignified human being. "Go shut them down," she said. "Nobody will be safe until you do."

"Aw, Porter," I said, and gently set her down. "Now be good and do whatever the people Harry sends tell you to do, okay? And I'll do my best to get in touch just as soon as I can."

She nodded firmly, and said, "I'm old enough to behave myself, Mr. Strang. But please go do whatever you're supposed to do about that base. I won't stop being afraid till those people are wiped out."

"It's a deal, kid," I said, and kissed her on her forehead. I turned to Skena, and said, "Okay, Harry, let's go get them."

We went out via a bathroom; Porter was running down the hall, when last I saw her, to call the police outside and get people untied if she could. God only knew what they were going to think when they found all the Blade of the Most Merciful dead with exploded heads, and nobody in there but the hostages. Especially because I knew Porter was smart enough to dummy up and not tell them anything.

It would keep some guys in Langley, Virginia, busy for a good long while, I figured.

As we stepped into the bathroom I said, "So they'd take over the world here, under some kind of dictatorship, and then put Closers in at the top of the hierarchy? Is that what they're after?"

He shook his head. "Basically this is a timeline they'd strip-mine, Mark. You guys are 'unclean.'"

He had been fiddling with a gadget on his belt; he grunted with satisfaction. "All right, good, they'll pop us from here in two.

Stand close to me, in the center of the room. There we go. Now, to continue . . . Closers are nuke phobes. Their language is akin to Phoenician, and we think what they are is Carthaginians. Probably in their timeline Hannibal took Rome and won the Second Punic War, and then they went on to conquer all of Europe and the world. And our guess is they fought a lot of nuclear wars in the process; so the only place a Closer will settle is in a timeline where no nuclear bomb has ever gone off. In the ones where nukes have happened, trusted Closer slaves run things, and they basically steal everything nonorganic for export back to the Closer timelines. We think it's a superstition, that maybe they had nukes a long time before they had genetics and that as a result they have some kind of visceral terror of nukes that we don't understand."

I nodded. "You don't know much about them?"

"After a hundred years of war, no. We'd love to find their home timeline—it's a disaster that they know ours, but at least we have many allies they haven't found yet. There's no way we know of to track a time invasion back to its source—but it does give off a special kind of radio pulse that we can easily detect. That's how I know that a whole bunch of things just crossed over in the Bellevue area near here, and if we had a car, we'd just drive but—"

It got dark and silent. I was beginning to feel like I was riding an elevator or subway—if you can remember the first time, when you were a child, it was pretty scary, all sorts of fascinating things happened, but by the time you'd lost count of how many times you'd done it, you were barely aware of it at all. I found myself waiting slightly impatiently for the gray . . . which came, and then the sounds came. We were back in the white room.

"Better reload—this may be heavy duty," Harry said. "Push on this stud."

I did, following his example, and little drawers like the drawers on a coffee grinder slid out of the sides of both our weapons. He grabbed an open can from a sideboard—it was filled with a heavy gray powder—filled the drawer full, and shoved it closed. There was a "beep" noise from his SHAKK. I followed his example.

"Is this some kind of gunpowder—?" I asked, but then it got dark and silent, again. The question went right out of my mind.

I've been to Seattle a few times, and it's hard to find a less appealing area (unless you're a computer dork) than Bellevue. The buildings all look like movie sets from B-grade science-fiction flicks, except for the ones that look like concrete building blocks used by a giant child who just happened to be a complete idiot.

What we were facing, just off the freeway, from a drugstore parking lot, was an immense blue cube. It was all glass on the outside, with just the fine tracery of metal wires holding the glass in place. The blue was very deep, like ink in water. Harry Skena laughed bitterly. "Jeez, they must have worked to keep this one out of the news. This is absolutely typical Closer architecture. They build buildings like this wherever they go. They must really have had substantial plans for this world, though god knows what. With Closers you never quite know."

"What do we do now?" I asked, dubiously.

"We start by walking toward it," Skena said. "The instruments I've got here—passive radiation gadgets, so there's no signal they can detect, I hope—show it's pretty much hollow inside. Nothing that looks like gun emplacements. But notice something about this parking lot?"

I looked around, and then the thought hit me. I ran to check and then came back. "There's nothing in any of the cars. Any of them. They're all different ages like a real population of cars, but nobody has any old McDonald's wrappers, or a shirt hanging in the window, or anything like that."

Skena nodded. "Yep. And I bet what happens every night is a bunch of low-level flunkies from their base come out in ties and jackets, drive the cars away, take a bunch of different routes to some hidden garage someplace . . . and then all park and transport back to where they came from. And do it in reverse the next morning."

I grunted. "A pity we don't have enough time."

"For what?"

"Ever driven in Seattle? The idea that someone is putting thousands of extra cars into the traffic for no reason . . . well, if you let word of that get around town, there'd be an angry mob here in no time, and they'd burn the thing to the ground."

Skena laughed. "It's a charming image. But, no, I'm afraid it's just you and me, and we'll have to do it the old-fashioned way; right now it's clear they're . . ." he glanced down at his gadget on his belt, and then started to trot toward the building.

"What—" I asked, matching his strides.

"They're powering up their transmitter in a big way. And there are a lot of human bodies in there. Probably they're taking the remnants of Blade of the Most Merciful back to wherever they stored them before. If we hit 'em now, we can kill most of Blade, and some Closers, and maybe toss a couple of bombs through the portal when it opens."

He said that last as he broke into a dead run. Any doubts I might have had about the kind of facility it was were erased when three men with rifles ran out of the building and started to level them at us; I fired a one-second burst of auto at them, and they went over with shredded heads.

But I could see a steel door sliding down over the entryway—the place was turning into a fortress before our eyes—and under my feet I could feel the rumble and vibration of immense engines, or maybe the generators, powering up to move great masses across time.

"How do we get in?" I shouted at Skena, as we rushed on, now only a few dozen steps from the steel-shuttered entryway.

"The good old-fashioned way," he said, pulling up. "Set for bursts." I did, and as I looked up he was opening up on the door.

I followed suit. The little slugs did nothing fancy, but they carried a huge load of kinetic energy, and six of them in a hex pattern were hitting a space no bigger than an ordinary double window with each burst. Visible ripples formed in the steel, and the door shuddered under the impact. Then, as we pumped burst after burst into it, one of the ripples snapped and cracked, and a few more bursts made a hole more than big enough to get in through.

I ran on ahead, and then an idea hit me, and I sprayed a dozen bursts at the huge blue glass wall that towered around the gate. Windows shattered everywhere.

Harry Skena followed suit, and as he caught up with me—glass was still plunging to the pavement all around—he said, "Great idea, for diversion?"

"Naw. I'm an art scholar. I've just always wanted to do that to a modern building."

He laughed, and I liked the sound of it. It was great to have a friend to do these things with.

We charged on through the gap we'd blown in the steel door, past the deserted reception desk, and down a corridor. All around us we could hear alarms going off. Skena dropped a few little tennis ball–sized objects behind us—"PRAMIACs," he said, "set to go off whenever we're both out of the building or dead, whichever comes first."

I was going to ask what a PRAMIAC was, but there was no time; we were turning the bend, and suddenly we were in the heart of the building, on a high platform overlooking a huge room that stretched to the top of the building ten stories over our heads, and at least that far underground. At its center there was a black column, beginning to glow a faint blue.

"That's a full-fledged gate," Skena said. "They could bring an army through there."

Machine guns chattered on the other side, and we dove for the deck. I crawled over next to him, squeezing off SHAKK rounds toward the gunners—stray rounds were doing things like knocking down pieces of guardrail and fluorescent lights, unfortunately, because my angle was so bad I couldn't really aim straight at the gunner—

I concentrated and put one into the machine gun, which blew to pieces with a gratifying roar. Then I rolled over next to Harry, some question half-formed in my mind.

But I didn't get to ask it. He was gasping for air and blood was puddling under him; he'd taken a round in the chest, and you didn't have to be a doctor to know he'd be gone in seconds.

"Harry!"

"Take a PRAMIAC from the hall. Leave blue knob as it is. Turn red knob to position *eight*—no farther! Get it close to the base of the column."

"Red to eight, base of the column, got it—Harry, can I—"

But I couldn't do anything for him, at least not anything except what he'd just asked me. His chest had stopped heaving, the blood that ran from under him was no longer gushing, and in the long second before I tore my eyes away from his, his eyes filmed over just a bit as they started to dry out.

For the first time, I had lost a client. More than that, I had lost a friend. And though I didn't know what exactly I was doing, I had a feeling if I followed his instructions, I could probably avenge him.

·7·

I scooted backward, ran down the hall, grabbed a PRAMIAC from the floor, shot the door off where it was marked EXIT, and ran down the stairwell.

As I ran I noted that the PRAMIAC was marked with symbols I couldn't read. I stopped and stared at it, and then the little symbols swam before my eyes and I saw which one the eight was, by the red knob. How did I—

A familiar voice in my head said, "Remember, they didn't remove me. I am still here to translate as needed—if I know the language."

"Thanks," I said, to the empty air, then the building started to buzz and shake like it might just come apart even before the PRAMIACs went off—I figured they were bombs of some kind.

The bottom door was locked, too, so I set for burst and fired five, experimenting with rotating the SHAKK. Sure enough, the bursts at angles to each other cut through the steel and concrete like a Sawzall, and the door fell into pieces in front of me.

I charged through, ducking low and rolling; bullets rang randomly around. I was about eighty feet from the base of the column, which was now that strange shade of deep purple that a working black light turns, and there was a whole gang of Bladers rushing around the other side. I could hear someone yelling at them, probably to come back, to judge from the way a couple of the more alert-seeming whirled and headed back.

I set the SHAKK on auto and sprayed the room in front of me; the last Blade of the Most Merciful went down like tenpins. I love my old .45, and I've won a lot of contests with it, but in a real fight you want high-tech, I decided.

I ran right up to the column and placed the PRAMIAC directly against the glowing base, which gave me an odd tingle but didn't seem to be hot or electrically charged. Two more Bladers popped out—that column was a good forty feet in diameter, so it was plenty to hide behind—and I SHAKKed them without a thought—except the thought that clearly most of them were on the other side of the column.

Which meant if I ran around there—

I flung myself around the column; something made me not quite want to touch it, especially since it now towered twenty stories over my head, all with that fierce blue glow. A few feet and I saw that the other side seemed to be bathed in red light; I pulled the SHAKK around to ready, but the gunfire I expected didn't come, and as I ran on around the corner—

I shot the last two as they entered the red, glowing door of the column. Faintly, through the door, I could see shapes moving— Harry had called this a "gate," and I realized it must be exactly that, some kind of open doorway that they could move big groups of people through. And to judge from the scream of the machinery in the background, this was about the limit of what it could move.

But the main thought that ran through my head at that moment was pathetically simple—

Blade of the Most Merciful was getting away! They were about to leave our timeline forever—before I was done settling the score!

So I know perfectly well what I did next was bone stupid. If you tell me that, I won't even try to argue with you. What's more, I know perfectly well that I would do it again.

Vengeance will move a man to all kinds of things.

Having shot the last two in line, I dove through the gate in their place; I hoped to open up on the backs of the crowd as they entered whatever Closer base they were going to, and then either jump back, get shot to death, or—

Or what? I hadn't thought that far ahead. Jumping back or getting shot seemed like the only likely options.

I hit the deck in a *tsugari* roll and came up with my SHAKK ready, but everybody in front of me was bent over on the floor in a deep bow.

Then the most amazing pain I'd ever felt tore across my back. I looked up to see a man with a flexible little metallic whip that looked like nothing so much as a plumber's snake. When I stared he lashed me across the forehead and pointed to the crowd that was all bent over.

The corner of my watering eyes told me there were hundreds of guards with whips all around, and every one of them was also carrying a sidearm. I wouldn't get half a shot out before they gunned me down. But clearly they'd mistaken me for—

The whip lashed my cheek. Shit, I got the idea; I ran and joined the ranks of Blade of the Most Merciful, bent over on the floor, kneeling with our faces to the ground and our hands locked behind our butts.

Guards walked around lashing the men and kicking them. If I hadn't been scared to death that the same was going to happen to me, I'd have enjoyed the spectacle.

I noticed that the whips drew no blood; probably they acted on the nervous system directly somehow. After the man on one side of me was whipped until he began to gibber and scream and sob, and the man on the other side was abruptly turned over, his pants cut away, and the whip applied to his genitals and anus until he fainted, I decided it was having a real effect on my nervous system, too.

I don't mind admitting I was ready to piss my pants with fear, and I had no idea how I was going to get out of that one. It was abundantly clear that these guards did not speak English, or possibly any other language from my timeline, and my translator wasn't volunteering anything about the strange grunting barks they made at each other.

It was also clear that they were just indulging in petty sadism— there was no point to the beatings and humiliations they were administering, they were just doing them to show they could, but the men who were obviously their officers made no attempt to stop it. In fact, when the guards tortured the man beside me, one young officer came over and laughed at the screams. When they threw him, still half-naked, to the floor, unconscious, so hard that I thought they might well have fractured his skull, the officer cheerfully flipped him over on his back, opened his fly, and urinated on the unconscious man's face.

Then they whipped the man on the other side of him into licking it off. The poor bastard threw up, and they beat him unconscious, this time with their fists.

Meanwhile, behind me, I could hear work crews going in and out, and tons of stuff rolled by. I figured it was loot from our world, and wondered how many art heists were going to go unsolved forever . . .

That woke a spark of anger in me. I'd spent years of training to conserve humanity's heritage of culture, and here a bunch of barbarians with a sadistic child's idea of entertainment were carrying stuff off as trophies. I still couldn't work up any sympathy for Blade—they were only getting what they deserved, and it was almost worth the risk of getting the same to be here while it happened—but that didn't make me like these guards any better.

One Blader just ahead of me was being tormented by their touching him with turned-off whips; I could tell when they turned them on by the way he jumped. They played with him in a way crueler than I've ever seen any cat be to a mouse.

Finally, the Blader couldn't take it any longer, and jumped to his feet to run.

I don't exactly know what they used on him. The Closers, I was to learn, have an all but infinite number of ways and tricks for inflicting pain. I think it was something that locked his legs and spine and paralyzed him from the neck down, because after they zapped him with it, leaving him a sort of frozen statue like a running cartoon character hit with a garden hose on a cold day, three of the guards carried him up to the front of the space.

Then they whipped us and kicked us till we were all sitting up straight.

We all watched the poor bastard as his face filled with terror; tears ran all over him, and he was screaming and gibbering for mercy like a madman.

He was about to discover that even if Allah was the Most Merciful, Allah's creations were anything but.

The Closers slowly wet him down with something. The smell permeated the room, and though none of us dared to make a sound, or to move, you could feel the silent shudder run through us all.

Gasoline. Or something enough like it as to make no difference.

He knew what was coming, and now he was raving, shrieking, blood running from his mouth because he'd torn his lips and tongue, but all that did was make the Closers laugh harder. Then they spent a long while teasing him with little torches, bringing the flame close, moving it back; twice they lit his pants and then squirted them immediately with something to put the blaze out, and then wet him down with the flammable liquid again.

Two thoughts ran through my head. One was how much I hated the Closers for being the kind of people who would do this.

The other thought was that I hoped to god this was the one who'd put the bomb under the van. I'd never been able to get over the feeling in my gut that Marie had been conscious when it burned. And if this happened to be him, I was finally seeing my number one fantasy, and as horrible as it was, as little as I liked the Closers for being the sort of people who would do it, if it had to happen, I wanted to be there.

They didn't stop their nasty little game until he finally gave up in despair. When he just stood there hanging his head and neither their whips nor threatening him with the little flames was doing anything to him anymore, they set him on fire.

It's amazing how long a human being can scream after you'd think he'd have nothing to scream with.

Vengeful satisfaction and nausea were fighting it out in me; I knew in a deep sense that this was the end of my fight with Blade of the Most Merciful, not just because they were all going to be dead, but because they were going to die in ways that I would have wished on them in my darkest fury, and because so many of them had died by my hand, and more because I'd helped to foil them.

Still, he was human. The screams tore at my heart, and however much my head might say he had it coming, I couldn't entirely feel that anything or anyone deserved this. And the smell—surprisingly like a barbecue—was making a lot of the men vomit. I felt a little like it myself.

All the while this was going on, the unconcerned workmen were passing by with their loads of loot. I saw crate after crate of stuff, some of it perhaps bought with stolen funds, other parts of it taken outright . . .

They will strip-mine your timeline, Harry Skena had told me, and now I knew what he meant.

The burning man had died, I think; the nervous system no longer held him locked upright, and he fell in a heap. They brought out a little contraption that was obviously a refuse-sweeper of some kind, swept him in, and took him away, without bothering to extinguish him.

Just after a large load of material went by, there was a change in the tone behind me; something was different about the machinery. They were just coming around to whip and beat us back into the position of kneeling with our faces on the floor, when quite suddenly I heard the machinery stop. They must be closing the gate.

Whatever a PRAMIAC was, it was sensing my presence through that gate, and not going off—until the gate started to close. That's what I think happened, and I've been told since it almost certainly is what happened.

I also didn't know at the time that a setting of "6"—what Harry had set his PRAMIACs to—is equivalent, roughly, to a World War II blockbuster, a one-ton TNT bomb. And the scale on it is base-10 logarithmic—going up by 2 means going up 100 x—so what blew up next to the base of the column was equivalent to 100 tons of TNT.

The gate was partly closed, but what that did was cause the force to take on strange properties as it moved through warped space and time. The shock wave that swept through the huge room in which we knelt twisted and broke everything more than a yard or so off the floor, and sheared the pieces off in a dozen directions. The guards were torn apart.

But we prisoners, kneeling on the floor, felt nothing, except the warm splashes of the guards' blood.

The blast had one other beneficent effect—for a long two minutes, it knocked out all the lights.

I crawled away in that time, looking for anything large enough to hide behind, getting the noise of the now-babbling Bladers on the other side of me, away from them, figuring that before they got it together they would again be targets. If I could put some room between them and me . . .

On the way I had a nasty turn as I realized I had put my hand down on a severed human hand. I gasped and moaned but kept crawling . . . too important to keep moving, and besides any noise I made was being drowned out in the general babble. It sounded, from the way they were calling to each other, as if they were trying to form up into their cadres, perhaps with the idea of going down fighting.

I finally got myself behind the remnants of what had obviously been a big crate, big enough to hold a full-sized car at least, and severed at about four feet off the floor in a mass of splinters and torn wire. They were still hollering at each other out there, and the racket was considerable.

It occurred to me to wonder how the homing system on the SHAKK ammunition worked, exactly. If it was entirely visible-light, it probably wouldn't do much, here in the dark, but if it was infrared, or radar—and my guess was it was, several different things . . .

Only one way to find out. I moved the switch to full auto and stood up in the pitch-blackness, then sprayed in the direction of Blade of the Most Merciful. The deep whoosh boomed through the huge room, and then there was a wonderful silence.

I had quite possibly bagged the lot of them, and if not, the survivors were probably good and scared. I crept along the wall, creeping from behind one wheeled cart and crate to another, until finally I found I was at a doorway, where a cart had become wedged, with the dilating door partly closed around it.

Just then the emergency lights—at least that's what I figured dim lights in such a situation had to be—came on, and I ducked, then peeked out. The heap of sprawled bodies told me that I had gotten the rest of Blade of the Most Merciful . . . my revenge, and Dad and Carrie's, and Porter's, too. It didn't bring anyone back, but it sure as hell made me feel better. I just wished there was a way for the folks back home to know what had become of Blade. I thought it might be a salutary example for a lot of terrorist groups.

Come to think of it . . . about "back home" . . . there was an obvious problem here. The gate was wrecked, and I had less ability to work any of the cross-timeline technology than a Stone Age tribesman in New Guinea had to fly a 747. A lot less—he'd probably at least figure out what the controls were, if not what they did. I hadn't seen anyone pull a lever or turn a wheel to do all this.

Well, now that I could see, I could also see that the door the carts had been going out through was bent and broken, and there was a hole I could squeeze through. I was just debating it when I heard the voices and saw the guards bursting into the place. It didn't seem like it would be wise to be there to discuss it with them, so I slipped into that hole and was into the space beyond before I had time to think about frying pans, fires, and all that.

Several of the carts in this hallway had also been wrecked by the whatever-it-was that had rolled out of the blown-up, collapsing gate. It looked like it was some kind of fold in space that just twisted everything as it passed; a picture in my mind developed of one guard whose skull had been wrenched into a bent oblong. I shuddered a little; whatever such things might be I would have to stay out of the way of them.

I wasn't sure whether I wished I knew some physics, so I could figure out what it had done, or was glad I didn't, so that I wasn't totally mystified.

As I went farther down the long cargo corridor, the carts grew less and less distorted and damaged, and the occasional body less horribly mangled though just as dead. I suppose it doesn't take much of a twist in the heart to make it nonfunctional.

Finally, when I had walked more than half a mile along the corridor with no sign of life other than a certain amount of shouting back behind me in the big room, I came to a cart that seemed to be undamaged, just abandoned, and a place where the scratching and scarring on the wall converged down to a triangular point. Within a few yards, the regular lights instead of the dim emergencies were on.

This meant a chance of running into living people; I went back to skulking along, hoping that anything that popped up would either not see me or not have time to sound the alarm.

I was in luck, for once, and when the corridor finally ended in what looked like a giant warehouse, I had still seen no one. I crept among the immense racks and the many crates, looking for anything at all to give me an idea on what I should do next. I was getting hungry, and I would be tired soon; there didn't seem to be much of anything I could do about the hunger, and I had no idea where I could safely sleep—I snore, for one thing.

Finally I just made my way out of the place, figuring that it might be a safe place to hide, but it could do me no good otherwise. I followed any corridor till it crossed a larger one, then followed the larger one, and sure enough in about twenty minutes I was facing a door with a sign over it in characters I'd never seen before, and that the translator implanted in my head was not equipped to deal with. I hoped they said "Exit"—there were just six of them, but for all I knew they were ideograms like Chinese, in which case they might well say "Door is alarmed," "Warning, hard vacuum on other side," or "Police Station."

No way to know unless I opened it, so I did. No alarm sounded where I could hear it, and I slipped out into a bigger space.

A cart rolled by, and the women running it appeared to have escaped from a dirty magazine, wearing high heels, bathing suit bottoms, and no tops. They looked bored to tears.

A moment later a cart going the other way was staffed by two guys with beards down to their waists.

Well, if I'd understood Harry Skena right, maybe the Closers didn't worry much about what their slaves looked like, or maybe there was a dress code for slaves. This would be one great time for me to discover that a tough "police sport coat" (it only looks like a sport jacket if you do all of your shopping at Kmart; what it is, really, is just a heavy vest made out of polyester, as padding and protection in the event of rough stuff) was perfect inconspicuous slave gear . . .

I walked farther up the corridor, and thought about it. This place seemed to be huge, and so far everyone I'd seen had been moving a cargo of one kind or another. My guess was that I'd found a major base here, probably a sort of Grand Central for shipping supplies to all their different wars.

Something big was coming up behind me. I looked for somewhere to hide, and there was nowhere. Then a bunch of men in guard uniforms came up behind me.

I had no idea whether it would work, but I just didn't think I could shoot my way out and run successfully, so instead I dropped into the bowed-over position on the floor, on my knees with my face near the floor and my hands over my butt. They ran by me without paying any attention, except that one of them sort of patted my head as he went by.

Another half hour of walking, and I'd seen another patrol go by and the same thing had happened; moreover, another group of slaves had been visible at the time, and they'd gotten into the same position. I must have guessed right.

It was clear that all I'd found was a bigger traffic corridor. I'd been passing doors and had slowly learned that there were about four different sets of characters that appeared on them; one was the set that had appeared on the warehouse door, which didn't seem promising, and the other three could mean anything from "Ladies" to "Darkroom—No Light!" to "Large Room" for all I knew.

If you're trying to be inconspicuous, unfortunately, you don't have many options in the way of nosing around. A slave opening doors at random would be pretty conspicuous; walking rapidly and firmly in one direction, just as if I knew where I was going, seemed to be the only hope until I decided to open one door, just as if I belonged there.

Something caught my eye—on a cart rolling by, crewed by three brown-skinned men who were all wearing what looked like short skirts, vests without shirts, and gigantic lace neckties. They were interesting enough, but what caught my eye was the eagle-and-swastika on every crate on the cart.

I'm not sure what made it add up for me. Maybe it was just that it was the first familiar symbol I'd seen in hours, even if it was that one; maybe I was remembering that Harry Skena had been pretty sure Blade's supplies were coming from a world where Hitler won. Anyway, I trotted up and jumped on the back of the cart.

They not only didn't seem to mind, they didn't seem to notice. I suppose it wasn't their cart or their crate, and there wasn't a lot of point in investigating. Whatever the case, they ignored me, and I rode on with them. We were clipping along at about five miles per hour, I estimated, and it was twenty minutes or so before they turned off, through a giant double door that had a set of symbols I hadn't seen before on it.

After some more rolling along, we came to a bend in the corridor, then into a wide area. There was a familiar blue glow, and when we came around the corner I saw that it was coming from a column that stretched several stories up into a covered space, like a missile in a silo; this was clearly a gate.

I got off and walked casually past. No one looked at me.

Then I crept quietly back and watched. The gate glowed red; out of it came many large, swastika-marked boxes, to be loaded on carts and driven swiftly away. Then a couple of small boxes of stuff were sent through the other way, and they powered it down and left it glowing blue.

Interesting. And to judge from the casual way of handling freight, with not all the outbound boxes thrown in this time and

with many of the inbound sitting around until a cart came for
them, it seemed a safe enough bet that this was always the gate to
Nazi-land. It wasn't exactly where I'd have picked to go, but it beat
staying here and starving, or getting caught in the open by a big
gang of these bozos.

If nothing happened, I'd be caught and either dead or enslaved sooner or later. And nothing was just what was going to
happen unless I made something happen.

All of which was the rationale I was mumbling into my own
mind's ear as I crept forward, got in among the crates that seemed
to be outbound, and saw if there were any I could lift the lid on.

Sure enough, there was one, and what was inside it looked
like—it was. Small transistor television sets. At least that was what
the picture on the box showed. All the way up to the top . . . but
plenty of room for me if I could find somewhere to hide the top
layer.

I sneaked over to the "inbound" group and discovered that
two of the open crates were only about half-full, with all kinds of
junk that looked a lot like stray merchandise, some of it obviously
broken . . .

Aha. Got it. Luxury goods they were either selling to the Nazis
or maybe distributing to the Closers over there. Which meant the
crate I had opened first was probably going to a civilian warehouse.
Perfect!

I hastily stripped off the top layer of TVs, still wishing I could
read Closer characters—but what else was a cardboard box with a
picture of a box with an oval screen and knobs likely to be? And if I
was wrong, I was sure I'd know soon enough.

Anyway, with eight perfectly good sets going back to the factory
(some poor slave would probably have to spend hours figuring out
what was not wrong with them), there was now lots of room for me
in the outbound crate.

I took a moment to quietly take a leak into the inbound crate—
I had to go, I needed somewhere to hide it, and besides I had no
desire to make life among the Closers any more pleasant—and then
got into the outbound. Not having anything else to do, I tried to
take a nap.

I must have dozed a little, because I only woke when the crate
started to move. They were jacking the pallet up with a little gadget
I had seen that was a bit like a hand-operated forklift, and then

there was a thud as they slid me and the TVs onto a powered cart. After a moment or two, the cart started to roll forward, and feetfirst and flat on my back, I entered another world.

Going through a gate is not nearly as nice as blinking in and out; I discovered why ATN used blink transmitters rather than gates. My first time, jumping through, I hadn't had time to notice the hard lurch in my stomach or the disorienting dizziness, let alone the strange, enervating tingle that ran up my body in a long slow wave. It felt like my leg going to sleep and the sensation spreading all over my body, and it seemed to last for hours, though really I think it was only seconds.

There was a series of hard bumps that I realized must be the crate being off-loaded. I suddenly had a terrible fear that every other crate would end up stacked on top, and that this crate wouldn't be needed for weeks, but no such thing happened. There were more thuds and crashes all around as other crates were laid in beside mine, then the sound of electric motors whirring, and a truck engine started somewhere and drove away.

After that it was silent for a long while. I figured my resting heart rate was around eighty; it had been the last time I gave blood, so I started counting beats . . . twelve hundred beats should be about fifteen minutes. I wanted to pop out when there was nobody there, but I also wanted to give myself as much time as possible before anybody came back.

Finally, I cautiously raised the lid and sat up. I was tired, hungry, and getting pretty discouraged; from what the ATN people had told me, there wasn't much chance of getting a ride home from here.

The warehouse, if that's what it was, was still brightly lit, but there was nothing moving around in it. I jumped down from the crate to get moving.

I suppose I could have died right there. I don't know what told me to look up, or how exactly I managed to point the SHAKK and pull the trigger before I knew what I was dealing with—

But the Doberman went to pieces as the round zinged around inside him, and fell to the floor in front of me, a bag of smashed protoplasm. I got the Dobe behind him, too.

There were shouts inside the warehouse—somebody yelling for Sieg and Frieda, which I suspected were the two Dobermans. I ran like hell from the direction of the voice, weaving in and out among the crates, hoping for a little bit of luck.

At first I seemed to be having it—it sounded like there was just one guy, who had noticed the dogs going into "attack" mode, coming in to make sure they were just after a rat or something. Probably I could get around behind him and find an exit.

I was thinking that right at the moment when I rounded a corridor turn and suddenly instead of dividers and shelves, I was looking out into an open space. The first thought I had was that this sure as hell wasn't the civilian warehouse I had hoped it would be, because the gadget in front of me was unquestionably a tank, and a pretty high-tech one at that.

It looked sort of like your basic idea of a flying saucer, silvery and clam-shaped, except that it had a long, slim gun sticking out of the side near the top; a crack below that showed where the gun rotated. There were many treads, on short little posts underneath the thing, some up and some down; I suspect it had something like ground-following radar and extended three legs at any one time so that it was always stable and at the same time able to move in any direction quickly.

Right now the part of the upper "clam plate" behind the gun had two big openings, both created by gull-wing doors like the doors on a DeLorean, and there was a big crew of men climbing around on it, a couple of them poking around in the thing's guts, and there were at least ten armed guards as well. Moreover, one of the men was looking straight at me, and he bellowed "look—over there" and pointed.

I turned and ran; I didn't like the way all those submachine guns were coming out. At least back among the goods there might be something too valuable for them to use as a backstop for bullets.

These guys were in shape, too, they weren't some stray garrison guard, gone to fat and sloth. I could hear them running out around and ahead, blocking the different ways. One popped into a corridor before me, and I gave him a round from the SHAKK; he fell dead and I leaped over him and kept going, hoping I had at least put myself on the outside of the net.

A burst of submachine gun fire chewed up the crate behind me and I dove to the floor, wriggling hard to back out of the corner I had run into. A moment later a head popped in, and I hit him with a SHAKK round; two down and god knew how many to go. There was a lot of shouting, and the occasional words I could hear (they seemed to be speaking English, which didn't make much sense to me, but maybe my translator was able to cover German? But why would it be?).

"It's English," the translator said in my mind.

Thanks, I thought back at it.

Sorting out I realized that first of all there was one guy who was upset by the condition Sieg and Frieda were in; later I learned that the ammo for a SHAKK isn't all that smart. It knows where to find the head on a human being, but on any other living creature it zings around everywhere, just staying inside the body. On a really big animal—an elephant, say—if you hit far enough away from a vital organ, the animal might even survive because the pathway through the body didn't happen to pass close enough to a vital organ, and so much energy would be expended in just getting through hide and surface fat. But on something the size of a Doberman—a lot smaller than a man—it had plenty of room to run, and it turned the insides of those dogs into sort of a nasty red jam that dribbled out of them all over the floor, leaving them as drained skins in the middle of a huge blood slick.

I could see why the fellow was a bit upset.

Yet another guard burst in on me, and this guy was shooting as he came around the corner. I felt something hot tag my calf muscle, and then I SHAKKed him like the others. He fell over with his finger convulsing on the trigger, the recoil driving him backward, and consequently knocked out about half the light fixtures in the immediate area and started a bunch of stuff that had been stored up in the rafters to slide and fall around.

It was a nearly perfect diversion, and, despite the stinging pain in my calf, I was up and running. By now I'd figured a set of directions and had decided that the side of the building farthest from me was the one that had the best chance of having an exit to the outside, which meant I'd have to find a way across the area where the tank was parked. Well, I'd think of something.

More shots chewed into crates beside me, and I zagged down an aisle, took the first right I could, turned again—and burst into the wide-open area.

The unarmed workmen there turned and stared, and I ran right into their midst, hoping the guards behind me would have at

least a little compunction about firing into a crowd that was mostly
unarmed civilians.

I should have figured differently, but I didn't know Closers or
Nazis nearly as well then as I was to know them later. Think of a
Nazi whose family has been rabid Nazis for twenty generations,
think of a guy who would toss a woman's baby on the fire because
he likes the way she screams while he rapes her, think of children
raised to execute their slave playmates so that they won't become
too "emotional," and you've got Closers.

There was a Closer among these guys, and the way I could tell
was that for one instant they refused to shoot into the crowd, and I
got away into the racks of stuff on the other side, ducking rapidly to
the left and jumping a low spot in the stored stuff, hitting in a roll
and getting myself back under cover. God, I was glad they hadn't
laid this out in nice neat rows, or I'd have been dead—

The voice had an unpleasantly sibilant accent; no big surprise.
Most Closers can't quite manage sh's or th's.

"You incompetent s-s-slaves, I'll have you s'ot! So you won't
s'oot because zair are s-slaves in ze way! S-s-s'oot zem all now!
S-soot zem, or I'll s'oot you!"

And to my amazement, I heard the chatter of submachine
guns.

It made me sick and disgusted; I was alive because those innocent workmen had been in the wrong place at the wrong time. All
thought of escape left my mind; I turned and crawled back toward
them.

"Now form a sssssskirmis'ing line and move forward!" There
was a whiny quality to the voice too; later I learned that Closers
who are running operations of this kind are often young teenagers,
getting extra training in ruthlessness.

I got a look at what they were doing, popped up with the
SHAKK set on full auto, and sprayed down the line, the deep
whoosh of SHAKK rounds going out into them, half the line falling
over and the high-tech tank suddenly flashing from a dozen places
and bursting into flames.

Half the line.

The SHAKK had stopped making a whoosh noise, and there
were four of them left. I glanced down and saw the readout on the
top was flashing "RELOAD BEFORE FIRING AGAIN," or at least
that was what the translator said it said.

I was out of ammo, and the only thing keeping me alive right now was that the four surviving guards and their Closer leader were too busy diving for the floor and trying to get their weapons pulled around to get a shot off at me.

· 8 ·

At least I had the advantage that I knew something was wrong a split second before they did.

I grabbed for my .45, and time slowed down as I found the deep concentration I needed. Pistol shooting is like any other martial art—once you're good at it, what you want is a clear, cool head.

I also had the advantage of a lot of backlight. Some stray SHAKK rounds must have decided to go into the engine compartment (if that was what it was) of the tank, and had made hash of a lot of things. Smoke was pouring out of the tank, and there was a strong flickering backlight from sheets of white plasma that skittered and ran over the silvery surface. The bright flashes nicely silhouetted the men in front of me, though since they were on the floor, the angle was bad.

I bagged the Closer on the first shot—he was just getting down to the floor, maybe because he didn't want to get his clothes dirty and, like most of them, wasn't so much an officer as a slavemaster.

It had taken one shot to dispose of the Closer; I got two more off, and I think might have wounded one of the guards, before the guy on the far right let off a burst with the submachine gun. I hit the ground rolling and running, and behind me I could hear them getting up.

I just hoped there wasn't another guy at the door.

There was a deafening roar, and the tank blew up. It flung me to the floor in a facefirst skid so hard that I barely kept from banging my head, and all around me the stacked crates, racks, and dividers were tipping over in all directions. I don't know what happened to the last few guards, but I would guess they had their backs to it and weren't quite among the stored goods yet. Probably they were just flung forward into the mess, and I would guess one or two of them were killed by what they hit.

Much of the stuff in the rafters had been stored on plywood sheets running rafter to rafter, and when the blast went off a lot of it went straight up, lifting those sheets and dumping their contents; all kinds of heavy junk rained down inside the warehouse, and if I hadn't been busy running for the door for all I was worth, jumping fallen objects and climbing over collapsed piles of stuff, I'd have been terrified enough to keep my head down. All around me the building groaned as the loads shifted abruptly; in other parts of the storage area, things that were supposed to be kept apart were apparently finding each other, for there were explosions and bursts of fire everywhere.

There was one confused-looking guard at the door, and when I burst out at him he went for his gun. I slammed my feet to a stop in the approved two-handed position and put a slug into his face; he fell backward. After all the exploding heads the SHAKK caused, it was almost a relief just to see a smear of blood, hair, and brains hit the back wall.

As I stepped over him I thought I saw an American-flag patch on his arm; oh, well, if he was working for these clowns, he wasn't part of the America I was. Just because you've got the uniform doesn't mean you play on the team . . .

At last—five minutes, ten or more deaths, and a lot of nervousness after getting out of the crate—I pushed through the door and out into the sunny deserted street, dashed across without checking for traffic, and ran down an alley. There was another alley at a cross angle and I took that route, then swung around one more corner, pressed myself into an inconspicuous corner of a doorway, and let my breath come down to calm and regular while I listened for signs of pursuit.

There was a thundering, ground-shaking roar. Given the variety of stuff that had been in that place, and how mixed together it was getting, I suppose it should have been no surprise. I saw a flicker of flame in the sky through the little opening of the alley

above me; I suspected any need to get rid of witnesses or evidence
had just been taken care of.

I drew a long, deep breath and took stock. I didn't exactly
know where I was, other than I was in a timeline where Hitler won,
and a timeline the Closers felt secure enough about to use as a base.
There were probably not more than two hundred or so Closers on
the planet, of whom I figured I'd just eliminated one, but there
were untold Nazis, and not just German ones either. I sure hadn't
felt like I could have turned to those guards and said, "See here,
I'm an American, too."

I was tired, hungry, without friends or money, two rounds left
in the magazine and no reloads, and the SHAKK was useless. I
wondered why I hadn't taken along a few pocketfuls of that sand
they were loaded with. And about ten extra magazines, two ham
sandwiches, and a cold Pepsi.

Worse yet, the alley in which I sat seemed to back up on an
Italian restaurant, because there was a wonderful smell of red
sauce. Not an easy place to do your planning when you were hungry.

Chances that they would take the money in my billfold—zip. I
doubted my credit cards would do much good either. Besides that I
had . . . well, I suppose I could stick someplace up if I really had
to. But totalitarian states are bad places to take up crime. They're
not awfully careful about the rights of the accused, and there aren't
a whole lot of situations in which you can just hide among people.

There were sirens wailing—fire crews headed for the warehouse, no doubt, and if there were any survivors there, I'd have
cops after me within half an hour. Time to get it moving. I didn't
know which way to go or where I was, but "away from the warehouse" seemed like a good plan. I got the SHAKK tucked under
my shirt (for all I knew there were reloads for it here) and the .45
to where it wasn't completely conspicuous, in the big inside pocket
of the jacket. I just hoped my clothes weren't going to be screaming
"arrest me" when I ran into people again.

I rounded two more corners in the tangle of alleys, popped
across a street—well, the people on it didn't look weird to me,
maybe I didn't look weird to them. I ducked into another block of
alleys, and repeated the process. Wherever I was, there was some
resemblance to Pittsburgh—I hadn't seen a bit of level ground yet.

All right, I could see plenty of daylight up ahead, and sooner or later I'd have to stick my head out; I gritted my teeth for a moment, listened to the explosions still going off back at the warehouse, figured I hadn't heard a siren close by in a while . . . time to take a walk down a real street and see what happened to me.

I popped out of an alley, looked quietly around. Most of the people seemed to be dressed from a fifties movie, the men in blue or gray suits and the women in calf-length dresses. Everything looked a little cheap but whether that was the way the country was or the way the neighborhood was, who could say.

I decided to walk uphill because there was a slightly better chance of finding a landmark that way. As I walked I did a little more study of the people; some of them seemed not to like me. Clearly there was something about me . . .

Probably that all the men were crew-cut, and all the women in tight little perms. My hair was pretty short, by the standards of where I came from, but I had it. Most of these guys looked like they'd just come from delousing.

On the other hand they felt free to glare at a stranger on the street. This version of America was not *that* totalitarian, then.

I also realized the crowd wasn't just men and women. It was just that anybody from puberty on up was either in a suit or in one of the three permitted dress styles. It occurred to me, too, that I had no necktie. Looked like everyone was wearing clip-ons. I wondered how they'd react if I asked to bum a spare tie from someone.

Well, the next thing to check out, then, was—

I came over the hill and one problem got solved right away. I saw the Golden Gate Bridge in the distance—or rather, about two-thirds of the Golden Gate Bridge. The center part of the span was torn out, and as I looked more closely I saw that there were many cables hanging loose from it; at this distance the reddish color on much of it suggested that it was rusting.

All right, so this was San Francisco.

"Hey, buddy, have a heart, will you, don't walk around like that over here!"

The man approaching me was paunchy, shaveheaded, and dressed in something that looked more like a brown-shirt uniform than anything else, but it had American-flag patches on the shoulders and a big white strip over the pocket.

It didn't look like this was a bust, and something about him didn't give off the flavor of cop, so I peered at him for a long

moment, reading "Good Neighbor Patrol" on the strip. It sounded
like the kind of thing McGruff the Crime Dog would be involved in,
but the closer look had also assured me that the American flag now
had a white swastika instead of stars in the blue field.

"Come on, buddy, you've seen this uniform before, especially if
you've been walking around like that. Let me at least put a tie on
you, and if you need the price of a haircut . . ."

So I had been right.

He got closer, then said, "You don't seem very, uh, connected
to things, there, pal."

If he started looking at me closer, instead of just hassling me
like the street bum he thought I was, I was going to be in deep,
quick. So I made myself focus and said, "Sorry—I—geez, where am
I?"

"You wandered over from Berkeley somehow," the guy said,
shaking his head. "And if you just wander back quick, I won't have
to do anything about you, and you won't have to have anything
done about you. I know you all walk around like that over there all
the time, but there ain't no chick houses or thump clubs here, fella,
and you're sticking out like a sore thumb." He leaned in close—it
took me a moment to realize he was sniffing my breath. "Well,
you're not drunk, and I don't smell any burning rope. So I don't
know what you're on, but"—he shrugged—"it's none off mine. I
just happen to have a perfect record for these blocks, and I want to
keep it. So—if you'll do me the favor—"

He reached out, buttoned my top button, and clipped a shoddy
little rayon tie to it. "And I got a barber right around the corner.
Listen, if I get you trimmed, put you on a streetcar—" A thought
seemed to hit him. "You got any dough? You didn't come over here
to panhandle?"

"Oh, no, not to panhandle," I said, since obviously that would
be the wrong answer. "I uh . . . this will sound stupid."

"Try me."

"Well, I put on the jacket and my good pants," I said, thinking
frantically, "to look a little more presentable because—you're right,
I don't have any dough—but I, um, was over here hoping to find
someplace I could apply for work."

His lips pursed, and he quietly whispered, "Vet, hunh?"

I wasn't sure what the significance was, except that pretty obviously it was going to change things drastically, so I hesitated and then he whispered, "That's right, don't talk here. Come on."

And he promptly led me around to a barbershop, but we went in by the back door and he plopped me down in a chair in the back. I could hear the barbers—there seemed to be two of them—cutting hair in the front, then a couple of low whispers near the cash register. I sat and waited.

About ten minutes went by. I was at least fairly safe here, and the guy had not acted like a cop about to make a bust. The trouble was, he'd assumed I was a veteran, and in this context I couldn't even be sure that I knew what war it was going to be. Not to mention that I'd never actually served a day in my life, and if anyone started quizzing me about military slang, I was going to have to rely on old movies . . .

Well, time enough for that when it came up. Meanwhile I could enjoy breathing calmly and safely.

The "Good Neighbor Patrol" guy brought a barber back with him, who said, "Okay, pal, we're gonna make you presentable on some of Bob's discretionary cash. Some system for suppressing vagrants you've got, Bob—dress 'em up to be respectable vagrants."

Bob, the Good Neighbor guy, grinned good-naturedly. "You know why I'm doing it, and it's the same reason you are." He looked at me closely and said, "You wouldn't have been Home Defense—you must have been Regular Army. Wim and me, we got captured halfway across Kansas and spent a long time moving rocks out by New *York* City." He punched the *York* pretty hard, and I realized there must be something different now. "Who'd you serve with?"

I didn't have a clue, but I figured what I'd do is tell him the only thing I could remember offhand, what was in fact where my father had been. I just wished Dad had been more inclined to tell war stories . . . "I was . . ." I swallowed hard. "I was with General Patton. Third Army. Spent a while in a Stalag—"

They stared at me, and I thought for one long instant that I'd blown it; then suddenly they were taking turns shaking my hand. "Then—you were at Gettysburg?"

Maybe I had just taken a hard hit on the head in that parking garage . . . but I played along. "Captured just after."

"Damn! Then you almost . . ." and his voice dropped to a whisper . . . "you almost made the boat."

I shrugged.

"You don't talk much, do you? You do stay over in Berkeley, it's all vets and poets and baxters, isn't it? Feel more at home there?"

I nodded. I suspected that if my hair and lack of tie had made that kind of difference, then I probably would have felt more at home in Berkeley.

"Well, we'll get you back there. Jeez, if the regular cops got you, they'd spend an hour kicking you just to stay in practice. No wonder he can't get work, Wim. His permit must be stamped that he's only employable as a last resort . . . and the last I knew the Black Mark guys were getting two cups of dry oatmeal, a cup of beans, and a vitamin pill per day from the Dole. When was the last time you had meat, son?"

"Couple days ago," I said, which was true, subjectively anyway. "Somebody gave me dinner."

They glanced at each other. "Well, you're getting a haircut, a hamburger, and bus fare back to Berkeley," Bob said. "And after that, *don't* come this way again. Your best bet, no kidding—I've known one or two this worked for—get a freight out of town and get out to the fields. Lose your papers and get another freight. Walk into a forced labor camp and act shell-shocked. It's three hard years, but they'll feed you, and at the end you'll come out as a John Doe, and you can get a job as a janitor or something. Beat the hell out of the way you're living now. And it works as long as you don't get caught."

I nodded. "Thank you."

"Repeat it back to me."

I did. He nodded, satisfied. "There's a train out of Oakland with a lot of empty boxcars most mornings, about four A.M. Catch it soon, pal. If you'd been one block over, you'd have found yourself a real Nazi for a Good Neighbor, and you'd be spitting out your teeth right now. Maybe on your way back to be extradited and put in another Stalag. There's plenty of folks over here who'd love to give you work and food, but they got to keep their heads down; most of 'em are like me, we never miss the VOA, but we sure don't take any chances about it. Maybe it'll all be different when the ship comes in."

Wim grinned. "When the ship comes in, Bob, I'm going to have to lock you up."

"Sure, if you let me shoot my boss first. I swear that's what keeps a lot of us hoping, is the thought that we can dispose of all these petty weiners that Reconstruction left in place."

It was all gibberish to me, but the point was that they were going to help me get to somewhere where I could be less conspicuous. And though I wasn't ready to give up the fight, I'd at least learned from them how I could make myself fit into this world if I needed to, and that was good to know—because I just might need to.

So without much further ado, Wim shaved my head, and Bob went out and came back a bit later with a hamburger, a huge basket of fries, a big slice of apple pie, and a thermos of coffee. He said it was compliments of a "guy up the street that was at the Azores," which at least gave me another battle to refer to.

I'm not bad at geography. The Azores are eight hundred miles west of Portugal; the Axis got nowhere near them in the World War II I knew. And I had about figured out why they were referring to Gettysburg . . . battles tend to happen in the same places over and over. The pass of Megiddo (or Armageddon) is up in the mountains of northern Israel, and the author of Revelations picked it as the site of the final battle because, probably, it had already been the site of so many battles. The same passes, river crossings, roads, and forests are attacked and defended again and again.

The reason Americans are less aware of this is because most of our continent has been at peace most of the time . . . but armies move on pathways dictated by terrain, and they run into each other in the same places century after century. Gettysburg is where an army moving north out of Virginia or the Chesapeake is apt to collide with one coming south from New York or Philly, or one coming east from the Ohio Valley. Pretty clearly Patton had made some kind of last-ditch stand there . . . and obviously, whether he'd won or not, it hadn't worked out.

All these thoughts were hitting me as I stuffed the food in; the other thought crossing my mind was that in an occupied nation— were they still occupied? It didn't quite sound like it—like the United States of this world, I would have to try not to get into any firefights. There were probably a substantial number of good guys like Bob and Wim around, and I didn't want to kill any of that kind.

The burger was great, the fries were great, the pie was great. Appetite is the best sauce, and so forth. I wish I could say the same for the coffee, but it was cut so heavily with chicory that I could taste no coffee at all in it. I realized, somewhere in my second cup, that the "chick houses" of Berkeley were pretty clearly not the massage parlors one might have thought.

Raw chicory . . . a guy would have to spend a while getting used to it.

Finally Bob took me down to the end of the street and handed me fare for a bus; he showed me one coming along that had a long list of destinations, Berkeley among them. "Just stay quiet till you get home," he said, and turned and went. I didn't get a chance to thank him.

And a good thing, too. When I got on the bus, the driver said, "where to?" and pointed to a schedule of rates when I seemed puzzled. I said "Berkeley Main," figuring that whatever that was it had to be somewhere reasonably close.

"You can take this bus all that way, but why don't you take the direct route? About six blocks and that way—half the fare and a third of the time."

The direction he pointed in was downhill, away from Bob's block . . . something seemed slightly funny. "I don't know the bus system at all well," I admitted.

There were about six riders on this one and they all looked pretty bored; the driver shrugged. "This is a featherbed route, bud. They have me driving long distances just so's I can finish out my time before retiring. The bus runs empty for most of the route, and I got no schedule to make. I get most of the way down to San Jose before I turn around and head the other way; the only regular riders I get are the cops coming off duty at the National Security station down by Moffet Field. I generally pull up there empty . . . and then it's a long time till I get back to Berkeley."

A bell went off in the back of my head. "Six blocks that way—"

"Is a bus that'll get you there in less than an hour. Pay one price. This thing ain't even good sight-seeing."

I thanked him, got off the bus, watched him pull away, then moved quickly and quietly into an alley across the street. San Francisco is kind of a tangle, but anyone who's learned to get around in Pittsburgh is hard to confuse about directions from then on. I got to the place he was talking about without poking my head out much, except occasionally to cross a busy street.

It occurred to me that good old Bob and Wim had learned a

fair amount about me, that the food had delayed me a long time, that Bob had had plenty of time to make a phone call. And I found myself thinking . . . if a vet was discriminated against, how did one end up as a Home Guard? There was a sort of obvious answer.

Whether Wim was in on it or not, I couldn't say. I never did find out. But I would bet he was . . . it's pretty hard to avoid knowing that your friend is a fink.

But there was a news broadcast on continuously on that bus, and just as it pulled up to Berkeley Main (which turned out to be one of the buildings on the old campus—now a set of office buildings and small shops, kind of a giant mall—)I heard that the police were looking for a man in a red-and-blue-striped tie and a navy blue jacket who had somehow escaped from a bus on its way to the National Security facility. There was a brief congratulations to Robert Christian, an alert Good Neighbor, for having spotted the man, and the news that the driver was being detained for questioning.

The red-and-blue tie went from my neck into the shopping bag of a lady getting off. I couldn't take off the jacket without making my personal arsenal a bit more obvious, but there were plenty of blue jackets around. And despite the impression I'd gotten as I got off the bus at Berkeley Main, I noted most of the crowd was shaveheads like me.

If I could find someplace to lie low for a bit, things might blow over.

Good old Bob. He'd seemed like every regular guy you met back home. He probably *was*—but this place wasn't anything like back home.

Checking menus in restaurant windows I figured out that I had the cash for two or three meals left over from that bus fare. If the ratio was what it was like back home, I could probably get things like bread and canned soup and so forth at groceries and stretch it out a few days.

I also had done a little more thinking and realized that if there were people looking for it, there was probably an underground to be looked for. The fact that they talked about my "just missing the boat" was extremely promising, too. There might even be somewhere to catch a boat *to*.

I needed to know a lot more, and the trouble was, I wasn't sure where to look for the additional knowledge.

Berkeley was different—everywhere was different, but Berkeley more so. I realized there had probably been a lot of fighting down here, because so much of the area had been razed; the kind of charm that it had had was about two-thirds gone, with most of it replaced with big ugly block apartment buildings.

Still, there were signs that Berkeley was still Berkeley. I passed three chick houses, and all of them had notes for "poetry reading" and "American folk culture nights." There was some odd graffiti on the walls; "1789!" was popular (I figured that was the year the Bill of Rights passed . . .) along with "BWRY—AA!" with the A's intertwined. That took me a long time to figure out, till I saw another bit of graffiti with the intertwined A's attached to the phrase "All American" and the word NO and a swastika below—so the AA meant "all American" and was a subversive slogan. Another anagram appeared on another building:

Y
RED
BLACK
L
O
WHITE!

Got it. The abbreviation was "Black White Red Yellow—All American!" Pretty clearly there was not only an underground around here, but one that was almost out in the open, at least a little bit. Moreover there was an enclosing arrowhead drawn around the top words, and that explained the little "bent arrow" shapes I'd seen in several spots.

That made me feel a little better, though no safer. There was an anti-Nazi underground, and one they weren't suppressing very successfully. But I hadn't found it yet, and I still had nowhere to sleep.

The other thing I noticed down here was that there were substantial numbers of men without ties, a few even wearing blue jeans, and some women with straight hair down to their shoulders and no makeup. There were also practically no cars on the street . . . probably nobody here could afford one.

A girl of maybe twenty-five walking by, hair to her shoulders, baggy sweater, dress not ironed, and sneakers, gave me a little smile, and I smiled back. At least she didn't look like the robot people over on the other side of the Bay. She looked like she might speak to me—

Then an old school bus came around the corner, and people started giving shrill shepherd's whistles and running into alleys. The girl turned and ran; I stayed for a second longer and saw the bus pull up.

It was a Boy Scout troop bus. On its side was a troop number, and what I guessed must now be the Boy Scout emblem—an American eagle on a trefoil, just as it was in my timeline, but here the American eagle gripped the twin lightning bolts of the SS.

The kids piling out of the bus looked like any other Boy Scouts, but they carried wooden sticks, what looked like pieces of inch-and-a-half dowel rod about two feet long. They were yelling at everyone as they came out, and they headed right for the stragglers—though not for me, it was pretty clear they were mostly after women and old people.

I froze for a second—I really didn't want to get mixed up in anything, with no valid papers, and anyway I suspected what they were doing wasn't illegal, but stopping them might be.

I turned as they went by me. The girl who had smiled at me had tripped over a curb, and before she could get to her feet, five of the boys jumped her, beating her buttocks with their sticks, whooping and hollering, grabbing at her to pull up her skirt.

Without thinking I waded in. None of them could have been older than thirteen; I noticed in an abstract way that they and all the other kids were screaming "Jooger, jooger, jooger!" at the people they were beating.

I grabbed the first one by the back of his shirt and the second by his scrawny neck, and slammed their heads together hard. They both fell down yelling with pain; the others jumped up in shock, and I treated myself to a trick roundhouse kick, getting all three kids in the face. All five of them ran screaming back toward the bus; apparently people hitting back was not in the script.

The girl jumped to her feet, glanced behind me, shouted something. I turned.

The bus driver—a guy who had "Scoutmaster" written all over him, one of those big hale-and-hearty types that you find with car dealerships or as school board members in small towns, was coming out of the bus with an electric cattle prod. Apparently he was the reinforcements.

He did not seem pleased with me. All around, the Boy Scouts were stopping to watch, and the people they had been beating on were getting away, so I guess I had accomplished something useful.

Mr. Scoutmaster Sir was striding along toward me, the prod half-extended, and I could tell he figured I'd break and run. Of course, I knew I had the .45, and he didn't.

But I didn't want to waste a round, and the way he was coming on I didn't have to. When he reached out with the prod, I had already lunged inside his guard, and I slapped the prod to the side. He had just time to look surprised before I kicked him in the balls, giving it everything I had. He dropped the prod and fell groaning to his knees; I brought both hands up over my head, clenched together in a fist, and whipped them overhead and down to the back of his head as I brought my knee up, trapping his head in the smashing blow and shattering his nose and teeth.

That seemed to be a signal; the streets were suddenly boiling with angry people, all closing in on the Scouts. If I hadn't seen the little bastards in action before, I might have felt sorry for them— but I had, and I enjoyed the spectacle of their being cornered and kicked bloody. Apparently these little defenders of public order and the New American Way had never found out about people hitting back.

The girl was at my elbow. "You've got to run. Come with me."

She was obviously right, so I followed her down several streets, zigging, zagging, and backtracking till we were far enough away so that we didn't see anyone else running or acting like anything was unusual. Then she took my hand and said, "Try to look like you're in love."

We walked slowly up the street together, then made an abrupt left into a small, older cottage that had a sign on the door: "Berkeley Free Library."

The inside of the front room was lined with books, with shelves visible through the doorways to the other rooms, and there was a big wraparound desk in the middle. The chairs and tables didn't even come close to matching each other, and there was just one person in there, a short, slightly built guy, shaveheaded but not wearing a tie, in a pink shirt and baggy gray pants. He looked to be about thirty; he could have been a mildly eccentric professor back home.

"Anybody been in while I've been gone?" the girl asked.

"Nope, Sandy, nobody. As usual, nobody wants to read what you have. But I see you've found yet another partner for your life of sleazy abandon."

"Glad to hear there was nobody—this time. Then we were never gone, and my friend here was with me the whole time."

The little guy whistled. His glasses were pretty thick, and they slid down to the tip of his big nose easily, revealing large dark eyes, so he looked sort of like a bewildered owl. "Yeah, what did he do? And what did you do?"

"Oh, the Boy Scouts were pogging Berkeley again. This guy decked the Scoutmaster, maybe hard enough to kill him. Started this medium-level riot . . . probably there'll be reprisals. Thought we better get him under wraps."

The little guy scratched his head vigorously. "Easier said than done, kid. Buddy, you wouldn't by any chance be the guy that escaped off a bus a while back this afternoon?"

"My name is Mark," I said. I'd gotten tired of being called buddy and pal; it was too much like hanging out with my father's friends. "And yep, I probably am. While I'm at it I had something to do with the warehouse fire over on the other side, too."

"You mean the one that all the cops went to, and there was a denial on the radio that there had been a fire, or in fact that there had ever been a building there? Anyone ever tell you you cause trouble wherever you go?"

I liked his voice—it was a little nasal, maybe, but there was something in it that told you he was tough underneath—he could look at anything and report it honesty, could be killed but not intimidated, didn't know how to see with any eyes but his own.

"I've heard that," I said. "What's our next step?"

He sighed. "Well, I'd like to make you wait three hours while I keep working here. I have a pile of notes I should make about Walt Whitman, if I'm ever going to get my little book about him done. Somebody's got to keep the torch of American scholarship alight . . . but then of course somebody's also got to keep the American resistance going. If I didn't have Sandy to run the library, I'd collapse under the load entirely."

Sandy made a funny noise like a horse that's smelled something it doesn't like. "Have you eaten lately?" she asked.

"Fairly recently," I said. "Actually the idea of just sitting down and reading is pretty attractive; if I can hide my coat someplace, I'll probably look less conspicuous, and I can sit somewhere well to the back."

"Good a plan as any," the small man said. He got up and walked toward me, extending his hand; his grip was firm and strong, for such a small guy. "Any man who can upset that many cops is a friend of mine. My name's Al."

We stashed my coat, and it gave me a chance to hide the SHAKK and the .45; then I went into a back corner. The first thing I did was pick up the day's newspaper, to discover that it was August 17, 1961. There were a bunch of notes about the new president being off to a great start; from the look of the editorial page, it had actually been a contested election, the first since Reconstruction was withdrawn. Reconstruction, I had figured out, was the Nazi occupation, and since they kept referring to "the fifteen years of Reconstruction," that seemed to imply that the Germans had occupied the US from roughly 1945 to 1960.

The current president was a Nazi; his opponent in the 1960 election had been Strom Thurmond, and the paper seemed to be in hysterics about Thurmond the "sore loser" having the temerity to criticize the government that had won the election. Their reference to him as an "ultra-liberal crazy" came very close to making me laugh out loud . . . I suppose context is everything.

I tried finding a history book—when you've worked in academia as long as I have, you know Dewey Decimal and Library of Congress pretty well, and it doesn't take much time to find a thing—but those shelves were all but bare of material that covered anything since 1940. I figured that was probably a political statement in its own right. The number of basic authors who were missing from the shelves was a long list, though I did note there was more poetry and literature than one would expect.

Most of the paper was propaganda. I noted that rents were low—ever see a thirty-five-dollar-per-month rental in San Francisco?—and roughly commensurate with the restaurant meal prices. There were several pages about how to establish "normalcy" in your household, community, and church. Normalcy seemed mostly to mean getting people to be very alike and have a positive attitude about it.

There was an ad for the Boy Scouts . . . "IS YOUR SON A SCOUT? IF HE'S NOT, WON'T YOUR NEIGHBORS WONDER WHY?" The picture showed a blond boy giving a Hitler salute, and down at the bottom of the page was the Scout Law. Having been an Eagle Scout myself, I knew that one by heart . . . and I noted they had added three laws to it: "A Scout is white," "A Scout scorns weakness," and "A Scout is normal."

I liked it better the old way.

Department-store ads featured about three styles of dress and did not mention anything about underwear. Suits came in four styles, one of which was "The Latest From New Nuremberg." It took me a little while to figure out that that must be New York.

I got bored or disgusted, I'm not sure which, put my feet up, and went to sleep. It was wonderful to be able to do that at all.

When Sandy woke me it was getting dark outside. "You looked too comfortable to move" she said. "Come with me down to the basement—it's where Al and I have our apartment."

We walked down the long flight of steps with her behind me, and when I came to the bottom of the stairs, she said, "Go left." I turned left and went into the living room.

Al was there, a gun leveled on me. There were four guys wearing hoods sitting around him. I heard the safety slip off and a hammer cock behind me, and I knew Sandy had me covered.

On the table there was my Colt Model 1911A1 .45 automatic, and the SHAKK.

"You've got a lot of explaining to do," Al said, "and we might as well hear the first part in comfort. Sandy will give you some bread and soup, but I'm afraid we'll have to shackle your legs to the table. If you'd like to use the bathroom first, that can be arranged. We aren't out to hurt you or scare you, but we do need to know the truth."

·9·

I took him up on the offer of using the bathroom, and then let them shackle me and put the food in front of me. "Eat first if you like," Al said. "And if you're thinking of anything other than telling us the truth, think some more while you eat."

I did think. Probably they hadn't made that pistol since about 1945—everything I'd seen on the guards had been some sort of German make. And it's trivial to check a serial number—this one would be absolutely, totally wrong.

All that I suppose I could explain. The SHAKK, on the other hand, was utterly inexplicable. Worse yet, it had that digital readout, and it suddenly occurred to me that I hadn't seen a digital *anything* since I got here; 1960 was too early for calculators and electronic watches to begin with, but I was realizing that everything looked vaguely old-fashioned; either the high-tech was back in Germany, or it wasn't in existence at all.

I seriously doubted I could convince them that the SHAKK was a toy.

There was the possibility that, somewhere out there, there might be a hidden base. Patton's troops had apparently made it there, or some of them had, if I had understood Bob's hinting around correctly, and if it hadn't been a line he was feeding me for some obscure reason—and both those things seemed like very low probabilities. I could lie and claim the weapon had come from the hidden base.

The trouble was, if anyone was apt to know anything about a hidden base for real, it was the people facing me. I couldn't possibly fake my way through that one.

I guess I could have said I was a Nazi agent with a new Nazi superweapon, and let them shoot me, but I didn't like that option either.

It also occurred to me that I liked these guys. I wanted their trust, and I wanted them to believe me . . . but I respected and admired them a lot. They couldn't possibly have been where they were, doing what they were doing, without a ton of guts.

So after I finished dinner, and Sandy sat down by the door, her pistol still leveled at me, I drew a very deep breath and told them the truth. I couldn't exactly tell it in order—it's hard to begin a story by saying "so anyway there I was more than thirty years in the future, not your future but a different future, when . . ."

But I got it all out, every fact and detail, and figured that if I got shot at the end of it, or more likely quietly drugged and dropped off by some quiet little asylum's gates, I would at least not add lying to all my sundry crimes.

When I finished, Al thought for a long moment, then said, "So, in your timeline . . . name me a few major American painters since World War II. Guys who would have been unknown at the end of the war but well-known by your time."

I blinked—it wasn't at all what I had expected—but then I sort of automatically started naming them. "Well, for sheer well-known-ness, there's Andy Warhol. Jackson Pollock's stuff wasn't well-known and really influential till after the war, really, but he had a bunch before. De Kooning, of course. But I'm really partial to one guy's work—I had several prints of his in my place—guy named Robert LaVigne."

The way two of the guys in sheets sat up straight told me I'd said something important, but whether it was right or not was a good question.

"Jazz performers?"

"Right after the war the famous ones, I guess, are Charlie Parker and Dizzy Gillespie. Dave Brubeck a little later. I don't know jazz well, I'm just naming the guys who got a lot of publicity."

Maybe a little too casually, Al said, "How about writers?"

"Since the war?"

"Right after the war."

"Well, if you're not counting pop stuff . . . oh, I guess J.D. Salinger, Jack Kerouac—"

"Well, I'm persuaded," one of the sheets said.

There was nodding all around. "Either that or they've completely penetrated us, and we're all dead anyway," Al agreed. He looked up at me. "Happens that we were all heavy into art—to use an expression that's officially banned for being 'too jazz'—and you've at least named some likely names."

"Definite names," the sheet said.

"Likely names," Al repeated. "Who was president during World War II?"

"Most of it, Roosevelt. His vice president, Harry Truman, finished it out—"

He had me recite the list of presidents as quickly as I could. I had to come up with all kinds of other bits of trivia as well. Finally he nodded, "You tell a very consistent story. It sounds like real history. Now comes the point where we have to decide to trust you . . . Sandy, you can unfasten him, and I think we can all put the guns away. If he's not what he says he is, it's too late anyway."

They all nodded, pulled off the sheets, put the guns away, and suddenly I found I was sitting in a room full of pleasant, intelligent-looking people without a trace of threat about them.

"All right," Al said, when everyone was comfortable, and they'd passed a plate of sandwiches around, "let me explain why we didn't just shoot you. We've seen one of these gadgets before." He pointed to the SHAKK.

"About two years ago a new member of the underground turned up in the area. She went by the name of Sheila. She didn't visibly do anything for a living but she obviously always had money; that's no surprise, there are plenty of rich people in the underground. Sheila seemed to have really uncanny intelligence information—when she said 'raid here on this date,' by god the raid scored big. At first we thought she might be a police provocateur—that maybe she was getting those results because they were planting targets for us. So we asked her specifically to find us a way to hit two old high-ranking Nazis that were about due to be rotated home.

"No problem. Sheila gave us a script, and we nailed them. There were hunts and reprisals all up and down the coast.

"Now, as you might guess, besides VOA broadcasts—did you have VOA in your timeline?"

"Voice of America is a government outfit in my timeline."

"Aha. Well, here it's the outlaw radio. Plays a little jazz to lure the kids, broadcasts some salacious scandals to lure the adults, and then gives a few minutes of hard news and some real music, usually just before the radio direction finders zero in on the balloon carrying the transmitter. It's generally on the air whenever we can get a transmitter up and running."

"And your not knowing that speaks more in your favor," commented one of the guys who had been sheeted, a big burly blondish guy with a sort of potato nose.

"Anyway, as you might guess, we have other major activities here, but the biggest one is to support the forces still in the Free Zone—which it will certainly not violate security to tell you is a big swath of territory running from Dutch Indonesia up through Indochina and into Burma, China, and Tibet, where there's all kinds of rags and tags of the old Allied armies. They've held out against Hitler, and now Himmler, for a long time, though in the process they eventually lost the South Pacific, Australia, New Zealand, and the Philippines . . ."

"Uh, in my timeline, a lot of that—the South Pacific and the Philippines—were in Japanese hands," I said.

"Not here. The Japs had to use everything they had to take Midway, the Aleutians, and Pearl Harbor right after the Germans took the Azores, and they didn't get much for it. They got about the same deal out of the war as Hitler's other allies like Italy, Spain, Turkey, and Hungary did . . . little dribs and drabs of land and the privilege of not being reconstructed. Then on top of that the Japs lost too much in their first attack on the Philippines—it had to be taken by Germans years later—and they are still bogged down in China, for that matter. A lot of us think, or hope anyway, that if Germany went down, her former 'allies' would turn on her instantly."

I nodded. "About this agent—"

"Well, she made it clear early on that she really, really wanted to be taken to the Free Zone. There's usually one of two reasons for that—either someone has a missing lover or relative there and is trying to get there to find them, or the person is a German spy. And the Free Zones have enough people, by and large. They don't need bodies as much as they need skills, intelligence, and stolen weapons. So you can only go if you've got an important thing to bring them or show them.

"Sheila said she did. It was a little bound volume, in black, with all kinds of physics equations and diagrams. She copied out three pages of it by hand and sent it over there, in one of our regular courier pouches. Three months later—not unusual, it takes a while to get there through channels—we got a note back saying they had to have her come out right away."

"You've seen it?"

"I have it here. Sheila got worried that they were closing in on her, and wanted to make sure that if anything happened to her, at least the book would get through. Part of it was, she seemed desperate to demonstrate to us that her knowledge was needed in the Free Zone, and of course the more desperate she looked, the more we suspected her motivations. So one night she took four of us out to the big rocket base out in the desert east of Los Angeles—the ones the Germans won't admit is theirs, and the US government won't admit is theirs, but that lights up the sky every third week or so—and as one of the rockets was taking off, she pulled out that gadget and blew it apart with four little 'whump' noises. It must have been four miles up when she did that; she said what she had done was to put very high-velocity shots into it—apparently they home in, in a pattern, just as you describe—and they tore the fuel tanks apart, spilling fuel onto the hot engine.

"The next day Sheila shot down a plane bringing the German consul back to San Francisco after a leave, from five miles off. That did a pretty good job of convincing us, and that's when we agreed to send the pages.

"But since she had shown us this gadget, it seemed like a waste not to use it some more. We had to be careful to use it only when there would be no direct witnesses, she said, and when the whole thing could look like an accident or when we could provide covering fire so that it looked like a lucky shot. So we had a lot of . . . well, fun, wasn't it, guys?"

Everyone nodded enthusiastically. "If we'd only been able to find a way for her to travel," one of them added, "we could easily have bagged the president, or even the Führer. It was one hot death angel of a gun."

"And when we asked her where she got these things, she said

only that . . . well, do you remember the war in Spain, back before World War II? She said something like that was going on, that the other side had help, and she was coming in to redress the balance. She described the help as 'what the Nazis were to Franco, these people are to the Nazis,' and she was pretty clear that she didn't mean just in technical or military help. And it sounds to me very much like she must have been—"

"A Special Agent, like Harry Skena," I finished for him. "Though I don't see why she couldn't just jump over to the Free Zone. Maybe she didn't have access to a base, or something. But—" the thought hit me hard. "You're talking about her in the past tense. Has she already gone to the Free Zone, or is she—um, dead?"

Al spread his hands; his bushy eyebrows waggled above his glasses. "To tell you the truth, when we found this gadget on you we figured either you'd stolen it from her or you were part of her team. And from the havoc you caused passing through the city— you wouldn't believe how tough it was to get the cell together tonight with Good Neighbors and cops everywhere, and apparently there will be USSS troops arriving on a plane tomorrow to help in the search—from all that beautiful, so-cool chaos you unleashed, we thought you must be a friend of hers.

"We're damn glad you're here, Mark, and one of us does some hand-loading, and we've still got some old .45s in action, so I think we can scrounge you a few magazines. We have a key to her place, and we've searched it a couple of times, but there's not the slightest clue to anything in there, and there certainly wasn't that blue-gray powder you were describing. Which I'm damned sorry about, because it would be fun to keep pulling those merry little pranks we were pulling before."

I nodded impatiently. "But where is she?"

"That's the point," Sandy said quietly. "We were really hoping *you'd* know. Because tomorrow night we make contact with a sub out of the Free Zone, and she's supposed to be there to go with the book, and she's been completely gone for ten days. It's like she just vanished into thin air."

"That could be exactly what happened," I pointed out.

"But if she was doing it of her own free will, why hasn't there been a message to us? And why couldn't she just pop back in whenever she got whatever it was done, and only be gone for five minutes in our time? And if it wasn't of her free will—"

"You think the Closers got her," I said.

"We didn't know what they were called till now," Al said, "but that's exactly what we think happened. So what I suggest is that we all get some sleep; tomorrow the library is boarded-up and closed because they'll have every Boy Scout in the city out pogging—"

"Pogging?"

"I think the word comes from 'pogrom,' " he explained. "What you saw happen with the bus today. Little bastards run out of the bus and beat hell out of 'joogers.' Which is a contraction of Jew and nigger, but officially there are no Jews anymore in America, and the black population is supposedly all on 'reservations' down South, being turned back into slaves. So the word 'jooger' is just an insult our home-grown Nazis use for anything 'abnormal.' And practically all of us in Berkeley are abnormal."

It was nice to know something was the same between the two worlds.

"Anyway," Al went on, "I vote for lying low and then trying to make the rendezvous. We take Mark along, and if Sheila doesn't show, we see if we can sub him in for her."

"I don't know any atomic physics," I protested, "and the SHAKK is useless without a reload. I might as well stay here."

Al shook his head. "Here's the part you're not gonna believe, Mark. You said that in your timeline the atomic bomb came along in 1945, and they really only started working on it in earnest after America got into the war, right?"

"Right, pretty much so. There was some research before then, but it got into high gear after Pearl Harbor."

"Pearl Harbor was—"

"Japanese sneak attack that started the war in my timeline. We lost a lot of the navy there. They bombed the harbor without warning on a Sunday morning."

They all nodded solemnly; it was news to them, I guess.

"So," Al said, "it took, what, four years to build the atomic bomb?"

"Yep. And the Germans were only about two years behind us, I remember reading once—the Soviets were in the race, too, but they were mostly running off stuff they stole from the American project, so they don't exactly count."

All of them looked at each other and shrugged. "And you're sure you remember *nothing* about atomic bombs?"

"A little bit from high-school science and from my science requirement classes, maybe," I said. "I told you, I'm not a nuclear physicist."

Al sighed. "The reason we're so amazed about this, Mark, is that obviously if the Germans had atomic bombs, they'd have cleaned out the Free Zone a long time ago. And they don't. In fact, 'atomic bombs' are on the prohibited list as 'Jewish science'—they were around in science fiction before the war, I can remember some stories I read as a kid, but they certainly never turned up in 1942 or 1943, when we really needed them, and the Germans never got them either. So this set of directions—well, Sheila said that's what it was and we thought she was kidding, giving us a code word for it."

Now it was my turn to goggle and stare. "You mean—I don't believe it. As I recall it was expensive and difficult but it turned out to be pretty simple in the long run. Hell, in my timeline by 1975 *India* had made one."

Al shook his head. "That's both the thing that makes your story convincing and the thing that makes it baffling. There is no such thing in this timeline as an atomic bomb. You say your friend said the Closers won't tolerate them? That's as good an explanation as any, I suppose."

"It's because of the radiation," I said. "Atomic bombs produce stuff called fallout, which gets everywhere—in the air, the water, eventually the food. It's radioactive."

They all looked a bit more puzzled than before, except for one guy who hadn't spoken before. "I remember radioactivity. I used to teach high-school science before the war. It was a hot new area—for that matter all the science-fiction magazines were full of it. But after the war we got told it was all a monstrous piece of—"

"Jewish science," Al finished. "Yeah, it all kind of fits. They want a world run by Nazis, and they want it without atomic bombs. So they came here, and played around . . ." Al groaned and stretched. "We have to go to bed. Tomorrow we have to get set to go meet that sub, and that will be a pretty full day of getting ready and then a long time up late. And besides, I've heard enough impossible things tonight to digest. Time agents, good and bad. Atomic bombs. A certain writer becoming a household name—"

They all laughed at that for no reason I could tell; one of them was blushing.

"—and on top of that, somebody that I think I actually hate more than I hate Nazis. Bedtime, boys and girls . . . we've got a busy day tomorrow."

It was a busy day; they'd pretty much decided that since nothing looked good, they'd fold down the cell and disperse before it got worse. One of the guys had a big old truck that he used to go camping up in the mountains—he was secretly a Buddhist and liked to commune with things, he said—and that was going to be our vehicle for the trip. He managed to slip out about midday, get back to his vegetable stand (which he found smashed to bits with "Jooger!" written in paint all over it, and all the vegetables hurled out in the street), and discovered they at least hadn't broken into his garage. As dusk was falling, he drove his truck back to the rear entrance of the Berkeley Free Library.

Meanwhile Al and Sandy and I had been getting everything incriminating into a small number of crates; the crates, in turn, would travel along with us, along with some gasoline and dynamite for destroying them if that became necessary. Our real security, however, was going to have to be not getting caught. There was just too much to destroy, otherwise.

The others had slipped away quietly during the day, except for one guy whose day cover was begging in the streets, a shaggy-haired (almost an inch long—a hippie by local standards) burly guy named Greg. He went along with one of the big tall ones to help out.

Dusk found us ready to load, and we did in about ten minutes; the truck bounced and thudded alarmingly in the potholed streets, with the three of us sitting huddled by the equipment. Al had assured me the homemade dynamite was fresh, and therefore hadn't sweat any nitroglycerin and was reasonably safe. This was very reassuring because I was sitting on a box of it.

We got the rest of the cell in without incident, and without any noise other than that of the truck. Jaffy, the driver (it seemed to be a nickname, and I never did find out his real one), kept the headlights out and stuck to back streets, just creeping along. I suppose that would look suspicious to a cop . . . if he saw it. But nobody else would phone the police, because in this timeline, America had become the kind of place where something creeping past the house, in the middle of the night, lights out, and engine barely turning, was probably official business, and you didn't want to know.

We stayed tense and quiet till we were out of the city, then, after a long while, Al said, in a quite normal voice, "We can probably talk now—no chance of a patrol out this way. We'll just have to shut up when we start to get close to Half Moon Bay."

Everyone chatted for a bit; nobody's day had been too terribly frightening, because the first day of a big dragnet search was usually given over to Boy Scouts, Jaycees, Kiwanis, and so forth pogging the bohemian areas, in the hopes that it would flush something out from cover. The cops had done the usual roundup of the usual suspects, but most of the usual suspects were "baxters," as Al called them.

"I've heard baxters mentioned before," I said. "What are they?"

"Honestly, when I saw that .45 I thought you might be one. They're people who've slipped the trolley a little bit; they start to imagine that they're living before the war, or during the war. They have a tendency to make speeches in public and to run around waving rusty weapons for which they don't have any ammunition. They're kind of sad . . . but proud, too. Magnificent madmen who won't let time kill their country."

I liked the phrase, and complimented him on it. "Thank you," he said. "I try."

"Al," one of the men sitting in the darkness said, "do you suppose—well, look, this might be our last time when we're all together, right? I mean it doesn't look good. Sheila probably *did* get caught, and you know what they say, after two days, *anyone* will talk. So . . . uh, could we all hear it one more time? I know you buried copies of it in a couple of places, but I like it when you recite it, and I'm afraid I'll never hear it again."

The truck bounced along on the rutted highway; it was clear that Reconstruction hadn't involved building anything like the interstates, or even keeping up what was already there. Under the canvas cover, it was warm from all the bodies, but cold drafts blew in from little crevices. Al was quiet for a long time.

"You really, really flatter me. Do you realize that?"

"We all want to hear it, Al," someone else said, then Sandy chimed in, and finally I said, "Whatever it is, my curiosity is over-powering now. I want to hear it to."

Al, beside me, nodded, and said, "All right then, let me get the trusty canteen beside me, so I can drink while I do this . . . and I think there will be time before we get to Half Moon Bay, for both parts if you want them."

"We want them," Sandy said, firmly, and it seemed to be set-tled.

He took a long swig of water. I got a funny feeling in my stom-ach, like something was going to happen, and then he began to speak.

It was *beautiful*.

·10·

I am not a poet, or even a poetry lover. Lit classes never taught me to like it. And I don't remember it well, so though I was to hear it a few more times, one way and another, I couldn't recite it or quote it.

So you will just have to trust me that it was beautiful, and let me tell you what was in it, and a little bit (which I mostly learned later) about how Al came to write it.

But if you want to imagine my first experience of it, you have to imagine this: Al is speaking right next to you, and his voice loses that strange, slightly whiny quality and becomes deep and resonant. Four others of the bravest people you will ever know are sitting so close to you you can feel the warmth of their bodies. The truck slams and bounces every now and then, and Al has to back up and repeat a couple of lines, but he does it so gracefully and stays so much on the beat that you feel like the bumps and jars are part of the performance.

Every so often you are reminded, by the back of your mind, that you are sitting on about seventy pounds of dynamite.

And as the truck winds its way down the peninsula roads, taking the least-traveled whenever it can, you get glimpses, through the open canvas back, of billions of bright August stars, and of silhouettes of pine trees and mountains.

The poem was in two parts. The first was called, simply, "The

Fall." It began with the assassination of President Roosevelt—a crime still unsolved—in 1936, right after the election. It narrated the following events:

Nobody was quite certain that it was the Nazis who shot Franklin Roosevelt as he rode in an open motorcade in New York City in June 1937. There was no suspicion of it at the time. Indeed, no one was even sure where the shots had come from; the street was noisy and there were so many windows open on so many high buildings that it was unknowable.

They seemed to be ready for it, all the same; within a day they had hate literature out blaming it all on the Jews, and there were anti-Jewish riots here and there around the country.

(It took me a while to figure it out, but it appeared that one critical variable in the whole thing—something that made me suspect the Closers had been working with the Nazis in this timeline for a long time—was that their subversion and propaganda was a lot more effective. They clearly were much more effective at stirring up race and religious hatred in the USA during that time than they ever were in our history.)

The new President was John Nance Garner, a Texas isolationist who was noted for devotion to the oil companies. As an isolationist, he refused to even comment on the Munich deal that surrendered Czechoslovakia to the Nazis.

But when, in October 1938, the coup by General Saturnino Cedillo overthrew President Cardenas of Mexico, and the Mexican Fascist Gold Shirts came to power, Americans found out just which of President Garner's loyalties came first. Cedillo immediately pledged to break up the Mexican government's monopoly on oil production, Pemex, which had been seized from American and European private corporations, and then to return the pieces to foreign investors, Mexico went up in rebellion—and Garner sent the army to back Cedillo. American planes bombed unarmed civilian crowds in Guadalajara; Cedillo kept power backed by one large part of the Mexican Army and by Garner.

The United States went up in a storm of political controversy—it sounded to me like the Vietnam protests but twenty times bigger. Garner had already canceled most of the New Deal, and there had been anger over that, but American troops fighting and dying to keep an avowed fascist and close friend of Goebbels in power was more than could be borne.

The Democrats had become isolationist; the Republicans out-flanked them by becoming ultraisolationist. In 1940, to everyone's surprise, the Republican candidate was Charles A. Lindbergh, prominent as a heroic pilot and public conservative—and member of many, many organizations with Nazi ties.

The situation was so bad that the only nonisolationist party by then was the Socialists, and they actually carried a couple of states. It didn't matter. On a platform of "peace with honor" and "bring the boys back from Mexico," Lindbergh won.

But the news from Europe was bad—worse than anyone could have imagined.

Al's voice recounted all this in a rolling, singing cadence, and through his eyes we saw America become imperialist, saw the army squandered in Mexico—Garner could keep the forces there but he couldn't get additional money out of Congress, so ammunition, aircraft, weapons, and lives were lost and not replaced—saw the horror of Americans presented only with a choice of an imperialist or a fascist sympathizer . . .

And gave us the horror that poured in over the radio from Europe.

(Again, it was much later that I learned from ATN sources that the Closers had been working with the Nazis since 1932. What they had done was to copy plans and devices developed by Germany at the very *end* of World War II, and transfer them back to the German Armed Forces of 1932; the easiest technology to learn is one that is an extension of your own.)

The Nazis began World War II with short-range jet fighters, a Focke-Wulf fighter plane called the FW-187 that beat the Spitfire by far in every possible category, big heavy bombers, snorkel submarines with underwater communication systems so that they could coordinate while submerged—and the V-1 "buzz bomb," modified into a television-guided homing weapon.

Al rattled it off in a litany; the Germans contemptuously ignored Poland in 1939 and struck west and north. France, Denmark, Norway, and Sweden had fallen before Christmas; every one of those nations had a long-ago-prepared pro-Nazi government ready to take power, like Vichy France and Quisling's Norway in our timeline, but far better prepared; within a year, France would be rearming—on the German side.

The British Army in France couldn't be evacuated due to the

stormy winter weather. There was no "miracle at Dunkirk"—most of Britain's combat-ready units ended up in German POW camps.

Again, with contemptuous ease, Hitler gobbled up Poland in the first two weeks of January 1940, after cutting his infamous deal with Stalin.

As in our world, the summer of 1940 was the Battle of Britain, but this time with a difference: the RAF was hopelessly outgunned. The V-1s could be shot down by airplanes, barely, but they were operated by remote pilots looking through TV cameras in the nose, and they hit with deadly effect; the London dockyards burned most nights.

And when the RAF rose against the V-1s, they rose to face Me-262s and FW-187s; they were hopelessly outclassed, and they fell out of the sky.

By late June, the Chamberlain government that had done so much to make sure Britain entered the war unprepared had collapsed, but instead of Churchill, the British got Lord Halifax—a man interested in negotiating a surrender.

It didn't happen, and here Al's voice rose in triumph, and I found my heart beating faster as I heard of the "miracle" that saved Britain.

It was only betrayal at the top that had made America useless to her traditional British friends, and there were people who did not like that . . . among them, Howard Hughes, the Rockefellers, and Alfred P. Sloan of General Motors. In defiance of the federal government, they organized a giant financial consortium to arm Britain against the Nazis. In a crash program, Hughes had produced the first Allied jet fighters by the summer of 1940, and Sloan had them rolling off the assembly lines at twenty per day—on money borrowed with no security from the Rockefellers. Moreover, they had copied the German use of drop tanks and gone it one better— the new airplanes, the P-100 American Eagles, could fly, just barely, all the way to Britain from Labrador.

The offer was straightforward and simple: the British government could lease as many P-100s as the Consortium could build, for a dollar a year and a promise to buy them at cost plus 10 percent within five years of the end of the war. They would cost Britain nothing while the fighting was going on.

The Halifax government, bent on surrender, tried to refuse the offer—and the Miracle of Britain happened.

The Labour Party had never wanted to surrender. Neither had the Churchill wing of the Conservatives. When it was announced that Halifax was opening negotiations and wasn't taking the Consortium's offer, British unions rose up in a general strike to put an end to that, and after an uproar in Parliament, within days Churchill was prime minister—months later than he was in our timeline.

During all this, President Garner thumped his desk, declared our business was in this hemisphere, and extended no aid to Britain. And presidential candidate Lindbergh went him one better by saying we didn't have any business in the hemisphere, either.

Garner tried to block the transfer of the planes, but the P-100s taking off from Detroit were far more than a match for the antiquated P-40s he might have used to stop them. They were touching down in Labrador within hours, refueling, and strapping on drop tanks—and what the British called "Miracle Night" happened on August 30, 1940.

Four hundred P-100s—more of them than Britain had ever had of Spitfires—arrived early in the morning, flying secretly into fields in Scotland and the northwest. Their pilots slept in pup tents on the fields while the mechanics who had flown over just two days before readied them for action.

That night, the P-100s screamed in to meet the German attackers. They overmatched the FW-187 by far, and sent them tumbling from the sky; they were about even with the Me-262, but the P-100s hadn't had to run as far and were flying over friendly territory. It was the first great battle of jet aircraft in history, and Britain won it. The surviving Luftwaffe raced back across the North Sea with its tail between its legs.

With P-100s covering, the old Hurricanes, Spitfires, and Typhoons swarmed into the sky to destroy the deadly V-1s. London slept well that night.

The British crews were exhausted, their planes pushing their safety margins, and yet they would never get a better chance; they landed and leaped from their planes to help the ground crews refuel, strap on fresh drop tanks, and rearm the planes. The bombers had been lost, mostly, in the futile and disastrous attempts to bomb the V-1 launching sites, but every bomber that could be pulled off submarine patrol was along on the mission, too, and every old plane that could fly and carry a bomb or a torpedo.

It was still night when they left; at dawn, they swept down on the invasion fleet being readied at Cherbourg.

They had caught the Germans napping, and in short order the landing craft, the stockpiles of ammunition and spare parts, the rank on rank of Tiger tanks parked and waiting for the landings Hitler had planned for September were in flames.

Britain was saved—for now. And with the P-100s, though she would continue to take a pounding, she could fight on. Moreover, there was an excellent chance that Russia would come in on the British side the next spring, for Stalin had finally realized that his deal with Hitler couldn't last.

Jaffy slowed down, turned up an old gravel driveway, and stopped the engine. "Patrol ahead," he called back to us. "They've got headlights on—I think it's just routine."

We sat with our hands on our guns and watched two German-built squad cars roll by, their machine guns hanging idle. We waited a long time there in the icy dark of the mountains, and a great field of stars danced above us. There was no sound at all when Jaffy restarted the motor.

"Keep going, Al," somebody said.

Spring held more surprises. President Lindbergh, too late and too little, offered aid to Britain, and not only brought the American Army home, but warned Cedillo to stay out of the European war.

But Congress was in a different mood, and many of them seemed to feel that if the Consortium was arming the British, Congress did not need to do anything for the USA. Lindbergh couldn't even get the weapons expended in Mexico replaced.

Hitler popped three surprises, one after another, in the summer of 1941. Under persuasion of his agents, and with the offer of German help, Franco joined the Axis, swept down the Tagus Valley into Portugal, and took Lisbon in a week; a week after that, Nazi guns were pounding Gibraltar, and the guided V-1 had closed off the western entrance to the Mediterranean.

Simultaneously, the Turkish government was overthrown by a Nazi-backed coup, and suddenly Greece and Yugoslavia were under a two-front attack. It was over quickly; in less than a month

Hitler's control extended from the Atlantic to Iran, and in a short time after that the attack was under way to close Suez. Unable to supply Egypt and Palestine by any means except around the Cape, Britain was forced to evacuate forces to India and Australia, and by July, Hitler had gathered up everything in the region, including the Persian Gulf.

The drive into Russia was nothing like what happened in our timeline. The attack was announced by Stalin's assassination; it was only six weeks till Moscow fell, and in the peace treaty the USSR gave up the Ukraine and the Baltics to Hitler. The German troops were not merely home, as they had been promised, by Christmas; they were home before the leaves turned.

President Lindbergh must have been sincere, and not a German agent, for he moved more and more to actively resist the Nazi onslaught. Al's poem called him that "poor, poor, well-meaning man, not a good mind, not even a good heart, but not bad, not evil, not yet captured, driven mad hysterical naked by the drum drum drum of evil." He proclaimed the Lindbergh Doctrine: The United States would fight to prevent any of the Atlantic islands, from which our shipping and Britain's lifeline might be threatened, from falling into German hands.

On November 8, 1941, German parachute and glider troops landed in force on the Azores, in a complete and total violation of the Lindbergh Doctrine. They were under command of Air Marshal Manfred von Richthofen; I was a little startled, since in my own timeline the "Red Baron" had been shot down and killed in WWI. Clearly the Closers had been working pretty hard for a long time in this timeline.

The Battle of the Azores is about half of Al's poem; he goes ship by ship, blow by blow. The story is grim from one end to the other; Admiral King's Atlantic Fleet was far from ready, but they linked up with the troop ships and set out anyway. It was clear the force was too small—King had only three operational carriers, all carrying planes that were worse than obsolete—and so Admiral Kimmel and the Pacific Fleet were supposed to run around to link up with him, through Panama.

But as the fleets were readying, a shipload full of fertilizer blew up in the Canal, and it was out of action. German or Japanese actions were suspected, but it hardly mattered now—Lindbergh had already declared war. And in any case, the Pacific Carrier Bat-

tle Group would have had to round the Horn—the ships were too
big for the locks.

The battle plan was foolish but politically necessary. Both King
and Kimmel protested, but without effect—King was to sit out in
the Atlantic, at the outer edge of where the P-100s could guard his
fleet, and wait for Kimmel; Kimmel was going to have to race ten
thousand miles as fast as his fleet could go.

But another player was about to enter the war. Argentina had
secret agreements with Hitler. Just off the Falkland Islands—part
of Juan Perón's reward for stabbing *los norteamericanos* in the back
was to get those islands—German JU-88s, effectively outdated but
more than able to carry the new air-launched guided V-1, jumped
Kimmel's fleet. In less than ten minutes on that dark night, the
carriers *Enterprise* and *Hornet* were ablaze, and before the remain-
der of the fleet escaped north they had to run a gauntlet of more
than two thousand miles of air attacks, covered only by planes from
the *Lexington*.

Brazil, already technically at war with the Axis because of the
invasion of her mother country, Portugal, struck south into Argentina; it was a measure of how desperate the Allies were that the
addition of Brazil seemed like a big gain. It was immediately coun-
terbalanced by the entry of Vichy France on the German side.

As Kimmel desperately raced north to join King, word reached
Washington of the terrible losses at the Falklands, and it became
clear that Japan was about to attack Hawaii. President Lindbergh
recalled the Pacific Fleet to San Diego and ordered King to press
the attack without waiting for Kimmel.

There is no doubt the Germans were reading American codes.
As the Atlantic Fleet pressed into striking range, now out of reach
of all but the briefest support from jets out of Britain, JU-88s and
heavy bombers closed in, and, in a hail of V-1 cruise missiles, the
carriers went up like tinder. Some of them launched planes; some
of the planes got through, and a few of the German allied ships,
from the Italian and French navies, took some damage. But it was
the end of American naval power in the Atlantic. Kimmel and the
survivors of the fleet that had run the gauntlet of the Falklands
turned back and put in at Rio, losing three destroyers and a cruiser
to the new high-speed efficient U-boats on the way. Al's poem
ended with Kimmel's fleet limping into Rio, and with the ominous
note that worse things were brewing far to the north.

The truck pulled over to the side and all but skidded to a stop; Jaffy was out and running around in a second, and we all jumped out to join him before we quite knew what was up.

"Something moving without lights on the road up ahead," he breathed to us. "No place near here to pull the truck over out of sight, so we're going to have to tough it out."

It was very quiet, but in those mountains sometimes you can see things a long way off. We sat and waited, and finally the low thunder of engines came to us. "Heavy haulers," Al breathed, "and a lot of them. I'd say we're going to see a parade . . ."

A few minutes later they came into sight. They were moving a lot faster than I would have dared, right down the centerline, big heavy tractor-trailer rigs each carrying a tank or an APC. I counted twenty-eight of them.

We waited a long time, and then Al said, "I don't think there's going to be a lot of the city to go back to. Somebody is really after Mark, or us, or something."

"Roll on?" Jaffy asked.

"Roll on," Al said. "Nowhere behind us to go, and I'm not optimistic about in front of us. But I know there's nowhere behind us to go."

Al's second poem was called "The Gathering of Nations," and it was the story of how the Free Zone got put together. I never got much of a chance to look into the history between when "The Fall" ended and "The Gathering of Nations" began, so there were gaps in it. Briefly, it told how Patton, Bradley, and Montgomery dueled with Rommel in the Shenandoah Valley, after the "great ships of ice in the Chesapeake."

That much, I found out, referred to the secret German weapon no one had any idea of. They had had the fiords of Norway, secure against prying eyes, for long enough to build two dozen immense artificial rafts of ice, big as small islands, onto which they moved whole air and submarine bases and divisions. When the ice islands grounded in the Chesapeake early the next spring, they carried most of the Wehrmacht.

There was another reference to Patton and the American Expe-

ditionary Force coming home to Boston on the Royal Navy—and to
the RAF coming with them—but exactly what happened, I never
learned.

At any rate, "The Gathering of Nations" began with Patton's
Army driven west out of Gettysburg, toward Pittsburgh, and Montgomery retreating northeast toward New York. What was in the
poem after that might fill many volumes—Bradley's defense of the
bridges at Wheeling, which allowed Patton's forces to escape in
their epic retreat, which was eventually to take them to San Diego,
to their rendezvous with Nimitz, and to the escape across the Pacific
to Auckland. That was exciting enough—but the Royal Navy had
gone them several better, picking up Montgomery's army from
Long Island and the New Jersey shore, running past the German
strongholds in Delaware and Maryland. (Al's poem has a passage
that brings tears to my eyes when I think about it, describing the
grim decision of fifty P-100 pilots to hold the air above the Royal
Navy long enough for them to get through, grabbing Marines and
some of the American Navy from Guantanamo Bay, skirting down
the South American coast with dozens of tankers of Texas fuel oil
that had managed to sneak unescorted out of Galveston . . .)

The rendezvous with Kimmel and the attack, with the Brazilians, that led to the revenge sacking and burning of Buenos Aires—
and the long voyage to Perth, Australia, straight across the Atlantic
and Indian Oceans . . . all that was in there. There were moments of comedy in it as well; the meeting of Patton and Montgomery, again, in Sydney, seemed to make everyone chuckle. ("Of
course you got here sooner, Monty, you rode the whole way!")

A few more verses sketched in references to other groups and
outfits that had found their way there. Soviet divisions that fled
over the Khyber Pass and slugged their way across Japanese-occu-
pied India rather than be disbanded as ordered. General Chen-
nault's Flying Tigers. MacArthur and much of the Philippines garrison. Anyone who could find a ship and get clear of the Axis navies
seemed to find a way there, often against terrible odds.

I'm no judge of poetry, but from the way people responded to
it, I'd say that the English-speaking nations had gained their equivalent of the *Odyssey* or the *Aeneid*.

The ending, with the litany of all the forces that were now in
the Free Zone—everything from the First Marines to the French
Foreign Legion to the Reconstituted Abraham Lincoln Brigade and

the Irgun—left me feeling better than I had in days. I was in with good people. If courage and goodwill could bring you victory, it ought to work for these people if it worked for anyone.

There was a long silence afterward; by now we were winding down from the crest of the mountains that run like a stegosaurus spine up the peninsula. The truck thudded and shuddered regularly, and once the box of dynamite actually rose a bit under me; people were sometimes thrown together in heaps. Jaffy was being careful, but the road wasn't much more than a track anymore, and there was no light at all among the trees and in the deeper ravines; he had a couple of tiny carbide lights with red glass in front of them burning on the hood, but whenever he got to a place where he could drive by moonlight, he would stop, run around, and blow them out.

At last the winding mountain road gave way to something a little smoother and easier to handle, and then to something that was merely a badly maintained country road. We were coming up on Half Moon Bay.

Jaffy knew a couple of ways to sneak around the town itself; Al, next to me, whispered that the town had sort of a vogue among the younger elite of the West Coast German expat community, because they had all gone crazy with surfing, and this place was sufficiently isolated so that they could slip off and do some not-quite-proper sex on the side. People who worked in the guest houses in the little, turn-of-the-century port town had become invaluable to the underground, because they could pick up so much blackmail material for the scandal files.

Half Moon Bay was also a great place to bring a sub in close to shore; they could paddle out in rubber rafts without much problem, because though the surf was reliable, it wasn't the sort of spectacular stuff that is also dangerous.

Jaffy was driving us around on back roads and sometimes through private farm roads where the underground had some arrangement; the idea was to get to the beach on the north side of town without being seen. As a result we did some backtracking and often went very slowly. It was too dangerous to talk now, so most of us just got caught up on our napping.

Finally he killed the motor. I could just smell a little bit of sea breeze. He came around and squatted in the back of the truck with us.

"We're still a long way off," Al said. "Did you see trouble?"

"Lots of it. Two groves of trees with men moving in them. Couple of guys keeping an eye on the road; one of them had a pair of binoculars. Stuff like that. I think they have the beach completely staked out."

"Shit," Al said. "Suggestions, anyone?"

What we had in the truck was more than enough to hang all of us if we were caught with it. In the aggregate it was far too heavy to move by foot. Thus we couldn't abandon the truck . . . but any hope of getting down to the beach depended on being silent.

"Well," I said, "I imagine most of you have the skills for a bare-hands night attack—"

They all nodded. "Everyone here has done a German or two, and more American quislings than you can count," Al said.

"Then why don't we each pick a direction, scout it, come back at a prearranged time, and see if we can figure out what's up? We've got hours till our friends come by."

Greg grunted. "Good as any other idea, and it won't be boring. Let's."

My target was one of the ridges where we'd seen some bored idiot lighting a cigarette; I worked my way forward carefully. This was a lot like playing Army as a kid; stay low, show no shadow, move as fast as you can without making noise. It helped that what I was going across was a huge field of pumpkins—there's a risk of tripping over a pumpkin or a vine, of course, but on the other hand it's all so damp that there's nothing to rustle, and it's so blotchy in dim light that there aren't very many shapes that show up well against it.

There were trees as I came out of the pumpkin patch. I was able to move just a little more quickly and ascend just a little faster.

There were two of them, both wearing the Good Neighbor Patrol uniform. It occurred to me that the Good Neighbors, and the local idiotic version of the Boy Scouts, probably appealed to a certain kind of personality that loved to wear uniforms and do violence but wasn't much into running any real risks to their hides.

I crawled up closer and discovered what I had was that perfect conversational pair, the Whiner and the Sympathizer. Whiner thought it was cold and damp out and he was going to get something and he had to have the cigarette to steady his nerves but if the fucking captain saw that he'd be in deep shit. Sympathizer agreed with all that and said it was really a shame that Whiner wasn't an officer himself. Whiner said, well, it was all political, what do you expect, and Sympathizer agreed.

I figured as soon as they were apart, Sympathizer was going to turn Whiner in.

Unfortunately, after I counted the thousand heartbeats I had estimated, all I knew was that they were generally watching toward the sea, when they weren't looking at each other, and that their organizational politics were like any other organizational politics; Whiner felt shafted, Sympathizer agreed, and I wondered why Whiner's shoulder blades were not itching right between them, where I figured Sympathizer's knife would go.

It was also pretty clear that these were not the last of the red-hot guards.

I came back down the hill quietly and slipped across the pumpkin patch, feeling pretty discouraged. I hadn't learned a thing, it seemed to me.

That was what everyone had found; a few younger members had been very spit-and-polish but no more effective, and mostly it looked like a bunch of disgruntled small-town back-slapping good-fellas, stuck out in the cold woods.

"They're more than enough to sound an alarm, though," Al said. "We probably ought to do something about them, so we can get the truck through. And I don't like the fact that they seem to be facing the landing point. That sort of suggests we've got big trouble."

Sandy spoke up. "I think I have an idea. Help me out with it. If you were using those guys as a guard, all you'd be doing is using them as a tripwire, right? I mean, if they run into something, they aren't going to stop it effectively, and they aren't going to do anything but run in circles and scream, right? So they're expecting to chase something that landed on the coast, and they want to make sure they don't lose it."

"Got you," Al said. "They aren't looking for anything from this side, for some reason. Well, hell, why don't we just drive the truck right into town and park by the fisherman's market? That will put us less than a mile from the rendezvous point, and at least we won't look as conspicuous as we do sneaking around in the pumpkin fields. And it will leave us a lot of time to send in a deep reconnoiter."

Driving into town was downright dull; there was a row of trucks sitting by the fisherman's market, and we just joined it. Sandy, Al, and I crept out; something made me take the SHAKK along, and Al brought the precious notebook. "We'll be back for all of you for sure," he said, "but this is because—"

"It's because luck can run out," Jaffy whispered back at him. "That's okay, man, we can understand that. Life is not always fair. Go in peace, and I hope it works out, but if it doesn't—woe to the wicked, you madman."

Al grabbed him and kissed him passionately on the lips, which startled me a little, especially since I'd figured Al and Sandy were probably an item, but like they say, some of your best friends and not always the guys you'd expect . . .

We moved up the edge of the beach—the grass came down there in irregular tufts and clumps so that there was lots of cover in shadows and hollows. It went faster than we might have thought.

Sandy touched my arm and pointed, and a moment later Al gave a little hiss beside me. There was a man patrolling the beach with a machine gun; he didn't look any more alert or better trained than the Good Neighbors, but he sure as hell was better armed.

I felt in my pockets and found one of the pieces of rope I'd cut for the purpose, tying a little bowline loop on each end. I'd never actually garrotted anyone before, but what the heck, I was new to the timeline. Maybe I'd get to like it.

I crawled forward, the cold sand pressing moisture up through my clothes so that between the sweat and the damp I was drenched when I finally reached the shoreward end of his patrolling. I crouched in a deep shadow and waited.

He came back into the shadows for just a moment, and I sprang. The gun hit the ground as I did, but in the deep sand it wasn't noisy, and praise god it didn't go off. I had the line around his neck, braced my knee in his back, and yanked it tight enough to shut off his air before he knew what was going on. I kept the tension up as I used my shoulder to drive him into the sand on his face.

I put one loop over the other, slid it down as my opponent struggled facedown in the sand under me, and then pulled the free end tight with all the force I had. It must have finally pinched a carotid, because after a flurry of scuffling around in the sand that seemed to go on forever, he finally lay still. I yanked hard to ratchet it that little extra bit tighter, and tied it off. If he was playing possum, he'd be pretty uncomfortable and have to move soon, and if not, he'd die soon. I'd made out the American Swastika insignia on his arm and was enjoying the thought of him dying slowly.

As I rose and motioned them forward, I found Sandy was right at my ear. She whispered, "Al saw another one and went on ahead. Let's move up to him."

When we got there, he'd done a neat little bit of knife work, but then I think he probably had had more practice than I had. Slashing the carotid like that drops blood pressure in the brain so fast that the victims are dead before they hit the ground—and Al had been quick enough about it to get practically nothing on his clothes.

We crept on forward; there was a dark, vertical shadow on the sand ahead. We had to get close before we could see what it was.

"Oh, *fuck*," Al whispered under his breath, about the time I saw, too.

It was a woman, nude, smeared with dark streaks that could only be blood, tied upright to a post, facing the sea. It wouldn't have fooled anyone under any circumstances—you could see she was either dead or unconscious, and the post stuck way up above her head. It was there to freak out whoever came ashore.

"Bush league," Sandy murmured.

Al glanced sharply at her. "Explain?"

"Everyone we've hit even up close is a Good Neighbor. This isn't a professional operation. They got lucky, caught her, beat her until she told them where her pickup was. Now they're doing this kind of petty bullshit. That's all. If we can get 'em off the beach somehow, we'll be right in the clear."

"Is it—" I whispered.

"Oh, yeah, it's Sheila. Jesus, those fuckers. Can we kill some more?" Sandy asked.

"Just about for sure," Al reassured her. "One good diversion would do it . . . if we just had somebody to kill one of them at a distance, we'd be in damn fine shape. They'll all either run toward the noise or start firing in the dark."

"I could go get one," Sandy suggested, "just to get things rolling."

Al shook his head. "We have to get to Sheila, see if she's still alive. And if she is, we need time there. We'll need a better diversion than that."

All of this was in whispers soft as breathing. I was gaining a little confidence—the patrols had not been set up in any way that would let them cover each other, so I thought Sandy was probably dead right. This was some overambitious local Good Neighbor captain—probably the same one Whiner and Sympathizer had been talking about—who had launched this operation on his own. "I just had an idea," I breathed. "I'm going to try something—just take advantage of it if it works."

They nodded, once—I guess they trusted me, which was pretty flattering in the circumstances.

I crept up the sandy beach to the brush line. The question I had asked myself was, if I had no brains or judgment, what would I think was the best place for my command post? I wasn't sure what I would do when I found my hyperambitious captain, but I did know that if I wanted to make a lot of valuable chaos happen, doing something to him was probably the most efficient way to accomplish it.

There was one likely spot, and as I climbed up the grassy side of the dune, I was gratified to find tire tracks. He'd even driven up here. Too perfect.

He was there on the hood of his car—having a car at all, of course, meant he'd spent some years of assiduous sucking up to the authorities. Probably thought of it as being realistic and honestly pursuing his self-interest . . .

He was sitting there cross-legged with his radio operator on the ground beside him, and as I listened I realized he was having a great time talking military-talk with the boys out in the field. He didn't know yet that two of his pickets were dead, because he'd put them out so badly; he had a lot of men scattered all over the place grumbling and hating him, and probably a division of marines could have landed without his men picking it up. He was smoking, himself, so that as I got closer I saw the tiny dot of red going back and forth.

The problem was there were two of them. If I could get them both, for sure, silently, I could have all kinds of fun . . .

I crawled in closer, and now I could hear the two of them talking. The radioman, I realized, was young enough to be impressed with his captain.

By now I was practically up behind the car from them, and could take a better look. The car was parked on an upslope, but I didn't think releasing the emergency brake would make it roll back—it was in soft sand.

I figured any burst of noise would bring people running in here, and it could well start them shooting each other, but that would mean regular cops out on the beach and make the contact that much harder.

There was a walkie-talkie, sort of—the thing was huge, backpack-sized—just leaning up against the car. In fact there were two of them . . .

An idea hit me, and the more I thought about it, the better I liked it. Very quietly I lifted the radio and crept on back. The captain was just explaining—way too loudly, "Well, you know, Jimmy, you do get a lot of time when all you can do is wait. That's part of being in the organization; it's the mark of real discipline . . ."

Probably the captain became a Good Neighbor because the Boy Scouts thought he'd make a lousy Scoutmaster.

It took very little time to get back to Al and Sandy. They saw what I had, and I wished it was bright enough for them to see me wink. "What kind of fun can we have with this?"

Al beamed; I could see the glow of his teeth in the dark. "Allow me . . . you said the kid's name was Jimmy?"

"Yep."

"Then it's Captain Alex Laban. A stuffed shirt and a first-order moron. Let's get some radio traffic . . ."

Holding the earphone so that all three of our heads could surround it, we heard three things; Jimmy requesting people to report what was happening at their stations, people reporting nothing, and Laban chewing them out for reporting nothing in incorrect form. "That's Command Post Command Post Nothing to report sir Over," he was telling one.

Al grinned, flipped the mike to talk, and said, "Jimmy, you tell us as soon as he tries to pat your butt."

There was an amazing spell of radio silence. Then Laban said, "Who was that! Acknowledge! Who was that?" It was really loud.

Al flipped the knob around, and his grin got more deep and wicked. "Emergency, Channel 100 Emergency," he said, crisply but softly into the mike. His voice was high and squeaky.

A voice responded at once. "Situation?"

"Good Neighbor captain exceeding authority. Beach north of Half Moon Bay. I have been ordered to do things contrary to my moral beliefs. My name is Jimmy, and he's just left me alone, but he's been bothering me all night—he said it was for field maneuvers, and I had to work the radio for him, but now he's got me out here all alone and he's—he's—I can't say. It's too icky." Then he rammed the mike against his neck and made a gargling noise, and rubbed it facedown in the sand.

The voice on the other end started frantically trying to hail "Jimmy." Al flipped the channel again and asked Jimmy a question that would have been pretty blunt in a leather bar. Jimmy didn't answer. Then Al asked him if he couldn't talk because of what he was doing for Captain Laban, and whether he really liked it. Jimmy's voice now came through high and squeaky: "Captain Laban is going around to the posts right now to find out who's doing it, and if you don't stop it, I'm going to have him *kill* you."

"Has he ever—" what Al suggested seemed a bit implausible, but now Jimmy was really raving, screaming almost. I could hear him perfectly well without the radio.

The regular cops had flipped over from the Emergency Channel and seemed to be convinced Jimmy was getting raped right there and then on the beach; they started trying to talk to him. Al did a deep voice and said, "Jimmy, this is the police. We just want you to know you are not to do any of that stuff with the captain. You are reserved for us, and you will do it with us."

That got Jimmy yelling that Al wasn't the police and he wasn't doing anything and Captain Laban was going to beat his ass in.

Al sat back, smiling happily. "Except on Channel 100, these things are all very low power, so they won't interfere with each other," he whispered. "Only base stations like Jimmy's have much oomph. So all they can hear is him raving. And I would bet any minute—"

Sure enough, the captain might not have been any kind of military genius, but he'd figured out that the cops would be out to investigate real soon. Considering he had kept a possibly important witness all to himself and that there were some pretty wild accusations flying around, he behaved like you'd expect anyone of his type to do—he ordered people to go home and jumped into his car. We heard him drive away.

"He didn't even check to see whether his whole command heard it," I said.

Sandy shook her head. "The regular cops were all trained by the Nazis during Reconstruction. He knows that anyone with any sense will be taking off to hide right now. Good Neighbors are always doing this kind of thing—a lot of them are people who weren't smart enough or brutal enough to make the regular cops. We can probably sneak up to Sheila now and see if she's alive—but I'm afraid she isn't."

She wasn't. She was as cold as the night air, and her poor body was bruised, battered, and cut all over. I figured they had probably not so much systematically tortured her as they had just improvised, the way a group of sadistic children will sometimes keep coming up with things to do to a dog or a cat until it mercifully expires.

She was tied to the post too tightly to unknot, but we cut her loose and at least laid her on the ground. There was no sign of her SHAKK or of anything else except her—along with her clothes they had taken everything.

Al swore and pointed at her mouth. "Look what they did to her."

A lot of the blood on her had come out of there. I didn't see what it was, and then Sandy said, "Oh, shit, shit, don't let Greg see this, I think he had a crush on her."

"What?" I asked.

"There's this weird belief they have that some agents on our side have radios concealed in hollow teeth. They pulled out all her teeth, either looking for it or to destroy it."

I felt pretty sick, but I said, "Uh, but—you *could* have a radio in a hollow tooth—"

Al made a face. "Please. I know your people are more advanced than mine, but even I know you can't make a vacuum tube that small work."

It was my turn to be baffled and irritated. "Ever hear of transistors? I'm not defending them, but if they've gotten hold of a Special Agent before—"

"What do you know about transistors?" a voice said, very softly, behind us. "Keep your hands away from your weapons," it added.

·11·

"May I turn around?" I asked, my hands kept high above my head.

"You may," the voice said, and I did—very slowly.

You know how sometimes a face of a public figure stays with you forever? You see him a few times, maybe you hear him speak, and—presto, with you forever.

I'd heard this guy twice, both times because I was deliberately crossing a picket line to hear him. He was the great *bête noir* of a rather large faction at Yale when I was there, and even though he generally irritated hell out of me, and more so out of Marie, he was always much too interesting to ignore.

That is, as much of him as you could get to hear before the whooping and shouting got too loud.

He was a broad-shouldered man with bushy black eyebrows and a sharp nose and chin, bigger than he looked at first, and he stood a little awkwardly, like he might limp or stumble a bit when he walked. At the moment he had a very convincing Thompson submachine gun pointed at me.

His Hungarian accent was not as thick as it had been when I'd heard him speak at Yale, he was twenty years younger, and even in the dim light reflecting off the sea I could tell he was heavily tanned.

"Dr. Teller," I said. "Are transistors unknown in this timeline?"

"You realize," he said very casually, "that your knowledge of transistors, plus your knowledge of timelines, means that either you are what I have been praying for, without knowing exactly what it was, for years—or else that I should shoot you and your companions right now."

"He's legit," Al said, and rattled off half a dozen passwords.

Teller nodded. "Then we had best get moving. Was this poor woman—"

"The contact you were supposed to have," I said. "I'm sort of the best that was available as a substitute."

"Let us pray you're good enough," he said. "Are we ready to go, then?"

"We can be," Al said, "as soon as we pick up our three friends from back in town. They've nowhere else to go and, there's a fair amount of incriminating stuff with them."

By that time a dozen soot-faced men in black turtlenecks, watch caps, and dungarees—the very image of the World War II commandos in the movies of my childhood—had emerged from the shadows.

Teller spoke briefly into a handheld gadget that looked like a cellular phone, and we hurried up the beach, back toward Half Moon Bay. But we had gone no more than three hundred yards when we heard the rattle of gunfire. We picked up the pace, but long before we got near the town there was a huge explosion. Flames shot far up into the air.

"Can we wait ten minutes?" Al asked, shuddering, as he stared at the flames. "God damn the god damn luck, Mark, Sandy, we could have taken them along with us."

Teller shook his head, and I could tell he didn't like it any better than we did. "This beach will be swarming with cops of all kinds in minutes. We've got to get off it. There's a good chance your friends died in that explosion, and if not, they will have to shift for themselves. At least they have been provided with a diversion."

Al nodded slowly and started to mutter something under his breath; we dog-trotted up the beach to where the rubber rafts lay concealed, guarded by four more tough-looking commandos.

There wasn't any surf worth talking about, but a beach that is able to have surf tends to amp up any wave that hits it, and the paddling out to sea was about as difficult, physically, as anything I'd done. They handed us all paddles, and we put everything we had into it.

There was no more gunfire behind us. Either the other three members of the cell were dead, as we hoped, or they were captured.

Al was still muttering next to me; I glanced at him, feeling sorry for him, and he must have thought I was curious. "Kaddish," he explained. "Haven't said it in years, not since I found out my mother died in a camp near Toledo."

Though there were no shots, there was plenty of noise from the shore—sirens, motors, people yelling. We could see many headlights on the road over the mountains behind us, as we topped each wave, and a little later there were headlights on the coast road as well.

Let all of ours be dead . . . please let them be lucky enough to be dead . . .

I was about to ask just how far out we were going to have to paddle—my arms were getting sore from the unaccustomed labor—when we came into the calmer water away from the beach, and I caught a glimpse of something long and thin sticking up from that water. By now there were all sorts of electric lights glowing on the shoreline.

Very swiftly, and making what seemed like a terrible lot of noise, the submarine broke the surface in front of us. I'd built some model ships as a kid, and I knew what a Salmon class sub looked like. In my time that thing would have been a museum piece, but here it was.

Lines were thrown out and tied off, and they brought us in fast. I'm no sailor, but it seemed to me that I'd seldom seen men who knew their business so well. In less time than it takes to tell, our rubber boats were up against the steel sides of the sub, and we were scrambling onto the slippery deck and down through the hatches into the close, smelly space underneath. They towed us into a cramped corner, sort of out of the way, and then the commandos were piling in as quickly as they could. The last man down the ladder was in a faded navy shirt and a pair of black pajama trousers, with bare feet, and as the hatch slammed shut he hissed, "Think I heard a plane engine, Cap'n."

"Take her down!"

"Aye aye, sir!"

The diving horn sounded, and I felt the steel deck shifting under my feet as the submarine plunged back beneath the waves.

I looked around. The commandos were sitting in a long double row, feet pressed together in the middle of the corridor, filling it completely. I heard the whine of the electric motors as the sub ran for the open sea.

When the commandos took off their knit watch caps, a second look told me something interesting about them—many were bald, or gray, or both. All had crow's-feet around their eyes, and though I could see hard muscle under the sweaters, most had at least a little bit of a paunch.

Every one of them must be in his forties.

The captain himself looked more like what you'd expect an admiral to look like where I'd come from. I suppose when a navy doesn't get any new ships or enlistees, this is what it gets to look like . . . on the other hand, they were probably the most experienced crew in history.

The silence was interminable, but I had no idea what kind of detection devices we might be hiding from, and I was not going to take any chances in my ignorance. The air got more and more stuffy, not from the failure of the recirc system—we had not been underwater for more than an hour—but from the tang of sweat and fear.

I looked across the corridor at Sandy; she was staring down at the deck, and tears were running down her face. She'd lost three of her best friends—hell, maybe one of them was her lover.

I'd been there; I knew what that felt like. My heart broke for her, and I reached out and quietly took her hand. She squeezed my hand till it felt like she'd break it, but I didn't take it back.

There was a change in the sound of the motors, and then we drifted silently. Overhead, there was a low thrum, which then became a throbbing sound.

Everyone seemed to hold their breath. Something thundered overhead like a freight train.

We sat perfectly still in the hot air, sweat running down our faces. The commandos, sitting next to me, who probably would have regarded a firefight at close quarters as all in a day's work, looked sick and drawn.

I didn't blame them. There was part of me thinking, *I don't know what a depth charge coming in sounds like, but I bet I'll know it when I hear it.*

And with that came images of the walls suddenly bursting in, icy water and high pressure, torn and bloody bodies and hands scrabbling against the pitiless steel surfaces bearing them down to the black depths—

We waited longer. The captain whispered a command, and the motors resumed for a little while, slowly pushing us forward. The commando next to me breathed in my ear, "Cap'n says we're under a cold-water layer and the tide can take us out, pass it on." I repeated it to Al, next to me. He nodded. It sounded like things were better than they had seemed to be.

The motors stopped again, and we drifted again. Twice more we heard ship's engines overhead, but never as close as the first one.

After another hour the captain started us forward again and said, "All right, let's not make too much noise, but we can talk a bit. We'll make the rest of this run submerged."

He turned to us. "I know we were a bit short on ceremony there. I was afraid the plane got a radar fix, and perhaps it did, but for whatever reason they didn't get on us fast enough. I'm Captain William Stark. Welcome to the USS *Skipjack*. I know the accommodations are not terribly comfortable, but you'll only have to bear with them for a day or so."

"A *day* or so? How fast does this thing go?" Al asked. "Or are you dropping us off someplace?"

Stark grinned at us, and we noticed how many other people were chuckling. "Well, you'll just have to see. But the short answer is, things are going to be much more comfortable than this, and the long answer is, if I told you how, you wouldn't believe it."

And that was all he said. Teller seemed very excited to get a look at the notebook Al had so carefully brought along, and as soon as he had it he was dead to the world; the commandos weren't supposed to know too much about us for security reasons. I tinkered with the SHAKK a little, but I still could not come up with any way to reload a gadget that obviously had to have a special substance that I didn't even know the chemical ingredients to.

Sandy sat in the corner, quietly weeping, and Al said he thought it wasn't so much for any one of the men who had died back on the beach at Half Moon Bay. It was more that she had lived so close to them for so long, and that some of them had been heroes to her. "Used to be a lot of those on college campuses, you know, boykids and girlkids who wanted to worship artists. God knows I was one. I kind of suspect my mother was, too."

"You—um, if you don't want to tell me, it's okay," I said, "but I'm really curious. You were saying Kaddish? I thought that after Reconstruction—"

"Oh, some of us survived one way or another. In my case I knew there were a couple of nutcase profs around Berkeley with theories about how to 'cure' people of homosexuality, and after the surrender they had been pretty fast to join the Nazi Party, even before the Wehrmacht administrative troops got there. And I knew their 'therapy' was basically tormenting people until they said they liked women. Well, women are okay with me—I'm sort of bi, anyway—and so I knew I could fake that part of it. And I turned out to be right—once they'd locked me up for being a queer, it didn't occur to them to come back and lock me up again for being a Jew. But there were parts of the country where they gassed everybody in both categories. I just happened to have this local dodge."

He stared off into space. "I wish I'd had a little more privacy, a little more time, gotten to see more of my mother before she died," he said, "partly because I just wish I had, like anyone would, and partly because I could have written a great poem about her, I think. One of the damned miserable things about all this is that instead of ordinary deaths, you have people who become martyrs, and their martyrdom matters more than who they are.

"I think I might have been very happy if I could have just been a poet."

I nodded, and then, feeling more tired than ever, I fell asleep. As I was drifting off I noticed Sandy had shifted around to use my shoulder as a pillow, and had the stray thought that I liked her, for her courage and common sense and all the rest of it. I'd have to keep an eye on her for a while; people who are in deep grief often do a very poor job of taking care of themselves.

When I woke up, Sandy was still sleeping on my shoulder, but something was subtly different. It took me a moment to realize the floor was sloping at a funny angle, and then that the motors were

making an odd noise and I could hear the hiss of compressed air
going into the ballast tanks. We were on our way up to the surface.

I sat up a little more, waking Sandy. "Where are we?" she
asked.

"Surfacing, I think," I said.

There were a lot of sailors swiftly, silently, running back and
forth, and all of us sitting in that corridor had to pull our feet all
the way in so that they could get past us. The captain appeared to
be talking to someone on a sort of telephone, and it didn't seem to
be anyone on board.

"Maybe we're meeting a ship?" Al suggested, next to me.

"Could be, I guess," I said, "but I can't believe they can get a
surface ship this close to North America. Maybe it's a plane? That's
pretty dangerous, too."

World War II subs were not terribly fast underwater, and they
had limited amounts of time they could spend submerged; even if
there had been an improvement or two, I didn't think we could be
much more than 150 miles off the California coast.

"Well," Captain Stark said, "I see we've awakened you at last.
You've all been asleep for most of the last fifteen hours; it's finally
dark enough topside to do the transfer."

"The transfer to what?"

"To what's going to take you people, and the commando team,
and Dr. Teller, to the Free Zone. I think you'll be pleased. Unfortunately our abilities to modify some things are limited; we've never
worked out a good way to do the transfers underwater."

We all nodded, just as if he'd given us real information, and he
said, "Do get your bags and things in hand, because we have to get
you out on the deck and then get you over the side very quickly."

After a few more minutes, the sub was at periscope depth and
cruising along slowly; they ran up a snorkel and the diesels started,
which made us go faster but was no advantage—it also brought a
strong smell of diesel fumes into the hull. Then, a long half hour
later, the captain gave the commands; the sub rose to the surface.

"All of you, topside, now," he said.

The commandos got up as one man—you could tell they had
done this before—and raced up the ladder, one after another. Dr.
Teller went next, more slowly and deliberately, and then Al and
Sandy, with me bringing up the rear.

The sun had set no more than two hours ago, and the night on the Pacific was warm and pleasant. There was a little fog blowing around, and, all things considered, I liked that; what I lost in star-light I was more than repaid in concealment.

There was a strange feeling, a shudder through the hull of the *Skipjack*, and it took a moment to realize that it was coming from the sea itself, that some vast force was moving beneath the water near us. The low, heavy vibration became stronger, and began to include a high-pitched component as well. Then the waves directly out in front of us took on a strange color.

Where it had had smokestacks, of course, it now had watchtow-ers and radars; those broke the water first, in a churning white disorder as they came out of the water, not yet connected to each other. Hundreds of gallons of warm greenish water sluiced from the sides of the rising towers and struts, and then, majestically, her bridge cleared with a booming roar.

By now the whole rising body was surrounded by a great mass of the water foaming and heaving, and there were choppy waves rolling toward us, making the *Skipjack* bounce and buck under our feet.

Then the gun turrets began to clear, the guns themselves shrouded in fabric of some kind, each turret big as a good-sized ranch house, breaking water one after another with a sound and effect like surf crashing on a great boulder. There was something about the effect that made you want to cheer, but if you did, you had nothing left to do when the main deck cleared with a thunder-ous roar, millions of gallons of water washing over the side as she came above the water like a ghost ship in a nightmare. It wasn't easy to keep your feet on the *Skipjack*'s deck, but you only felt sorry for anyone who had to be below and miss this.

By then the Stars and Stripes had broken from her mast, and at the upper levels there were men running around, getting things in order. The lights of her bridge were visible.

We all waved; it was impossible not to, the way it is for a big ocean liner.

Though nothing could top the huge sixteen-incher turrets and the main deck breaking the surface, there was something awe-in-spiring in quite a different way about the manner in which she continued to rise steadily from the waves, foot by foot, until she floated before us on the now-calm ocean.

I knew what she had to be, and a part of my brain was ready to gasp it out—a ship whose picture, heading to the bottom, was famous from Pearl Harbor in my world; the ship that in Al's poem here had carried Patton and Admiral Nimitz to New Zealand and eventually to the Free Zone . . . and then I knew how it was possible, and I turned to Dr. Teller and said very softly—"She must have been the only hull you had that would stand the pressure and could be sealed up that way . . . once you had the atomic reactors to put into her."

Teller nodded, like a proud papa, and added, "It wasn't the easiest job we've ever done. We'd have fabricated a new hull if we could, but since we couldn't . . . the worst part of the job, really, was figuring out what to reinforce and where to seal, since if we'd made a mistake and she'd sunk, we could never have raised her."

The little boat from the *Arizona* came out to us, and there was a certain amount of naval pomp and ceremony in getting us transferred to her. We all shook hands with Captain Stark,, but like any decent sub captain, I could tell he was eager to get back under the waves and away from such an obvious target.

Finally we were on the *Arizona*'s boat, whirring over to the side of the battleship.

When we arrived, there was a long, complicated process of getting netting down for us all to climb, but still, in less than half an hour we stood on her deck. From the way the commandos were grinning, I could tell they were looking forward to being dismissed belowdecks, something that happened as fast as their officers got a nose count.

Meanwhile, we three and Dr. Teller were met by a pleasant young Asian man in black pajamas who said, "Captain's compliments, Dr. Teller, and I'm to conduct you and your party to dive stations and then to the bridge once we're down and under way."

"Lead on, then," Teller said.

We crossed the steel-plated deck—I noted how heavy the gray paint was, and that now that I was looking around a little more, I could see scars here and there, places where things had been taken off or modified in a dozen ways.

We went through a double hatch, with two doors about ten feet apart. The outer one had probably not originally been in that position and might not have been on the ship; the inner one looked like it had been carefully cut from some other steel and made to fit. I realized as the man with us dogged the second hatch down that it was an airlock.

The maze of winding passages inside the battleship was utterly baffling; to judge from the number of welds and the diversity of surfaces, I doubted that anyone from my timeline who had served on the ship would have been able to find his way. They had kept the hull, the bridge, and the turrets, and I guessed they had kept the steam turbines as well, but that was about all.

Diving horns were sounding everywhere, and we felt the decks sinking below us. The young man who had guided us here grinned. "I always feel a little nervous at this point," he said. "I've been on almost every dive since the first one, but this is always the point where I realize this poor old girl was never designed to do any such thing."

We could feel thuds and bangs through the hull, and all of us must have looked a little nervous, because the kid winked, and said, "You saw her come out of the water. You know she's not stream-lined. What do you suppose happens when you submerge all that steel in such irregular shapes?"

We all relaxed until Teller added, "Mind you, you're getting that groaning and thumping in the structure because it *is* a high-stress process. If she ever fails, this is when she would be likely to."

He appeared to be enjoying the thought, so I decided I wasn't going to let him scare me. That was one of those decisions easier to make than to carry out . . .

After a while, the young man said, "We have cabins for each of you, and all four of you will be sharing a head. If you'd like to freshen up before I take you to meet the captain . . ."

We followed him through more winding corridors and down a few ladders, and eventually found ourselves looking at four coffin-sized compartments with bunks—actually they might better have been described as being bunks with a door—and a phone booth–sized space with a toilet and sink, arranged so that you could use the sink if you practically stood in the toilet, or the toilet if you didn't mind a sink on the back of your neck. It looked great to me—it was certainly better than anything I'd had in a while.

We all took turns making use of the facilities, and then the young guy took us up to the bridge to meet the captain. It was another climb through a winding passageway, this time one with a lot of traffic, where many times we had to stop and press ourselves into crevices to let various sailors get by.

The crew seemed to be multiracial and multilingual, and many of them were younger than the commando unit. Probably it was easier to rotate new guys onto a big ship than to put them into a tightly knit combat unit.

At last we came to a spiral stair, and, following it up, we found ourselves on the bridge.

In some ways it was the most altered part of the ship, in some ways the least. The heavy glass of the windows looked even heavier than what I had seen on a tour, once, of the *Missouri*, and, of course, at our running depth it was all but pitch-black outside anyway, with just a faint overhead glow. The screens the men were watching were sonar and hydrophone, and there were rank on rank of instrument and gauge boards that no one had ever planned should be here when the ship's keel was laid down.

The man who turned to us was dressed in old uniform parts, often mended, but there was something—well, *stylish* about him. He looked like a guy you'd follow anywhere.

Then I got a better look at him and realized with whom I was dealing.

I suppose it was natural enough to work your way up—he couldn't have stayed in PT boats forever, and there were no offices to run for out in the Free Zone. His hair was short but still managed to be a bit disorderly; the famous, wide-set intelligent eyes were still there, and they looked right through you in a way that made you want to do whatever he asked of you.

I started to understand the reactions of some older people I knew.

Understand, I'm a little too young to really remember John F. Kennedy from my own timeline, but there was a certain kind of magic about him anyway, and of all the things I saw and people I met over in that timeline, this was the one that stuck with me. There were famous people I got to know better, and certainly there were many closer friends, but when I think back on that particular adventure across time, it's the vision of him standing there, leaning slightly on his cane because his back was bad, staring out into the black ocean depths before us.

He took a little time to show the place off—he was very proud of his strange command, and whatever didn't have to be kept secret he was happy to show us. Dr. Teller, of course, had worked on getting the nuclear power plants built and on working out pressures and top speeds—the *Arizona* wasn't fast, couldn't be fast, for though her engines could push her a lot harder than they ever did, her superstructure had enough to do just to keep the terrible pressures below the surface from rupturing her, and there was so much drag that they didn't dare to move fast. The *Arizona* could circle the globe submerged—it turned out that Captain Kennedy had taken her under the North Pole more than once and had run the length of the Atlantic in her—but her top speed was low, and her vulnerability to depth charges something that no one aboard seemed to want to talk about.

For all the slowness and vulnerability, I was to learn in the next few days that the crew had come to feel invulnerable after some of the things Kennedy had taken them through; on the run through the Atlantic, they had surfaced off Jutland, run in close, and shelled Wilhelmshaven and Bremen—"You should have heard the variety of stories the Jerries kept coming up with to explain that one," one of the intelligence staff said. "Simultaneously they had to denounce it as barbaric, cruel, and a justification for whatever reprisals they wanted to take, and declare that it had no effect, and announce that there was no such thing as an Allied warship anyway and it was just an industrial accident in Wilhelmshaven getting picked up and becoming a rumor that was also misattributed to things happening in Bremen."

This was a day or two later, and I was having dinner with him in the officers' mess, where we all had permanent invitations as a courtesy. It had taken me a long time, even after seeing it surface, even after having to travel around inside it, to realize just how large the *Arizona* was.

Besides her occasional surprise terror raids around the Axis-controlled world, and her operations in support of various rebel groups around the world, she also acted as a floating intelligence and research base, a guided missile platform, a flagship when in combined operations, and when operating by herself far from base, a sort of super-subtender. She could tow up to five submarines behind her—in fact that was where *Skipjack* was right now—while supplying them with fresh air and electric power.

All this I learned over a couple of days as I got rest, food, and a certain amount of the simple feeling of safety. We knew we were making for the Free Zone, though exactly where was secret even from us.

It was different here. I had seen Axis America only through the eyes of the rebels and as a hunted fugitive, but that was the most accurate way to see it, and its most notable feature was the cloud of fear in which you lived. Even people in the Good Neighbors and various other fascist organizations had to be afraid of each other. But on the *Arizona*, once you were aboard and it had been determined you belonged there, you were automatically part of the accepted circle. I found I could talk to anyone about anything that wasn't classified; there was an atmosphere of freedom that, in just my short days away from my own timeline, I had all but forgotten.

I spent quite a bit of time with Dr. Teller, trying to figure out the SHAKK, but all we could determine was that it wanted to be reloaded, and we had none of whatever it was that it was loaded with. "It's a pity," he said, "because what you and the two resistance people describe as its effects are things we could really use. We'll have to make sure you get a chance to work around some of our materials science people; maybe you or they will find whatever it is."

Two other things became clear from the conversation; first of all, Sheila had probably not been a Special Agent. "Officially her rank seems to have been Time Scout, whatever that might be," Teller said. "That was part of the coded material she sent us. If I were making a guess, it's that she was more or less dropped off here and told to report back every now and then. We can only hope that this means they will come looking for her, and that they have the means to come and look."

The other was what had happened at the beach. "Understand," he said, "here I was expecting one woman on an empty beach. First I find the beach guarded, then the guard departs and an armed party comes down to look at the naked, tortured corpse of the person I came to see. I was more than suspicious—I was ready to shoot—but then you mentioned transistors."

"I don't understand," I said. "Are they a secret password or something?"

Teller laughed. "No—or yes. Your choice. We've been making them in the Free Zone since about 1950, but they're a closely guarded secret. And the important thing is that they work by principles of quantum physics—or what the current masters of the

Earth refer to as 'Jewish science.' The same branch of physics is essential to understanding nuclear energy as well. So if, as you are guessing, these Closers who control the Nazis are phobic about nuclear power, they probably suppress quantum theory, which is why the Nazis have no transistors."

"And no lasers," I said.

"And no *what*?"

It had never occurred to me that I might meet a physicist, let alone a world-class one, who wouldn't know what a laser was. Unfortunately, I didn't really know myself—I knew sort of what they did, but had very little idea how they did it. At least I remembered that they were monochromatic, and the light didn't disperse at all.

Teller sat and scribbled frantically, scratching his head the whole while. "Wonderful," he said finally. "Absolutely wonderful. I shall be sure to cite your assistance."

I was a bit startled. "Do you have any way to publish?"

"Oh, eventually, eventually. The war is not going to last forever, you know, merely for a very long time." And we were off to some other subjects.

It took the *Arizona* almost three weeks to traverse the Pacific submerged, and I suppose if I had had anything that it was urgent for me to do, I'd have been screaming with impatience. But the fact was that I was very much stranded in this world, and therefore until someone found a job for me to do, nothing could be really urgent. Moreover, being here meant time enough to do a little reading in the ship's library and to do some hard thinking about what I would do when I got to the Free Zone. Other than being dead certain I would volunteer and try to make my contribution in the struggle against the Nazis and the Closers, I had no idea, nor did I really know what my options might be.

That left me with one other thing to consider—me and my place in the universe. One problem with time to rest and think is that all of a sudden things start to come into clear focus.

First thing to notice, I decided—nobody really needed me back home. The fact was that Dad looked after himself well, and even Carrie managed to do so. Robbie and Paula would miss me but would find other agencies to give them work. I was a good bodyguard, but there were other bodyguards as well. Maybe Porter would write me from camp . . . that was about it.

So there was no urgent reason for me to go home. Blade of the

Most Merciful were gone—I'd had the satisfaction of bagging most of them with my SHAKK, back in the Closer base. I had liked the few ATN people I'd met, and I wouldn't mind linking back up with them, but it might happen anyway, and I didn't have to be at home to do it.

No, it was clear I not only could make a place for myself here, but I probably should, because it was also quite possible that I would be stranded here for a long time. Even if another Time Scout or Special Agent came through, it seemed to me that the chances of their finding me, or of being interested in me if they did, were pretty slim.

So I was here for good, and I was going to act like it . . . and that led to some hard self-reflection. I realized I hadn't acted like it in my own timeline. Waking up fantasizing it was somewhere else had just been a symptom—the real problem was that, miserable as my new existence as a widower was, however much I had only been able to assuage my despair by constant violent action, that existence *was* mine, and I had gone through it sleepwalking or like a tourist, not letting it touch me enough for it to fix me.

I had missed a lot of pain, but I had been avoiding life.

This would have to change; I couldn't make this new lifetime be a copy of the old, nor could I drop out into a comfortable if barren existence as I had at home. If I was going to have to live here, I would have to *live* here.

All this took me quite a while to arrive at, and if I had had anything significant to distract me, I'm sure I would have managed not to think about it.

The day that Captain Kennedy announced we were only ten days from port, I noticed there was something new and different on the bulletin board—an announcement that Al would be performing his poems that evening, in one of the larger messes. I wasn't going to miss that—having heard it once, and now having read enough to get more of the references, I probably couldn't have been kept away at gunpoint. But I did think it was kind of a shame that they had put it in such a big space, because poetry was never a popular taste as far as I could tell, and I figured maybe a dozen people plus me, Sandy, and Teller would show up.

I had badly underestimated the power of boredom; for most of the crew, one voyage was a lot like another, once you got used to the idea of cruising below the ocean in a rebuilt battleship. They had seen the films and read the books and heard the records in the ship's library; the idea of anything new, anything at all, was enough to draw them out in droves. The room was packed to the walls, and though I was not late, I couldn't find a real seat of any kind, and ended up in a corner where I couldn't quite see Al, my back wedged a bit uncomfortably—though for this, I was more than willing to put up with it.

The room fell to a dead silence; I thought Al was beginning, and then I saw people struggling to their feet and realized Captain Kennedy had come in. I heard that gentle, deep New England voice making everyone else sit, but whether he liked it or not, they were going to make room for him in the front row.

Then there was a little more excited buzz, and then a very deep silence. Al cleared his throat, took a drink of water, and said, "All right, then, the first of these is called 'The Fall.' "

It didn't have quite the same impact as the first time, for me, but it still brought tears to my eyes before he was done, and as I watched the men in the room—Asians, Polynesians, Caucasians, and blacks jammed together, all listening intently, no one making a sound, tears trickling down cheeks and eyes shut to hear better—I knew I wouldn't have missed being here for all the world.

But if "The Fall" hit them like a hammer blow, "The Gathering of Nations" was a nuclear blast; by the end of it some of them were shaking with stifled sobs, others had mouths open in wonder. I have never heard wilder applause.

They had Al read again and again, five times in all, so that everyone on board could hear it—indeed, Captain Kennedy decided to require it, I suppose in the same spirit that George Washington had made all the troops listen to Tom Paine's *The Crisis*.

After about the third reading, I bumped into Sandy; she looked much better, and without exactly saying that I asked how she was.

"Okay," she said, idly, a little distracted. "God, it's so good to see Al like this. I've been looking out for him for a couple of years and to have so much acceptance from so many people listening to his poetry—well, I think it must be something he's wanted for many years."

"Those poems are going to live forever," I said.

Sandy smiled sweetly and tucked her legs under her on her chair. "And of course the other thing . . . well, Al's a great man, but . . . you know, I've been getting a lot of attention from Captain Kennedy—which he doesn't really have time to give me, but he's such an interesting man, not like anyone I've ever met before—"

I bet, I thought, and for one moment couldn't decide whether I was more jealous of him or her. But the jealousy passed, and then I mostly felt amused; I had to admit that it was almost as interesting to see what *wasn't* changed between the timelines.

·12·

It wasn't until we were actually approaching that Captain Kennedy let us know that we were going into the harbor at Haiphong. That seemed to be very popular with everyone aboard; Vietnam was the heart of the Free Zone, both physically and politically, and was about as far from Axis bombers and raiders as you ever got. Then, too, there's something about being able to take leave in a city, and a city where you can feel safe . . . Hanoi was just a short trolley ride away, and I remember being a bit disoriented by the number of American sailors who kept telling me about all the places to have a good time in Hanoi.

Dr. Teller had been spending a lot of time by himself with the notebook Al had carried aboard, and as we were putting into the harbor, he said to me, "I just wanted to let you know how significant your efforts were. This notebook is exactly what we have needed for at least three years—so many things in it which are obvious once explained but couldn't possibly be learned other than by painful trial and error! You've given us a huge leap forward—"

"Sheila did," I pointed out, "and Al carried the notebook—"

Teller grinned. "I know that—in fact I've already told Al my feelings on the subject. Also that he's the great American poet as far as I'm concerned."

"It would never have occurred to me that a physicist would have much of an opinion about poetry."

His brows furrowed, and I realized he was a bit angry; his hands flew around excitedly. "You damn silly Americans! God! The only nation on earth where they think that if you're smart, you won't be interested in literature or art!"

That made me laugh, and I apologized, which seemed to help.

He calmed down, and said, "But in particular I wanted to thank you for something else. This 'laser' idea of yours—it's pointed me in a number of exciting directions."

"It's not really my idea," I pointed out, "and besides, all I told you was that it was possible."

"All!" He laughed at that. "All! That's *all* any decent physicist wants to know. What you've done is assured me of a place in physics of my own—"

It was my turn to be startled. "Then wasn't that notebook—"

"Hah! Oh, sure, I was a footnote. The guy who read the textbook and got it sorted out for everyone else. But I've wanted an independent area to open up ever since I got into this. I had thought it might be this nuclear bomb thing, but so much of that has been concerned with just getting things accomplished at all in a setting where doing any kind of science is so difficult—and then suddenly *this* comes along—well! I've seen a dozen ways in principle it might all be done, you see. At least a dozen. I've filled a notebook of my own thus far. You've given me something new and interesting to work on, just when this other project was about to play out . . ."

He went on like that for quite a while, and I was driven to reflect that he seemed like a pretty happy guy as he got off the boat. I just hoped he'd remember to finish up on the Bomb before he got going on lasers.

It was sort of good-bye for me at the dockside. At Captain Kennedy's strong urging, Al was going around to read his poetry, sort of a micro-USO tour, and Sandy would be going as his assistant and bodyguard. Nobody exactly knew what to do with me, so I was being sent up to Hanoi for the generals to worry about.

Kennedy gave me this big, warm, toothy smile when he shook my hand for the last time, and said he was sure it would work out, that the Free Zone needed every good man it could get. It made me feel good, and between the firm grip and the big smile I realized I might easily have voted for him myself.

I wasn't particularly alarmed when they put me in a closed

compartment on the train to Hanoi, and stationed a guard outside the door. There was a war on, and I was an anomaly, and if there was anything I'd learned as a bodyguard, it was that anything anomalous, anything that just didn't fit into the pattern, was something to be watched out for.

The secure barracks in Hanoi was Spartan but livable, and the food was mostly rice with a few vegetables and some fish, but perfectly palatable. I've had better Vietnamese food in Vietnamese restaurants, but then nobody goes to French prisons to sample French cuisine either.

The next day they loaded me into a truck with a bunch of other people, none of whom spoke English, to go over to the government building and be sorted out. I figured out from what the guards were saying that it wasn't unusual in the Free Zone to have people of highly indefinite status around—Japanese who had fled their homeland and its Thought Police to float down the China coast on rafts, Hindus and Muslims from India fleeing persecution there, pilots who deserted the air forces of the Soviet or American puppet regimes and took their planes with them, Brazilians who had forged papers to get out of occupied Brazil . . . the list went on and on. They all had to be processed for loyalty risk, with the ones who seemed least likely ending up in prison for a while and the ones who seemed most likely offered a provisional citizenship in the Free Zone and put to work on some nonstrategic project for a few months to see what happened.

On the other hand they hardly ever processed anyone who claimed to be a traveler from another timeline.

They kept me waiting most of the day in a beautiful old colonial palace in Hanoi. The walls were thick and heavy, which was how it had survived a number of Japanese and German bombing raids, and the high arches in its walls were graceful and allowed quite a bit of air and light into the room. I had a pitcher of water, and they brought me a bowl of rice and fish around lunchtime, so I wasn't at all uncomfortable, just bored.

The most astonishing thing to me was how green it all was outside. There were tall palms—Hanoi was far enough from Japanese bases not to have taken too terrible a pounding, especially because (one of those funny coincidences between timelines) it had a very strong and effective set of air defenses. So the trees mostly still stood, and though you could see bomb damage here and there looking out over the city, it was still mostly what it had been in old *National Geographics*—a city of graceful French neoclassical official buildings, bright pagodas, and thatched-roof cabins, through whose crowded, busy streets the palm-helmeted people streamed all day long. The ruckus outside the window—children screaming, barking dogs, crowing chickens, pigs grunting, vendors crying their wares, bicycle bells, and everywhere the excited babble of busy human voices—was wonderful music after the pulsing mechanical silence of the ship. I hoped that soon I could be out there tasting and smelling some of the sensory delights.

It even occurred to me to wish Al and Sandy hadn't departed quite so fast—I'd have liked to have seen the city with them, Al for his passionate enthusiasm, Sandy for naïveté—both of which I was a bit lacking in, but this Hanoi in the Free Zone was my first real taste of the Orient, and it occurred to me that to see it as a burned-out, world-weary cynic was not to see it at all.

Finally, after a very long time, a physically slight, neatly dressed Vietnamese man came in; he spoke perfect English with a very slight accent. "Mr. Strang. I am General Giap. I must say, we have heard a number of very unusual statements from a number of very unusual people, but yours are the most unusual I have ever seen. Moreover, we have the odd fact that you have a certain amount of support and corroborating testimony from many people we would dearly like to believe. So you pose us quite a dilemma. This device you call a SHAKK"—he pulled it from a box beside him—"will you help me to examine it, please?"

He handed it to me, pointed to the readout, and said, "You claim to have an implant behind your ear which allows you to read this text?"

I bent forward and showed him the implanted device.

"Hmmm. Can you remain in that position? Thank you . . . now read to me the words displayed here?"

I hesitated, then translated, using the chip on the back of my head. "Reload before firing again."

Something felt slightly funny in my head, and he asked me to translate the characters next to the fire-control switch. I looked but couldn't read them, and said so, "But I've used it enough. All the way forward for single shot semiauto, middle position for hex bursts semiauto, all the way back for full auto."

"All right, now hold still—" he said.

Again my head felt extraordinarily strange, but this time more so; I almost fell, and he steadied me. "What did you just feel?"

"Very dizzy," I said. "But not like I'm ill—"

"Look at the fire control switch again," he said.

" 'One shot per pull, hex cluster shot, stream of shots,' " I read. "I don't—"

"I pulled out your translator chip, then put it back in. It proves nothing, of course, you might just be a superb actor for all I can tell, but at least it proves you are good enough to fool me. If you are acting, the slight dizziness when I put the chip in and took it back out were superb touches." He sat down and pressed his fingers together lightly at the tips, clearly thinking. "The physicists assure me that the material they have received is genuine, but of course it was not entirely received by your agency. A colleague of mine is looking at another piece of evidence; provisionally I am forced to believe you may be who you say you are."

I nodded. "I'm glad to hear that."

"So are we. We are the Free Zone only in the sense that we are not under the heel of the Axis. Some day we hope to make it mean a good deal more than that, of course, but for right now it really does not. There are no guarantees of the rights of the accused here, and if, for example, we had become convinced you were not who you said you were, we would not hesitate to use drugs, torture, or whatever coercion stood the best chance of working. We are the side of the right, I believe, Mr. Strang, but for the right to be right it must first *win*—and that is our goal just now." He got up and paced slowly over to the window. "I do hope you understand that. Should we conclude that you are working against us or dangerous to us, we would take swift and possibly violent measures to deal with the problem . . ."

"And if you become convinced I'm on your side?"

Giap smiled slightly. "One of my first postings here was in intelligence, and I retain an interest in that field. I am never entirely convinced that *anyone* is on my side." The smile he added to that was utterly without compassion.

I nodded, understanding he meant to frighten me and frankly agreeing that yes, if he wanted to, I could hardly stop him, but then I said, "Just the same, if you decided the risk of my disloyalty was low—"

"Then we have a hundred possible billets to put you in, assuming you want to join the Free Zone Forces, as you said you do."

The door opened. The next man who came in was large, strong, and looked like a comic-strip boxer, his nose a little flattened and bent, his whole way of moving as if he were looking for a fight. He wore what had to be the only perfect GI battle dress I saw the whole time I was there, and twin ivory-handled revolvers graced his hips.

He was carrying my Colt automatic. "Giap," he said, "damn all if this thing isn't perfectly consistent with the story the bastard is telling. According to his debriefing the States had two big wars after World War II, in his timeline—if you believe in all that bullshit about timeline—and shit if the serial number here isn't right up in the two millions where it ought to be. And the cops just got done checking his jacket and it's a synthetic they don't recognize. And not least, that silly watch of his is displaying consistent time but there are no moving parts except the buttons, and when we looked inside all we could find was something that looked like a complicated midget crystal radio."

Giap nodded. "After my examination of him I'm inclined to think he is telling the truth, George."

"I'm sure he is. I guess that should be I'm sure you are, Strang. How the hell are you after all this probing? We'll get your stuff back to you later today."

"I'm fine," I said, "and I'm not sure whether in your place I'd have believed me, sir. I do have the honor of speaking to General Patton?"

"You do indeed, and I'm damned glad somebody realizes it's an honor. It's an honor to speak to Giap, here, too, though he's quiet about it. Well, the question now is what we do with you. You look like you're in decent shape, and from what that crazy poet you brought with you says you might make a soldier, so I guess we can just enlist you, but it seems like something as unusual as you are would have a better use than just lugging a rifle."

I shrugged. "I don't know, sir, if you've read the interview, then no doubt you know that all I have training to be is an art historian or a bodyguard. I'm good at both, but I don't imagine you've got much need for either."

Patton nodded and handed me back my .45; he said, "You seem to take good care of your weapon, and that's another plus for you. Since you're a bodyguard, why don't you come to lunch with us? About when I started to think you might really be what you seemed to be, I started to want to hear about your world."

"Shouldn't you take other guards—"

"Oh, I'll have them whether I take them or not. Certain other generals around here insist on having me followed. How about you, Giap?"

The Vietnamese blinked innocently. "I have never followed you, George."

"I'll say!" Patton grinned; I suddenly realized that these men were very old friends. "Will you come along to lunch with us?"

"Gladly."

"By the way," Patton added, "there are two fewer rounds in there than usual. We pulled the two you had left over from your own timeline. They looked like we should copy them."

"They're called Black Talons," I said, "and I don't know how they do it exactly, but they're supposed to have maximum stopping power."

"Well, we've got some whiz kids in our labs, and they'll figure it out. But I'd be damned surprised if a 1990 round isn't better than what we're using."

We were out on the streets now, and I had to admit I was amazed—and that I felt like I was going to earn my keep as a bodyguard. Giap and Patton walked through all the swirl of bicycles, vendors, shrieking kids, handcarts, oxen—with just me as their apparent guard—like any two tourists anywhere.

As we rounded one corner and actually went deliberately into a narrow alley, Giap turned to me and muttered, "He refuses to be afraid. And to be fair, people love him for it. As for me, I have to follow him like this because I will not let him make it look like I am afraid of my people!"

He stopped for a minute to let a little parade of waddling ducks go by, and we caught up with him. "There's a noodle house over here I like," he said. "Mac introduced me to it, and I like to visit it now and then in his memory."

To my astonishment, the place was a Japanese restaurant. Giap and I exchanged glances, and Patton explained, "Here, watch . . ." and as we went in, he said, "Hey, Jimmy, where's my baby doll?"

The Japanese man behind the counter grinned and bellowed—

in a thick Bronx accent—"You keep your white devil paws off my daughter! Ruthie, get out here and wait on these gents!"

The girl who came out to lead us to our table was about eighteen and terribly cute; her Bronx accent was as thick as her father's.

"Jimmy's from New York, if you haven't guessed," Patton explained. "Used to be a steward on a Navy cruiser, then drove a landing craft, then was an artillery spotter for me in Australia, then spent a year or so sparring with Krauts on New Guinea before they gave that up for a bad business. Now that he's a little older, he's settled into being the noodle king of Hanoi."

We found ourselves conducted to a table in the back; no menu ever appeared, nor did any bill I noticed, but what did turn up, again and again, were plates full of all sorts of wonderful food. I ate sparingly, and so did Giap, but we were both a little logy by the end of the meal.

Then, as the tea was poured for us, Patton said, "All right, now all I need from you is the whole history of the USA from your timeline."

Even when you're reasonably well educated, that's not easy to do. Unfortunately for Patton, too, military history is off in one small corner of academia, art history in another, and the twain touch rarely. He was glad to know my father had served in the Third Army and that he had commanded it, and glad to know he'd won distinction.

Patton had a certain generosity of spirit, too . . . when I told General Giap that he had defeated first the French and then the Americans in a deeply political war, he said, "All wars are political."

Patton grunted. "Not the ones that are any fun."

"Nonetheless," Giap persisted.

"Yeah," Patton grunted. "I know you're right, Giap. Ah, hell, I'm glad you got the glory, friend, but I wish to hell you hadn't had to beat my side to do it."

"Here, we are on the same side, George," he said. "Now, if you could tell us once more, a little more about this space program . . ."

The afternoon passed pleasantly enough. Two hours later, the two generals seemed ready to go. "The strangest thing of all," Patton said, "is that just now there's not much work for either of us. Though a couple of the projects we will be putting you to work on just happen to be the sort of thing that might get either of us employed again . . ."

Giap nodded. "Who did you say, again, was the first American to orbit the earth?"

I was getting puzzled by how often he'd returned to that point. "John Glenn. A Marine Corps pilot, I think from Ohio—at least that's where he went to get himself elected to the Senate."

The same flock of ducks started to cross the street in front of us, but something was different this time—

There. Under the canvas of one booth, someone had pushed *those ducks out to walk in front of the generals.*

I'd had a lot of practice at noticing things that weren't quite right; I had tackled both of them, the tall burly American and the frail Vietnamese, in a moment, and then was standing above them, the Colt in firing position, just as a too-late shot screeched wildly by. I'd seen the muzzle flash in the dim tent, and fired back—what came back out was a flurry of shots, and then there was a scuffle and the tent itself went over.

Police had been near the tent on the other side and had jumped on the men inside—there was a struggle and a shot or two more, but it was clear that matters were under control.

Patton was on his feet as well, his famous pistols drawn, but Giap seemed to have vanished—for just an instant. Then the booth from which all the trouble had started tipped over, and I saw him locked in a knife fight with the man who had been under there. They rolled over my way, and I stepped on the attacker's knife arm at the wrist and placed my .45 against his temple. The man let the knife fall, and we pinned him down and flagged some more of the police.

After they had taken him away, Patton said, "Well, he could be one of our bodyguards."

"True," Giap said. "But in all truth, I think I'd rather send him over to Engineering Seven. As a bodyguard. And I certainly hope he has better luck with those lunatics than we do."

"Engineering Seven is—"

"Not for discussion here in the street," Patton said firmly. "But I do believe Giap has the right idea. Come along, then, Strang, I think we've found a place where your mix of skills can be some use."

I had been bewildered at having that much attention from two senior generals; it was only later that I came to understand that because in the Free Zone officers kept the commands they brought with them and units kept their weapons, by and large, high-ranking generals like Patton, Giap, Montgomery, and the rest were usually not wanted for anything but sliding counters around on maps and talking about what could be done next.

The exception to this was an organization called the General Council, which was as much of a coordinated command as the Free Zone really had. (The local legislatures and governments that raised taxes and ran civil affairs had no military power whatsoever—they had only the choice of either raising levies to pay for the armed forces, or of starving their own forces, letting the Axis win, and then seeing what deal they could come up with. It's wonderful how a serious situation can introduce the spirit of cooperation into a legislature.)

The General Council had one hundred engineering projects going at any one time, scattered around various parts of the Free Zone. Of these one hundred, at least half were dummies, but which numbers were dummies varied from year to year as well. It turned out that Giap had mentioned Engineering Seven for me only because it *was* a dummy. "Actually," Patton said, "we'll send you to Engineering Fifteen. That's the one that's being supervised by General LeMay, who's all right if you don't mind maniacs, and has a bunch of good people working on—well, you'll see. And you have one additional duty—write down everything you remember of your home timeline. We have no way of knowing what's going to be useful, so we want all of it before any of it can fade from your memory."

"Yes, sir," I said, and took the orders that were to get me on a plane out of Hanoi to Engineering Fifteen's offices in Singapore.

"Oh, and Strang?"

"Yes, sir?"

"Thanks for saving my life. And old Giap's, too. I'd miss the old commie if anything happened to him."

"My pleasure, sir, but you should be more careful."

The general looked at me a little incredulously. "Are you aware whom you're asking to be careful?"

I thought about it for one long instant, realized he was right, said so, and took my leave. The last I saw of him, the palm-frond ceiling fans were turning over his head and he'd pulled on a pair of pince-nez to study a map.

The flight was all space-a, meaning whenever there was room on an airplane and a more important sack of flour was not ahead of me in line, I got to move toward Singapore. The first hop was right down to Saigon, but then I was stuck there for a day, tried jumping to Bangkok, and ended up coming back on a DC-3 that was going on from Saigon to Ipoh down in the Malay Peninsula, before finally catching a flight to Singapore.

Once, on my way to a dig in India, I had passed through Singapore, and in my part of my timeline, it looked sort of like a chunk of Manhattan torn off, wrapped up in bits of Hong Kong, and stuck out into tip of the jungles, protruding into the sea. But in my world Singapore had been fought over just once in the twentieth century, and had been utterly undefended from the land side; the Japanese took it with no trouble at all.

Here, it had fallen to them at the outbreak of fighting, been retaken almost at once by Aussies and New Zealanders (able to get there because the Japanese fleet was busy with the invasion of Hawaii), fallen again when the Japanese made their brief counter-attack, fallen again to the Free Zone forces . . . and so it had been worn down by shellfire and fighting until it became one vast, grim, forbidding fortress complex, nothing like the exciting trade entrepôt it was in my timeline.

When the old Ford Trimotor I had managed to hitch a ride in touched down at Singapore, what I saw was about as attractive, esthetically speaking, as East Berlin used to be. It was from here, just three years ago, that an air sortie had sunk the aircraft carriers *Kaga*, *Graf Spee*, and *Gloire*, but only after the island had taken yet another pounding; bomb craters were still visible here and there.

I was met at the airport by an older guy named Bob, who practically talked my ear off on the way back to Engineering Fifteen; he didn't know where I'd come from and my official new title was "chief of security," so as far as I could tell what he was trying to do was make sure I knew how important Engineering Fifteen was.

He kept referring to "the future of humanity itself," which after all was pretty much what the Free Zone was all about, anyway.

It wasn't until we reached the secure bunkers that I finally found out what I was guarding: the Free Zone's space program.

Just as Patton had scooped up and run with most of the American nuclear program in his long run that went past Oak Ridge and through Los Alamos, Marine General Puller, stationed on the West Coast, had had the presence of mind to grab the advanced research projects from the Consortium's Hughes Aircraft facility. One of those projects had been a group of men around Robert Goddard and Willy Ley, and they had been working on rockets.

What they might have done had they had another year or two is an open question. What they had done here, starting from scratch with miserable equipment, was nothing less than astonishing—they had to hand-build each one, and there were innumerable false starts, but they had produced a whole series of rocket engines.

The problem was, the kind of people who could do that sort of work were exactly the kind of people who were impossible to guard. Remember what I said about hating to guard kids, except for Porter? Well, creative scientists and engineers are large kids. They want to do everything when they want to do it, and they don't see why they can't do it their way, because after all they're the smartest people in the room.

I've heard the theory, too, that being childlike enhances creativity. I couldn't say, really, except to note that I was never around adults so childlike—or so creative.

Goddard had died not long after the Free Zone was established, but Ley was here, and Wernher von Braun had escaped the Nazis to come here (partly sickened by what he saw of slave labor—he'd brought several slave workers with him—and by his own admission also because the V-1 had been such a success that long-range rocket projects had withered on the vine). There were a lot of brainy types from Hughes Aircraft, and Kelly Johnson from Lockheed was in the crowd, and some really odd characters from the Philadelphia Navy Yard who had hitchhiked to LA, missing the departure of the Pacific Fleet by no more than a few days, and then managed to sail clear to Tahiti in a stolen yacht—Bob, who picked me up, was one of that gang, and they were far and away the strangest of all.

And my job was to keep this silly gaggle of visionaries out of trouble, because they were on the brink of giving us working ICBMs and spy satellites.

To do this, besides myself, I had about twenty Thai and Malay cops. I got along with them all right.

My major job most of the time was to back them up when they tried to stop some key person from doing something stupidly dangerous. The attack on Patton and Giap had not been isolated—Japanese agents had tried to get about twenty key personnel that day, and had actually badly wounded Mao Zedong, who was pretty much in retirement these days but still valuable as a symbol for the Chinese resistance. We had given them a short, succinct answer—the *Arizona*, and the other two submersible battleships USS *Tennessee* and HMS *Resolution*, had slipped in close to Honshu on a moonless night, surfaced, and unleashed their big guns on the harbor at Yokohama, setting fire to the dockyards and leaving many ships on fire in the harbor, during a state visit from Himmler. Reportedly dinner had not been a success.

But the attack meant that once again the Axis was getting ready to move against us, and every such attack was a painful reminder of the fact that the Free Zone had once been almost a fifth of the Earth's surface, even after the loss of the Americas, and it was still dwindling. We weren't beaten yet, but we had to depend on new weapons to save us eventually.

Von Braun actually was the one who finally made it clear to me why the Germans had not closed in to destroy the Free Zone, and why they hadn't developed their weapons much beyond what they had been at war's end. "Don't forget," he said, "that Hitler may have rallied his armies around being supermen, but he came to power promising the Germans that every German would be rich. They're still"—he shuddered, and looked down at his plate—"the German translates as 'digesting.' They've got so much of Eastern Europe where they've exterminated whole populations, and then there's the rump of the Soviet Union to be pressed into service, and they're already making noises about *Anschluss* with Canada or the United States—they're busy giving their citizens the payoff. Once they had the world in hand, that was enough for them, at least for the time being."

Six relatively pleasant months went by; Singapore was still a grubby fortress, the scientists and engineers were still loony and helpless as kids, and my assistants got more and more efficient.

I had gotten a letter or two from Sandy, and written back in a friendly way without much expecting to hear from her again (attractive young women didn't stay single long in the Free Zone, and my pursuit was at best halfhearted). On Thursday nights I played poker with the Philly Navy Yard crew, on Saturday I did some pistol practice with my guards (the newly copied Black Talon rounds were indeed superior because they spread out in a star shape inside what they hit), and usually on Tuesday I went to one of the twenty-year-old movies at the Ex Sell Lent Theetre, often with Ley and von Braun, who both had a thing for German expressionist sci-fi flicks, of which there were many. In between I stayed in shape, worried about infiltration, looked for holes in fences, and the like, and wrote out at length everything I could remember of the history of my own timeline up to the point where I stepped out of it.

At first that made me homesick, then it sent me into a period of introspection where I started to come to grips with Marie's death, and then finally it was just one more chore.

Once in a great while I'd look at the SHAKK—I had discovered that for some mysterious reason besides the drawer to feed in the powder it had another drawer next to what I was guessing was the firing chamber, but otherwise I had learned nothing more. The translator in my neck continued to work, but it didn't know the word for either of those drawers; the readout continued to say "Reload before firing again." I thought it made kind of a nice paperweight.

My new world wasn't what I would have chosen to make it, but I was fitting into it, I was useful, and, frankly, I was better adjusted there than I had been at home. And I barely thought about home, anymore.

·13·

What saved us finally, at Singapore, was that my whole guard force for Engineering Fifteen was there. And that only happened because it was first launch day.

FZSS *Human Rights* wasn't what I'd have recognized as a spaceship, but that was what she was.

Sitting there waiting for launch, anyone would have said she looked like an upside-down pile of airplanes hanging under a dirigible, and they'd have been right. But all four stages of the craft were necessary—miniaturization and cryogenic fuels weren't very far advanced in this timeline, so the ship had to be big, and it had to use every possible trick to get up there.

The day was almost windless when the *Human Rights* was towed out of her hangar by a motley collection of old trucks, was brought around into the wind, and started her engines. I had snagged a spot on the dirigible stage, rank having its privileges, so I was standing there next to von Braun when the ship rolled out.

Dirigible takeoffs are neat; they just rise, and as long as the props aren't on the gondola, you barely feel the engines at all. It's like floating in a dream.

Singapore looked about as good as it ever had; it was still a giant steel-and-concrete turtle sitting astride the strait, but the jungles and the dim blue mountains beyond them were beautiful.

We were going up to fifty-five thousand feet, and to make this thing work at all, we had had to decide to use hydrogen—yes, it's flammable, and it's why the *Hindenburg* burned, but on the other hand one cubic foot of hydrogen will lift four times as much as a cubic foot of helium. Moreover, hydrogen is cheap and easy to make, while helium is complicated, tricky stuff, even if you do have it coming out of natural gas wells. If there was time to get another model into the air, most of the engineers wanted to go to helium— but we'd need much better engines before we could do it.

It took almost an hour to get up to altitude and cruising speed. Singapore sits almost exactly on the equator, which means that if you take off headed east, you get almost a thousand-mile-per-hour extra boost from the Earth's rotation.

As we reached cruising altitude, the steadying cables hooked to the eight-engine prop plane below us were released, so that soon we were towing the three-plane combination; General LeMay was on the phone to the crews of the three locked-together craft, and they all seemed ready to go.

The engines of the big airplane began to turn. "Here, we may begin to get just a little nervous," von Braun said. "If all her engines do not catch, we will all look very foolish."

But they all did; as they came up to speed, the huge airplane moved forward, until it was towing the dirigible. We cut her loose, and General LeMay stepped back and saluted. "God, I'd give anything to have that kid Glenn's job," he said, and we all laughed; it broke the tension.

All of us scrambled, packed close together, up the eighty feet of ladders and stairways through the body of the dirigible to the observation bubble on top. Rank has its privileges, and being one of the least important people present, I was one of the last up the ladder; by the time I got there everyone was already pointing and talking.

Ahead of us the eight-engine plane soared upward; it could not have left the ground on its own, but its engines were more than adequate for what was to follow. A mile or so above us, and perhaps twenty miles ahead, when it was just a dim dot to the naked eye, it plunged downward over the South China Sea, building up speed. At the bottom of its dive, near the water, it released the remaining two linked-together craft. The twin ramjets of the "third stage" caught, and we saw her soaring up on a stream of flame as the huge mothership swung away and headed back to Singapore. "Let's stay on this course just a little longer," von Braun suggested, and Le-May said, "Try to make me stop watching."

The twin-ramjet craft had gotten up to about Mach 3, still climbing, and was fifteen miles above us—the merest arrowhead on a great pillar of flame and smoke rising above the blue Pacific—when it released Major Glenn and the orbiter. The powerful rocket engines cut in with a flare we saw from where we waited, and the dirigible's observation deck echoed with cheers.

The ramjets of the "third stage" had cut out, and through binoculars we saw her loop over and head back to Singapore in a long fast glide; she would have to land with her tanks empty, for her ramjets would not operate at the low speeds she would need for landing. I didn't envy the pilot—he'd have no chance to make another pass.

I swung my binoculars back to the uppermost, space-going stage of *Human Rights*; it was as big as a modern fighter jet from my timeline, and rode a huge plume of fire and smoke; as I watched, she dropped her first strap-on tank.

"Go, baby, go!" LeMay yelled, and the bridge echoed with cheers again. "Guess we might as well head for home—we can see about as well from there."

The great dirigible swung slowly around, her engines a distant thunder through the body. It took much longer to get downstairs than it had coming up, with everyone stopping to talk and slap each other on the back.

"Got a message, General," the radioman said. "I'll put it up on loudspeaker . . ."

"Mama Bear, this is Ocean City." That was mission control on Singapore. "That crazy kid is all the way up. Says he sees the stars and the curve. And radar from Big Dog confirms. He's made it!"

Everyone cheered and clapped some more; LeMay grumbled about being stuck on a "damned hydrogen gasbag" that wouldn't let him have a cigar to celebrate.

Glenn was to make ten orbits, experimenting with the attitude controls, photographing German and Japanese strategic areas, and experimenting with radar from space. Then he was to come in for a landing on the hard-packed airfield on the north side of the island, by the Johore Strait, where the twin-ramjet stage had also landed; the eight-engine piston prop stage was a seaplane and would land right in the harbor at Singapore.

All in all Glenn would be orbiting the earth for fifteen hours; time enough for people to rest, to wait for his return, possibly to catch a plane over to the airstrip to see him come in for his landing.

It had been a thrilling day so far, and the prospect was for more excitement before it was over.

If only, somehow, it could have stayed the same sort of excitement.

We were getting relayed messages from Glenn most of the way back to Singapore, and the news was all good; the ship was handling well, he could see what he needed to see.

It takes a dirigible a long time to fight up a headwind, so Glenn had completed one orbit just as we made it back to base. LeMay got a private channel with him for the few minutes he was overhead—and then we all saw him grow pale. "You're sure that's what you saw," he said, three times. "Confirm with radar as soon as you can. We'll be in touch."

He turned around and said in a low voice, "Gentlemen, we may be a little late. I will want all those of you with top clearances in my office as soon as we're on the ground."

The big dirigible thumped and hummed as she came in for her landing, and a band was playing, not well but good and loud, loud enough for us to hear it as we approached the mooring mast. LeMay was on the radio a lot, and he didn't sound pleased, whatever the matter was.

I've said that in that timeline, from up above, Singapore looked like a giant turtle. When you got closer it looked like a giant turtle with a massive skin problem—there were bumps and blisters everywhere, low thick towers and heavy bunkers, any structure that had proved impossible to bomb out. A kind of evolution had happened to them—only the strong had survived—so that there were no tall thin spindly structures of any kind, no steeples, certainly no skyscrapers. Dead ahead of us was the "Cake Pan," the big stationary radar for this end of the island—and the place where the first V-1 hit.

There was a great flash, and flames leaped up from the Cake Pan.

They had fired them in salvos, and they had found ways to jam us; first the radar tower blew up, then the control tower, and then, suddenly, the great fortress was rocked with explosions, everywhere.

People were shouting, LeMay was trying to get anyone at all on the headset, and the pilot must have decided to try to run for it, though where you could run in a dirigible is beyond me. I don't think we took a direct hit—had we done so it would have ended in one great fireball—but when I looked outside I saw the skin of the dirigible rupturing and the blue hydrogen flame burning across the surface.

The loss of pressure sent the great airship drifting slowly toward the ground, as the wind carried it toward the roaring fires that the salvos of V-1s were starting all over the island.

I grabbed von Braun, merely because he was closer than anyone else, and shouted in his ear "got to get to the outside catwalk." He nodded, and we started our struggle that way—the floor was too smooth to climb easily and just now the door that had been only steps away moments before was a steep climb on that slick floor. We threw ourselves upward; I got hold of the door handle, he got hold of my belt and climbed up my shirt for a better grip, and we both managed to get ourselves braced above the door.

The dirigible was still sinking like a brick, and bucking up and down as her gas cells ruptured. Flames were pouring out above us.

I yanked the door open, and we both slid out onto the catwalk; for one heart-stopping instant I started to slide down the rough corrugated iron, as if to plunge under the railing and out into the sky, to drop three hundred feet onto the concrete runway. But I grabbed a post on the railing, and again von Braun grabbed me, and we fought our way up the railing, climbing hand over hand, once having to make it past a blazing gas cell that seemed to singe our backs through our shirts.

At last we reached what we were looking for—one of the securing cables that had kept the giant plane steady during takeoff. There was too much noise to talk between the thunder of the burning hydrogen, the wail of sirens and explosions of bombs from below, and the scream of the tormented propellers, for no one had been able to shut off the engines, and as the keel warped and buckled, no longer supported by inflated cells, the propellers were being brought into strange angles with the wind.

We had just taken a grip on the cable together when one of the engines, with a shriek like a coffee can thrown onto a table saw, ripped loose from its pylon and dove down to the pavement, now just a couple of hundred feet below.

Relieved of the weight, the airship shot upward for a moment, dragging us sixty or seventy feet higher as we clung to the cable and tried to keep feet braced on the catwalk.

The extra strain must have ruptured other cells, for we found ourselves sinking faster this time, the dirigible now drifting over the end of the airfield and heading down toward the harbor, some of the dragging cables already touching housetops.

We had little choice; we could stay aloft to avoid being smashed, and thus be burned alive whenever the cell next to us blew. Or we could climb down the cable to get away from the flames, and in all probability be dragged into the wall of a building at ten or twenty miles per hour, two stories up, or scraped off on an electric power line.

Something about burning does not sit well with the human mind . . . we couldn't have discussed it in that terrible din, but we were both immediately climbing down as quickly as we could go, hand over hand, the cable whipping horribly.

After a few moments I was motion sick; I leaned over my arm and threw up, but I did my damnedest not to get a drop on the cable, which could become slick.

Something nasty went by my head; I assumed it was von Braun's lunch.

I hadn't wanted to look down, but the news was slightly better—our cable was now trailing down a smashed-up street, and though there were three large rubble piles, there were clear spaces between them. Moreover, we were sinking fast now, and only about fifty feet off the ground.

Fifty feet is still an awfully long way. I climbed downward as fast as I could, taking a risk I couldn't have believed I'd be taking less than ten minutes before, for it had been no longer than that. Von Braun's shoes, swinging to and fro on the cable above me, gave me an incentive to climb all the faster, and the sinking dirigible carried us farther downward.

I was drenched in sweat, and my best suit was never going to be the same; all around me, now, the smoke of the great fires raging on the face of the old fortress was making it hard to breathe, and I couldn't see anywhere clearly enough to be sure of exactly where we were or what might happen next. But there was less than twenty feet to go, and I took a calculated risk and burned my hands a little sliding down the rope—at least right at that moment there wasn't anything too terrible to run into. My feet scraped pavement, but I hung on for an extra second so von Braun could slide down, too. We let go at the same time, but the dirigible didn't bounce up much; the cables whipped by us like mad pythons, and then we felt rather than heard or saw the great dirigible crashing to the pavement, a block of houses beyond us.

A great burst of red flame blossomed over the street and belched upward in a low, deafening roar. Every house in front of us caught fire.

"Well, we're not going *that* way!" von Braun shouted in my ear.

"Deal!" I shouted back. "I think Engineering Fifteen is *this* way from here, anyway!"

It's not a great place to be lost. We were out beyond the permanent buildings and in the free-floating shantytown that surrounds so many Third World cities; at least the area wasn't a target for the cruise missiles now pounding the main citadel, but on the other hand much more of what was around here was flammable. Already the streets were beginning to jam up with people seeking to flee, but on that densely settled island, with no real cover except in the fortresses, there was so little place to flee to that only those who were burned out were sure they wanted to run.

Many simply came out in the street and stood around; the bombardment wasn't happening right here, by and large, and they desperately needed to know what was happening.

I caught a glimpse of one radar tower and of the stump of one of the prewar office buildings, and now I knew where we were. Holding hands like scared kids or lovers in the rain, we rushed on toward Engineering Fifteen, taking any route we could, crashing through water-filled potholes, switching to one side or another to avoid blazing buildings.

The fire and smoke were getting thicker—later I realized that some of the cruise missiles had passed over the poor parts of the city spraying hundreds of pencil-sized incendiary submunitions, starting fires everywhere at once, overwhelming the fire crews, starting pathetic columns of refugees fleeing in all directions to block up the roads.

For a short distance we made good time following behind a militia unit that was trying to get formed up and get to its station, but after that we had to fight our way across a pile of stalled carts in

a little public square. We had just made it across when we heard the
Dopplered rising roar of incoming jets.

The fighters screamed in over the square, little high-speed Gatling guns on their wingtips spraying death into the unarmed
crowd; as each peeled off, it let loose a bomb.

I knew before they hit what they would be, and von Braun
clearly did, too, for both of us piled up against the wall. There was
a hideous thud, and the jellied gasoline—napalm—sprayed into the
crowd, sticking and burning wherever it went. People on fire ran in
all directions, and no one fought the hundred fires that sprang up
all around. From the next block we could hear the rattle of automatic rifles as the militia company tried to put up any kind of
opposing fire.

"This is no raid," von Braun said. "They are going to invade.
This must be what Glenn saw from orbit. Dear God, where is that
man going to land?"

We fought onward through the crowded streets, struggling
through panicked crowds. Twice more fighters roared in at low
altitude, wreaking whatever havoc they could. There were bodies
in the streets now, and the sky that had been a perfect soft blue, just
an hour ago when we were off to launch a man into orbit, was now
black and gray from the smoke, tinged pink underneath with the
blazing fires.

But Singapore had evolved. We were in the bad part of town,
and the poor were stuck, but the fortress, after having changed
hands six times in twenty years, had been rebuilt and rebuilt until it
was awesomely tough. As we reached the perimeter we found well-
organized authorities getting people under cover, moving the frantic refugee convoys into the safety of the special tunnels, giving first
aid, tagging lost children to make sure they could be matched up
with their frantic parents.

There was very little panic, if any. We showed our priority
badges and were given access to one of the covered tramways; in no
time at all we were back at Engineering Fifteen, far inside the complex.

Bombs were falling now, and cruise missiles were still hitting,
but there is something about a yard of concrete between you and a
bomb that makes the bomb so much less upsetting. "You think it's
really an invasion?" I asked von Braun. "Could they have made it

all the way here from India—right down the coast of Sumatra—without getting spotted?"

He shrugged. "There are many ways here. But if it's not an invasion, it's a terribly big raid. German bombers out of Japan couldn't have run the radar fence, and the fleet couldn't have come from India—and those were carrier fighters—the most likely thing is that they slipped up here out of western Australia and the carriers are over on the other side of Sumatra. And these improved cruise missiles worry me. The Nazis haven't improved *anything* since they won the war. If they're getting the research habit again, and they keep it, they could bury us—they have a hundred times our facilities."

I doubted very much that they were doing research; I suspected the Closers had merely gotten impatient and slipped them some technical improvements. But since von Braun did not know of my background, this hardly seemed the time to explain it to him.

Besides, if the Closers got serious about technical aid to the Nazis, then we would probably get buried anyway.

The tram had dropped us off at the concrete blockhouse that covered the entrance to our area; a lull in bomb hits let us chance a run to the main building. As I came in, several of my Malay and Thai employees saluted smartly, and the sergeant of the guard came up to me in haste. "Sir—we've had one attack by agents trying to penetrate the compound, and we're cut off from the metallurgy building and mission control. We've heard shooting, but we can't get out that side of the building; I've got a team that's going to try to go around and get behind them—"

"Damn good," I said. "We'll go with your plan—carry on. I'll join your sortie party."

He gave me the biggest salute I'd ever seen in my life and started hollering orders. I jumped in with the ten men who were going to go around; the plan was to use one firefighting access tunnel that we had to get to a small instrument shack, then try to burst out of the shack and get to the back side of the metallurgy building. The trouble with it, other than an exposed run of about sixty yards, was that it would put us right between metallurgy and mission control—and we knew for sure the enemy was in the metallurgy building.

If they were in mission control as well, we were dead. But there had been a lot of our people in mission control, and nobody in the

Free Zone ever went anywhere without at least a sidearm, and many people habitually carried a rifle or a carbine. So there was an excellent chance that mission control was out of touch but still with our side, and if we could get them to sortie—

It was worth a shot. Right now anything was worth a shot, actually.

We raced down the tunnel at a breakneck pace; I was in the middle of the party, not wanting to disturb my assistant's plans by joining the van or rear guard. Everything would depend on speed—

I hit the concrete steps under the instrument shack and leaped up them—and almost fell over the body of one of my men. I jumped to the side, went prone, cursed the fact that all I had was my .45 and the shots were coming from—

Plenty close enough. I realized I was looking into the legs of a group of Nazi paratroopers charging the shack. I fired at them, upward, through the instrument shack door, which was propped open by the corpse of the lead man, who lay in the doorway. There were just two of us alive, besides me, and only one other man fit to hold a gun.

Praise god our team leader, Prasad, was the next one through and had three vital things: a tommy gun, good luck not to get hit right off, and lots of presence of mind. The enemy were totally out of cover and virtually at point-blank range, so he got virtually all of their rush in one long burst. Prasad emptied the drum mag at them, and that gave everyone else a chance to get up there and start laying down fire. The enemy fell back to the alley between the metallurgy building and mission control.

It was then that I got a clear look at the side of mission control, and if I hadn't already thrown up from that ride on the dirigible, I would have had to now. They had dragged out everyone in mission control, put them up against the wall of the building, and shot them. Black smoke poured from the building.

Between the dead from mission control and the dirigible, our space program was gone, or would be as soon as Glenn landed.

Prasad gave quick, crisp orders; we dropped back into the tunnel, set the time charge on the other side of the door, and ran like hell. We were most of the way back when it blew behind us; we could be pretty sure it had blocked the tunnel, but it would have

made us feel better to know that it had taken a few of the enemy
with it.

When I got back, von Braun was crouched at the phone. "I've
got a patch through from a guy in the control tower, and I'm
talking to Major Glenn," he explained. He talked just a little
longer, and then groaned, "Okay, fading out, we'll talk again when
you come back around."

It looked like the building was being well defended, and there
wasn't a lot of need for my attention; nobody was low on ammo yet,
and since my whole guard had turned out for the launch, there
were about three times as many armed men on our side in the
compound as we'd normally have any right to expect.

"Well, then," I said, "what's the news?"

"Well, the one piece of good news—" A bomb blew somewhere
near the roof, but not on it, and though the building shook, it held.
We both heaved sighs, and von Braun went on. "Glenn was able to
spot their fleet from orbit. They're over on the other side of Sumatra, just as you guessed, down by the Barisan Mountains in fact,
where the Coast Watch wouldn't have gotten much warning of
them. They must have flown in through the canyons and ravines to
avoid detection. What they don't know is that we've got a wolf pack
on patrol down that way—their carriers will be getting hit within an
hour, and the bombers are already on their way from Borneo.

"But the bad news is a lot worse. He saw something in Florida
as he passed over. There's a cape somewhere along the north
coast—"

"Canaveral?" I asked.

"That's the one. Strange name—can't imagine anyone would
ever work there, but it is a perfect launch site if you're going to go
out across the Atlantic. And that's just what they're doing. They've
got a launch facility there—looks like they have big multistage rockets. Perhaps from a career advancement standpoint I should have
stayed at Peenemünde.

"Glenn saw one of their rockets take off as he was going over;
the plume is unmistakable from orbit. And his radar now tells him
he's got a little shadow. They're closing in on him; if he turns
around and uses his engines to brake, he's going to have to drop
right across their sights. If he doesn't—well, they're in a lower orbit. That means they move faster than he does. They're going to
pass under him soon, and anything they shoot upward will come

right into his path . . . and since orbital velocities are in thousands of miles per hour—"

I whistled. "They could bring him down with a brick."

"Exactly," von Braun said. "Could and possibly will. He's going to keep relaying intelligence to us as long as he can, and then take his chances with them; he said something about 'every fighter pilot knows there's one way to be sure you don't miss.'" I shuddered; von Braun looked at me curiously. "This disturbs you?"

"You bet it does. I think he'll try to ram them. Which is good as far as it goes, but I suspect they've got more than one ship, and we don't."

We never heard from John Glenn again. After the war we found out the Germans had in fact lost the capsule that flew pursuit on that mission, but didn't know how or why. I like to think it's because he didn't miss.

There wasn't any chance to talk about any of that anyway; I heard a shout from Singh, my sergeant, and ran to see what he was pointing to. There were at least a hundred paratroopers coming down. "Not an invasion but a raid in force," I said to von Braun. I told him what I had seen from the instrument shack, and had to wait a minute for him to calm down after the string of oaths poured out of him. Some of those people were ones he had lied to get out of death camp, taken with him in his flight, done everything possible to save—and now they were gone.

The paratroopers were hitting the ground before I got von Braun calmed down enough. I turned to Singh, and said, "This is hopeless. They aren't after your men, and you can't save whatever survivors we have here. *Sauve qui peut*, man, that's all we can do."

Singh shrugged. "It's not a bad way to die. My family will hear of it soon. But those of my men who wish to flee, none of us will stand in their way. You, Captain, you've got to run for it, and you as well, Dr. von Braun. And I do think we can give you a few minute's start if you can grab or destroy anything that shouldn't fall into their hands."

Swift, silent, and grim as death, the paratroopers—close enough now to see the SS thunderbolts on their uniforms—were closing in on the building. Von Braun laughed. "Chances are they are ahead of me, but I'll go do what I can." He was off at a run toward the front part of the building, where his office was.

I thought I had nothing, then realized. The SHAKK. Just because I had not been able to figure out how, or rather with what, to reload it, didn't mean that the Nazis wouldn't. Moreover, I had no idea whether the SHAKK was a common technology between ATN and the Closers, or whether it might be something bad to have them capture.

I pounded down the hall to the office, grabbed the SHAKK, stuffed it into my shirt, and turned around to find myself facing a small, cruel-looking man who had a Luger leveled at my chest. "What is that?" he asked.

"Uh, cereal box prize," I explained. "My favorite toy when I was a kid. I didn't want to leave it behind. After you . . . um, you know, *do* me, could you leave it on my body so maybe it will get buried with me? It's got to be the last real Flash Gordon Ray Gun on earth, and . . . well, I just really loved it. As I guess you can see from the way I ran back here."

He seemed totally unconvinced, and extended his hand to take it—just before he fell forward. He hit the floor, quite dead, and blood spread out from under him.

General LeMay stepped into the room, putting his service .38 back into its shoulder holster. His clothes were burned and he was sooty, but he seemed all right otherwise. "Von Braun said you'd be down here; figured when I saw the gent headed this way maybe I should see what was keeping you."

"Thanks," I said, and followed him out the door. We rushed back up the hall toward where I had left von Braun.

"Singh has a line of retreat opened up, and we've got an autogyro we can make a run in, if you're game."

"It beats staying here and getting shot," I said. By that time we were headed down the steps.

"Yeah, my way of looking at it, too," LeMay agreed.

After all the trouble leading up to it, getting out was ridiculously simple—Singh and his men covered our retreat, we ran to a hangar, and there was an eight-passenger autogyro warmed up and waiting to go. We kicked the doors open, opened a gate onto a service road, got in, started her up, and rolled down the service road to get space for a takeoff.

Autogyros are one of those things that never took off in our timeline and probably wouldn't have in theirs, except that the Free Zone couldn't do much research and the Axis didn't. Basically it's an airplane with a freely rotating wing—the wing turns like a windmill, or like helicopter blades, just from the forward motion of the aircraft. It isn't as versatile as a helicopter, but it's a lot easier to make it work, since you only need to put the rotor blade on a pivot and use a regular piston-prop engine up front. It can't hover, it won't fly backward, and it has a distressing tendency to bounce as it lands, but it will take off from a short runway, and the fuel economy's okay.

Shortly we were airborne and headed out away from the city, across the island, and on up across the South China Sea to Saigon. As we got farther away, I looked back; a great pillar of black smoke, lit by the sudden flares of storage tanks and ammo dumps blowing, towered over us, but in a few minutes, we were out over the South China Sea, the fire of blazing Singapore was not the whole of that side of the sky, and we were no longer under that black cloud. The sun came out, the sky was blue—

It was the same day on which we had launched John Glenn to orbit. I didn't know it yet, but probably he was already dead, and when I found out he had not reported in, I was hardly surprised. The whole catastrophe had taken less than a full afternoon, and the future looked miserably bad.

•14•

If it looked bad for me, I couldn't imagine how it looked for von Braun. To have lost the physical facility was one thing, but between the deaths on the dirigible—LeMay, like us, had thought he was the only survivor—and the massacre of technicians, Engineering Fifteen was dead for good. They had delivered rocket engines to several other projects of one sort or another, but the effort to get into space was going to be over for a long time.

LeMay's escape had required both more guts and luck than ours; he had clung to the railing until the last moment, then jumped onto a corrugated iron roof, falling about ten feet, causing the roof to bow in and deposit him in an empty house, the residents apparently just fled.

He had seen the end of the launch stages because he had been down nearer the harbor; the dirigible had scraped off its now-burning gondola onto a warehouse roof. The gondola fell into a street with a sickening smash and the fuel in the auxiliary tanks blew; he doubted anyone had survived, though you could never tell.

Freed of so much mass, the gasbag and keel structure had leaped up into the air, in flames, rolling over, and blown completely with a great roar, the burning wreckage falling back into the dockyards. "Did 'em more good than twenty bombers could have," he said.

All this time, as we talked, we were whirring up the coastline of the Malay Peninsula; there was a fuel depot at Songhkla, and if we could gas up there, we could make Saigon in the early evening. We had no way of knowing whether or not Singapore would be taken—I still thought it was a raid, von Braun still suspected it was the lead force for an invasion—but at least, for the moment, von Braun and LeMay wouldn't be captured.

I was not feeling particularly good about my performance as chief of security, though both of them pointed out that what I was supposed to do was defend against the occasional infiltrator or assassin, not against a fully armed military assault.

There was really nothing for von Braun or me to do except watch LeMay fly, and though autogyros are interesting gadgets technically, riding in them is not necessarily any more amusing than riding in any other aircraft. We sat down, and I pulled out the SHAKK to have a look at it.

That meant telling von Braun and LeMay my story—which didn't seem like a big deal since their clearance was higher than mine—and showing von Braun the chip in my neck. He nodded for a moment, then he said, "I have a thought, if you'd like."

I said sure; he took the SHAKK carefully, opened the reloading drawer, pulled out some change from his pocket, dropped it into the drawer, and closed it. The message changed instantly.

"What's it say now?" he asked me.

I looked at the display, which was now scrolling a long message horizontally, and read " 'MORE RELOAD NEEDED. COPPER 35%, ZINC 12%, IRON 0%, SILVER 87%, CARBON 0%, SILICON 0%, RARE EARTHS 0%.' Well, you made it do something, but I don't know what."

"Read the numbers to me again," he said, taking out a pad and writing them down carefully. He reopened the drawer, and his change was gone. Then he rummaged in his pockets for change and started counting around in it, finally finding four copper pennies. "These are all prewar, should be all copper, right?" He set them in the SHAKK's drawer and slid the drawer home again. "Now read."

I did again. " 'MORE RELOAD NEEDED. COPPER 42%, ZINC 12%, IRON 0%, SILVER 87%, CARBON 0%, SILICON 0%, RARE EARTHS 0%.' I don't see—oh, wait, it's like the Minimum

Daily Requirement on a cereal box! I mean—well, never mind. It's telling us how much it has of each thing it needs!"

Some random screws from the tool kit brought iron up above zero; slivers of a broken drinking glass (we found it under a seat, apparently some VIP had had it along) got us the silicon. The carbon and some of the rare earths came from my handkerchief and the back cardboard of von Braun's notebook. LeMay cheerfully informed us we were crazy and pointed out that modern explosive powders tended to contain some rare metals; I slid in a whole clip for the .45, and it digested that, and one odd-looking pair of pliers from the tool kit, and then . . .

I looked at the message. "MORE RELOAD POSSIBLE. ROUNDS: 23."

"Gun port to your left," LeMay said. "Let's try it out."

The gun port was really made for a man with a rifle or submachine gun, but I shoved the SHAKK up against it, set it for a hex burst, and watched as LeMay brought us down to treetop level over a deserted beach. We flew low and slow as I picked out a particular palm tree, squeezed the trigger—and heard the wonderful sound of a SHAKK burst going out. The palm tree burst into splinters halfway up and fell over.

"How did you know that would work?" I asked von Braun. "Obviously when I get back on the ground all I have to do is shovel a bunch of junk into it, and it makes its own ammo."

Von Braun nodded. "Well, I didn't know that it would work at all, but I thought about the guy who must have designed it, and the people you said would carry it. They clearly could not all go back to reload every time, so they must be carrying spare ammunition— but that wasn't true. So it seemed to me that powder had to be something commonly available, but if as you say ATN operates in places where there is no technological civilization, it couldn't be anything you had to make—and yet from your description it wasn't a natural material either. So if it wasn't the finished product and it wasn't the natural source—it must be a raw material. And then it occurred to me that a gun you can reload by putting rocks and metal scrap into it would be a very useful thing indeed for one of these Special Agents or Time Scouts you were describing. At that point I had an idea to try, so I tried it."

It made sense to me when it was explained; I wondered why I hadn't thought of it. I consoled myself with the fact that I was not, after all—and here I almost laughed out loud—a rocket scientist, and, besides, art historians use a lot of scientific gadgets but we don't exactly do experiments—no matter what you feed a rat he won't start drawing in perspective.

The fuel dump at Songhkla was able to take care of us quickly; we were flying out over the water as the sun went down behind us, and before midnight the sparkling city of Saigon glowed beneath us. We had reached the command by radio, and they were expecting us.

That night was spent answering questions for the intelligence guys, over and over and over, while they took more and more notes. It was irritating, but I saw the point when I learned that the forces landing on Singapore had hit every active weapons project, bypassing all the fake "Engineering" sections that had skeleton crews and empty buildings.

"I don't honestly think they cared about anything other than getting your group," said the tall, thin, balding man with the Russian accent. "I think they didn't mind hitting some of the others, but that was a cover. By far the largest force hit Engineering Fifteen, at exactly the time when they could kill the most personnel and destroy the most material. They wanted us shut down in that area. I think there is no question."

Von Braun groaned in frustration. "Don't you see it? Don't you see it?"

The man leaned forward. "Tell me."

"They have space launch themselves already. That means they can look down on everything we do, and they can target accurately and at will. There are half a dozen sites I can name, and I'm sure a hundred that I don't know about, that are potentially their targets. They hit the facility at Singapore because they already knew it was there—and they know where everything else is. In a dozen raids or so they can destroy whatever hope we have of besting them; after that they can slowly pound apart our means of making modern war. We may linger on in the jungles for another ten years, but our real threat to them is over."

"Not quite over," the tall man said. "We will see what we can do."

We had been up all night, and we were pretty frustrated; I didn't know what we could do about anything right now, and when

I went to bed, to sleep through most of the next day, I had bad dreams and thrashed around a lot.

The next couple of days were dull in another way; when the intelligence guys weren't asking me just one more time to see if maybe I remembered something this time that I never had before, I was being processed in the great paperwork swamp that had built up in Saigon. A security chief whose facility has been destroyed doesn't have a job, and since I didn't have the position, the one thing I really wanted to know—whether Singh and Prasad and the rest of them had come through, how many killed and wounded we'd taken—was now classified information that they could not tell me.

That meant floating from desk to desk a lot, and quite possibly getting myself written up as an obsessive nut who was a security risk since he seemed to want to know classified information. I wasn't doing my prospects for another posting any good, but I had to know.

Three days later, as I was walking along one of the broad boulevards, trying to enjoy the sunshine and the feeling of safety that Saigon gave me in those days, and not succeeding because I had just been trapped between two petty clerks who each thought I should have talked to the other one first, I heard a voice behind me say, "Hey, kid, you still a straight shot with a .45?"

It was Patton, big as life (which was pretty big) and striding out of the crowd to say hello. Before I knew it I was off to eat with him and his staff; he knew all about the disaster in Singapore, and, being the kind of generous and effective leader he was, suspected that I might be blaming myself.

As a result, I got to tell him about my frustrations, and in only the time it took him to bellow into a dozen phones, I had the answers I wanted—Singh and Prasad were all right, we had lost seven guards to death and two were missing, and there were about a dozen wounded, none on the critical list anymore.

It wasn't great news, but it was news.

After that he wanted to talk about my next posting; I had not been thinking that far ahead, since my present occupation seemed to consist of talking to intelligence types. He made a couple more calls, then said, "You know, Strang, you might have told me that a little force of auxiliary security guards you trained held off an SS paratroop force three times their size. It's hard to help a man who won't blow his own horn! I'm just going to have a little chat with old Giap—I have a feeling he's apt to have a use for you. And no more hiding your light under a bushel!"

I had just about enough time to thank him for straightening the mess out for me, and for lunch, before he and his three junior officers were piling into his jeep to race away. "Mims," he said—I was not to hear his voice again for a while—"I do believe we are late at the airport, and I think in all likelihood that Monty will be angry and will stamp his little footie and pout about it. Shall we thank the gentleman for helping us be late?"

Sergeant Mims, the driver who had been with Patton through all of the years, right from the start of the AEF, turned around and grinned at me. "Sir, you couldn't have known, but taking care of your problems has made the general late. This is going to make Field Marshal Montgomery very angry. So thank you for making General Patton's day!"

They roared away; the captain and lieutenant riding in the back waved a little sheepishly. I suppose they were used to this sort of thing but could never be sure who else might or might not be.

Two days later I received orders and space-a pass to take me up to Hanoi for a meeting with General Giap the next week. I wrote a thank-you note to Patton—and I *never* write thank-you notes, Mom always had a terrible time with me about that—packed my single suitcase, squared my bill at the *pension* I was staying in, and caught the next bus to the airport.

When I arrived at General Giap's office, he was just finishing up some sort of staff briefing, so I had to cool my heels outside a bit. There were a number of delicate little watercolors on the wall, quite good in the Annamese and Hmong traditions, and I studied them carefully, letting the analytic process shut off more worrisome matters for the time being.

"I sometimes wonder—does our art say anything to an outsider?" Giap asked, behind me.

"It might not say what you intend it to, but it does say something," I said. "It's a way of seeing the world, and it's interesting to see other people's ways of seeing."

He nodded, as if I had said something profound, and showed me into his office. "What I am about to tell you," he said, "is a matter of highest confidence. To be honest about it, we are giving you this post not so much because we think you can do it—we think perhaps no one can do it—but because you did rather well in a hopeless situation. General Patton was impressed with how you had trained your men; I was impressed with the fact that you actually managed a counter-attack, even if an unsuccessful one.

"What we have for you to do is to guard our last possible key to victory. We will have to depend on you to be resourceful; your job, if you are willing to take it, is to think of every possible way some enemy might try to knock out the facility, and to make sure that way is blocked. Technically you will be a staff officer under General Minh, but he intends to give you a fair amount of autonomy and ability to command resources.

"What you will be guarding is the facility designed to give the Axis its death blow. The code name for the place is Engineering Forty-six. You will see one familiar face there—Dr. von Braun has accepted a position.

"As you know, we've made considerable use of nuclear energy here since the Free Zone was established. In fact we've even tested a couple of atomic bombs in underground caverns, using their neutron production to make more plutonium.

"The information you brought has allowed Dr. Teller to make a more powerful kind of bomb, the 'fusion' or 'hydrogen' bomb. How it works, I have no idea. But they say it will. And we have enough rocket motors left so that Dr. von Braun has been able to assure us he can build enough missiles to deliver two dozen of these superbombs to anywhere in the world we select.

"When those missiles fly, our forces will attempt to break out of this hellish pocket in which we have been cornered for a decade. We know we can count on uprisings around the world, and what we hope to do is to catch the Nazis with their leadership cut off, local forces paralyzed by indecision, and supply lines in complete disarray. They were never really able to occupy all the vast territory they control, especially since they decided to allocate very little of it to their French, Spanish, Italian, and Japanese allies; this is why they had to leave your country in charge of its home-grown Nazis after so brief a Reconstruction. In many, many places the underground is ready to break out and take over, so long as the local fascists cannot get support from the Luftwaffe and from the world headquarters. And once these missiles hit, they will not be able to.

"We have only a very limited amount of time. The rockets are being set up and the bombs hauled out to them as quickly as we can

go. The raid on Singapore has shown us that the Nazis know we are
up to something which could bring them down; and with these
artificial moons of theirs, despite our best efforts, they will undoubtedly know all about what we are up to within a short while.
We are getting as much air cover as possible for the area where you
will be working, but we have to be alert for a possible ground attack, and, of course, we are critically short of radar capabilities—so
although we can spot a high-level bombing run, airborne commandos might well get through.

"Your mission, Mr. Strang, is to make sure that nothing whatsoever happens to the missile field."

"Glad to be of service," I said.

"Understand, no one can tell you where or how the threat will
come."

"That's usual in my line of work."

"I knew you would say that." He stood up; I was always startled
when he did that, for he was a small, physically slight man, but his
dignity and intelligence, and his fierce approach to everything,
tended to make you forget that until you were standing right next
to him. He smiled slightly. "And I do hope that you and I will meet
again when the world is at peace. I had always hoped to be a professor of history, you know—circumstances dictated otherwise. I
should like to hear what you think of my paintings sometime, over
sherry in a faculty club somewhere, where the most serious violence is on the soccer field."

I shook his hand, bowed, and agreed. It had taken a very short
time, and I was eager to get on with the mission. "Can you tell me,
or should I wait to find out, just where this missile field is going to
be?"

"I think we can safely tell you. It's in a little place you've never
heard of, a provincial town north and west of here, called Dien
Bien Phu."

General Minh was a big, easy guy with a big, hard job. He was
happy to turn me loose on it. The next week, the only break I took
was a brief dinner one night with von Braun. He wanted to know
what had happened to the security forces at Singapore, just as I
had, and I got from him the accounting of whom we had lost at

mission control—I couldn't quite imagine that the whole Philly Navy Yard crew was gone, but they were.

I spent much of the time just walking the ground. The village of Dien Bien Phu itself had had about a thousand people before the war, but it had swollen to six times that size with crews and technicians. They were hiding as much as they could from the air (and though few of them knew it, from space), but there was no concealing the fact that Provincial Highway 41, which had been a good-weather gravel track, was now a four-lane highway. Nor, really, could the launchpads sprouting like mushrooms up in the hills be entirely concealed, though the control bunkers were at least hidden under what looked like houses from the air.

Everyone knew we would be better off putting the missiles into silos, because freestanding as they were they could be blown over by a bomb a hundred yards away from them, and if they tipped over, the damage would put an end to their usefulness. But everyone knew we didn't have the time, the resources, even the concrete, to put them in silos. So we just kept our fingers crossed; it was all we could do.

Or almost all. The other thing I did was walk around with a French major, a guy named Bigeard, who had managed to make it to Britain and traveled all the way here with Patton. Or possibly with God. I wasn't sure Bigeard could tell the difference.

He'd been a paratrooper, made the landings behind the German lines that had slowed them down at York to allow the AEF to escape, jumped again at Cumberland, Maryland, and Petersburg, Virginia, in the spearheads of other failed counterattacks. He'd made about ten more jumps in various raids.

"No question," he told me. "There are only four decent places to jump into here. The SS might be crazy enough, you know, to jump somewhere else, but they will be no better off for it if they do. The airfield, the land across the ditch from the airfield, or along the Nam Yum below the town, up on the flatland above the river on either the west or east side. That's all. If they cannot land there, they cannot land at all."

There were a lot of kids in the village, and nobody had time to run a school, so I put the kids to stringing barbed wire around in the bushes in the drop zones, to digging pits and setting pungee sticks, and, where possible, to digging deeper holes that could be expected to flood. I did nothing to hide this from the satellites; I wanted them to think about it a lot.

That left me two holes in the defense; I couldn't very well dig pits in the airfield, but I got a bunch of proficient snipers trained to cover it. At least there was always plenty of small-arms ammunition, and we had enough people from the Himalayan fringe to ensure us all the sharpshooters we could want. I could make them very sorry they landed there, make it impossible to set up the artillery, and the airfield was away from the launching pads by some margin.

Part of the problem I was facing, too, was that if they came in overland, infiltrating from some more distant landing site (our radar fence just wasn't good enough to cover against that possibility), I needed to have patrols out, but if they landed in the middle, I needed forces concentrated. Moreover, I had to figure the enemy were likely to all be half-crazed, since there was no way they could expect to be extracted once they hit the ground, and thus this was a one-way trip to prison or the grave for them.

At dinner with von Braun, I was talking about all of this. He had kind of an abstract, distant stare, and then suddenly he said, "Did you ever continue our experiment with the SHAKK?"

"Gee, no," I said, feeling stupid because of course it was a far better weapon than the Colt automatic I was still lugging around.

"There's something I'd very much like to see about it. If it's in your quarters, do you suppose we could conduct an experiment or two more before we call it a night?"

"Happy to oblige." We got the SHAKK from my bunk, and then went back to the Materials Science Lab.

This was a much better place to work than the back of an autogyro; we were even able to figure out just what the rare earths *were*, and soon we had all the percentages moving up toward 100.

"Now let me try my experiment," he said.

Although copper was already at 100 percent, the next thing he put in the drawer was a coil of pure copper wire. There was a brief humming noise, and from the base of the grip—where the magazine slid in on my .45—a tube extended, and pellets of copper dribbled out. When the copper stopped coming, the tube slid back into place, and a cover slid across it.

"Amazing," he said. "You realize that to reshape it that way takes a lot of energy—and yet the SHAKK isn't warm anywhere, which means it somehow put out all the energy it needed without producing any waste heat at all. Now watch closely . . . next trick . . ."

This time it was copper sulfate with which he filled the drawer. Again the tube extended, and this time it spit out pellets of sulfur, followed by pellets of copper. "I suppose the oxygen in the sulfate just goes out to the air," he said quietly. "It's a large favor, but could I possibly borrow this for—oh, a week at most? I can't promise it will be unharmed, but I'm not planning to do anything to harm it."

I agreed, he borrowed it, the next week he brought it back, and that was as much thought as I gave it. At the time Bigeard and I were busy with figuring out where to dig holes.

It did occur to me that evening to try a few experiments of my own. I discovered that plain dirt, some local stone, fistfuls of hardware, and a bit of charcoal seemed to be a workable mixture; there were excesses of a few things that rolled out the tube. Then I got curious about what the drawer next to the "firing chamber"—if this thing had a firing chamber—might do, so I opened that up.

There were tiny transparent pellets in there, smaller than BB shot and looking like nothing so much as cheap caviar. They were arranged in neat rows. I touched one gingerly and it rolled onto my hand; it felt light there. I could see what appeared to be nozzles on every surface, and the inside had a strange, complicated pattern, visible by holding it up to the light, that resembled nothing so much as a microscope photo of a nerve cell.

The drawer had been empty before; I figured this must be the ammo.

I tried to return it to its place, but it wouldn't stick; a thought hit me and I pulled out a bunch more of them, closed the ammo drawer, and checked; sure enough, it said it was "93% loaded" rather than the 100 percent it had been before.

Then I took the extra shot and fed it into the raw materials hopper; in just an instant, the SHAKK display changed back to 100 percent. Now I understood what the loading powder Harry Skena had used had been—it was just the right chemical mix to produce shot without any waste. And I also knew how I could store up a lot more than the two thousand rounds the contraption held in ready. All I had to do was make pellets, in quantity, and have a few buckets of them handy. It was so simple that I did it that night; from then on I had four galvanized iron buckets of SHAKK shot always in my office.

A few experiments showed the SHAKK shots would go right through the system to become usable as ammunition again in a second or less, even while the SHAKK was also firing full auto. (Ever try to find a good backstop for hypersonic ammunition that likes to loop around inside whatever it hits? I finally found that an empty, rusted water tank filled with sand worked pretty well.) That meant, I estimated, that me and my four buckets had just over 300,000 rounds available.

I was pretty sure that if I could get to a good place with those buckets fast enough, I could make hash out of anything coming in. The trouble was, the outer range on the SHAKK was about six miles, and that didn't allow me to cover all the drop zones, quite, let alone all the launchpads and control bunkers. So I rigged up a centrally located tower that would give me a clear view of as much as I *could* cover, and kept my kids digging holes and stringing wire. (One clever little bastard who was good at catching poisonous snakes started "farming" them in the holes of one drop zone—I figured that ought to surprise the occasional SS man.)

The day the tower was done, I decided to move my buckets of spare ammo up there, and some impulse or other made me fill up two more. I now had 450,000 rounds, give or take, for the SHAKK. I couldn't be sure it would be enough, but any more would start to take up floor space I had to have on my "flagpole," as General Minh dubbed it.

He had his own hassles—a series of long-range patrols in the back country had run into occasional Japanese infiltration, and although we had the advantage of having the peasants mostly on our side, we still had to get men out there to catch the bastards, and in operations at that distance it wasn't easy.

It turned into sort of a party, for Bigeard showed up with wine, and then of all people von Braun dropped by. Minh's patrols had reported some success, so his mood was a bit better than usual; Bigeard had been given some secret mission he was ecstatic about; I had my tower, and von Braun was all but glowing.

"I do wish I could tell you," he said. "Oh, god, how I wish I could tell you. By late tonight you'll know anyway. And in an odd way, Mr. Strang, we owe a lot of it to you. It will all be much clearer when—"

There was a roar and rattle of trucks approaching the village on Highway 41; it sounded like as many as a hundred. Von Braun raised his glass, drained it, and said, "Gentlemen, when next we speak—well, you'll find out!"

It occurred to me as he dashed away, that blue-eyed blond muscular German, that he looked like every stereotypical Aryan in every Nazi poster. His sense of humor, though, was pure twelve-year-old; what do you expect from a man who wants to go to Mars, the basic dream of so many twelve-year-old boys? I suppose it was a lesson about judging by appearances . . .

The truck convoy swung immediately into the secure compound, the area south of the village where the top secret work was done, mostly in underground bunkers. Men were running there from all over, so whatever this was, it was big.

Bigeard sighed. "Not that this is particularly fine wine, you understand, but it's the last of the Australian, and there are no good places left for grapes in the Free Zone. I suppose I shall have to kill it all myself—"

"Happy to help you," I said, and Minh smiled and extended his glass.

"I hate to see a party break up too soon," Bigeard said. We all toasted the afternoon, the minor successes of the day, and the fact that there was still some hope in the world.

There was so much commotion from the secure compound that at first I didn't realize a distant siren had sounded; by the time I was scrambling to my feet, there were sirens everywhere. Minh was on his feet, hollering for his jeep and driver, and an instant later Bigeard was forming up his battalion to get a perimeter thrown around the secure compound. The raid we were waiting for had come.

·15·

I climbed my tower, SHAKK in hand, and phoned central radar.

"What's up?"

"Planes coming in low from the north. Lot of big ones. Bombers or transports. Air Def Com says they've got fighters on the way." He hung up; I don't think he'd heard my question, I think he just knew that the answer would be the same for everyone.

I lifted my binoculars and looked; it was a minute or so, and then tiny dots swam in over the mountains.

I got the SHAKK into my hand while I watched, and the planes swept down toward the village. It was still too soon to tell bombers from transports—the Germans tended to use the same body shape for either—but it seemed odd for an attack to be led by big, slow planes unless it was paratroops.

It was. As soon as the first one was in range, I gave him four hex bursts, moved to the next one, moved to the next one, but now there were more than a hundred coming, and I couldn't sight or pull the trigger that fast. Dimly, I was aware that the ones I had shot had started to fall out of the sky, wings and engines dropping off, troops blocked by their mates trying to get out the door with their chutes. The first transport hit hard enough to blow her fuel tanks, and in the last fifty feet or so she dropped three paratroopers with no room for chutes to deploy; they hit the dirt and lay still, streams of silk billowing behind them.

I looked away in haste. The sky was beginning to fill with chutes, and I carefully swung the SHAKK from body to body under them, squeezing the trigger precisely each time. High above, the bodies pitched hard once as their brains were torn to pieces, and then hung still on the end of the line.

I could work the SHAKK fast enough to keep up with this wave, but not fast enough to hit the planes, too. I crouched, grabbed a fistful of shot, popped the drawer on the SHAKK, shoved it in, and was up shooting again; a couple of paratroopers had made it to the ground on the airfield by then, though.

I heard the rattle of rifle fire and knew my sharpshooters would keep them busy; meanwhile I concentrated on getting caught up at hitting them before they touched down.

You would think it would be like pointing your finger, but the reality was that the SHAKK round went exactly where you pointed it. I took to firing short bursts across each paratrooper, which sped the process up, and probably nine out of every ten of them arrived dead. What that must have been like for the ones who were alive on the ground is something I avoid thinking about.

Not that I'm squeamish. Whatever compassion I ever had was cut out of my heart by Blade of the Most Merciful; I had never made a secret of the fact that my favorite thing about being a bodyguard was having a license to hurt people and a good excuse for it as well. But even I, when I think of a man finding himself landing in a firefight, in a tangle of pits and wire that he can't safely move in, trying to make his way through while the bullets are pecking in at him . . . and finding only his dead buddies, with their heads exploded, shrouded by their chutes . . . well, I have to hope that the sharpshooters at least got them pretty quickly.

The first wave had obviously been intended to secure the airfield and the area north of town; it was just as obviously a failure. What came in next, I assume, was supposed to be close air support for the invading force of corpses laid out in front of us.

That was a lot worse. The jets came in very fast, and I sprayed at them with full auto, but I didn't have much luck—only two of the ten or so augured into the empty fields behind us without releasing their weapons loads. Another let go his bombs and then blew up, which was satisfying only from the standpoint of revenge.

Bombs crashed into the village, and there I was, up on that silly "flagpole"—the shock waves made it bounce around in a way that was completely terrifying. I nearly lost my balance, and one bucket of SHAKK shot did fall off.

When I stood back up everything was in chaos—buildings on fire, walls blown down, frantic rescue efforts in progress everywhere, and I could hear more transports coming in.

If they had been intending to drop on the airfield, as the first wave had, they might have taken it then, for the wind was blowing the smoke north and I couldn't see. But their target was the secure compound, and that meant they all passed directly over me as they began their drops. I pointed the SHAKK upward and sprayed two full magazines into the sky; some rounds hit the few paratroopers who were already out the door, most rose harmlessly to a height of more than ten miles and floated back to Earth to become marbles for the next generation of kids, and maybe half of one percent of them found their way into the transports.

But that was what really counted. It helped that the few para-troopers who landed arrived dead, but it helped more that rounds found their way in through the door, or through the fuselage itself, and slaughtered them inside the transports before they could ever step out. It helped that wings fell off, engines sheared away, and the planes themselves disintegrated.

Again, I'm just as glad I know nothing of the experience of anyone who wasn't killed in the air or in the plane, for what it must have been like to be surrounded by all of your suddenly dead friends, in an airplane falling to pieces and catching fire around you—well, if I really knew, I might pity them, and I feel no desire to pity Nazis.

I reloaded again and turned back to fire at the oncoming wave of close air support; this time I was luckier, because I had a slightly longer time to aim, and four ships fell apart on their approach, decorating the hillsides behind me. I tried laying a curtain of fire between the dropping bombs and the village, but there were only two early explosions—and one water buffalo, peaceably watching us humans kill each other, fell dead in the street. I had let my hand jump a bit as I fired.

There was a rattle of rifle fire from the other side of the cloud of smoke that now kept me from seeing what was happening on the airfield and in the northern drop zone. There was nothing for it—I would have to leave the tower and take my chances that there were no more coming in from any other side.

I grabbed the phone and asked for a status report. Fighters were to be there in twenty minutes, which wasn't bad, but we needed them now. There was another wave behind this one, closing in fast at higher altitude.

It didn't necessarily look like the good guys were going to win. I jumped down the ladder, one bucket of SHAKK ammo still in my fist, and ran through the village—most of the civilians and dependents had headed straight down into the shelters at the first sign of trouble, but it was still a Vietnamese country village, and so after the first bombs had hit the streets had filled up with panicked chickens, ducks, goats, dogs, and practically everything except water buffalo; they were there, too, but they weren't particularly panicked, just wandering around as if it was too much work to wonder what the noise was all about.

The smoke was thick, sharp, and bitter, for the village was mostly palm and bamboo, and in the dry season there's not much to keep it from turning into tinder. For some reason that made me angrier than ever—the thought of all these people losing everything they owned in the fires—and it seemed to put wings on my feet.

I burst from the smoke to see that there were a hundred of them on the landing field, now, taking cover behind two wrecked Gooney birds. The sharpshooters had them surrounded and were plinking away at them, but the SS men had submachine guns and could spray enough bullets to make our guys keep their heads down, and it was clear they were about to get organized to make a break for it. If they did, the line was thin enough that they might well carry forward into the village.

I leveled the SHAKK at the underside of the nearer DC-3, set it for hex bursts, and began pumping the trigger as fast as I could. In about ten seconds, the plane began to fall apart; first a landing strut fell off, then parts of the fuselage came down, and finally with a great rending crash the whole thing fell into small bits. The SS men behind it tried to run for the cover of the remaining plane, but the conventional fire pouring through the gap got some, and SHAKK rounds eliminated the others. I turned my attention on the other plane, and it, too, went to pieces, but before I had completed the job I was out of ammo. I tossed fistfuls of slugs into the drawer, as I crouched there behind a stone wall at the edge of the field, but the SHAKK did take a second to turn each fistful into ammo.

I had just thrown in the third and final handful when a German leaped over the wall, his submachine gun at ready.

My hand fell onto my Colt, the automatic flicked onto the target, and I turned out to have faster reflexes than he did. I squeezed the trigger four times in all, and the first two rounds went in right above his eyes. He was dead before he hit the ground.

There are things to be said for low-tech, too.

The interruption had given the SHAKK time to get fully ready, so I popped up and hosed down the ten SS men now running directly toward my position; they fell dead on the pavement, and I climbed the wall, hearing more fighter planes coming in.

The fighters were jets, moving very fast at the outside edge of my range, orbiting a perimeter around the village, but I fired a hex burst at each one as it passed by, and I was happy to see that by the time they had circled twice, I, or ground fire, or just the perverse nature of mechanical things, had caused two of them to have engine flameouts and to disappear over the hills trailing smoke.

There was a field telephone nearby and I used it; the man said it looked like the last wave of troop transports in this flight would be coming in on the southern side, probably trying to land below the secure compound. In a way that was good news—the secure compound was well defended and getting more so—but it sounded like I could be most effective in that direction, so I snatched up my bucket of ammo, ran back through the smoke—the village was beginning to get firefighting under way—and stopped for an instant at the tower to throw a few handfuls from the spilled bucket into my still-almost-full one.

I came out of the smoldering village just in time to see them coming over the more distant mountains.

They were not troop transports. The Nazis had taken another big leap in technology, or more likely their Closer masters had done so, and what these things looked like was a sort of distant relative of the B-52. They were coming in fairly low, and not yet in range, but I didn't think I was going to be able to get all of them. Moreover, three of our launchpads were out that way, and if they let loose with their bombs, they would get at least those pads, and probably several more. Even with the SHAKK, I could hurt them, but I could not stop them.

Bursts of heavy firing came from behind me; I ran back to the tower and bellowed questions into the field telephone, but it was nothing to be worried about—merely Bigeard and his troops sweeping the landing field clear of the remaining resistance. The enemy in the northern drop zone were already surrendering.

I dashed back, out of breath, smoke searing my lungs and making my eyes water, so that when I got into fresh air the first things I had to do were to retch and wipe my eyes.

The bombers were closer still, hanging like metallic vultures above the distant blue-green hills. They would be able to hammer several of the launchpads before I could even get one shot off, and, in fact, if they split up and circled, they could probably get every missile in the valley—and with the missiles, the last hope for this timeline.

Behind me, the gate of the secure compound opened, and the damnedest thing I had ever seen in my life came rolling out. It was a plain old GM truck, of the kind we saw a lot of here, probably shipped to Russia, captured by the Germans, donated to Japan, captured by the Free Zone forces. The engine was hammering away trying to drag the outsized load on its back.

But the truck itself was just a frame of normality around the deep weirdness of what sat on its bed. It might have been half of a "Martian invader" from some old fifties sci-fi flick, or the metal clam-plate top of the Closer tank I had blasted, glued to a lot of old auto parts, or possibly an entire junk sculpture collection rammed together, welded at random points, and placed under an aluminum awning to keep the rain off. Behind it trailed a cable as thick as my waist, winding off a spool ten feet tall. The top had something on it that looked like a telescope poking out of an observatory in an old cartoon, except that there was a dark hole right in the center of the lens.

And just above the dome of it, three radar antennas were spinning madly. It couldn't have looked any screwier if it had had six eggbeaters, a set of Christmas tree lights, and a steam whistle attached to it; it looked like what happens when somebody scrambles all the parts of thirty modeling kits and hands a chimp a tube of glue.

Or two tubes of glue, one of which the chimp sniffs before beginning.

Driving this whole mad contraption, wearing a shabby black

suit and pair of sneakers that made him look like he was trying to
dress up as a punk rocker and not succeeding, was Dr. Edward
Teller. As they reached the end of the cord—that was the only way I
could explain that huge thing trailing off the end—Teller braked to
a stop, leaped out, and ran around to an instrument panel
mounted on the side.

The whirling radar antennas sped up. The dome itself crept
about, moved up and down, and a bright light flashed a few times
in the muzzle of the "telescope." Then he nodded, appeared to
hesitate an instant, and pushed a button.

I've heard thunder up close and been on mountains during
thunderstorms. Once in Oman, on a dig by the sea, I got to see a
waterspout, and once in Iowa, had to take cover in a ditch when a
tornado passed close by. I'd heard more big explosions than I ever
wanted to hear again.

This dwarfed them. It was a brief, stuttering roar, over in less
than two seconds, but in that short time it made my ears bleed;
some of the older land mines around the valley were detonated by
the vibrations.

I looked up to see that all seventeen of the bombers had exploded. There was no one part of them that went first—a fuel tank,
bomb, or engine—spreading to the rest. Each whole bomber had
become so hot on its surface that the air next to it was superheated
and flashed outward, which was the first part of the explosion, and
the reason why there was such a bright flash of white light first;
then the heat, conducted inside in milliseconds, detonated all the
explosives, the fuel, the liquids in the hydraulic lines, the lubricants, the plastic seat cushions, creating a yellow-red explosion that
swelled into a great, pulsing fireball, which then evaporated into
dark smoke and a rain of bits of melted metal and charred cinders.

Dr. Teller's little device fired ten shots per second at ten separate targets, under radar control, so presumably the whole thing
took 1.6 seconds for the bomber squadron.

There was a very long pause while the implications sank in.
Then all those of us who could see Dr. Teller began to cheer. He
got up on the truck, clenched his fists over his head like a
prizefighter, and jumped back down.

He walked straight toward me, for some reason or other. His
hand was out, and since he extended it to me, I shook it. From the
roar that his gadget had made when it fired, I was still a bit deaf,

and so was he, so he leaned in close to say, "And we owe this one to you, Mr. Strang. Not to mention that I'm quite confident about the results for me as soon as the Nobel Committee convenes after the war."

"The Nobel . . . owe it to me . . ."

"Of course. You're the one who told me about the whole idea, remember? The lasers of your own world. Once you told me what they did, building one was easier than I thought it would be. The biggest problem was coming up with the device to pump it, and it took me forever to realize that you must do it with nuclear fusion— nothing else would have the power density I needed—and that it couldn't be fusion in a plasma, had to happen in a normal state of matter. Once I got the cold fusion idea doped out—took me the better part of a week, and if I hadn't gotten it last Wednesday I was going to call you and ask you for a hint—"

"Cold fusion?" I said. "This thing runs by cold fusion?"

"The amplifier does," he said. "I still need a huge current surge to start it, which is why I have that silly cord rigged up to the back there. Now, come on, there's no other way a device of this kind could be powered. That's crystal clear from the equations. You said it was coherent light—I know you didn't say coherent light, but that was clearly what you described—and commonplace in your world—"

"I don't think I've ever seen a laser one one-thousandth the power of this," I said, almost whispering. "This is like some-thing . . ." I was going to say "something for SDI," but I sus-pected it was bigger, and, anyway, the term wouldn't mean any-thing to him. "This is like something out of science fiction. I mean, I've seen ten-watt and hundred-watt lasers—"

Now he stared at me. "But didn't you say—oh, god, no, you didn't. I've been doing weapons work so long I just assumed that if you couldn't shoot it at someone, no one would build it." He sat down; he looked as dazed as I felt. "The first day back on the *Arizona* I hit on the idea of something that would work like that, but it would be so difficult to make it big enough to use as a weapon that I gave up on that line, especially because when I thought of this other way . . . then you don't have anything like this?"

"We don't have cold fusion, either."

"Good thing I didn't call you for a hint, then," he said. He still looked a little dazed.

He was right, though. The next year when they had reorganized the Nobel Prizes, they gave him three years' worth at a clip, for 1958–60 inclusive. By that time he'd gotten over the shock a bit.

When Teller's laser destroyed the oncoming bombers, von Braun's group was only hours away from loading the warheads onto the missiles. I've found that when I describe my feelings to people, they just don't understand, but that night as I watched twenty-four columns of fire rise into the sky, I was only happy. I knew they had equipped them with huge warheads, gratuitously big to, in Churchill's phrase, "make the rubble bounce." In that timeline, Berlin became the site of a crater you could easily see from the moon, and Germany itself a radioactive wasteland for generations after.

Al and I had a sizable argument about that one, though we stayed friends; he just didn't have a bitter, hateful bone in his body when you came right down to it. I figured I had more than enough for two of us. Anyway, there are those who think his "Pillars of Fire" is as good as "The Fall" and "The Gathering of Nations," but I suppose I'm too partisan to see it that way. No ear for poetry, as I've said.

As the missiles tore Nazi Germany from the face of the Earth and the pages of history, the other fascist nations were not spared, either. But Germany took the brunt, and then the major Axis military facilities. Moreover, the Free Zone Forces had hundreds of tactical nukes, and they weren't shy about using them; in a few weeks' time, they had retaken the Philippines, Australia, and New Zealand, driven the Japanese out of China and the Axis puppet regime out of India, and accepted the surrender of the Empire of Japan.

Everywhere people rose against their tormentors. After Buenos Aires vanished in a mushroom cloud, Brazil rose as one nation and struck southward, avenging the wrongs of twenty years; I was privately amused to hear Brazilians blame the Argentines for the destruction of rain forests, and to see Brazil acquire a reputation as a nation of environmental nuts.

Patton's invasion of the United States ranks as a political masterpiece in its execution; his terms were so unrelentingly harsh that most of the quiet Nazis and cryptofascists, the people for whom the occupation and Reconstruction had been excuses to practice the bigotry they had believed in all along, were too frightened to allow the puppet regime in Washington to accept.

I once heard a man in a bar complaining that Patton could have taken the country back without a shot fired—but if he had, the fascists would have been voting in it. I made that point clear to the gentleman by slugging him, and used my political pull to beat the rap.

Instead of trying to mollify the fears of the eighteen million strong American Nazi Party, he provoked them into meeting him head-on. Patton announced he was going to free all the remaining black Americans in the labor camps and give them first choice of land confiscated from the Nazis. He promised that no former Nazi would ever vote, hold office, or own property again.

Then, to tempt them to try their luck, he pledged he would not use nuclear weapons on American soil—and didn't.

It still took him less than a hundred days to trap their army in the desert and tear it to pieces, and the huge losses he inflicted simply meant that any of them with the courage to fight was probably dead. It was swift, brutal, and did the job—it was like him.

Anyway, I voted for him in the first free election. It was a hard choice; I had gotten to like Captain Kennedy, too.

·16·

The story could have stopped right there. I learned long afterward, from von Braun, that what they had used the SHAKK to do was to chemically separate plutonium—they had simply put high-level reactor waste in the drawer, closed it, and let the weapon spit out all the things it didn't want, separately. In a week of this they had obtained many tons of weapons-grade plutonium, and that had made the difference.

The Closers who had been in that timeline probably died in Berlin, or were now so far underground we hadn't a prayer of catching them for a few generations. At any rate, they would never want this timeline or any of its descendants to colonize again—too many nukes had gone off. It was about the equivalent of an extra dental X-ray per year, spread around, and well worth it from my viewpoint.

But one day, two years later, I was at a Victory Day celebration—just as I had the year before, I told my class at Yale that I hated having to take time out to go to that thing. They never believed me, and they were right.

Patton had won the election the fall before, and there were more American flags—with stars and not swastikas—than I had ever seen before lining Pennsylvania Avenue. The postwar problems were setting in—everything was either in short supply or needed to be done now—but spirits were up.

I was walking along in the crowd and noticing that attractive women running out to kiss me was more fun than it used to be, when one very attractive woman slipped her arm into mine and said, "Hi, remember me?"

It was Ariadne Lao, the ATN Special Agent.

"I sure do. So you found this timeline again."

"Unhhunh. Where can I meet you to talk with you, say, later in the week?"

I told her my new address, and she quietly wrote it down. "Enjoy the parade—I don't think anyone's earned it more thoroughly." And she vanished into the crowd.

It was three days before she turned up; in that time, I did a lot of thinking but reached no conclusions.

She was dressed like any female colleague would be, in a simple skirt and blouse and sneakers. There was sort of a cultural uproar happening out there, as America rediscovered jazz and everything black, and as fashions stopped being either military or "normal." But it hadn't much hit the campuses yet.

She sat down, let me make and pour coffee for her—one wonderful thing the old Free Zone had had in abundance, and which they were happily exporting to the free USA—and said, "Goodness, where do we start? First of all, I really must apologize for the entire situation—you were supposed to be a local assistant for poor Citizen Skena and instead you ended up in all of this. For what it's worth, we've given you extended hazardous duty pay that's still piling up for you back in the ATN timeline."

"Do I have to spend it there?"

"You might *want* to—there are many nice things that aren't available in a lot of other timelines—but no, it's fully convertible. You can take it in gold, silver, plutonium, germanium, platinum, or gallium and turn it into the currency of wherever you want to go; in fact we can handle that for you. In your home timeline, converting to platinum and then to dollars, you've got about ten million dollars; in this one, with postwar inflation and so forth, more like a billion."

I gave a low whistle, and I meant it; that was a pretty impressive deal.

"The question," she said, crossing her legs, which were great legs in my opinion, "is what you want to do. Let me explain it to you simply. We don't recruit a lot of people from outside the ATN timeline, and when we do it's generally someone who has been an agent for us inside their own timeline and has a lot of promise, Mr. Strang.

"Your case is truly strange. There are three categories of agents we maintain—the Time Scouts are the ones like Sheila, who go into timelines that have not yet been explored to find out whether there is any Closer presence and any possibility of getting the timeline to join the Alliance. Their skills are mostly at blending in without very many clues as to their surroundings, and then at finding the people closest to the ATN viewpoint.

"Special Agents like Harry Skena go in after Time Scouts have reconnoitered; they go in very well prepared and with specific missions—in Harry's case it was to block Blade and to find out what the Closers were up to in your timeline. They have much greater resources at their disposal, but they only stay a short while to accomplish a particular thing.

"And then there are the ones like me—Crux Ops. We have to be a bit of both, because what we are is Search and Rescue. Every so often a Time Scout or Special Agent runs into bad luck or gets careless—or sometimes is just a little incompetent. When that happens, they disappear and stop signaling. That's when we send in a Crux Op. A Crux Op always has a simple mission, three parts. One, find out what happened to our missing agent. Two, retrieve the agent or, if the agent is dead, retrieve the agent's body. And three, accomplish the agent's original mission.

"Now it occurs to us, in Crux Recovery Operations, Mr. Strang, that you have essentially done the job of a Crux Op with no training, no mandate, and no requirement that you do so. This impresses us very much. More than half of Crux Ops wipe out on their first missions, and only one out of ten people makes it through Crux Op training, and yet you—somehow—managed to be a very effective Crux Op with no training at all and no knowledge of the job."

"What was her original mission?"

"To move this world toward eliminating the Nazis and to prepare the way for friendly contacts with ATN. And, incidentally, to hand the Closers a big defeat, because they've been very arrogant lately."

I had to concede I had done at least that much.

"So here is the deal, Mr. Strang. We offer it freely. You have a job with us if you want it. We would be happy if you wanted to be a Time Scout or a Special Agent, since to do a Crux Op's job you have to be able to do either of the other as well, but what we really want you for is a Crux Op. The pay is superb, as you might have figured out from what accumulated while you were gone, and some people actually like the opportunity to see how many other ways history could have been. You have your choice of basing—here, your home timeline, or any other—and a certain amount of freedom in visiting other timelines.

"Since you are a widower, I will caution you that it generally does not work out well if you try to find a timeline that contains your spouse but in which you never met her; we won't try to stop you, but we will warn you that the results are usually emotionally disastrous. You approach her already deeply in love and knowing a great deal about her, but she is not exactly the person you loved, and you are not, perhaps, so much to her taste, and you assume too much . . . it is better to let the one you knew go than to look for another. So hunting for your lost spouse, alas, is *not* one of the benefits you can expect."

I nodded and thought about it for the first time in ages. A lot had changed for me since coming to this timeline; Marie had been part of an innocent, younger me, and I was chagrined to admit how little I had really known about her—I had known her body, her background, and her eccentricities, and I had told myself I was in love with her, but I was in love with the trappings—I never really knew the person under them.

It can happen, even in marriages that later grow deeper.

If I were to look her up now, I would want to know more before getting involved—and what I learned could easily destroy my memories.

"I wouldn't try to look up any version of Marie," I said.

She nodded, and her eyes softened a little. "It happens that my lover was killed while I was in Crux Ops training. I disobeyed orders to find another version of him. I have never regretted trying, but I have always regretted succeeding—it poisoned some memories I wish I had left pure. Once an illusion is past relevance, there is no point at all in shattering it. So I try to be very firm with possible recruits about it—because I know what kind of error it is."

I nodded; it spoke well of her, and I was noticing how much I liked Citizen Lao.

"Now, whether you join or not, we have two other proposals for you," she said. "The bare bones one is that besides the cash, we feel we owe you a free trip home, either a round-trip to say good-bye before you move here permanently, or a one-way trip if you wish to go back where you came from."

"I know I'll want to take the trip," I said, "and I assume I have some time to decide which form."

"Yes. Now, for the third . . . Crux Ops do not go directly from mission to mission. You could, in theory, you know, because the time machine would allow that easily, but we find that for mental stability, you need to have people at home—and those people should have lived about as many days as you have by the time you get back. Thus we *strongly* recommend that you return to your home timeline about three years after you left it. We can arrange to have your family and friends believe that you were on a top secret mission for the government, and we can also go back and plant documents and records so that your affairs are well taken care of in your absence, including using some of your pay to cover any debts or obligations."

"I'm much obliged," I said.

"Now, if we do that, it so happens that we have something to suggest to you. You may recall that when you left, Harry Skena had one other non-Blade person he was keeping an eye on besides yourself. Her name is—"

"Porter Brunreich," I said, "and the poor kid was having terrible luck."

"One year after you left," Ariadne continued, "her luck got worse. Her father got into a brawl in prison and was killed."

"Sounds like him."

"She has been shuffled from foster home to foster home, and institution to institution. She's thirteen, she's been out on the streets far too much, and though there's plenty of money waiting in trust funds, her relatives and their lawyers are working hard on getting their hands on it.

"Porter Brunreich is vital to the future of more than fifty time-lines that are already members of the ATN. And we think there are two or three great 'trunks'—groups of related timelines—that she may be the root cause of."

I was astonished, even though I'd heard it before. "She's really smart and a terribly nice kid," I said, "but I had no idea—"

"Well, there are plenty of timelines where she doesn't do so well. In some of them she's nobody, in some of them she ends up—badly. There are a lot of ways a child who has been traumatized as Porter Brunreich has can go wrong, or disappear forever."

I thought of that and digested it for a long moment. "So there is something I could do about it?"

"Several times in her early teens she runs away from a foster home, in your timeline. Many things happen after that, some bad, some leading to good timelines. We never know everything that went into making any one timeline, you know . . . but we do know that in a few of them, you end up as her guardian."

I goggled at her. "How does—"

"It turns out that she wrote to her father while he was in prison and asked him to name you as her guardian if anything should happen to him. He did so. And thus you are."

"He, uh, had some help in this?"

"He did, she didn't." Ariadne Lao sighed, then smiled at me. "Your sister Carrie is lonely, you know, and her internal injuries won't allow her to have children, aside from all the difficulties she has in meeting men of her own caliber."

"There never was anybody good enough for her," I said.

"Spoken like a brother." She beamed at me. "I've heard my brother say the same things about me—what a charming idiot. But it is also true that not only does Carrie not meet many men who would be good for her, she simply doesn't meet many men. It's the opinion of our psychological team that if you were to take in Porter Brunreich—*and* you wished to be a Crux Op—this would be good in several regards. You would be around to take care of her, and between your fighting skills and our intelligence service we could keep her safe. She could learn to trust people again—you, Carrie, your employees, your father could become a second family. Carrie would have someone who needed her, and that's very important to your sister—who *also* is important in a number of timelines."

I got up and looked out the window across the broad green common area. "The trouble is," I said, "you make such a good case that I feel as if I'm almost being ordered to do it. And I look around here and find myself thinking, this world is so poor and so damaged by the war. They're going places, but it's going to be a long time, even with the explosive development of science. They need all the willing hands they can get. And I have a lot of friends here, some of them people I never knew in my home world."

"Nor ever will, in your home world," Ariadne said, quietly. She put her hand through my arm and stood next to me; it made my heart thunder, but there was nothing romantic in the gesture, just friendliness and concern. "You have to remember that these people are not the same people; they were formed by different experiences out of different pathways in history. The George Patton, Edward Teller, Curtis LeMay, or Wernher von Braun you know here are not at all the same ones as existed in your world; they look like them, they may share some behavioral tics, but truly they are not the same; they just have the same name. Likewise, should you ever learn of the doings of any of your alternates, you must not be upset. Almost everyone has alters who died stupidly young, alters who were wildly more successful than themselves, alters who turned criminal. These are the possibilities in a life, not your nature—your nature is formed and expressed only in what *you* have done."

"Do I exist in this timeline?" I asked.

"Both your parents died as Resistance fighters early on. They never met."

I nodded. "That's a bad thing, but I can live with it."

"Name a crime and a person, and I can show you a world where they committed it."

"Helen Keller and voyeurism."

"Easily," she said. "There are thousands of timelines where she never lost her sight or hearing. There are thousands more where she had far more influence than she did in yours." Then she punched my arm, very lightly. "But it was a good try."

"So," I said, "are you telling me my friends here are less real than the ones at home?"

"People are real in whatever world you are in. That's all."

I thought about that for a long time. "This timeline will be kind of cold and hardscrabble for a long time to come," I said. "They have little use for an art historian. And they have all sorts of things to live down. I, uh . . . well, I have friends here. But in my own world, the heart of Europe is not glowing with radioactivity, America did not kill fourteen million of its own citizens from 1952 to 1960 . . . and I do miss Dad and Carrie, and, oh, crap, I miss Porter, too. Let me finish out the term here and then go home?"

"To quote you, deal." She withdrew her arm from mine. "And do you want to become a Crux Op?"

"Give me a little time to think. Ask me three months after I'm back."

Going home was the merest blink; I had said my good-byes, put what I wanted into a case. The Crux Ops team had fixed things for me at home, so Dad and Sis thought I'd been off with the DIA in the operation that nailed Blade, Robby and Paula had kept the agency running, and things were more or less waiting for me on return. I had even composed a telegram that they arranged to have come in the day before I landed.

I had said all my good-byes. I was going to miss Al—Sandy had found herself a straight poet and settled down a while past—but that was about the only close friend I'd made here. At least he understood where I was going; other people got the impression that it was something top secret.

I returned to my office for the last time—or at least the last time till I got my dissertation finished and got hired, things that might never happen in my own timeline. In the privacy there, three people, one of them Ariadne Lao, popped into the space. They handed me the boarding pass; I blinked into existence in an airliner bathroom, from which one of them had just emerged, after having checked a bag of my belongings for me earlier that day.

I returned to my seat, fastened the belt, heard the captain announce landing.

Something strange happened at the airport. I cried and told my family I loved them. And they broke into the most beautiful smiles; it wasn't till then that I realized how much they had been worried.

Three weeks later I had just gotten in from a simple little job of keeping Keewee the Family Klown from getting mobbed. (A man in shoes so big he can easily break an ankle falling must have someone to keep children from tackling him.) When all the potential Bad Guys have bedtimes before nine, it's not hard to get the evening over with.

I had moved back in with Carrie and Dad. Dad was already in

bed, and Carrie and I were watching an old movie on TV, when the doorbell rang.

I opened it, and there she was.

She was wearing a pound of makeup badly applied, she'd obviously stuffed her bra with toilet paper, and her skirt was more like a wide belt than anything else. But her blonde hair was matted and dirty from the spring rain, and she was shivering and looked like she might burst into tears.

"Porter!" I said. "God, come in, you'll freeze."

Her face lit up, just a little, with just a hint of hope. "You remembered me," she said. "You remembered."

"Of course," I said, and whisked her in for a scrubbing and a feeding. Sure enough, somehow it turned out that the legal papers making me her guardian had been hidden by an aunt bent on getting Porter's trust fund, and that somehow things just worked out. I recognized Ariadne Lao's gentle hand—or one very like it—and thought how I might feel about that kind of operation.

She started to improve pretty quickly, but the nightmares were something else. I never asked her what she had done to survive on the streets, except by letting her know, in the most indirect way, that I would see that she got medical or psychiatric help if there were any lingering problems or things to worry about.

It had been almost two months when I woke up—as more often than not—to Porter screaming. I knew this was going to be a bad one, because she was screaming for her mother. I threw a robe on over my pajamas and headed down the hall. Porter stopped screaming just as I arrived.

Carrie had beat me to it; she was caressing the girl's face with her single hand, leaning way out of her wheelchair to do it. Porter lay there, silent, her face streaked with tears, and I came around to her other side and held her hand. "You're dreaming about your mom's death again," I said, gently.

Porter snuffled. "She died for me."

"Yes she did, honey. She loved you very much," Carrie said, which let Porter start crying, something that we figured she probably needed to do after all that time in institutions. She held on to Carrie for a bit, and sobbed, like so many other nights, but then she turned to me and said, "We had a deal."

I thought for a moment, then remembered. "We did."

"Did you get all the bad guys? Are they all gone?"

"Blade of the Most Merciful is extinct to the last man, Porter," I said.

"But were they all of them?"

I sighed. "No. Porter, I can't keep my promise to you; there are billions of bad guys, at least, and even if they were all tied up in a row and I just walked along shooting, I could never get all of them. I'm sorry."

Carrie looked at me, baffled, and Porter said, "So you won't keep your promise."

"*Can't*, kid. It's not quite the same thing." I knew Ariadne Lao would be coming for my answer soon, and I knew that here were the two people I most cared about on Earth—the two who needed me most. I sat down and said, "I'll tell you all about it if you like," and then I took both of them downstairs, made a fire in the fireplace, and I made hot chocolate. I talked for most of the night and told them everything.

As I finished, I explained, "So, in about two weeks, Ariadne Lao will be coming to hear whether I want to join the Crux Ops. I would be away a lot, Porter—"

"It's okay, I've got Carrie to take care of me and Robbie and Paula to guard me."

I nodded. "I have to think about it. I'm not sure what I'll tell her, even yet."

Carrie said, "Porter, if I act just like a rotten bastard grown-up and go talk to Mark in the other room, will you promise not to listen in?"

Porter said, "Sure. Is it really important?"

"It's really important." Sis rolled her wheelchair out to the kitchen; I followed.

"Mark," she said, "can I ask you one question before we talk about anything important?"

"Anything you like," I said.

"Didn't you realize who your friend Al was?"

I shook my head. She told me his full name, which was accurate, I'd seen his papers, but it was still a common name. "I don't get into poetry, Sis, I never read it or remembered it. If I ever read anything of his in this timeline it was in the Cliff Notes."

She groaned in frustration; she's loved verse ever since she was a kid. "All right, never mind, here's the important part. Porter is a child. She has a child's concept of promises—she can't imagine that an adult would be *unable* to keep one. But if you don't want to be a Crux Op, don't—and I'll handle it with Porter. If you do, do.

"All I'm asking you to do is make up your mind. You've thought for two months. You know your feelings. Just *decide.* Whichever way you do, you're aces with me, and you will be with Porter, too. But make up your mind and come and tell us."

And the chair spun around—she had gotten into doing stunts on it to annoy Dad and me—and peeled out of there before I could answer.

So I thought. I thought of places to see, and the chance, maybe, to get a feel for how the world might be different.

I thought of the Closers, and Blade, and how they had managed to make the Nazis even worse, and all the other things I knew about them. And the thought that came to me was how wrong I had been, consistently. I had thought, right up into being married and having students, that there was no real malice in the universe; nobody was out to hurt me or my loved ones just to hurt me.

That had been shattered by the bomb explosion that claimed half my family.

But I had dreamed, even then and ever since, of a safe place, where I could sit out the wars that raged across all the possible times.

And that was sheerest folly, I realized, standing there with the corner of the refrigerator pushing into my back. The Closers were everywhere, everywhen, expanding in all directions in time. That they had not intruded into most of my past did not guarantee they wouldn't strike again and again.

For that matter, those bastards were looking for Porter. I could guard her till I died, and others could guard her afterward, but it would make no difference—the Closers only had to get lucky once per timeline.

ATN was the outfit that was doing the right thing, I realized. They were carrying the war to the enemy, wherever they could. It had been the grim determination of the Athenians—and the fact that once they had repelled their own Closer invasion, they didn't decide to sit safe at home—that had saved, was still saving the many universes as places that, if not exactly beautiful or even decent, had some potential for good. With the Closers, there was none.

And I thought of what the Closers were like, finally, and of what I'd seen them do personally—and that in two million time-lines they were doing similar things or worse.

You could never pay all that back, but it would be fun to try. Something had twisted permanently in me, but I wouldn't want it straightened out now, for anything. The longing to sit home by the fire was more sentiment than anything else; I wanted to carry the fight forward. Other people could be noble about it; I wanted to go bag some Closers.

I went back to the fireplace and said, "I'll only be gone for three weeks before I get first leave—"

"Told you," Porter said. "He promised."

• AFTERWORD •

One of Napoleon's better generals observed that God is generally on the side of the big battalions; nowhere is this truer than in World War II. The fact was that Germany, Italy, and Japan faced not just one nation with greater resources than their own, but three (if one counts the British Empire as a unit). By D Day, American factories and training camps were turning out enough men and matériel to *completely replace* every ship, gun, man, tank, plane, and round of ammunition expended in that invasion within six months. In late 1944, the U.S. government *canceled* more battleships and cruisers than the Axis ever had.

And the Americans were merely the largest force in the mixture; though the Soviet Union was badly prepared and (especially in the early months) badly led, it also had enough to beat Hitler all by itself (or rather, aided only by "General Winter"). By the time Marshal Zhukov entered Berlin, he was suffering a major problem with "artillery traffic jams"—he had so many cannon that he could not park them all within range of the enemy.

British aircraft plants and shipyards far outproduced German ones, even under bombardment, and by late 1941 the UK was shooting down bombers and sinking U-boats faster than Germany could build them.

Once the greater weight came to bear, the result was inevitable . . . unless the Axis could win very quickly.

Thus, when you set out to write a "Hitler wins" scenario, you must make him win before Allied war production can come on line, and thus you are driven to one of two possibilities:

1. Give him the atomic bomb.
2. Make up something thoroughly implausible.

I have chosen the latter, and I hope we've all had fun with it.

To make wild implausibility convincing demands mad imagination combined with a thorough grounding in fact. In this case, I had the help of the inspired madmen and madwomen of the GEnie Science Fiction Round Table, in the "Alternate Histories" area. These are people who know more strange esoterica, dispute more points more passionately, and who are more willing to help a fellow writer or alt-history freak than any others I have found. If you're on-line, drop by sometime and join the fray.

This book would have been much more difficult—and much less fun!—without the assistance of the following members of the SFRT:

Tom Holsinger, Trent Telenko, Robert M. Brown, Bill Seney, Ben Yalow, P. "Rascal" Rivard, Pete Granzeau, Leigh Kimmel, Jim Brunet, Tony Zbaraschu, J. "Oakfed" Johnson, Lois Tilton, Al Nofi, S. "Meneldil" Schaper, J. "Digger" Costello, C. Irby, Bill "Sapper" Gross, Robert Mohl, Kevin O'Donnell, Jr., Steve Stirling, William Harris, Gary Frazier, John Johnston, J. Filpus, Mic Madden, Rick Kirka, Jules Smith, Vol Haldeman, Susan Shwartz, S. "ET" Elliott, Oz Osmanski, D. "Moo" Mohney, Alan Rodgers, Ariel, Steven Desjardin, and N. Glitz.

Very special thanks, for assistance far and above the call of getting acknowledged here, are due to Bruce Bethke, Tom Holsinger, and Trent Telenko, whose extreme generosity with their time and expertise kept me out of thousands of stupidities. Any remaining stupidities can be attributed to me.

Washington's
Dirigible

*This one's for Nathan Hurwitz and
for Ron Richards.
God, won't they be embarrassed.*

·1·

Chrysamen ja N'wook has big, dark eyes it's real easy to get lost in, cheekbones high enough for an elf, wavy hair black as coal, and skin the color of fresh coffee with a lot of cream. At the moment she was looking into my eyes and smiling, and what she was saying was, "Remember how happy we were when we got this assignment?"

I did my best to grin back at her. "Remember who said she'd rather ski than swim?"

We shook hands and got into the doors of our separate drop-wings. Back where I come from there would have been hundreds of technicians clicking around behind us, reading boards and checking lights, and somebody called Mission Control would be drawling instructions to us. Here, at ATN Crux Operations Training Area (COTA, or at least that's how most of us pronounced it), shots into orbit were so routine that they were handled automatically, like getting a Coke from a machine. They figured, I suppose, that if you were dumb enough to get into a spacecraft unprepared, you were probably too dumb to be a Crux Op anyway.

My gear was already in my pack, strapped to my chest, balancing my parachute; between all that and the winter-weather coverall, I had about fifty pounds of gear on me. It's a good thing that the little throwaway ships are so reliable that you don't bother with a space suit. The only special requirement is that, since a drop-wing's boost is in the direction of your feet, if you're male you'd better be wearing a jockstrap. (I didn't know what special equipment Chrys might have to wear under her coverall, but even now, with a lot on my mind, I would have been happy to investigate.)

I stretched out in the coffinlike slot in the dropwing, facedown, so that my chest pack fit into the depression. There was a window in front of me but right now all I could see through it was the side of the booster, a scant couple of inches away, and dark because the lander was tied on with a fairing to prevent the wind from shearing it off. I grasped the overhead handles and pulled the trigger to close and seal the bubble doors above me.

Chrys's voice came over the speakers. "So, ready to zoom-bang?"

The autotranslators embedded as chips in our heads were a constant source of amusement; they allowed her to speak her native Arabo-Polynesian, and me to speak English, and us to understand each other—but words and expressions that didn't exist in the other's language tended to come through in a very strange fashion. From talking with her before, I knew what she had said was the equivalent of "Ready to party?" so I said, "Let's blow this Popsicle stand, dudette." From the shriek of laughter I figured her translator had come up with something interesting.

"All right, enough silliness, we have the Dalai Lama to rescue," she said. "Cuing to go . . . *now.*"

Acceleration slammed into me as if the floor had leaped up to hit me in the soles of the feet. It yanked my guts downward and seemed to press the air in my lungs against my diaphragm; I felt for an instant as if my face would run down the front of my skull like molten wax. Then it steadied down to about two and a half g's, and I became aware of sounds again—mostly the thunder of the engines, mixed with Chrys going "Whoooo!" through the speakers. All right, she wasn't *quite* perfect. She wasn't decently scared out of her mind like I was. I'd taken four dropwing flights in training and never gotten to like it one bit.

A long three minutes clocked by as we shot on up and out of the atmosphere, and then finally the booster stage blew clear, as the explosive bolts in the fairing kicked it away. I blinked hard, saw Chrys's dropwing fall off to the side and roll away, and looked at the display projected on my window. Beyond the display, the Earth rolled by, as it did in billions of other timelines.

This was an Earth without human beings—I had seen the

herds of woolly mammoth in Kansas and the blue whales in the Gulf of California to prove it—and thus a perfect training ground. For two years, we and the rest of our class of cadet Crux Ops had climbed untamed mountains, sailed empty seas, trekked across empty deserts—and practiced with every weapon invented in a million timelines, from the SHAKK of the High Athenians, to the boomerang and atl-atl; driven and flown everything from Piper Cubs and Stanley Steamers to spaceships and chariots; ridden on horses, camels, elephants, killer whales, and moas. It had been a little like military basic (or so the vets in the group assured me), a little like fraternity hazing, and a lot like every kid's fantasy of the perfect summer camp.

Now we were two weeks from graduation, and I was looking down on that empty world, where no lines of highways showed and no cities burned like jewels in the darkness, and found myself thinking a just slightly sentimental good-bye at it.

For that matter, it was also the world on which I had met Chrys, and she was the first woman I'd cared about at all since my wife had been murdered, back in my home timeline.

I suppose I could have gotten much more choked up if I hadn't had that terrifying feeling you get, of falling forever, in orbit. I've heard all the old lines, and I don't care. I know that in orbit you're falling *around* the planet, and not into it, and that after all the fall doesn't hurt, the landing does, and all that. I'm scared of the falling, thank you very much, and that's that.

But being scared doesn't mean you get out of doing your job. I watched the green vector line till it hit the target point, then triggered the burn. At once I felt more comfortable—I had half a g pushing me—and in parallel with Chrys, off to my port side and below me, I rose into a higher and more inclined orbit. We were to come in from the southwest, which meant getting an inclination of almost fifty degrees; there were to be two more burns after this.

Cutoff—the engine shut down—and I was falling again, frightened again, and my eyes were locked on that green line. The green line entered the circle, and I pulled the trigger again—once again there was gravity, once again I could enjoy the spectacular view as we swung up over empty Europe, looking down across the forests of Italy to those of Lebanon and Syria—man had indeed left no mark here.

There was one more heart-stopping lurch of weightlessness, a short one this time, and then our engines blazed briefly as we got into the right relative positions, about 140 miles above the North Pole, and swung around to face backward. Now it was just twenty minutes till we started the retroburn.

Twenty minutes of falling without end, but scared as I was I did my best to enjoy the view of the Americas and the Antarctic ice cap.

Then the engines roared to life one more time, and there was weight under my feet as we slowed, slowed, started to plunge . . .

Our dropwings rotated, using their positioning jets, and now we were nose-down into our descents. One each side of me, through my window on the underside, I could see the long white wings curving down under the ship, the steep curve of the Earth beneath us, the Cape and Madagascar spread out before us, with India smeared out near the horizon and the great bumps of the Himalayas—where we were going.

There was the tiniest tug of "gravity," and I knew the wings were beginning to bite air, and that I was decelerating toward the target. From here on out I would have to trust the machine, until very late in the flight—at these speeds no human pilot could cope with the job.

Abruptly my view of the Indian Ocean was closed off by a bright orange curtain, and I felt a throb in my body. A shock wave—a sort of captured sonic boom—had formed in the enclosure under the dropwing, and the blazing heat of reentry would be directed against that wave, not against the surface of the dropwing. The drag became stronger and stronger, the deceleration greater, and the plasma before me glowed a painful white before the window automatically darkened.

This went on for quite a while—seventeen and a half minutes by the clock, to be exact.

It was our final field problem, and the fact that we had had to propose it had not made it any easier. The final exercise before you graduated was to construct a plausible mission that Crux Ops might have to accomplish, carry it out in mock-up, and then write a lengthy critique all about how you could have handled it better, what else might have gone wrong, and what you would have done then. You proposed them in teams of two, and I had been flattered beyond words when Chrys had asked me to partner with her. I didn't think it was anything romantic . . . but I wasn't dead certain it wasn't, either, and I had looked forward to it because of that.

It was all a daydream, anyway—it would be years, normally, before two Crux Ops would have any say in who they partnered with on missions. Besides that, most missions were solo. And on top of everything, normally they posted us back to our home timelines, and ours diverged somewhere around 500 a.d. I guess we could be pen pals or something.

I realized that I was letting myself get into a mental loop here, and I should know better. Besides, I could also look forward to seeing my father, my sister Carrie, and my ward Porter in just a short while . . . no, that led to other trains of thought that would take me far away from the mission again . . .

Repeat to self. Practice drill. Chrys is just my partner for a practice drill. We are going to land at the site of Lhasa, walk north-ward into China for a pickup, while carrying weapons enough to take on a light division back home. This is to simulate a mission in which we rescue the Dalai Lama and an ATN advisor from a world with a technological level about that of 1890 A.D. That's all I need to think about. Land, ski, climb, ski some more, climb some more. Nice to have Chrys along for a partner because . . . because she's very good at this, of course. Especially she climbs a lot better than I do, and I ski better than she does, so it's a good combination.

At eighty thousand feet, the plasma in front of my face went from white back to orange, and then disappeared, leaving me with a literally breathtaking view—I had to remind myself to take a breath some seconds later—of the peaks of the Himalayas below and ahead of us. It was a full moonlit night as we plunged over into Tibet.

The high peaks all around reflected so much light that only the ground below us seemed dark. The sky was full of light and stars. I saw Chrys make her eject at seven thousand meters, then ejected myself a moment later; the ice-cold sky leaped into my face, my harness yanked me straight back and up, and I was lost in the job of steering the parawing. The thing is like a big awkward kite, and it swayed from side to side ominously.

At least it usually swayed side to side for me; there were people at COTA for whom they worked a lot better, and some, including Chrys, who even claimed they liked them. For me, the best part of the thing was that I had so much trouble steering and holding on to lunch that I didn't look down very often, and therefore wasn't quite as scared by the ground rushing up.

Meanwhile, of course, Chrys was going "Whoooo!" and zooming all over around me for fun. I did kind of hope she wouldn't do that on a real mission.

The peaks were getting closer, but the sky was still light. The snowy mountains were like high islands around us, as if we sailed just above a great sea of darkness that sank away from our boots as we descended.

The parawings worked more efficiently close to a flat surface, and we leveled off as we approached our drop zone. Finally we came gliding in like immense owls about twenty feet over a wide, flat field of snow. That is, if you can imagine a gorgeous Arabo-Polynesian owl gliding in gracefully going "Whooooo! Come on, Mark, lighten up, this is fun!" and a square-built muscular owl flailing around, swinging from side to side, going "Oops, oops, oops," under his breath, just before doing a face-plant into a snow-drift.

By the time I had backed out, wiped the snow from my face, and begun to wrestle my parawing into behaving, Chrys had hers furled and was standing by. I gulped hard at my pride, and said, "Er, I could use some help."

She didn't even smile, just moved in close, pulled on a line here and a flexrib there, and presto—my parawing was furled neatly. In another minute, I had earned my keep by digging a stash-hole on the windy side of the drift. Our parawings went into the hole, along with a bacteria mix that would destroy them within hours, leaving only a thin water solution of fertilizer.

"The Sierra Club would love this gear," I mumbled.

"You have a political party devoted to mountains?" Chrys asked. "For or against?"

"Translation problem," I said. "It used to be a hiking club. Now it puts people out of work."

The translator chips, as I said, are great, but they're not perfect. I mentioned a "Baptist Ice Cream Social" once and everyone wondered how you baptize people with ice and what that has to do with public ownership of the dairy industry. It's a good thing Crux Ops normally only have to say things like "Watch out!" "Behind you!" and "Cover me!"

Not that good a thing. It would have been nice to have a reliable language in common with Chrys . . .

I told myself to forget those thoughts again, but I took it as a sign of health—I'd been widowed for some years, back in my own timeline, and any interest at all was probably healthy.

Anyway, now that we were down on the ground with our kits intact, the job was to walk from here, about where Lhasa was in many timelines, to a point 160 kilometers away for pickup three days later.

In most ways it was really just an orienteering problem. Crux Ops normally operate alone or with just one partner, and we do our own planning (something like packing your own chute). Most of us are crazy enough to win the fights we get into, but nothing is as likely to cause a mission failure as trying to carry too much or do too much, and nobody is more likely to plan too much than a bunch of overachievers like typical Crux Ops. Thus our final exercise—work out a plan and see if the one you had worked out was one you could do.

With everything under wraps, Chrys and I started the long trip. We unrolled skis and sprayed them with the stuff to make them rigid, then extended the poles, swung our chest packs around into the backpack position, and glided out into the emptiness of Tibet.

An hour later, Chrys said, "It's very beautiful in the moonlight."

I agreed, and asked, "What's Tibet like where you come from?"

She made a face. "Completely overrun with tourists; Lhasa is where everyone goes on their honeymoon. How about yours?"

"A little underpopulated country occupied by a big power," I said. "Not a good place."

We skied on in silence, and I had a lot of time to wonder just how different our worlds were. I knew that in hers, Islam had overrun Europe in the 700s A.D., conquered all of Eurasia before 1000 A.D., and then turned Sufi and pacifist; she was from about 2400 A.D. in her timeline, so presumably she was a long way past war (except, of course, the war against the Closers). Had I shocked her with mentioning things like that? Would she hold it against me?

It was like being back in junior high. I desperately wished we had more to do.

It was getting near daylight and time to stop when our earphones crackled. "Provisional agents Strang and ja N'wook—attention. First added problem."

We rolled our eyes at each other; they were going to complicate it for us, to teach us something about unpredictability, I guess. Considering I had gotten into this line of work, once, by getting into a shoot-out in a parking garage, and later by diving into what looked like a hole in a void, it didn't seem to me I needed such training, but that wasn't mine to decide.

"We're going to simulate two complications in your mission: the Dalai Lama was wounded severely during the escape, and the Special Agent you were rescuing was killed. To simulate this, please dig a shallow grave and refill it; then fill a GP bag with rocks and snow to simulate the weight of the Dalai Lama, take it with you, and continue."

They clicked off. We groaned, but it was their game and their rules. We dug that hole and filled it in, there in the dark, in frozen ground. "At least they said a *shallow* grave," I said. "Couldn't we just agree that the Special Agent was a midget?"

Chrys laughed, but we kept digging. Then when we got all done we filled the hole in.

"I don't suppose any rule requires us to fill the bag with more dirt than we've broken out of the frozen ground," I pointed out. "Let's make our Lama out of dirt from the grave."

"Good idea."

In short order we had laid out a sled and sprayed it rigid, dropped the Dalai Lama (a very unconvincing sack of rocks) onto it, and started on our way. As the stronger skier, I got to pull it over the level ground until we got to the first bout of climbing, where Chrys was to take over.

The sun was coming up now, the pale sky suddenly turning blue, light blazing off the mountains around us. "Come on, Lama," I muttered, as we skied the last two hundred meters to the first cliff we would have to climb down.

"Not much of a talker, is he?" Chrys commented. "We'll need to take a rest break up here, because it's going to take some time to get the climbing gear in order for this job. So you'll at least get a breather then."

"Good," I said. "Are we running far behind?"

"We already made up most of the time we'd lost—you ski about as fast towing that sled as I do with just my pack, Mark. We might as well stick to the original plan. It's just not as likely that we'll get in early, is all. I'll let you have the honor of dumping out the Lama when we get there—bet you're looking forward to it."

"Yep. Hope we don't have to be politically sensitive to his feelings."

"Obviously he fainted from wounds. Is there anything we should do differently for the next stretch on the sled, right now while your muscles are telling you about it?"

"Not a thing. The harness works fine. It's just that between the bag and the sled, I feel like a reindeer."

That got us into a half hour conversation about Santa Claus, Christmas trees, hanging stockings, and mistletoe, none of which her home timeline had. We talked about a lot of things like family traditions and holidays and so forth while I got the ski stuff stowed and she got the climbing stuff out. Apparently in her timeline Ramadan was a fast, just as it was in ours, but it was followed by a feast that commemorated a bunch of miracles that had something to do with world peace.

"How did your people ever beat back the Closers and join ATN?" I asked. "It sounds like you were pacifists by the time you were invaded."

She nodded. "We had been for fifteen hundred years. We'd already settled large parts of the solar system and had probes on their way to the stars. Then the Closers crashed in. We call it the Bloody Generation—the thirty years before ATN found us. Fortunately we at least had a long tradition of nonviolent action."

"How can you passively resist an army that never takes prisoners and kills for fun?"

"Mostly we just died. There were only about a third as many of us by the time ATN agents showed up. By that time tradition had weakened, a lot. The rebellion was pretty ugly, and my grandfather, who fought in it, still won't talk about it. The Closers, the collaborators, all the people who had gone over to them in the slightest way . . . well, it was gruesome. How about your timeline?"

"The Closers just started infiltrating about twenty years before I got into it, and ATN was maybe ten years behind the Closers," I said. "But we're still very divided politically—there are about 180 countries, most of them armed to the teeth. And the operation in which I was recruited destroyed the timeline the Closers were planning to stage their invasion from—or destroyed it for them, anyway—I expect they'll eventually join ATN. So my guess is they're going to be looking for a softer target . . . besides, Closers don't want timelines with nuclear energy, they're phobic about it. My timeline has more than a thousand reactors running worldwide, and what with all the testing, several hundred nuclear bombs have been exploded in my timeline." I figured I'd better not tell her about Hiroshima and Nagasaki . . . it seemed like bad publicity somehow. "From the Closer standpoint we all glow in the dark."

"I'd have said 'spoiled meat,' but it's the same idea. The signal to start our rebellion was nuking a big Closer holiday celebration on the Riviera."

"Nice job," I said.

She grinned. "Thank you. Perhaps we can do a massacre together someday. Okay, if you've got all the ski stuff packed away, I'm all set to rig us—and the Lama, here—for climbing. I suppose we should get on with it before they think of something else for us to do."

"You're the captain, Captain," I said. "I'd a lot rather climb with what you rig than with what I come up with." Supposedly all of us can do whatever is needed, but reality is a bit different. Most of us have seen most things done and are willing to try, all of us have several things we are experts at, and a very few of us—those with twenty years in, those teaching at COTA—really can do anything.

Vertical face climbing was in my "seen it and willing to try" category, but it was one of Chrys's strongest points, so as far as I was concerned, she was in charge for this next leg of the trip. (She had a bunch of other strong points, too—notably parawing. In our line you'd better not be a narrow specialist!)

Thus the job of getting us and the Lama down was all hers, and she went about it a lot more quickly and efficiently than I could even understand what she was doing. ATN climbing harnesses are made out of some miracle stuff that hangs on to you wherever it can get a grip and knows how not to hurt you, so you put them on by stuffing them down the neck of your clothing and pressing a button. An instant later you feel exactly like a marionette on a string. The little "walker" that comes down the cliff face above you steers itself and the climbers it's belaying according to the captain's orders; the whole thing looked like two toy soldiers and a bag of garbage hanging from one of the Willie the Wall Walker toys I had as a kid.

The first thing for which I was really useful was hefting up the

Dalai Lama and pushing him over the side after Chrys had tied him off to the walker. "Oooogh," I gasped, "couldn't we just decide he'd lost, oh, say, thirty pounds of blood, and pull out the rocks?"

"People don't have thirty pounds of blood."

"Okay, we had to amputate his legs."

Her eyebrow was up, and I could tell she was teasing, but all the same she seemed a little irritated. "Does your culture have the concept of 'sportsmanship'?"

"Uh, yeah, but we also have a concept called 'Nice guys finish last.' "

She looked startled, then thoughtful. "I just heard you say something like 'Decent people are there to be eaten,' which is a pretty strange translator error."

"I'm afraid that all that got lost in the translation was the politeness," I said.

"Hmm." She seemed thoughtful, and I was afraid I had offended her, but whether I had or not, her attention was now all on the steep descent in front of us. It was a series of cliffs and ledges, like a steep staircase, with the ledges cutting deep into the face, so that we were actually shooting for only very small patches of accessible, level ground, and there was a great risk of fouling a line from the walker. I suppose she must have wanted all her concentration for the job at hand.

Then she reached over to my harness and said, "If you'll excuse me, I do want to check you out as well. Partners falling to their deaths is just the kind of thing that could get me a bad grade." She ran her hands over the harness, and then said, "Now, what could this huge thing be? Could it be the thing Mark Strang is most known for at COTA?"

I snorted. "You can make fun of it all you want, but it makes me feel secure just to be able to get my hand on it when I need to."

We were talking about my Colt Model 1911A1, the .45 automatic I carry with me everywhere. I had carried it in my job as a bodyguard in my home timeline, carried it through three years of being accidentally stranded in another timeline, and I had lost count of the number of times that this little habit had saved my life.

"I wouldn't dream of depriving you of it," she said, "but you know the harness only accommodates itself to your living body, and it doesn't realize that it can't attach to your shoulder holster. I've got it pulled away now, but if it slips back, it may bind and cause trouble. Are you sure you wouldn't rather just put it in your pack with your SHAKK and NIF?"

"Call me superstitious, but no. I know perfectly well that there's nothing dangerous anywhere around and that we're the only people for a thousand miles in any direction. And I don't care. I'd rather have it at hand." I was doing my best to smile as I said all that—while, of course, carefully not relaxing on the basic point: I wanted the Colt to stay where I could grab it.

She sighed. "I'll just have to think of it as a religious object. All right, let's go."

We didn't talk at all as we started the descent. With the ATN belay, you really just climb downward as if it were a free climb, but taking more chances because your belay is perfect and has electronic-speed reflexes. If you hit a stretch where you need to descend on the line, you just speak to the walker via your mouthpiece, show it where you're trying to go with your optical designator, and it will pay out for you as you push out, keeping your speed reasonable and helping you steer to your target.

I had asked once what we would do if the climbing equipment failed us, and they explained that it failed safe—if anything went wrong, it just worked like regular climbing gear. The next day we started a week of practice with plain old "dumb" climbing gear. All of the other trainees blamed me for that. I decided that after that experience, I wasn't going to ask any questions unless I was fairly sure the answers did not require demonstration.

It was actually a good season for climbing—late summer, with most of the stuff, snow and loose rock, that was going to fall, already fallen. We made quick progress despite our lack of sleep.

By around 8 A.M. local solar time, we were most of the way down, just about twenty meters above the level area on which we planned to camp before resuming our skiing the next night. We were most of the way down to the next ledge, and I was already trying to think of something clever to amuse Chrys, when the walker blew to pieces.

The bag of rocks that represented the Dalai Lama plunged past me and dropped onto the rocks below; it was only then that I realized that when the walker dropped my line, my line promptly snagged the rocks and shortened up enough to catch me before I fell far. I now had a belay line twenty feet over my head with about fifteen more feet to go. I hit the emergency reel—I didn't understand how that worked, either, there was no actual spool, but it seemed to take up or pay out a few meters of line as needed into a small black box—and sank rapidly to the ledge below, Chrys running out her line beside me less than a meter away.

As our boots touched the narrow, boulder-choked ledge, and we found our balance, the thought finally formed. "I think they blew up the walker as part of the test," I said, looking out at the vast empty plain in front of our cliff. "I guess we're supposed to—"

There was a slim dart of silver in the morning sun, high above us in the blue vault of the sky. It was falling, and though it wasn't big, it was coming very fast. I hadn't yet thought about it in words when I dove on Chrys and pressed both of us back behind a large boulder, against the rock face behind us.

A great shock leaped through the stone to our bodies. A huge clatter of stones, some bigger than our bodies, fell past our opening in the cliff and into the empty space beyond. "Missile," I shouted in Chrys's ear.

"Closers!" she responded, and I realized she was right. The stuff that had been thrown at us had not been the kind of thing they do in training, at all. This had been stuff that could easily have killed us, even just by accident . . . and that meant hostiles. Which meant Closers.

They had found the timeline of ATN's secret training base, and they were after us. For all we knew everyone at COTA was dead. If we were going to get out of this, it would have to be just the two of us.

I pulled my .45 from its shoulder holster and started looking for a target, or at least for whatever had shot at us. Out beyond the rim of boulders, the sky and land were empty.

·2·

I didn't have to wait long. There was a strange low-pitched thrum in the air, and then I spotted the small aircraft coming in low. I said "helicopter" and Chrysamen said "ornithopter"—what it would have been in our home timelines—but it wasn't either of those.

It flew on four spinning plates that pumped up and down on their axles beneath it, and the axles came out of four long spidery arms that extended out at right angles from the cab. The cab itself was a windowed box of what looked like yellow plastic, and inside it, three guys, with firearms (or at least it looked like they had a stock and a barrel) slung on their shoulders, held on to straps like the ones on a city bus or subway. A fourth guy standing at the back was hanging on to a horizontal bar, pulling it back and forth and twisting it.

Since then, for the heck of it, I've asked six engineers in a few timelines how such a thing could fly. I've gotten three different explanations, plus three other explanations of why it couldn't possibly have worked and how I could not have seen what I did.

As the gadget swept in toward us, I leaned forward across a boulder, braced the Colt in both hands, made the guess that the guy holding the horizontal stick at the back was the pilot, and put four rounds in the direction of his chest, hoping one of them would connect.

I don't know if I got him or just scared him into letting go of the tiller. The little flying machine veered sideways in a spin, then abruptly flipped over and plunged cab-first onto the frozen ground below.

I braced for an explosion. There was none. Maybe it didn't have fuel tanks, or maybe it just happened that nothing caught fire. Anyway, nothing came out of it alive, and the cab seemed to have smashed like an egg.

That was comforting but no help. I had gotten myself behind a rock as soon as I'd fired my last shot—if you're fighting anyone with homing AP ammo, you never get exposed at all if you can help it.

If they'd been on the ball, the two seconds it took me to use the automatic would have been my last. But the good thing about fighting Closers—maybe the only good thing—is that they have very little initiative and little ability to get off the plan.

The plan must have been that the missiles—the one that got the walker and the one that followed it—would kill or disable us, and the guys in the bizarre flying machine would then land and confirm we were dead, or make sure of it, or maybe take any survivor prisoner. The others out there in the plain were just there as backup or to do scut work afterward, and no one had told them to provide any covering fire or retaliation. By now, of course, some Closer officer was screaming orders at them, but it was too late.

The Closers teach their slaves, even their very highly trusted ones in their armies, not to make decisions without checking first, and always to do exactly what they're told. It makes for great slaves, but lousy improvisers. And in combat, there's a lot more call for improvisers.

The delay not only gave me time to get back under cover after having gotten a good look at the landscape; it also gave Chrysamen enough time to get into the packs and get out the SHAKKs and NIFs.

The SHAKK is my favorite gadget in all of future technology. When I had gotten stranded in another timeline, I practically won World War II all by myself with a SHAKK. The initials stand for Seeking Hypersonic Ammunition Kinetic Kill, and the weapon itself looks a bit like one of the super squirt guns painted silver—but there the resemblance ends. Point it, squeeze the trigger, and the ammo—a spherical translucent bead about half the size of a BB shot—finds and hits whatever was in the sights at the time you pulled the trigger, out to about six miles, at Mach 10. You have two thousand rounds in the magazine, and on full auto it fires four hundred of those per minute.

I unclipped the remote sight from underneath my SHAKK and cautiously crawled over, staying under cover, to set it on a boulder a few steps away. Now I could look through the little screen in the recess the remote sight had left, move a cursor, squeeze the trigger, and as long as I had left a meter cubic space for the shot to turn around in, let the shot find its way to the target.

How does it work? You got me. I just use it. My sister Carrie, the physics prof, says she can see nine ways it might work, all of them impossible. But then she also thinks she can prove that time travel and multiple timelines are impossible.

Possible or not, I love the SHAKK. I didn't expect to see anything at first—they'd probably all been told to stay under cover, and they were probably more afraid of their officers than they were of us. Sure enough, nothing moved for a while.

The remote sight scanned back and forth over the broken country below, all rock, snow, and hillocks, much too high up to have trees. There were no signs of life for two long breaths, so I flicked to infrared. Another three long breaths went by.

A hand glowed for a moment as it set a remote sight up on a rock. I moved the cursor with the tiny slides until it overlapped his hand—indeed, thumbing the enlargement upward, I took the shot specifically at his wrist. When I squeezed the trigger there was a sound like a whip cracking, another like a furious hornet, and then a high-pitched scream, all in less time than it takes to blink twice.

The sound the SHAKK makes is not from the pressure released from the muzzle as the projectile is expelled, like the guns of our timeline—what you're hearing is the sonic boom as the tiny engines on the shot propel it up to Mach 10 within less than a meter. The high-pitched scream, a little like a ricochet from an old movie played on a sped-up turntable, came from the engines braking and curving the shot almost 180 degrees within that short distance, then reaccelerating it.

Sis assures me that that can't be done either, and that the reason they told me that the shot doesn't leave a glowing tail like a meteor—that it recovers and reuses most of the energy from atmospheric heating of its surface—is even more impossible. I fall back on the position of flying-saucer nuts and miracle-cure enthusiasts: but it *did*.

The scream of the departing shot had not yet faded out when I saw the hand in the sight fly up into the air, jerking as the round entered his arm, and steered up through it (the shock wave making the arm first bulge and then collapse, like a toy balloon hooked to a compressed-air line).

Too fast to see that it happened at different times, blood sprayed from the shattered wrist, burst from his shoulder as the shot crossed to his head, sprayed once more as the shot went in through the eye. Then, in less than a hundredth of a second, it used up its remaining energy spiraling around inside his head. The shock wave in that confined space turned everything from his spine up into runny jelly.

I had to imagine that last part, but I enjoyed imagining it—if that sounds too horrible, well, Closers are horrible, and I like to see bad things happen to them. I knew that the watery goo that had been flesh, bone, blood, and brains would spray in a fine mist out through his nose, mouth, ears, and eye sockets, leaving his head to collapse into a bag of skin.

First time I saw that I upchucked. After I got to know Closers . . . . I could do it over dinner and still order dessert.

My remote sight vaporized in a bright flash-and-bang.

An instant later Chrysamen's NIF was spraying fléchettes in a black streak like a swarm of wasps into the open space before us. It occurred to me I was a bit of an idiot—the NIF was a much better weapon for this situation because the fléchettes home on human bodies within the target area and thus can find their targets without being aimed.

Maybe I'm just a caveman—the SHAKK is a much higher-powered weapon, so I prefer it. But by using the NIF in this situation, Chrys was probably taking out 90 percent of the enemy.

NIF stands for Neural Induction Fléchette. The gadget itself looks a lot like a cordless electric drill, and makes a squealing noise that's downright unpleasant when fired. The fléchettes—tiny needles no bigger than pencil points—fly for about three miles in about half a minute. But those three miles are only rarely in a straight line—normally the fléchettes circle the target area till they find the target people. When they do, they hit, burrow into the skin till they find a nerve—and then they take control. That is, they induce signals that make the nervous system do funny things—knock you out; give you terrible pain all over your body; turn your heart off; or temporarily blind you and make you vomit, lose bowel and bladder control, and itch all over (no kidding—that particular setting is very useful in riot work!).

So by setting her NIF to spray the area, Chrys had probably gotten the great majority of them—which unfortunately left a minority that was sighted in on us. The Closers don't seem to have NIF, but their homing gear, if anything, is a little better than ours (somehow they seem to be able to detect any sight we aim through, which was how they got my remote so quickly). Moreover, they like brute force. I was expecting them to blow the whole mountainside apart any second.

I carefully slid to the side, then tossed out my second (and last) remote sight. I wasn't eager to fire again, but I wanted to know what was going on.

Long seconds went by without motion. The thing about these future weapons that was really eerie was that since they only hit what you aimed at, even though a battle had just flared across the lumpy, snowy plain in front of us, even though somewhere out there a dozen Closer troops might still be sitting with fingers on triggers, or getting ready for an assault—the rocks and little hills looked just as they had before. No shell craters, no ripped lines from machine-gun fire, just one splash of blood, bright red in the morning sun, from the man I had hit. If not for that, the frozen waste in front of us could have been empty.

After more time, Chrys breathed, "I couldn't have gotten all of them. They must want us alive for some reason."

"Except they could easily have killed us with those first missiles. I think they're trying for definitely dead, so they want to have our bodies in hand for sure, which is why they can't use anything that won't leave them enough to prove they got us. Did you set off a help beacon?"

"First thing. I bet you forgot again."

"Sure did," I admitted. "Reckon it'll come out of my grade?"

I had only the corner of my eye to enjoy Chrys's grin with; most of my attention had to be on the remote sight. "You're incorrigible," she whispered. After a long pause, she added, "How long do you expect we'll have to wait for help?"

"Well, we've been fighting . . ." I checked a time on my

SHAKK. "I shot that man twelve minutes ago. Figure we started five before that. So I'd say there's three possibilities . . . One, this is part of the exercise, those are androids and not real Closers out there, and we're supposed to improvise our way out of this. Two, those are Closers, COTA Main Base is already halfway down to hell, and we're stuck here. In which case, we have to improvise our way out of this."

She nodded. "And three is, 'something you haven't thought of'?"

"Bingo. You know my methods . . . but anyway, the point is, if this isn't part of the exercise—and I don't think it is, because it's way too realistic and expensive to waste on our field problem— then it's a real Closer attack, and what are the odds they'll attack two trainees out in the middle of a field exercise, and *not* go after any of the larger bases? My guess is they hit Main Base and everything else that shows from orbit five or ten minutes after the last time we talked to COTA, right after we got told to fill that silly bag with rocks and pretend it was the Dalai Lama. So if I had to bet, I'd bet we're the last two ATN agents alive and at large on Earth in this timeline. The ATN will be back but it could be days, weeks, or years."

She nodded solemnly, then suddenly heaved a baseball-sized rock up against the ledge above us, so that it bounced down onto the steep cliffside in front of us. On its third bounce it was blasted into gravel, stone chips flying all over. I got the position of two weapons from that and squeezed off ten NIF rounds, set to kill, toward each hiding place, but I wasn't optimistic. After all, those guys were in holes that had evaded Chrys's earlier shots, so chances were they were in pretty good cover.

"I don't think it's a training exercise," Chrys said. "That was less than two seconds to track on the object and blow it apart. And moving as eccentrically as it was, that's about the time you'd expect a machine already sighted in to take."

"Yeah." Another reason my shots had probably had no effect . . . most likely I was shooting at a weapon that was running on automatic control, and the soldier was somewhere else by then.

"I wouldn't bet on it either," I said. "Chrys, it really doesn't look like we're getting out alive; what's the most effective thing we can do before they get us?"

"Record what we've got, but our recorders have been running

right along. Maybe get a couple more of them. Damn, Mark, I had
a grudge against these people, and it looks like we'll never get a
real shot at them."

"I had one real shot at them before I was recruited," I said,
"and the revenge was just as good as you're imagining."

"What'd they do to you?"

"Killed most of my family. My mother and wife among them.
Listen, I've got a ward—"

"A what? Translator problem—"

"I've got a kind of adopted daughter, back in my timeline. If
you get out, and I don't, nag ATN about seeing that she gets taken
care of. Poor kid lost her mother to a Closer operation."

"Sure," Chrysamen nodded emphatically. "And there's a guy I
want you to look up for me, if you get out and I don't."

How is it possible at a time like that to feel your heart sink as if
you were in eighth grade? But that's exactly what I felt, there,
wedged into those cold rocks in Tibet, eyeing the remote sight and
waiting for the final attack.

"He's my brother," she added. "He's quadriplegic . . . he was
a Special Agent until the Closers did that to him."

Despite the fact that probably we would be dead before the
hour was out, the world suddenly looked a lot better. "Of course I
will, if the need comes up," I said. I chucked another rock, this
time sideways down the slope, and they blew it apart again, from
the same two positions. Whatever was down there, the NIF wasn't
working on it.

"Note for whoever reads the recording," I said, "unless you're
a Closer, in which case let me say I'm sorry I didn't get a chance to
stake your mother out on an anthill. It would be very nice if in the
next version of the SHAKK there were a way of recording a target
position, then turning off the remote sight, and then firing, so that
we didn't have to give away the remote's position when we shot.
Right now I can see them, and if I wasn't going to lose the sight as
soon as I tried it, I'd be firing hex bursts from the SHAKK to get
them out of their holes."

Chrys nodded, and added, "Mark's teammate enthusiastically
agrees." Then she thought for a moment and said, "What would
happen if you shot those hex bursts and then I knocked the sight
off its rock? It seemed to take them a couple of seconds to hit it the

last time; maybe they'd hit where it was, rather than where it had been knocked to."

"You're not going to try to move sight? They'd sight in on your hand."

"I just planned to hit it with a rock. If it doesn't bounce anywhere where we can get it, we still have another SHAKK left with two remote sights. We'll just have to be careful in setting it up."

"Unh-hunh. Well, it's a lot nicer than sitting here and waiting for them to bring in more forces. Okay, let's try it. I know which two rocks they're behind; I'll sight in, squeeze off, oh, say, four hex bursts, do it again. At the end of my second group of four, you chuck a rock at the sight."

Chrys nodded, and said, "Probably it won't work, but it's better than sitting on our butts. But before we do that, let me see if I can get the other remote set up, so we can see what happens." She detached a remote sight from the other SHAKK, crawled down the ledge, then carefully took the bowl from her mess kit, balanced the sight on top of it, balanced that on top of a tent pole, and raised the whole thing to the top of a pile of scree. The sight fell off the bowl, but it landed facing outward, and when we checked we found we had a decent view of the country in front of us.

"Okay," she said. "You'll fire four bursts, reaim, fire four more. On the fourth, I knock over your remote with this." The rock in her hand was the size of a tennis ball. "Then we see what happens. Just to liven it up I'm going to spray the target spots with the NIF right after all that, in case you've flushed anything human from cover."

"Deal," I said. "Let's see how this one goes."

I sighted carefully on the better of the two targets, a narrow cleft between a couple of boulders; I figured there was some kind of microcave there, probably our boy was lying in under a slab of rock held up by two boulders, and that the NIF fléchettes just hadn't been able to see him in there. "Ready?" I asked.

"Ready," Chrys responded.

I squeezed the trigger four times, as fast as I could. There were four deep roars. A hex burst is the middle setting on the SHAKK; it fires a group of six rounds that fly in formation to the target, then strike in a hexagon pattern about a meter across. There's about as much kinetic energy in a SHAKK round as there is energy in one of our hand grenades, and so the effect is pretty spectacular.

I wasn't watching; I twiggled the cursor over to the other target. This one was a crevice under a large boulder; I wasn't at all sure how he was managing to fire from under there. Maybe he was sitting behind the boulder, sighting with a remote sight that I hadn't spotted, and then firing through a hole that led under the boulder and connected to the crevice I could see. Anyway, I moved the cursor to the crevice and squeezed the trigger as hard as I could four times.

Beside me, Chrys's wrist and elbow snapped in a hard sidearm throw. The rock flew straight and true and knocked over the remote sight—which promptly fell forward and rolled down the cliffside.

There was a hail of shots as the remote sight was chewed to bits by Closer fire, but as we watched on the other remote sight, we saw it was coming from other locations. "Great," Chrys said. "We got two, and three more are revealed. At this rate we only need about a dozen remote sights to be sure we get them all."

I nodded. "Pity we only have two left. Did you see what happened to the targets?"

"The little cave collapsed when the boulders in front of it blew apart. You probably buried that guy under a twenty-ton slab."

"Good," I said. "I hope he's still alive under there."

"Mark, sometimes you turn my stomach. I don't like them either, and I'm glad to do them harm, but spare me your bloodthirstiness, please . . . I don't see any reason to rejoice in pain and suffering." She sighed. "Anyway, I saw the other one take a NIF hit—he was trying to crawl out from the rubble where his hiding place got torn up."

"So . . . want to hit those three hiding places and then see where matters stand?"

"Sounds good. Let me find the right-sized rock. We cut that one pretty close last time—if you're going to do three, I think you'd probably better keep it to three bursts each."

"Sounds right to me. My turn to set the remote sight." I crawled forward and to the side with it, then very gently pushed it over the side of a boulder so that it fell onto a lower one, facing outward. "You want to do the honors with the SHAKK, or shall I?"

"You go ahead. Let's not break up a winning pattern."

This time it went a little better, at least at first. The nine hex bursts whizzed out toward the little cracks and crevices where the

Closers had dug in, and Chrys said that the ground exploded nicely around every one of them. She NIFfed at least one more of them, and another hidey-hole sprayed blood, indicating that probably a round had found its way to the warm human body concealed within.

This time she got the remote sight with the rock so that it fell into a concealed place, a little spot behind a rock, but to get to it we would have had to climb down through two whole meters of open ground, and it was pointed facedown into the ground, so it might as well have been on the Moon for all the good it did us. I was just about to say something when it suddenly blew to pieces; that better Closer homing ammo had done its trick.

"Just one place shot—but that might only mean there was just one target," Chrysamen said, looking through the screen of her SHAKK. "Maybe we should—"

With a flash and bang, the last remaining remote sight blew up. Now we couldn't look at them without being shot—I remembered how easily I had hit the hand of the Closer setting his sight, and what had happened to him, and shuddered a little. To shoot a SHAKK at them now with any chance of success, I would have to poke my head out. It would be only an instant until it was blown apart; it didn't give me any additional sympathy for the Closers, but I couldn't help wondering what one of those slugs spiraling around in the brain pan at hypersonic speeds would feel like. Probably like nothing at all . . . it would happen too fast. I hoped.

"Got any ideas for last-ditch procedures?" Chrys asked.

"Move back as far as we can into the best cover we can find, spray with NIFs at intervals to slow them down, and SHAKK anything that pops its head up at us." *And try to look brave while they kill us,* I added mentally.

"That's what I thought of," she said. "And we'll have to not talk, since we'll need our ears."

"Far back" wasn't much—the hole in the cliff we were in wasn't more than twenty-five feet deep, and so all we could really do was move from our position behind the boulders covering the ledge in front of us, into the rubble at the back. It gave us maybe fifteen feet, which was nothing at all. I crouched behind one boulder, watching the line of rocks in front of us with my SHAKK in hand and Chrys's beside me; a scant six feet to my right, Chrys squatted behind rubble, her NIF and mine ready to hand, watching her watch. When she judged enough time had gone by, she sprayed the NIF once, in a short burst, out over the outer rim of the boulders; this far back in the shallow cave, the squealing echoed weirdly, like a flock of rabid bats bursting from the bowels of the Earth.

We held our breaths, listening for anything—and then suddenly there was a wailing, ululating, sobbing sound far out beyond us, followed by the booming report of a SHAKK-type weapon.

I glanced at her curiously; she let loose another squealing flock of fléchettes, and then we waited a long time, but there was no further sound.

"I set it to start at high pain and keep adding pain till blackout, then kill," Chrys said. "Hoping it would give us some idea how many of them were moving around out there."

"At least two, before," I said, "and now probably still at least one."

We couldn't talk any longer—we had to keep our ears open for the danger approaching us. The cave was amazingly cold, and my position was getting cramped and uncomfortable; I realized the sun probably never penetrated this far, and these rocks hadn't been warmed since they'd cooled from their making. It was still midmorning, less than an hour after our battle had started.

I crouched, looked through the sight of my SHAKK, and waited.

Chrys counted off another time interval—I knew without checking that she was smart enough to vary them—and sprayed again. This time there were no screams, and we sat still. More minutes ticked by, and again she sent a flight of fléchettes squealing into the space in front of us. This time there were screams, probably from two or three people; they went on for quite a while, and no shot ended them, but one screamer stopped abruptly, and then the other. She sprayed again, and no sound came.

I glanced sideways at her. She was listening with all her attention for the sounds that did not come. Her coverall was grimy from climbing, and under her hard hat her soft black curls were beginning to escape in little, untidy ringlets. Her breath hissed out in a white cloud, and finally she said, "That might have been it. Now we wait and stay on the drill for a while."

I nodded. "How's the supply of fléchettes?"

"One NIF is almost empty. I've given it a load of dirt, two

candy bars, and an earring I didn't want anymore, and I'm using the other."

Because Crux Ops often operate in primitive conditions, far from supply bases, our weapons are always capable of manufacturing their own ammunition—but the worse the raw materials you start with, the longer it takes and the more waste it produces. "Is it giving you any numbers?"

"Looks like I'm short on copper and iron."

Keeping my eyes forward through the SHAKK, I pulled a spare clip of .45 ammo out, emptied it into my hand, and edged sideways to her, exposing myself for a brief instant as I did so. "Here, add these."

She did, and the NIF reported it had everything it needed to reload itself completely. Meanwhile, she had the other one with a full charge. Since it had been a few minutes, she sprayed again; I was beginning to find the squeal of the NIF more than a little unnerving. But then I can't imagine that anyone alive out there liked it much, either.

I waited in the silence. My shoulder was within an inch of Chrys's; now that we were physically close together, given just how bad the situation was, it seemed too comforting to move away from her, and she seemed in no hurry to move away from me, either. At best our "cross fire" would be no more than ten feet of separation, anyway.

Time rattled on, marked only by our steady breathing. She checked her watch, fired the NIF again. No sound came from the slopes below, but that might mean only that they were under cover.

She kept firing at irregular intervals, but the intervals grew longer. Just before one, she explained, "I'm spacing them wider to give the enemy a chance to get overconfident and stick their heads up. Of course, if they're smart—or all dead—they won't take the bait." She fired the squealing burst. There was no response after a full minute.

"You know," I said, "we can't stay here. If they're still out there, they called for help, and it will get here sooner or later. And even if they didn't, someone will come looking for them. The longer we stay here making sure there's no one to shoot us, the less time we have to escape and get a long way from here."

She nodded. "Yeah. Well, are you ready to try?"

I checked my watch. "Since the last time anyone screamed,

they've had three hours to get up here, and it shouldn't have taken them twenty minutes, even in a very careful buddy rush. Hell, if I were as ruthless as they are, I'd have let the screaming cover my advance and gotten here sooner. Even assuming they're out there and really taking their time, there shouldn't be more than three or so of them left, anyway. Why don't we at least move back to our old front line?"

We did. Nothing happened.

Chrys wanted to flip a coin, but I insisted that since she was the one who was any good with the NIF, I be the one to peek out and see what happened. I crept a little distance from her, took my SHAKK in hand, and peeked. I took a couple of long swallows to count the six visible corpses out there—against the dingy gray-white background they were not hard to spot. I pulled my head in, counted off a full minute.

My head did not explode in a nasty pink mist, and my body did not suddenly leap and jump with pain. I took a deep breath and did part two of the plan—I stood straight up.

It had been so long since I had done that, that I felt light-headed, and my legs ached. I took a long deep breath; took two more; and let myself relax a bit. Chrys, still from cover, sprayed the landscape thoroughly. After the long shriek of the NIF died out, I stood and watched for some minutes; out there, I knew, the neural induction fléchettes were seeking, cross-cutting, patrolling a few inches off the snow for anything at human body temperature. In a few minutes they would begin to run out of whatever their fuel was (nobody ever seemed to be able to explain that to me, and I couldn't understand even whether they were telling me that the information was classified or that I didn't know enough physics to understand it). Then they'd glide down into the snow, bury themselves, switch off permanently (unless Chrys was setting them to function as mines, and she hadn't been), and start the chemical process that would, within a day at most, turn all the tiny darts into indistinguishable little lumps of organic matter that would fade into the soil without much trace.

As I watched, hundreds of little puffs of snow popped up in the sunlit field; the fléchettes were gone.

Tentatively, Chrys stood. She, too, needed to stretch out a little. We reloaded our packs, made sure our weapons were ready to hand, stuck a line to the cave wall, and did a fast rappel down the face to get to the bottom as soon as possible. Nothing moved except tiny puffs of wind-driven snow; there was no sound but our breathing and the wind itself.

At the bottom we hurriedly stowed the climbing gear, unshipped the skis, and got ready for an afternoon of fast, hard skiing. With little hope that our pickup would be there for us, we were going to head off at almost a right angle to our original direction, both to put them off our track if possible, and to take advantage of the direction in which we could move farthest fastest.

"Well," I said, as we strapped up, "here we go. With two days' rations we ought to be able to make it to somewhere where we can start living off the land. I suppose eventually—"

"Eventually we'll be dead," Chrys said. "But maybe we can delay it a long time."

I grinned; she was right. "Okay, let's go."

At least I wasn't pulling a bag of rocks behind me, and we were moving in a direction that the ground favored. In a short time we had logged a couple of miles, and the future was beginning to feel just a little brighter. Chrys was puffing a bit, so I slowed the pace, figuring in a while she'd want to talk. After another mile, as we wound through a narrow defile, I ventured to say, "We seem to be doing all right. Want to get a few more miles?"

Before she could answer, a male voice behind us said, "Keep your hands away from your weapons. Now raise your hands. Now turn around slowly."

•3•

They had us perfectly; we couldn't do anything except what we were told, at least not if we wanted to stay alive.

We turned to find six men facing us in the snow—all of them in COTA coveralls and holding NIFs on us. There was a startled instant of realization—and then we recognized several of the instructors from COTA.

"You can put your hands down now, ja N'wook and Strang, if you've recognized us," Captain Malecela said, grinning at us. "We don't want to end up like all those Closers you dealt with back there."

I wasn't sure which was more remarkable—that Malecela was here or that he was smiling. He was commander of combat training at COTA, and most of us were more afraid of him than of anything the enemy could throw at us.

Physically a remarkably strong man, he would have turned a lot of heads on any beach in any timeline if it weren't for the faint lines of scars that stretched across his face. I'd heard a lot of stories about where he got those, and I believed all of them. He was black, and from some timeline where Zanzibar was the capital of the Earth; it was said he was some relation to the Emperor there and had given up titles and wealth to enlist.

I had seen him do a number of things, physically, that I would have reckoned impossible. Malecela had caught two students trying to steal a bronze bust of the founder of COTA, as a prank, to move it onto the ad building roof. He had shown them "how to do it right"—tucked it under one arm and took it up the four stories one-handed, then brought it back down the same way, and then demanded that they either do the same, or give him a thousand sit-ups. They did all thousand, then and there.

He had a standing offer that if there was any weapon of your home timeline and you gave him one day to practice, he could do better than you with it. It had only taken him half a day to shoot a better round than I did with the Model 1911A1, three hours to throw the razor-edged boomerang better than Simil Patapahani, and about a day to get better with the *linea mortifera*—kind of a cross between a lariat, fly rod, and garotte—than Marcellus Guttierez-Jenkins.

Of course we were relieved to see him there—but if it was going to be anyone from our side, it would be him.

"There are some minor details to discuss," he said, "but you two did pretty well. It wasn't the field problem we set you, but we think you improvised pretty well. I'll give you a passing score, anyway."

"The Main Base—" I asked.

"Completely untouched, so far. We're getting an evacuation under way. But you two were the only ones actually attacked by Closers."

Chrysamen looked as startled as I did, I'm sure, but Malecela just grinned some more—maybe he was just getting it out of his system before he'd have to be in front of other candidates again. "All right, the way for you two to look at this right now is that you're going to get hot showers, real food, and comfortable beds a couple of days early, and that you're about as safe as anyone else is right now. Let's get you home."

The liftwing turned out to be waiting less than a mile away, and in less than an hour we were flying back to COTA Main Base itself, not far from where Perth is in Australia in our timeline.

"We got the help beacon, and then no words, so we shot up a reconnaissance satellite, and it dropped a ground-observer package," Malecela was explaining to us. "You can imagine our surprise. That was excellent shooting for nonhoming ammunition, by the way, Strang, and it's good that you had the foresight to use nonlethal instructions in the NIF, ja N'wook, because the med teams tell me we might very well get ten or more for interrogation."

"You did what?" I asked her.

"I wish I could take credit for brains," Chrysamen said, looking down at her hands, "but it really doesn't come easy for me to set a weapon to 'kill' unless I know I have to. It was just what I did naturally."

Malecela shrugged. "Part of the secret of success is learning to take credit for your lucky guesses. And anyway, it probably didn't occur to you, but once you won the fight and started to run, anyone you were leaving knocked out was going to be frozen solid by nightfall anyway."

She shuddered. "No, I didn't think of that."

"Anyway, I would bet neither of you will ever let your more modern weapons get out of your reach again, if you can help it," Malecela said, going on without acknowledging her reaction. "And thanks, by the way, Strang, for pushing to make the SHAKK more programmable when it's being used on remote sight. Clearly the Closers have figured out some way to home on its wireless communication. If they can hit the remote sight today, figure in two weeks they'll have a way to hit the SHAKK itself—which is going to be damned unpleasant if you're holding it. I've been telling them about all that for years, and it's good to be able to show them that any old candidate can see the same thing."

He leaned back in his seat. "We have a big job ahead of us. Construction battalions by the dozen will be coming in to get COTA moved across to another timeline, and to convert this facility to a surprise for the Closers in case they turn up in force. But the situation is different for you two . . . you're going direct to Hyper Athens, to the Crux Ops center there. We'll be putting you two into the transmitter about an hour after we land. Orders of the high command."

For the rest of the liftwing ride, we didn't say much. After the ship had risen vertically, like an elevator, until the sky was black in the daytime, the stars were out, and the Earth's curve showed below us, it began to accelerate at about a g; somewhere over Sumatra it whirled around and fired its engines to decelerate, then smoothly spun again to ride down like the space shuttle. It was one terrific ride, and since we had nothing to do but enjoy it, we did.

In this timeline, Australia had an inner sea, probably because the sea level was a lot higher, and there were thick forests around it, so the view down below us was pretty wonderful, and I was kind of lost in it when Chrys abruptly said, "If we're supposed to go to Hyper Athens, why the delay here? You could have packed us and just thrown us in after our stuff."

Malecela grinned again. "You'll see."

All right, so I'm sentimental. I still get a little choked up when I think about it. They held a special graduation for us, right there at the airfield, with all our classmates there, and gave us a little time to shake hands and accept congratulations.

But it was only brief. They had other things to get done, too, and in almost no time we were standing in the now-familiar booth of the transmitter.

Malecela nodded one more time, and said, "That was excellent work, both of you."

"All we did," I pointed out, for some perverse reason, "was save our own lives."

"You're valuable ATN assets," Malecela said. "So you prevented valuable assets from falling into Closer hands. I think that's pretty respectable."

Then he stepped back, and we got into the booth.

Then there was no light. The world fell away, as if we had dropped back into the weightlessness of space, and our surroundings were silent as vacuum. I had no sensation of being in my body for a long instant that might have been half a second or a thousand years for all the difference it made. Then I was facing an even, dim gray light in all directions, which got brighter, began to differentiate like a photograph developing, and abruptly burst through into color. As this happened there was a low humming that was about an octave lower than the sixty-cycle hum you sometimes hear on stereo systems.

The world started to take shape again.

We were at Crux Ops Central, on the giant space station of Hyper Athens, in the thirty-second century since Perikles founded the Federated Democratic Poleis; or if you want, what would have been in the twenty-seventh century A.D. if there had been a Christ in this timeline, or the twenty-first century since the *hegira*, if there had been a Mohammed. I had been here three times before, and though nothing quite equaled the experience of being dumped here unexpectedly after a firefight, as I had the first time, it still impressed me.

The platform we arrived on was open to the "sky," the miles-wide space inside the great wheel that was Hyper Athens. From where we stood, we were on the roof of a low building, between what at first glance looked like great rows of mile-high skyscrapers, but were actually the working and living areas that formed the sidewalls of the huge structure. Far above us, we could see through the glass centers of the sidewalls, and watched as first the Moon, and then the Earth, rolled into our view. Hyper Athens rotated about every ten minutes, to supply a gravity of about one g at its edges; at that speed, you could see a lot of sunrises.

"Friend-daughter ja N'wook?" a familiar voice asked, "and I do believe Mister Strang, as well."

I turned and smiled. "Citizen Lao. It's good to see you again."

"And you, Mister Strang. Someone had to meet you here, and since I was in the base, it seemed reasonable."

Ariadne Lao is something over six feet tall and built like a serious triathlete. Her features are Eurasian and heavy-boned, extremely well formed but not at all the delicate kind of thing that's in fashion in our timeline. Hollywood would cast her as a prison matron or the bad guy's assistant, but they'd be wrong; she's startlingly attractive with her ice-blue eyes and black hair, even if she does look like she could deck a bear.

"It's a pleasure," I said.

She nodded to Chrysamen, including her in the conversation. "It happened I was the Crux Op on duty when Mister Strang first got involved in crosstime affairs, and later in recruiting him into the service." And turning back to me, she added, "I was absolutely delighted to hear that you had decided to join and that you were doing well in training. But this latest set of events absolutely justifies my faith in you."

She might have said more except that at that moment the sky darkened above us; a passenger dirigible was coming in. I wondered how Chrys was reacting to all this; I knew her home civilization was spacefaring, but after some roaming around in the timelines you realize that's a bit like knowing that a civilization uses counterpoint in music or the arch a lot in architecture—it isn't the fact that they use it, but what they do with it, that really matters. Some civilizations—like the one I come from—just do engineering and stop there, so that our space facilities all look like industrial plants, with a lot of machinery slapped together any old way that fits. I've seen pictures from many that seem to do everything in very simple geometries—all spheres, lines, annuli, pyramids, triangles, and cylinders. And then there are the ones like this one, the headquarters of ATN, the place where the battle against the Closers began . . . where if something is worth doing, it is worth doing beautifully and gracefully.

The timeline was currently going through an artistic period that was a bit like our Art Deco, and so the inside of the dirigible, like the shapes of the "skyscrapers" surrounding us, was made up of Z- and S-curves, with a lot of rounding and simplifying, elegance for no other reason than that it was elegant. As Chrysamen and I sat over juice, and Ariadne Lao gave us the quick tour of the station, I noted once again what a spectacular place Hyper Athens really is.

Traffic was heavy that day through the center of the great wheel-shaped space station, so we went around the rim, between the walls of mile-high buildings. Hyper Athens is sixty miles around the outside edge, and our destination was about a third of the way around from the transmission station, so it would take us a little time.

Above the tops of the buildings, and well down into the space between them, I could see a dozen dirigibles and perhaps twice as many little silver airplanes. In a space station that uses centrifugal force for gravity, the gravity falls off rapidly as you move toward the center. Thus very little energy is required to fly, even though gravity in the "street" is Earth-normal.

Beyond the building tops I could see the great clear space of the windows, and through it, when the angle was right, the Earth on one side, covering almost a fifth of the sky, and the Sun and a crescent Moon close to each other on the other side. It's a pity that kids have ruined the use of the word "awesome" to mean nothing more than "good" or "impressive," because this view was really awesome.

As we watched, a big space freighter, delicately woven of ellipsoidal capsules joined by curved and recurved girders, came into the transparent airlock that sat like a bubble on the Earth side of the station, and space-suited workers moored it with cables.

Chrysamen seemed oddly quiet, and there wasn't actually

much catching up to do with Citizen Lao, so conversation lapsed until the dirigible dropped us off on top of one of the skyscrapers.

We were to meet with some higher-ups the next day. The building we had been taken to was the equivalent of a hotel—actually a wealthy person's house with a group of guest rooms, because the Athenians think of having guests as an honor. Since, Hyper Athens time, it was about time for supper, as soon as we were shown to our rooms we were given passes to a local restaurant and told to make ourselves comfortable until the next morning, when we would have some sort of meeting over breakfast.

In the Athenian timeline nobody ever invented the menu; you eat what the restaurant has. This time it was something that looked and tasted a little like sweet-and-sour pork with a lot of pepper poured over spaghetti, and a side dish of apples and cucumbers chopped into yogurt. It was good enough to keep us both from talking much during the meal.

Afterward, as we sat over coffee, Chrysamen said, "Citizen Lao seems to like you."

I nodded. "She recruited me; I suppose I'm sort of her protégé, and when I do well it reflects on her."

Chrysamen nodded, and asked, "How did you end up getting recruited? You said you went crosstime accidentally . . . ?"

"It's a very long story," I said. "I can abbreviate. Back in my own timeline, I had been an art historian. It happened my father was a Middle East affairs specialist. He was investigating a new terrorist group . . . which we didn't know was a front for the Closers."

"What's a terrorist?" Chrysamen asked.

God, there were times I wished that I, too, had grown up in a pacifist timeline. "Uh, military forces or guerillas that attack civilians. In order to scare the hell out of people, which gets them attention and also pressures the authorities."

"Doesn't it also make them angry?"

"Well, yeah. That's certainly how it worked out for my family." I took a long, slow drink of my coffee, reached for the pot, and poured myself more. "Anyway, they set off a bomb that killed my mother, brother, and wife and left my sister with just her right arm. Happened right in front of my father and me, at a family celebration."

"Oh, god, Mark—" Those huge dark eyes looked a little damp, and she reached out and took my hand.

The trouble with sympathy is that if you're not careful you get to enjoy it, and before you know it you spend all your time getting it, so I said, "It was nine years ago, at least as I've experienced the time. You never get over it, but you do go on. And anyway, if we're going to be . . . uh, friends, then you had to know sometime."

She started a little at "friends." I mentally marked that for future reference, and went on, "So, anyway, I sort of found something else I could do for a while that made me feel better—I became a licensed private bodyguard."

Chrys sat back a moment. "Your timeline must be terribly violent if people can make a living at that."

"I'm a rich kid—I could run the business as a hobby. But yeah, it's a terribly violent timeline. If you're good at hurting people and not letting them hurt you, you can always make a living." I had some more coffee; this was probably shocking her, and I already had a feeling she thought I was a barbarian. "Well, to make it really short . . . I had two cases that turned out to be related. One was a little girl I was guarding for another reason, who turned out to be important in . . . well, at the time they said fifty timelines, now they say more than two hundred. I don't know much about all that, by choice, because I don't want to put any load of pressure on her, and from my viewpoint she's just a nice kid. She's my ward, back in my own timeline."

"You miss her?"

"Oh, yeah. When I return she'll be about fifteen, which is kind of a difficult age, or so I'm told. Fortunately she's got my father and sister on one side of things—and two of the best bodyguards in the business as well, my assistants Robbie and Paula. So no doubt she's just fine, but I really miss her anyway.

"Well, the other case turned out to be a Special Agent who was supposed to be keeping an eye on me and on that girl, and who got into a messy situation with the Closers. There was a lot of shooting, and a lot of people died, including the Special Agent, and I sort of kept falling through things. Finally I ended up—just improvising, mind you, because ATN barely knew I existed and had no idea where I was—stowing away through a Closer gate into a world where the Nazis won World War II. Since you didn't have either

Nazis or World War II in your timeline, that probably doesn't mean much to you . . ."

"Not a lot. The Nazis sound a lot like what the followers of Suleiman the Butcher could have turned into, if he hadn't dropped dead of a stroke in a very embarrassing situation. One of those timelines where there's a tiny little group of masters and everyone else is a different degree of slave?"

"Right. Anyway, I was there for two and a half years till they found me again, and I just kind of improvised, and, uh, things broke right. That whole timeline was turned to ATN—and now it's an important new ally, I understand.

"But I have to admit all that does something to you. I'm afraid I'm pretty cold-blooded . . . well. No, not really. Actually, I *enjoy* killing Closers. I got to see enough of them and their stand-ins to feel about the same way I would killing a nest of copperheads under my house."

She nodded. "I can see how you could get to be that way. Er . . . there's something, too, that I want you to know. You know that I'd never killed anyone before, uh—"

"You didn't kill very many," I pointed out. "You set it for stun. Just the few who died of cold and the ones we got with the SHAKK died."

"Um, yes . . ." She was quiet for a long time, looking into her coffee and stirring it slowly. "Anyway, what I was going to say . . . well. I had kind of thought that tonight we might . . . uh, that is, I might drop by your room and we could be . . . "

The word didn't translate. Damn this not knowing each other's language.

"Uh, maybe the closest thing would be 'bed-friends'? It's not like it's marriage or anything but . . ."

"I'd be honored," I said.

"The problem is, religiously, I can't do that unless I er, well, I guess purify myself. I've taken human life. The prayer and ritual take about an hour or so. If that's, um, getting too late—"

"I can wait," I said. "Do I need to be purified as well?"

"No, it's just for . . . people of the Faith. Or at least for our version of the Faith. Er, maybe I should . . . go get started with it? We want some time to sleep tonight, too."

"That sounds reasonable," I said, and we headed back to our rooms, enjoying the walk through one of the many little parks in the Hyper Athens station. Chrys went off to her room to meditate and pray and do whatever else was involved in getting purified, and I stretched out for a quick catnap. I was excited about the fact that a beautiful girl was coming to share the bed with me, but I'd learned from bitter experience never to pass up a chance to sleep. Or to eat or take a leak for that matter.

As I drifted off, the one other thought that occurred to me was that this was would be the first time I'd made love—as opposed to getting laid—since my wife Marie had been killed. It seemed like it was about time. I curled up on the bed and let myself relax into a warm, happy state—

I woke abruptly when I heard a SHAKK being fired two doors away. I had left the lights on, and I rolled sideways; it was only a heartbeat before I held my own weapon and was standing upright.

I'd have had to get up anyway, because at that moment the door blew in with a roar and landed all over the bed. The light in the room went out. Something moved in the doorway, and I popped it with a SHAKK shot; I heard the body hit the floor.

I heard another SHAKK burst; it had to be Chrysamen, and thinking of her reminded me to pop the help button, the little tag we have that calls for a backup. Then I crept closer to the door, SHAKK at ready.

The next guy cleverly tried to just stick a gun in and squeeze off a homing round that would find me; but that meant exposing the muzzle, and a SHAKK round, pointed at any tube weapon, is smart enough to go in the open end and look for the round and firing mechanism. It blew apart in his hands, he screamed and fell forward, and a second shot converted his head to an empty bag. I flopped down on the floor and watched for feet; of course, sooner or later one of them would think of firing through the wall—unless the ATN had armored these against—

There was a clatter of bangs and pings and the wall beside me shook, but it held. Apparently I was in an armored box—

Something hit the floor and bounced, and I sprayed it with SHAKK fire, hoping it was not—

It was. There was a boom and flash, and I was temporarily blind and deaf; they'd tossed a PRAMIAC, a sort of smart grenade, into the room. The high-tech gadgets, if you get SHAKK rounds into them fast enough, will sometimes just fizzle—they don't work like old-fashioned high explosives. I'd been fast enough, I judged, since if I hadn't, that wing of the house would likely have been blown right out through the floor into space. In the dark I couldn't tell if it was an ATN or a Closer model

I couldn't see or hear well at the moment, but something was moving, so I fired. An instant later there was a painful jolt in my left hand; someone had gotten a homing round down the muzzle of my SHAKK and it had blown to pieces. I couldn't seem to get my left hand to do anything, but I groped for my shoulder holster with my right, drew out the Colt, swung my head from side to side, and perceived something in my peripheral vision near the door—

It was fine shot if I say so myself; I knew where I was, where the door was, and sort of where he was relative to the doorway. I pointed the .45, squeezed the trigger gently, and put a round up into his chest. I later found out it went right through his lungs, cut his pulmonary artery, and blew out through the back of his neck, shattering his spine and brain stem. He was dead before he slammed against the doorframe.

Something shoved in front of him, and I squeezed the trigger again; the Colt roared.

When the flash, bang, and acrid smoke cleared from my perception, someone was screaming. At least it wasn't me. I saw no more motion, but that might only mean they were being cautious; then I glanced down at the pistol and gulped.

Smokestack jam.

Every so often a spent casing doesn't clear, but ends up jammed by the slide, sticking out of the top of the weapon like a smokestack. When that happens, you've got to pull it back to clear it, which normally takes a second.

If you don't have that second, you're in a bad way. If you don't have that second, *and* you don't have your left hand in working order to do the job, you're dead.

I was trying to work it with my teeth—and noticing how badly my left hand hurt where it was getting squashed under me—when hands came down on my shoulder, something stung my thigh, and I slipped into unconsciousness.

A moment later the world was turning gray around me, and then shapes were forming. My left hand hurt like it was on fire, and my head seemed to have the Mother of All Hangovers, whereas my stomach wanted to eat without stopping for a week. I was in a set of restraints; had I been taken prisoner or—

"Some men will do anything to find a polite way out of a social engagement," Chrysamen said, standing over me. I looked up and saw that she had a bandage over one eye, her hair looked strangely mauled to one side, and there were several plasters and bandages visible on her bare arms. She was wearing a hospital gown. "Here, drink this," she added, bringing a glass to my lips.

It was strong, sweet, orange-and-strawberry, and I gulped it down. That told me once and for all that I was still in the ATN timeline and hadn't been taken prisoner; it's one of the favorite flavors there. Closers would never stoop to doing anything decent for a prisoner.

I finished the drink, and said, "You can release the restraints now—I know where I am and I won't come up swinging."

"Good," she said, letting me loose. "I'm afraid they put these on you because of what I did."

"What did you do?"

"Punched out the doctor when I woke up. It was their silly fault anyway; they knocked me out right at the end of a fight and then expected me to wake up realizing I was among friends."

I sat up and looked at my left arm. It was practically all pink, and when I touched it gingerly I found the skin was still a bit sensitive. "That must have been almost gone. My SHAKK blew up in my left hand," I said. "No wonder I'm starving. The nanos must be running on overdrive. How long have I been under?"

Chrys nodded sympathetically. "They said it was pretty bad; I know they had to give you a lot of IV to keep the nanos supplied. It's been about two days since the attack. They say we each have about a day to go. In another few hours I get to try out my new eye."

"Just so it matches your old one," I said. Nanos are tiny machines—small enough to pass through your capillaries—that work like little robots. They put a few million into you, the little rascals read your genetic code, and they start fixing things to fit the code, kind of like building supers for the body, except I've never seen a building supervisor get anything up to code. It has its weird effects; typically they get rid of scars, tattoos, trick hips and shoulders, old injuries of any kind. The first time I got treated at Hyper Athens they not only repaired bullet holes, and got rid of an old football injury, they also gave me my appendix and my tonsils back. "Were you hit badly?" I asked Chrys.

"Oh, if we hadn't been at Hyper Athens, we would probably both have died," she said, and sat down in a chair close to the bed. "They were wearing our uniforms and carrying SHAKKs, so the rounds homed on my weapon, not my head, and I got these holes in me from when my SHAKK blew up. I lost the eye to shrapnel. But my score was pretty good, too—I had to do another purification—I got six of them."

"Ahead of me," I said. "I only recall getting four."

"They told me five—you must have been too busy to count accurately," she said. "Malecela seems to be very pleased, to judge by the letter he sent. Eleven of them dead and both of us alive, or at least salvageable. Not bad for a couple of trainees, especially since this was one of their assassination squads."

"What the hell were Closers doing at Hyper Athens, anyway?" I asked. "And those assassination squads are supposed to be suicide missions, and eleven is a lot—that's *two* assassination squads."

"Exactly what we're trying to figure out," Ariadne Lao said, coming in through a door that had just formed in the wall. "We wish we knew why they're so determined to kill both of you, but now at least we can be pretty sure it's both of you." She nodded at Chrysamen, and said, "Friend-daughter ja N'wook, clearly you're feeling better."

"Still itches a little around the eye, Citizen," Chrys said.

"And you look like you're able to be up and around, Mister Strang?"

"I think so."

"Good then. To tell you both the absolute truth, we don't have much of any idea what's going on; Closers trying to assassinate trainees like this is way outside of normal behavior. So we're going to sit down with the intelligence analysts and do our best to figure out just what exactly is going on—as soon as we get enough food poured into you two."

Nanos run on your blood sugar, the same as you do, so when you have them in there you're generally eating for ten million or so; I've long figured if I knew enough to know how to make them and patent them in our timeline, I'd sell them as a weight-loss system. It takes a lot of energy to rebuild an arm out of hamburger.

The meeting room was a short walk away, and when we got there, there was an enormous supply of noodles, bread, rice, and chapatis, and a huge array of sauces to put on them. We didn't say much as we ate until we were stuffed; as I was having the last of a whole pastry that sort of resembled a football-sized éclair with pumpkin-pie filling, and Chrys was having a last bowl of clear noodles in sweetened cream, the ATN people came in, nodding polite greetings and talking among themselves. With a sigh, Chrys and I poured ourselves huge mugs of the thick coffee, added condensed milk to it, and joined them at the table. After a short spell of everyone telling us how glad they were that we were still alive, we got down to business.

The discussions went on all afternoon, which is what you expect of a committee no matter what timeline you are in. Finally it all boiled down to three facts: One, the Closers knew something or other that made them consider it worthwhile to eliminate Chrys and me no matter what the cost. Two, I had already been assigned a first mission, so it seemed likely that if the Closers were trying now, something about that first mission was more important than anyone on our side had guessed. And finally, we had no idea what was so important.

The puzzling thing, too, was that Chrys had not yet been assigned a first mission, so whatever important thing she was going to do was much more up in the air than it was for me.

One puzzle for them was what to do now. Mission assignments certainly were not random—they were made carefully and systematically—and now that it was known that Chrys's mission was important, it was simply not possible to make the decision in the same way it would have been made before. In that sense the Closers had already scored some points—knowing we would do something to damage them, they had forced us to change that decision. That didn't mean we wouldn't come up with something else to hurt them, merely that whatever it was we had had before was now lost to us.

Weighed against that, though, was the fact that Chrysamen and

I were still alive; the Closers must be worried pretty badly back at their headquarters, on whatever Earth that might be. Moreover, we had at least the start of a plan—do whatever we had been planning to do before.

The drawback to that, of course, was that if we stuck with it, clearly they would know what our next move was.

And yet they might not, for the one thing they could not know was whether we would stay on our original plan or not. . . .

The arguments went on and on. They kept circling back—if you ever try to think about time travel for any length of time, you'll notice that's what your thoughts do, keep returning to their original point—and finally they settled on the fact that they had a mission already planned for me which they knew was at least potentially going to hurt the Closers, and with a bit of luck what use they were to make of Chrys would soon turn up as well.

So, finally, after all the discussion, it boiled down to their doing exactly what they would have done anyway—sending me home for some leave, prepping me for the same first mission they'd have sent me on anyway, and putting Chrys into the pool of agents waiting to be assigned missions. It seemed like a lot of discussion to get to that point, but then I'm either a professional esthete or a professional thug, depending on which job you count as primary, not a politician, and maybe a politician would see matters differently.

One thing I'll say for ATN, when they make a decision they make it, and they put it into practice, and there's very little nonsense in between. Of course, from the standpoint of Chrys and me getting some hours together, this was no advantage at all. We had about fifteen minutes to say that we liked each other, we didn't think we'd see each other again for years, and it sure would have been nice but we'd write when we could. Then Chrysamen ja N'wook was headed to the new ATN training base (in a timeline the Closers hadn't found yet), and they were getting me dressed in the clothes for my home timeline, handing me all the materials I was supposed to have, and briefing me as quickly as possible about everything that had happened that I needed to know.

The big surprise was that another governor nobody had ever heard of was president, and again, after electing him, people mostly didn't like him. Porter had turned out to be unusually talented musically so she was getting a lot of private piano and violin lessons. My sister Carrie was apparently continuing her career in physics and getting some kind of acclaim for it, my father was on some consulting gig in the Middle East, and everyone was pretty much fine.

Oh, and with accumulated pay converted first to gold, then to marks, and finally to dollars, I was now a millionaire twenty times over, after taxes. Not a bad thing to know . . .

The transfer was simple. An ATN courier who looked something like me got onto an airliner headed into Pittsburgh, with a ticket in my name, checking all the bags I had taken with me to the alternate timelines. The courier went into the bathroom, locked the door, and signaled; then the ATN crew opened a portal between the two timelines, right into the airliner bathroom. He stepped out and handed me the ticket; I got in, they closed the portal, and I walked back to my seat.

I noticed one bored-looking man, balding with a bushy beard and huge black eyebrows, a typical college-prof type, who looked up from his book and watched me closely, as if he didn't quite recognize me. He shrugged, as anyone would; after all, there's no way for one guy to go into an airliner bathroom and another to come out, right? Still, the fact that he had noticed at all would have to go into my report. No point getting sloppy—the Closers know where our timeline is and there's always a risk of reinvasion.

If you like giant shopping malls with high prices and a lot of very upset children, the Pittsburgh air terminal is terrific. Otherwise, it's a place to hurry through. I got off the plane, not really expecting there to be anyone to meet me, and to my surprise Robbie and Porter were waiting for me. Robbie Wilmadottir looked her usual self—small, lean, dark-haired, with a crew cut, eyes darting around all the time. She was in skirt, flat shoes, and sweater, dressed more like a woman than usual, though I noted that the jacket she was wearing over the sweater was the usual heavy-grade polyester thing that hides (not well) a thin sheet of Kevlar and provides enough space to make a shoulder holster less conspicuous. Go to any rock concert, any place where a prominent politician is speaking, or any time a big movie star has a press conference, hang around looking crazy and talking to yourself, and you get to meet people who wear jackets just like that.

Porter Brunreich, my ward, seemed to be three inches taller. She was wearing ripped jeans, a sweatshirt for Oxford University (I wondered for a moment if Oxford actually *had* sweatshirts), a backward tractor cap, and a pretty amazing number of earrings in each ear; it occurred to me that after all the trouble I'd gone to keeping her from getting holes in her body, she'd probably put more holes in her ears than the Closers would have in the rest of her. I told them they both looked terrific, and I meant it about Robbie.

"Nice to have you back, boss. Do I have to stop embezzling from the till?" Robbie asked.

"Hi, Mark," Porter said. "You look pretty good yourself. Who picked out your suit?"

I grinned at her. "I don't suppose the court would look on it kindly if I locked you in your room for the next five years, but think of the studying you could get done for college." I draped an arm around her shoulders, and we went off to catch the silly little train that takes you to baggage claim.

Robbie had the Mercedes convertible waiting for me in short-term parking; knowing she likes to drive it a lot, I suggested she drive us home. Porter got into the backseat, we rolled the top down, and we were off.

It was a bright, clear, not-cold October afternoon, the kind that makes you think about football and hayrides and all that other Americana, when you know it will get cold that night but right now the air just has a pleasant bite to it. Porter leaned forward to get her head between me and Robbie, and we conversed in occasional shouts.

"I'm legally required," I bellowed, "to ask you how school is going."

"*Ça va,*" Porter shouted.

"You're taking French?"

"No, but all my friends are. I'm taking Latin."

It was a typical Pittsburgh fall day, all right; people were lurching onto the Parkway like maniacs, and Robbie was veering around all those pop-up roadblocks gracefully. I saw a couple of surprised old codgers suddenly realizing we had been there as we roared past. Public conveyances eight hundred years in a more advanced future may actually move faster and be safer, but there's a lot more romance in a plain old piece of German iron with a ragtop.

A lot of Porter's blond hair had escaped from the back of her cap and was whipping around in the wind; it occurred to me that uncool as it might be to be seen with adults, when I was her age I'd certainly have been delighted to be seen in a car like this.

"Okay, so school's okay. Now I'm supposed to tell you that you can bring all your problems to me."

"Sure, if anyone's trying to shoot me!" she said. "Violence to you; math, science, and love life to Carrie; Latin and history to the Prof [that's what she calls my father]; and athletic coaching to Robbie and Paula."

"I wasn't aware you had a love life!" I kept my tone light, but I have to admit that the idea made me a little nervous; first of all, it's bad enough to be the de facto father of a teenager, but when she's a target for an organization which could, if it wanted, infiltrate an assassin who looked for all the world like a ninth-grade boy . . . well, let's say it doesn't really add to the normal Dad-paranoia, but it sure gives you a great excuse for it.

"Not yet!" Porter said. "But with Carrie's advice, there's always hope."

Well, Sis wouldn't steer Porter too far wrong, anyway. Not necessarily in the direction I'd pick, but not *wrong*. Always assuming you could steer Porter at all. I tried not to assume that.

"What's this I hear about you and music?"

"Well, they say I have talent," she said.

"Hah!" Robbie said.

" 'Hah' she has talent, or 'Hah!' they say that?" I asked.

" 'Hah!' Porter has talent like water is wet and the sky is up." Robbie downshifted, shot us around a truck through a hole that I wouldn't have said was there, whipped us back into the right-hand lane, and added, "Let me steal her thunder. She's performing with the symphony tomorrow night. One piece each, piano, violin, cello, and flute. The critics are calling her the phenomenon of the century, and they're right, whatever you might think of them."

"You don't even like classical music much," Porter pointed out. "And, okay, yeah, I'm pretty good, but I know I could be a lot better; I've got a lot of work to do."

By now I was gaping. "You learned all four instruments in the two years since I saw you last?"

"No, I started Suzuki violin when I was three and did it for five years. But I didn't have much idea what music was all about when I was eight, and my hands wouldn't do what I wanted them to, so I got bored." That last sentence came out as a shriek; Robbie, who always drove with the radio on, had heard that the Fort Pitt tunnel was closed, and made an across-four-lanes last-minute diversion to

51 South, to take us through the Liberty Tubes and into the city that way. "Yeah, I know I'm supposed to be good and all that," she added as we began to rocket down the highway again. Fifty-one winds a lot, working its way along the back side of the ridge that separates it from the Allegheny, and it's in comparatively lousy shape; Robbie was being held down to not more than twenty over the speed limit. A lot of cops knew me, knew her, and knew the car, and it was a good thing most of them liked us.

"It sounds more like you're a genius," I said, and from the face she made at me I knew she'd heard that particular word too often.

"Yeah, right," she said. "You know what a genius is?"

"A chick who stays home on prom night," Robbie volunteered.

"No kidding," Porter said. "And not only that, it's also somebody that teachers and everyone act completely weird around. I mean, I love you and your family, Mark, and Robbie and Paula are great, but . . . you know, I want some friends who are . . . uh . . ."

"Your own age," I finished for her. "Understood. I hope I've at least got a ticket to see you play. I promise I'll wear a suit and behave myself at the performance."

"Of course you have a ticket!" she said. "Um, um . . . there's this one other thing, too."

"I'll be sitting next to a boy, and you don't want me to act like a geek in front of him."

"Don't I wish! No, it's just something else . . . Carrie said I could ask you after the concert but I thought if maybe you got a chance to think about it first. . . . Well, anyway, I just don't want to sneak around and surprise you or anything, I wanted to ask permission . . ."

"If it's marriage, heroin, or enlisting, the answer is no; otherwise, we can discuss it," I said.

"I want to have my nose pierced."

"Then again, if it's marriage, heroin, enlisting, or getting your nose pierced . . ." I tried to keep the tone light because I really didn't want to have an argument with her about it. It also occurred to me that I'd better see what Sis had come up with in the way of answers to that one; Porter was a good kid, but any kid will try to play both ends against the middle.

"Aw, Mark . . ."

"I didn't actually say 'no,' " I pointed out. "I was teasing you till I get used to the idea. I know a lot of women younger than me—a lot younger than me—do that. It looks horrible to me, and I hate like hell to imagine having a cold with one of those. But I also know that if you change your mind later the hole will heal up pretty fast, so it's not like a tattoo; I figure chances are that there aren't many infections or I wouldn't see so many girls doing it; and besides, you aren't interested, really, in how your guardian reacts to it, but in how kids your age do. So I'm going to wait and think a little, okay?"

"Okay. I knew you'd be reasonable."

"If I'm being reasonable, it's only with an effort. Bear in mind that your guardian also thinks of it as 'mutilating your nose,' okay?"

"'Kay. I won't bring it up for . . . oh, a week?"

"Deal," I said. "By that time I'll try to have an opinion instead of a reaction."

I'm not parent material, and getting stuck being one was not the best of things that could have happened to me. Still, if you have to do it, I recommend the way I got into it—Porter already knew me and trusted me long before her dad died and left me as her guardian, and she didn't move in with my family until she was thirteen. That meant nobody had a habit of thinking of her as a little girl to overcome, and moreover she didn't have any past memories of thinking of us as omnipotent.

She thought of *Robbie* as omnipotent . . .

It left me smiling a little to think that. From the first day we'd been guarding that kid, Robbie had been her hero.

"What?" Porter demanded.

"What what?"

"You were smiling."

"Well, I'll never do that again, then."

"Mark!"

"You're a terrific kid, Porter, I'm very proud of you, and I love you very much."

"Oh, sure. Pull out your sneakiest tricks," she said, but she was smiling, and she didn't hassle me again about my mystery smile.

Robbie took a second to wink at me—I'm never sure how I feel about her taking her eyes off the road—zipped around to the left, and took us into the Liberty Tubes.

Say what you like about Pittsburgh, coming into it from any

direction, the view is amazing. From either of the tunnels, you come bursting out of the dark and there's the whole mighty array of skyscrapers in the Golden Triangle right in front of you across the Monongahela. From there it was only a few minutes home to Frick Park.

Dad came bustling out, a big healthy guy with a mane of white hair, and a moment later Paula (Robbie's partner and the other reason my agency keeps functioning in my absence) came around the corner pushing Carrie's wheelchair. The gathering was complete.

There was a certain awkwardness, glad as I was to see Robbie and Paula, for they always had the impression that I was doing secret work for a federal agency that couldn't be named, and thus I couldn't exactly talk about where I'd been or what I'd been doing. Dad had set up sort of a small party that afternoon, and we all sat around and talked about nothing and laughed.

Finally, at dinner, after Robbie and Paula had gone—and for Porter's safety, I had made sure the .45 was ready for action and that the SHAKK was in easy reach—we all sat down around the table, and I told them about what I'd been up to. I wasn't sure whether I should be pleased or embarrassed at the interest that Porter and Carrie took in Chrysamen. I explained again that I wasn't likely to see her for a long time, that we were actually from centuries apart, and that anyway Crux Ops age at different rates from each other because we get different durations and schedules for missions. "Chrys and I could end up thirty years apart in age or more, within just a few years," I explained. "And it's just . . . well, it's a very close friendship," I said, "but it's not exactly a romance, yet, and we're going to write, but it's important not to have too much hope about that."

They both nodded solemnly, which immediately told me that they didn't believe a word of it. It figured. Carrie had been twenty-three when the bomb went off, which made it a lot tougher for her to have a love life. Porter was still too young to have any idea. That is, they were both naive enough to believe that love conquered all.

After Porter went off to do some homework, and Carrie was enlisted to help her through it, I was left alone with Dad. Now that there were just the two of us, he said, "Welcome home again, son. Sounds like you've given a good account of yourself."

"Fair, I'd say," I said. "Dad, what the hell do you suppose all this means? I know I'm smarter than most people, and I'm good in a fight, but why, out of all the tens of thousands of Crux Ops scattered across a couple of million timelines, would the Closers dedicate themselves to killing just one rookie?"

"Well," Dad said, "my first thought is that the Closers who have attacked you are from somewhere in the future of the timelines you were in. There's something they know will happen because of you and this Chrysamen ja N'wook. That's about all I can say."

"But what am I going to do?" I asked.

"You may not even know when you do it," Dad pointed out. "Suppose you were a machine gunner for the Brits in World War I. One day things went just a little differently, and you bagged Adolf Hitler; a month later you were with an antiaircraft battery and you got Goering with a lucky shot. World War II would be a pretty different affair, and all because of you, but how would you ever know that? Even if you knew about the existence of other time-lines—how would you know which, of the thousands of things you had done, had made the difference? Grant, Sherman, Lee, and Stonewall Jackson all served near each other in the Mexican War. Get them all into one bar and give them bad liquor, and what would have happened to the Civil War? And would the guy who distilled the liquor, or the unimportant lieutenant who invited all of them to come along, have ever known what he'd done?"

I sighed. "Yeah, I know. Still, it's a pretty oppressive thing to have hanging over your head. I'd a lot rather have been insignificant."

"Wouldn't we all. Nobody gets that choice, Mark, nobody. If you're a king or president, it might be very obvious that you're significant, but think about what I just said. You never know. The guy that washes a windshield doesn't do his job right, a smear on the windshield picks up the glare, a car goes off the road, and the girl who would have been mother of a Nobel Prize winner dies at age ten. That windshield washer doesn't know.

"You don't even get to pick which way things go, or whether doing your job well is the best thing you can do. Suppose you're a bus driver and you're careful to be on schedule. A guy running late for the bus doesn't get on yours—and he never meets the people who would have given him his start in business, and a whole giant corporation doesn't happen. You can only see a short way into the future, and absolutely not reliably. You don't have to have traveled across twenty timelines to know that."

I leaned back and thought for a long moment. Dad had sort of a sardonic grin under his halo of white hair. Sourly, I said, "That's not fair, all the same."

"Unh-hunh. If we had any choice, none of us would go to the future without a firm contract."

I had to grin at that. *If we had the choice* . . .

Anyway, I quit worrying and let myself relax into my old life. At the bodyguard agency, I answered the phone, talked to people, set them up with guards, and did no work myself. I spent a fair amount of time walking in the park with Porter, talked with Dad about various alternate worlds I'd visited or heard about, tried to get Carrie to explain a few things to me about what she was do-ing—apparently what I had told her was possible was having some kind of influence on her work, and she was trying to figure out how a projectile could draw on the heat of its passage for propulsion—and, in general, spent two glorious months of working out to stay in shape, shooting a lot to stay sharp, and unwinding till I was comfortable, healthy, and bored out of my mind.

Porter played her date with the symphony, and offers started to come in from everywhere. There was a brief period of reporters tromping through the house, because besides Porter's status as a prodigy, they connected her with me, and me with my father's long battle with Blade of the Most Merciful, the Closer front group in our timeline, and with the "heroic recovery" stories they used to do about Sis. They dredged up the fact that Blade terrorists had killed Porter's mother before her eyes (in fact, Closer agents had been trying to kill Porter, but her mother had switched passports) and that her father had died in prison. There was even a little bit in there about me; just who I worked for that caused me to be absent for so much of the time (and made me so well-off) was a regular matter for speculation.

I didn't worry about that. Nobody in my timeline was going to figure it out, and the Closers already knew who I worked for and where I was. If they wanted to try to come and get me, well, they'd had a shot or two at me before, and it hadn't gotten them very far.

There was a letter from Chrysamen every day, and I wrote back every day, too. The letters appeared and disappeared from the small safe in my office; sometime during the night a tiny crosstime port would automatically open. Outgoing mail would leave and incoming mail would arrive. For weeks there was just Chrysamen's letter, and every other week a large paycheck in dollars (which I deposited locally) and an obscenely large paycheck in Swiss francs (which I mailed to a bank in Zurich, via a drop service in Amsterdam that looked like an art history journal).

We talked about a lot—family and friends, how bored she was waiting in Hawaii to get her assignment, how we never quite had enough time to get to know each other. At least we were still in sync, one of her days corresponding to one of mine.

One day Porter and I were coming back from the airport after a trip out of town. She had gone to St. Louis for a concert with the symphony there—and to demonstrate the three new instruments she had also acquired in less than a month's time. Thanksgiving had been a few days before, and mostly we were talking about Christmas plans.

"They won't call you up just before the holiday, will they?" she asked.

"They try not to do that to anyone. But I'm expecting to have to go in the first week of January or so."

She nodded. "There's something I was going to talk to you about. I've been thinking I want to cut back on the concerts . . . there's something I'd like to work on."

I nodded, being careful not to apply too much pressure, in case this was a momentary whim. "It's very much your choice, Porter."

"I know. But I'm a little nervous, and I'd like to make the change while you're here."

"Make what change?" I asked.

"I'd like to work more on composition. Now that I understand so many instruments . . . well, I'm realizing part of the problem I'm having with not always liking what I play is that there isn't much music written that's really what I want to hear." She turned a little sideways in the car seat, to face me more. "Do you think that will be okay? Are people going to get mad if I cut back on public appearances? And will it make the reporters come back?"

"No way of telling, but I don't think it will be a problem. Especially if you don't cut it back to zero." I shrugged. "You're the one who knows anything about this, Porter. If you say you want to do, say, just a few concerts a year, and put more of your time into composition, I think mostly you'll just get a very attentive hearing."

"Good." She took a long pause. "And can I get my nose pierced?"

"It's your nose, kid."

I never did get used to that little lump of gold on the side of her nose, but I was as good a sport as I could manage. I even got her a tiny gold hoop for it for Christmas.

Letters kept getting longer between Chrys and me. She finally got notified that she was being put in command of a standby combat team—ten people that would come in shooting when a big situation demanded major action. If you figured how many targets they could actually *hit* per minute, those ten people had greater firepower than one of our infantry divisions. But since it cost a lot, even by ATN standards, to move much mass back in time, they would probably not go at all during the year she would be assigned to the team. It was fundamentally a training command—the officer was at the top of her class, but the other fighters were at the bottom, people who were good enough to pull a trigger but had to be watched. She was bitterly disappointed.

On January 3, I got my orders. I had two days for good-byes, and then I was off to the crosstime port in Manhattan; in the timeline where the mission was, I would be landing in colonial Boston, 1775.

At least I figured I knew the basics of what would be going on.

·5·

"Excuse my asking, but what language is that?" The woman in the aisle seat looked kind and grandmotherly, but she was leaning way over the middle seat to look at the Crux Operations briefing I was reading. The flight to La Guardia is short, but some flights aren't short enough.

"I am your pardon please?" I replied.

"What-a language-o is that?" she asked, very broadly and loudly. Some people believe that any foreigner will understand them if they just talk slowly and loudly enough.

"Tilde umlaut?" I said brightly.

She peered at me closely and then, with a slight click of the tongue, went back to her airline magazine. I got back into my briefing.

I'd read it before, but you never know which little fact is going to turn out to be important, so you try to get as much of it into memory as you possibly can.

The timeline I was going to was one deliberately created by ATN, one that would eventually (it was hoped) become a powerful and well-armed ally. Though crosstime travel was fairly cheap, if you went forward or backward in time, the cost went up enormously, so that when either the Closers or ATN started most new timelines, they usually did it by sending a single agent back in time to a crux, a period when things could have gone very differently.

Even then, the agent had to work pretty hard. Timelines like to remerge with each other, so it's generally only possible at a crux to get a new timeline started fast enough, and make it diverge far enough from its "parent" line, and at the crux you still have to do everything you can to make matters different. History can stay perfectly on track with slight discrepancies. (Ever find yourself arguing with someone about something you remember perfectly? A little micro-crux may have opened in your life at that point—and closed up afterward, leaving two people with slightly different memories.) Thus the new timeline not only has to be made different, it has to be made *drastically* different, or the timelines will reconverge, leaving nothing but puzzles for historians. Ever wonder about Pope Joan, Prester John, Atlantis, the Seven Cities of Cibola? Or why it's so difficult to find cities like Camelot and Tarshish archaeologically? All of those, I suspect, were failed crux changes, either from ATN or Closer operations, or just maybe from other organizations or individuals that we don't know about.

Rey Luc, the Special Agent on the job, had really taken that lesson to heart. He had arrived in London, in the same timeline our history comes from, in 1738, as a man in his mid-twenties, and set up shop as a doctor, investor, and eccentric scientist. With some judicious use of antibiotics and nanos, he had achieved a reputation for miracle cures.

In 1751, in our timeline, Frederick, the Prince of Wales, son of George II and father of George III, died after a brief illness caused by an abscessed injury. George II lasted till 1760, and was replaced by George III—the "Fat George" that the American colonies were to rebel against, "Mad George" who was to pose such a problem to British politicians during the Napoleonic age.

Now, George III wasn't a particularly stupid man; he was headstrong and had bad advice, and once he formed an opinion he tended to stay with it. He'd have fit in perfectly in the Johnson or Nixon White Houses as a staffer in charge of Vietnam policy. But he was generous and loyal to his friends, perhaps a bit too easily led in his younger years, maybe a little too easily manipulated—none of these needed to be fatal character flaws. His real tragedy was probably only that he came to the throne at the age of twenty-one, when he had many of the common failings of young men, and because there were few to tell him no, he never really outgrew them.

Still, his record as king was mixed, not atrocious; Britain had worse monarchs as well as better ones, and there were many places where he showed some real talent for government.

If his father had just lasted a few years longer—and his grandfather had lasted not quite so long—George III could have come to the throne as a mature, self-confident man. If he could have gotten a better education, instead of being spoiled by the tutors his mother found for him (mostly for political reasons rather than their knowledge or wisdom), he might also have been a capable and effective person.

So that was the first thing Rey Luc set out to change. He cured Frederick in 1751—probably just some penicillin would have done it, but it sounded as if he'd used the nanos to really fix the old guy up. He managed things one way or another (that's a part of the job I'll never get to like) so that within a year of that, George II died nine years early.

(I've known many Special Agents, and that's a part of the job they just won't talk about. Usually it's done with tailored viruses aimed at one particular individual to produce a sudden, painless death in sleep—their heart just shuts down. And of course when a historical figure is "erased"—the euphemism most of them use—he or she is still alive in the main time frame, so in a sense they are just killing one of the alternatives. But killing is killing, and most of them always feel a little sick about having to do it.)

Frederick was a smart man, and an efficient king. He saw to the education of his son—and Rey Luc saw to it that it was a different education. Most fundamentally, Luc arranged to get a special tutor hired for the future George III, a man who would have been a good influence on anyone: Benjamin Franklin.

When I hit that part I nearly choked with laughter. Franklin, of course, was already known in Europe by the time, and had made a good name for himself in a dozen ways; he was an obvious choice, and one could hardly imagine a better teacher for the young prince.

Meanwhile, Rey Luc had not been idle in other areas, either. Britain and her American colonies in the 1700s were among the most progressive, forward-thinking, and innovative societies on Earth, but that was still only by eighteenth-century standards. Ideas developed very slowly by the standards of even 1850, and it wasn't even very clearly understood that technological changes could make big differences in life.

Through a dozen fronts and hidden organizations, Rey Luc set out to give technology a big push. Better steels were introduced, and cheaper ways of making them; the steam engine came along quickly. The Minié ball made breech-loading rifles possible and was an idea that could have been invented any time from the mid-1500s onward; in our timeline it took till almost the American Civil War, but Rey Luc had the British army equipped with breech-loading rifles at the beginning of the Seven Years' War in 1754. By 1760, there were electric motors and generators (though they were crude), and by 1765 the first dirigibles were flying regular service in the Thirteen Colonies and around Britain.

The Seven Years' War wasn't called that, because it had lasted just two; the better ships and cannon of the British Navy had swept the French from the seas, frontiersmen equipped with bolt-action rifles had chased the French and Indian forces back to Canada and taken every chunk of French land on the mainland, and on Christmas Day 1755, Paris had surrendered to British invaders. Thus instead of the Seven Years' War (as Europeans call it in our timeline) or the French and Indian War (as we call it), it was known simply as the Conquest War. After some strategic purchases, it left Britain in possession of North America from the Nueces River and the Columbia River north, all of India, and great parts of France itself.

In the aftermath of the war, the young George, as Prince of Wales, had taken an extended tour of the American colonies. He had visited Boston, Charleston, New York, and Baltimore. With Colonel George Washington as his guide, he had gone up the frontier road through Ticonderoga and Saratoga to Canada, come back via a ship across Lake Erie and through Fort Pitt, met town merchants, farmers, frontiersmen, and ordinary people, and been cheered wherever he went. In one of Luc's reports he had noted, with justifiable pride, that in this timeline, George III was the most passionately pro-American person in Britain.

Luc had been a busy little devil—all Special Agents starting timelines are—and he'd also managed to introduce the ideas of Adam Smith, David Ricardo, and the other early free-market economists more than a generation early; not that they were the last word, or that their solutions would work for all purposes, but by tying the British Empire together into a vast free-trade area, he had managed to create fast economic growth and the basic conditions for peace—merchants are not big fans of war, France was disarmed, Russia not yet a serious foe, Spain and Holland too weak to challenge Britain, and thus the whole world had a very small number of men at arms, and trade rather than war was the major activity.

Last and not at all least, he was encouraging George to have a lot of kids, and maneuvering those kids onto every throne he could find—a step not unlike the one that Queen Victoria took naturally, a century later, in our timeline.

The plan was that by 1800, there would be railways from Savannah to Quebec City and all over Britain, dirigible service across the Atlantic, and a British-controlled telegraph net from Rangoon to the American Pacific Northwest. By 1850, there would be airplanes, telephones, and a world federation of peoples built around the British royal family; and by 1900, human beings would be settling the Moon and Mars, ocean farming would abolish hunger, and the ATN would have a new powerful and prosperous ally.

The one catch in all of those splendid plans was a great big one.

After a routine report in 1771, detailing the first actions of King George since Frederick had died the year before, and explaining that he himself was going to go to Boston to move along the dawning railroad industry and push the movement to change the Empire into a Federation, Rey Luc had disappeared. There were no further reports and no word of any kind. Moreover, thus far ATN's Time Scouts had been unable to find any of the descendants of the new timeline, which meant that it was still in a state of "chronflux"—whichever way it was going to go had not settled out, and there were at least some high probabilities that it wouldn't go in the direction ATN had been aiming for.

Time for a Crux Op, then. Chances were that Rey Luc had died, been taken sick, or otherwise gone off the case, and things had slipped in his absence. Another possibility was that matters had simply turned out to be very delicate indeed, and his communications were being lost in the chronflux—in which case the attempt to transmit me would get nowhere, and I'd be on vacation for another month.

There was also, always, the possibility that the Closers had intervened, but normally that was a low probability—even though the two sides were at bitter war, time, with all its parallel tracks, is *big*. Agents only rarely ran into each other—most of the time ATN and Closers developed their own set of timelines without the other side even being aware of it. Of our million and a half timelines, the Closers knew about perhaps six thousand; of their two or three million, we knew of only ten thousand or so.

This was a different case, though, because the Closers had taken such an interest in me. It was quite possible that they had found and invaded this time track, and they might well be there waiting for me in force.

I sighed and put the briefings back in my case. The pilot was just announcing the approach to La Guardia; I had flown into it in another timeline where it was called Jimmy Walker, and in one where it was called Charles de Gaulle, but given the size of the flat patch in Queens, and the rarity of such in the city, if they had airplanes, there was usually an airport there. Moreover, it was usually a boring, routine place, and all the ones I had been to had been old and beat-up.

The cab ride was dull, the city seemed drab in the gray January midafternoon, and nobody was around on the quiet floor of the midtown office building that was my destination. I used my key, walked in, checked my watch—half an hour to go—and went to the can, sitting down to read the briefings again. By now I figured I could even spot Rey in any wig, which was going to be important— his introduction of rayon had led to the spread of wigs down the social ladder (when they didn't have to be made of human hair, and would stay white without powdering, they could be a lot cheaper). Rey would probably be wearing one, and there was no telling what the fashionable shape for them would be by the time I got there, so I needed to know his face in any hair.

When the portal opened, I was ready. I stepped through into a prep room—there was nothing to indicate the century or the time-line, it was just a white room with nothing in it except a table with the things I needed arranged on it. I picked up a backpack that held more supplies, a freshly charged and loaded NIF and SHAKK, and a large array of technical information in very small electronic storage (not just the *Encyclopedia Britannica* on a pinhead, but several of the great libraries of a variety of timelines in a con-tainer the size of a matchbox). I set my old SHAKK down on the table for the routine maintenance guys to pick up, changed quickly into a period outfit, and glanced through my trunk to make sure I had decent clothing for where I was going, indicated I was ready by saying so, and felt the world go abruptly dark, darker than it ever is except in a deep cave.

Sound and weight disappeared together, and then the sense of having a body. A pale gray halftone light, even in all directions, swelled up around me, and the low rumble that always came at this point, and then the world began to swim into existence around me, first shapes and vague sounds, then colors and tones, and finally with detail and precision.

I was in the upstairs room of the Quiet Woman tavern, on Arch Street, in Boston, April 1775. At least that part had gone right—by dropping a note with a couple of gold pieces into the local postal service, Crux Operations had set up the room for me. Well, it was the right place, there was no one here, and a note on the pillow of the small bed said that the owner hoped it was all in accord with my wishes. Thus far thus good.

I moved my trunk to a better location and began to get things into some kind of order. It was midafternoon when I arrived, and I figured the first day would be a matter of looking for anything big and obviously wrong, but I wasn't expecting to find anything like that. Usually, at least according to the training, it took a while to see what wasn't the way it should be.

Of course in my own experience, I had just lunged out into Nazi-occupied San Francisco, and been attacked by crazed Boy Scouts, but then what did I know? The odds of anything big happening the first time I walked out the door were practically zero.

I made sure everything was in good order, and all the stuff that was supposed to be concealed was well concealed. Then I sat down on the bed to think for a moment.

There was a knock at the door. "Come in," I said.

The woman who came in looked strangely like a high-school pageant version of a colonial woman, because though the clothing style was not much different in general line from what I remembered of fashion history, some of the materials were obviously synthetic, and the dress itself hung a little strangely—I suspected that undergarments had changed and perhaps were not as voluminous.

"Oh, hello, Mr. Strang, I didn't see you come in," she said. "I was coming up to ask if you'd be with us long?"

"Well, I have business in the city," I said, "and so I might be here some months."

She giggled; now that I looked more closely I saw that she was about seventeen or eighteen at oldest. "Business in the city? And so you do. I was wondering, sir, if perhaps your quarters at Province House were in need of repair or some such, and as I'd heard nothing from tradesmen about that, I thought perhaps you might know how long you'd need this room."

"Oh," I said, completely baffled. There had been a message to Rey Luc but he hadn't acknowledged it; had he perhaps set me up with a room elsewhere in the city and then for some reason not told anyone else? But then why would anyone else know I might have been there? And anyway, the translator chip behind my right ear had just supplied the information that Province House, in Marlborough Street, was where the Royal Governor's residence was.

It was a bit like checking into a Motel Six in Washington, D.C., and having them assume you normally stayed at the White House.

All that took just a moment to think. "I suppose then that you hadn't heard. Well, I was hoping to keep the matter quiet—a little disagreement, you know, one of those things where it just seemed best—"

"You can count on me," she said, and winked broadly. She set down a large pitcher of water, which the thing in my ear told me was for washing and drinking, and then went out. From the way she had smiled and the interest she took in my business, I concluded that whatever it was that she thought was going on would be all over town before I ever got downstairs onto the street.

Well, there was clearly no reason to delay and a lot of reasons to get moving. I tucked my .45 into my shoulder holster, concealed the SHAKK in a special pocket inside the coat between my shoulder blades, and tucked the NIF into a special slot in my left boot. I was ready for a lot.

Then I pulled out my transponder tracker. All Special Agents, Time Scouts, and Crux Ops have a surgically implanted radio transmitter that charges up off your body heat and runs for ten years after you're dead. It's a low-powered weak affair, and it only transmits in the event of a coded signal, to prevent the enemy getting any use out of it, but if you're within about two miles, you're wearing a transponder, and a tracker switches on, it should be able to get at least a direction and an estimate of distance on you.

There was nothing. This didn't necessarily mean anything—he could be back in London, or over in New York, or anywhere else. His last three messages had said he was making Boston his headquarters, but that had been four years ago. For all I knew he'd decided to take some time off and go find himself with a guru in Tibet.

There were voices on the stairs. "Well, gentlemen, if you have business with him, you can ask him yourself." It was the voice of the girl who had come in to check the room.

A soft voice said something I couldn't hear, and then a louder one added, "How the deuce did he get all the way here so quickly anyway? Unless perhaps his engagement up in the Mill Pond went faster than he imagined it would. And thank God we ran into your father, Sally, or we'd have gone over to Province House instead—"

Three possibilities. Mark Strang is a common name; maybe they just had the wrong one. Rey Luc was doing fine but for some reason couldn't even manage to leave a note in an emergency drop box; thus these were men to take me to him.

Or they were Closer agents, and I was totally blown—my mission and I were hopelessly un-secret to the enemy.

If there was another Mark Strang, and he was an important guy in the town, the odds that nobody had talked to him about this room reservation were zip. And I could think of no way that a man could pick up signals from base, arrange meetings and deliveries, and yet be unable to put a note inside any of a dozen locking boxes, for ATN to retrieve.

So it was probably Possibility Three: the Closers were here already.

All that I had in that room was a change of clothes, all the weapons were already on me, so I checked the view out the window. By now their footsteps were reaching the top of the stairs.

There was a large overhang under my window, and it seemed to reach a third of the way into the street. I rolled out my window, slid down the roof of the overhang, clutched the wooden-trough rain gutter, let myself drop into the street, and walked away in a hurry. Whenever you do something weird, get away from the witnesses as fast as you can.

People seemed very surprised, but I avoided making eye contact and hurried through an alley that wound about as it led away.

The alley made two more bends and came into a small dark

courtyard. It was what you expect in a preindustrial, or just barely industrial, city—a muddy, filthy space ringed by two- and three-story buildings in bad repair, in which wash was hung out to dry and into which garbage pails and chamber pots were emptied. Fortunately someone had laid a board sidewalk around it to where another alley led away.

As I went around on the boards, which rolled and bounced beneath my feet, I heard odd scurrying noises. It did seem strange that there were no children watching me, or at least none I could see; normally a place like this is full of kids, housewives, goats, and chickens . . .

No one spoke to me, but now that I looked around I could see a ball, a hoop, and stick, and something that probably was a hobbyhorse on a stick, much handed down. Moreover, I had to step over smeared areas where a goat had probably been tied. It was as if everyone had left just seconds before I came.

The next alley wound to the north, and I figured I was probably making toward what's now Franklin Place. I had been there a few times in my own timeline, but this was going to be different—so much land had been filled in, especially around the Neck, that the peninsula was a completely different shape.

Sure enough, there was a bigger street there; there were no street signs to identify it, but I doubt that any eighteenth-century cities had street signs anyway. I slipped quietly out of the alley and merged as inconspicuously as possible into the foot traffic.

Or I tried to, anyway. As I passed two distinguished-looking gentlemen, they tipped their hats and greeted me by name. A woman nodded and wished me, "Good day, Mr. Strang."

"Thursday at one o' the clock, Mr. Strang," another called out, tapping his forehead with the palm of his hand, clearly reminding himself of an appointment he believed that we had.

I nodded and waved back; no one seemed to find these things unusual. I let myself slow a bit, took a coin from my pocket, and turned to buy an apple from a street vendor. The apples were small and scrawny by the standards of a twentieth-century supermarket, and had probably spent the winter in a cellar, but good "keeping apples" are usually sweet.

"Oh, no, Mr. Strang, just take one if you like," the vendor said. "Gift for His Majesty's servant. Always glad to be of help."

It was on the tip of my tongue to just ask him outright what I was doing for His Majesty these days, but I nodded, took the apple, and thanked him warmly.

The apple was what I expected—mealy but sweet and with a strong flavor. If someone could persuade this timeline to hang on to its genetic stocks for a century or two, they'd have at least one terrific export ready to go.

Another advantage of eating an apple: you can keep your hand over your face. Fewer people seemed to recognize me.

Now to do some thinking. Clearly not only did everyone here think they'd seen Mark Strang before, but they thought they knew Mark Strang well, and they knew him by sight. A common name is one thing, but an identical twin in another timeline . . . wouldn't be odd at all. But not in this century, surely?

All right. Facts I knew. Something was seriously wrong in this timeline. Somebody who was apparently me was already here. He lived at Province House, which was the governor's mansion.

That was where I needed to go, then; for what it was worth, I wouldn't be conspicuous there, or at least not until my doppelgänger turned up. Whatever the answers were, they were more likely to be there than anywhere else.

I was on the brink of asking someone for directions when I realized that *that* would really be the height of conspicuousness—a prominent citizen, probably a government official, asking where the governor's house was? No way.

It wasn't as bad as I thought it might be. After a while I noticed that a few buildings every so often would have a street number plus a street name on their placards, and by dint of a lot of wandering around, and keeping in mind that Marlborough Street was one of the largest in town (it was part of the old High Street that was now known successively as Orange Street along the Neck, Newbury Street as it neared South End, then Marlborough and finally Cornhill), I eventually found, after walking nearly to the Long Wharf, what I hoped was the right direction. It was a good long walk, and my shoes were unfortunately much too authentic—this was a long time before the development of the concept of right and left shoes, and my feet were beginning to kill me.

I could see, ahead of me, one of the few buildings that the little interpreter in the back corner of my head seemed to recognize. The gadget told me it was the State House, and I realized that, with a modification or two, I was looking at something I had seen in my own time.

A light went on in my head; Cornhill, Marlborough, and the rest were actually Washington Street. Now that I knew where I was, I could just go there, and I began to walk quickly, even though my feet hurt, and I had been walking for a couple of hours.

I had expected Boston to look Georgian—it was the Georgian era, and had been for decades, so I was expecting a lot of red brick and tall white columns. Instead it was more like what you would see in a movie set for something in Shakespearean times, lots of lumpy buildings with rough plastering on the outside, mixed with unpainted clapboard. It was one of the biggest English-speaking cities in the 1770s of our timeline, and it was three times bigger here—but it still looked poor, dumpy, and squalid.

I had just come into Marlborough Street proper when I noticed graffiti on a building—something you didn't see in Boston at that time. It was just three words: SONS OF LIBERTY.

There shouldn't have been any such movement in this timeline. I stood and stared at it. One of the most radical patriot groups from my timeline, a driving force for the revolution . . . what was it doing here? The British regime was benign and pro-colonial; there wasn't supposed to be any Revolution at all.

I was just considering that question when a pistol shot buzzed by my head and sent a shower of brick chips spraying outward, stinging my face. I spun around to find I faced four hooded men, all with muskets.

·6·

Only one musket was leveled, and it had just fired. The others waited at ready. One of them started to say "You had better come with—"

Adrenaline and training cut through the situation. The .45 popped out of my shoulder holster and I braced and fired four times before I drew a breath, some of the fastest shooting I'd ever done. At the range—less than fifteen yards—you'd have to be a lot worse shot than I was to miss. The man who had fired, and had nothing to shoot with, was my fourth target, and he didn't quite have time to turn around before my shot flung him, turned half-around, facedown onto the muddy brick street.

There were screams and people running everywhere. I looked at the crowd running toward me from both sides and vaulted the wall.

"Mr. Strang, I *beg* your pardon!" a young woman said. I had just managed to miss her as I came down into a secluded back garden.

I jammed the Colt back into my shoulder holster and did my best to manage a bow. "I hope you'll forgive me, but I've been attacked," I said, "and forced to defend myself. We'd best get away from here before—"

On the other side of the wall there were screams, groans, and moaning, shouts of "Help! Murder!" and what sounded like fistfights and screaming matches breaking out. It was going to be a full-fledged riot soon, and one concept that the eighteenth-century English-speaking world didn't have was a police force. I remembered someone, Orwell I think, said there was no level of force possible between closing the shutters and volleys of musket fire.

Obviously some thought like that had crossed her mind, too, for she hurried up the garden path as I followed. "It was the Sons of Liberty, wasn't it?" she said. "Of course it was. Papa had just sent for men to scour the brickwork—we'd only just found out that was on our wall—"

Behind us there was more shouting, the sounds of breaking glass, and cries of "Fire! Fire!" and "The Redcoats!"

This house obviously belonged to somebody with money, and I was just as obviously known here. I just hoped it wasn't my brother-in-law or something.

Even in our hurry, I managed to notice that the small garden was formal in a very English way, that there was glass in the windows, and that the combination of red brick and white woodwork and columns was what I'd have called Georgian. Clearly this was someone who paid attention to English fashions.

It was just as clear from the look of his daughter; if I remembered right, bustles and low necklines were just coming into fashion in Europe, and she was definitely wearing both.

We hurried into a high-ceilinged room, and she told a black servant, "Fetch my father at once." He bowed and hurried away.

With a loud pop, she shot out a fan and began waving it in front of her face. "Entirely too much excitement," she said. "The doctor will be very unhappy with me."

She looked to be about twenty-two or twenty-three, dark-haired, moon-faced, with a pouty red mouth and not much of a chin, pretty but not exceptional. A quick estimate was that she was probably brainier than she was given credit for, almost certainly didn't have enough to do, and, if I were any judge, was her father's pet even though he never listened to her.

The man who came down the stairs wore a large, old-fashioned full-bottomed wig that made him look more like a British judge than anything else. He was fat by our standards, or healthy-looking by theirs, and his red face looked like it got that way from beer and wine rather than the sun.

"Mr. Strang leaped our garden wall, Papa, to get away from a mob," the girl explained.

"Well . . . hmmph. It's certainly better than getting murdered, now isn't it?" the old guy said. "You honor me with your visit, sir, even if it was no choice of your own. I trust you are aware that the sentiments upon my wall are not my own. Now I suppose I shall have to have a man or two stand with a gun to protect the workmen erasing that mess from my wall. The Sons of Liberty, faugh and damn 'em, are inclined to think every wall is their own."

"I shot four of them," I said, "and I'm not sure what the results were. At least two of them were still making noise as we ran to the house."

"Quite good shooting, that, and lucky you had a second brace about you."

Single shot pistols normally come in braces of three, the translator in my head supplied. "Er, yes," I said. "I'm not sure how much effect I really had on them all—it's just as likely as not that they're all alive but frightened."

"I should hope so, Mr. Strang" the girl said. "It would be such an inconvenience to you and to the whole colony if you should have to stand trial."

"Hah," her father said. "Inconvenient indeed, sir, but not at all a bad thing. We might establish a precedent that permits the shooting of vermin, and there's something to be said for that. And I should think, speaking as a judge, that any reasonable judge would see matters the way I do, and if any damned jury doesn't, well, we'll see how they like the pillory and the stocks. Now, tell me, were they—"

There was a crash of breaking glass. Shutters began to slam all over the house, and I heard the servants running frantically; a moment later the butler burst in to announce, "A mob, sir, they say they want—"

"Me," I said. "I'd better get out of here and let you show them that I'm not here."

"What, and invite a rabble into my house to inspect it? Thank you, sir, but no thank you, I like my silverware where it is, in my possession. My servants are tolerable marksmen, and I think we might have some good shooting from the roof if you like—see if any of those hooded rapscallions has escaped you, eh?"

"Papa, they might all rush at once. They might set fire to the house."

"Honoria, they might also all decorate the end of a rope. I daresay you've been right all along, Strang, for all our arguing in the past."

"Uh, right about what?" I asked, as I looked around for an escape. Apparently this old judge intended to put up a fight here, and I hadn't seen any evidence that the house could stand the fight. It seemed a poor way to pay him and his daughter back for taking me in. Presumably if the mob wanted me, they would follow me when I left—

"Why, right, sir, in what you've always argued before me and my daughter, at many an evening of whist."

Oh, hell, I have no idea how to play whist, was my first thought, but then he went on:

"The natural arrangement of mankind is masters and their servants, and this country should have been settled by a few wealthy men and their trusted overseers, plus all the niggers we needed from Africa. It was allowing free white paupers into this country that has made all the trouble, for you can't shoot 'em when they're wrong, you're at the expense of a trial every time one needs hanging, and most of all the filthy bastards *will* go thinking themselves your equals. That's what you've said and by god the events of the last year have convinced me."

I was spared from hearing any more of my opinions—just who the hell was I in this timeline, anyway?—by a rattle of gunfire from the upper floors. There were wild yells up there, so either they'd hit something or they thought they had.

"Just the same," I said, "if you'll hold them briefly, I'll be over your garden wall again, dash around, get the crowd's attention, and get them away from your valuable property. I can get away quite safely, I assure you; it'll only take a little nerve and luck."

"Oh, godspeed, sir," Honoria said, and extended her hand to be kissed. As an art historian, I knew she was premature—the Romantic Era wasn't due to start for another half generation—but still, if you grew up on movies, how could you resist a moment like that? I kissed her hand, smiled at her, and said, "All right, then, over the wall and I shall see you sometime later."

It was just a quick dash back to the brick wall, and it was a lot easier to make the jump from this side, since there was a bench in the right place. I bounded over, dropped into an empty street—the whole mob must have been around the front—and raced around the block, yanking the NIF from my boot.

There's a setting on there for "temporary hallucinatory panic," a fancy way of saying the dart gives you six hours of nightmares in broad daylight. I figured in an age like this one, when every kind of raving lunatic was let loose to wander in the streets, it might pass unnoticed, with a little luck.

They actually weren't much of a mob, and I saw why Honoria and the judge hadn't been very frightened. When I rounded the corner and crouched behind a wooden horse trough, I saw that there were really only about seventy of them, and almost all of them were hanging back and shouting, trying to egg on the few who were considering throwing rocks. Not one even had a firearm in hand.

None of them were on the ground, so I figured that the volley of fire from the house had frightened them but not hit them; the translator in my head explained quickly that though the Minié ball had made firearms more accurate in this timeline, and with cartridges they loaded faster, they were still no great shakes as weapons, and a few of them going off was frightening but not a reason to turn and run. Better machining, and thus more efficient human slaughter, wasn't due to be introduced for another generation in the master plan—they wanted to get a couple of wars over with first, apparently.

At least it was nice to know that the shot that went by my head had probably been aimed at it. I'd been thinking that if it was a warning shot, perhaps shooting at and hitting all four of them had been an overreaction.

I set the NIF for temporary hallucinatory panic and squeezed ten shots into the mob.

There was an instant change; a few fell to the ground and others began to shout. When you give someone hallucinations, he sees things that are part of his culture, things his culture thinks about a lot. A man who knows nothing of elephants doesn't hallucinate pink elephants no matter what he drinks; a Muslim doesn't see Jesus.

These people were definitely not Muslims.

I should have figured that in a Puritan city—especially since in most places the poor are more religious than the rich—what I'd touch off was a whole series of religious revelations. And sure enough, that's exactly what happened. One old codger with a lot of stains on his trousers, and a pale thin young girl with a big basket of buns, began to talk loudly to Jesus, who seemed to be very angry with both of them, to judge from just the side of the conversation I could see. A younger man, who looked like he'd been spending time at the tavern drinking on someone else's tab before he joined the crowd, thought that Catholics were sending devils to torture him. A plump, dowdy woman began to scream that Quakers and Anabaptists were coming out of the sky to roast and eat her children.

Moreover, they all sort of fed ideas back to each other, so that in short order they were all having the same vision, and then a bunch of people who hadn't been hit got the idea, too. There's a certain prestige, in certain circles, about having been god-attacked, and, besides, some people are naturally prone to it, so that although I'd only fired ten fléchettes, it was only half a minute before there were twenty people having visions.

The idea was screamed by a red-haired freckled boy, everyone else took it up, and then they were all running down to the harbor to try to walk to Charles Town, across the water (and *not* via the bridge) for some reason or other. I stood and watched them go; none of the crowd seemed to remember me.

They had gotten almost out of sight when I heard the gunshots. I ran to see what was going on, and there in the street was—

Me.

He wasn't dressed exactly like I was, or like I would have been if I still had my trunk, and his wig had fallen to the side, but he looked like me, he had several braces of pistols slung over his shoulders like an overgarlanded Christmas tree, and he was busily emptying the first brace into the crowd. As I watched helplessly, the young boy who had started them in motion toward the Charles, a kid of not more than ten, fell over, clutching his abdomen.

The "Mark Strang" in front of me pulled another pistol from the brace, cocked and pointed it. He squeezed the trigger, and with a boom an old man fell dead to the sidewalk.

Everywhere people were scrambling for cover. The man who looked just like me pulled out another brace of pistols and began to fire again—first a shot into the now-fleeing crowd that caught a handsome young man in the back and flung him face first into the mud, then a wanton shot between the shutters where a young woman was peeping out at the action on the street. I couldn't tell from the shriek whether she had been hit and hurt, or perhaps she had only been terrified.

He raised the last pistol in the brace, this time leveling it on—

A little kid, I realized, too dirty and small for me to say boy or girl, dressed only in a smock, running frantically away from him.

Instinct took over. The NIF in my hand shrieked before I was even aware that I was holding it or pulling the trigger. I had not even taken the time to reset the fléchettes, so the one that went into him was still set for temporary hallucinatory panic—not something you want to do to a man who is holding a loaded gun.

Abruptly, the loaded pistol still in his hand, the other "Mark Strang" began to scream and gibber, moaning with fear. He fired wildly at something that wasn't there, then turned and fled, leaving four bodies stretched in the street.

I didn't think it would be smart to hang around and try to explain things, especially since I did not understand any of them myself. I darted into an alley, ran down it at full tilt, and veered to the side. I could hear wailing and keening beginning back behind me, which was probably the friends of my doppelgänger's victims coming out of shock. I zigged and zagged between alleys, got myself completely lost, and made a point of staying off main streets.

At least it was only April, and the sun would go down early. For three more hours I moved quickly from hiding place to hiding place; twice I heard parties of people looking for me, but too far away for me to make out exactly where they were or anything they were saying except that it sounded like if I surrendered right now, I at least wouldn't be lynched.

I was crouching between three barrels—one rain barrel and two filled with kitchen slops and chamber-pot dumpings—when a small party of men with pistols and clubs came down that alley. By now the sun was nearly down, and I had begun to think I might stay there till it was full dark and then see what I could come up with. I was tired, footsore, more scared than I wanted to admit, and completely baffled, and for a guy who was supposed to have such a promising start, somebody the Closers would go out of their way to eliminate, I sure didn't feel like I was having much effect, at least not in any direction that I was supposed to. If I was a big threat to the opposition, you couldn't tell it from where I was squatting.

I sat all the way down and set the NIF to stun; I didn't want to murder anyone innocent, and I figured these guys were probably just a local posse.

It took me a moment to notice that the spot on which I had seated myself was foul with wet street muck and the stuff that leaked from the bottom of the waste barrels, and cold besides, and it was soaking into the seat of my pants. I gritted my teeth so as not to shiver.

"Ah, Nathan, he ain't going to turn up. He's a madman they say. He'll have shot hisself somewheres, or run into the bay, or they'll find him moaning and weeping somewheres."

"It's not our job to know where he is," a reedy, nasal voice responded, "but to look for him. And we need to look for him here."

"Well, he ain't here. And it's nigh on to dark, and the wife will be stone angry with me, she will, and there ain't no point in us being here in this empty way. You know he's got to be a madman— a Royal Customs Commissioner, to do a thing like that? First to stand about in the street when the damned Sons of Liberty are about, then to shoot—and not once, but twice, and the second time not the Sons but just a crowd—"

"Ah, the crowd was whipped up by the Sons," one of the men said, "and I told *my* son if he ever joins a mob like that, I'll by god have his guts nailed to the fence post."

"I'd watch how you talk of the Sons of Liberty," an older voice said. "They've got ears, you know—"

"And you're one of them ears, is that it, old man? They're thieves and ruffians, the type that ought to have an ear cut off so decent folks knows 'em by sight, and if you're their ear, then that ear ought to be cut off—"

There were two sharp thuds and groans, which I figured was a pistol butt being used hard on each of the arguers. "Next time I'll put a pistol ball in each of you and claim you by-god fought a duel," the sharp-edged voice I had identified as Nathan said. "We ain't here to talk about customs, nor taxes, nor the Sons of Liberty. We ain't here to talk at all, and a good thing too, because if we was drawing our pay for that, the whole colony couldn't afford you two jibber-jawers. Now what we're here for, in case you forgot, is to find a man that shot down citizens in the street. Self-defense or madman or whatever, that's for the law to decide. We're just to take him, alive if we can, and bring him in. If we find him. Which we ain't going to do by standing here and jawing."

"We ain't going to find him at all," one of the voices said, sullenly, and with the kind of tone that comes through a bruised mouth.

"We don't know that till we look, I said. And I'm the captain here."

There was a lot of grumbling, but they went off, following Nathan.

I stood up slowly; if the patrol was going west, I might as well go east.

Mark Strang, Royal Customs Commissioner? The last we'd heard from Rey Luc, there wasn't even supposed to *be* any Customs—the Empire had declared free trade, which is what you're in favor of if you're in a position of strength. It was supposed to be France, Holland, and Spain that were doing the smuggling and passing the restrictive acts in this timeline. Clearly in four years a lot could go very far wrong indeed.

I checked my transponder tracker again, but there was nothing to indicate that there was any transponder (other than mine) on Earth. Wherever Luc might be, he was at least a couple of miles away, or under or behind something that really blocked radio.

Half an hour later I found a dry, dark corner under a flight of steps behind a dry goods store, and curled up to go to sleep. Things were just plain not going well, I said to myself.

I ran over the inventory of conditions when you were supposed to call for backup. When you arrived and discovered a sizable Closer armed force. When you arrived in the wrong timeline, indicating that chronflux had carried away or destroyed the timeline we were aiming for. When you were badly hurt or in imminent danger of death, and "such condition might tend to jeopardize your mission." Nothing in any of those about being cold, dirty, tired, hungry, hunted by posses, beset by doppelgängers, or just having had the most confusing day of your life. I decided I was probably going to have to tough this one out.

You know how so often things look better in the morning? When they *don't*, it's because they're really bad and not getting better. I woke up to the crashing thunder of cart wheels in the street, right at dawn, and noticed that I was even colder, that the feel of whatever had soaked my clothes in places was indescribably slimy, and that I was a lot hungrier and coming down with a cold.

I coughed hard, spat out some phlegm, said some words that were the same in both centuries, and groped in my pocket for the first-aid kit. I jammed a self-injecting ampoule against my arm and gave myself one of my three immune boosters; for the next few days I'd have an accelerated immune response, which meant I might be sick as a dog this afternoon, and would need to eat like an ox to get energy back, but I'd be fine by tomorrow morning. For that matter, temporarily just about nothing could infect me or cause me to get cancer; if I wanted to take up smoking or whoring, and had money for either tobacco or a woman, this was the time to do it, as the humor ran in the training center.

God, I missed everyone, and I really wished I had a letter from Chrysamen. To read over the coffee and breakfast I wasn't going to get, after the shower I wasn't going to get either.

It was probably about forty degrees out. I've slept rougher than under those steps, but not much rougher.

I drew a deep breath and coughed it out. *All right, Strang,* I said to myself. *Now that we've got self-pity down cold, we work for some other possible responses, like maybe some effective ones. Let's get going on something. First job is stop looking like this, get some clean clothes, and find Rey Luc. After that, fix whatever turns out to be wrong. Merely a big problem, not an impossible one.*

The pep talk did me about as much good as a pep talk ever does. I felt better for having given it but not much for having gotten it. I shook off my clothes, decided I looked like a bum, decided I could do nothing about that yet, and slouched down the alley, pulling my tricorne down low to hide my face a little.

The trouble with alleys is that sooner or later they lead to major streets. I had known that I was moving toward the Common the night before, but hadn't realized how close I was; in just a few minutes I had popped out onto Common Street, with the wide green space to the west of me. I crossed over into the Common itself, where a group of boys and dogs were just driving the sheep in to graze, and headed for the Charles. Walking along the river might give me a chance to cover some ground inconspicuously and pick up some clues about what was actually going on. And at this early hour, other than the sheep and the boys, there was nothing and no one here.

I let myself pass close enough to two boys to hear what they were saying; they were talking about whether or not "Seth's sister" was too ugly for any man to marry. Why is it in the movies you get all the information by overhearing two minor extras, and out in the timelines you have to get it a little bit at a time. The major thing I learned was that "Seth's sister" had a nice chest and bad acne; I supposed it might be useful information in the event of being offered a blind date sometime.

Another couple of boys were talking about three public hangings coming up; none of them seemed to be mine.

The Common was a beautiful place, and without any real traffic noise, I found myself thinking that one of these days—once things were a bit more in hand—I'd have to come here at this time just for pleasure. Spring was far enough along for the grass to be bright green and a thin haze of leaf buds to be on the trees, and though damp and squishy in places, the ground wasn't really muddy anywhere except right where the sheep had been concentrated.

Eventually I hit Charles Street, which at the time was nothing more than a mud track. Nobody seemed to be walking on it this morning—it didn't serve much purpose just yet other than as a bypass for carts and wagons from Cambridge to the South Boston Bridge—and took that west to the river.

Now that I was up and moving I was warmer, and though I had no plan as yet, I had at least determined that I was going to get one. The sun was coming up fast now, and the air had that glow it gets in early spring, when it still holds the damp and cold of winter but the sun is warming it fast.

It occurred to me that, as they tell you in training and as anyone in my line learns, disguise is mostly a matter of not looking like yourself, and that can mean very simple things. I let myself slouch a lot, inclined my head forward, and in a burst of inspiration, undid the corners of my tricorne so that I was now wearing my hat wide and floppy, more like an Old West sombrero. Two hard discreet shakes, and with the brim flattened out, my translator assured me I now looked like a Methodist preacher or possibly a schoolteacher. I'd have considered going over and applying at Harvard, as a cover, but they never take Yale men there.

At least this way I would only be spotted by people who got close to me. The extra feeling of safety, plus the gradual warming of the morning, made me feel steadily better, and I picked up my pace a little.

I decided to give the transponder another shot, and this time, much to my surprise, there was a faint signal. The direction seemed to point southward, along Charles Street, opposite the direction in which I had been walking, and not having any better plan, I turned and went the other way.

The sun was getting higher now, and there was more noise of people getting to work. Probably the biggest factory in Boston, even in this altered timeline, didn't have a hundred workers in it at a time; typically people were working in little shops of three or six, a master, a journeyman or two, and a couple of apprentices. As I drew nearer to Boston Neck, I could hear more noise in general— the bank of the Charles River had some wharves and a lot of small businesses going there.

After a bit there was a fork in the road, with Boylston Street going off toward town, to my left, and Charles Street continuing near the river, to my right. The transponder tracker obstinately pointed right up the middle of the fork.

I shrugged and decided so far Charles Street had been lucky for me, so I took the turn to the right. This meant coming into some of the new "industrial" part of the town, the part that had been built up from the new technologies that Rey Luc had introduced; to my eye, it didn't look industrial at all, with its many small barnlike structures and individual workshops, but it was in fact one of the biggest manufacturing areas on Earth in this timeline.

I noted that there was a shop that built "Engines of all Kinds" and another for "Electricks"; there would have been no such thing in Boston in my timeline, so at least I could see that Luc's handiwork wasn't completely undone.

I heard a big, slow "chuffing" noise, and saw puffs of smoke rising from the direction of the river. Pretty clearly someone was starting up one of those engines; since Luc didn't seem to be going anywhere, (triangulating off past readings from the transponder tracker hidden in my sleeve, I found that he seemed to be in just one place less than a mile away), I decided to get a slightly better look at this timeline and see how things were coming along. I walked away from the signal of Luc's transmitter a little, but it was now strong enough so that I didn't worry about it going out, and went to get a look down by the river.

The belches of smoke had consolidated into a gray-black stream, and they were coming from a paddle wheeler. That also told me that things were still on track here. In my timeline there hadn't been much in the way of steamboats on the rivers until well after the War of 1812; here, they had arrived seventy years early.

As I came down toward the wharf, I saw that it was a tugboat—the engine was huge in proportion to the boat, and it had the kind of snub prow they have to have—with the paddle wheels on the side. But it didn't look much like anything out of Mark Twain; Greek Revival and Victorian gingerbread had not yet hit the design world here, if it ever would. Rather it was boxy and flat-sided, painted deep red (the cheap color in those days), and looked like nothing so much as a large shack on top of a capsized barge, with the engine and its stack of wood sitting behind the shack, and two big crude paddle wheels on each side of the ship, so close together that their vanes almost meshed. It wasn't graceful, but it looked powerful.

There was a crowd of about sixty people around the foot of the gangway leading up to the tug, and after checking to make sure that I hadn't lost Rey Luc yet (he seemed to be staying in one place), I moved into an alley and worked my way cautiously forward. A Customs officer is likely to be recognized around a waterfront, but I was wondering what could possibly draw a crowd to the departure of a tugboat in a busy harbor. For that matter, why had I heard so little noise from Boston Harbor the day before? I'd been close enough so that I should have heard more shipping or seen some masts moving—

I crept closer, staying in the shadows, doing my best to look like a preacher or teacher that was just wandering in from idle curiosity . . .

The tug captain—at least he had a coat and hat that I thought made him look like the captain—came to the head of the gangway and was promptly pelted with rotten fruit and vegetables. He ran back into the shack, and two of his men—big, ugly, dumb-looking guys—came out with muskets. The crowd started to back away, and the captain came back out, and proclaimed loudly, "I takes no sides! No sides at all! I just takes pay to move what people pays to have moved, and I follas the law!"

There were hoots of derision, but nobody threw anything, so he seemed to gather his courage. "And besides, I'm commanded by the Royal Navy, anyway! Now, I'm goin' out to bring in the *Terror*, and that's that!"

There was more hooting, but he stormed inside, and the crew started to bring up the gangplank.

Terror is a not uncommon name for a warship; this didn't sound good at all. It looked like, if I hadn't been so busy running for my life (and being mistaken for my double, who seemed to be a murdering nut, among other things) just possibly I'd have found out that things were falling apart all over. Luc was going to have some explaining to do, anyway.

I checked the transponder and saw that if I followed the street I was on now—a sign on the Brown Dog Inn said it was Hollis Street—I should pass very close to Luc. I walked down the lane, doing my best to look the part of a wandering preacher or something of the kind, facing the now-risen sun. It was getting warm, I'd had no breakfast, and the smell of sausage frying from the inn had made the thought of some kind of lunch urgent.

A half mile later, as I was nearing the harbor again, I checked the tracker and found I'd passed him; since I had checked it just two hundred yards before, pretty clearly he was somewhere very near, though the signal was faint. The only significant building there—assuming he wasn't hiding in a storage shed or warehouse—seemed to be a big, new church that sat in a block to itself at Hollis and Orange. I approached it, checked the tracker . . . no, Luc was somewhere to the side—

It was a shock, but obvious. He was in the churchyard, which meant unless he'd been working as a gravedigger all morning, he was dead. It took me about five minutes to find the grave; he'd Anglicized his name to Raymond Luc, but it was clearly him. Moreover, he'd been killed in 1771, according to the stone, "shot down in anger/O passerby, let not your Jealousie rule you!"

I stood by that four-year-old grave and sighed. Well, first part of the job was done; a team could come out here and quietly remove Luc's body and return it to his family, if in his home timeline that was a religious duty or a matter of honor. But clearly he wasn't going to be a lot of help in the matter of getting the timeline back on track.

And even though I'd turned one timeline around before—not many rookie Crux Ops had had that experience—the major thought running through my head was that whatever was wrong, I was just one guy, probably wanted by the authorities, no friends, not enough money to get out of town on, hungry, tired . . .

A hand fell on my shoulder, and a voice said, "Good friend of yours?"

The voice had something a little like a Southern drawl about it, and a bit like a clipped British accent, and the timbre of the voice was like gravel rattling in the throat. I'd heard one human voice like that before, though not with quite that accent, and that had been in another timeline . . . the hand that gripped me was firm and strong, too, and the man it belonged too seemed to be over six feet tall. There was one funny instant, just as the martial artist decided for me that spinning and kicking would be uncalled for, when I thought it was the man whose voice it sounded like— George Patton.

I turned and stared for half an instant; the jaw, bunched with pain from bad teeth, was the same, but the face was a young, vigorous forty-three, not the old man one sees on the dollar bill. "George Washington," I said directly.

·7·

"Mark Strang," he said. "Are you of the faction of Perikles, or that of Hannibal?"

"Perikles," I said, and the light went on.

No one in ATN is really sure, but we think the Closers were descended from Carthaginians; for one thing, they seem to worship Moloch, the great god of Carthage. Perikles, of course, was the great Athenian; Hannibal the great Carthaginian.

And if Washington was asking me that, it was because my double really *was* me—from some other timeline where (god, what disgusting thought) I must have become a Closer agent.

I wanted to call him "General," but in this timeline he certainly wasn't, so instead I said, "I'm very pleased to meet you, sir."

You could see the resemblance to Patton, and that was no great surprise—a lot of the old Virginia military families were heavily intermarried. I wondered, distractedly, if there would be a Patton in this timeline. Washington was taller and thinner, his face more finely formed, and of course his hair was still dark. But the characteristic heavy jowls and wide-set, piercing eyes were pure Virginia aristocrat.

He nodded and extended a hand. "You'll pardon my asking a few questions," he said. "What did Dr. Franklin learn from Dr. Luke?"

"The principle that an electric field is always at right angles to a magnetic field."

"How was King Frederick cured of his abscess?"

"With penicillin, I believe. Otherwise, he'd have died in 1751."

Washington nodded slowly. "I think we need to get you somewhere where we can't be observed, sir, and following that I might suggest a bath, a change of clothes, a disguise, and some food. In whatever order seems best."

We walked up Orange Street in silence; I knew from casual reading that Washington wasn't much of a talker, so I didn't worry about it. He'd taken care of most of what I was really worried about, and I certainly didn't expect him to entertain me on top of that.

"You might keep your head slightly bowed and appear to be striving for the salvation of my soul," Washington added. "That would make you very unlike the other Mark Strang, I should think."

"Quite agreed," I said, bending my head farther. "Have we far to go?"

"I have quarters in Essex Street," he said. "There, that looks a bit more parsonly."

I nodded. "I seem to have dropped into nothing I expected; our last report from poor Luc was apparently shortly before he died."

"Then you're not aware, for example, that you shot him?"

"*I*—oh, my, uh, double. The Customs Collector."

"That one. It was in a duel, very shortly after Mark Strang arrived here. I was not present at the time, but I knew Luc from many years' acquaintance. It was a matter of honor, a challenge, a duel . . . and a death. A most peculiar matter, for Mr. Luc was known to be very passionate about taking care of his health, you see . . . that alone made it strange that he should engage in a duel. The claim that he had seduced the sister of Mr. Strang was, of course, stranger still; he'd always been an honorable man. There were those of us . . . those who had been deeply in Mr. Luc's confidence, deeply enough to know who he really was and where he really came from, felt something might have gone deeply wrong. Adams in particular was concerned, and wrote to me and the others at once."

"I see," I said. At that moment a cart came around a corner

and passed us; as it was going by I added, "But of course in Leviticus the matter is far less clear, and surely you must agree with me—" the cart passed out of earshot. "This is John Adams?"

"That question alone marks you as our man. His useless cousin Sam is a passionate Son, I'm afraid. They're so taken with the idea of running a nation that they can no longer see how much of our wealth comes from our life in the Empire. Anyone who could confuse Sam and John is not from this time . . ." He sighed, very slightly. "As I understand it, these agents of . . . other times, other histories?"

"We call them timelines."

"Thank you. These agents of other timelines arrive with a list of people known to be important, but apparently not any idea of why they will be important. Your name was on such a list, but as an agent for the, er, friendly faction, not for those other sorts. Mr. Luc apparently was beginning to fear that his health might fail, and if it should do so, that we might be left without support."

That was pretty much what I would have expected; Special Agents generally get a station in their mid-twenties to mid-thirties, and then stay there until they die or retire. They're guys who change the world—that's their mission—but they do it as peacefully as they can, with ideas and teaching and information, and they stay with that world, often, until they die there. What they get from home is an update to their orders every six months, and—if they stop sending or call for help—a Crux Op to rescue or avenge them.

I could never imagine the kind of day-to-day courage and self-reliance that must take.

"There's no way of knowing exactly what will happen," I explained. "Whenever they can, timelines will collapse back into each other, so to separate two timelines requires enormous changes. Even then it only works at a crux, one of the places where there's a natural dividing point. And 1740–1780 is a large crux, so although there are many timelines out there where various of our people figure into the future history, so many different things could happen that it's not possible to say what we will actually do here. It's only after it's all done and the crux is over that matters will begin to settle out."

Washington nodded. "I am told this is confusing even to those of you who live with it all the time." There was a clatter behind us, and I looked around to see group of women with baskets of live chickens in each hand; as they passed us Washington added, "So it's your position, then, that anything in Deuteronomy that is not specifically reaffirmed in the New Testament cannot be binding upon a Christian?"

"That would seem to be the position of St. Paul," I said, though I hadn't the foggiest idea.

The women went by with the chickens, and we continued walking. "I'd have thought," I said, "that you'd have been in Virginia at this time, near your home."

Washington snorted. "I admit I was very tempted to retire completely after the Conquest War. I had entered a major, come out a colonel, started a world war when I was in my twenties . . . General Braddock's drive through the Ohio country and all the way to Fort Detroit had made me famous, the land grants and the knighthood His Majesty King Frederick was pleased to bestow upon me had made me wealthy—I hired a splendid man named Boone to run matters out to the west for me—and between prestige and wealth, I could settle to do almost anything I wished. I had very nearly resolved to do so, but Mr. Luc seemed to feel there was some service I could be to the new king, and since we had gotten to be friends . . ."

"Of course," I said.

"Not to mention it is very hard to say no to a sovereign who has made one a duke," Washington added. "I don't suppose that was in Mr. Luc's reports?"

"No," I said, "it wasn't."

Washington smiled. "I've been granted the Duchy of Kentucky. I don't imagine I shall move there for ten years yet; Boone writes me that there is much to be done."

Washington's house in Boston turned out to be a decent wood-framed building with a couple of spare bedrooms and an honest-to-god bathroom; it turned out that Rey Luc had introduced the flush toilet and the shower to these folks, for which I was deeply grateful. I found myself immediately believing all the stories I'd heard of Washington's consideration for his men, because once we were there, he immediately suggested that I ought to go down to the kitchen for a meal, and that "my servant will ready you a shower, sir, and a bed and a change of clothes. I think a few hours will not hurt the business of one who has all of time at his command, and you look in need of food, rest, and some cleanliness."

The meal was wonderful—marred for me only by the fact that there was no coffee, for in this timeline there had been no resistance to tea. It was a great big slab of apple pie, a plate of scrambled eggs with ham, and a pork-and-vegetable pastry whose name I didn't catch, all washed down with a lot of tea and a nice heavy breakfast porter. The person who served all that to me was a tall, handsome, black woman, who seemed amused at the company the duke was keeping and the quantity I ate; it took me a while to figure out that I was probably being waited on by a slave. Abolition was supposed to happen fairly soon in this timeline—though if the Closers took over, it never would.

The shower, too, was a lesson in how far this century had to go—a slave had had to pump the tank full and build a fire under it—but I was so grateful for it that I managed to overlook the gross incorrectness of the whole thing. When I got back, Porter or Carrie could lecture me about it.

Besides, I tipped the guy, and he seemed pleased to be thanked. It might not have been the peak of social justice, but it was a start; at least they didn't seem badly mistreated, and I remembered from somewhere that in my timeline Washington had been a relatively decent master, making sure his slaves received an education and freeing them in his will.

I fell asleep in a clean, comfortable bed, woke up in a few hours hungry again, and got dressed rapidly. The new outfit didn't have the special pocket between the shoulder blades for the SHAKK, or the boot pocket for the NIF, so I ended up just wearing the .45 and tucking the more advanced weaponry into a little leather bag, like a doctor's bag, they'd provided for the purpose.

The servant came in and summoned me down to supper; I found that besides George Washington, there were also John Adams, and two young doctors—Joseph Warren and Tom Young—present in the room. Adams was a tough-looking little guy, despite being from one of the best Boston families; Warren was tall and handsome, and Young a square-built, muscular guy. While we were sitting down, Samuel Cooper, a local minister, came in; like Adams and unlike the rest of us, he wore a white-powdered wig, which didn't diminish his sharply etched strong features. Visually with a change of clothes any of them could have been a dockworker or cab driver, and they reminded me more of an American Resistance cell I had once known in Nazi-occupied San Francisco than they did of the stiff, posed paintings of Founding Fathers from my own timeline.

Dinner was a roast turkey, mashed potatoes, and corn bread; the available seasonings seemed to be salt and pepper. It occurred to me that this was before any of the waves of South European immigration, and therefore the diet was going to be pretty bland this trip out. Naturally no one noticed except me, and I was hungry enough to eat eagerly anyway.

I was also a little surprised at how much everyone drank; there were several kinds of hard liquor and a number of thick red wines available, and most of them were drinking mixtures of those, usually with some sugar and some hot water stirred in. I tried one of those myself and ended up sipping it for the rest of the evening. The mixture didn't seem to hit any of the other men nearly as hard.

After we'd all finished, and tea had been set out, Washington began the meeting by explaining, "To some extent it was pure chance I was here, for I am due back in Virginia in the fall, and after that I've some business in London; with the new steamships one may much more safely undertake a winter voyage, you know. But as for how we knew to watch for you, that's easily explained; your counterpart from the—did you say Closers?"

"That's them, the Closers," I said.

"Ah. Well, your Closer counterpart has been a very unpleasant fellow in many regards, but undeniably he has been popular, at least among the more drastically Tory crowd."

It took me a long moment to realize that in this timeline Tories and Loyalists were not the same thing; the King in London was a Whig, Parliament was Whig, and the Tories were thus the rightwing opposition to King George, not his staunchest supporters as in my timeline.

"Popular and inflamma-Tory," Young said, and there was a mild groan from everyone at the table. "He's made himself the darling of young men that I suppose you would call intellectual macaronis—the sort who change their ideas for exactly the reason other young men change their coats, to make themselves conspicuous and give them an importance they would not otherwise have. And like any true macaronis, they are, of course, given to calling attention to themselves by adopting what is most extreme. So where a more sensible young fellow would simply wear a wig that was too high, a hat that was too small, shoes that pinched his feet, and buckles and buttons big enough to weigh down a sail, these fellows around Strang have been vying to see who can be more Royalist than the King and more Imperialist than a tax collector. They've brawled in the streets dozens of times with the Sons of Liberty, and they've organized the King's Own Undertakers, as they call themselves, to kidnap and murder Whigs."

I shuddered a little. "All that around someone who looks just like me. No wonder the Sons of Liberty were so quick to take a shot at me."

"They're just as bad a lot," Warren said, morosely. Later I was to realize he did almost everything morosely. Though he was a gentle and kind man, he seemed to expect the worst in every situation. "The Sons have a good sixty murders to their credit, if that's the word. It's gotten so that the Common is deserted in the morning, because people are afraid to see who may have been butchered and left there 'as an example' by either the Sons of Liberty or the King's Own Undertakers. There've been many rumors that there are Redcoat officers working with the King's Own, and I rather suspect it's true; certainly the Mark Strang we've all come to know and loathe is at the heart of it."

Cooper was nodding vigorous agreement. "But no one would have thought him mad, and what he did in Bishop's Alley yesterday was madder than anything we've seen, even poor old James Otis included."

I knew that Otis had suffered from insanity after being a major Patriot leader in my timeline; I must have looked puzzled because Adams explained, "It's that damned new explosive; we don't know if Luc introduced it through one of his many front organizations and covers, or if Strang brought it in, or perhaps it was actually discovered by one of our own chemists. It's a niter of glycerin mixed with a special white clay—"

"Dynamite," I said.

"Yes, I think that's the name it's sold under. A lump the size of a loaf of bread goes off like a barrel of common gunpowder; a small box of it can level a fair-sized house. And that's just how poor old Otis died—he was carrying a box of it into a tavern, and it's quite touchy stuff and this had gotten old enough to sweat out some of its niter. It destroyed the tavern and killed a dozen soldiers and Royal agents, and it also left almost nothing of Otis." Adams stared off into space. "It's a bad thing, you know. When you had to haul in whole barrels of powder to make something like that happen—well, then it was hard to do. With this stuff a bomb might be made and concealed anywhere, and both factions are beginning to use them in just that way." He sighed. "Otis and I were friends, you know. Without that accursed dynamite, he might be mad as a March hare and confined somewhere, but he would at least be alive."

There was a long silence at that. The candles that flickered and danced made no sound, and the dark April night outside, though it had been threatening rain as I came down to supper, held no hint of wind or rain.

"You see," Cooper said finally, "we're all more than a little disheartened, or we have been. In a bit over thirty years the world came along very far very fast. And though the information brought by Mr. Luc was what made it possible, we ourselves have done the work; Rey Luc showed us how to do things and how they might fit together into a scheme, but it was our work and our effort that brought us to understand them, and it was our further work that made them become real. We know of his influence in many places—it was he who got the King out of Bute's keeping and got Franklin appointed his tutor . . . and though George has prospects of being as fine a King as ever good old England's ever had, no one will deny that he's a little slow at times, especially when it comes to the more abstract sort of thinking, or that he is remarkably easy to lead. Mr. Luc brought out the best in him, partly by his personal contact and mainly by letting the young Prince come over here and see what sort of country he had."

"I'm surprised," I said, "that the King hasn't acted more to abate this crisis."

"No one's more surprised than I," Washington said. "For five years after his visit here, he and I corresponded frequently, and I think I may fairly say that we had become quite good friends. Indeed, Cooper, the one thing I would add is that whatever you may think of his brains, George the Third has a passionate desire to do the right thing and to know what the right thing is. I find it quite inexplicable, therefore, that in the past three or so years the King has stopped answering my letters, indeed communicates with no one in America despite all the many friends he has here, and even the London social crowd sees him only at public functions." A thought struck me; I was about to speak when Washington raised a finger. "Alas, too, Mr. Strang, from what I have been able to learn there's no possibility of a double's being substituted—too many of our Whig friends have seen him closely enough, and he has recognized and acknowledged them sometimes with a word or two. I fear he is changed; there was a brief period, you know, of fits while he was over here—"

"I had the honor of treating His Majesty at that time," Young said, "and the fits he suffered, even if they should eventually devolve into full-blown madness, were in no way consistent with any such change in him. He might be in great anguish, and even suffer hallucinations, true, but his feelings for his friends, his affections, his opinions—these would be left untouched, if I am any judge. Moreover, if he were suffering such a condition, any hypothetical Tory captors he might have would not allow him in public, and further they would have every reason to apply to Parliament for a Regency, most especially because the Prince of Wales is still a child and thus by controlling the Regency they might control the kingdom. No, what exactly is going on is impossible to say from here. It's a great pity that they didn't make their move a year earlier, in my judgment."

"Why?" I asked.

"Because then Luc would have died in London, and his last report would have come from there. You'd have been dispatched there. I'm afraid you're a good thirty-five hundred miles from where you need to be, Mr. Strang. We'll have to get you aboard a ship somehow, and not from Boston—the port's been closed by Royal order."

I looked from one face to the other, there in the wash of red light from the candles on the table, and all were nodding solemnly. It seemed reasonable enough to me.

"What's my best way?" I asked.

Adams shrugged. "The most common way seems good enough for the purpose—and I can't think of any that would be faster. The port of Boston is closed, and so are most of the other port towns in Massachusetts and New England, but they are allowing coasters out of Providence, in Rhode Island, and from there you may easily get to New York, where we have many friends and the port is open. From New York to London, then, and good luck to you at every step."

"And Providence is only about forty-five miles," I said. "With a little effort I can walk that in three days if I have to—"

"Walk? Egad, sir. You are not the sort of maniac that Mr. Luc—I should say Dr. Luc—proved to be? Your whole timeline is not like that?" Young seemed to be peering right through me.

"I'm not sure what sort of maniac that is, Dr. Young."

"Bah! The man believed that every pleasure of life—liquor, tobacco, a good wench—was a danger to the health, and moreover he wanted us to eat more vegetables, which are of course well-known for causing flux of the bowels, and to do this thing he called 'exercising,' when any fool can look and see that it is exactly those classes which do heavy physical labor which live for the shortest time. Begging your pardon, of course, Joseph," Dr. Young said, turning to the slave who was bringing in a pot of hot, seasoned cider.

"No pardon need be begged, sir," Joseph said, and I noticed that his accent was not Southern at all, as one might have expected, but very similar to the New England accent I had been hearing here in Boston. "It's well-known that when Master Washington freed us, he most likely added five years to all our lives."

Oh, well, *judge not that ye be not judged,* I reminded myself. I had assumed he was a slave because in my time Washington had kept slaves right up to his dying day.

"Freedom is good for people," Adams commented. "But before Young got off on his track of denouncing your medicine—I'm sure he'd have started on your morals and religion next, sir"—there was a lot of laughter at the table about that, and Dr. Young blushed slightly—"what he should have said is that one of the new traction engines is now plying a route from Jamaica Plain to Providence. The line would have been extended here by now if the Royal embargo had not been interpreted to mean that there must be no easy access to the other ports. So it's just a short stage ride, and then an uncomfortable trip by traction train, and then ships all the way. Nothing to it but a bit of discomfort and the need for some patience. Certainly no need to walk like a peddler!"

That seemed to take care of all the issues as far as they were concerned; they told me that I'd be stopping at the house of Gouverneur Morris, a young Whig in New York, for the time—anywhere from a day or so to two weeks—until I could book passage on a ship for London. They also assured me, repeatedly, that costs were covered, finally explaining that one of their sympathizers in the inn where I had first landed had quietly made off with most of the money from the trunk I arrived with. I wasn't sure they were telling the truth—whoever claimed George Washington never told a lie, Warren was to tell me later, had never played cards with the man or watched him run for office—but it was plausible enough, and anyway I didn't have much of any way to pay for anything myself.

Dr. Warren had business in New York and would see me to Morris's house; it all seemed to be arranged. I was in bed early that night, and up with the sun the next morning. At breakfast together, Washington and I mostly talked about camping and hiking—he was a passionate advocate of getting exploratory expeditions launched to the Rockies, and my descriptions of what was actually out west just whetted his appetite for it. "No doubt there will be time," he said, "once all the current infernal nonsense is done with. I hope that by that time I will not be too old; my memories of the Ohio country when I was much younger are still fond ones, and I should like to have a chance to walk to the Pacific. And in your timeline—"

"It was done in about 1806. Of course, you've already got dirigibles. It would be hard to fly east-to-west, with the wind against you, but still, if a dirigible can make it here from London without refueling, which you all say one is expected to do any day now, it ought to be able to make it from here to the mouth of the Columbia—and you could have a ship waiting for it there."

"It's indeed a thought," Washington said. "If only I still had His Majesty's ear! But oh, well, time enough for that when the world is back on track. Meanwhile if I'm not mistaken, here's Warren with the trap."

As I tossed my bag in beside Warren's, he commented, "I see that Washington also shops at Goodwife Pelster's." The two bags were identical on the outside; nothing could have told you that Warren's contained tools for saving lives, and mine contained tools that could slaughter three thousand men.

The drive down to the Jamaica Plain station was pleasant enough; Warren and I were alone on the road for a lot of it, for with the embargo and blockade the port was not busy, and thus there was much less land traffic to and from it, and most of what there was was not urgent. This early in the morning only a few farmers going into town to sell vegetables could be seen.

From Boston Neck we could make out two of the British iron-clads in the harbor, big ships with the new submerged screws in-stead of paddle wheels, and with turrets instead of banks of guns. They looked, to me, like kids' crude pictures of warships, the kind of thing that second-grade boys like to draw, but it was just such ships a dozen years before that had put the whole main line of the French fleet on the bottom in less than an hour.

It was a nice day again—and how often does that happen twice in a row in Massachusetts in April?—and the time went quickly. Warren, too, was interested in everything and had opinions about everything and everyone. He was one of the most highly regarded men in Massachusetts, part of the informal aristocracy of Charles Town, and though he knew everyone and everything about them, he didn't so much judge people as enjoy them. It might sound dull to listen to a couple of hours of gossip and wit about people you didn't know, unless it were really nasty and salacious stuff, Warren could not only entertain in just that way, but he could entertain while mostly talking about the good side, or at least about the mi-nor vices. I had a feeling after a while that he just plain liked the human race, and that was why most of them were returning the favor by liking him.

It was getting near lunchtime when we reached the traction-engine station. You could see it some distance away—if I had walked all the way out onto the Neck, I'd have seen the billows of smoke in the distance, and even eight miles off you could see the big smokestack.

The traction line was sort of a compromise, a little something that Luc and a couple of cunning engineers—notably Boulton and Watt, whom he had found and recruited—had dreamed up be-cause pretty clearly real railroads were going to take too long for the essential job of tying the colonies together and speeding up communications enough to hold the Empire together; Luc's last plan had had the first locomotives available about ten years from now, but the first need for a mechanized road had been in getting forces from New York City to Ticonderoga during the Conquest War. Thus the "traction line" had been created as a temporary expedient.

It worked a lot like a cable car, except that the cables ran overhead; every few miles there was a great big chugging multiple-cylinder reciprocating steam engine, with ten cylinders as big as wine barrels, a boiler the size of a house, and a transmission and gearing that took up a barn-sized building linking it to the running cables. Between these stations, there ran a set of wooden tracks, like railroad tracks but made of wood with just a tinplated iron top, and on the tracks were wagons and stagecoaches with iron-rimmed wheels. Because the engine didn't have to drag itself along with cargo, it could be as big as needed, and because the gears could be made so big, they could be made of wood and didn't have to be made to precise tolerances—both very important at a time when good-grade steel was made in small crucibles and the best steels were literally worth their weight in gold.

In another ten years, if Luc had lived, there'd have been Bessemer converters and a whole steel industry—the giant steam engines would make it possible to power the blowers that the converters needed—and in very little time after that there would have been a railroad from Savannah all the way to Nova Scotia. Lewis and Clark, in this timeline, would have been able to take the train to St. Louis before starting up the Missouri, probably in cars with aluminum doors and window frames, for even now Ben Franklin was hard at work on large generating plants.

Well, we would get it back on track. Meanwhile, the ride was jerky, and there was a lot of soot from woodsmoke whenever we approached stations on the way to Providence. Splitting wood and not atoms is a smelly, dirty business; the air would get cleaner around here once they started getting decent Pennsylvania anthracite, and by the late 1800s they should have nukes and all the clean power they wanted, not to mention a bogey to help scare the Closers away (we think they're terrified of nuclear energy because their home timeline was trashed by repeated nuclear wars; if so, it couldn't have happened to a better bunch of guys).

It was still daylight when we got to Providence, and there was more than enough time to get a decent meal at an inn—I was sort of figuring if I got a spare minute in this timeline I was going to introduce the idea of a restaurant with a *menu*, but the food was good enough—and then catch a night steamer, an elegant little paddle wheeler called the *John Locke*, to take us into New York, just about eleven hours away. Unfortunately the *Locke* didn't have sleeper accommodations, and we wouldn't get into the harbor until morning, but we had telegraphed ahead, Morris was expecting us early in the day, and, besides, there was nothing we needed to do the next day, and we'd be able to sleep then.

The funny thing was that even coming from a world of jet planes and rapid transit, it all seemed like a kind of a miracle to me. Once you've walked for even a few days, your sense of distance is very different. For Joseph Warren, who had grown up with horses and sailing ships, I supposed it might have seemed like a miracle.

There were more miracles on board; the *Locke* was a luxury ship, and it had a small "tour of wonders" which included going to the ship's radio shack to meet the radioman, and to watch him try to catch one of the daily radio broadcasts from London—so far there was just one station on the air for twenty minutes every day, but in just the right conditions you could get it anywhere in the world. Home crystal sets were already down to the price of a printed book (which unfortunately was still about $45 if you were converting it in gold to dollars from my timeline). More than anything else, I figured, radio—or the Franklinphone, as it was called, was going to make a difference.

There was also a small casino of sorts; Puritan New England did not allow gambling but once they were out of Providence Harbor they could open up the tables. I'm not much of a gambler—when I've visited casinos I've stuck to blackjack or to the crap table pretty much—but Warren wanted to get in a few hands of whist, there were hot sausages, bread, and coffee there, and I could amuse myself with the newspaper or with idle conversation.

Warren and I had noticed already that his medical bag, and the bag that contained my change of clothes and specialty weapons, were pretty similar, so I piled both bags under my legs to make a sort of footstool, sat down on one of the hard-backed chairs, and began to absorb the local *Dispatch-Intelligencer*; as was common at the time, the first few pages were advertisements, which mostly told me that the changes Luc had made in the economy had really taken hold—there were ads for electric-generator windmills, crystal sets, toy "electric carriages" for children, the dirigible line from New York to Philadelphia (actually they just hooked onto the traction-engine line, and the dirigible's Sterling-cycle engine was used only for maneuvering in takeoff and landing), and a variety of crude lightbulbs, though to judge from the fact that nearly everyone seemed to be using candles or gas, the new technology was more a novelty than anything else.

The other thing, though, that the ads told me was that a depression was settling over the colonies. There were many, many auctions of farms and factories, and because Luc had introduced credit buying to get the economy stimulated, many more ads looking for people to assume payments. There were many ads that began "position sought" or "land for sale," and none at all looking for workers.

It took me a couple of hours to figure all of this out because the ads weren't classified, as in our newspapers, but just fit in any old way the printer could get them to go. That was fine with me—I needed to kill time, after all, and was sort of hoping that counting ads would be dull enough to send me to sleep even in that uncomfortable chair.

The news of London was unimpressive as well; many people were sitting for the new photographic portraits, there had been many parties in the past season, and a remarkable number of rich people were marrying each other and were expected to foster happy lineages of many children of breeding and distinction. A traction engine had been built in India, and a line would shortly be opening from New Delhi to the coast.

I had just about decided that stern duty wasn't going to keep me at this any longer, and even the dullest news wasn't going to send me to sleep, as the clock struck midnight. I turned a few pages, and was about to start reading Dr. Samuel Johnson's column from London, when something across the room caught my eye.

I looked up and saw myself, leaning over the crap table. Apparently both of us had had enough skill to get out of Boston. I glanced toward Warren, but he was deep in his game of whist, and there wasn't much hope of getting him out of it without stirring up a fuss. Keeping my eye on the other Mark Strang, and doing my best to keep the newspaper well up in front of my face, I quickly scribbled a note to Warren, flagged a server, and sent the note. Then I quietly leaned forward, setting my paper to the side, and grabbed the bag with the SHAKK and NIF from under my feet.

I was about to get the NIF into my coat sleeve—this seemed like the kind of job I wanted to do without making noise—when my target abruptly collected his winnings and went out the saloon door onto the deck. Grabbing the bag, I followed him.

Fog had blown in since we had entered Long Island Sound, and it was hard to see even to the end of the deck. Had he seen me? If so, then he was undoubtedly in the shadows somewhere close by, waiting to take a shot at me; if not, then I very much doubted he was out here for any good purpose. If he was being met by a boat from shore, he might show a light, but otherwise I didn't think there was much reason for him to give himself away.

I looked both ways, again, and checked behind me, and still there was nothing. I stood and listened for a long time, but between the chugging of the engine, the splashing of the paddle wheel, the light slap of the waves on the side of the *Locke*, and the wind in the radio aerial, there was far too much sound out here for me to make out anyone quietly walking across the deck or climbing steps. He had had plenty of time, and he could be anywhere on the ship by now.

The moon came out up above, but it only helped a little; the fog was still on the sea, and though it was bright now, visibility was not much extended. I crept along the side of the main cabin, back past the saloon and toward the stern, because one direction was as good as another. I tried setting a couple of ambushes by crossing in places where my back seemed exposed but the shadows in the murky moonlight fell in front of me; either he wasn't buying it (would I? I wasn't sure) or else he wasn't behind me. I started a slow search of both decks, outside.

Of course by now he might very well have gone in the other door. At least if Warren was still in there, he had been alerted to what was going on and might be able to take some action.

I slipped farther along the side of the steamer; the chugging was driving me crazy. In the dark you depend on your ears, and I couldn't hear a thing. Moreover I had gotten to a point just back of amidships and was now near the bearings of the paddle wheels, which were screeching softly—petroleum and silicon lubricants were going to be a great thing when they came in!

"Please, sir, do not do that," a soft voice said ahead of me. It sounded like a woman.

There was an unintelligible mutter.

You know how hard it is to recognize your own voice? I couldn't be sure.

"Oh, please, sir, stop, sir, please," the voice said again, softly.

I slipped under a staircase leading up to the bridge and peered into the darkness.

"Oh, god, sir," the voice said. Something was writhing in the darkness.

I pressed closer and listened; the male voice suddenly groaned.

"That's good, sir," the voice said. "If you're in town, I can be louder there—"

The male voice muttered something, and the woman then gave her address and said, "Eight shillings, as we agreed, sir. And I did indeed make a show of resistance, but you recall, sir, we agreed I was not to make too much noise."

The muttering got surly, and there was the clink of coins.

I crept away. In any century, more people than spies are sneaking around in the dark. It occurred to me that if I had thought that poor guy sounded a lot like me, unpleasant things might have happened. At the least, we'd all have had some explaining to do.

I descended to the lower, crowded deck, which was largely open, loaded with barrels of cargo and stacks of finished wood from the New England sawmills, plus all the people they could cram aboard her. It took a lot of crawling around, and it must have been an hour, before I gave up and admitted that if my doppelgänger was there under a blanket, I could have stepped on him three times without knowing it.

I headed back up. I had seen him, I knew I had seen him . . .

Someone was crouched on the deck in front of me. As the moon had risen higher in the sky, the light had gotten better, but the fog had thickened, and now I could see only a dark outline, like a badly developed black-and-white photo. Staying in the shadows, I went nearer; I was almost on top of the figure before I saw that it was a man, stretched out at full length on the deck, peering over the side toward the lower deck. In his hand there was a pistol.

Something about the hat made me suspect, and I crept forward; when I was a bare three feet away I saw enough of the face to be sure. "Warren," I whispered. "Did you see him, where is he?"

There was no response; his concentration on the deck below was absolute. I crawled closer.

"Warren. It's Strang. Are you—"

There was no response. Knowing what I would find, and shud-

dering from much more than the icy spray-covered deck on which
I lay now, too, I reached out and touched his face.

The unseeing eyes never blinked. He was cool to the touch, not
yet cold, but that would come soon enough, and already the flesh
was beginning to stiffen.

·8·

I crawled back slowly and carefully, though if my counterpart was watching the body, he surely would have fired by now.

Damn, and I had liked Warren, liked him quite a bit. I had this idea of myself as being tough, an ice man, bent only on revenge and slaughtering Closers . . . and it wasn't entirely true. I felt like bursting into tears; I'd just lost a friend.

But if I had normal feelings after all, I also seemed to have my full complement of desire for vengeance. We were going to settle accounts soon, I decided, and with that my brief wave of mourning was done. My heart was cold as the fog and as dark as the night, and I crawled forward, determined either to find my man or eventually have a shot at him as he disembarked.

He was nowhere on the upper deck. I even went back inside the saloon to check, with no better luck. By now a few determined gamblers were still playing in the casino, but he wasn't among them, or among the disorderly heap of men in coats and knee breeches piled together and trying to sleep in the armchairs.

I had been around the upper deck several times, as well, and the more I thought, the more I doubted he had been there at any time that I had; one of us would have seen the other, there would have been a shot, and that would have been the end of it. That left the lower deck, where he could hide forever, and with a moderately good disguise probably get off the boat . . . or just slip over the side and swim to shore, as long as he waited until the very last minute and had someone waiting with a change of clothes and a hot fire . . . I knew in these waters in early spring you could die in minutes from exposure, but how many minutes? And would he know? When would I have to start waiting for the splash?

I shifted the small black bag in my hands a couple of times. It, too, had slowed me down, but I had no better way to carry the weapons I needed. The hand that clutched the handle tended to get raw and numb, so I'd been using my left hand, trying to keep my shooting hand in decent shape.

There's an old Sherlock Holmes line about "When you have eliminated the impossible, whatever remains, however improbable, must be the truth." There's also an old joke about a drunk looking for a lost quarter under a streetlamp, even though he lost it in the alley, because the light was better where he was looking.

If that other Mark Strang were hiding out on the lower deck, I wouldn't find him until he tried to get off, and quite possibly not then. He wasn't on the upper deck. I doubted he would have been admitted to the bridge or stayed there so long if he'd come up with some pretext, and I didn't think he was likely to know any more than me about how to steer one of these things. And there was nowhere to hijack it to.

That left one significant space I hadn't investigated—the engine room and fuel hold. What he'd be doing down there, I didn't know, but if I could find him there, I could do something about it, and I couldn't find him anywhere else.

The best way was probably back through the saloon and down the opposite stairs, so I went forward again. I was almost at the saloon doors, and just passing around a little wind barrier they had to protect the deck chairs in nice weather, when something moved in front of me. I stepped sideways silently.

"Please don't hurt me," the voice said softly. It didn't sound like the working girl it had been before; I thought it was probably the steward, and who else—other than us agents?—would have been out on deck at this hour?

"The key," a voice said. It sounded like my own voice on the answering machine.

"Yes, yes, sir, but there's nothing down there, the passenger valuables aren't locked in the engine room sir—"

"The key," it said again, and I knew the voice for my own. In the dark I could not make out which shape was whose, but sooner or later they would separate, and if need be I could stun them both, and then revive the steward—*after* I made sure my counterpart would never wake up.

Doing my best to keep it silent, I turned the catch on the black bag and reached inside, feeling for the NIF, which should be lying on the right, with the SHAKK on the left. Something hard and the right size for a handgrip met my hand. I began to draw it out slowly, but something felt wrong.

With great care I set the bag down on the deck and braced, but it took a hard pull that was nearly impossible to keep silent.

Neither of the figures noticed; there was a jingle as one handed a key to the other, but the hands were hidden behind the nearer one, and I still didn't know who was who in the dark.

I felt with my left hand, and then bit my lip in pain. Something had seared into my left hand . . .

I forced the case open wider and felt more carefully, looking out for blades, to confirm they were there, not to cut myself on them again—

And I found them. There were bone saws, scalpels, and now that I felt more, bottles of medicine in there. I had taken Warren's doctor bag by mistake, and god only knew where my SHAKK and NIF were now.

I wanted to scream and throw the thing around in a rage, but I bit my lip, closed the bag, and set it down on the deck. Time enough to pick on myself later.

My left hand wasn't cut badly, but it was slick with blood; I wrapped it in a corner of my coat and squeezed down hard to stop the bleeding.

The two figures finally parted. I drew my Colt from its shoulder holster; this wasn't so finely discriminating a weapon as the NIF, and I would want to be right about who I shot. Unfortunately, the builds were similar, the light bad, the fog thick—

Abruptly the more distant of the two figures brought up a pistol and shot the other in the back. The steward fell with a scream, wounded and probably dying—when you're hit in mid-back like that, in a world without antibiotics or blood transfusions, you're a goner.

My alter turned and ran. I shot at him twice, unable to hit him even at the close range because I could barely see him, and I couldn't seem to adjust for the roll of the deck—

And he shouted, "Help! Murder! Murderer on the deck!"

My real position was instantly clear. There was one fresh corpse and one dying man on that deck; the dying man, if he could talk, would describe me. And I was standing here holding a smoking pistol.

I turned, darted into the shadows, and fled down the stairs, jamming the gun back into the shoulder holster as I went. Nobody was going to be listening to me if I tried to explain.

There were screams and shouts from above, and I realized they had found the dying steward and Warren's body. That would at least slow most of them for a moment; I needed to get under wraps here somehow or other.

The problem, of course, in this chilly April night, was that every blanket that could possibly be found on that deck was in use. Moreover, my clothes were too nice and too clean—a leg with stocking showing anywhere, or my relatively new and decent shoes, almost anything of the kind, could easily betray me as not belonging where I was. And this was the kind of America where if they bothered to take me into New York for trial—the captain no doubt had the authority to hang me right there—the trial would be next morning and the sentence carried out ten minutes later.

I squatted as deep into one shadow as I could get, between two bundles of blankets that seemed to be a sleeping couple, probably a farmer and his wife taking some choice part of the crop into the big city . . . lucky bastards, I thought, be content where you are, it's a big nasty universe—in fact it's millions of big nasty universes—and if you can find love in just one place and time, stay there.

That made me think of Chrysamen, which was distracting if I thought about her as a person and discouraging if I thought about whether it was time to call for a rescue yet. The mission wasn't quite in danger, just me . . . and if I died, the signal would go off automatically. I still had the button in my pocket, but I didn't yet have a good excuse to push it.

There were lanterns being lit all over the place above, a lot of people were beginning to order each other around, and some of the sleeping bodies were beginning to stir on the deck where I was, not yet very aware, but their consciousness sort of crawling to the surface to see what the noise was about. I couldn't stay where I was, and there was no diversion readily available, at least none I could think of—best to get moving before they came down here with the lanterns.

I had known my counterpart had come down here with the key to the engine room, and you couldn't miss your way to that—the deafening racket as you got closer to the stern was unmistakable. As swiftly as I could move without making noise, I headed for the stern, stepping over bodies, pistol already drawn because it was too late to worry about looking suspicious, and I wanted it handy.

The noise grew louder, and now there were no bodies on the deck—no one could have slept there.

In the moonlit shadows, there was something on the deck, something too small to be a person, and yet it had what looked like two human arms flung out from it. For one horrible instant I thought it was a human torso, that my counterpart had dismembered one of his victims for some obscure reason, but then I saw that it was too flat to be a body.

I crept forward and found a complete set of clothes at the rail—clothes that would have fit me perfectly.

I stared at them for a long second. Had he stolen a uniform and boldly dressed in it right here, was he naked for some reason—

I looked over the rail to the dark, brooding bulk of Long Island, still farm country where it wasn't outright wilderness, and my thoughts came together with terrible speed. I leaped to the engine room, found it locked, beat on the door, and shouted for a moment without any response.

There could be no more than a minute to spare. I yanked the Model 1911A1 from its holster, thought, *Don't jam now!* and laid it against the lock and bolt. I wanted to make sure a single round would do the job—I had only the round in the chamber, one fresh magazine in the Colt, and two magazines in my pockets; when you're trying to change all of history it's a good idea to make sure you have enough ammunition.

I pressed the muzzle hard against the surface, to get the round angled to shatter the lock and, with a little luck, then cut the bolt as well. The trigger squeeze was slow and smooth, the kick against my hand was ferocious as a little pressure backed up into the barrel (and amazingly, it didn't jam as I'd half expected it to).

There was more shouting behind me now, and they'd be here in seconds. I kicked the door open—it bounced a foot or so open and then bounced back. I shoved hard with my shoulder, against some resistance on the other side.

It was what I might have expected. The engineer was in there, and both stokers, and all had rolled against the door from where the bodies had been piled on an overhead fuel bunker. All three of them had round holes in their faces, the size hole a pencil might make if you jabbed it hard into a watermelon, and all three of them had baseball-sized chunks torn from the backs of their heads and sprayed on the walls; there was a smell of cooking meat where one such chunk had smeared across the hot face of the boiler.

Apparently my Closer doppelgänger also liked the Colt Model 1911A1.

All that I saw in a short glance, in the vivid red light pouring from the firebox, so that even now in my memory I see it all in reds and blacks, the shadows deep and hard and everything else stained shades of red and orange in the flaring, dancing light. It was a scene out of hell, and yet none of it was interesting, at least not compared to what I was looking for, not at that moment. I was looking for something in particular, and unfortunately there were twenty or thirty things it could look like . . . a lump of clay, a black box, an irregular package, an old barrel, but it would be—

There. On the side of the boiler there was a silvery cylinder, about the size of a can of tomato juice or a two-pound can of coffee, stuck onto the iron surface with what looked for all the world like black roofing tar. It did not look like it belonged there.

I had seconds to work, and chances were I was dead anyway. Since that other Mark Strang had gone over the side like that, into water cold enough to kill you in minutes—even if he had a wet suit and scuba gear at his disposal, he was in a hurry. And if he was in a hurry, he hadn't set the timer for very long.

So, with no time for anything better, I did something I *really* don't recommend if you find a bomb—I grabbed it with my bare hands, braced a foot for an instant on the burning-hot surface of the boiler, and yanked that silver cylinder with all my strength.

There was a sucking, tearing noise, and it came off as if it had been stuck on with very old bubble gum. I pivoted on my remaining foot, put my other foot down, and was about halfway through a crude pitch-out when I realized there were two big goons with pistols in the doorway. They raised the pistols, staring at me; I held the bomb in front of me, and said, "Dynamite," with as much control in my voice as I could manage.

Their eyes got wider, but their pistols didn't move. I began to walk very slowly toward them, and said, still keeping my voice level and slow so that they would understand what I was saying, "I don't understand the fuse on this thing. It may have a clock inside, or go off when it is bumped." On my third step I was pushing the bomb toward the point where their shoulders overlapped. If they had wanted to take it from me, I'd have let them, but they backed out the doorway.

Out of the blazing heat and red light of the boiler room, the air rushing out around us making yet more fog, we must have looked like three shadows in a complex dance. I had lost my night vision from my time in the boiler room, and I was stumbling just a little, taking short steps and trying not to fall in the sudden dim, blue fog. My hands were hurting incredibly, and I knew that the cylinder was burning them; if that had been a modern high-pressure boiler, I'd have had third-degree burns if I didn't just lose my hands, but fortunately a wood-fired low-pressure boiler doesn't get much above the boiling point. It was merely like grabbing a pot of boiling water off a stove with your bare hands and then slowly walking twenty feet with it.

I knew I wasn't far from the aft rail, anyway, and as I continued toward the two big guys, they parted before me, and when they slid sideways to be out of my way, that told me about where the rail had to be.

This time there was nothing to prevent my pitch-out; the cylinder rose over the railing in the smeary, gray-red light, etched against the fog, faded and blurred in outline, and was gone into the fog; an instant later there was a splash.

I turned to face my captors, holding my hands over my head. I could feel my hands stinging in the salt spray, and I didn't want to think about what that indicated; I would have to give myself one of my two remaining injections of nanos to heal that, and I wasn't at all sure, offhand, whether the kit with those was in my pocket, where I hoped it was, or in my bag—which was god knows where.

The two men closed in gingerly, and one said, "You would be the Mark Strang wanted in Boston for wanton murder?"

"I am in fact his twin brother, Ajax Strang," I said, "but I know how much like a lie that sounds, and you might as well take me in, for I'm sure I'll have to prove it in front of a judge sooner or later."

"And was it your brother who murdered Dr. Warren and Steward Little?"

"It was."

"And the engineers?"

"Yes."

"And where is he now?"

"His clothes are beside the railing back there," I said, "and I can only assume that he has gone over the side and swum for Long Island. It's very cold, but if he has confederates ashore—and I am all but certain that he does—he can probably live to tell of it."

"Mr. Strang," the shorter one said, "since you have already said you don't expect us to believe you, I will only say that of course we don't. If you'll please keep your hands up, sir, then we can—"

The light was so bright, even through the fog, that my first thought was that lightning had hit, and my second was of a nuclear bomb. I was facing away from it when suddenly the fog flashed in my eyes, and it made my eyes hurt and my head ache; the men facing me were facing the light, and they were temporarily blinded.

I guess that was why they didn't shoot me when I flung myself to the deck on my stomach, ignoring the agony of my burned hands slamming onto the hard surface. The truth was that I wasn't thinking at all; I just knew something really bad was about to happen.

In the time we had been talking, the *John Locke* had gotten more than a mile from the point in the Long Island Sound where I had heaved the bomb overboard. Sound travels at twelve miles per minute, or about a mile every five seconds; I had a long breath or so, there on the deck, to listen to the screams of fear and pain from those who had been awake and looking the wrong way, to watch the boots of the men who had arrested me take a few aimless pain-filled steps around on the deck, and to feel the swollen agony of my hands on the rough, cold, salty deck. I even had time to say to myself that at any moment the sound would come and that I had better get my hands over my ears to prevent ruptured eardrums.

I felt my elbows begin to press on the deck to move my hands to my ears—

I had forgotten that sound travels much faster in water, the concussive effect from an explosion is nothing but a giant shock wave. The deck below me slammed up into me with terrible force; it felt like being pressed against a door that was being taken down with a headache ball, like being a mouse flung into the air by some sadistic kid and then hit like a ball with a baseball bat.

There was a long dark second of knowing nothing, and then it was terribly, unbelievably cold, and I couldn't breathe. With all my strength I lashed out in all directions, but things were holding me, my movements were dreadfully slow, and—

My hand broke out of the water over my head, and I realized I was floating, with a big bubble of air between my shoulder blades trapped under my coat. I stroked down with my arms and raised my head, just like they teach you in Boy Scout swimming classes, and sucked in a big gulp of icy air. It was wonderful stuff, even though it set me coughing, so that it was three or four more bobs upward before I got my breath for good.

Even in that short time I had become so cold that my arms and legs were numb, but I managed to tread water and, using my stiff, burned hands, get my pants off. Fortunately they were just knee breeches and two hard yanks were enough to tear out the buttons near the knees, though it skinned my already burned hands under the salt water, and I came close to fainting. With one more yank I got the belt off, and with another the pants came down. It took forever to knot the legs into a loop—maybe a whole minute or so— but then I was able, with a hard kick in my treading water, to whip the tied breeches over my head, filling them with air, pull the open waist down into the water, and stick my head between the tied legs. The pants inflated beautifully, another thing that worked just like in Boy Scout camp, and now besides the air in my coat I was being held up by the air-filled "collar" formed by my pants.

That meant it no longer took any muscular effort to keep my head out of the water. I began to kick, slowly, looking up often, trying to make for the black bulk of Long Island by the shortest way I could, though in truth from my position, with my eyes only inches above the water, I could only see that some parts of the horizon had a dark band of land above them, and not which of those was closer. I had not kept any sense of direction between the explosion and finding myself in the water.

I figured that two thousand strokes of my legs ought to bring me to land if I kept pointed in the right direction, and so I started kicking, resolving to count to three thousand before pausing to take stock. This was not a good time to start the kind of thinking that leads to seeing the world as futile, let alone for noticing that if there are billions of timelines and hundreds of millions of galaxies in every one of them, one life doesn't matter much, and I was cold and tired, and that my hands really hurt. Pain kills endurance—that's why in collision and combat sports you try to land some blows on your opponent even if those blows couldn't be effective enough to win, just so that the poor bastard gets tired faster.

Two hundred and fifty strokes later the shore was about where it had been, my hands hurt more, and my legs were beginning to ache. I shifted to a sidestroke kick and kept going. Do this twelve more times and then think about it. Jeez, the water was cold . . . good thing I was in shape, but even so I could easily have had a heart attack hitting this stuff at this time of year. . . .

The night had finally turned clear, or maybe the shore breeze was tearing the fog away. The moon was incredibly bright, with no competition from the ground, and the stars seemed to blaze rather than twinkle. It was dark enough so that I could see the colors of the stars easily . . . so nice and dark, and now that I was keeping a steady beat going with the sidestroke, I was warming up quite a bit. I could almost just go to sleep in the nice water for a bit.

What was the count? I thought I had counted six hundred a while back, but maybe it was only five, or then again perhaps I'd missed a hundred a couple of times and it might be a thousand. How could you keep track when it was so boring? At least it was . . .

Warm.

There are three major warning signs for hypothermia. You stop feeling cold. You stop being able to concentrate on even simple, important tasks. And you have an overpowering desire to sleep.

And once you do, you never wake up.

Really, I was doing pretty well; during World War II a lot of men died of hypothermia in less than ten minutes in the cold water of the North Atlantic, and I'd probably hung on for half an hour or so, so far, and I wasn't really beaten yet, just tired—

Back when I was a kid my brother Jerry and I used to go see movies about World War II every chance we got. That was before Jerry was killed, of course, but then he'd been out of college a year or two before . . .

He was killed with Mom and my wife Marie. I remembered it vividly; I was so tired, and if I dreamed of that, I'd have nightmares, I knew I would even though I was so comfortable . . . so comfortable even in the cold water of the North Atlantic where my ship had gone down but Humphrey Bogart would be coming along any minute in the rubber raft with some hot soup for me . . . or was it Katharine Hepburn? Or would he have Katharine Hepburn for me?

That made me laugh so hard that I sucked in what felt like half a lungful of water, which set me to retching and coughing. The blast of pain in my chest and the heaving of my guts brought me back to consciousness enough to realize how much I had drifted. I was back in the real world, even if not very coherent. There's something about getting close to dying, and realizing it, that brings you right around, if you're not completely gone.

Had I been kicking? I didn't know and began to kick harder to try to make back the time—that wasn't right, I knew it wasn't right, I'd tire myself out but I couldn't think—

I churned onward; maybe the effort could raise enough heat to ward off the last stages of hypothermia, and at least this way if I sank, I would go down fighting. I avoided thinking about Dad, Carrie, Porter . . . about Chrys . . . about warm beds and big bowls of hot cereal and soup . . . there were an awful lot of thoughts to fight off, when you came right down to it.

My left foot felt like it burst into flames, so much so that I yelled, and it set me to coughing again, and in the convulsion whatever had gotten my left foot promptly got my right, and now both of them were in agony. I doubled over an instant, putting my head all the way underwater, and the diving reflex cut in and panicked me, groggy as I was, so that I lurched wildly, thrashed frantically, and then stood up to get a breath . . .

I had coughed and spewed half a dozen times, getting the last of all that out of myself, before I realized. I was standing in chest-deep water, and only two hundred yards off there was a stony beach with pine trees behind it. I lurched forward in the water, stumbling over submerged logs and boulders, and finally staggered up onto the gravel, my pants deflating around my neck as I came out of the water. I made myself keep going—I needed food, shelter, something—and just beyond the trees I found a winding wagon track, probably leading to some farm or small town.

It was a warm night, and now that I was out of the water, shivering and walking were doing some good.

How long I staggered, I don't know, but the sun was up when I finally came around a bend and found myself looking at a fallen-in barn and an empty house. There was at least a roof on the house, and I staggered in and found a corner with a big pile of leaves in it, reasonably dry.

Finally I allowed my burned, peeled, bloody hands to fight into the pocket of the breeches and find one of my two remaining ampoules of nanos. I jammed it in my arm and lay back, panting; they would rebuild me, but they took so much energy from the body that I had been afraid that while I was moving they might make me collapse, and even now I was afraid they would be the final push into hypothermia and death.

Something came into the room; my vision was getting dark though there was bright sunlight pouring in through the door. It got closer and I leaned down to see. . . .

I was down on my chest, I realized, face-to-face with a live chicken. It had black feathers and a red comb, and it was turning its head from side to side and clucking a little, now and then, wondering if it remembered people or not, and perhaps thinking that people used to put out corn for it. I reached very slowly forward—I doubt I could have done anything quickly—and it came a step closer to see if maybe I was about to throw the corn. The expression of stupid curiosity, of being focused only on the hand as maybe something to feed it, might have made me laugh if I'd had the energy.

There was a practical difficulty or two to consider, I realized, as I grabbed the chicken by the neck. I could make a fire but not trust myself to tend one, and the field-butchering lessons from training school were kind of hazy in my mind, and anyway I didn't have hours to pluck it—

And then the one important thing I needed to remember from training school kicked in. The nanos in my bloodstream would last about twenty hours. During that time if I were cut, the wound would close up within hours, and if I became infected with anything, the infection would quickly die out. It was like having a superñimmune system, though paid for at a huge cost in body energy. But right now, with the nanos fresh in my bloodstream, I could drink out of sewers, eat roadkill, and lick every used bedpan in a hospital, and nothing would happen to me—

The thought is father to the deed. My hands clenched once and broke its neck, and after that I don't remember much, or at least I prefer not to remember much. I woke up late in the afternoon with the sun going down, blood and feathers all over my face, and an amazing mess of discarded bones, feathers, beak, and feet scattered around. I seemed to have lost five pounds, which I figured was probably the body consuming whatever it didn't get from the chicken. I yanked the now half-dry breeches on and staggered out into the yard.

There was still a bucket in the well, so I cranked it down and up—it was work but not difficult. My hands were covered with new pink skin and quite a few other places seemed to be fresh and healthy new flesh as well; I noticed that some of my fingernails had grown an inch during the night, probably the places where I'd hurt a fingertip or cuticle, and when I looked down at my feet I saw that not only were all my toenails really long, but apparently the nanos had sensed that I needed calluses there, and I had the kind of hard, horny feet you get from going barefoot in all weather, though again all the flesh was pink and new.

When the bucket reached the top, before I quite took a drink, I caught sight of my reflection. There were still blood smears everywhere, and a feather or two that I hadn't brushed off. My hair was a tangled, uncombable mess, and where the nanos had rebuilt skin on my face they had also caused big tufts of whiskers to grow out. And I was so happy to be alive, and feeling well, that I was grinning like a complete idiot.

"That's *Mister* Geek to you," I told my reflection.

·9·

It wasn't so much knowing how to get to New York that was the problem—after all, I was on Long Island, on the side facing the Sound, with the water a scant few hundred yards off. All I had to do was face the water, turn left, start walking, and keep walking.

My guess was that the *John Locke* had blown up at about 3:45 in the morning, local time, and since it was due into port at about 5:30 A.M., I was probably thirty miles, as the crow flew, from Manhattan, which was all there was of New York at the time—the whole settled area was what's just Lower Manhattan today, Greenwich was not only still a village, but it was separated from town by farms, and the other boroughs were pretty much farmland and little villages. According to the information they'd dumped into me, in this timeline Boston was not only still the biggest city in the Thirteen Colonies, but would stay bigger longer. The faster things grow, the more they concentrate near pre-existing sites, and thus it would probably not be until the middle of the next century that New York would become America's largest city.

All of which meant that there weren't going to be any buses or trains along soon, and even when I got to Brooklyn I would probably have to wait a while for a ferry.

That put me in mind of another problem, and I checked my coat pocket. I still had the purse of silver and copper coins, and there was enough in there to get me food, lodging, and a ferry if I was careful. It would be nice to afford new boots as well, but maybe Morris would be able to lend me a pair or to extend a loan . . .

It did seem pretty bizarre that with the resources of almost two million Earths, the ATN was borrowing petty cash from private citizens. Maybe I could do something to get everyone reimbursed. . . .

If your feet have ever been in shape for barefoot walking, you know there's still a limit to how much of it you can do. After seven or eight miles, I was getting footsore and, moreover, skirting around villages was getting to be a hassle. I figured I was far enough away, and my clothes were at least dry, so that people wouldn't immediately wonder if I'd been on the *Locke*.

I was in luck; the next place along the road, a little tavern called the Dog and Pony, had fresh bread and sausage and decent beer for not too much, and was willing enough to let a traveler sleep in the yard for part of the afternoon. I got fed and rested, borrowed a scissors, and trimmed my nails. For a copper coin I rented a basin and razor and made myself all but presentable; if I had just had shoes and stockings, I might merely look like I needed new clothes.

The owner was a little surly guy who didn't seem to have the slightest curiosity about me; as I finished another beer for the road, and was tucking some bread, cheese, and sausage into one of the coat's big pockets for later, though, he asked, "You'll be going up to New York Island, then?"

"I will," I said. "I've friends with money up there."

"If you don't mind working your way, the stage is coming, and I know they'll have need for a porter; bunch of folks swum to shore up the coast after the boiler blew on that *John Locke* yesterday, and the money to pay the passage for the rich folks just went by t'other way this morning. I know Fat Richard that drives the stage is short a porter-boy, for his usual one broke an ankle, and with so many well-off folks, even if not much floated to the shore, there's bound to be need for a porter-boy coming back, especially what with some of them bound to be injured."

"That's a great opportunity," I said. "How soon do you expect him?"

"I expected Fat Richard an hour ago. That means he either broke a wheel and won't be here today, or more likely he was held up getting all the quality-folk"—he said *quality-folk* the way my father used to say *terrorists*—"into that stage, with them all fussing and some of them hurt and wanting special arrangements."

I nodded. "So it might be worth waiting around for an hour."

"Aye. And if you'd like to dig up a potato bed for me, I have an old pair of boots you might have for it, that I think would fit you."

We checked, the boots fit, and I got to work on that stony patch of ground. One nice thing about the times, there was no paperwork to fill out, and if you weren't fussy, there was at least some kind of work. I remembered reading that it was only after the Civil War that it could be proved that anyone ever starved to death during an economic depression in America; before that the countryside was always close, and most people could do enough work to get themselves a space in the barn and a little food.

When the stage pulled up it was the silliest-looking contraption I'd ever seen. Luc had introduced vulcanized rubber to this timeline a while back, so it had inflated tires with wooden spokes, like what you see on old Ford Model T's in our timeline. That meant a lot of the shock from the bumpy, rutted road was being taken up by the undercarriage, and to make that work in turn there was an elaborate double system of springs, much more complex than on any old-movie stagecoach, with individually pivoting and counter-weighted arms rather than axles. So from the wheels up through the suspension it looked like a moon buggy.

Above that it got weird. The passenger compartment was small and looked like it was about half the size it should have been for the wheelbase; it was shaped like a can of ham lying on its side, and held on to that silly suspension with a system of guy wires, as far as I could tell.

In front of this thing was what looked, more than anything else, like a bicycle built for four, or two bicycles built for two welded together side by side, in which each front cyclist pedaled the front wheel directly, like the way a kid's tricycle works, and each back cyclist pedaled the back wheel directly. All four of them sat way back, so that the rear cyclists had their heads only a couple of feet from the front of the stagecoach behind them.

Or, I realized, three cyclists. The rear seat opposite me wasn't taken. And just as abruptly I realized what the other duty of a porter-boy must be. Well, I didn't mind working, and it beat walking for speed if not for ease.

A few minutes later introductions got made. The guy on the

left front was Richard, "driver, captain, and company man," as he described himself. He was fat only by comparison with the other two, and I'd actually have said he was just muscular. I suppose it's all relative.

I sat behind him. The one who sat on his right was Abel, the guard, who had a short carbine strapped over his shoulder and a pistol at his belt. To my right was Seth, the conductor, who grinned at me as we got onto the seats; there had been the minor task of carrying one man with a broken, splinted leg to the outhouse and back, but there was no one getting on or off at the Dog and Pony, so I didn't have to load any additional bags.

"It's a clever porter that signs on where the guests have lost their luggage," Seth said.

I smiled back at him. "Except for some work on my legs, I think of this as a free ride."

"Wait till we climb that hill down yonder, from Whitstown to Flushing. That's when you'll see how free this was!"

I nodded and laughed, and then the driver said, "All right, now, gentlemen . . . we're all introduced, our passengers are all aboard . . . now, porter-boy, Strang, have y'ever did this here before?"

"Not at all."

"Right, then you're as fitted to the work as Abel here and better than Seth, for him's learned it wrong. Y'see where my left foot is here?"

"Yes, sir."

"Well, now you see where your own is. And see that your own comes back to that place when mine comes back. Not just afore, not just after, and not pritnear, and if y'do get it wrong—and ye will, ye will, ye've these two t'show you how to get it wrong—don't you try to catch it up, but take your new mark and mind you keep it where it is."

"Got it, sir."

"But will y'do it?"

"I'll try."

"That's what I was afraid of hearing, ye're just like the others."

"We ain't moving at all while we talk, Richard," Seth said.

"True enough. And . . . one, two, *stroke*."

If you've ever ridden a bicycle built for two, you've got an idea of what this is like; your legs work pretty hard and it takes a while to get in sync so that you're pushing forward but not doing all the pushing. This was both easier and harder—harder to stay on Richard's beat, but much easier to tell when you were off it. In half a mile or so, I wasn't exactly an old hand, and I could tell my muscles would complain later, but I was pulling my own weight and then some, and we were clipping along at something like four miles an hour or better.

The other men settled into the rhythm comfortably, once it became clear I wasn't going to be impossible, and soon we were bouncing along that dirt road, the little scoop seat at my back thumping my butt, the pedals pushing against my legs but not painfully hard. I could probably, if I'd had a decent pair of running shoes, have run the distance in a bit less time, with maybe a little less overall effort, but it was interesting, anyway, to see the little villages roll by and to swing by the occasional farmer out doing his spring plowing.

I even saw one steam tractor, an immense chugging thing that slowly crawled across the field on big steel rims, which got everyone talking for half an hour; Seth and Richard were very much in agreement that it was the wave of the future, that with steam you could plow deeper and faster, and so forth, but Abel inclined to the view that the horse was cheaper, oats grew faster than wood, steam tractors did not make more steam tractors, and anyway no one had proved to him that plowing deeper really brought that much more wheat.

"You've all got strong views on it," I noted. "Are you all from farming families?"

"Aye, each of us," Seth said. "Alike as can be in that way. We're all third or fourth sons, there was no more land to take us, and the frontier is a long way away. Oh, we dream about it, but mostly we work. The pay's good, and the Flushing Line is a good outfit, you know, and so it's not so easy to decide to pack it all up and head for Ohio or Kentucky. Nothing keeping us here but decent pay, but that's a lot, especially when a man's got a family."

In my timeline, there had been almost no settlements across the mountains yet, and many people who weren't in line to inherit a farm had been angry about the frontier being closed to them. It occurred to me that even after the Revolution, only a tiny minority of people had ever packed up from settled regions and moved west; the only difference in this timeline—but it made a big difference in terms of peace and quiet!—was that the normal force of family and community, and not the authority of the state, was perceived as holding people back.

I wondered what was happening to the Indian nations, and whether they'd get any better deal out of it this time. Supposedly there were going to be treaties of alliance and development and all that, but the fact was ATN was in a war, they wanted timelines to develop fast economically and technically because more sophisticated timelines made better allies, and people who just wanted to live the way they had been living tended to get stomped flat.

We claimed we had allies who had joined ATN while still in the Stone Age, but the truth was that once we found them, they didn't stay Stone Age long. And even now teams were jumping farther and farther back into the past, despite the enormous expense, to get industrial civilization going earlier and earlier in more and more timelines, and thus to create allies who were ever more advanced in science and technology up at the 2700s A.D., where the fighting was going on.

That meant that if you were, say, a Polynesian in 800 A.D., in any of billions of timelines, with hardly any risk at all that the Closers would attack your timeline in your lifetime . . . you were not necessarily made better off when ATN agents showed up and leapfrogged Japan into the Industrial Revolution, bringing steamships out to the South Pacific hundreds of years early. Very likely you died of disease, or you quite possibly got shot by not-yet-fully-culturally-sensitive Japanese, or failing all that, anyway, a pleasant life went out the window.

I wondered just how much good we actually did . . .

I also wondered why I was having such thoughts. I figured it must be partly having the luxury for thought—these were not guys who talked a lot unless there was something to talk about, the work was repetitive and strenuous but not killing if you were in shape, and so I had my mind and eyes free. It was a nice spring day, and those are the best kinds of days to be outside with nothing to think about that has any immediate relevance.

The villages were getting larger as we got farther south and west, and the country was more settled. In a little while we had reached the point where there were no more woods between the farms, as such, just one farm after another shading into villages and back to farmland, and the road was actually a little crowded—that is, there were people, wagons, pedal stages like ours, and so forth in sight all the time. I took a deep breath at that; it occurred to me that my counterpart was out there somewhere, and that given that he was me he'd not believe I was dead until he saw the body. Therefore, he'd be looking for me, just as I was for him, and whichever of us saw the other first would have the advantage.

The hill outside Whitstown, leading up to Flushing, was everything Seth had implied it would be. When you push a wheel directly with pedals, if there's any resistance at all, the resistance has all the leverage. For my own sour amusement I started to figure it out. . . . The stage behind us probably weighed 1500 pounds loaded, we and the pedal gadget probably 850, and on a 5 percent grade like this that worked out to probably (near as made no difference) a backward drag of maybe 120 pounds. Okay, so each of us has one foot pushing at any given time, thirty pounds against the foot—except the wheel multiplies it. If the pedal radius was about half the wheel radius, that would come to—

"I worked it out once," Seth said, "and I make it that we're pushing sixty pounds on a stroke."

Well, he'd had more than one chance to do this, I thought to myself. Richard said, "Just hold your stroke as even as you can; this part is where ye earn your pay. And remember at least ye won't get pedal-kicked as we do comin' down."

The push went on for quite a while, but there was a reward I wasn't expecting at the top of it; I had wondered why everyone was emphasizing getting to Flushing, and I hadn't realized that it was the end of the line. As we neared the top I saw that the woodsmoke marking the clear spring sky was not from a village, but from a power plant, and that there was a traction line starting from here.

I still had all the bag unloading to do, but all it was was work, and Seth, as conductor, helped a little. Besides, a coach full of shipwreck victims doesn't have a lot of bags and certainly doesn't have anything very heavy.

The passengers inside the coach were pretty quiet—not surprisingly, since I'm sure many of them were still in shock. Three were injured badly enough to need carrying, and that was the toughest part of the job, not so much for the weight as the caution I had to put into it.

"You're good with the public," Seth observed. "Stick with work like this, and you might make conductor some day—though it's not so easy as it looks."

I grinned. "I've other business, but it's good to know I could take this up. Though I doubt I'd make conductor quickly—it looks like there's a lot to learn." No matter where you go or when you go, you'll never give offense by telling a guy his job looks difficult.

"Well, that's what Richard told me when I was a porter-boy and he was a conductor," Seth said, grinning. "Good luck wherever you're bound."

By now it was almost dark, but there was still a seat on a passenger car just starting out on the traction line, so I rolled into Brooklyn that evening just as it got dark. A quick walk down by the wharf assured me that the ferry would start again at first light and told me how much cash I had to hang on to to get across to Manhattan; there was enough left for a bed and two meals at a tavern nearby, though if I'd had anything worth stealing that I couldn't keep under me, I'd have thought a long time before staying there. As it was, the fleas attacked pretty fiercely at first, but I was so tired that it didn't matter to me, until morning anyway.

Breakfast was a big bowl of boiled potatoes and beef, plus all the corn bread I could cram in, which was quite a bit—the nanos had presumably expired, but I was still paying back the energy they had consumed.

It was chilly and gray but not raining when I walked down to the wharf and caught the ferry. The East River was as gray and flat as the sky, and there was no wind this morning, so we went over pretty quickly. Less than four hours after I'd gotten up, right about midmorning, I was on the wharf in Manhattan, completely broke and knowing only Morris's address. It was even less impressive than my entrance into Boston. I hated to imagine what arriving in London would be like.

Well, nothing much to do for it; Morris, like most of the rich people, lived up higher and away from the water, so I started the short walk from the wharf up French Church Street to Broadway. There was more brick and stone than in Boston, and in general everything had an air of comfortable prosperity; I remembered that in my timeline Thomas Paine had said that the British moved the war to the Middle Colonies because there were more Tories there, and there were more Tories there because more men had more to lose. I could believe it, looking around me; here were thriving businesses, big new houses, all the signs of growing wealth in a city, and a lot fewer beggars than you would see on the same streets in my timeline. Hardly anything makes a city more attractive than enough work for everybody . . . I hoped that the progress we had created here would at least continue to provide that much.

The only problem with all this was that I was still broke and ragged.

I had just rounded the corner onto Broadway—and that was really a surprise, for Broadway at the time was a wide, tree-lined mall, thick with elms and chestnuts just budding out—when something caught my eye, and I quietly slipped over toward the trees and the traffic on my right to get a good look without being seen.

Sure enough, there I was again . . . it was my double, this time getting into a cab a block away, headed the other way on Broadway from where I was going.

Instantly I was turned around and headed for the wharf again; I wanted to know where he was going and what he was up to. Besides, I was fairly sure that he had not yet spotted me, and one of the best ways not to be spotted is to be behind the guy, not in front of him . . . if I didn't let him go, then he couldn't surprise me later.

I could have saved myself most of the walk; he finally arrived at the Exchange, at the foot of Broad Street, not three blocks from where I'd gotten off the Brooklyn Ferry. He didn't stop there, however, but turned to the left and headed for the wharves.

I had little trouble following him in the crowd, for his one-horse cab had actually moved more slowly than I could walk in the crowded streets, and there were so many people down around the markets that it wasn't difficult to stay concealed. Even after he got out of the cab, I wasn't afraid of losing him, because he was making such a direct path through the crowded market stalls and down to the wharf that there was kind of a cloud of disturbance around him—he seemed to have no problem with just shoving people out of his way.

When he reached the wharf, he headed straight for one big, modern liner, and I realized I was about to have a major problem here—its stacks were already puffing smoke as she built up a head of steam, and from the look of the tides coming over, I guessed they'd be sailing about noon.

The liner was the *Royal Hanover*, and it was another strange contraption, a product of the way that Rey Luc had goosed the technology of this timeline along. There were four tall, thin stacks that looked more like the stacks of a Mark Twain–kind of riverboat to me than anything for an ocean liner. Each of the stacks had two wooden masts running parallel to it, a scant foot or two away; presumably those held up the stacks in high winds, since they were all bolted together, but just as obviously they could be used for rigging sails in the event of an emergency.

The *Royal Hanover* had what was pretty clearly a hybrid between paddle wheels and screws; probably the better metals developed so far weren't available in quantity enough to make drive shafts that wouldn't buckle under the load, so it wasn't possible to just put a bladed propeller on the back. But paddle wheels are pretty inefficient in that you're moving most of the wheel out of the water most of the time. So they had compromised by putting a huge cone-shaped wooden screw on the stern, with hundreds of slender wooden blades arranged like a shallow spiral staircase.

The whole ship had been hung with so many fake columns and pilasters that it looked like a storage room at a theater where they did a lot of the Greek tragedies.

And, from my standpoint, the most notable feature was that there was a man at the gangplank checking tickets and signing people in. The ship would probably depart within three hours, and when it did, there went my best chance to track my doppelgänger—not to mention that he would get a head start of several days in London. I didn't even know if there were any more berths available on the *Royal Hanover* . . .

I had just about figured that out, and sidled up one little alley while doing it, when I saw the other Mark Strang come down off the ship again. He checked a pocket watch and talked with the guy taking tickets, then set off in a considerable hurry—probably getting some last-minute thing for the trip, or maybe just finding a quiet corner to send a message back to his superiors in one of the Closer timelines.

I watched him go, and a thought dawned on me—a beautifully simple thought. I wanted to be on that ship. And there was no problem at all with that, because I already *was* on that ship.

I let another five minutes go by, to make this convincing, hoping desperately that he wouldn't turn out to have gone somewhere a block away and already be coming back. Luck was with me for once, so when the five minutes had passed, I strolled up the gang-plank.

The ticket taker, of course, took one look at a man in a ragged coat and breeches, ruined shirt, no hose, and obviously old and worn boots, and got ready to heave me back down the gangplank. I walked up very close to him, and then said, "Do you recognize me?"

He stared for a long minute, and then said, "Mr. Strang, is it? What on Earth are you doing in them clothes, sir?"

"Keep your voice down," I said, keeping mine very low. "You know I'm a Customs agent, of course, but in fact I also do His Majesty's business"—and I dropped my voice very low—"as a mumble mumble rhubarb. Lord Harumph takes an interest in these matters, you might say."

He nodded and laid a finger beside his nose. "Ah. We carry many such passengers lately."

"I'll warrant you do. Well, I shall be coming on and off a few more times in the next few hours. Most of the time you will not see me—believe me, sir, I am good enough at my trade for that!—but should it happen that you do see me, it would be a very good thing for your King and country if you did *not*, if you take my meaning; just, er, wave me through, if you could. I just wanted to make sure you had a good look at my face so that you could—"

"Recognize without questioning. Of course, sir, go right aboard and do whatever you need do. But we still do sail at 12:15 sharp, sir, so make sure you're aboard."

"I shall certainly make sure I'm aboard," I agreed. "Thank you so much for your understanding."

"Er, for that matter," he added, "I should assume then that you have means a bit, er, beyond those of your occupation?"

"You may assume it."

"Well, then, sir, I shan't worry about the deposit you've put into ship's safe; just see that a man comes round to pay the *Hanover* when we make port, and see that he, er—"

"Is able to compensate you for your trouble and assistance. Very well, and thank you!"

Not only had I gotten aboard, I had just opened an unlimited credit account with the bad guy's name on it. I was pretty proud of myself.

It took no more than ten minutes to find a good, out-of-the-way corner and get to sleep under a pile of canvas there. With any luck at all they wouldn't be using the sails this voyage—this might make a good place to sleep for several days.

I stayed down there, getting hungry but being cautious, until long after I had felt the ship start to move.

·10·

It was late afternoon when I finally let myself emerge on deck, and I was careful to come up slowly. Unfortunately, I couldn't very well ask, "Has anyone seen me around? Where am I?" and I really did not want to meet myself—not yet, anyway. I had had some time, besides sleeping, to do some thinking, and I had a better idea of what I wanted and needed to do to get the mission accomplished.

In the first place, there *had* to be something that the Closers had done besides just dispatch my counterpart to stir up trouble in Boston. I mean, I'm a bright, talented guy and all that—who should know better?—but I am *not* Superman, and this guy was exactly as capable as I was, but not any more capable. He couldn't possibly have created a situation teetering on the brink of war just by covertly financing a few hotheads on both sides, stirring up hatred here and there, and that sort of thing. That's a harassing action, not the main process.

Moreover, I'm not a subtle guy, the Closers are noted for liking brute force, and yet somehow whatever was being done was being done invisibly. . . .

That meant the Closers had somebody a lot more subtle and shrewd than I am on the case, and most likely that person was in London. So almost for sure the other Mark Strang would be going there to meet him.

Now, that left me three options. The first one appealed to me because it was action and it was simple: kill my alter before he got to London and take his place at the rendezvous, then play it by ear and try to penetrate the Closer operation that was probably active there. Easy to do, and I'd supply my own alibi doing it; as soon as the body was over the side and out of sight, there would be no evidence that anything wrong had happened.

Two, stick close to my alter, spy on him, follow him, and eventually figure out what was up; then use the knowledge when I got to London. That other Strang might even get away, though I kind of hoped not; he was pretty clearly not the biggest fish in this particular pond anyway. That was the prudent and intelligent thing to do.

The third thought, which I kept pushing to the back of my mind, was this: the Mark Strang they had looked so much like me, and had so many features in common with me, that he could not have been from a timeline at all far from my own. Chances were that he and I shared a lot of background, and that meant perhaps that we shared many values.

It was far too much of a gamble, but in principle—after all, a Crux Op on mission is only evaluated by results, not by how he gets them, I told myself, and then had to shove the thought away, but it kept coming back.

In principle it might be possible to turn that "other me" to our side. He could not be so very different from me, and if he was not, then his heart should go to the ATN, as mine had.

Just where that piece of lunacy was getting into my brain from, I really could not say. My best guess was that I was thinking of the many discussions of values that Chrys and I had had in our letters; her timeline believed in changes of heart very deeply, and many of their favorite stories and plays had villains who reformed at the last moment, usually for the sake of sheer pity. I thought those were lovely fairy tales. . . . but then she thought our stories, in which violence finally settles the question, were naive because violence usually just means more violence.

If I could win by changing his heart, it would please Chrysamen a great deal.

I suppose if I'd been stuck with him on a desert island or something, with no clock running and without so many lives at stake, I might have considered it or even given it a try. After all, it couldn't hurt that much to try. . . .

But there was just too much at risk. And the fact was that I hated Closers, hated them for all that they had done, and to see a version of myself working for them was altogether too much. Whatever might please Chrys, if it were just up to me, I'd have already fed my doppelgänger to the fish, and if I'd been able to put him in alive, and watch a group of small sharks gradually consume him, I'd have stood there laughing with glee while I watched.

So, since there was that idea I couldn't get rid of, which seemed dumb, and the thing I wanted to do, which seemed rash . . . and the most prudent course—I decided to go with the most prudent. I would let him live, spy on him, and see what I could learn.

And *then* maybe if I was lucky, I would feed him to the fish.

So when I came up on deck, I was mentally prepared for the worst possible case—I'd pop out and he'd see me—but no such thing happened. I had noticed, and had heard from some of the men in Boston, that my counterpart was a little more decadent than I, had more of a taste for liquor and fine food, gambled with more enthusiasm, and so on. Warren had assured me he had a reputation as a "whoremaster," which is what the eighteenth century, with its keen sense of calling things by their right name, called what we call a "stud."

On the other hand, unlike me, he hadn't shown much interest in books or etchings or anything of the sort. Boston at the time should have been a spectacular place for finding all sorts of Early American crafts and arts—after all, Paul Revere wasn't being distracted so much by politics and was getting to concentrate more on his silversmithing—and if I had been stationed there on a long-term basis, my house would have been full of such things. This version of myself, though, seemed to own neither art nor books.

So I figured with nothing much else to do on shipboard, and not being all that good at entertaining himself, my counterpart would probably be attending the "rum and gambling in the forward saloon" that was scheduled. Meanwhile, there was a great big tea in the rear saloon—and in the fine old British tradition that would mean a full-fledged buffet meal.

I filled my plate four times, leaving it on my counterpart's bill, and each time crouched in the corner, looking as crazed as I could manage, and wolfed it down. It wasn't so much a matter of having lost my manners, though I was hungry enough not to be too fussy, as not wanting anyone to look too closely and perhaps later ask my counterpart how he had changed his clothing or his behavior so quickly.

At any rate, the mutton sausage, corn bread, and sweet cakes were all quite good, and I managed to slip a lot of the last plateful into my pockets for future reference.

Since the afternoon was very fine, and I suspected my other self of being the kind that did not come out till dark, I let myself enjoy a brief view of sunset from the stern. It was cold out there, and I was still pretty ragged, but it was nice to get a breath of fresh air, and once you're out of sight of land the sea is about the most restful thing human beings have ever found to look at, even when it's wild; a lot of the Romantic painters were fond of it for just that reason, and standing here on the rolling deck, realizing that some of those painters had already been born, I found myself hoping that this timeline would still have its Romantic period.

I had just decided that I had best get back below-decks when the steward came by and exchanged glances with me; then he smiled and said, "Sir, I might mention that if you want to be inconspicuous here, your dress as a beggar is a giveaway. No man dressed as yourself could afford to be aboard . . ."

I nodded. "Unfortunately it's the only disguise I was able to bring with me from the city."

"I might arrange something; several of our sailors are tailors as well, you know, for on long voyages there must be such, and they draw a bit of extra pay for it. I could look about and see if someone might be found to make you another set of clothes . . . something to conceal your appearance, so that you did not look yourself."

"It's a magnificent idea," I said, and I had to admit it was. The steward was undoubtedly going to mark up the price by several hundred percent, and he knew there were deep pockets to pay the bill. "But the tailor, or yourself, must not bring the clothes to my cabin—I have reason to believe that certain people who are no friends to the King are searching my cabin every time I am out of it. There's a pile of canvas—I believe it's the auxiliary sails—just below us here, is there not?"

"You've a sharp eye, sir."

"Sometime when you see me up and about, place the clothing just under the port, aft side of that pile." It was the farthest corner from where I was sleeping. Even if he happened to synchronize it by my doppelgänger, that should be all right. "It need be nothing fancy; indeed the main thing that would help is if it concealed my face, and looked like something a man might wear on shipboard. I should be happy to pay full price for old clothing if it got it to me the sooner."

The steward couldn't quite keep his eyes from lighting up at that point; the deal just kept getting better. "In that case, sir, I think we might well have something under there tomorrow morning."

"Absolutely splendid! Your King will be grateful!"

"If he ever hears of it, I suppose, sir. Will you want anything else?"

"Hmm. Now that you mention it . . . I will be in the forward saloon for much of this evening, dressed, er, differently from this fashion, shall we say. I would like it very much if a large gin punch—very sweet, with the gin doubled—should find its way to me. Make that two, actually . . . but only if you can find me one other thing . . ."

"Yes, sir?"

"A fellow gets lonely on these damned voyages, and the service from which I draw my pay is understanding, but not *that* understanding. Do you suppose there might be, among the women on board, someone who would like to be my companion for this evening, one who would come to me and make it appear as if she were drawn to me, and to, er, do my pleasure for the night? If you could draw on some of my private money, which is in the ship's safe, to pay for this and arrange it—so that, you see, I need not be conscious of handling money . . ."

"Why, surely, sir! I should be delighted. I've one with red hair, plump, and nice in the chest, and another that's young and just learning, very thin and dark—"

I knew my own tastes well enough to say, "Thin and dark should do it. But anyway, if it is arranged, see that she doesn't mention money, that she merely acts as if she were fascinated with my person. It's a whimsy I like to indulge."

"And a very good one, sir, and popular. I've handled such things before. Indeed if you like she can play the virgin."

"Oh, that won't be necessary. Let her be, even, a little coarse in her approach. But see that I have two of that sweet gin punch first—say it's from an admirer. Gin, you see, tends to enhance my prowess."

"It can all be as you've said, sir—"

"And naturally while you are in the safe I should expect you to take some handsome fee for services rendered and arranged. Shall we say one third of whatever the young lady gets?"

"I get that already sir, but you mean in addition?"

"I do indeed. My employer, you will see, shall make all good— as we enter port, I'll give you a note to send to them that will bring them at once to the dock with the gold required." Another thought occurred to me. "Oh—and if you'd be so kind—I have reason to believe they watch me constantly and closely when I am 'myself' and not while I am in disguise. Therefore, if you could avoid speaking of any private arrangements whatsoever when I am not in disguise—"

"Of course, sir. Very good indeed, sir, everything will be as you ask." He was bowing and scraping, and I think he was fighting the urge to rub his hands together with sheer glee.

We parted company then, and I went below to catch a nap before the night's festivities. Things were looking very strikingly up.

When it was dark above, I slipped silently back to the deck and began to do some real exploring. I needed the other Mark Strang to be out of his cabin for a while, and then I needed him to be in there and not likely to come out. Sending him a load of gin (his head was like mine, and gin goes straight to mine—and in a warm sweet punch like that he'd have no idea how much of it was hitting him), and then a hooker, ought to guarantee the latter part, and the setup ought to keep him out of his cabin long enough.

We'd learned a lot about picking locks at COTA, and this one wasn't tricky; the main protection for shipboard cabins was that you were at sea for almost three weeks, and in the event of theft they could search the whole vessel, thereby at least finding the property and quite possibly also catching the thief. Though pricier metals could be used on the lock, the technology wasn't at all far advanced; a little jiggering and the end of a knife was enough to flip a couple tumblers and let me pop the thing open.

Now, here was something strange . . . I'm a pretty neat guy, and always was except during the half year or so after half my family was blown up in front of me. It isn't so much that I try as that it comes naturally; everything tends to have a place, and it's easier to put it there than elsewhere. So I was more than a little startled to find that the little chamber was a complete and utter mess, with clothes, books, papers, and whatnot strewn everywhere, covers from the bed on the floor, and even a plate with a mostly eaten dinner on it sitting in the middle of the unmade bed. Moreover, I've never smoked—I hate the smell—and there were two overflowing ashtrays in here, along with a stale smell of tobacco. All that since just this morning? I wouldn't make a mess like that in a week.

My first thought was that I had broken into the wrong chamber, though I'd been very careful about confirming it from the passenger list . . . but no, a quick search turned up the complete giveaway—a .45 caliber Colt Model 1911A1. There weren't any of those in this timeline yet, except the one that I was wearing (which might or might not work after the swim it had had—sometime tomorrow I was going to have to strip it and clean it thoroughly, and even then I had no way of knowing how dry the cartridges had stayed), and the one my counterpart had brought with him.

That, too, seemed pretty strange. Me, I don't go anyplace, not even to the toilet—hell, especially not to the toilet, it's a classic place for a hit—without that good old piece of Army iron. If I had to jump out of a burning building and the choice was between bringing my .45 or bringing my underwear, there's no question. After all, you can shoot perfectly well without underwear.

But apparently he had gone unarmed to dinner, and was very likely getting drunk there and messing around with a girl he'd never seen before. This other Mark Strang really did not have my instinct for self-preservation.

More searching turned up a few familiar Closer weapons. There were three more of the "tomato juice cans," adjustable bombs a lot like ATN's PRAMIACs—you could set an explosive power anywhere from about "big firecracker" to "ten megatons." There was a long, thin wandlike thing with a tall sight, a bulge at the middle, and a rest that fit over the big muscle of the upper arm. I'd seen them in training; you extended the sight to eye level, gripped it by the bulge, and squeezed the bulge to fire. It hit whatever was in the sight.

It was a slightly better weapon than our SHAKK, in several

ways, and we were trying to get it reverse-engineered and improved still further.

All that I had found out so far was that I was in the right room and that my other self was a Closer agent. I had been searching thus far in the little bit of moonlight that came in through the porthole, going by feel until I found something in the mess and then holding it up to look at, but now I pulled the curtain over the porthole closed, jammed some clothing against the crack of the door, and lit a candle.

I almost gasped, but if there had been any possibility that this was the wrong room, or that the other Mark Strang was from a timeline close to mine, all the doubts were erased now. There were small hooks for pictures on the side of the room opposite the porthole, and the other Strang had used virtually every one of them, all for pictures of the same thing.

My wife, Marie.

She was the same one, and clearly he had branched off my timeline sometime after the marriage. I remembered a couple of those pictures from my own dresser drawers and albums.

It had been nine years in my subjective time since Marie had died. I had been a very different man at the time—one of those all-around guys, brainy but an athlete, too, nothing ever too difficult for me or even really hard, married to the best-

looking woman I'd ever met . . . I had been one of those guys for whom the whole world constantly goes right.

We had flown home at my father's expense, as the whole family always did, for a Fourth of July gathering at the big house by Frick Park in Pittsburgh. Marie and I, Carrie, and her twin brother Jerry were all to fly back that Sunday, so we were all getting into the van; Marie and I had only that morning broken the news to the family that Marie was pregnant.

Mom was driving, Marie got in, Jerry got in, Carrie was about to get in, Mom turned the key—

The van exploded.

The bomb was so big the van flipped over and rolled down the lawn, slamming most of the frame and floor up into the ceiling.

Carrie was flung back against me, her legs gone below the knees, one arm severed and torn to a bloody mess that was later found in the bushes.

I got my belt off and made a double-bind tourniquet for her

legs, used hers for the stump of her arm, and stopped the bleeding.
She lived, and being tough as she was, she found a way to go on.

When I finally looked up, it had been maybe twenty seconds
since the bomb had gone off.

Dad had run by me, but when I turned to follow him I fell—
somewhere in getting hit by Sis's flying body I had broken my
ankle. So as I pushed myself up off the blood-slick pavement with
my hands, I could only look toward the van, where the blast had
flipped it and rolled it down the lawn. It lay on its side, flame and
smoke pouring from it. The underside was toward me, and I could
see how it had been slammed upward, bending into the body everywhere it wasn't tied down.

Dad, forced back by the heat, was dancing around it like an
overmatched boxer, trying to find a way to the still-open side door
now on the top of the van. From where I lay, I could see it was
hopeless—the frame had been bent and jammed up into that space,
and even without the fire he couldn't have gotten anything out
through there.

He said he saw something or someone moving in there in the
long second between when he got there and when the gas tank
blew. The coroner said, though, that to judge from the shattering
of the bones that remained afterward, there was nothing alive in
there at the time; he thought Dad was probably hallucinating, or
perhaps had seen a body sliding down a seat or falling over on its
side.

Anyway, if the coroner was right, Mom was probably crushed
against the ceiling instantly; Jerry was impaled on a piece of chassis
that must have ripped up through the seat at the speed of a bullet,
entering his body somewhere near the rectum and breaking his
collarbone on the way out. His whole body cavity must have been
torn to jam before the first time the truck rolled, and the sudden
pressure loss would have meant he was unconscious before he
knew what happened.

Marie's skeleton was twisted and coiled. The coroner thought
that the whole seat had been hurled against the ceiling, fracturing
her skull, breaking vertebrae in all three dimensions, ripping both
femurs out through her leg muscles, rupturing many of her internal organs. The coroner said chances were she was dead before the
van rolled down the lawn.

But Dad saw something moving in there, just before the gas

tank blew, and if Mom and Jerry had both received unquestionably instantly fatal wounds . . . what did that leave? Hallucination, a body falling over, or . . . ?

And yet Dad said he saw something moving in the van, before it burst into flames, before it burned completely, while he danced around it trying to find out what, or who, had moved, and while I crawled miserably down the lawn, my clothes still drenched in Carrie's blood, and long before the fire trucks and rescue crews got there.

It had sent me into that very special part of hell known as severe depression. I had spent half a year doing nothing, staring bleakly, trying to wish the world away.

But I had eventually come out of it. Gone forever was the trendy, brilliant young academic I had been; I had not looked at my partly finished dissertation in art history in a long time. A chance came for me to carry a gun and get even with Blade of the Most Merciful, the Closer front that had butchered my family.

And I found that I was not the same fellow at all. There was a cold black core of glassy, frozen hate in my heart, and I took a deep pleasure in hurting the kind of people who needed hurting. Ex-husbands who beat up their wives, loons who attack singers, losers and creeps out to hurt someone famous, that sort of thing. I came to appreciate the deep, booming thud my boot could make on a deserving human rib cage.

The scar in my heart that was Marie came to me sometimes in dreams. Sometimes I thought, just for a moment, that our child would be in third grade, if Marie had lived to give birth. But the pictures of Marie were mostly off my desk, mostly out of my living quarters . . . not because I chose to forget, but because that was the past, and the past needs to be kept behind us, so that it doesn't devour the present and future before we get there.

It had taken a while, though. And part of what had helped had been when I had stumbled through the rabbit hole in time that let me find out that my real enemies, always, had been the Closers. During my time in the other timeline, when I remembered Marie, it had tended to be with a certain fond warmth—just after I had pulled the trigger on a Closer, just after another one of the self-styled Masters of all the timelines had been blown apart. I kept one picture on the wall as a remembrance and never looked at it.

This was more than just a remembrance. This was a shrine.

And in a strange way it went with the sloppiness of the room. I hadn't even bathed most of the time that I was in the deep depression after the murder. Had this version of myself had not ever really come out of the catastrophe, not learned to go on? God knew he was active enough; he had none of the depressive's inability to move. Had he lost Marie in the same way? Had he lost her at all?

It was a complete mystery, and not one I was likely to solve by standing there and staring at it, I decided.

The great thing about sloppy people is that when you toss their rooms they rarely notice. The bad thing is that often there are just a few objects—and you don't know which ones they are—that they knew the exact location of, and if you get one of those out of place and they notice, they've caught on. It's so much easier to get a neat person's place back together.

I had been pretty much around the horn of things to look at. He didn't have anything written down, but then I would not have either. I wanted to sabotage his weapons, but the only one I understood was the .45; a thought occurred to me, and I traded him my wet and probably rusting one for his clean, well-maintained one. At least he was taking care of his gun even if he wasn't making his bed. For good measure I swapped him ammo, too.

There was nothing else. It was about time to go, I figured—and then I heard my own voice. "It's over this way, so just come on and be a good girl."

She squealed and gave a high-pitched giggle; I would have put her at two years past puberty at most.

I had had a plan for this in mind since the first instant I had been in there. I blew out the candle, yanked the clothes away from the door, jerked the porthole curtain open, and slid swiftly under the bed. I might have to count on the other Strang to fall asleep, but I'd heard him stumble a time or two as he approached, and his speech seemed a bit slurred. And if his body was like my body, he would be sound asleep right after sex anyway.

Though no matter how you try, it's kind of hard to maintain any mental dignity while you are hiding under a bed spying on yourself.

The door opened, and I could see his boots and her slippers. "A light so you can look at me?" she asked, and he said no.

I'd've felt a little funny about laying a kid prostitute in front of twenty pictures of Marie, myself. And there wasn't much to report about all that. He wasn't especially nice or especially rude, and I wasn't all that sure that he was excited at all. He told her what he wanted, and she did it, and that was about all. When I thought about it, during my bodyguarding days there'd been one "working girl" who had hired me to protect her from her ex-pimp, and paid me partly in exchange of services, and that was about what it had been like—sheer biological relief and not much attention paid to the partner.

About as soon as he was done she was yanking her clothes on and out the door; there wasn't a lot of romance around here to spare.

I waited till I heard him snoring, then crawled forward very slowly and carefully, a hand and a knee at a time, until at last I could stand and look down on the sleeping, drunken man. There was enough moonlight through the portal to see that his face was wet, I suppose from crying in his sleep, and that a trickle of snot traced its way over his upper lip. The room smelled like an old locker room, and it was oddly cold and clammy, and not just from the April sea air.

I could have killed him then and there, any number of clean and quiet ways I knew, and I'm not sure he'd have cared. But I needed to know where he was going, who he was meeting, and why; and more than that, to my slight disgust, I found I pitied him.

I slipped through the door as quietly as a shadow does, closed it, and turned to breathe the clean sea air. When I got back to my pile of sails, I found that the steward had already put my change of clothes in there, and once again I was to be dressed as a scholar. At this rate I might have to think about finishing my dissertation . . .

I spent a few hours moving quietly from corner to corner, finding ways to listen to conversations. I wanted to get whatever idea I could of what impression this other Mark Strang had made, and of what people were expecting to find in London. I learned nothing about either subject; mostly I discovered that the two prostitutes the steward had smuggled aboard were busy, that the man mixing gin drinks was busier still, and that the celebrated "wit" of the period wasn't much of anything to listen to cold sober. After a while, with everyone else asleep, I went back to my pile of sails and got some sleep.

·11·

In a line of work like mine, you can learn to relish the dull times, even the *frustrating* dull times. The steamer took twenty days getting across the Atlantic and swinging around the south of England to come into London, and I would honestly have to say that I enjoyed most of it. I spied a lot on my other self, and mostly I found that he was bored and depressed, he didn't appear to be communicating in any way with anyone in this timeline or elsewhere, and he did pretty much the same things every day—ate, exercised enough not to lose muscle tone, began to drink late in the afternoon, and then either spent the evening at cards (he cheated, just a little, not so much to win I think as to make the situation a bit riskier) or drank himself into an early stupor and went to bed.

That helped me considerably, because he didn't usually go into the aft saloon, where the main meals were served. He ate at the gaming tables or sitting in a chair in the forward saloon, and he ate only enough to keep himself alive. Meanwhile, I was free to go wherever he didn't—deck promenade in the afternoons, a big breakfast before he got up, a huge tea while he got his start on the afternoon's drinking. I suppose that of the crew that tended to the passengers, about half thought Mark Strang was that morose, silent man who appeared to be working hard at drinking away some small personal fortune, and the other half thought Mark Strang was that burly man in scholar's clothes, hat brim always pulled low outdoors, who liked to sit in corners and read, and ate immense meals.

As to which of us was really which—well, I leave that to the philosophers. I know who *I* was, anyway.

The last day of the voyage, we entered the mouth of the Thames and a steam tug, one of those paddle-wheel contraptions like the one I had seen in Boston, came out to drag us into London Harbor. The afternoon was fine, but I had sent my counterpart a lot of rum punch, a lot of gin punch, and the girl the night before, and he was still asleep in his cabin. Just for fun, once he was really asleep, I had slipped in and done some some random damage to his Colt, then carried off his hypervelocity gun, since when he woke, to a series of surprises he would know I had been there anyway. We'd all fired them at COTA, and I thought it might do better things in the hands of the good guys than it would where it was.

So he was asleep belowdecks when the bum boats came out. Those were little boats, mostly operated by women, that came out to sell trinkets, tourist stuff, fresh fruit, and anything that people might want at the end of a sea voyage. More importantly, from my standpoint, they generally carried off mail.

I had my envelope and letter ready to go, the address selected after listening to half a dozen gentlemen discuss various difficulties in their lives, and the first bum boat to pick up mail and leave was carrying that envelope. The steward glanced at me, and I grinned at him. "That's the letter that will get your gold fetched here, sir. You should find that I've been more than generous. Now, let me add, it is desirable that I not be seen leaving the vessel, and to that end, I shall contrive to appear to be drunken and ill in my cabin. If you could refrain from waking me—pretending to wake me, that is—until half an hour after our gangplank is down—"

"Not a problem at all, sir, the *Royal Hanover* is a busy vessel at such times, and I'll have no time—I'll see to that."

"Thank you," I said.

The toughest part of the whole thing was finding a good time to go over the side on the side away from the gangplank; when there was finally a chance to do so quickly and quietly, I had been pacing around nervously there for half an hour. At least this time I had been able to change back into my rags, and had swiped the equivalent of a GP bag from my counterpart so that my scholar's clothes and weapons stayed dry. The water was not just cold but filthy—London's system for handling sewage was to let the rain wash it out of the streets and into the river, and the city was huge by the standards of the day, and, of course, though steam was coming in, there were still large numbers of horses.

I dragged myself out underneath a pier, nearly retching from the smell, and began to look for some stairs or a ladder up, preferably farther away.

There was a loud clatter and some shouting; after a bit I heard my own voice, bleary, raw, hungover, and in a rage. The note I had sent had fetched a detachment of Royal Marines with the note that I was wanted for murder in Boston, and had added debt-skipping to the list of offenses. Moreover, it had added that I was a dismissed Royal servant "still trading on His Majesty's name for financial credit."

My badly hungover doppelgänger was being arrested; he would be in jail for a while, and given how much I'd spent on his account, would undoubtedly be remanded to debtors prison. I had little doubt that he'd break out of there in short order.

Meanwhile, I was free and armed. Unfortunately, I also stank, and the little bit that had been returned to me from the ship's safe wouldn't get me far. Still, it should cover a room at an inn, a meal or two there, and the most urgent need—a bath and a shave at a barbershop. Getting all of that should take the rest of the day, but I was no longer in quite the hurry I had been in.

A little shopping allowed me to find a place where the bathwater was fresh and hot and the soap newly made and soft—a big consideration if you visit any version of the eighteenth century, believe me. It's not to be assumed that you will get bath-water that hasn't had other people in it, or get it warm, let alone that you will get any kind of soap that you want touching your skin. But this place was quite nice—they'd been hoping to get the sailors off the *Royal Hanover* and had been beaten out by a special price reduction on used hot water down the street—and very willing to make a deal.

It takes a little getting used to, to take a bath in front of everyone who happens to be in the barber shop, but once I got past the modesty issue (which I did by ignoring it till it went away), it was marvelous to sink into hot water and take a good stiff brush to my skin. There had been baths available at a very high rate on shipboard, but though the Closers were paying for it, I had not wanted to take the chance of being out in public, out of disguise, in such an exposed position for so long. So I had had no bath since the one in Boston almost three weeks before, and I'd had a couple of saltwater swims and a good dunk in sewage in the interim, not to mention wearing the same clothes through much of the time. I was good and ready for this bath, and it was about as wonderful as experiences come.

Afterward, dressed, clean, and relatively presentable, I set out to see what the biggest city in the world had to offer. For an art historian, the effect was very strange, for much of what there was to see in the city was still something you'd recognize from Hogarth, Rowlandson, or Gainsborough, but in three dimensions, with full color, and vividly noisy and smelly—but at the same time there were great thumping steam-driven factories, small Sterling-cycle cars rolling in the streets, a few electric trolleys, and in the great squares, electric lights just coming on. It was a scrambled mixture of everything; as I watched, the *Great George*, first of the Royal Navy's new dirigibles that were eventually to cross the Atlantic, passed over the town—the newspapers on the ship had said it was due to begin field trials. There were telegraph offices in all the better-off districts, and it was very much like seeing bits of London in the 1920s wander into a collage of the London of Tom Jones and the London of Sherlock Holmes. Every so often I'd note some landmark from my own time—St. Paul's, or the Tower, or one glimpse of Westminster far away—but mostly it was as confusingly different as Boston and New York had been.

There were a dozen Whigs that Washington and Adams had told me to look up, and after I had strolled around a little, just for the pleasure of being off the ship and somewhere relatively safe, I stopped a boy and asked him what street I was in. His accent practically screamed "Cheapside"—it was the old Cockney accent, not the one you hear today but the one that you find in Dickens's novels—but I managed to gather that I was on Threadneedle Street.

A moment later I felt like a complete fool, when I passed the Bank of England, a landmark at the time and so much a part of London that it was like having been on Pennsylvania Avenue in Washington, D.C., standing in front of the White House, and asking where you were. Oh, well, fortunately this was a century in which lunatics and the feeble-minded were turned out to wander around, when they weren't being beaten, tortured, or exhibited to amuse the gentry. No doubt the kid merely thought I was one of them.

That realization, anyway, allowed me to know where I was going at once; the coffeehouse where I stood the best chance of meeting any of the people I was looking for (and where I could at least get a newspaper and see what was currently going on) was very near St. Paul's on Ave Mary Lane, a place called the Chapter House. The Society of Honest Whigs, Society of Supporters of the Bill of Rights, and a host of other reformist organizations met there; I was supposed to find Joseph Priestley, the noted scientist and friend of Franklin (and where in my timeline he'd discovered oxygen, in this one he had discovered valence and the periodic table; at least in my timeline I'd have understood what he'd done).

Failing to find Priestley, I was to look for Catharine Macauley or for Thomas Hollis. All of them were from the radical wing of the Whigs, but where in my timeline they'd had very little influence, here they were leading figures in the city, at least as important as Adams and Warren were in Boston. After conferring with them, I'd try to figure out what to do next.

Chapter House was severely crowded, which I might have expected in the evening, and no one had seen Priestley or Hollis; Catharine Macauley would have been conspicuous, as the only women in there at the moment were serving.

Besides coffee, Chapter House served sandwiches and various kinds of cold dinners, so I decided my best bet was to get some dinner and wait out the evening; there was an excellent chance of catching someone I wanted to meet. I found a table—a little circular thing barely big enough to hold a plate and cup—with an armchair, sat down, and waited for one of the girls who waited on customers.

From her, I got a *Times* and a *Daily Advertiser*, both used (which meant they were that day's paper but about one-quarter the price of new), plus a plate of bread, cold sliced beef, and cheese, and then she went off to get me a pot of coffee and a cup.

When she got back with that, I slipped her a coin to do some inquiring around and to make sure that if anyone I wanted to see came in, I'd know about it.

Then I settled back to enjoy myself. So this (despite modifications) was the London of Dr. Samuel Johnson, Goldsmith, Hogarth, Adam Smith, Rowlandson—and with added features like electric lights and flush toilets. It was really a pity that I couldn't tell anyone, back home, or have them believe me if I did tell. I could have traded on this in the English or art departments for a good long while.

The *Times* had mostly news of Court, most of which was that the King made very brief appearances but seemed quite concerned to make sure that his old friends knew he was merely busy, not ill and not avoiding them. This led to all sorts of odd rumors which were lovingly reported as almost fact.

The *Advertiser* was radical Whig, and it was much more sharply critical, but since the King himself had been quite Whiggish till recently, and no one knew what had caused the change, there was a certain strange tone in all the stories of trying to get the King to come back to his senses.

In neither paper was there the faintest pretense of objectivity, and I appreciated that fact quite a bit; you might not get the truth from your newspaper, but you would never mistake your newspaper for the truth.

The coffee was very strong by my standards, like barely filtered Turkish coffee, and gave me sort of a caffeine buzz; the food was generally good if very plain. A man could get to like London, I decided.

I had been half-listening to the conversations around me—two young men discussing horse racing and which brothels in town offered the best bargains, a couple of men arguing about electricity and phlogiston, one grumbling owner of a theater explaining for the tenth time to a playwright that if there were not enough songs, the police could close him down and therefore the play was not acceptable without more songs.

There was a certain odd silence for an instant, and I looked up from a theater review in the *Advertiser*—it looked like Sheridan's *The Rivals* was a big hit in this timeline, too, with Mrs. Malaprop much the same, but now parts of it took place in a traction-line car—to see the other Mark Strang.

"Brother Ajax," he said calmly.

Over his right forearm, which he held level in front of him, he had a newspaper, and under the newspaper, only I could see that he had a .45 automatic pointed right between my eyes. "Why don't you invite me to sit down, and while you're at it, avoid moving in any way that makes me nervous?" he added.

I moved my hands farther away from my body; the gesture was invitation, surrender, and above all else a way of demonstrating that I didn't have any weapon right to hand.

Of course if I had, I'd have used it already, and chances were he knew this.

He sat down, and I noticed, glancing around, that everyone in there was staring at us. They'd probably never seen a set of twins who looked so much alike. So far, so good; right now I really wouldn't want to be alone.

While I had been reading it had gotten dark outside, and though the coffeehouse was now fairly brightly lit, the light came from dozens of candles and some gaslights, so that it all flickered strangely; the clouds of tobacco smoke in the air were thick, warm, heavy, and oppressive, and I suddenly became aware that for all of its comfort, the place had the unmistakable stench of bodies that didn't wash often enough, at least not by the standards of my time in my timeline.

The thought that came to me was that I knew him, literally like I knew myself, and if our situations had been reversed, knowing this was an effective and dangerous Closer agent, I'd have been happy to pull the trigger.

I could not imagine that he was going to be any kinder about it to me. The only question was whether he wanted witnesses, and if he didn't, and told me to come with him, I wasn't going to have much choice.

So there was a good chance I would die in this place, thick with its human stenches, or not far from it, in a history where I didn't belong . . . a timeline where there was no Chrysamen, no Dad or Porter or Carrie, and where there would never be.

I'd have felt sorry for myself about it except I was too disgusted—to get caught at a table in a public space, reading a newspaper—and that made me too angry; life had been all right before Closer bastards had wrecked it, over and over again. Even then, there might have been some purpose in knowing that I was fighting them, that I would get my licks in . . . and now I was face-to-face with the fact that I was at least as much on the other side. Moreover, that other side seemed to be winning . . .

It made me crazy with rage, more furious than I'd been in a long time, angry and reckless and willing to do almost anything.

Almost.

I looked at that automatic, under the folded newspaper in his hand. I knew I had carried it through a couple of good swims in salt water, the one thing that was mostly likely to ruin it, and that I'd done no maintenance before I switched guns on him. I knew his ammo had taken a similar dunking, but it was good modern stuff that shouldn't have been too badly bothered.

That afternoon I'd also taken a handful of dust from under the bed and sprinkled it into the works, spitting on it to make it stick. But I had not dared to damage it more than that and possibly give my presence on the ship away before I had the full benefit of my head start.

Clearly I had just lost my head start, and although I'd done my best to make sure that gun was unreliable, the Model 1911A is tough. It wasn't *that* unreliable. It looked like it was his call, and all my anger would do me no good at all.

"I do want to say, Brother Ajax, that the bit of billing all that to me—and then sending the Royal Marines to arrest me—was pretty good; I'd have been here much more quickly if you hadn't come up with that one. As it was, I finally understood why the steward had been acting so weird around me for the whole voyage, and not only did I get matters straightened out with the Marines, I also got the steward carted off for stealing my gold, and gave the Marines my deposition. I should guess they'll be hanging him tomorrow morning, or, if you like irony, perhaps they'll let him off with transportation to the colonies. We're alike enough that I'm sure you rather got to like him; just think about him at the end of a rope, and the way the neck makes a crunch like a breaking chair, or perhaps imagine him in some nice swamp in West Florida or Georgia, chopping brush and living on bread and water. Oh, am I making you angry? Well, it's just possible, just very possible, that I'm rather angry myself, Brother Ajax. I think you had better come with me."

Suddenly, as I got up and carefully kept my hands away from my sides, and waited while he got my bag, I noticed that for all the bad smells and dim light, for all that most of the people in there were talking about things that didn't matter to me . . . for all of that, I really liked Chapter House. I wanted to stay there.

Mostly because as soon as I was out of it he was going to blow holes in my body until I was dead. And I'd used that particular weapon often enough to have a really good idea about what kind of holes they'd be. Little and smooth going in, big and raw coming out.

It was dark when we went out of the Chapter House, and he didn't bother to hire a lantern boy; instead he just told me to turn left and walk, then to turn into a deep alley. I started to wonder if maybe it was dark enough to make a move, and then realized that I just didn't know; bad idea to try unless I knew it would work, since there was no real point in getting shot early.

Then again, if he was thinking, he might realize the best way to get me for sure would be to get me somewhere reasonably concealed—like where I already was—and to leave me thinking that he was going to do something else, or had something he had to find out from me . . .

And then just pull the trigger by surprise.

If I knew for sure that it was about to go down—that I was a few feet from the place appointed for my death—I would draw and turn and fire, maybe taking him with me, counting on dark and luck and the rust that might be in the weapon, if he hadn't cleaned it yet, or the dirt that might jam any of the working parts—it was a lousy gamble, of course, to bet on a gadget to fail when it was made to stand abuse, but it would be the only thing to do if I were six steps from him pulling the trigger.

But if I weren't . . . if he intended to keep me alive for a while . . .

There was no way of knowing. And with no way of knowing, in that uncertainty, I couldn't do a thing, except notice everything around me and keep looking for a logical way out of it.

My feet were slipping in the slimy mud of the alley, and it was getting cold back here, where the buildings were so close together that the sun probably never shone in here. There was a strange smell I had not quite recognized, and then I stumbled a little, and he barked, "Hands up!"

My hands stabbed at the sky and threw me so far off-balance that I nearly fell, but at least I knew now that he could see me moving, and that if I was going to get out of this one, it wouldn't be by pulling the .45 from its holster.

I had to appreciate that the guy was as smart as I was and knew me pretty well. He had figured out that if he asked me to extract my .45 and drop it, I'd want to see which of us had a better reaction time. But if he made me hold my coat open and reached in to get it, he'd risk getting a foot or fist in the face and a quick test of one of the nifty pistol disarms I'd learned at COTA.

So it was better to leave the gun where it was. He could always take it off the body later.

It was how I would have thought of it.

Okay, shooting him was out. Temporarily at least. I didn't think he'd appreciate idle chat, either. Better just keep doing what he said.

"Feel the ground in front of you but don't bring your hands too close to your body. I'm wearing infrared goggles now, and I can see you even if you can't see me."

Damn. In the instant that he must have been putting them on, I could have turned and bagged him. But of course—he was good enough to not let me know.

I felt the ground in front of me. I found something with a blade—

"Don't even think of throwing that, but hold it in your hand."

The knife was big and heavy, something a surgeon might have used in that day and age, when they amputated legs and arms with no anesthesia and, therefore, speed was the most important thing.

I held it by the hilt, just as if it were good for something, but in my left hand; if I got a chance with my shooting hand, I wanted to take it.

"Just in case some eighteenth-century Sherlock Holmes should realize that it's odd for a man to hold a knife in the hand he doesn't use—and the position of the shoulder holster would give away that you are right-handed," the other Strang said to me, "perhaps you should move that to your right. Do it slowly. And yes, I do remember that you, or I, or we, are a lousy shot with the left hand. While you are at it, turn over very slowly and sit, so that you are facing me."

I did as he said.

"Now take that left hand and feel to your left a few inches," he said.

I did and I found something under my hand—something thin, and warm, and wet. A little more feeling around and I knew that what I had was a human leg, a small, slender one—and that though still warm, it had begun to cool. I felt slowly up the leg and found knee—and then a ragged place where it was severed at the thigh.

My stomach was heaving, but with no more expression than if he'd been telling me where to catch a bus, he said, "You can find the rest of her around, near your hand, if you're interested in examining her further."

"Who?" I gasped out.

"Does it matter? No one you know. I promised her a few small coins to come back here and do what I wanted. I didn't have to offer her much because she was so young. Then we walked back here, and I asked her to close her eyes and tip up her chin, as if I were going to kiss her. I got her larynx on the first stroke, so she gave no cries; then I cut her up. I think she died fairly early in the process, actually, so I suppose if you're worried about suffering, there wasn't much. You *do* worry about suffering, don't you?"

I felt sick and sorry. I wanted the .45 that was so maddeningly close, right there on my shoulder. I wanted to empty it into him, again and again and again, especially into the face and head, until I had erased any resemblance between us.

"You do, don't you?" he repeated.

"Yes, goddammit, I do, and this is fucking horrible, and I'd be damn glad to see you hanged for it." It might not have been the smartest attitude to take with a guy who had a gun pointed at my head, but it was about the only thing I could manage to say. Throwing up might have been a more accurate expression, but I was too angry and too focused on finding a way to get at him.

"There was a time when I cared about suffering a lot, too," he said. "I can remember it, pretty much the way you remember the pain after the wound is all healed; you know it hurt very badly, and you know you don't want to do it again, but no imagination or memory can really bring it back for you."

"Why?" I asked. "Why would you do something like this to someone you don't know? Damn it, I know you, and I didn't diverge from each other more than—"

"Just about nine years ago, both our times, I think," he said. "So you're thinking we should somehow only be nine years different. But think how different that can be. Your wife . . . mine, too, for that matter . . . your Marie . . . her remains are in a cemetery somewhere near Baltimore, I imagine, near her parents' house?" There was a long pause, and then he said, "You can answer or I can put a shot into your leg, and have my .45 back up and aimed at your head before you can get yours out."

"Yes, she's buried there." Knowing what my counterpart was, I had not wanted to share with him anything of myself.

"Much better, much better. Well, then, she's very different now, nine years later, isn't she, from what you remember? A box of decaying pieces, formerly burned. That's quite different. And your sister Carrie—"

"You made your point. So we're different. So nine years can be a lot. So *why*, dammit? *Why* did you cut up a little girl and then bring me to her body?"

"Because when I finish talking—ah, but you won't know when I'm done—I'm going to shoot you, and leave you here with her body, and then go summon some men from Bow Street, who will come out, discover that I have slaughtered my twin brother Ajax Strang—it was so good of you to come out with that alias and explanation, for one of those detectives on the ferry survived and as a result there are now warrants out for both of us—discover, as I said, that you are dead apparently after you did all this to a little girl. Your case will be closed, and mine will be resolved by a Royal pardon, and then there we are, all safe and sound. You will be dead for a good reason, I will be alive for the good reason that you are dead—"

"But what did *she* ever do—"

"Oh, what did that steward ever do? And yet by implicating him and leaving him in the lurch, you've either sent him off to die of malaria in the American South, or just possibly to his hanging. And what did the people you've shot on your past missions ever do? They got in your way, or they shot at you . . . it seems very fair to me. Pretty clearly, the only thing anyone ever 'does' is to be in the wrong place at the wrong time—and then, presto, they are in a crime, a war, a terrorist bombing, and wondering what they ever did, without realizing that if it hadn't been them, someone else would have been wondering."

Now there was a long, long silence, and finally, very softly, he said, "I want to be understood. You may consider that appalling, but I want to be understood. But you remember what you—or I— used to say back when we were teaching Intro to Art History. 'Art is man's way of explaining himself to himself.' So what we're getting to, here, is the art part. After all, who can resist a chance to be really, really understood . . ."

"I don't think I want to understand you," I said, my guts still filled with disgust, still trying to find a way to a weapon and an even shot at him.

"Perhaps not. But you're going to hear an explanation of it all, from me, now. As I said, I don't know when I'll get this chance again. Which I think you will understand whether you want to or not. And then, once it is explained, I'm going to kill you. So I would say, offhand, that either you can be dead right now, or you can hear me explain, and then be dead. The choice, really, is all yours."

Well, if nothing else, he had made his point very clearly. "Explain away," I said, "and take all the time you want."

·12·

He drew a deep breath and sighed. I felt the cold stones of the alley pressing up against me, the foul black mud oozing in through the seat of my trousers, and the blood congealing on my hands, and let my eyes roll up for just a second to see a few stars through the narrow slit the top of the alley made in the blackness.

I suppressed a shiver and resolved to stay alert. There was always a chance, if only just a chance, that he would slip, or I would get a chance . . . but only if I was alert at every second. And just now the only tool for staying alert was probably listening to him, little as I really wanted to do that.

When he finally spoke it was like a whisper. "The last time you and I were the same person was Christmas Eve, Mark. The Christmas Eve after Mom, Jerry, and Marie died. Do you remember it?"

"Yes." I could hardly forget it. That night there had been an attack on my father's house that had been stopped by the guys from Steel Curtain Guards, the bodyguard agency that had been watching us survivors. It had been hard, bloody fighting, in which I had taken no part—because I had been hanging around the house uselessly, lost in another world, living in my bathrobe and eating cold cereal, bathing only when someone insisted, leading the half-dead life of the severely depressed. Somehow, having missed the chance to put a bullet into one of the terrorists responsible had been the final step; I had wanted to live in order to kill them, and that had brought me back from that cold wilderness of despair.

"Well," he said very softly, "in your timeline, I understand, you started to change at that time. But the timelines bifurcated because the Masters stepped back through time to intervene at that point."

The Closers call themselves "Masters." It's just part of their charm, I guess, because of course it implies that all the rest of us are slaves, or meant to be slaves. I didn't like hearing the word used that way, coming out of my mouth, but the guy was still holding that gun on me.

"They came back and made the attack succeed. All the Steel Curtain guards died in the fighting. Then they came in and . . . well, they took me and Dad and Carrie away to one of their bases. And they made me an offer. We could all die, or we could live in a different world. One that had Marie, Jerry, and Mom still alive. One where we three had been killed."

"So you all went," I said. I felt disoriented, dull, and heavy, and I mustn't feel that way—not if I was to have a chance of getting out of this. "I can understand that."

"No, that's one of the parts I don't understand," the other Strang said, and for the first time he didn't seem to be angry with me or about to kill me, and there was a little, desperate edge of sanity in his voice. "Dad chose to die. Carrie chose to die. I don't know why they did that. They . . . *left* me."

As far as I could tell, though he had nearly sobbed, the .45 in his hand had never wavered.

"And then the Masters took me to another worldpath . . . I was a wreck by then, I don't mind telling you that . . ."

"You were—I mean I was—well, both of us were a wreck *before* you were kidnapped," I pointed out.

"Hunh." It was a strange little grunt, with more recognition than anything else in it. "Yeah, I sure was. You're right, of course. Anyway, what happened then . . . well, they took me to a world where there had been no bomb, but I'd been shot in front of the family as a 'warning.' And where they were all glad to see me . . . I spent several days doing nothing but cry from being so glad to be with all of them."

I could understand that. My eyes were getting a little wet. But it also occurred to me to say quietly, "You realize, of course, that they probably produced that worldpath for you to move into. Another Mark Strang died so you could have his family."

The other Strang had been raised the same way I was, and Dad had always had that big poster hanging in the downstairs hallway, that quote from George Orwell that to write anything worth writing you have to be able to "face unpleasant facts." He didn't hesitate long before he said, "Of course that's what they did. I gave it very little thought at the time. And it made very little difference after I figured it out. Well, actually, that's a lie. Two lies. I didn't figure it out, Marie did, and then it made a big difference."

"She didn't like the way you'd chosen."

"Of course not. They'd shot her husband. And I wasn't the same guy. I wasn't the 'real' one. The 'real' one didn't have shattered nerves. The 'real' one didn't have nightmares. The 'real' one hadn't . . . betrayed everyone in the family." There was a funny tone in his voice, something that it took me a while to place because it had been so long, and then I realized there was a strange little whine in it—something I hadn't heard in a very long time.

What he was doing, unconsciously, was imitating the way Marie talked when she whined. Not that that was often, I hasten to add, but Marie and I were married right out of college, and we were two people for whom nearly everything had nearly always gone right. That gives you a pleasant disposition—you're used to people "being reasonable," which is what most of us call it when we get whatever we want, and you generally assume that if there are hitches or delays, they are temporary. But it also means that *if* it does become clear that you are not going to get what you really want, you think there's something drastically wrong with the universe.

When things didn't go well for long enough periods of time— and after all, when you work on archaeological digs together, normally the past has not been obliging enough to leave you exactly what you wanted it to in perfect condition—Marie and I had both reacted less than perfectly. I got sullen and irritable, and she whined.

It occurred to me that with a real grievance as deep as the one she had in this other Strang's timeline, she might have developed that tone that I heard maybe once every other month into a constant, grating, nasty sort of sound that could easily drive a guy half-crazy . . . if he wasn't already half-crazy to begin with.

There had been a long silence. He had said he wanted to be

understood and that when he was sure I'd understood everything he would shoot me. Was it better to give him some sympathy and see if I could make him hesitate, or to play stupid and make him explain it again?

There was a cold, unpleasant something dripping off the timber wall behind me, and it was slowly soaking my collar. I wanted out of there; I decided to gamble on sympathy.

"Well," I said, "it wasn't entirely your fault. You were a wreck, you'd been through hell, you'd seen them kill everyone, and you just wanted some comfort from your family—"

"Exactly," he whispered. "But bad as the situation was, they couldn't leave well enough alone—"

"They?" I asked. "You mean—"

"The Masters. Yeah, they won't like what I say next, and you know we all wear a recorder, so they'll hear it. I don't care now, but they'll make me care later."

There's physical courage and there's moral courage, and they are not always found in the same people; there are men who can face gunfire who can't resist peer pressure, and people who can face being martyred more easily than they can deal with a high diving board. "Then tell me while you still can," I said.

"Right." He sighed. "They claimed they were keeping their promise to make it all right again. They . . . intervened. They did things—and threatened to do more . . . to make all of them, Mom, Dad, Jerry, Carrie, Marie, behave like I wanted them to. I tried . . . that's the thing I most want you to believe, and it is true, I tried to tell the Masters that what I wanted them to do was to stay out of it, let the family find a way to accept me as I was, as who I was, to understand that I hadn't ordered it, hadn't realized what was going to happen, that I just needed a lot of help, and I needed it from them . . . I don't know. I really don't know."

"You really don't know why they didn't listen," I said. It was obvious enough to me, but I'd spent a long time hating Closers and not having to do anything about them but kill them when they turned up. Hatred, like love, requires you to focus a lot of energy and attention. I knew their style.

It had not been enough to create a potential agent for them by restoring his family to him. They had to make that as painful as possible, so that when they bound him to them—as they were bound to do, when you make a deal with the devil he's never giving they'd no longer have been able to get at him—I might have felt my heart wrung by that groan. Or perhaps I might if I hadn't been sitting there in cold mud waiting for him to blast a series of holes in my body. Or if I hadn't been sitting there smelling and almost touching the corpse of his victim. It was a very convincing groan . . . but nothing could have been convincing in the circumstances.

To this day I wonder if he realized that. Maybe the groan wasn't for me, but only to convince him.

"So they made you one of their agents."

"It was that or see everyone tortured to death. And then . . . well, there are things they make you do in training camp. Things that some men and women just won't do. Things that sort of . . . strip you down. Get you to your core. Get you to where you understand what you're really made of."

At that moment I began to hope that he would pull the trigger.

No such luck; he continued. "I refused things, at first, and they had no concern at all, they knew I would refuse, they expected me to refuse so that they could show me what would happen if I did.

"And I started to change, to *really* change. Or rather I started to become myself. I found things out."

There are times when you can't stop even your stupidest impulses; I asked, "What things?"

"Oh, the same things you found out, Mark, working for the other side. That you're good with weapons and with your bare hands. That you like to kill human beings. That you enjoy causing pain. That when you push deep enough down into the core of either of us, all you find is hate."

I fought down the urge to scream and leap at him, kept myself in place, but I don't quite know how I did that. It seemed important, so I managed it, is all I can say even now.

I drew a long deep breath and made my voice stay flat and level. "You're wrong," I said. "You're absolutely wrong. Think about yourself. You just wanted love from your family—"

"But that's not at all the same thing as loving your family," he said, and there was a nasty, gloating *smile* in his voice that made me—

Hate him. Want to kill him. *Listen* to him.

I began to be afraid that there were things worse than dying.

"You see," he went on, "to love is to be vulnerable, to let them hurt you again. And you and I, we know, we've been hurt enough.

you a loss leader—this other Strang would experience it as a horrible pain that it was impossible to escape from. The "Masters" don't want love; that's freely given and unpredictable, it makes people loyal, but it doesn't make them slaves. No, they want pain and fear. Those are reliable. Once they've made one of their slaves feel that—and then do their bidding—the slave is really theirs.

From that standpoint, better still if the slave hates them. Hatred breeds understanding, and a good slave understands his Master.

I had the fresh body of an innocent child beside me as all the evidence I needed that this other version of me had come to understand them much too well.

"So you lived in a house where they were being forced to turn into robots," I said, "probably growing to hate you more and more, while they were being forced to act like they loved you, probably forced to do things you knew they wouldn't naturally do to 'prove' they loved you . . ."

He did sob, then, but he also extended his right arm just a little and braced the wrist with his left hand, as if he might start firing then. There was still no chance for a move. My buttocks were getting numb from the alley, and the smell of that poor kid's blood—and there's an amazing amount of blood in even the smallest human body—was somehow getting stronger with time, so that with every word he spoke I was weighing those self-justifications against the consequences here beside me.

"At first it mattered a lot. I kept trying to find ways around it, ways to tell my family that it was me, that I was a prisoner as much as they were. That didn't work at all; the Masters always intervened to make them agree that they accepted it and believed it, so that I couldn't tell whether I was getting through to them, couldn't even tell how they really felt because all of them, always, were stiff with anger and fear at being made to say things. It isn't just a matter of torturing them so much that they deny their own real feelings—it's more than that. Torture people enough, force them to play a part for long enough, and they *have* no real feelings.

"And it was then that they came to me for the rest of the deal." He groaned, then, and if I had not been thinking very hard about the fact that he had made choices all along—he could have decided to defy them, he could have decided to die, no matter what condition he had been in, all he needed was one instant's courage, and

We have all the pain we need from that bomb going off. We don't need any more of that. And think about how good it is to see a human head blow apart. Think about having—what do you call us, the 'Closers'? It's a silly term, Mark, they didn't 'close' anything off for me, they opened doors in myself I'd never have known were there. I might be injured or feel pain and sooner or later I will die, but I'm no longer vulnerable. That's the discovery their worldpaths made. The greatest gift of all is not love, but hate. Think about yourself for the last few years. You've killed and killed, fought and run and fought again, lived on adrenaline and strength. Have you really felt alive anytime you didn't have your finger on a trigger? Don't you find you'd rather see a man's head blow apart than hold a naked woman?"

I sat and listened, and I tried hard to think. And strangely enough what I thought of was not my lost wife, brother, and mother, not of Carrie and Dad never seeing me (or me them) again, not of wondering what would happen to Porter, but of something Chrys had said to me. *"Mark, sometimes you turn my stomach. I don't like them either, and I'm glad to do them harm, but spare me your bloodthirstiness, please . . . I don't see any reason to rejoice in pain and suffering."* And she had said that in the middle of a fight . . .

It had made me angry that Chrysamen, who I liked so much, who I wanted to understand me, had said that. I'd been really annoyed to feel so—

So *ashamed.* Because she had been right. And because I had known it and been unable to admit it. And just now it seemed so important to be able to say that to her, to say that she was right, I was wrong, and that I would try to do better, not for her or because she'd like it, but just because she had seen what I should be, instead of what I was, and that I didn't want her to understand me as I was nearly as much as I wanted her to call that good part of me out into the open.

And now chances were I wouldn't get a chance . . .

He was still talking, too. "There's a sense in which I'll never get you to understand. What it's like to hold the little pain control that can send Marie into agony in your hand, and tell her exactly what she's going to do for you; what it's like to have her do it, see that look in her eyes like a beaten dog, have her obey perfectly and then give her a jolt anyway . . . and see her accept it without resentment or surprise, because she's learned that that's all she's for—"

My hand was about to leap for my holster when a pistol roared in the alley, and I heard the other Strang cry out in pain and surprise.

My hand finally leaped to my shoulder holster, but the light was dim, he'd been careful to sit in a shadow, and that first pistol flash had all but blinded me—I fired at the sound the other Strang was making as he scrabbled through the alley, but I heard the shot scream off something hard and fly harmlessly away. The muzzle flash revealed one of his legs pulling away into the shadows, and I fired again, but it did nothing, and he got clean away.

"Are you all right, Mr. Strang, and just which Mr. Strang am I addressing?" a voice asked. It was a young male, with the upper-class London accent, and it had the kind of pleasant sound to it that you get by a lot of training in public speaking.

"You've got the one that was being held at gunpoint," I said, "and I'm about as well as can be expected. The other one got clean away, I think—or if he's around, he's lying low, and since I haven't moved and he hasn't fired, I would guess he ran for it. Probably because he doesn't know how many of you there are."

"Well, then I'll chance a light," the voice said. A lantern un-shuttered just twenty feet away, and I stood up and moved toward it—not quite fast enough to avoid seeing the little dismembered and mutilated body beside me. My heart sank like a rock, and I thought again I might throw up; my counterpart had done that as casually as I might have cleaned my .45 or prepared a cover story.

There are people that there is no shame in hating; hate might not be all there was at the core of me, I hoped it wasn't after seeing him and what it had made of him . . . but I didn't have much feeling for him except hate.

"I think I actually hit his pistol," the man who had rescued me said. "His shooting hand may be a bit sore. I was aiming for the hand, but . . ." He shrugged.

"Even at the distance, hitting the pistol was a damned fine shot," I said, meaning it. The brace of pistols I saw across the man's chest were simple dueling pistols, better than anything that had been around in the 1775 of my timeline, but not at all as accurate as even a Civil War revolver would have been. It was also a very lucky shot, and luckier for me than for him.

The man was quite young, about twenty-five or so, and re-markably handsome. His hair was thick and dark, his eyebrows heavy and arched, eyes wide with intelligence, and he had the kind of jaw and chin that Hollywood never finds enough of. "Well," I said. "You know my name—"

"But you don't know mine," he finished, and stuck out his hand. "Sheridan, Richard Sheridan. Sometime agent for Mr. Priestley, my literary career not yet being thoroughly under way, and my political career thus far a matter of humor."

I nodded. "And did you hear much of what we were talking about?"

"All of it. I had followed you in here because, before your counterpart pulled that gun on you in the Chapter House, I had in fact just determined that you were the Strang that I had been sent to find, the one that Colonel Washington had asked us to look for and to assist. Unfortunately it was not until he began to extend his arm to shoot you that I had a clear shot; that gun glinted distinctly in the starlight, and then I could do something. Till then I could only wait. I trust you won't hold the intrusion on your privacy against me—or the fact that I was fascinated."

"Considering how matters turned out," I said, "I have no complaints."

"Well, then, at least one mystery has been resolved, as far as I am concerned. I'd been wondering for quite a long time, sir, about certain aspects of our work, and I do believe I've heard them answered tonight. So there are a multiplicity of these 'worldpaths' that he refers to, and in each of them history is different—"

"We call them 'timelines,' but you've got the idea," I said.

"And plainly there is war across them, as comes naturally to man," Sheridan added.

"Yep. Or at least there's war. I don't know that I want to think of it as 'natural.' "

"As you wish, sir. And apparently there is one faction that wishes to see all men their slaves, and another that opposes them? And you work for the liberating faction? Am I right in that?"

"You've got it."

"Well, then, sir, I am very pleased to make your acquaintance. Most especially because you have just unraveled a mystery regarding the King and his strange behavior."

"Glad to hear it," I said. "Can we get out of here?"

"Of course, sir." He held the lantern higher, which was a mistake, because it meant that behind me, he saw what my double had done to that poor kid prostitute. Sheridan's eyes bulged, his jaw went slack, and I just had time to take a step back before he threw up all over the place.

I didn't blame him at all . . . but I was also very careful not to look back.

"I thought you'd heard everything," I said.

"I knew it was back there, but knowing and seeing are two different things," Sheridan said, sighing, and then, drawing a large handkerchief, he wiped his tongue. "There's blood on you, a great lot of it. Let's go to my house and get ourselves a change of clothes, a good scrub, and some coffee and brandy. There's a lot to tell you about, and I would rather not discuss it in this setting."

We stayed in the shadows while Sheridan flagged down a cab. I had been trying to think of who he was for a while, and then I remembered the theatre reviews in the paper. I asked him, as the cab pulled up, "I do presume that you are the author of *The Rivals*?"

He was delighted and clapped a hand on my shoulder, then grunted and pulled out a rag to wipe the nasty smears from his hand. "Yes, I am. So the thing has had some success in your time-line as well?"

"Or something by someone like you, with the same title," I said, carefully. "That's one of the confusions of this kind of travel; you don't actually meet the same people that were there in your own history, you meet the people they would have been in the history you are visiting."

"Perfectly clear," he agreed, grinning. "Remind me to avoid discussing such murky matters and stick to clear subjects like theology and political intrigue."

The cab was fairly nice inside, and I felt a little guilty about spotting up the guy's upholstery, but clearly this wasn't the time to argue about it. The little space inside would have seated about one and a half modern people on each side, so the ridge between the seat cushions dug into one side of my bottom a little uncomfortably, but it was so pleasant to be in a seat outside the weather that I wasn't complaining much.

The cab ran on a little Sterling-cycle engine that was hooked to something that looked a lot like the derailleur rig on a ten-speed bicycle. The Sterling engines were one of Rey Luc's more clever introductions; they're known by a lot of names in a lot of different timelines, and in fact here they were called "Dr. Luke's Patent Engines." It's a simple gadget and perhaps the real miracle is that, like the hang glider, telescope, horse collar, or paddle wheel, they weren't found back at the dawn of civilization in every single timeline.

It's about the most efficient kind of small engine you can make without precision machining. Any piston engine works by heating some fluid—a liquid or gas—so that it expands in the cylinder, pushing the piston out; in gas and diesel engines the heating is done by burning the fuel inside the cylinder, which is why they are called "internal combustion" engines. In those engines you get rid of the hot gas by venting it to the outside, which is why there are a lot of days when you can't see very far in Los Angeles.

In steam engines, of course, you have a boiler to make hot steam, the heat gets supplied by some kind of fire somewhere, and the steam either gets vented, or else you cool the cylinder somehow and get some extra energy by having the steam contract and suck the piston back down—thus providing a power stroke in both directions.

The Sterling engine goes the condensation engine one better. One way or another, it brings the cylinder alternately into contact with the heat source and with something to cool it. You get power on both strokes. Usually you don't even bother with putting water in there—air will work just fine as the working fluid.

In this century, Ben Franklin's student—the Joseph Priestley I was supposed to meet—had invented the electrical process for making aluminum. The stuff still wasn't cheap . . . but it so happens that aluminum is about the best stuff in the world for Sterling engines. It's lightweight, it holds pressure at the right temperatures, and it conducts heat rapidly, which is important since the faster you can heat and cool the cylinder, the more power you can get out of the same size engine. Thus chances were pretty good that by the time this timeline had automobiles and airplanes, they'd be running on Sterling engines.

Besides, they're kind of fun to watch. The easiest way of all to make them work is to have the cylinders spin around a stationary crankshaft, so that the motion of the engine itself brings the cylinders close to the heat and then moves them away from it. It doesn't turn out a lot of rpm's, but there's a lot of force in every stroke, so it has to be geared *up* to the speed you want to run at, not *down* like our automobile engines.

Thus Sheridan and I got in on one side of the cab, and the driver up top got Sheridan's address and threw a fresh scuttle of coal onto the fire on the roof of the cab. The whirling cylinders were attached to a big ring, which in turn was on an axle that drove a little wheel that stuck out to the side away from the door—and that little wheel turned a belt that turned a wheel almost as big as the cab itself. It looked like a cartoon of a mad inventor's dream.

It also had a suspension that would be thought a little crude for a toy wheelbarrow, and the London streets jounced and slammed us as we went, but I had to give it credit—we zoomed along at almost 20 mph, and at the end of the ride, at Sheridan's house near the Drury Lane Theater, we were certainly less tired than we'd have been walking the same distance.

Sheridan's house had such modern conveniences as flush toilets and a shower that didn't require human pumping; I decided once more that Rey Luc had been one hell of a guy.

After we were clean and dressed again, the doorbell began to ring; pretty soon some of the city's more prominent radical Whigs were sitting around Sheridan's fire, many of them looking a bit morose. Since it had long since been decided that this would be a "conscious" timeline—that is, many people right from the first would be aware of the war across the timelines and of their place in it—I didn't have much trouble with spreading the knowledge around farther. Sheridan, for reasons I couldn't fathom, had me tell most of the story of my adventures here, as if he really wanted to make sure that everyone knew everything.

There was a long pause, and then Priestley said, "In fact, Dr. Franklin has told me about matters of the kind several times. I'm quite sure Mr. Strang is telling the truth. And you are absolutely right, Sheridan, you've put your finger on just what this implies. We have our puzzle solved, but now we must decide what needs to be done."

"Your puzzle?" I asked. "Perhaps it's your turn to fill me in."

"Indeed it is, Mr. Strang, and if we've hesitated, it's only been because for these past few weeks we've been unable to speak of this in front of strangers. Perhaps you should tell him, Fleming, since you were the first witness."

The man who spoke was dressed differently from the others,

and though his accent was not Cockney, I knew at once he was from a lower class than the other men. It took me only another instant to realize it was a very slight Welsh brogue, one he had been at pains to suppress. "Well, sir, it's really a pretty simple story. I was working at the new Queen's House—Buckingham House, it was, the place His Majesty moved his family to after his coronation—and it was a simple job, as I'm a pinner by trade and all that had to be done was to fix up a few joints to get a wainscoting to hang straight upon its wall. And that was when I saw the King go stamping through and shouting back and forth with his lords—shouting like a madman, I might add, sir—and he kept talking about one room, some upper closet in the St. James Palace, the old royal residence where good old King Fred lived and his fathers before him. Now, it happened I knew that wing as I'd worked there before, and there was some furniture work to be done there just a bit later that week. So naturally I kept my eyes open while I was there . . . and what I saw there, just walking about a bit during dinner and nobody watching—was the King again, the King in a small room, sitting up in a stiff chair, and his eyes wild and glaring—not like the King I knew at all . . . his skin all blotchy and not healthy-looking at all . . . and yet, sir, I knew he was downstairs at the time, receiving an ambassador."

"It makes sense, then," said Priestley, shaking his head. "Strang has supplied our missing piece."

"*What* missing piece?" I asked, feeling stupid.

"Well, if there are these timelines or worldpaths or whatever, and if that can result in your having a double . . . why not our King? And my guess would be that the one Caleb Fleming saw up in the tower in St. James is probably the one we used to have, the one who had been so splendid in the first years of his reign and then deteriorated into the vain and unpleasant creature that we now deal with. I think your enemies, your Closers, have switched kings on us."

·13·

The question of what to do about that took almost a day of discussion to settle, and unfortunately this was a century that truly enjoyed discussion, so there was very little hurrying them along. The first question, and the one that between Sheridan's imagination and Priestley's scientific precision took the longest, was the question of why the original George III was still alive. Fleming, with his common sense, eventually came up with a simple enough explanation—it would have been all but impossible to smuggle anything remotely resembling the corpse of King George III out of the Court of St. James at any time of day or night. That meant not only that they couldn't kill him, but in all probability they couldn't let him die, either; his body was bound to be detected before they could cover it up, and "once it is known that there is a double for a king," Sheridan said, "depend upon it, there will always be rumors that it is not the real King that sits on the throne. And this King they have brought us has made himself exceedingly unpopular, sir, with every class of society. Let the word get out, and the people will rise up to put the rightful King back on the throne."

"Then couldn't you just put rumors out and let matters take their course?"

Tom Hollis, who was an alderman, shook his head. "Nothing is certain, and both sides know that. Right now it's better for them to take the chance that he won't be found, or that their replacement

King will come to look different enough from the original with time. But if there were serious doubts out there, while it might result in their getting caught, it also might make them decide to gamble—and even if they do get caught, if the rightful George III is dead, well, we don't win either."

It was a standoff, obviously.

Just as clearly, there had to be very heavy Closer penetration of the Court and quite possibly of Parliament as well.

"Our best bet," Sheridan said, "is to get the King out of there, into the hands of the Royal Navy, and thence to America. From there he can rally support and bring down the false regime. I'd suggest Ireland, but the Irish hate us; the French would be happy to lock up the King forever . . . and the false King undoubtedly has already extended his influence back into his ancestral domain of Hanover. Indeed that explains why, after so 'British' a start, the monarchy has become so suddenly 'German' again. No, it's America, the Navy, and then the Army that can save the King and kingdom."

"Agreed," Hollis said. "Once he's aboard ship somewhere we will be in far better stead, but how to get him to a ship?"

Priestley had been staring off into space, and now he smiled. "And the problem would seem worse than that, would it not, gentlemen? London is a port on a river, and the larger warships cannot get past London Bridge. We would not only have to free the King from St. James—a very heavily guarded place indeed—but we would also have to get him down to the river, and then downstream to a large enough warship to get him to America, with a real possibility of being killed or captured the whole way, and with the whole city in an uproar after shooting starts at St. James." His smile got bigger and wider, and he stared farther off into space; he looked like a grinning idiot.

"Dr. Priestley, if I didn't know by your manner that you had some idea in mind for resolving the whole matter, I'd punch you in the eye," Caleb Fleming said, firmly.

"And we'd hold you down so he could do it without interference," Sheridan added. "What in the sweet name of god do you have in mind?"

"Well," Priestley said, "how many shots are left in that remarkable gun of yours, Strang?" Sheridan and I had retrieved my bag from the checkroom at the coffeehouse and found that it was intact;

one test shot had brought down a seagull three miles away, convincing everyone that it would do what I said it would.

"If I'm reading the Closer hieroglyphs right—and maybe I am and maybe I'm not—I'd figure it at 331," I said. "That's enough to kill every guard around St. James and blow the doors down, if you just want to go in by brute force."

"And its range?"

"Around six, seven miles, about the same as the SHAKK I'm used to," I said. "I wish I knew exactly."

"No problem at all. I was merely wondering if you could hit Buckingham House from St. James Palace."

"Ah . . ." I thought for a moment and then recalled from trips to London that, at least in my timeline, St. James and Buckingham Palace were not at all far apart. And this would be much easier, because the Buckingham house wasn't nearly so built up yet—not yet a "palace," at all. "There should be no problem at all," I said.

"Well, then," Priestley said, "if you'll permit me to be more overoptimistic than my position as a scientist would warrant, strictly, then I do think we can manage the whole matter pretty handily. It will merely be extremely dangerous and difficult."

"What isn't?" I said.

I noticed Sheridan scribbling frantically when I said that, but since Priestley was then launching into explaining his plan—something that turned out to take a couple of hours—it was not until later, at dinner, that I found myself with time enough to say to my host, "Er, by the way, Mr. Sheridan—"

"Do call me Dick," he said. "And may I call you Mark?"

"Er, sure, no problem," I said, "I'm from a very informal time myself, but what I meant to ask—"

"It must be delightful to be from an informal time. More of the goose, sir? I think this is quite the tenderest we've had."

It was very good goose, in fact, so I took some more before trying to press the subject any farther. "Now, anyway, Dick—"

"Oh, yes, the informality definitely makes a difference. I feel much more closely the sentiments of true friendship with you, sir."

It didn't surprise me to remember that in my timeline this guy had been a member of Parliament, and a prominent public speaker, for more than thirty years . . . or that he'd had a relatively successful business career as well.

"Now, Dick," I said, "one way in which we are *extremely* informal is that we quite often use an expression that I'm sure you'll understand." I helped myself to a bit more mustard and spread it on a terrific piece of steak, figuring that if I was going to offend my host, I might as well do it while fully appreciating his food.

"And that expression would be?" he asked, looking mildly amused.

"The expression would be 'cut the crap,'" I said, "which means—"

"Oh, I know what it means, it's current in my stables," Sheridan said. "I suppose, Mark, you intend to ask me just why I have been taking notes on what you've been saying. And you don't think it's because I'm a spy, because others with a like chance to see me have plainly seen me doing it and not asked me."

"Uh, yep, that was the question." I smiled as nicely as I could manage; I really didn't want to offend him, but I really did want to know just what the hell he was up to.

He snorted and shook his head. "Well, you know, this house and a good part of what else I own is all a matter of *The Rivals* having succeeded. Now, it so happens that I've another comedy I shall be presenting soon . . . a splendid little thing called *The School for Scandal*, which is even more a work of genius than the previous—"

I nodded. "In my timeline it was thought to be so." And then, smiling broadly, I added, "And your modesty is very becoming."

"Modesty, sir, is for men who cannot assess themselves accurately. Or perhaps for those who assess themselves too accurately. In any case, it has no place in the temperament of the artist, who needs to see clearly. At any rate, it is good to know that my *School* will, as it were, bring in some handsome tuition. But that can only be the start, you see . . . there's also the matter of becoming wealthy enough to buy myself election to the Commons in an appropriate district. That is going to take money, for all that it will make a great deal once I am in."

It occurred to me that in my own century when artists lived on grants and Congressmen on graft, I'd never seen anyone combine the operation, but there was no logical reason not to. I nodded approvingly, figuring it was the best way to get him to tell me the rest.

The gaslights flickered, and his smile deepened into a smirk; I

had a vision of looking at—for lack of a better expression—a handsome devil.

"Well, then, has it not occurred to you that your life is the stuff
of which melodrama might be made? And that once victory is won
we are going to be public with what has happened, no doubt you
recall that since you explained it to us? Well, sir, I do believe that
with the right actor to play the role of yourself—and with a Bibiena
or two, which I think I can command the price of, to paint the
scenes of the time you come from and the wonders of twenty-ninth-
century Athens—that you will do very nicely. I should be happy to
cut you in for a share of the profits except that the thought did
occur to me . . ."

"That I'm on duty, and, besides, you'd have no way of getting
them to me," I said. "Oh, well, it's an entertaining thought, I guess.
And if I do happen to make it back here, I'm expecting to be shown
the town," I added.

"Nothing would give me greater pleasure. Well, we'd best get
on to coffee and the trifle; they will be here soon enough."

And that was the nearest thing to business we discussed during
that last dinner. There really was nothing else to talk about anyway.
Priestley's plan would work or it wouldn't, and the preparations
were already made and things set in motion. We might as well
enjoy the pleasures of a sweet dessert over coffee and a good, comfortable stretch by the fire before we started off on what might be
our last night alive.

So we had our coffee and dessert, and we talked about comedy
and Molière, and about Hogarth and Rowlandson, and why some
centuries have better cartoons than others, and if it wasn't what I
had come to this time to do, it was certainly the kind of thing that
the century delighted in, and it was what I needed to do.

We had just let it get comfortably quiet, and I was letting myself
daydream a little about Chrysamen and the letter I would write to
her when I got back, when the delicate little clock on the mantel
chimed quarter of eight with its brass bells. The two of us stood and
picked up our small kit bags—very small considering how much
traveling we had ahead of us—and started for the door. At that
moment the whistle on Priestley's steam-engine coach sounded outside the door.

" 'Harper calls, 'tis time, 'tis time,' " Sheridan said. "And 'When
shall we three meet again?' "

I followed along after him, muttering, " 'I coulda been a contender.' "

"I beg your pardon?"

"A line from another sort of play . . . one your timeline hasn't
come up with."

"Ah."

Priestley and two others were waiting in that coach; others
were to arrive out at St. James by trolley or on foot. We had forty-
five minutes to get there, which in the crowded streets of London
was not as much as it seemed.

The whole way there, Sheridan kept muttering, " 'I coulda
been a contender.' Fascinating sort of rhythm it has. 'I coulda been
a contender.' "

I had a feeling I had intervened more than I intended in these
people's culture. And since in this timeline Marlon Brando would
probably never get born, the chances of having him play me
seemed pitifully slim.

The coach jounced and thumped its way across Blackfriars
Bridge and through Southwark, its carbide-gas headlamps stabbing
into the darkness ahead of us. It was an experimental model that
Priestley was hand-building for some nobleman—he and Watt had
some kind of rivalry going for who could most revolutionize industry, I gathered, and this gadget was part of it. It was probably one
of the most recognizable moving objects in London, and we were
counting on that fact.

The two men Priestley had brought were strong and burly, and
they had something you didn't see much in that century—deep
suntans. Chances were they were officers of some regiment. They
were being kept in the dark about all of this. If things went wrong,
they couldn't turn us in, and if they had an alibi of ignorance, it
might save them from the firing squad. So we didn't speak to them.

After a long interval one of them raised a window, leaned out,
and asked something of the engine tender. When he came back, he
said, "As you had guessed, sir, there are now three coaches following us with their lights out."

"Steam, Luke's Patent, or horse-drawn?" I asked.

"Luke's Patent, all three, sir."

That was a nuisance. Steam carts could have been put out of
action with a hole in the boiler, horse-drawn by killing the horses.
Now I would need to fire enough shots, and make them go into the

right places, to put that very simple and clever steam engine out of action.

We wound deeper into the tangle of streets that was South-wark; the area was in fact one of the older parts of the city, Shake-speare's theater had stood there, and it had been old then, and so there were plenty of alleys and niches. We wanted somewhere truly narrow. Priestley's coachman had grown up down here.

We hoped his memory was accurate.

Finally, as we wound down a narrow, dark alley that we were assured had an opening on the other end, pursued by all three carts, I opened the bag, got out the Closer weapon, and then opened the window. I climbed carefully through the window, grasping the little ladder that was supposed to let you get to the roof, and climbed up, hoping all the while that the little brazier that heated our Sterling engine wouldn't tip on me.

Crawling past the coachman, I sat down on the tail. The coach bounced horribly in the rutted streets, and I really needed both hands for the weapon, but eventually I got the sight folded and pulled out to a comfortable height, and the rest of it unlimbered so that it rested in my forearm. I was ready to shoot.

Some twiggling at the scope control let me find the setting for infrared, and now I could plainly see the rims of the cylinder as-semblies on the three coaches following us, since those rims were heated in the braziers.

Moreover, by a little fine adjustment I discovered that I could see the wheel hubs, for the friction produced just enough heat to illuminate parts of the axle and wheel assemblies to the weapon. That finally gave me a thought.

There had been a lot of stories back at COTA about the fact that the number displayed did not seem to correspond accurately to the number of shots a Closer weapon would still fire. This proba-bly meant that we didn't actually understand how the weapons did what they did. You could use them like a SHAKK for a while; then they would begin to whoop, and you had to throw them away or they would go off like grenades. Their power source was clearly not the little baby nuke that a SHAKK carried—Closers didn't even want to share a timeline with nuclear power, let alone carry around a little direct-power reactor with them—but just what it was was another good question. Possibly an antimatter device of some kind, but those were at least as radiation-prone as the nukes; was it only fission and fusion the Closers were afraid of? Or maybe somehow they were making atom-sized black holes and drawing power by throwing matter into them; according to that theory, the "whoop whoop whoop" noise was triggered when the Hawking radiation got too intense, indicating that the black hole was about to blow apart. It seemed quite impossible to say, anyway; all we knew was you could shoot for a while, then it would begin to malfunction unpredictably, and then finally it would start whooping and blow up.

Anyway, it wasn't whooping yet, and it had not yet malfunctioned in any other way. I thought for a long instant about just how long and dark and winding this alley was, and then waited until I got a clear view of the last coach pursuing us.

This wasn't exactly *The French Connection*—none of these buggies could do any better than about twenty-five miles per hour and all of them were bouncing around in the muddy London alley as if they'd been Jeeps racing through Baja. I was going to have to count very heavily on the homing properties of Closer ammunition.

I finally had a long breath of clear view of the last carriage. The rim of the cylinder assembly on top glowed where the brazier heated it. The brazier itself was one bright mass of light in the infrared scope; the occasional glimpses of the bearings were like fireflies.

I sighted on the rim and squeezed off one shot. There was not the slightest recoil against my forearm—even the SHAKK has a tiny kick—and god knew how the ammo was doing what it was doing, but it hit that whirling iron rim and apparently steered right around through it, peeling it off like the skin off an apple.

I saw that in my peripheral vision as I aimed and fired at a wheel bearing; an instant later the coach slumped sideways as its wheel came off, and it plowed into the side of a building. Then I turned my attention to the coach nearest us, from which two pistol shots had just roared in quick succession—the boom you get from a .45 is unmistakable, so I knew my counterpart was in there—and gave it three quick shots, one each for the rim of the cylinder assembly, the bearings on one wheel, and the bearing on the main drive wheel. The coach fell into pieces and slammed another wall.

We were gone before I got a shot at the middle coach.

It was as if I had felt a silent hug from Chrys—they were

jammed in the alley, immovable coaches in front and behind, with a very real risk of fire that they would have to fight (not because they were nice guys but to avoid losing their whole party and baggage)—and I had not fired a shot at one of them. So far as I knew, though they might be shaken up, they were all still alive.

It was a strange feeling, though; a few days ago I'd just have shot all the coachmen and enjoyed every moment. I wondered what kind of fighter I would make without a love for the taste of blood . . . and wondered what I had ever seen in the taste of blood.

It was a fine night, and I wasn't needed back inside the coach, so I sat up with the engine tender, a dour and silent Scot who was supposed to be highly reliable but about whom I also knew nothing. After a while we rolled across Westminster Bridge.

In my timeline, that's an impressive experience—everything is lit up, and Westminster itself is a grand sight, especially at night with the light coming from underneath. But in this timeline there were just a few crude arc lights that were used for special occasions, and this wasn't one of the special occasions. We rolled over the dark Thames, the engine chuffing away beside me; it was heavier than a Sterling and a little bigger, but it was whirring along at a much higher rate of speed and as a result the transmission was just that much more effective and modern; the driver was constantly yanking the clutch in and out and trying to find a better top gear. Priestley claimed to have had it all the way up to thirty miles per hour twice, though never while being officially timed.

We rumbled and thudded over the cobblestone pavement of the bridge, and now we were well on our way. We could assume that warnings had been radioed or sent by runner all over the city, and that we were being treated as the main body of the approach. With luck, the body of men moving silently down Swallow Street would attract much less attention; the group that had gathered by St. George's Hospital and was now coming quietly up Piccadilly would likewise gather no close inspection.

We hoped, thanks to the attention we had gained with the shooting we had done and the ruckus in Southwark—tied to such a conspicuous vehicle—to find them ready, waiting, and excited to see us. And since there was no official business tonight, and the King had become so secluded, whatever force there was, hidden or visible, would move to get between us and Buckingham.

They would probably not worry much about St. James Palace, though undoubtedly some would be left on guard there. None of the royal family except the rightful King was there, and after all if he started to escape, there would be time to move forces back into place. It was only a matter of a few hundred yards, and St. James Palace, in those days, was surrounded by open ground. The King could not possibly get away.

Or so we hoped they'd reason. These "assisted" timelines were disorienting—the wrong things were there at the wrong times—and that was what we were counting on. The *Great George*, if things were still on schedule, had already slipped off her mooring post near Bethnal Green, and was cruising through the sky toward us. If she could meet her date, Priestley assured us, the naval officers he had talked with had figured out the mechanics of the rest of the escape.

We were betting that they wouldn't think about the aerial route, that it would still not seem quite logical to them.

St. James's Park was dark as pitch, and though we knew it was popular spot for assignations, if anyone was making love out there they were doing it quietly. We were taking the swing to the south and west of the park, aiming to put ourselves between the Palace and Buckingham. The carbide lights blazed out ahead of us, making the trees throw strange shapes into the darkness, and the moon lit the more distant shrubs, bushes, and hillocks as we went on through the night, but no sound came to us over the relentless noisy pulsing of the engine and the roar of the coal-burner.

As we rounded the corner to turn toward St. James Palace, I stretched out almost prone, with my head next to the driver. The engine tender had picked up a Pennsylvania rifle, and I heard the windows sliding open under me as Priestley, Sheridan, and the nameless officers readied themselves. We had been making plenty of noise and running with lights on; we had shot it out with Closers less than fifteen minutes before. We expected half the Royal Army at any moment.

We turned the corner and it was just as dark and quiet as it had been before. Through the trees, which did not yet have their leaves, we could see Buckingham House and St. James Palace, and there were a bare few lights burning in each. There was no trace of the armed opposition we were expecting, and even less of the armed irregulars that were supposed to free the real King and get him to the roof for the *Great George* to pick up.

There was nothing but silence and the darkness, the sputter of our lamps, the chugging of our engine, the grinding of our wheels on the pavement. We might as well be driving into a stage set.

Then suddenly there was a single man in front of us, waving his arms frantically and shouting. The steam-carriage slowed and swung wide; I flipped the Closer weapon to infrared and scanned for any possible ambush, then shouted to the driver that there was no one else. We slowed to a stop just beyond the man, and he ran up to the coach window.

"Dr. Priestley! Mr. Sheridan! Mr. Strang! Sirs, it's bad news, the worst, and for the love of Christ put out them lamps if it's not too late already!"

Without waiting for Priestley's barked "Do it!" the driver killed the lights; the engine tender began to stoke the now-idling engine, getting it hot and ready to run fast if we needed to.

"Sir," the man said, still panting, "Sir, listen, we're betrayed, I think. Or some such. They got our main columns, sir, they got us in the street far from here—"

"Who got you—"

"The King's Own Scots Machine Guns, sir, and the King's Riot Cavalry, them new forces, they met us in the street, sir, it's a massacre, there must be hundreds dead, and they knew right where and when to find us. We didn't get near to St. James's, sir, you're here without friends, and you've got to turn and run—"

He coughed violently, and it was only then we saw that his shirt was stained with blood. "Good Christ, man, are you—"

"Dying, I think, Gov'nor. Had to warn you or we'd have—"

The men were hauling him into the carriage; I crouched upright and began to sweep the landscape with the spotting scope set on infrared plus visible light boost.

Below me I could hear the muffled cries of frustration as the man died despite their best efforts; he was hit in the lungs, might have made it if he hadn't run a mile to get to us, or so Sheridan said that the small, pale man, who turned out to be a surgeon, had said.

I swept twice more without seeing anything. If they had found some way of getting at us, they must be invisible. I turned the scope back toward St. James Palace.

There were at least a hundred guards moving swift and silent as shadows out of St. James Palace—men who were moving in a quick, stealthy "buddy rush" that meant they had to be the First Virginian Rangers, one of the deadliest forces in the Royal Army— tough frontier riflemen who had scouted for Braddock in the War for Quebec and later raided far behind the lines in France itself.

I whispered the news down to the men below; we had no more than half a minute till they got here, and they weren't moving like they were looking for us—clearly we hadn't killed those lights soon enough, or maybe a glow was showing from somewhere on the steam engine. There was no time to get ourselves turned around and in motion the other way; we would have to stand and shoot.

And nobody at COTA had ever told me—maybe nobody had known—how you got a Closer weapon to fire on full auto.

"This looks like business," I whispered to the men below.

·14·

The carriage squeaked and shook as the door opened. One of the two nameless Royal Army officers, a tall, thin man with a beaky nose and a strange, piercing stare, got out and walked silently toward the oncoming force. He had gone about twenty paces when the first rank of the oncoming Rangers froze; then all of them did. Then he whistled a strange little tune, and one man in the middle stood up and whistled something back.

There was another exchange of whistles. I was beginning to wonder if maybe we were going to hold choir practice here or something when our man, and theirs, ran forward and embraced each other. Silently, the Rangers stood up; just as silently, our little party got out of Dr. Priestley's steam coach and walked over to join them.

"I suppose this destroys my pretense that people don't know who I am," said the officer who had ridden out with us.

"If I admit I don't, will you explain what's going on?" I asked.

The Ranger officer laughed. "We damned near attacked and killed our commanding officer. This is Colonel Dan Morgan, and we were wondering where the hell he was when we got orders earlier tonight."

It rang a bell, again . . . Dan Morgan. In my timeline, he and Benedict Arnold (back before Arnold had changed sides) had nearly taken Quebec for the Americans.

It didn't take long to explain the situation, oddly enough; the Rangers would go wherever Morgan said they should, so he simply said that the guards inside St. James Palace were holding the real George prisoner, that the George in Buckingham was a pretender and an agent of a foreign power, and suddenly we were about to make the attack with the best infantry we could possibly have had.

I got myself positioned near the front. God knows I'm no soldier—I've never served a day in any uniform other than a security guard's, and "right face" means about as much to me as "keelhaul the poop deck"—but given a nice simple job like "stay out front and shoot anybody who isn't on our side," I could handle it.

We relied on deception for the first step; Morgan and Major Marion walked up to the door and asked the captain, his lieutenant, and his top sergeant inside that wing of the Palace to step out and look at something. Two paces from the door, they abruptly pistol-whipped them and flung the doors open.

The Virginians next to me were on their feet in a silent bound and running for the Palace doors. We were going in through doors in the side of the tower, not through the main part of the Palace, but this did not bring any special relief—there were lots of windows from which we could be fired on.

It didn't take the guards inside long to recover. There was a muzzle flash from a window. A man running beside me stumbled and fell. An instant later I heard the bang.

I popped a shot through the window and heard the wet sock of a hypersonic round going home and turning bone, flesh, and brain into red jam. I scanned other windows, fired at the barrels.

It was a Closer weapon, all right. Our SHAKKs, if you point them at the muzzle of a projectile weapon, will set their projectile to home in on the open muzzle, scour its way up the barrel destroying it from the inside, and finally smash the round backward through the firing chamber to destroy the weapon. The poor bastard who's holding it might lose a finger if he's unlucky, and the way the weapon blows up in his hand isn't going to be any fun, but he's around later to complain about it.

This was a Closer weapon. Aim it at the weapon and it finds the brain of the person who is holding it.

I squeezed off eight shots and eight of them died. That probably meant three more Virginians, or so, got to the door alive.

Once they were inside, there was no stopping them at all.

These were men who were used to fighting with knives in the dark, unexpectedly, out in the middle of the forest. Given lights, untrained opponents, and plenty of others to watch their backs, the Virginia Rangers smashed their way through. The guards inside began to throw their weapons down, first in ones and twos, and then by the dozen, until suddenly this tower of the Palace was ours.

I raced up the stairs to where Colonel Morgan and the rest were talking excitedly to the King, who looked thin and ill but functional. "I am so glad to see all of you," he said. "Now we need only get my family and we can—"

There was a loud crash from downstairs, and the thunder of gunshots. I darted out and was halfway down the stairs when I saw that a counterattack was under way; grenadiers were trying to force their way in down a long hallway, and were being held back by Virginians crouched behind overturned tables. I popped two of the grenadiers with rounds from the Closer weapon, and that seemed to make them retreat.

A Ranger strode up to me, his soft leather boots thudding strangely on the hard marble surface below him. "Sir," he said, "we have a major problem. It looks like there are troops coming out of Buckingham, and some of the forces that went out to suppress the mob in the streets are returning as well. We're going to be cut off and surrounded very quickly if we don't get moving soon."

He probably wasn't supposed to salute a civilian advisor like me, but what did I know about that? Besides, he was standing there looking like I should know what to do. "I'll let the Colonel know," I said. "Meanwhile make sure everyone is ready to move."

He nodded, so it must have been the right answer.

I raced back up the stairs—this was four flights of marble steps, past a dozen paintings that really ought to have had some attention and more fine furniture than you can imagine; there's plenty of exercise in my job, but, though you travel, there's no chance to sightsee.

When I burst back into the room, I discovered several people— Morgan, Priestley, and Sheridan among them—looking very carefully at the floor or off into space, clearly trying to appear to be listening to the King and actually trying to come up with some overwhelming argument.

"It's quite impossible," George was saying. "I can't leave my family to the mercy of these scoundrels, and most especially I can't leave my eldest son—and heir!—to their attentions. So we *must* cross over to Buckingham House and rescue them."

"Your Majesty," Morgan responded slowly, "I am sorry to repeat myself, but we just don't have the forces. We'll be lucky to hold the roof till the *Great George* gets here, if it gets here, and after that it's anyone's guess. I would go after the Queen and your children myself if I possibly could, but we can't risk doing it."

"It's no longer a risk," I said. "It's impossible." Quickly I told them about the troops pouring out of Buckingham and the returning forces from the city.

The King turned and looked out the window, across the low middle of the Palace on the opposite side of the inner court, toward the city itself. Flames were showing in places, and in others there was the unmistakable distant twinkle of muzzle flashes. There was fighting raging across the city tonight.

Major Marion said, "I do believe those troops were sent with orders to hang any Whigs they could take, without trial."

"Oh, God," George groaned. "These bastards have my subjects killing each other."

"Exactly, Your Majesty," Sheridan said, very smoothly—maybe too smoothly, I thought. "This is why we need to get up to the roof, so that when the *Great George* comes we can whisk you away to—"

"Nonsense," George said, just as firmly. He was thirty-seven and looked younger, despite his years of captivity; there was something about the set of his pouty lips over his cleft chin that made you think of a stubborn small boy and feel like spanking him, and yet at the same time his clear, slightly outsize eyes seemed to be looking at and weighing everything, constantly searching for the right thing to do. That was just the way he was; once he locked onto an idea, there wasn't much use in trying to talk him out of it. I was to realize later how hard he worked to make sure he locked onto *good* ideas.

Unfortunately, hard work has never guaranteed success. "The Queen must be frantic with worry, especially since she has had cause enough in the past to fear for my sanity, and it's impossible not to reassure her on this point just as quickly as I can. And then, too, has it not occurred to any of you that they have the Prince of Wales? If I die, they will have a perfectly legitimate Regency that they control. In that case all the effort you have made will be wasted."

The other obnoxious feature of the King, I realized, was that every so often he would hit on something he was right about, and those ideas would be a thousand times harder to shake him off of. I had just had the sinking realization that this was shaping up to be one of those operations they pick through at COTA ("Now how could this blunder have been avoided? Given that the situation was already a disaster, what could they have done?"), when three panes of glass blew in at us. The other side had gotten riflemen onto the roof of the wing we were facing.

Everyone took cover, and Morgan dragged George to a fairly safe corner. I took a look outside, saw a few of them, and popped them with the hypersonic weapon. Sickeningly, I realized that "popped" was more than just COTA slang—these guys went to messy pieces like squeezed pimples.

There was firing now from windows on all sides of the tower, but there were muzzle flashes all around as well. We were surrounded and cut off.

I heard Morgan pointing this out to George, who made an impatient, hissing grunt, and said, "Then do the best you can. I'm at your disposal, sir, if anyone has a good idea."

By now I was running from window to window, trying to get riflemen whenever they fired. I had probably killed twenty men, besides the ones killed in the first rush on the building, and every one of them had doubtless been quite certain that he was dying for his country—that is, he would have been if he'd had time before he was torn to bloody rags. In the whole city there were probably not actually twenty people consciously on the wrong side of all this—it was all over a deception and a misunderstanding.

Damn, but my counterpart and his cronies were talented. I was going to have to find them and reward them. . . .

Morgan gave a low whistle, and I crawled to his side. He'd been using one of the new bolt-action Pennsylvanias, with a sniper scope, and I'm not sure he hadn't killed more men than I had with homing ammunition. When a frontier marksman like Morgan pointed a gun, something died.

"Strang, the news just got worse," he said.

I could hear the crashes, booms, and screams far below as the Virginia Rangers held the ground floor—for now.

I peeped out the window and saw. The Palace was beginning to burn.

"They're lighting it," he said, answering my question. "It's probably worth it to them just to get rid of us, get rid of the real King—and with any luck this way there will be plenty of bodies to hide his among—"

"Yeah, and I'll be burned beyond recognition," George said, crawling over to join us. "I don't suppose there's anything useful I can do except not die, just now."

"That will be useful, and it may be quite an accomplishment," I said. I looked up and managed to bag a man with a torch before he could apply it to the house; it made the others hesitate. Dan Morgan's rifle barked, and another of them fell. The rest broke and ran, but after all, there were fires already burning that we could not fight, and the air was fast getting thick with smoke. The way gunfire was echoing in the stairwell suggested that we weren't going to hold the ground floor much longer, or the floor above it—too many doorways, too many windows, this was a palace, not a castle or a fort, and it had not been designed to take a siege.

"We're going to have to retreat to the roof in any case," Morgan said. "I hope the damned Navy turns up with that airship, or we've really lost."

It's hard to describe how well the Virginia Rangers handled the retreat—I was too busy to see much of it, it was so confusing that no one could have managed an accurate picture, and besides, it breaks my heart to talk about it. But they managed to bring along their wounded and even most of their dead, and they made the enemy—who should never have been set up to be the enemy!—pay dearly for every step, room, and hallway.

It took the better part of half an hour, while St. James Palace blazed around us. I guessed that in this timeline Buckingham would become the important one much faster and sooner.

Whenever I could get a glimpse out the window, I did, and I hated what I heard and saw—it looked like much of modern London was going to burn down before this was over. How much of that was obstruction of fire companies by the struggling factions, and how much of it just the fact that the cities of the time were flammable and fire-fighting techniques were crude? I don't suppose we'll ever know.

The lower floors of the tower itself were on fire by the time that those of us around the King were getting him onto the rooftop, and the strong updraft was going to turn the place into an inferno at any moment; as soon as a draft broke through with enough force, the whole tower would become one big chimney, and we'd all be cremated. The only positive thing you could say about it was that the fire was now so hot that the enemy couldn't close with us.

Besides myself, Priestley, Sheridan, the surgeon, and Morgan and Marion, there were eighty-three living men on the roof. Rifle bullets were pocking the surface of the roof as sharpshooters tried to kill our men up there, but a shot across a burning roof is extraordinarily tough from below—the smoke and flames are in the way of your aim and the strong, unpredictable drafts will distort your shots. It was frightening, but most of them were not even managing to hit the roof.

The noise between the shooting, the burning, and the screams of the wounded and the dying, was completely deafening, and that was why we didn't hear the *Great George* at once. It was only when she turned on her spotlights that we actually realized that rescue was at hand.

The *Great George* was a dirigible, but if you start picturing the kind that were around in our timeline from about 1890–1940, you won't imagine anything like it really was.

To begin with, it was right at the edge of what was feasible for its day; it had an amazing all-aluminum keel with good pine ribs, but it couldn't have fully round ribs the way a full-blown dirigible does, so it was flat on *top* where spacers were put in to keep the ribs in the right position. So it had a strange "flattop" look, which was exacerbated because for fire safety the six big gas-fired Sterling engines were put on top of the ship. So start by imagining a dirigible with the top half cut away and with wooden propellers up on trusses, so that it looked like there were six old-fashioned farm windmills sticking out of the top.

Then, too, there wasn't anything they could use cheaply to make that much hydrogen, and though they had vulcanized rubber and latex, they didn't have enough to cover the gas cells inside the ship—so they compromised by using producer gas, the stuff you get by passing steam through a bed of glowing coal. It's a fifty-fifty mixture of carbon monoxide and hydrogen, both of which are lighter than air, and both of which will burn.

Besides, keeping the gas in the cells warm greatly increased its lifting power, and the ballast of water and coal underneath helped keep it upright and on course. And finally, since to make producer gas you burn the coal in a sealed vessel, there was less risk of sparks—the engines simply burned the same producer gas.

So in addition to all that other stuff, imagine the same object with a big, heavy aluminum vessel, the coal burner, the size and shape of a large apartment building Dumpster, hung under it, and two tanks of water attached to the sides of that.

It was a dreadfully silly-looking gadget, even before they painted a big Union Jack on each side and an image of George III on the prow, and even before they put the little hanging pilothouse with all its Georgian gingerbread and columns up under the prow, with what looked like a steamboat cabin hanging behind that, where the troops and passengers went.

And just to top it off, there were the half dozen machine guns (big crank jobs like the early Gatling guns) and tiny cannon that studded the catwalks around the outer edge.

It looked, in short, like what an airship would have looked like in a science-fiction movie of 1875, if there had been any such thing.

It had to be just about the most beautiful thing I had ever seen, and I was yelling and hurraying like everyone else. It made a big, graceful turn, and as the people inside realized which side it was on, a fusillade of shots screamed out toward it.

Gravity is not on the side of an upward-bound bullet, but it is on the side of a cannonball moving downward. The cannon on the *Great George*'s starboard side boomed and roared, one after another, and the other wings of St. James's, already in flames, flew to pieces, taking the sharpshooters posted there with them. The cannon boomed again, dirt roared up from one clump of bushes, and bodies lay there like broken dolls. We saw dozens of men flee from their spots on the lawn and grounds; the thought of becoming a choice target was simply too much for them.

Give everyone involved credit for guts; the airship had to sit there for several minutes while just about its maximum possible load of people walked across narrow gangplanks to the entrances on the top, sometimes carrying other wounded people. Getting the King across made him good and furious, for he fully intended to be the last off the roof and had to be swayed by arguments that if we lost him, we lost everything. And the last few of us running across the gangplanks had an experience that I'd just as soon have missed—fleeing across something twenty inches across, rocking up and down, bridging the gap between a burning tower and the rocking airship. There were hand lines about ten inches above the gangplank, and believe me, I held on to them.

I was only stupid enough to look down once, and notice how much my gangplank was dancing around above the blazing wreckage below. Then a stray bullet, from somewhere far off (they were too afraid to get close) burst through the gangplank less than four feet in front of me; had I been there, I'd have been injured or killed. I looked at the bobbing airship, her underpowered engines desperately trying to keep her in position, and at the burning tower that was now shedding blazing pieces into the court and open yards below, and at that bullet hole, and thought, *Boy, am I lucky*.

The laughter from that thought carried me right on across the gangplank, scuttling like a monkey climbing a shaking stick, clinging to the ropes for dear life, bent over and coughing.

They just cut the gangplanks free—they had spares and there was no way that anyone was going to untie them at the other end—and we started to rise into the night sky. Producer gas is flammable—it's a fuel, after all, and it's what the engines were burning—but it doesn't blow up quite so easily as hydrogen. Even so, the crew had been climbing around madly, with all the healthy Rangers pressed into service along with them, getting sparks put out before they could burn through the heavy canvas fabric.

The heat from the fire had warmed the ship steadily, making it tough to keep *Great George* level as the gas cells on the side nearer the fire warmed more; the moment they cut loose, the captain dropped a load of ballast, perhaps in the hopes of nailing some of the people running in under to shoot at us, but mostly just to get us up above the flames and the sparks.

It was a strange sensation; there was almost no forward motion, and the starboard side, which had been nearest the flames, distinctly rolled upward as the whole great airship tilted on its side. The propellers were fighting to catch the air, and all of those of us who hadn't yet gone down the tunnels through the inside to the gondola or the pilothouse found that we had to grab whatever was handy and cling to it.

The black smoke was all around us, so at first there was just a sensation of rising through the choking cloud, and only my own grip on a line in front of me and a peg beside me seemed real.

Then we broke from the smoke, and sweet, clean air filled my lungs. I sucked in a few wonderful breaths, coughing and hacking the dirty taste of smoke off my tongue and lips, and then began to breathe more deeply. It was a cool night, and our ship was warmer than usual; we had a lot of lift, and the ship climbed swiftly into the icy, clear night sky.

It felt wonderful to be alive.

The men around me, most of whom had never flown before, were exclaiming and pointing. I sat up on the little platform that surrounded the main hatch, my bottom on the tiny wooden deck so that I was looking through the railing, and got a good look around.

The Moon and stars were far brighter than they ever are above a modern city, but there were odd palls and wisps against them, and as I got to my feet, I saw why. The city had caught fire at four points—besides the blaze at St. James Palace, which would probably burn itself out, there was a fire in Southwark (guiltily I thought about my wrecking of the Sterling-engine coaches, and how proud I had been not to have killed anyone in stopping them; just possibly I would have made hundreds of families homeless before dawn, despite my being so carefully humane. It seemed like intentions ought to count for something, dammit).

The other blazes were on Piccadilly, about halfway from the hospital to the Palace, and on Swallow Street, clear up by Hanover Square. They were clearly getting out of hand already; this was going to be one of those truly bad fires in the city's history, maybe as bad as the one in the 1660s. London would be a different place in this timeline because of what had happened tonight, and that, too, made me sad.

And yet the rightful King was now at large. Moreover, word would be out in the city right now, and the rumors would have the city ready to rise on our behalf when we needed it to.

If it hadn't all burned to cinders, of course.

I stood for a long time and watched the silvery Moon shine off the dark Thames, and the streaks of smoke from the great, leaping fires. Airships are too quiet and fly too low; every so often I could hear the shrieks of those fleeing the fires or the crash of houses coming down. It was going to be very bad, I figured.

The Rangers were slowly filing down the hatchway behind me, a little sheepishly because they weren't the sort of men to get lost in the scenery quite so easily as all that.

The airship came about and began to work its way southward; to fly into any sort of head wind would have been very difficult and slow with her enormous cross section and relatively weak engines, but she did well enough at heading south into Kent to get herself over open water. I looked around once more, at the Moon and stars, at the dark land below unmarked by any farmyard lights as yet, and then again at the distant, burning city, and shivered with the cold of the early-spring night so high up.

When I finally descended through the long tube that wound between the gas cells—the big, spherical balloons that held the lifting gas—to the outside catwalk, and then walked along it to the gondola, I was chilled to the bone, and bothered, too, by the strange new sensations I was feeling about having been in a fight. I wasn't just tired and sore, as usual, but there was also a feeling of sadness at the lives cut off. It was hard for me to shake the feeling that someone might have loved someone I killed, or that someone might have treasured a house I had accidentally set fire to. And the Palace of St. James was absolutely irreplaceable; they'd lost some of the finest art their timeline had, and a library of rare books besides.

I wasn't sure, just then, that Chrysamen's improvements in my character were actually doing me all that much good. There was still a long fight ahead of me, and feeling bad after the last one is not a positive sign. I would have to talk with her about this.

Or about anything else in the world. Hell, as long as it was with Chrysamen, we could talk about raising parakeets, recipes for stewed bananas, or common indoor houseplants, and I'd love it.

As I came into the gondola, the King turned to me and smiled. "Oh, there you are, Mr. Strang. Please join us—we're having a sort of a council of war."

"Sure." I discovered there were a bunch of people around a tiny desk with a map, and an empty chair, but no one was sitting on it—probably because the King wouldn't sit when so many others were standing, and no one else would sit in the presence of the King.

The captain, a quiet, polite man named Richard Pearson, was showing us all how it looked on the map. "Now, we can set down several places in Kent," he began. "There we can unload the Virginia Rangers, at least their wounded, but I would think the whole lot of them if possible—they're extra burden and there isn't much we can do for them aboard, nor anything much they can do for us while we are airborne.

"Now, after that the matter begins to get genuinely complicated. As pure theory we are carrying enough coal and water to get us across the Atlantic, but of course we cannot take that chance with the King in so dangerous a situation—the first crossing of the ocean by dirigible, and not even in the easy direction, with the west-to-east winds, as we had intended. When Admiral Howe first informed me of the situation and our mission, he stressed to me that he would have some ship or other meet me in the Channel, but as yet I've neither the name of a ship nor a position for one; our man on the radio is trying to raise the Admiral in order to get some orders on the subject.

"Once I've deposited His Majesty with whatever vessel will take him across the sea to New York, then I would say . . . I beg your pardon?"

The King had turned to whisper something to a young officer.

"Ah, no, Captain Pearson, excuse *me*, please," King George said. "I was indulging in some calculations of my own. I am told it will be more than an hour before we touch down in Kent?"

"It will indeed."

"Then if I can get pen and paper, I can send off a load of letters with the Rangers—each of the letters containing some little thing that only I might remember about some lord or politician, plus the vital information that it is indeed I who am at large. That should fix that usurper on my throne."

"It should indeed, Your Majesty," Sheridan said, grinning. "And it might well allay some of the worrying of your family—"

"Or delight William, the young scamp," the King muttered, but he was obviously pleased to have everyone think his idea was a good one. We found him a surface to write on, a pen, and paper, and he set to work.

The empty field in Kent where we set down was broad and dark, but Captain Pearson had seen the highway from above, not far from there, so that the Rangers would be able to move quickly once they disembarked. The King had managed, writing as quickly as he could, to come up with fifty-nine messages, plus a short open letter to his subjects, and these were divided among the Rangers, who undertook to see that the mail got through. Priestley elected to go back with the Virginia Rangers, to use his political influence to help make sure people believed the truth.

We had carefully hauled ourselves down on our anchor lines and banked the fires, and that had taken the better part of an hour

in its own right; now Sheridan and I stood on the catwalk and
waved good-bye to the forces we'd fought beside. There was a long
moment of a kind of salute, as the assembled Rangers waved back;
then we cast off our lines, the stokers began to pile coal into the gas-
making vessel beneath the ship, and we were off into the night sky
again, climbing after the now-sinking Moon. It would be daylight
soon. It had been a very long night, and though it hadn't gone as
planned, it was going pretty well.

When we returned to the pilothouse, Captain Pearson was
muttering under his breath and appeared angry. "What on Earth is
the matter?" Sheridan asked.

"Oh, it's just the vessel we're to meet," Pearson said, glaring
around him. "That man irritates me. He's annoyed me since the
day I met him, and so of course it *would* be to his ship—well, his
boat, really—that I'm transferring our King. I understand Howe's
thinking perfectly, and I wouldn't dream of arguing. But how annoying, how absolutely annoying—"

"What's the vessel?" I asked, hoping to divert his attention.

"HMS *Nautilus*, also known as Bushnell's Folly," Pearson said,
"the only ship on Earth where men above a certain height are not
welcome, which is why the best-qualified man in the fleet is that
annoying, scrappy, quarrelsome, bowlegged *little* Welshman—"

At that moment there was a shout from the forward lookout. I
ran out onto the catwalk and looked where the lookout was pointing.

All around me people were muttering in wonderment, not
knowing what that could be or what it could mean. But though I
didn't move, it wasn't because I didn't know what it was. Quite the
contrary.

I didn't move because for a few long moments I was frozen in
shock. What was coming at us was one of those Closer flying machines like the one that had attacked Chrysamen ja N'wook and me
not that long ago (subjective time, anyway) in the Himalayas. It was
a little smaller, but it had a cabin that stood on legs that rested on
four spinning disks, and it was closing in rapidly.

I pulled the Closer weapon onto my forearm and took several
shots at the oncoming craft. Nothing at all happened. I had just
time enough to figure out what that might mean before the weapon
in my hands began to make whooping noises, and I hurriedly
pitched it over the side. It vanished into the night, and the airship

lurched upward several feet; Pearson was going to be mad at me for dumping weight without warning.

Down below the calm sea lit up as the device flared into brilliant light; long moments later a deep boom came up to us. But I had no eyes or ears for that—I had grabbed my Colt .45 Model 1911A1 and was standing on the catwalk in the standard police academy firing position. The first time I shot down one of these things, it had been on sheer dumb luck; I hoped the luck of the Strangs was continuing.

Or, considering who was almost certainly at the controls of that gadget, I hoped the luck of *one* of the Strangs was continuing. And I hoped it was the right one.

The craft whirred closer, and I could see that it had just one person aboard. I leveled my pistol, calmed myself, and waited.

·15·

The thought of Chrys wouldn't leave me alone in that long few seconds, and then I realized why. There was something she always did that I always forgot. My hand leaped into my pocket for a moment, and I turned on the help button. If this wasn't Closers turning up with a major technical advantage, I didn't know what was. And if nothing else, maybe an ATN team could get the King off this airship before we all demonstrated that you can cook anything better with gas.

The enemy ship was very close now, closing to within pistol range, and I realized the craft itself must be unarmed, or we would already be on fire and dying. It veered to the side, and I saw the other Strang—it had to be him, of course—pull down a window and draw his own pistol.

We shot at each other several times on that pass. As soon as I fired I became his chief target. But his aircraft was so little—that cabin was smaller than a Volkswagen Bug and the whole assembly not much larger than a big pickup truck—and bouncing around the sky like a crazed bat, and I don't think I came close to a hit.

If he'd had tracers in that pistol, he'd have finished us for sure—all he needed to do was to set one gas cell on fire, and we were all dead—but he didn't. The bullets were the special hollow point that deforms into a star shape that rips flesh into hamburger—I should know, it was my gun and ammo he was using—

but nothing in their path was even giving them enough resistance to make them do that; his shots cut through the thick canvas into the inside, but even when they pierced a gasbag, all they did was make a tiny hole. And at the low pressures this thing operated at, it would take a long time for the gas to leak out.

After his first pass, I had considerable help on the rail; there were a half dozen Royal Marines on board the *Great George*, and they took up posts with rifles, plus of course there were the ship's machine guns. His first try had told me he was desperate, but "given the outfit he's working for, that only means he's afraid of what they'll think of him. He's more afraid of his bosses than he is of us. So there could be thousands of them on the way, but he may need to shoot us down single-handed to avoid death by torture, or worse," I shouted, explaining it to Sheridan. "How far does Pearson say we are from the rendezvous?"

"He's started our descent!" the younger man shouted back. "If we can only—here he comes again—"

This time we were ready, and I think his .45 jammed on him after the second shot—given all the abuse the thing had been through, I was surprised it had held out this long. One of the machine guns managed to rake the disks on which his strange, spidery vehicle sat, and abruptly one of those shattered and stopped.

The effect was dramatic. At once the craft fell sideways toward the stopped and broken disk, and then it began to turn slowly in a circle and rise gently upward. Two of its windows shattered as our ship's Marines found the range, and abruptly it climbed up and away from us.

There were a couple of premature cheers, but I wasn't about to believe he'd given up.

Sure enough, in a moment we heard that high-pitched whir, almost a whistle, that the strange little flying machine made, and it came back, flying not quite level and not quite straight, zigging and zagging as it approached, until abruptly it darted between our propeller towers. We fired at it as it came in and as it went out, the red blazes of our machine guns and rifles lighting up the silvery sides of *Great George*.

But the airship had been designed to bombard things below it or to fight other airships that moved as slowly and clumsily as it did. There had never really been any provision for firing much above our own heads, and in any case we didn't want to hit our own propellers. By coming in high and climbing on his getaway, he avoided most of our fire, though if a stray round had gotten one of those disks as he was coming in, we'd all have died together—I suppose that didn't matter as much to him as it did to us, and that was one advantage he had.

In the wash of his passage, two of the propeller towers twisted and bucked, and the whole ship shuddered, but they righted themselves—for now.

"He's coming in again," Sheridan said, drawing one of his useless little dueling pistols.

He'd figured it out now, and this time his dive was steep and directly over our bow, where only two machine guns could be brought to bear. Moreover, it's very hard anyway to aim accurately at a diving aircraft from underneath it, and it's harder the faster it comes at you, so our forward speed worked to his advantage. In moments the strange disked flyer hurtled down upon us out of the starry sky, grew huge, slammed through barely off our upper deck, and climbed away swiftly, futile rifle shots chasing after, as its great wake of air shook and battered our propeller towers.

With a shuddering scream, we lost the forward port prop, the structure that held it twisting just a little too far, and the big pieces of wood crashed and fell across the upper deck and dug into the surface of the *Great George*. The bulk of it slid over the back, taking one cannon with it as it shattered part of a catwalk, and fell away in a tumbling array of junk that would eventually crash into the flat black sea so far below us.

The big gas-heated Sterling engine at the base of the tower, suddenly relieved of its load, thundered as if to tear itself free of its moorings, but the tenders jumped on it and shut it down; it merely shook the whole ship for a few long, frightening moments, and then coughed and died as they turned off the gas flame that supplied its heat.

Far out there, the black dot that was the other Mark Strang in that weird craft was coming around again. If you didn't know where to look, you could easily lose him until he crossed a star—or until the instant the dark shape flashed across the Moon.

Then he was above us, climbing, getting ready for another pass.

Pearson came out onto the catwalk, briefly, megaphone in

hand, and shouted word to all of us—if there were more damage, we'd find it hard to make our rendezvous; as we were going lower, we were losing our maneuvering room.

There was nothing much, really, to do about it except to try to get him again. He came in at a different angle this time, across our bow so that he zoomed across the top of the ship diagonally; the three Marines crouching up there with rifles fired at him as he tore through the space.

He surprised us that time by diving farther *after* he passed the ship; in the long moment it took to depress the guns, he got out of range.

The towers were shuddering and twisting violently, and with a horrible crack, the two propeller towers amidships got close enough to each other to bring their props into contact. There was an instant spray of splinters everywhere and a wobbling, thudding noise as the prop that had lost one blade yanked its tower around like a drunken sailor with a greased walking stick. The other tower recoiled and went over the side; chunks of debris hit the starboard amidships machine-gun crew from behind in a deadly hail of chunks of wood bigger than ball bats; then a piece of the truss, as big as a small car, carried off the catwalk on which they stood. They fell away into the darkness.

Was it only my imagination that I heard one of them screaming on his way down? We were still almost a mile above the sea, though Captain Pearson was bringing her down rapidly.

Then I heard a whoop from a ship's Marine, and turned to see him point; someone had gotten a hit on one of the three remaining disks, for the distant flyer was now shedding bits of it. As we watched, squinting at the distance, the little ship abruptly flipped over, so that it now hung from the disks like a helicopter; it dropped precipitately toward the water, then bounced back upward a little and seemed to stabilize, still hanging upside down from its two whirling disks.

The *Great George* was bucking and rolling like a whale that was slowly deciding it didn't like what was riding on its back. The three remaining engines, overloaded and not arranged symmetrically, could not keep the ship in trim or on a steady course.

Pearson bellowed more bad news through the megaphone. "We've got bad leaks in three gas cells. We'll be sinking toward the water. All crew not fighting or running the ship, get to stations for the lifeboats. And no one is to fire any weapon near any rent or hole in the ship! It could blow us all to kingdom come!"

The dying airship sank slowly toward the water, and all around I could hear the bustle of men readying the life rafts, shutting down the inessential services; there was a rattle of telegraph keys from the radio room in the pilothouse as they called in a last position, hoping to help rescue crews find them in time.

We drew lower; there was nothing for me to do in the evacuation, so I decided I was one of those people who was fighting.

The engines above were backing down to half and lower, trying to find a mix of speeds and positions where they would stabilize us instead of making matters worse, and perhaps just as importantly getting some of the producer gas burned so that it wasn't around to fuel an explosion.

The only thing you could say for that was that we were only yawing slowly back and forth, and we had been in some danger of actually spinning.

The water wasn't more than four hundred feet away when my counterpart came back at us one more time. I'd have to give him some kind of credit for his performance under the circumstances—he was flying upside down, and I don't think he'd had very much training as a pilot—but it was still a sloppy, messy approach, for whatever reason.

Maybe at that moment he just didn't want to live, figuring that the Closers were not particularly sentimental, and if he failed on this mission, whether he lived or died, they'd probably kill the version of his family that the other Strang had sacrificed everything to preserve. At least if he died in action, they were less likely to "make an example" by torturing them or selling them off as one of the lower kinds of slaves.

He lurched through our three remaining propeller towers, the cabin of the little ship mere feet above our top deck. Sheridan managed to empty his brace of three pistols at the cabin, breaking a window, and I gave him the rest of the magazine in the .45, but veering around as he was, and protected to some extent by the cabin, he seemed unhurt.

Then the little craft plunged wildly out of control—maybe one of us had gotten him after all—and swept through the port aft propeller tower and engine housing, carrying all of it away in one big sweep, slapping off the shack that covered the engine and the wooden tower in one blow and hurling the whole wrecked mass to the water below.

The shock to the body of the airship made it turn and pitch, and a great convulsion ran through it as if it were alive; structurally, after all, it was built like a big spring, and so much weight being removed and so much force applied at the end made the whole thing slam and jump like a coil bedspring hit into the air with a tennis racket. Sheridan and I were thrown to the catwalk, and the walk itself tore partway away from the *Great George*.

Suddenly we were hanging by a twisting, turning, smooth-surfaced rope ladder, a thousand feet off the water, as the *George* rolled back and forth. Sheridan clawed for a grip on the line next to me; I reached for him, got him by the collar, and wrenched him over toward the line.

He got his grip, and we began to climb upward in parallel. The line above swayed alarmingly, dancing and wriggling like a poisoned snake, and it was all you could do to work your way forward a handhold at a time. Below us, rungs were dropping from the catwalk, and then whole sections of plank. Twice, we heard the bellow of a man falling from the airship.

Each time something fell, the ship lurched upward and rolled again. Even though it was losing gas quickly and sinking because of that, an airship is always in a delicate balance—after all, what keeps it in place and holds it up is that the air density at the top is just that much less than the air density at the bottom, and the difference is just enough so that the buoyant craft cannot rise into the thinner air above or sink into the thicker air below. The difference is no more than three or four stories of an ordinary building, or the height of a moderate sledding hill—you never notice a pressure differential across that short distance, but it's real, and it's there.

Change the mass of the dirigible by even a few pounds, and that alters the density; alter the density and the equilibrium height—the altitude at which the dirigible is stable—will change.

So as things fell from the airship, even with gas spilling out as well, the equilibrium height rose rapidly, and the airship, single-mindedly chasing that abstraction, wobbled and lurched its way upward, shaking the ladders, catwalks, decks, and everything else to which most of the crew was frantically clinging. Moreover, when weight falls from one side of the ship, the ship rolls to get the heaviest part downward; thus as it shook off pieces of itself like a dog shaking off water, it spun now this way, now that, on its axis.

Far below, the craft and tower had made a huge splash, big enough to throw water up against us even as the *Great George*, unburdened by the weight, swung up into the sky. I don't recall thinking at that moment that it was the end of my counterpart; I know that I stopped worrying about him and concentrated on staying alive.

It had been a long climb up the twenty-five feet or so of the broken catwalk, and Sheridan and I were almost at the top. It was a good thing we were both fairly young, fairly athletic, and not at all overweight, because this had been tough, but we had only about five feet to go.

Then a line parted, and my side of the catwalk and his were abruptly separated. Sheridan suddenly swung clear out to the side, just as the ship rolled. I was swung, too, but not far and not hard, and I just brushed against the heavy canvas side of the main body.

Sheridan swung out almost to horizontal, still just five feet or so away—I was reaching for his hand, but he was holding on with both—and then the piece of catwalk he was on snapped like a whip, and his hands began to slip just as the airship itself surged sideways. He slammed into the side, right where one of those hard pine ribs pressed out against the outer wall, and his head snapped sideways; he might have only been dazed for an instant, though I hope he was knocked unconscious.

I grabbed at his coat, but I got only the tails. He was limp inside it, and so, with a horrible yank, his arms withdrew through the sleeves the way a kindergartner's do when he takes his coat off over his head, and I was left holding Sheridan's coat, still warm from his body, still strong with the smell of his sweat, by its tail as he fell into the blackness below.

The airship again lurched upward, though as it died it was lurching with less vigor at every loss of mass.

For a long moment I clung to the coat as if he might somehow come back for it; then I let it fall, and it whirled away into the night, sleeves flapping.

This timeline would never have its own *School for Scandal*.

Sick at heart, I climbed the last few feet in seconds, and then scuttled along, always holding on, toward the bow and the pilothouse.

Pearson was still keeping some semblance of order, and the ship was going down fairly gently. His biggest worries were keeping the King from jumping in to help in dangerous situations, and the danger that the coal-gas generator, which was still burning—there was no way to put it out quickly—might ignite a gas cell and cause the whole airship to blow. "And Jones should be here any moment," he said. "He's irritating, but he'll manage. We only have to get to where . . ."

There was another hard slam, but this time we began to sink rapidly; a crew had finally succeeded in cutting the two most-damaged gas cells free, and they had broken through the surface of the dirigible and climbed high into the sky.

The ship was slowly spiraling downward, its keel now almost level, spinning end for end just a little faster than it would have to make perfect circles, because the propellers that were giving us headway and letting us make some use of the rudders were a bit off-center.

"The main gondola is designed to float," Pearson said, "and it has the lifeboats. The sea is dead calm. I think our best chance, almost surely, is to get it set down on the water, to begin to release as much gas as we can, and then to cut first the gas generator and then the bag free. The generator will go right to the bottom, where it can hardly do any harm, and if we get the gas cells deflated far enough, then the weight of the gondola alone should be enough to keep her down; at that point we can cut ourselves free, let the body float up and away from us, and then get into the lifeboats."

I hate feeling useless, so I volunteered for grunt duty on the crew cutting the gas generator free; there were five of us, and the job was simple enough—severing every other line holding it on. It was a little frightening because even though the generator had been sealed for more than an hour, since we got into trouble, it was still radiating tremendous heat at us, and though we were now on a mostly even keel, we were still settling rapidly enough to warp the frame up above us, and thus things bucked and swung unpredictably.

Thus, as we cut it more and more free, there was the constant danger of having it swing and brush against one of us, giving us massive burns immediately. "It's worse than that, sir," one sailor commented to me as we swung in close again. "We'll be closest to it if it goes."

"If it does what?" I asked.

"If it goes, sir. The water in there is enough to keep the coal burning, don't ask me how, I ain't a scientist, without no more air getting in. That's why it's still hot. And when coal burns in steam it makes gas, sir, and that's what it's doing. But with all the vents shut up in it, the pressure just keeps building and building—and the gas in there is so hot we don't dare vent it, for it would go off as soon as air got to it. So you leave that thing to itself, sir, and it will go off like the biggest bomb you ever seen, sooner or later. I do suppose the old man could have ordered it vented and run the risk of starting a fire from that, but I rather fancy he's gambling all or nothing—if we get this away and into the sea before anything happens, we win it all, and if we don't—well, sir, where we're hanging, there's suddenly going to be a lot of nothing, and I don't imagine even those in the gondola will feel much."

Ever been in a lightning storm when someone points out to you that if you get hit, you'll be the person who *never* knows it happened? It doesn't help much. I kept climbing around, and we kept cutting lines—we were down to just a few, and after that we would have to wait until the generator was actually sinking into the water.

Sailors at the time weren't noted for their long life spans to begin with, and the conversion of the Royal Navy to steam—many decades before it would normally have occurred—had cost even more lives. The survivors were a little too . . . well, let's say philosophic for my tastes. During the ten minutes as the great dirigible finally sank to the calm surface of the Channel south of Kent, my coworkers developed a set of bets about whether or not dunking the hot vessel in cold salt water would distort it enough to make it rupture (and thus blow us all halfway to the Moon, I added mentally), whether when it sank it would blow up near enough to capsize lifeboats, and whether the dirigible would hold together long enough, under the strains of settling onto the waves, for us to get back to the gondola and lifeboats.

I didn't ask anyone how they intended to collect if they won; they were all betting fractions of their life insurance. I did notice that no one seemed to be betting that it would all go just as Pearson said it would, but when I ventured that opinion they all shook their heads.

"The Old Man's as good a skipper as you could wish, and he knows the *Great George* as well as any man, and if she could do what he wanted her to do, she would, but she can't. Not possibly," the sailor beside me explained.

By now the sun was coming up, and we could see that the water was flatter and calmer than one would expect at this time of year, though of course it was no warmer. In the morning light we could see just how much wreckage hung from the sides of the *Great George*, and the many rents in her fabric where things had pulled away or fallen over.

"She's been a fine vessel for all that she flew rather than sailed," one of them said, "and I hope the King—now that we got the right King—will build more like her, for she's a majestic thing."

We were now just seventy feet or so over the water, and the tail—the end we were at—was sinking just a little more quickly than the nose. The airship came back into trim a minute or two later, but now we were down to forty feet . . . and the ship continued to sink toward the water. "You men there, hold off with your axes," Pearson bellowed through the megaphone, "till we know there's enough gas out of her. We don't want you sailing off on what's left."

"Aye aye, sir," the chief of the crew answered. "We don't want that much ourselves."

Pearson nodded and turned back to his preparations. We were barely ten feet off the water, and now he was shouting to the crews aloft, "Bleed her port forward . . . now hold, port forward . . . starboard forward, bleed her . . . now hold—"

We were working our way down a foot or so at a time, the engines stopped, just drifting ever so slowly on the bare breath of breeze.

The gas generator touched first, in a great hiss of steam; the ship bounced up just a little, for the buoyancy of the water took up some of the load, but then settled steadily. Steam bubbled and curled around us in a thick, warm fog. "You're going to have to pay up," one of the sailors beside me said.

"You wait till we cut her free. She might take some time before she blows," one said, and another added, "Hush, listen."

There were creaking and thudding noises, and the moan of metal doing more than it should, as the gas generator settled into the sea. It was the kind of sound you heard in sixth grade when they did the old demonstration of heating up a gasoline can and then capping it and letting it cool, but amplified hundreds of times, and it occurred to me that the metal I was hearing buckle and warp was almost two inches thick.

People on the gondola were whooping and cheering, but the fog from the rising steam was so thick, and the noise from the distorting gas generator so loud, that we couldn't make out why.

Then a little whiff of a breeze carried off enough steam so that we could see what they saw—and we cheered, too.

Floating just two hundred yards from us, the Union Jack waving proudly from her conning tower, was the first submarine in His Majesty's Navy, HMS *Nautilus*, and there on her deck was a small man bellowing back and forth with Pearson about arrangements for taking off, first the King, and then all of us. "Captain Jones," the sailor beside me said. "Him and Pearson don't like each other much, never had, but they're the two best captains His Majesty has, and I hope he sees that."

"Jones?" I asked.

"Captain John Paul Jones, that's him. The man who fought for ten years to get submarine boats built; that one in front of you, the *Nautilus*, has been to America twice, and once ran a hundred miles without coming up, though I understand half the crew was blacked out by the time they did come up. It's said he ain't going to be happy till we have a war that lets him take that gadget out and fight; he's only half a man till then in his own eyes. But that half is more than most folks' wholes, sir."

Whatever Pearson and Jones were yelling at each other about, after a short while Pearson turned to us and said, "The gasbag crew says we're low enough, now, so they'll be coming down off her. Then you cut your lines and *run* here along that catwalk."

"Aye aye, sir!"

A long couple of minutes went by; Jones stood on his tower, arms folded, watching patiently.

Then the crew from aloft emerged from the main tunnel through the body, and one by one climbed onto the gondola. There were eleven of them, and I noted that Pearson counted twice before he gave the order. "Cut the gas generator free!"

We jumped onto the job with all the energy we had, hacking one line after another. The big piece of metal was still not entirely submerged, and baking heat was still coming off the top surface. For that matter it was still groaning and thundering, and the sailor who had a bet down that the contractions would rupture it wasn't giving up yet.

I cut the last line on my side, and the corner of the gas generator under me sank into the water. The chief reached to cut the last line, opposite me, when it parted on its own; the generator floated for an instant, and then the top burst with a boom, spewing flame and glowing metal up into the bag. The chief died instantly as something from the explosion hit him, and he fell onto the top of the sinking generator. The man who had bet it would rupture was thrown into the water; I didn't see what happened to him after that.

The airship bounced above us, yanking the catwalks to which we clung this way and that, but Pearson had figured correctly, and it was not enough to lift the gondola. Instead, it swung and twisted as the gas caught fire. Producer gas doesn't blow up easily at atmospheric pressures, and though the gas pouring out of the cells was blazing, and the airship above us had flames licking through dozens of holes within seconds, it didn't go off with an explosion.

We scrambled along the catwalks as Pearson yelled for us to hurry; I was on the port-side catwalk, which had a hole in it, so I was a bit behind the others as I had to jump that hole.

Then several people were pointing and yelling, and others were shouting for me to hurry. Ten more steps and I would be there—the crews were already cutting through the last of the cables, and the blazing structure, filled with flammable gas, was bouncing on its last couple of cables, eager to float free into the bright morning sky. Eight more steps—why were people pointing and shouting—and I would be—

Something caught my ankle. I fell headlong on the catwalk, my only thought to get those last twenty feet covered before the lines parted, the rescue sub was *right there*, I could see the expressions on everyone's face in the gondola—

And I heard the deep boom of the last lines giving way. I tried to get to my feet so that I could run and dive to safety, but something still held my ankle, something that would not let go, and when I turned to get rid of it—

The face could hardly have been more familiar. It was the other Mark Strang, and he was gripping my ankle tightly with both hands, probably getting ready to twist my foot. He must have jumped from his aircraft and been hanging around in the rigging ever since—it wouldn't have been hard with everyone so busy.

"Oh, there you are," he said sarcastically, when he saw me see him. "Well, it looks like this is where we're going to settle the whole matter."

I looked over the side of the broken, swaying catwalk; the sea was now at least two hundred feet below, and the dirigible was still rising. Blue-and-yellow flames were playing everywhere on the framework above us.

He applied pressure to the foot, just the way he, and I, had learned in the dojo so many years ago. My ankle stabbed with pain, and before I could control the impulse I had flipped right over the side of the gangplank.

·16·

My hands caught the side rope, and I twisted my upper body hard, getting some slack in the ankle, letting myself swing out into space over the water, counting on his not being willing to follow me into the void.

I was right as far as it went; the trouble now was that I was hanging from the catwalk rail with hundreds of feet of absolutely nothing between my boots and the deep blue sea. Furthermore, with the fire raging through it, so many lines cut, and the whole thing rolling because most of the weight had been lost from the bottom, the remains of the *Great George* were coming apart and tumbling down to the sea rapidly. If I could live through the next ten minutes somehow, the dirigible would probably be returning to the ocean surface . . . though how fast or in how many pieces was up for grabs.

His hands were groping for my fingers, and I had no desire to have him start breaking them one by one—and no doubt that he would do that if he could. I grabbed a line running under the catwalk, yanked it hard to make sure that it at least sort of held, and let myself swing out into space.

It was smarter than I knew. Though I looped out alarmingly into space, and there was a sickening lurch in my stomach, I had in fact gotten on the line used for a quick release on the walks, a little trick Pearson had dreamed up for the event of being boarded.

It was a great trick; the far end of the catwalk came free, and suddenly the other Strang, too, was dangling and swinging, in huge, dangerous, whiplike snaps, from the still-rising airship.

Each of us hung perhaps fifteen feet below the body, which actually was no refuge but at least had more things to grab on to in the event that what we were holding on to gave way. I shinnied up that dancing, whipping rope a lot more eagerly than I'd ever done at COTA, or in gym class for that matter, and over to the side of me I could see the other Strang just as eagerly climbing the broken catwalk.

My rope and both catwalks hooked to a long, thin truss on the bottom of the gasbag itself; it was probably a safe bet that whoever got to the other guy's anchor point first would be able to cut the line and send the other guy to his death in the ocean far below.

I was climbing as hard as I could, and so was he; we both knew the stakes. I had a slight edge for just two reasons—I had known that I was going to be swinging out into nothingness and he had been surprised by it, and also a rope tied solidly to a truss is much easier to climb than a slick catwalk that was intended to carry a few sailors, walking very cautiously, on its surface.

I got to the top first and began to swing along the truss like a kid on the monkey bars, being careful not to look down because we had been rising all this time, and I knew perfectly well that every dizzying swoop was now high above the cold sea. In just a few swings I was at the top, where his catwalk hung, ready to cut the line—when I realized that I was not wearing preprepared Crux Op gear. I reached and found neither knife pocket nor knife. Moreover, the pistol in my shoulder holster had been emptied at this clown's aircraft, and I had no more ammunition.

I tried hanging by one hand and pistol-whipping him as he approached, but though I could make him keep his distance, I couldn't deliver any kind of an effective blow with the pistol. And the moorings of the broken catwalk he hung from were unfortunately quite solid on this end.

Just to be annoying, I suppose, he was grabbing at my feet and legs, and trying to slam one of my knees with *his* .45, which told me it was as useless as mine. Meanwhile the vaguely sulfurous stench of burning gas—there was all kinds of contamination in the producer gas here—was getting thicker, and my arms were getting tired.

I went to switch hands, tucking the pistol into my holster before I did so, and just then he swung at me; I lost my .45 (or his, depending on how strict you are about property rights) as it tumbled from the holster. I fought back with my feet and reached behind me to take a big swing back; the combined motion must have been what sent the Colt out of its holster and down to the sea below.

I was gratified that it smacked his shoulder on the way; it wasn't a terribly hard blow, but it was solid, set him back a second, and made him grab on to that catwalk and cling to it with both hands again, at least briefly.

That instant gave me a chance to at least try the butterfly nut on the little gadget the catwalk attached to; it didn't turn easily, but I got it half a turn loose before I had to kick at my counterpart again. The trouble with fighting a man who is below you when you're both swinging free is that there's so much "give" in both of you that very few blows, even hard stomps to the face, land with any force.

On the one hand, if he climbed up higher, he might be able to get hold of my foot or leg and stop me from kicking him; on the other, the higher he climbed, the harder I could kick him.

At that moment, he came up with something—he threw his automatic straight up between my legs. It was a good toss—it hit right where he intended—but there wasn't much force in it, for the same reason neither of us had been able to land much of a blow. Still, it hurt like hell and made me double up and gasp.

Unfortunately for him, throwing the automatic had upset his balance, and it took him a moment to grab back on to the ladder. When he did, he grabbed one rung higher, putting his fingers in range, and I got my foot down on top of his hand and began to grind his fingers with my heel. He didn't have enough grip to let go with the other hand and grab at my foot, so I was able to keep working at his hand for quite a while, feeling the hard little knucklebones rolling around under my bootheel.

But again, in that position, there was only so much I could do. The force I could apply was excruciating, I'm sure, and I was wearing off skin, so that it must have stung like crazy, too, but the fact was that I couldn't actually break the hand unless I stomped on it, and to stomp it I would have to pick up my foot—at which point he would get away from me.

Far below, the broken end of the catwalk whipped around; I

saw planks breaking loose, saw them flung out end over end into
the bright spring-morning sunlight, and watched them tumble
down toward the Channel below. We were higher, now, maybe at
four hundred feet, but I did not think we would rise farther—

Until I realized we were rolling. The dirigible was rotating on
its long axis; the loss of the last half of the catwalk must have just
tipped it far enough so that the top was now heavier than the
bottom. As I hung there from the truss, the starboard side came
around and began to press against me, harder and harder, until it
scooped me up, tilted me over, began to lift me. Gingerly, I put my
feet on the surface.

Scant feet away, the other Mark Strang was doing the same
thing. Behind him, I saw a curtain of blue-and-yellow flame rise, as
the rising gas flowed through new vents, and new fires caught. The
surface shuddered underneath us with great ripples, as, twice,
pockets of gas blew up in low-velocity explosions, and the pressure
wave traveled the length of the ship.

"We end it together, eh, as we began it?" he said. "I just want
you to know you're a fool before you die."

"All right, I'm a fool," I said. "So now try to kill me."

"You've spent your time fighting for things that won't make
you happy. What everyone wants is power, power over himself,
power over others, the ability to get what he wants."

"Sure, that's why you're enjoying having Marie be a slave," I
said. "It must make you feel great to have her give you a thousand-
yard stare and say things she'd never say naturally."

That must have struck the target, at least a little, because he
came after me then, in a neat T-stance skip that I recognized because it's exactly the one I use. His foot lashed out, my thigh coun-
tered, my foot thrust, he gripped it and turned, I dropped into the
Crab and thrust him backward, and he did an inside turn to bring
his hands to my throat just as I brought my elbows up to rake his
teeth. We spun away from each other, staggering awkwardly on the
fabric-covered surface of the aluminum keel, seeing if we could lure
the other onto the softer, unsupported fabric nearby.

He was a little more injured, and perhaps with his drinking
habits he might be a hair slower. Neither was enough to make the
difference. To use my martial arts skills on him was like using them
on myself; we knew each other's tricks deeply, viscerally, and we
could no more surprise each other than you can tickle yourself.

I was looking, as hard as I could, for rubble I could throw, but until seconds ago this had been the undersurface—nothing loose was available. I backed toward the main interior tunnel entrance; maybe if I could fight him down there—

"You love to pull the trigger," he said, as he pursued me a step at a time. "You kill and it makes you feel good. Or if it doesn't, it's only because somebody has shamed you into feeling differently. But the truth is that you kill, and you like to kill. Ever had a woman and then killed her while you came, Mark? You and I are the same guy, we have the same nervous system, and I'm telling you, it would make you glow—"

"I'm surprised you haven't done that to Mom yet," I said. Maybe if I could get him mad enough, it might make him miscalculate.

Or it might make him faster and stronger than I was. There had to be a difference between us I could use, a difference bigger than the little bits of skin missing from his left knuckles.

"You know," he said casually, "I'll probably do it to all of them sooner or later. You get that way when you begin to have real freedom, you know, and I'm not far from having it." He took a long side step that might have been a lead-in to a flurry of punches if he got a little closer.

I took a countervailing side step to put myself out of reach. It brought me almost to the edge of the hard keel, to where the canvas bulged. I saw more gas flare and burn behind him and noticed that we were beginning, very, very slowly, to sink downward. "Must be wonderful to have that kind of freedom," I said. "Freedom to enslave, torture, and kill people you love. Gosh, why didn't I ever think of it—"

"Because you never had a chance to learn, which is why you're a fool," he said, implacably, and closed in on me again. "You haven't found out that after all the sentimental warm fuzzy stuff, the only reason people will give you all the sweet talk and hugs— and don't misunderstand me, I know we need cuddling as much as we need sex—the only reason people give you affection is to get what they want. Romanticizing it doesn't make it any different. That's what it's for. If they cuddle you and hold you, it's because they're getting something for it, even if it's just to congratulate themselves on how well they're doing it . . . and that's why they do it. It has nothing to do with you." He took a big jump forward, and I skittered back.

This wasn't the way I'd been taught in dojo—you're supposed to always attack even when you're on the defensive—but it occurred to me that just now I had no ideas about what might work, and I wanted whatever I did to work. Meanwhile, maybe he'd make a mistake . . . like talking too much, for instance.

"You know, it's funny," I said, "You obviously want me to understand you. As if it mattered for someone to understand you and say that you're right. And yet I don't care if you understand me. I think I'm plain as day. You don't suppose you want to be understood because you know you've got a problem, do you?"

"What problem do you think I have?" He was still working his way closer; in a few moments I would be near enough to the main tunnel entrance.

Behind him, there was a great boom and a puff of flames, all gold and yellow in the clear morning air. It was almost beautiful, even the flickering and dancing fires above the torn fabric and the sudden shine of the exposed aluminum keel.

Just a few more steps, and I could jump down a hole and see if he would come and get me . . . but for right now I did not dare to turn my back on him.

"Well," I said, temporizing, "you know you and I are not judgmental people. We weren't raised that way. But I'd say we are what we make ourselves, wouldn't you?"

Three steps more, just three steps more . . . the flames behind him were dwindling, probably meaning that one gas cell had blown but not all of them. We were definitely drifting downward fast now . . .

"You see we do agree," he said, and now he had seen the mouth of the main tunnel and was trying to prevent me from reaching it, moving to cover me more. He couldn't quite block it, and I couldn't quite get to it, and neither of us was a gambler by nature. The flames died down behind him, but he never looked; I have no idea what might have been going on behind me, because I never looked either. "We are what we make ourselves," he said, repeating me, "and thus the important thing is to have the freedom to work, is it not?"

"If you say so," I said. "I was just hoping to ask why I chose to make myself a fairly ordinary guy with a peculiar job, and you chose to make yourself a vicious, lying, psychopathic bastard."

His face twitched, but I got no answer from him then. The corner of my eye noticed a rain of fabric pieces and bits of wood off to one side, and before I had time to think, I had taken a hard dive for the entrance to that tunnel. He didn't quite catch me, but that wasn't only because I'd distracted him with an insult.

It was because suddenly the sinking wreckage of the *Great George* began to roll over again, and just as suddenly it lurched back upward into the sky, this time tilting up at a crazy angle.

My gut reactions had realized before I had that the rain of debris was coming from something, and then that the something was very likely that fire had burned through or into one of the propeller towers and engine shacks, allowing the huge, heavy engine, its bunker of coal, the massive propeller, and the whole wooden tower to tear loose from the pine ribs of the ship and fall to the ocean.

With such a heavy weight removed from that side, the burning hulk was able, very briefly, to climb again and to right herself, so she was rolling 180 degrees, tilting up toward where the propeller and engine had ripped off, and slowly climbing.

I hit the ladder going head down, caught myself on my hands just barely, and scrambled along it as it rapidly became, first level, and then vertical, swinging back and forth in that dark, dizzy space with only the light at each end of the tunnel—

And suddenly my head began to pound, and I was having trouble breathing—a lot of trouble. I gasped for more air, but it only got worse.

One of those annoying parts of the brain that is right too often pointed out to me that I had gone inside the hull, where lots of producer gas had been leaking for quite a while. Producer gas is half hydrogen, which supplies most of the lift if you use it in a balloon, and more than half the power when you burn it.

But the other half of producer gas is carbon monoxide. The stuff is deadly, and I had just climbed down into a thick cloud of it. I felt an overwhelming desire to sleep, even if I fell off the rungs of the ladder, even for just a few minutes—

I tried to climb down, the way I had come. Carbon monoxide is lighter than air, and it rises; there would be more oxygen below, and though my counterpart was probably still down there (I hadn't gotten rid of him by any trick so simple, had I?), he was only dead eventually; the carbon monoxide was going to get me right now. I climbed down farther, and while I climbed I looked around at each landing I came to and fought the urge to just stretch out on one of those landings and go to sleep. Carbon monoxide kills you by tying up your hemoglobin chemically so that it can't deliver oxygen, but there's some oxygen already in the tissues, about thirty seconds' worth of moderate effort or fifteen of all-out, that's what they told us at COTA, and if I hurried I would not black out . . . I would not black out . . . I would not black out . . .

The bottom landing revealed great gaping holes in the sides of the airship, some timbers still smoldering, a couple of gas cells not yet burst, and the twisted wreck of the keel; how this thing was holding together was a mystery. There was air enough, here, so I dragged myself onto the landing and breathed hard and deep for a few minutes to get some of the carbon monoxide out. My stomach rolled, and I leaned over to throw up—

It came down right in the face of the other Mark Strang, who had been climbing up the main tunnel after hanging on god knew how. He screamed with rage—you try having someone vomit on your upturned face if you don't see why—and started to scramble up the ladder.

I whirled, sitting down on the edge of the landing, braced my arms overhead and my back to the ladder, and kicked him in the face with both feet as hard as I could. Still blinded by the mess I had dropped onto his face, and with his hands slipping in it on the rails, he fell a few feet before he could brace himself in the chimney position in the tunnel. He was about ten feet beneath me, rubbing his face, probably still blinded by pain, tears, and vomit, probably still trying to clear his head.

It had reached a point where my decisions—even if they were completely crazy—were absolutely clear. I wanted to get rid of the other Mark Strang much more than I wanted to live myself. After all, this overgrown gasbag could blow up at any time when a cell rocked against a burning timber, or might fall apart in midair, or might land so hard that I could not survive anyway. The chances of getting out of here were very slim, and in those circumstances you do whatever is going to accomplish the most good in the world. And getting this asshole, this so-different mirror face of me, this thing I could have become—indeed, you could say it was a thing I had become, for our pathways had merely parted in time—getting that out of the world, really, definitely, and completely, seemed like the best thing that could happen.

I jumped down the tunnel onto him, landing boots first on his chest and belly, which gave under my shoes like sandbags. It knocked the wind out of him and sent him thumping downward, so that now he hung by his hands, his body mostly out in the empty space below.

I grabbed the ladder and continued to climb down.

With a deafening crash, the *Great George* tore in half, and the other side end—weighted down by the remaining engine and the forward coal reserve—fell away into the sunlight as we climbed still higher; we might well reach two thousand feet before we finally descended for good.

The force of the motion yanked him harder; I saw his fingers slip a bit. Slowly he managed to close his hands around the rungs—

"All I wanted was not to hurt," he said. "All I wanted was the freedom to live the life I wanted."

"Well," I said, "you know the song." I stamped on his fingers and felt them giving under me; this time I wasn't hanging, and I could apply the full force of my body; a few stamps, and he would fall into nothingness. " 'Freedom's just another word for nothing left to lose.' You're about to lose, which means you're going to be nothing—so enjoy your freedom."

The hard heels of my boots slammed down on his fingers again and again; blood sprayed the side of the tunnel with the force, and he moaned.

"Understand, at least!" he screamed, just at the end.

The only response I gave him was a series of hard kicks in the face, breaking his teeth and nose into a bloody pudding. His eyes were wide, first with terror, then with some sort of rictus, and finally they saw nothing, just before he let go and fell silently away. I watched the twisting, turning body, like a stuffed animal thrown from a great height, until I lost it in the sea below.

I had understood him just fine. That was why I had stamped so hard on his hands.

He was gone, for what that was worth, and now it was just a question of whether or not this thing would bring me down alive. I wondered if I could vent some gas to descend faster, and if that would really be wise. Right now all that was left was a middle section; the tail had burned off, the nose had fallen away, and now I was in a tube open at both ends. At least gas was unlikely to build up in here.

I had stopped rising; the airship was beginning its descent. This was a relief as far as it went; the way it was drifting, it might well make it to France before it touched down, and in that case I could probably come up with some way to get home. Of course it could also blow up at any moment.

I climbed down to look around some more; the Channel was narrow enough here for me to see both the British and the French coasts, so at least my odds weren't bad if there was no explosion. I was some hundreds of feet up, and descending, but I had no idea how fast, and it looked like I was probably seventeen or eighteen miles from France and a little farther from Britain—the narrowest part of the Channel, the Straits of Dover, was visible north of me.

A little searching around inside turned up some completely useless mallets and a couple of wrenches that fit things I didn't see anywhere; the gas cocks themselves turned with a key, which was hanging beside them, but I could see no special reason to descend faster until I knew something about my current descent.

I was definitely lower now than before, and somewhat closer to France, I thought. Not enough closer to give me any assurance of making it there, however.

Well, if you ignore air resistance, a body falls at sixteen feet per second squared. I had a pretty good digital stopwatch still in my pocket after all the knocking around, and finally a good reason to use it. Very carefully, I started the timer and dropped a mallet straight down the tunnel, watching it till I lost sight of it, the way you lose sight of the coyote in the Road Runner cartoons as he falls from a cliff.

And very much like that same coyote, the mallet eventually sent up some evidence of its impact—a big white splash appeared in the calm water below. It was a good thing it was a nice day.

It had taken just thirteen and a half seconds to fall. That was about 181, squared, and times sixteen feet per second squared gave me around twenty-nine hundred feet.

I timed off ten minutes, dropped the next mallet. If the dirigible had been fully functional, it would have lurched upward—they are terribly sensitive when they're actually flying—but as this one was drifting downward, not much happened; I could neglect whatever effect losing the weight was having.

Thirteen point three seconds; that meant around 178 seconds squared, or 2850 feet. Round it all off and say I was coming down at fifty feet per ten minutes, which was three hundred feet per hour, and thus I'd be up here for . . . hmm. Probably about nine more hours.

The galley had vanished with the gondola, and there were no bunks inside the dirigible; besides, if another leak developed, I didn't want to asphyxiate while I was falling to my death. So I couldn't eat and didn't want to sleep. Instead, I took a deep breath and climbed up to the remnants of the top deck around the top of the tunnel, then sat down to think.

That other me had been half-right, which is just about the worst possible position philosophically, since it's harder to see your mistakes. I certainly knew I could enjoy suffering, knew I could enjoy destruction. Hell, I had enjoyed destroying *him*.

But I had not gone as far as he had . . .

It was only that I had never quite realized before that I could. I didn't want to . . . but I could.

I found that I didn't hate him, but I couldn't make myself sorry about his death. It seemed to me that maybe he had overlooked another possibility about himself. He and I each had no way of knowing how many times the Closers had kidnapped me and offered me their particular deal with the devil. I was descended from the timeline where it had never happened. He was descended from one where he had gone along with it. In how many had Mark Strang resisted, and died for his resistance?

It made me feel better, but not much. I had seen some potentials I really did not care for or like, and I would have to do something about it.

I reached that resolution as I sat up there on my fragment of dirigible, a body bigger than a couple of houses, and as we settled down, crossing the coast of France and drifting steadily onward. After a while I noticed that I was being followed by a regular parade—a couple of cavalry troops, plus more carriages than you could shake a stick at. *Great George* had not made a call in France during its trial phase; now of course it never would.

I wondered if the King would put up with having one called *Great George II*? He had hated his grandfather . . .

Well, it didn't matter much. As the sun was setting, I found myself descending into a freshly plowed field in northern France, and an amazing number of Frenchmen were coming out to meet me. I just wished I spoke French.

The middle part of *Great George* bumped along over the soft, wet soil, and then settled like a dying animal that had been run to death. I slid down the side, along one of the ribs, rappelling by a line tied off to the ragged upper deck. There were some noisy huzzahs, to which I responded by waving, which invited more of them, and then finally I jumped down into the muddy field.

I surveyed the crowd; they looked friendly and even enthusiastic. "Does anyone here speak English?" I asked, very loudly.

"I do," said a familiar voice, just behind me, "or near enough." Partly it was familiar because it was a voice I'd dreamed of hearing, and partly it was familiar because it had activated the chip behind my ear.

"Chrysamen," I said, just as she stepped forward and slipped her arm through mine.

"Come on," she said, "it's time for me to take you home. Way past time, in fact. But first we've got a parade to make it to in London, and that's just two days away, and in this miserable century and country we'll have to spend most of that time traveling."

·17·

After the relatively paved roads of England and the Sterling and steam carriages, travel in eighteenth-century France took some getting used to. The stagecoach was miserably uncomfortable—they designed the things for four people (four small French people who had their own built-in suspensions and seat cushions, apparently, since the French stage had neither) but there were six of us in there. Fortunately we were the only English speakers in the coach (though there were two English scholars and a Welsh poet among the nine people riding on the roof), so we had a lot of time to talk and to get caught up on news.

The great thing about working for an agency that uses time travel is that they can take a quick look, see how things are really going, and pick the best time to intervene. Once they knew I was going to win the fight with the other Mark Strang, and that the dirigible wasn't going to blow up, they had literally weeks to prepare a cover for Chrysamen, as a planter's daughter from the West Indies (I thought she looked terrific in the very low-cut styles of the day, a thought which made her look down at the floor in a completely captivating way when I expressed it). Then they dropped her into Paris and had her take the stage out to the little village, only about forty miles from Calais—which, with the roads of the time, amounted to just about a day's travel.

The stagecoach made an ungodly screaming rumble, and a

wheel came off twice during the trip. My seat slammed into me constantly, and when I peeked out the window on one occasion I noticed we were running in ruts about two feet deep. April, of course, was a muddy month, so if anything it was worse than usual—though Chrysamen, whose translator chip understood French, assured me that most people were talking about how mild the weather had been and how much nicer mud was than dust.

There's a strange idea out there somewhere that because many of us like "traditional" cooking, the food must have been better in previous centuries, but the sad truth was that April was a lousy time for a meal—most of it would come out of the root cellar, where it had lain all winter, or it was dried or pickled, and in any case the meat tended to be what we'd think of as tough and stringy. I recognized the meal we had at about two in the afternoon, and I assured Chrysamen that we would have to go to my timeline and visit France if she wanted to know what it was supposed to taste like.

At last, after a day of kidney-battering and bun-slamming excitement, we pulled into Calais. By then Chrys had told me most of what had happened after I was out of it, so I was not quite so surprised at the reception we got there.

King George was a serious, hardworking fellow; apparently he was that way in every timeline. He wasn't particularly smart, and he wasn't necessarily the most amusing wit of the day, so he tended to be about as good a king as the advice he got.

Here, where ATN had intervened to try to create an accelerated and better world, the advice he got had been very good indeed, and the kingdom had been in good shape before the Closers moved in. One thing my counterpart had underestimated was just how strongly the difference was felt between the George III that secured himself in St. James, and the George III the Closers had specially created and trained for the job.

"Somewhere out there," Chrysamen said, "they've got a timeline where George III was mainly interested in expanding the slave trade, promoting wars, and in general running the country into the ground. But when they moved that one over here—Allah only knows what they left behind him in that timeline—he was truly in hog heaven. We've captured all kinds of documents, and four other Closer agents alive. It's the best look we've ever gotten at their plans for anywhere.

"And what we found out they had in mind was to take the

We talked of other things as well, and most especially, though it was painful, we talked about just how tough it was going to be if I wanted to change . . . if I didn't want to end up the mirror image of the man I had killed.

I was glad Chrys was there to talk about it with.

I had said Calais wasn't a complete surprise, but it was still pretty impressive. The Royal Navy had dispatched a fast steamer to take us over to London; the next day there was to be a major parade, and then the King was going to begin the process of revealing the existence of ATN, the sources of help they had had . . . and to start the long, fast march toward full membership in our league of civilized and free timelines. They'd be there before my home timeline was ever even found; in a way I envied them that, and in another way I was glad we were spared the crosstime wars as long as we were.

The parade and ceremonies were impressive, but our work here was done—a new special agent would be coming out to replace Rey Luc, and we were due to return to headquarters.

Captain Malecela himself was there for the debriefing; that, more than anything else, told me that what had been captured was vital.

"It's the first major link," he said, with a deep smile cutting into one corner of his face, yet at the same time with a ferocity in his eyes that I would have found frightening had I been on the other side. "It is just possible that their whole reason for hunting you, Strang, is that they had established that the series of disasters we are preparing for them began from intelligence captured due to your mission. That is one hypothesis, anyway." He sat back and sighed, opening a refrigerator door; Athenian offices are designed to be comfortable places to eat a meal rather than to work, because Athenians think of paperwork and that sort of thing as something you do at home, and the office is where you entertain guests. "If you two would care for beer, we are officially off duty; I've also got a wide range of cold meats and cheeses, and more kinds of bread than I would have imagined existed."

We made sandwiches and poured beer; then I cautiously said, "Captain, you said that that was one hypothesis. It sounded very much like it was one you don't believe."

"That's absolutely right," Malecela agreed. "I don't believe it at all, in fact. I think this is the first step, but your close connection advanced technology we had brought in and turn it against these people. If there had been an American Revolution in this timeline, and that's what they were trying to start, there would have been literally millions of deaths—it would have looked like the Civil War of your timeline—and the development of all sorts of charming things like machine guns, barbed wire, and poison gas, plus bombing cities from aircraft, in the European phase of the war. Britain would have conquered the world and left the world bitter, bruised, and ready for more rebellions. You'd have ended up with a single absolutist British monarchy holding down a world empire by sheer bloody force . . ."

"And that's the point where the Closers would have moved in and taken over the top of the operation for themselves," I said. "Yep, that's what they always do. Well, in light of their known behavior it makes sense."

"We've gotten ten times the documents on this that we've ever had before, Mark. The intelligence people all want to kiss you."

"Hmm. Well, I could take applications, maybe—"

"Or you could abjure quantity for quality, and take me."

"Deal." It was a good deal, too, though I think we slightly annoyed the other passengers. It wasn't a very demonstrative century.

It turned out that because the two Georges had been so different—one so obviously trying to put people at their ease and make them feel appreciated, the other so clearly brutal—that the allegation, especially in the wake of the disastrous fire and the more than a hundred deaths in the protests, had sent the country up like a powder keg. Every single one of the fifty-nine lords and politicians the true King had written to had declared for him, and the Navy had gone over immediately. The invasion and civil war that they had thought they might have to fight had in fact collapsed completely as the Army, in turn, went over; before the real George III had even stepped off the boat in Dover, the false one was under arrest.

"He's got a terrible mess to clean up, but there's a huge reserve of goodwill," Chrys said. "It looks like this timeline is back on track—and in fact they think they're already getting signals when they're looking for its descendant lines, way up in the future. You've probably helped bring billions of people into freedom and prosperity."

with all the timelines descended from your own that seem to be of so much importance—and that one of the few names we know for sure will be vital coming out of your home time is Porter Brunreich, who of course is your ward . . . well, my guess is that in some way we don't quite understand, you yourself are a point of temporal discontinuity, a place where history itself can change in a big way. If you like, you're a walking crux, Strang.

"We've also noted that you improvise very well, you get missions carried out, and perhaps most importantly—you seem to be *lucky*. That might just be significant in its own right. History is constantly trying to find its own channel and to move in its own way. That's why some timelines are so hard to start, and some are so easy; there is something up ahead, many centuries in the future, something that is beautiful or wonderful or terrible—but it's calling all the timelines to itself, and when it finds someone who will help it go where it wants to, he becomes *lucky*."

"What if it's on the Closers' side?" I asked. "I mean, maybe the future that is calling is calling them, not us."

"If that's the case, we might as well all lie down and die. Or just find somewhere to party until they come and kill us. Does either of you feel like that?"

Chrys and I had to grin.

"Now," Malecela said, "I have one simple issue and one complicated one. Mark Strang, by virtue of the fact that when you are out and working in the field, good things appear to happen for ATN, we are going to make you a Special Crux Operative. It's a new designation. What it means is that we'll be dropping you into much hairier, more dangerous cruxes, with a much wider latitude of action—but also with more resources available. That's the simple issue."

"I'm very honored," I said. "But really all I did was—"

Malecela grinned at me again. "Now, now, in the first place, you don't have to tell me it's an honor. I can only say I envy you the contribution you'll be able to make, and I think it's wonderful for someone at the beginning of a career to be given this. But the fact is that it was a pure engineering decision—we didn't decide that we ought to do this, the scientists looked at it and said you're a good bet. That's why it's such a simple decision—I'm not making it, I'm just informing you of it.

"Now, it happens that there's another and more complex decision. We would like to assign one other Crux Op who will work with you closely, as your personal assistant, on a permanent basis. This would also improve security around Porter Brunreich, of course, but the main purpose is to have an additional observer wherever you are. But despite the fact that we counted your first expedition retroactively, giving you several years in grade . . . well, we realize you don't know many Crux Ops. There are really only two you have ever worked with closely . . . Ariadne Lao— who by the way has said she would happily accept such an assignment, despite being ten years senior to you in the service—and Chrysamen ja N'wook. Now, there are arguments either way; a relatively new agent can more quickly become used to your way of doing things, a more experienced agent may have additional information you will find valuable . . . but I thought there was the possibility, since you may be working together for decades, that there might be some personal preference involved . . ."

"There sure as hell is," I said, and then realized Chrysamen's interpreted voice in my earpiece had said the same thing.

It took us a while to get everything together, but finally the day came when I stepped through the gateway at ATN Crux Operations Central and into the locked bathroom of an airliner bound from Denver to Pittsburgh, trading places with one of our couriers, who had gotten onto the flight. I returned to my seat and had just settled in when Chrys slid into the seat beside me.

She was thoroughly nervous, but I put my hand on her arm and said, "Now, it's the best possible start. The Fourth of July dinner is sacred to Dad and Carrie, and Porter has gotten to be just the same way. And I've missed more of them than anyone else, so now it's always regarded as a treat when I'm there. You're going to pick up a lot of points just for attending."

She squeezed my hand and whispered under her breath, "Just remember, I come from a culture with arranged marriages."

"You've always got the option of just being a working associate," I pointed out, gently. "I don't want you to feel pressured—"

"Bite your tongue. I'm nervous, that's all," she said, and moved closer to me.

Dad's a rotten driver, so Robbie drove to pick us up at the airport; Carrie and Porter had come along. This was the scary part for me, too, I realized, and wondered why I wasn't nervous. Maybe history was letting me know it was on my side again or something.

"Dad, Carrie, Porter, Robbie, this is Chrys," I said.

They all said "Hello," except for Porter, who said, "Yeah, right. Bring in the most gorgeous woman in the universe and introduce her like she's someone you met bowling. It's good to have you home, Mark—you haven't changed a bit."

▪ AFTERWORD ▪

Once again, this book comes with a deep debt of gratitude—to the inspired loons of the Alternate History discussions in the Science Fiction Round Table of the GEnie electronic network. Special thanks this time are due to:

Kevin O'Donnell, Jr., Jon Bunnell, P. "Calamity" Drye, Robert Brown, William Harris, Steve Stirling, Dana Carson, S. "Lemming" Weinberg, G. Tan, and Al Nofi.

And again as always, mistakes, errors, and anything you caught me at should be attributed entirely to me.

Caesar's
Bicycle

This one's for Ashley Grayson—
my agent,
my friend
the guy Calvin probably grew up to be.
With a sense of relief that he will probably never
get his hands on any such hardware
as is contained in this book.

•1•

Chrysamen was looking sad, and since she has huge dark eyes, she's good at looking sad. Though we were running just a little late if we wanted to get to the Met without rushing, I knew, after some years of marriage, that it was better to talk about whatever it was than to try to brush it off until there was time to talk about it, so I sat down next to her, and said, "Is something the matter?"

"Not a lot, just a minor case of frustration." She tossed her dark curls with her hands and shook her head, as if working out a kink in her neck.

"Anything you want to talk about?"

"Oh, just realizing I'm probably never going to lose back the three pounds I put on after we had Perry, and that even if I'm physically a lot younger, I'm almost fifty."

I shook my head. "On the same scale, I'm fifty-three. That's what a lot of time travel will do for you. And in this timeline we're both still under forty, legally; heck, in *this* timeline you're minus seven hundred something. Figure that if the life-extension drugs work as well on us as they do on Ariadne Lao—"

Mistake to mention our boss. Ariadne is a charming, pleasant, usually polite person, but there was once a slight spark of interest between us—long before I met Chrys, mind you—and Ariadne *is* pretty stunning, thanks to the long-life drugs, even though she must be past eighty. Consequently "Ariadne Lao" is an extremely bad thing to mention when Chrys is feeling unattractive.

A few years of marriage gives you enough experience to recognize that you've said something stupid, when it's only a *little* bit too late. I put an arm around Chrys, and said, "Look, we're actually only about a fifth of the way through our life spans. I mean, through what our life spans would be if we were in a normal line of work. We both might be shot dead next week, of course."

"You certainly know how to cheer a girl up."

"Well, damn it, it's hard to work up sympathy for you when half the women on the planet would kill to look like you."

"That's more like it," she said, smiling, and stood up and stretched. That was a view I enjoyed a lot; she had on all the lingerie but hadn't yet put on her dress (one of those little black things that seem to be part of the dress code for women at the opera). She has a mass of dark curly hair, high cheekbones and a full mouth, very light brown skin, and an athlete's body that I know, in several different ways, is all hard muscle, no matter how well shaped it is.

"And as far as self-confidence is concerned, Mark, that leer from you is all I needed."

"I am not leering."

"You're right. It's more like the way a lion looks at a gazelle."

"Rrrrr."

"Not now, dear, but hold the thought. You look pretty terrific in the tux, yourself." She slipped into the dress and turned to be zipped up, and I figured we'd gotten past this little attack of the blues with no harm done, but then she said, "I was just thinking . . . well, it may be silly."

"If it bothers you, it's not silly," I said, pulling up her zipper.

"Well, it's just . . . you and I are doing our part, certainly, in the war against the Closers. And ATN seems to be doing pretty well in the fight, though with millions of fronts it's hard to tell. But even if we're really clobbering them, as far as I can see, we'll still be fighting them a thousand years from now. You and I will grow old and die—or get shot or blown up—and so will Porter and Perry . . . and the war will go on, and more people will be born and grow old and die, and the war will go on, and maybe we'll be as far in the past as the time of Christ before the war is won."

"You can't let yourself think like that," I said. "We have a lot to do, and we're just two Crux Ops; ATN has thousands like us, and we just do our parts and hope for the best. I'm sure somewhere there are generals or field marshals or something who are paid to worry about that, but it's not our lookout."

She sighed. "Oh, I don't mean I think it's being badly run, and I know as well as you do that it's the fight in front of us, and the *next* one, not the last one, we have to worry about. All I mean is . . . well, why haven't they sent back word about who wins? Does the war just go on forever?"

"Maybe they're afraid of changing the result by letting us know," I said. "We need to get moving if we're going to get to the opera in time for me to show you off to the other guys."

We had imposed a firm rule ages ago. Since this timeline is not aware of the war that rages across a million timelines, we don't discuss ATN business anywhere where we might be overheard. If you think waiters and cabbies are nosy about your marriage or your job, imagine what they'd be like about the fate of whole universes. So we went to the opera, chatted mostly about my ward Porter Brunreich's career (at eighteen she was having a very successful European tour, and nowadays she was mostly performing her own compositions for organ and piano), our three-year-old son Perry (we both agree he's a genius, and handsome, too), and that sort of thing. We were pleased to note that the cab driver agreed with us.

Placido Domingo was wonderful as always, *Rigoletto* was terrific (the director and designers stuck to the story), and for that matter the coffee and cheesecake afterward were great. (Sure, Lindy's is a cliché, but they got to be a cliché by being worth going back to.)

Chrys came from a timeline where opera had never developed—it was good that the special language chip behind the ear allowed her to speak English without an accent, because if anyone had asked her nationality, "Arabo-Polynesian" would undoubtedly have raised a lot of questions. Three days after she came here to marry me, she was idly playing with the radio when she hit WQED in Pittsburgh, the local classical station—and that was it. Hopeless addiction. There aren't a lot of Pittsburghers with season tickets at the Met—that's a lot of airplane tickets in addition—but we're two of them.

As Dad said to me, if you find you're married to a junkie, your choices are to try for a cure, which rarely works, or to take up the needle yourself. At least it was only opera she'd gotten hooked on. It could have been heavy metal.

I thought she'd forgotten all about her early case of the blues. But that evening, as I closed the door on our hotel room again, she said, "It's such a beautiful world, Mark. Yours, and the one I came from, and all the millions of others. And if there weren't Closers, we could open the gates between them and let more people see them all. I'm sure we'll win. I just wish we could win during my lifetime, or our children's. I'd like to be around to enjoy it."

"Me too," I said, surprising myself a little. I'd always been the much more eager killer of the two of us—Chrys came from a timeline that had been conquered by the Closers, and then liberated a couple of generations later by ATN forces, and you'd think she'd have more hate for them. But Chrys's people were largely pacifists when they were conquered, and the bitter war of liberation afterward had sickened them so much that there were only a few aberrant ones, like Chrys, who could bear fighting at all.

Me? I'd lost half my family, including my first wife, to them, and a lot of friends along the way, and there had been a time in my life when nothing gave me a rush of pleasure like pulling the trigger on a Closer bastard. When ATN agents—including Ariadne, the first Crux Op I'd ever met—had turned up and recruited me, shown me who was behind the terrorist group I was after, and armed me to hit back at them, I'd become a kind of killing machine for a while.

But that had been before Chrys, before the birth of our son . . . before a certain bitter fight on a blazing airship, when I had faced a version of myself from another timeline, a version that had gone to work for the Closers—and seen that hatred was *their* weapon, not ours, and that when you got down to the last moment of choice and the last ounce of will, it wasn't a match for plain, ordinary courage. I had seen the kind of broken, poisoned thing I could become, and turned away.

Mostly. The old feelings came back now and then, and if I occasionally found myself enjoying a battle with the Closers a bit more than was good for me, well, so it goes. Nobody changes overnight.

So I was more than a little surprised to realize that Chrys's ideas had gotten into me to that extent. I, too, could imagine a future where you could visit the thousands of beautiful things and places that exist across the many parallel timelines. There were timelines out there where Beethoven didn't go deaf, where Marlowe didn't die young and lived to be Shakespeare's great rival, where the great library at Alexandria was never burned.

There were dozens of different Parises, Athenses, New Yorks, Saigons—all beautiful in their different ways. There were timelines where there had never been human beings, where you could still find herds of buffalo that stretched farther than the eye could see, great herds of elephant and rhino in Africa, flocks of moas and dodoes. Worlds where elegant white cities shone in the wilderness, where you could walk from the equivalent of the Met right out into the equivalent of Yellowstone.

All of that was out there, just a quick flip of the time machines away—but every time a traveler crosses, the pulse can be registered in many other universes. Cross often enough, and the Closers get a fix on that timeline—and then suddenly they're there, vast armies pouring in out of nowhere, and another world falls beneath their iron heel, only to be won back at a cost of millions of lives and vast destruction. So travel between timelines is restricted, as much as we can, to timelines that they already know the location of, and those timelines are defended as heavily as can be managed.

Of all those wonderful doors, only a few can be opened . . . and only for emergency military purposes.

I knew how she felt; so much wonder, hardly any time for it. We could go anywhere and anywhen, but we had to spend all our time jumping into places where rude strangers shot at us.

"Well," I said, though the joke was feeble, "we'll just have to hurry up and win the war."

"Yeah, right." One great advantage of the ear gadgets is that you only have to move toward speaking the language gradually, but you don't make any mistakes on the way. Chrys's English was now as good as her Arabic and Attikan—and mine were equally good—and she said, "Yeah, right," with the true Pittsburgh spirit, the way that lets the world know that no one is going to fool *you*.

I stepped into the bathroom for a second, and when I came out she was removing the little black dress very slowly, which pretty much killed discussion for that night. Ever had a fantasy about sleeping with a beautiful female agent? I do every night—though there was a period of sharing responsibility for two o'clock feedings in there as well. The job's risky, but there are fringe benefits.

On a New York weekend, you're always running out of cash, which is probably why New York is so fond of tourists. So after breakfast in the Wellington's coffee shop, we went around the corner to a bank to get more. It was a pretty typical Saturday morning—everyone looking bored and a lot of huge-haired tellers with bright blue eye shadow desperately trying to pretend that they had a date for Saturday night, in order to keep away the guys who might figure the girl at the bank was the last possible chance. The security guards were a couple of bush-league rent-a-cops rather than off-duty NYPD, so the bank could save a few bucks on a time when there weren't likely to be many robbers.

I wondered about that idly. In our line of work, jumping into all sorts of violence all the time, you get such a habit of casing the joint that it's easier to do it than not to.

Maybe they figured all the robbers would be at home watching cartoons or something, because this place was really pretty wide-open. There was one amiable guard, a very young-looking man with a big nose, pasty white skin, and black hair, who was trying to talk to the rightmost teller, a girl whose hair was dyed platinum blond and piled into a huge meringue. The other guard was middle-aged, a black man with gray hair and mustache, and a distinct gut; the way he stood and shifted his weight suggested he also had a bad back, but at least his eyes were on the door and the customers. As I scanned him, he yawned. I noted also that I'd been looking at him for a while and he hadn't looked back or noticed he was being scanned.

This was one of those modern, friendly banks that have a lot of low tables and just a counter for the tellers, not one of the old 1920s ones that looked like a tough prison or maybe a fort, or one of the more recent ones that looked like a biolab where they expected every customer to be infected with something deadly.

"You're really checking the place out," Chrys muttered to me as we stood in line.

"It's something to do."

"Have you checked the four that just came in?" she muttered. "I know you see everything in New York, but it looks like a new flavor of everything."

What was coming in was one woman with thick butt-length red

hair and the kind of body that men turn and stare at, wearing a tiny little sprayed-on white dress and heels halfway up to the sky, and with her were three dignified older guys in three-piece suits.

"Ha. They threw a party with the little lady last night and came up short on cash; now they're going to get some additional so they can pay her, probably so nobody comes around to threaten them. No big thing—"

As I said it, the girl turned from the men and clattered over toward the younger security guard and the teller he was trying to pick up. The teller had a clearly displayed CLOSED sign in front of her window and had been counting bills very slowly.

That was the first warning bell that went off in my head. If this was a high-priced good-time girl collecting from a bunch of johns, the last thing she was going to do was move away from them, until they paid her. Nobody heads for an obviously closed teller, not when the line is already long. And besides, she took two big clacking steps and deliberately shook her shoulders before she started out.

Which, aside from letting everyone in the room know she wasn't wearing a bra, also got almost everyone to stare at her, the women because most women stare at someone who is really overdoing it, the men because . . . well, you can imagine.

Anyway, she made enough noise for a cavalry troop on a tap-dance floor as she crossed over to the guard and the teller. The teller looked up in obvious relief, clearly glad to have anything get the guy away from her, and the guy was busy staring holes in the woman's little white dress.

"Hand on your NIF?" I muttered to Chrys.

"Always. Ready when you are."

It so happens Chrys and I were both the kind of nasty kids for whom magicians hate to work birthday parties. You know how stage magic always works by getting people to look in one place while you do something somewhere else? Well, we were always the kids who were saying, "He's really putting it in his sleeve," "He moved it while he was waving the flowers," or "That's not the one you started with." And this woman's little routine was screaming, "Hey, look over here!" so naturally we were looking everywhere else, as unobviously as we could.

What I saw was one of the guys in the three-pieces stopping to tie his shoe by a potted plant—and getting into a perfect position to draw a pistol from an ankle holster and blow the younger guard away.

On the other side, she told me later, Chrys was seeing one of them heading over toward the manager's desk, and number three approaching the other guard as if to ask him a question, but also reaching into his jacket.

"Excuse me," their woman accomplice said, with that loud, cutting New York accent that goes right through crowd noise, "but I really need sex right now." The corner of my eye showed me that she had whipped the dress off and was now naked except for the heels. "Would anyone like to—" It was quite a list, but I was too busy to listen.

I put a NIF round into the wrist of the one I was looking at before he quite got the pistol out of the ankle holster. Chrys nailed the guy with his hand in his jacket, and he hit the floor with an extrahard double thud—his head and the pistol. Then she got the one approaching the manager (who had just gotten up to deal with the disturbance, and appeared to be pretty perturbed by it, at least to judge from the way she strode toward the naked young woman) with a clean shot in the back of the neck, and he fell over, but he'd actually had time to draw his pistol.

NIF stands for Neural Induction Fléchette, which is the projectile it fires. The fléchette is a self-guiding dart, so small that on a sheet of white paper it looks like a dust grain or a gnat, that homes on body heat and flies at just below supersonic speeds. When it connects, it finds its way to a nerve, and does whatever it's programmed to do. Chrys and I usually set ours to knock the person unconscious for a few hours and then let him wake up slowly with the mother of all hangovers, but a NIF could do anything from making you itch all over to stopping your heart right then to giving you strong enough convulsions to break every bone in your body.

The projectile itself would dissolve in a few minutes, leaving no evidence that a doctor in our timeline would recognize. This was going to make *News of the Weird* for sure.

There was a long pause; the robbers' distraction had been so good that no one was noticing three unconscious men with guns just yet, because everyone was still gaping at the naked woman. She really wasn't all that pretty, I decided, just big in the chest and very made-up, and from the way the hair had slipped, I knew it was a wig.

I considered whacking her with the NIF, too, just for tidiness and that aesthetically important sense of completion, but I figured it was too amusing to see what she'd do now.

The NIF is almost silent—it makes a noise like an electric drill, but just for the instant that the tiny fléchette it fires is going out the barrel, and only about half the volume. Since we'd fired just three single shots, very fast, and gotten them back under cover, no one had noticed the three brief squeaks, or even the three men going over.

"Miss, you're, uh, going to have to leave the bank," the manager said, still unaware of the man, collapsed and motionless, on the floor behind her, a gun still held in his limp fingers.

"That's not a bad idea," Chrys said to me. "We could go up the street to a bank-card machine. Might be a lot faster than hanging around here—there are going to be cops all over the place soon."

"Yep," I said. We turned and went, doing our best to look like any middle-class couple whose day has been mildly disrupted by something that they will talk about for weeks afterward—but that fundamentally doesn't matter.

Just as our cash came out of the automatic teller machine, the screen began to flash at us. Abruptly, it glowed with three words of Attikan that were the current password, and a PRESS ENTER in English below that. With a sigh, I did.

The screen lit up like a full-fledged video screen, and a grainy image of Ariadne Lao said, "Please acknowledge. Report to the mid-Manhattan gateway immediately. Please acknowledge."

There wasn't any microphone on the automatic teller machine, so I figured she couldn't hear us; I nodded my head at the security camera and pressed the ENTER/YES button.

"She doesn't look happy," I said.

"We aren't supposed to use ATN ordnance on local events," Chrys pointed out. "So I guess we compromised security. Probably we're just going to get chewed out."

"Very likely." It was the kind of thing that could spoil a day but not more than that; and at least we would be returned to the same time and place we had departed from. That was in our contract.

We were almost there when my beeper went off. "Damn. Just a minute, Chrys, it's probably nothing much—"

I found a working public phone—always a small miracle in Manhattan, and it took me about five minutes—dialed the private line to my bodyguard agency, and waited a long second for the connection to Pittsburgh.

Mark Strang Bodyguards is a real agency—it was my real business before I started working for ATN, even if it was never a particularly lucrative one. Nowadays it was actually making much more money than it used to, but I didn't do much work in it; it served as a cover for the large payments that came in from my real employers, and, to maintain the fiction, my two assistants, Robbie and Paula, now ran the place. They'd built the above-ground part into quite a respectable business. It helps to be obviously affluent and have a reputation for being exclusive. People think you must be guarding a lot of celebrities, and they're willing to pay accordingly.

Paula answered the phone, as I expected. "Boss, it's Porter. She was attacked after her Oslo concert. She wasn't hurt, but Robbie was—it wasn't serious, but they've got her in the hospital for observation, in case it's a concussion. I've made sure your Dad and Carrie are covered, and I'm going over there as soon as I can."

My gut sank like I'd swallowed a frozen brick. "Right," I said. "What's the situation on coverage for Porter?"

"Three reliable backups are on it, and as soon as she's over into Germany we have full police security. She got on the chartered plane because Robbie insisted, so she's in the air right now."

Not great but better than nothing. "Okay," I said, thinking furiously. "Tell Robbie to get better fast, or she'll have to answer to me. Do you know what the injuries were?"

"Just a bad beating, it sounded like. No kidney damage, one cracked rib for sure. They want to hold her for observation. I think she'll be okay." Paula and Robbie have been the closest of partners since I've known them, and that's some years now. Paula must have been frantic, but she didn't let it show in her voice.

"Well, get over there and make sure," I said, completely unnecessarily. "And you be careful, too, you hear? I want both of you up and well."

"Probably you should know, too, boss," she said, very slowly and carefully, "that Porter is why Robbie is alive. She, uh, made use of that .38 you trained her with. Took down two of them while they were busy beating Robbie."

"Is Porter okay?" I asked.

"As okay as you can be, I guess." I could hear the resignation in Paula's voice. "She's not one of those people that enjoys killing, boss, I suppose you'd say. And she didn't damage her hand either. She's planning to play tonight. If I can get Robbie transferred or released, I'll cover Porter at that concert myself."

"Don't hesitate to wave agency money around if it helps," I told Paula, "but it's a shame we're dealing with this in Norway—too many honest civil servants, and they're too well paid."

"Yeah, one more complication. I've got to get on a flight, boss, I'm most of the way out the Parkway West to the airport right now, and if I get the commuter flight to Kennedy, I can make a Concorde if that's okay."

"Of course it is! Use whatever money you have to. We can always get more."

That was one difference between them; Robbie is a small woman, very strong for her size but mostly just fast as a whip, and when there's action of any kind, she moves too fast to worry about what the rules are. Paula's nearly my size and probably stronger, and if it were up to her, we'd have a manual of procedures for everything. ("Terrorist attack: 1. Agency personnel are to avoid getting shot . . .")

"Thanks, boss. We'll get it under control." It was more from the gratitude in Paula's voice than from anything else that I understood how worried she was. "Got to run—just turning off the Parkway now."

"Take care of yourself. Bye."

I hung up the phone and turned to Chrysamen. "Bad news, and I think we better get to the gate right away." I summarized it quickly as we rounded two corners and entered one of many midtown office buildings.

"Shit," Chrys said. "What did Al Capone say? 'Once is happenstance, twice is coincidence—' "

" 'Three times is enemy action,' " I said. "But I'd bet on it already. Two of those robbers were in great positions to whack us—I think we'd each have taken the round after the guard did."

"Good thing you're not the ogling kind," she said, with a little smile.

"I'm a speed ogler. Got her all ogled before I had to do any shooting. Not that there was much to ogle—all packaging and no product. Anyway, here we are."

It's one of those anonymous midtown buildings with offices on the lower floors and apartments above, the kind of place where you always wonder if you saw it in a movie sometime, and you never did. There's an automatic elevator that goes up a few floors and dumps you into a space where you are facing a glass door with a bunch of names in white on it that looks vaguely like an architect's partnership, a brokerage, or a law firm. No lights are ever on, so you wonder if it's closed.

The door unlocks only when an ATN agent, like Chrys or me, or the Special Agent for our timeline, approaches it; just where the gadget that recognizes us is, I've never figured out. I never know how any of this stuff works, I just use it. Think of me as a caveman with a VCR; I like the show, but that's all I can say.

The door clicked open as we stood in front of it, and the lights came on as we opened the door. We closed and locked the door behind us and went down the hallway where, in a normal set of offices, the private offices and the conference room would be. Instead, there was just a blank wall, which turned gray and faded as we approached it, like a perfectly smooth, backlit fog. We walked into it.

It was dark as a deep cave, we were as weightless as you are in orbit, and there was no sound at all, not even the ringing of ears or nervous system. For a time I couldn't define I couldn't feel that my body was there.

Even, dim gray light came in from all directions, brightening, swimming into focus first as dark patches and then as lines and shadows, color adding suddenly. At the same time a low rumble, an octave below a sixty-cycle hum, swelled in my ears, and then cut off abruptly when the colors came back.

The world around us turned into the early-twenty-ninth-century Athenian timeline, in a perfectly ordinary reception room for a gate.

Ariadne Lao was waiting for us. She looked grim, and worried—and not at all like we were about to get reprimanded.

"We're under some kind of Closer attack," she said, "and whatever it is, it's put all our connections to our own future into flux. I'm getting the senior Crux Ops together to try to formulate a plan of action, and it's a relief every time any of you comes through the gate. There've been attacks on Crux Ops in almost every timeline so far."

"Ours too," I said. "We think on us, and for sure on Porter Brunreich."

She nodded grimly. "We've lost nineteen Crux Ops that I know of, dead, injured, or seized. Six critical people have died in time-lines we were watching. *And* we can't contact our own future much beyond the next few weeks. Whatever it is that's happening, it's big."

·2·

There were more than a thousand Crux Ops in the auditorium for the meeting, and security around us was amazing. Instead of the usual meeting place, the giant space station Hyper Athens, which hangs over the equator on the same line of longitude as the city of Athens, we were on the back side of the moon at the Earth System Defense base. The whole moon was under guard—heavily armed warships orbited it in a complex dance, every ship on red alert, waiting for trouble. The base itself was ringed with robot and human defenses, and the building the auditorium was in was crawling with crack security forces.

And then again, the strongest security of all was what was in the auditorium itself. Crux Ops are deadly in a fight, and there was no nonsense about checking arms at the door—first of all, most Crux Ops would rather check their pants, or kilts or togas or whatever. Secondly, if we weren't capable of making faster and more accurate decisions about what to shoot and when than anybody else, we wouldn't be Crux Ops. So if anyone, particularly any Closers, were stupid enough to come in shooting with ground forces, there was going to be a hell of a fight, and they were going to lose.

On the other hand, if they knew our exact location, a gate might pop open and a tactical nuke might take care of the whole thing. Closers have a horror of nuclear weapons in any system they might occupy, but in purely enemy territory that position tends to be flexible.

A few of the Crux Ops filing in were old comrades, people Chrys and I had worked with on one mission or another, but mostly they were strangers. ATN operates across millions of timelines, and for most of them it can only spare the once-in-a-decade or so visit of a Time Scout; an important one might have a Special Agent assigned to it permanently. Crux Ops normally go in only when the regular forces are put out of action, like when expected transmissions from a Special Agent fail to show up. So the half million Time Scouts and fifty thousand Special Agents are backed up by fewer than ten thousand Crux Ops, and since it's an occupation in which people tend to die, living long enough to get to be a senior Crux Op is rare.

Generally we operate alone or in pairs—Chrys and I had been lucky enough to be assigned as a permanent pair, partly because it seemed like a good idea to Ariadne Lao and mainly because they had owed us a whole lot of favors, and we'd insisted on it.

Even though few of us knew many of the others, all of us knew a few, and the room was buzzing with conversation and little, happy noises as people greeted each other. There were four people there from our class at COTA, the Crux Op training camp, but they were all talking to other people. Over on one side was Roger Buckley, a guy about my age who happened to be from a timeline descended from the very first timeline in which I had intervened, a guy who had at first approached me about the same way I would approach George Washington.

In fact, George Washington was there, from a timeline where we'd recruited him because there was no United States to need a president, and the Empire was at peace, so King George didn't need a general. I knew him slightly—I waved to him, and he nodded in his usual formal, correct way. He looked to be a bit past fifty, but with ATN's advanced medicine, he had all his teeth and was as strong and healthy as anyone. Scuttlebutt among the Crux Ops was that now that he wasn't the father of his country in his own timeline, he'd been fathering a lot of other countries in other timelines, and from the way Chrys muttered, "God, he looks *great*," I was inclined to believe rumor.

Over to one side, unsmiling, grim as death (but that was usual), and looking just a little worried (which was new), was General

Malecela, Ariadne Lao's boss whenever he wasn't personally supervising training, who most of us held in awe.

There was the usual array of social stuff—several hundred flavors of tea, coffee, chicory, maté, chocolate, and tisane, a dozen different kinds of breads, and, for those who wanted them, more kinds of beers and wines than you'd ever have imagined possible. For Chrys and me it was still early morning—we discovered they had grabbed everyone we talked to from sometime shortly after breakfast—so we weren't particularly inclined to get alcohol, but I noticed that even people from timelines where booze at breakfast is normal were passing it up. People wanted to be alert; this was an unprecedented event.

We found seats. "It's been a long while since we've been back here," Chrys said. "At least we know they're not bringing us in here for a chewing-out."

Another hour went by as people trickled in, but none of the additions were people we knew. I realized after a while that no one was going to ask anything—"Whatever happened to X" or "Surely Y must be a senior agent by now"—because the likely answer was grim.

That got my mind turning back to the things Chrys had said, either last night or eight hundred plus years ago or however many years that was sideways, depending on how you counted. Look around the room, and you could figure that though there were a few hundred of us here, very few would die peacefully. Most of us would be blown up, burned to death, shot, skewered, poisoned . . . it was a room full of targets-to-be. Hell, I had killed a version of myself that had gone over to the Closers, stamped on his fingers as he clung to a ladder until the bones broke, and he fell to his death.

Or should I have thought, Until I fell to my death?

It's the nature of people who face danger regularly that they're convinced that bad luck is something that always happens to everyone else. They can look at statistics that say that every single person in their line of work dies by violence sooner or later, and shrug and say that after all, *I'm* still alive, *I'm* not dead yet, many times I've been places where I could have been killed, I could have died a lot of times and I haven't, and so on and so forth. After all, they're fighters and adventurers, not insurance actuaries, not statisticians. . . .

And the thought that came to me then was that I had been thinking "They." When more accurately it should have been "We."

I was like that myself, and so was Chrys. If we were rational, we'd have known that the way we lived was more dangerous than skateboarding on freeways. As it was, we both figured that the life-extension drugs would give us our full two hundred–plus years, instead of figuring the obvious thing—that ATN gave us the drugs because that way we could be young, fast, strong, and sharp for as long as we lasted—and that still would be a matter of a decade or two at most.

Most of us senior Crux Ops were like the old people you sometimes run into, heavy smokers and drinkers who are pushing ninety and therefore figure they're never going to die. The fact is that if you put enough people through a process that only kills most of them, there will be a few that last a long time, just as, if you roll dice long enough, you will come up with any roll you like as many times in a row as you want. You just can't say when it will happen or how long it will all take, and you certainly can't say which it will be. But the lucky dice are not the especially virtuous or smart or strong dice—they're just lucky.

And the three-pack-a-day man who makes it to ninety-two is just the last one of his group to die, because everyone dies eventually, and his group died early. In a normal group the last guy to die would have been over a hundred.

So a senior Crux Op . . . I decided I didn't like the trend of thought, and told myself to give it up.

Now, none of us was a volunteer "for the duration"—at least half the people in the room had enough time in to resign or retire if we wanted to. Chrys and I did, for that matter. But the war with the Closers is a total war, about as total as it gets, and neither side recognizes retirement. You can decide to go off somewhere, even to go across time to some timeline the other side has never discovered—and chances are still pretty good that one day your car blows up, or in your luxury suite on your spaceliner bound for Mars someone barges in and shoots you, or the stirrup cup some groom hands up to you is poisoned.

It doesn't matter to them that we retire. Why should it? It doesn't matter to us. If I had known that the other Mark Strang, who worked for the other side, had retired to grow roses and learn the harpsichord, I'd still have been perfectly happy to cut his throat.

The only difference retirement or resignation makes is that nobody is looking out for you. They no longer check to see if you're okay, and when the inevitable happens there's no revenge for you, no investigation . . .

You're going to die the same way regardless, so you might as well get a few licks in.

Chrys saw an old friend from COTA that I didn't know very well, and we went over to talk with her. I stood beside them, alone with my thoughts, occasionally distracted by the animated way Chrys was talking and gesturing with Xiao Chu.

My wife was very beautiful. In the time since I had known her, she'd had an eye and two limbs regrown by the advanced ATN medical technology; I'd had the same done for three limbs and a large part of my liver. She was very full of life. In our line of work it was really just a question of time before one or the other of us was blown apart so badly that they couldn't do anything for us, because although they can practically regrow you from your head and the stump of your neck if they have to, once the enemy bags your brain you're gone. And sooner or later they get your brain.

She was the mother of my child, and like a second mother to my ward, and chances were excellent that we would never see Porter's college graduation, or even see Perry enter school. Chances were also that one of us would live out some lonely years as a widow or widower—crazed and living only for revenge. I had done that before, and I didn't like the thought of doing it again, or of having Chrys do it.

The Closers had made me a widower once before, long before I ever heard of ATN or the Closers. They had killed my wife Marie, brother Jerry, and mother in the same car-bomb blast that had cost my sister both legs and one arm . . . and very nearly cost me my sanity.

There had been a long time during which I lived only for revenge and pleasure of killing Closers. It had been a time when life seemed pretty simple, if ugly.

Things had changed, a lot. I had a few other interests now . . . and most of them demanded living longer.

I did not want to see Chrysamen die and have to go on without her, and, for that matter, I did not want to die myself and miss so much of life together.

And as Chrys had pointed out, the war was nowhere near over, hadn't even reached a point where we could say which side was winning. In all probability there would be many thousands of years more of fighting, and long after I was buried and forgotten in some timeline or other, probably far from home, the fighting would go on. Perry's grandchildren, for all I knew, might end up as Crux Ops.

It wasn't putting me in a very good frame of mind.

The last of us filed in, and after a decent interval so they could get refreshments and find seats, the people up front started to shuffle papers, adjust lighting, and generally do all the things that are the same wherever or whenever you go—hinting strongly that it would be a good idea if we all took our seats.

Chrys slid back into her seat next to me, and I took her hand. She seemed agitated and nervous; a second later she whispered in my ear, "At least half the people I talked to just survived an assassination attempt or a major fight. Everyone is getting pulled in out of very heavy action. A couple of them were badly shot up and just got here from treatment."

"We already knew that whatever this is, it's big," I whispered, and then the room got too quiet to keep talking.

The first person to address us was General Malecela. "Crux Ops," he began, "I have no doubt that all of you will have figured out six things that this meeting might be about, and rejected all of them as implausible. I won't keep you in the dark any longer; you are here because we've lost touch with a very large number of futures, and because we think we know why and we're going to need all of you to do something about it."

There wasn't a sound from the room. As yet he had not said anything that required any response, and we all wanted to hear what he said next.

Malecela nodded to us, as if he took our silence as a courtesy, and said, "Citizen-teacher Zouck will explain matters further; then Citizen-senator Thebenides will discuss our plan of action. After which there will be time for lunch and questions. But to allay whatever concerns you may have—you have been summoned here, I know, and you have been attacked in many cases, I'm fairly sure, because the news is *good*. They are hitting back as hard as they can because they are being hit very hard indeed. We have an opportunity to alter the balance of power tremendously, and with a bit of luck, that is just what we shall do."

"Citizen-teacher" isn't exactly a title like "Doctor" or "Professor." The Athenians don't see much connection between research and teaching, so the title implies only a lot of familiarity with the subject and an ability to explain it clearly. It's a highly honored title, and the little implants behind everyone's right ear explained this to us in the quick, abrupt way they usually did—*Stand up and bow your head.*

I'm used to doing what the implanted gadget tells me; they're carefully programmed to talk only when they know more than you do, and then only when it's urgent or you ask a question. Everyone else's is pretty much the same way, so we all stood as one and bowed our heads.

"Return to your seats, please," said a soft, gentle, woman's voice.

We all sat again—with almost no sound, for Crux Ops are all athletes of a high order, and we don't waste motion. The woman facing us at the podium was just slightly gray at the temples of her crew cut and had small, wide-set eyes and high cheekbones; her smile seemed warm and kind. I figured that she never had very much trouble keeping a class of students in line.

"I am honored that you honor me," she said; it was a polite phrase used between experts in different fields. "Let me try to take as little of your time as possible.

"You know, better than any of us who merely teach, what a crux is. Timelines don't naturally divide, or at least not often; whenever they can, they close back up with each other, leaving, perhaps, a few anomalies in the record. You all know a case or two of such things, I suppose—the couple who cannot agree on what evening they first danced together, the police files in which the same person appears to have died in an accident and to have committed a series of crimes afterward, the mysteriously scrambled records that drive historians half-mad trying to find out if a given ship was at a given battle or what rank an officer held, with clear evidence on more than one side.

"Those are cruxes that closed, places where things could have gone two or more different ways, and because finally it didn't matter, the diverging timelines sealed back together.

"But if the timelines are pushed farther apart—if one of our agents, or one of theirs, intervenes, or a time traveler comes back to force a change—then the crux widens until the two timelines will no longer reconcile, and at that point a new timeline forms. Such a timeline is always unstable in the great scheme of things, for whatever formed it at the crux can always be altered further, making it disappear, or reconverge, or go somewhere else entirely.

"Now, at first, when we found ourselves at war with the Closers, we were playing catch-up. They had found out how to travel across timelines and forward and backward along timelines. We had not. They had been operating for a long time. We had to invent things quickly.

"But we've come to realize that they tripped over their own idea of superiority. It never occurred to them that they might encounter serious resistance, so during the fifty years or so of head start, they didn't put nearly the effort they needed into developing other timelines to be allies.

"In fact their very nature may have precluded it. We have pretty good evidence that the Closers all come from just one timeline, that the only relation they will tolerate with any other timeline is complete control and subjection. As you all well know, when the Closers take over a timeline, a few hundred of them move there, and the native population is kept as slaves of one kind or another. Thus, as you all have seen, though Closer forces are often well trained, if their officers are killed or they get beyond supervision, they fall apart quickly. Once we realized this, we began to capture them in large numbers, and we've learned steadily more about the Closers themselves.

"The biggest revelation is that the Closers proper—the ones who call themselves 'Masters'—are universally trained from birth as fighters and officers; by the time he's twenty a typical Closer male has commanded a full division somewhere. Apparently there are many positions for which they won't use even their most trusted slaves. Thus the war is taking more of a toll on them than on us, even though they began with many more timelines, for they simply can't mobilize as many forces as we can. That's part of why we've been gaining steadily in strength relative to them.

"Our other big advantage has been in our diversity; because we don't make every timeline alike and run it from the top down, we discover more things. Thus ever so slowly, due to the cross-fertilization of so many different ideas, we have been pulling abreast of them, and in a few areas we are now definitely ahead."

She paused and nodded at all of us. "Now, no doubt some of you are impatiently waiting for the status report to be over so that you can hear the news. But I'll have to explain one more part of what we've been doing first.

"When a crux is embattled—when there are Closer and ATN agents fighting there—quite often all the timelines from which it is descended become inaccessible. Our signals and cargo won't travel crosstime to them because it's not settled whether they exist or not. Eventually, the embattled timelines open up again, or they vanish forever. Sometimes they're just somewhere else in time, somewhere that we can't find because there are so many or somewhere that is simply inaccessible because the volume of paradox we'd have to tolerate to contact it is just too high. Either things settle down, and we can then reach that timeline, or they don't.

"Well, for the last eighteen months, everywhere in the ATN more than twenty years in the future has been out of reach in just that way. And, in fact, the distance into the future we could reach has been steadily shrinking. We are down to being able to contact our own timelines only about fifty days into the future."

A buzz ran through the room, but when Citizen-teacher Zouck raised her hand, we fell silent again.

"This might be taken as bad news, but instead, what we are finding is that the opposing timelines seem to be in a very different state. Everywhere, where we know the addresses of the Closer time-lines, our agents have been able to penetrate with little difficulty, and universally we've found that those timelines are up in rebel-lion. In many of them the Closers have already been slaughtered and—because they tend to keep time travel and cross-timeline tech-nologies only in their own hands—the gates are closed. The armies left in those timelines have generally mutinied and shot their Closer officers. Sometimes democratic revolutions are under way, sometimes civil wars, sometimes the army is taking over and trying to keep things going without the Closers, sometimes you have 'warlordism'—all the military units fighting each other for control. Nowhere did we find an intact Closer society.

"So, tentatively, our conclusion is this—whatever is about to happen apparently involves destroying the Closers entirely, but it also involves changing the societies of the ATN so completely that we are unable to reach them from where we stand. And just to complicate matters, way out at the fringe of what we can detect, we seem to be seeing many, many more timelines than have ever arrived before—we have probes under way to a few of them even as we speak, but the effort and expense in locating and landing in them are enormous. We don't even know if those are ours, theirs, some third force's, or what.

"But still and all—I believe I bring you good news. The overthrow of the Closers, at least in the hundred thousand or so of their timelines we know about, is right around the corner. I cannot believe a great victory of that kind is causing anything bad to happen to us, however strange it may be."

There was a round of applause when she sat, though it was sort of strange applause since only about half of us were from cultures that applauded speakers, and maybe half the ones who applauded clapped their hands—there was also whistling, barking like dogs, shouts that sounded like "Oh—wah!", and people making the "bibibibi" sound with fingers on lips. I was pretty sure we all approved anyway. Citizen-teacher Zouck nodded politely, acknowledging our approval, and sat down.

General Malecela stepped back to the podium and gestured for quiet. As the room fell silent, he said, "To complete your background information, here is Citizen-senator Thebenides."

Thebenides was a small, dark-haired man with light brown skin—which is what just about half of humanity looks like across all the timelines, palefaces like me being fairly scarce—who seemed just a little nervous, as if he wasn't quite sure he should be up there. I suppose standing in front of a room filled with the most lethal people in millions of universes will do that to a guy.

"Well," he began, "Citizen-teacher Zouck's news, as you might guess, has caused quite a stir in government circles. We, too, find it very hopeful that the Closer timelines seem to be disrupted and destroyed by whatever is just ahead of us in the future, but naturally, to us these concerns are something more than just academic."

I did not like the way he said "*just academic.*" Now, I knew I was a bit sensitive on the point, because way, way back, when I had no idea that I would ever end up as a professional killer, when the world was a happy playground for people like me and my first wife Marie, I had been headed into the academic life as an art historian, which is about the most unemployable thing you can be outside of academia. So the notion that professors and academic issues are somehow less important than "the real world" always irritates me a little in the first place.

But in the second place, it sounded like he had just patted the previous speaker on the head and told the silly little dear that now that she was done, the government man was going to straighten matters out for everybody. The lack of respect shown for someone with considerable knowledge bothered me, especially coming from a politician. She was trained to think; he was trained to smile. I knew who *I* trusted more.

And then, too . . . something about the way he did it. When people paint their opponents as theoretical dreamers, and themselves as hardheaded realists . . . well, at least, whenever I had done that, it was because I was about to do something brutal. And brutality is something governments tend to do, especially when they're nervous and don't know what's going on. I had a deep, deep feeling that whatever he was about to propose wasn't going to be anything I would feel good about.

Somehow all of that crystallized into feeling that this guy was whiny and devious and not to be trusted. That at least activated my Crux Op instincts—I leaned forward to listen and watch more carefully.

While I had been thinking, he had been blathering on in vague generalities, about how he was so glad to be among practical people of action who could take the necessary steps. It was a real bad sign as far as I was concerned, and utterly unnecessary—none of us could vote, so we had nothing to give him; we already knew what it was to be the best fighters there are, so he had nothing to give us.

By the time he got down to the meat of his speech, I wanted to frisk him for small arms and toss his room for child pornography. Chrys noticed how I was reacting and glanced at me with a little puzzlement, then turned back to continue watching Thebenides.

"There are several possibilities about what is going on," Thebenides was saying, "and with all respect to my esteemed academic colleague, she has presented only the most hopeful of them. It is possible that the new timelines coming in are bringing with them some superweapon, some new way of organizing ATN that brings about a swift and sure victory, and we must be open to that possibility. But it is also possible that what they indicate is the appearance of some catastrophe that spans all the timelines we know, including those of the Closers.

"I need hardly remind you that if, for example, there were a rogue planet out there about to smash through the solar system, none of our known timelines would be capable of dealing with it, and so it would arrive in millions of timelines at the same time, and the chaos it caused could well produce these effects. Against such a situation there is naturally little we can do except try to ensure that the methods exist for getting our high-tech resources back on line as quickly as possible."

It occurred to me that what he meant by that was probably something like "getting the time machines and the crosstime equipment running again," but the way he had said it would justify almost anything the government might want to do. Zouck might have been academic, but she had managed to talk plain language to people who spoke it; "high-tech resources back on line" was a collection of weasel words to justify any old thing.

He went on. "Another possibility is that the impinging timelines do in fact represent a third force, one that is hostile both to us and to the Closers, and that we have been hit even harder than they have. In such a case, a certain kind of flexibility might be warranted, and toward that end we must explore—"

"Horseshit," I muttered. People turned and looked at me; Chrys looked embarrassed.

Whatever words he used for what we were supposed to be exploring was lost to me in the little stir around me, but I knew damn well what he was hinting at.

"And still another possibility," he added, "is that although those timelines are hostile to the Closers and friendly to us, they are in effect so advanced and so alien to us that their advent is like the arrival of a high-technology industrial society into a Stone Age back-water, as has happened in many timelines. It will do us little good to be free of the Closer menace only to end up permanently as the 'little brother' in a paternal relationship."

In the first place, you have a paternal relationship with something that looks like your father, not your big brother, and at least an academic wouldn't have abused language quite that far. In the second place, while I could see that it would be bad news (as in having to do something useful for a living) for Thebenides and the other citizen-senators, the Citizen-archon, and a whole lot of citizen-bureaucrats, I didn't exactly see having people who knew what they were doing take over the show as a complete disaster. There were parts of my own timeline where arriving American armed forces had found people in the Stone Age and left them operating airports, universities, hospitals, and all the rest. Even if they came to dislike the Americans, I never heard of any of them saying, "What a relief! Now that the Americans are gone, we can go back to washing clothes by pounding them on a rock, letting every other kid die before the age of five, and worshiping the chief as a god!"

"Thus," Thebenides was finishing, "we must be aware of the wide range of possible dangers and opportunities and be ready to move in any direction."

I was a little disgusted that my fellow Crux Ops seemed to applaud him more than they had Citizen-teacher Zouck, but maybe they were just more psychologically ready for it.

"What was that all about?" Chrys whispered to me.

"What was *what* all about? That speech? Hell if I know except—"

"I'm talking about the way you behaved. People noticed."

I blinked, hard, and realized my wife was angry at me, and obviously I had embarrassed her. "What did—"

General Malecela was back at the podium, and he was doing the usual things, thanking everybody and assuring us all that we had just heard things we really needed to hear. I did my best to pay polite attention to that, gesturing to Chrys that we would talk in a minute. I figured there would be assignments announced, and if I'd already embarrassed myself somehow, I didn't want to compound the problem by not knowing where I was supposed to be.

Malecela finished the platitudes and handed things over to Ariadne Lao, who gestured at a large screen that appeared behind her. "As you can see—"

At that moment the screen blew into bits, and a fusillade of projectiles roared into the room. I could see bodies falling over; something or someone was firing on us, and even in this heavily guarded room, we were under attack.

I was firing back at whatever was coming through the space where the screen had been before I even had time to note that so was everyone else; the big auditorium rang with the fire of a thousand weapons.

·3·

Where the screen had been there was the blank grayness of a gate, and a dozen figures in black uniforms, masked and goggled, each firing a long, spidery gadget that looked more like a broken-off television antenna folded into a child's idea of an Uzi than anything else. My NIF was aimed and firing before I thought it in words, but I recognized the weapon—Closer standard issue, a gadget something like our own SHAKK—and I sprayed the lot of them with neural induction fléchettes in less than a heartbeat.

So had a lot of other people, I realized, before my finger was entirely off the trigger, and as my eyes probed desperately into the grayness of the gate, watching for whatever might come in next.

Each of those initial dozen raiders must have been hit by at least a hundred rounds from SHAKKs alone. I could hear the deep bass whoosh from a vast chorus of them—all of those rounds had homed in at Mach 10, found the bodies of the Closers, entered them (with more than enough speed and force to kill with the internal shock wave alone, even if they entered a hand or foot) and then spiraled to a stop within the body. The Closers had simply, instantly, turned into bags of red jam.

There were probably a hundred-plus NIF rounds in all of them, too, but none of them had enough nervous system left to feel them with, and it takes twelve times as long for a NIF round to get there—probably the set of fléchettes arrived an entire eyeblink late.

My thumb found the selector on my NIF—I was still set for temporary unconsciousness, as I had been in New York—and naturally flipped toward instant death before a better thought struck me, and I flipped it to severe convulsion.

Holding the trigger down on full auto, I sprayed a deadly stream of the tiny, gnatlike projectiles directly into the grayness of the gate. Gates are two-way, and if there was any unprotected human flesh on the other side, the fléchettes would find it and burrow in.

I pictured what would happen to the Closer then. The muscles of the body would lock against each other with sudden, brutal force, hard enough to shatter the bones and tear them out through the flesh, the jaw smashing the teeth to red ruins and driving them up into the sinuses, the scalp muscles crushing the skull, arm, and leg bones ripping out through flesh and clothing in great, sharp splinters, hands and feet bursting into shredded meat, all in an instant before the heart locked down and burst from internal pressure, and the chest muscles collapsed the rib cage. The ripping, dissolving figures would emit one unbearable scream as the air and blood from the chest was pushed with enormous force through slammed-shut vocal cords and crushed jaws.

It was a horrible noise and a terrible sight, which is why I was trying to cause it over on the other side. If that starts to happen around you, even the toughest fighters tend to suffer a loss of morale. And if they began to hesitate—

There was a scream from the screen that cut right through everything else—one of the Closers coming through must have stopped one of my rounds, and air-foamed blood sprayed everywhere for an instant before everyone else's SHAKK rounds tore him apart.

The second rank had managed to arrive in a body, stepping out all at once and diving and scattering, so they returned some of our fire, but now that their surprise was gone, the advantage was all with us—we could see them coming out before they could see to shoot, and they were only coming through one narrow aperture.

They got off a few stray rounds, and because both sides have homing hypersonic ammunition, some of their rounds found targets. Perhaps a dozen more of us died, torn to bloody rags around us. The man in front of me, a tall guy with Oriental features who had been pumping SHAKK rounds at the screen in a steady rhythm, suddenly burst apart backward, his heart and lungs driven out through his rib cage and coat to spray Chrys and me.

I wiped my face, but I kept sending fléchettes into the hole where the screen had been.

Still, even though they scored on us a few times, and much as I was sorry anytime one of us died (or one of them didn't!), they lasted for only a few seconds before they, too, were mowed down; they looked more like criminals trying to make a break from in front of a firing squad than a body of organized troops. Their bodies flopped around and sprayed blood, and they were still.

Whatever the third rank was supposed to do, all they did was die. I don't think many of them even made it out of the gate—there was a storm of SHAKK and NIF rounds pouring in there by then, and what it must have been like on the other side is hard to guess.

I saw General Malecela rise cautiously from the deck up there and toss two things through the gate before he fell down, hugging the dirt again.

A moment later, the surface of the gate—with shadowy figures still half-falling through it—glowed red, and then there was only blank wall where it had been. There was a long moment while we all checked to make sure that all the Closers who had come through were dead; then another burst of activity as people grabbed their fallen comrades, hoping—though with the weapons of that future, it's hopeless—that someone had somehow survived a hit.

I suppose I should give the Closers some kind of credit—obviously it was a suicide mission, which takes guts, and they certainly kept coming. But after the initial explosion into the room, and the first hail of deadly projectiles that killed sixty of us, they barely managed to get forty fighters through the gate they had opened, and our total deaths were under a hundred. I call that amateurish and sloppy, and since I wasn't used to seeing either from the Closers, it told me in part how desperate they must be.

Within a minute or so, the ATN staff were back in action and had opened an emergency gate. We all filed through it in quick, silent order; they were popping us to a concealed base deep inside an asteroid in an uninhabited timeline, one of many sanctuaries that ATN maintained for times when absolute security was imperative.

As I stepped through the gate, I glanced back and saw that a detail was taking the bodies out; there were several bodies lying in the aisles or in seats with living Crux Ops kneeling or sitting beside them. I thought of how I might have felt had Chrys died in the attack, and realized I'd have been doing the same thing—saying good-bye, getting it into my brain that she was gone. As we went through the gate, I shuddered.

It got gray, weightless, and soundless; as always, light came back first, color last. At the end of the process we were walking on a seemingly endless steel walkway that curled around over our heads; the asteroid was spinning to provide artificial gravity, and the walkway ran around the outer edge.

The assembly hall here wasn't nearly so comfortable. There were no refreshments, but I doubt that anyone was hungry or thirsty.

We milled around for a moment, and then General Malecela came in. When he took the podium, everyone fell silent.

"Let me begin," he said, "by asking you all to take a moment to reflect on your fallen comrades, to ask any deity in which you believe to take care of them, and to calm yourselves and get ready for the next step."

The room was plunged into excruciating silence for a long time; finally Malecela spoke again. "First of all, I want you all to know that I'm proud to be one of you. Collectively your quick reflexes and speed in maneuver held our casualties far lower than they might have otherwise been, and, moreover, the returned fire was very intelligently executed—some of you may have noted that I tossed two PRAMIACS through that gate. I had set one for ten megatons, to go off whenever the gate closed, and the other for a couple of tons of explosive in hopes of destroying the generator. I discovered that the rest of you had already tossed in at least forty PRAMIACS set for the maximum, to blow off when the gate closed, and, moreover, several of you tossed various charges and fired various programmed rounds in there that collectively must have ensured that the gate generator would fail. In other words, we couldn't have done that better if we had planned it.

"Another detail is more significant, if you think about it. There has been no further attack on the base on the back side of the moon, and our probes into the immediate future show none as far as we can trace. Yet, having lost the battle, why did they not toss a bomb through at us? It would have taken almost nothing at all, compared with their known resources, to open another gate from a military facility somewhere, push through a nuclear bomb or a large mass of antimatter, and switch off the gate.

"The answer to that can only be one thing. They didn't do it on the first shot because they wanted to capture at least some of us—several of the bodies had stun weapons among their equipment. They know by now that we don't negotiate for hostages, so they were looking for someone to interrogate—and they chose to try to get prisoners from the most dangerous possible time and location they could have picked. That means that, from the standpoint of whoever planned this thing, the prisoners *had* to be taken from that meeting—probably the only place they could identify where the information they needed could be found.

"Moreover, there's only one reason we can think of that the Closers would mount such an inept expedition, and then not even follow up with a bomb . . . we think that it's because they *couldn't*. What we were attacked by was something thrown together at the last moment, a last-ditch effort by some isolated Closer base. Which, thanks to you all, just received about four hundred megatons in return."

There was a very long, stunned silence.

"Yes, you are thinking accurately," Malecela said, repeating himself, then looking up and grinning at us. "That attack was from the last Closer base capable of mounting an attack. The evidence is that sometime very soon—and god knows we don't know how just yet—we are about to win this war."

The place broke into the wildest applause I've ever seen in my life; even people whose faces were still streaked with tears for their dead were cheering. It took a long time before there was enough quiet for Malecela to be heard again.

"Now," he said, "we've managed to get enough staff and personnel into this base to get some sort of quarters ready for all of you. We'll give you a couple of hours to settle in and clean up—which also gives us a little time to do some planning and arranging—and then, after that, we'll be meeting with you individually and in small groups. Right now I don't have the foggiest idea of what you will be doing, but I do know that given the number of timelines we must investigate at once, there won't be enough of you.

"That's all for now. If you'll file out to my left and place your thumbs on the reader, you'll receive directions to your rooms."

There wasn't much to say, but everyone was saying it loudly and rapidly. Chrys and I could barely hear each other and gave up trying, figuring it would be easier to talk once we got to our room.

The thumbprint reader told us that we were on Level 8, Wing 4, Room 80; before we had time to ask where that might be, we saw a bank of escalators, labeled with "Level 2" up through "Level 8."

"They put us in the penthouse," I said.

"Not much of a view here," Chrysamen pointed out. "That means eight levels up from the outer edge of the spinning asteroid. We're deeper inside than anyone else."

"People get penthouses either for the view or for the privacy," I pointed out.

"You're incorrigible."

The escalator ride was a strange sensation because when you use centrifugal force for artificial gravity, the gravity falls off very rapidly as you move in toward the center, and at the same time the apparent Coriolis force gets more noticeable. The total effect was that if you shut your eyes, it felt like the escalator was twisting upward to the left, about to curl right over and dump you off. We both hung on, though Chrys seemed to be getting a kick out of shutting her eyes and letting go momentarily.

But then she enjoys parachute drops and roller coasters. Chrys is close, but nobody's perfect.

"You really ought to try this," she said, grinning at me.

"No thanks. I prefer only to be scared to death when there's actually something to be scared of."

She shrugged. "Think of it as staying in practice."

At the top of the escalator, there were moving sidewalks like the things they have in airports, fanning out from the escalator head, and one of them was clearly marked for "Wing 4." It was enough to make me wonder if all this had been sitting here waiting for centuries (it might well have been) or if they had suddenly realized they would need it, dropped a construction team back five years in time, and then built it right after the attack on the back side of the moon. In principle the only way to tell would be by asking.

The room was in that gray range between hospital, barracks, and hotel, clearly not a place intended as anyone's home but not entirely devoid of comfort either. They had provided us with some simple tunic-and-pants uniforms, since we had no bags—those were "still" back at the Wellington in New York in my home timeline, god knows how many years crosstime but at least 850 years back. Supposedly after this mission we'd be returned to that time and place—where Paula was on her way to cover Porter, where Robbie was in a hospital bed in Oslo, where with Paula gone, the second team would have to cover my son, father, and sister.

Time travel costs a lot of money; probably if it hadn't been for the Closers, it would have been millennia after it was discovered before anyone did it regularly. *In principle* they could have sent back a probe to see how it all came out and let me know whether my family and friends were all right. *In principle*, if it's before noon, you could be in Paris tomorrow morning from almost anywhere in the United States. It would merely cost you so much that you wouldn't think of doing it. In the same way, unless there was a remarkably good reason other than the nerves of two senior Crux Ops, they weren't going to do that. And being able to know is not at all the same thing as actually knowing.

I was about to work my way up into a fine fret, since there was nothing else to do until they called us, and I don't respond well to having a lot on my mind and nothing I can do. So I took a shower and changed, as Chrys did, and *then* I started to work on developing a fine fret.

Maybe because she recognized the warning signs, Chrysamen abruptly asked, "So, just before the meeting was extremely rudely interrupted"—the funny twist in her mouth told me the joke was supposed to make me a little more relaxed and easy to talk to— "you were acting like there was a snake in your pants leg. And you were focusing a lot of your strange squirmy energy, my dear husband, on Citizen-senator Thebenides. So I think you didn't like what you were hearing, but unfortunately I think you made that very clear to everyone else."

"Hmmm." I sat down on the bed, kicked off my shoes, and stretched out. She did the same and lay in my arms. After a couple long breaths and a false start, I began, "So I suppose that if I start out by admitting that it's just a funny feeling, even if it's a very intense funny feeling, you're not going to be pleased?"

She made a face, twisting her mouth a little sideways, and then said, "Mark, you know I know you, and you know I love you, and by now I know you don't act up in public without a good reason. And you were really acting up, and I really couldn't see the reason. So if it's purely a gut feeling, I assume it's a very strong gut feeling, and if it's something more than that, it's probably important, but anyway—what I want to know is, *what did you see that bothered you so much?* You and I stay alive on our hunches and our feel for evidence, sweetheart. If there's something the matter, share it. I trust you."

I hunched up onto one shoulder so I could look at her face more closely, which also gave me an excuse to push some of her dark curls back from her face a little. She was so beautiful, even now . . . after all those years, after all the usual marital hassles . . . and, of course, after more than a dozen dangerous missions together. We'd seen each other shot and bleeding, fought side by side in worlds you can't imagine, and all I had to do was explain to her that Thebenides gave me the creeps. How complicated could that be? As she said, if I couldn't trust her . . .

"Look," I began, "I think part of it is a matter of where and when I grew up. In my time and timeline, we weren't great trusters of politicians. I know that nobody is, but us particularly. We knew a little too well that when someone starts talking about how principles are all very well, but you've got to be practical, he means that he's going to do something he thinks you won't approve of, and he wants to head off your argument. Nobody ever says, 'Look, let's just get practical here' if he's talking about feeding or housing people, or about giving good jobs to vets or something. The 'I'm just a practical guy—let's all be practical together and not pay too much attention to those pointy-headed intellectuals' dodge usually only comes along when a politician is cooking up something so disgusting that it can't be justified in the normal way. It's the way Truman talked about dropping the bomb, the way Johnson talked about getting into Vietnam, the way Nixon talked about law and order, and the way Bush and Clinton talked all the time."

"And boy, did they talk all the time," Chrysamen said, grinning. "Okay, lover, I can buy that explanation. You think he's trying to put a fast one over on us, morally speaking, right?"

"I don't so much think that as I know it in my bones. And look at what he's saying, too, Chrys. 'Oh, sure, maybe we've won, and that's swell, but what if we didn't beat the Closers in a way that we would approve of.' Meaning, what if he doesn't approve of the way the ATN would have to change to win. But the only reason ATN exists is to fight back against the Closers. ATN never meddles in the affairs of a member timeline, or at least that's what they always tell all of us. Don't you see how peculiar that is? If I had to make a guess, it's that the Athenian timeline has a big bureaucracy, by now, with quite a bit invested in keeping the war going. I would guess the timelines war is big business for a lot of our good, generous, civilized Athenians."

She looked more than a bit startled. "Mark, you can't be serious. Your timeline and mine both owe everything to the Athenians. If they hadn't fought back, and developed the time machines themselves, and then organized and helped everyone else, we'd all be under the Closer heel. We even named our son after Perikles!"

I nodded. "You see how uncomfortable it is? But let's face facts, wars involve a lot of money, and the money flows through a central point somewhere. The central point always gets its hands on a lot of the money. That all makes common sense, doesn't it? So somewhere in the Athenian timeline, there are people with jobs or property who are going to lose out when the war ends. Since that wasn't supposed to happen for thousands of years, nobody thought about what to do when it was over. Now there's the scary prospect of peace real soon. And nobody is ready for it.

"But our boy Thebenides knows a voter's interest—or maybe a campaign donor's? I don't know how they finance their elections— he knows what they have at stake. Any good political hack does. And he's not going to let them get hurt. That's the first given. And the second given—well, so whatever timelines are now drawing close to our own, they seem to just possibly have it in for the Closers. That strikes me as just fine and a high personal recommendation.

"But good old Thebenides sees it differently. He's afraid that whatever is out there might not like ATN either. Which is quite possible. And considering we have member timelines that are absolute monarchies, and Communist dictatorships, and hell, there's even a couple of reformed Nazi timelines that joined up . . . well, maybe we just don't look all that good to the Intertemporal Good Guys. Maybe all the other little compromises that Thebenides and his crew have made would make us look not different enough from the Closers . . .

"Or maybe the new timelines are actually really bad guys, even worse than Closers."

I sighed and shrugged, holding Chrys tight. "Don't you see how much of a mess this is, at least potentially?"

"Maybe," she said. "Do you mean you're afraid Thebenides wants to make an alliance with the Closers?"

"I'm afraid he wants to leave the door open to it, anyway, and I don't like that one bit. I'm also afraid that he may have worse than that in mind. Like he wants to bargain out some balance-of-power deal. Like he suggests that if the new guys do turn out to be friendly, we keep the Closers around 'just in case' or 'for the balance of power.' You see the kind of thing I mean?"

"Maybe."

"Well, jeez. It's not easy to put into words. The whole idea of having a principle is that it's something to guide your actions, isn't it? And if at the first sign of things getting complicated or difficult, you decide to throw the principle over the side, there's only two reasons—either it was always a bad principle, or you've decided to do a bad thing. I don't think he wants to do anything consciously evil, but I think he's like politicians in my timeline—he wants to have the option. He doesn't care enough about right and wrong to let them get in the way of anything he wants to do."

"Well, it *is* practical politics, Mark." She looked straight into my eyes. "I mean, I come from a very impractical timeline. We were completely pacifist. We were taken over, exploited, slaughtered, wrecked, and we never varied from our principles until we finally made one huge massacre. And if we hadn't been willing to do that when ATN showed up and armed us . . . well, you can imagine. I'd probably have never been born—we'd have died out a generation or more before I was born. You can't be completely principled about these things."

"You can't be completely unprincipled, either," I said. "Look, it probably is just the experience of history. When I think about the deals my nation made to win World War II—deals with Russia that gave millions of refugees back to Stalin, deals with France that eventually got us into Vietnam, deals with Britain that got the USA into the business of preserving a colonial empire . . . well. During my lifetime we were so practical that we backed any murdering dictator who said he wasn't a Communist, and turned a blind eye to torture, murder, and repression anywhere that they'd let McDonald's sell a hamburger or Disney put on a movie. That's what 'practical' got us."

She nodded, and her face looked serious and far away. "I understand the problem, I guess. You think he talked like one of your politicians, and you don't trust them at all."

"You don't know 'em like I do," I pointed out, "and there's a certain analogy about the whole thing, too. In my timeline, we had just won a huge war, and we were sitting on top of the world, and then the wealthy and powerful grabbed the whole show for themselves and managed to make us roundly hated everywhere within a generation. Nobody was more liked and respected in 1945, and thanks to a few thousand dorks in suits whose only interest was in making money, nobody was more hated by 1965. I'd hate to think that after the war is over ATN would do anything except hunt down whatever Closer bases are still hidden, and then dissolve."

"Hmm. And Thebenides set off all those feelings in you?"

"Yeah, all those and more. See, the other problem is, the son of a bitch just comes across as a greasy liar."

At that, she finally laughed a little, which I found encouraging. I put an arm around her waist, and we kissed, long and slow. It occurred to me that there was at least one good way to kill an hour or so in a room alone with Chrysamen. Gently, I stroked her skirt up her thigh; she kissed me more firmly.

We were both most of the way naked and beginning to get to the intense parts when the little loudspeaker in the room said, "Agents Strang and ja N'wook, please acknowledge."

"Here," we said, together.

"Report in ten minutes to Conference Level 2, Wing 3, Conference Room 7," the voice said.

Oh, well, getting dressed in a hurry always gives me more energy for a long boring meeting. We caught the escalators back down and discovered that they deposited us right by the door of the conference room; we were even about half a minute early.

In the conference room were Ariadne Lao, Citizen-senator Thebenides, and General Malecela. I figured my confidence in whatever was to follow was at just under 67 percent.

They were polite, but they got down to business right away. I had already realized that if three people that senior were explaining the mission to us, it must be unusually important even for senior Crux Ops.

Without preface, Ariadne Lao said, "The new timelines that are going to assist us in this war—"

Thebenides cleared his throat and Malecela glared at him.

Ariadne Lao began again. "It seems to be clear that our new allies will contact us through timelines which are derived from the ones in which Porter Brunreich becomes a figure of major importance. I therefore must apologize for assigning you to your own time, but it's become abundantly clear why they are targeting Porter Brunreich—the timelines that are our bridge to our new allies all spring from her."

"And let me underline and highlight that," Malecela added. "She must not only survive, but she must survive as the sort of person whose legacy will include trust rather than suspicion.

"Therefore—and I know it's not as interesting or exciting an assignment as it could be, but it's certainly the most vital—both of you are assigned at once to return to your own timeline and organize around-the-clock in-depth protection for Porter Brunreich."

"She's had that since she was thirteen," I pointed out, "but we can step that up several levels. And don't worry, it's the job we'd rather be doing. How soon can we leave?"

"We thought you might like a decent meal and a night's rest," Malecela said, "but you can go right after breakfast tomorrow if you like. We've sent one of our on-the-spot fronts to get your things from your hotel and get them shipped over to Europe; we can have you meet her in Weimar, just before her concert there. We've arranged, via your bodyguard agency, for her to get to Weimar by helicopter—you'll go by ground transport, but you'll get there a bit before her."

"Good," Chrys said, and since there wasn't anything more to add, we both got up to go.

But Citizen-senator Thebenides still had something to add. "And do your best to recall that not only are the Porter Brunreich timelines vital to our defense and to our contact with, er, the other new timelines, but since so often the culture of a given timeline is simply one person's prejudices writ large, I would hope that when you talk to Citizen Brunreich you will keep in mind the values of ATN and of Attika generally, and—"

"We usually suggest that she ought to do what's right," I said, without much trace of patience.

We were all the way back to the room, and beginning to mess around where we had left off, when Chrysamen whispered into my ear, "Okay, I see your point about Thebenides. Still, it's obvious that Ariadne Lao, and for that matter General Malecela, despise the man. I don't know how much harm he can do in the circumstances."

"Ever hear of civilian control of the military? He's the boss."

"He's one of a lot of bosses, Mark. Not necessarily the most important one, either. I agree, if he were really in charge, I'd be worried silly. He's slippery and greasy, and that's his most attractive feature. But right now we have a lot more to worry about."

"Funny," I said, "but it's easier to worry about Thebenides, who is merely an asshole, than about Porter and the future of all those timelines."

"I wasn't going to worry about Porter either. We'll be there to meet her plane, and if the Closers can't get a bomb to a Crux Op meeting, when they know the location and time, and when it would only be across time—they aren't going to get anything that can shoot down an airplane all the way back to a couple of critical hours in the twentieth century. We've got other things to worry about." She kissed me, then, very firmly.

"Such as what?" I knew she was right—Thebenides was minor, Porter was important but not anything we could do anything about—but now I didn't know what she thought we *should* be worrying about.

"Such as that a few weeks ago Perry wanted to know why he was an only child and suggested we get working on it." Now she slipped her arms around me and pressed her body to mine.

"Should've named that kid Aristotle," I muttered. "His major interest seems to be biology."

•4•

The next morning breakfast was what it usually is in that timeline—dense, heavy bread served warm, big chunks of feta cheese, olive paste, and coffee so strong it etches your teeth. We ate quickly and reviewed instructions; they would be putting us in through the usual channels, our bags were already in place, our briefcases and passports waiting on the airliner. They had appropriate clothing waiting for us as well.

"Will you look at this?" I said to Chrysamen. "I look like a yuppie instead of a goon. I think they set me up with Brooks Brothers Number Four, Corporate Boring."

She grinned at me. "My feeling exactly. How are they going to tell me from the flight attendant?" She gestured at the blue suit with its simple skirt, silk blouse, and string tie. "They must have gotten this out of a costume handbook or something. Though I have to concede I'm at least going to be inconspicuous. I'll look like every other female biz nerd on the flight. All the ones that everyone suspects are being exploited by their bosses."

A few minutes later we made the crossover. A gate opened in front of us, and the ATN couriers stepped through, handing each of us our ticket and passport. I noted with amusement that the male courier was about four inches shorter than I was and that the female courier was about three shades lighter than Chrysamen in skin tone—and had her hair tied up tightly in a scarf, which probably meant she didn't wear it anything like Chrys did. Well, supposedly this was a short commuter flight from Frankfurt to Leipzig; probably everyone would be reading, and no one would look closely at us.

We stepped into the gate. The world faded to gray, weightless silence; there was a timeless interval when we didn't exist; then light came back, and sound, and weight, and finally color—though there was little enough of that in an airliner bathroom.

We came out of the bathroom and everyone was staring at us; it then suddenly occurred to me that they had noticed a man and a woman going into an airliner bathroom, staying there several minutes, and emerging out of breath.

It was a very long walk back to our seats; fortunately our opposite numbers had left English-language newspapers for us there, though we felt more like hiding under them than reading them.

By the time the plane landed, people had mostly stopped staring at us, or at least stopped being quite so overt about it. Almost you might have imagined we were any other passengers—though a lot of the men on board certainly stared holes in Chrys's clothing on our way out.

Leipzig Airport is one of the world's uglier airports, thanks to a remarkably uninspired set of Communist architects, and it's extremely busy all the time. That's a bad combination because one thing a Communist architect never figured on was heavy traffic. They do all seem to have figured that people would be standing in line a lot and would want some nice blank gray walls to stare at, and wouldn't want to wonder about where the seats were, so they didn't put too many of those in . . .

As always, the ATN couriers had been much too efficient, and gotten our bags on the airliner in Frankfurt first, so of course they were last getting off. While they were getting off I surreptitiously checked our passports and determined that we had officially been stamped through the day before. Once again those guys had thought of everything.

Which made me suspect that the trick of having us both come out of the same bathroom after a delay was a function of their sense of humor rather than their carelessness. "You know," I muttered to Chrys, "I won't have time to write a report on those guys for days and days, and by that time, I'll probably think it was funny."

"Then you'd better let me write the report."

"Absolutely. Is that your suitcase?"

It wasn't; just the third one like it on that flight. But the next one was hers, and then there was mine, and at last we were on our way.

The Fodor's people say that rail service in what used to be East Germany still has "one foot in the steam age." Every time we take a train through that area—and Chrys and I do often, because if you have money and an opera-crazed spouse, there's nowhere more attractive on Earth than that area where what used to be East Germany borders what used to be Czechoslovakia—I wonder just what age the other foot is in. Possibly the Late Stone Age.

The trip to Weimar was mercifully brief, all the same, and the fact that it was Weimar was a compensation. That little city is so small compared to its importance in art, theatre, and music that if you know any of its history, it's a constant shock to realize how close together everything happened . . . Goethe and Schiller didn't just live here at the same time, their families probably borrowed sugar from each other.

Porter was playing at the National Theater; we had been there a few times. The place has a strange effect on the visitor; the building is beautiful, and about as good a smaller auditorium as you're apt to find for opera, concert, or theatre—then suddenly you realize just how much of European intellectual history happened there. There's a statue of Goethe with his hand on Schiller's shoulder out front, and that reminds you . . . but you still have to think for a moment to realize that Franz Liszt and Carl Maria von Weber lived and made music here, both Cranachs painted there, Wagner's *Lohengrin* opened there, Gropius came up with the designs that half the modern world is built to—it goes on and on. All that in a little town smaller than Great Falls, Montana, and a lot of it right there in the National Theater.

The cab from the railway station carried us on past, and I finally looked down at the note they had given me to show the driver. "Upscale all the way this time," I told Chrys. "They're putting us up in the Elephant."

We had always figured sometime when we came here for a concert or opera, we'd stay there, but only as an indulgence—the place is expensive. What do you expect for a three-hundred-year-old hotel that can claim, "Hitler always stayed here when he was in town?"

It was about two hours till Porter was due, so we got checked in and had the fun of playing dumb tourist, checking out the appointments in the room, for a while before we got down to business.

Naturally the NIF in my coat pocket and the SHAKK in its special holster between my shoulder blades didn't require a permit—or rather they would have if anyone had known what they were, but since they wouldn't be invented for centuries in my home timeline, they weren't exactly against the rules. Not exactly within them, either.

Oddly enough, as part of my cover, I had to go to the bother of having a permit to carry my old Colt Model 1911A1, the basic "Army .45 automatic" you see in too many old movies. Sure enough, both the pistol and the permit were there in my bags, the pistol carefully disassembled and labeled in six different ways to get it through European customs. I carefully reassembled it, checked it out, and slipped it into my shoulder holster.

"Pretty silly," I grumbled, "when I'm better armed by far with stuff they wouldn't even notice, to have to call attention to myself with this."

"You're a bodyguard," Chrys pointed out, being practical. "And someone took a shot at your ward. It's what people will expect."

"Yeah, yeah." Actually it felt good to have the old overweight piece of iron back on, and at least in my home timeline it does have an advantage that the NIF and SHAKK don't. If you look at a NIF, you think, "cordless drill" or maybe "kid's ray gun"; if you look at a SHAKK you think, "super squirt gun sprayed with aluminum paint." Never mind that the former can knock out an infantry platoon with a burst and the latter, in a pinch, can blast its way into a bank vault or bring down a bomber. (I know, I've done both with it.) They don't look like real weapons, and you have to *use* them to convince people, and a lot of times you don't want to use it, you just want to convince them.

If you look at a Colt .45, however, you think, "This will blow big holes in people." Which can mean you don't have to pull the trigger.

There was a knock at the door. I moved to one side of it and asked, "Who is it?" in English.

"A friend from Athens."

That wasn't the password. It also wasn't *not* the password; it was the kind of thing a field agent might improvise, and also the kind of thing that a Closer agent might try.

Chrys drew her NIF and covered the door. I gingerly reached out and flipped the dead bolt.

"Come in very slowly," I said, holding the .45 level at head height.

Something was wrong the instant the door opened. Just what was wrong didn't register, but it was enough to know we were in a fight, and I pulled the trigger.

A .45 makes a deafening roar in an enclosed space like a hotel room, and that added to the confusion. The door swung wide, and I saw that the body falling onto the carpet was in a short black dress; Chrys's NIF whined, and something fell backward in the hall. She fired twice more, hitting nothing, though I could hear her rounds wailing off like tiny bees down the halls, looking for other targets. I hoped they were set on stun, so she wouldn't kill—

Oh, hell, a maid. Whoever was barging in had pushed a maid in front of him, and I had shot her—

There was no sound from the hall, and I crept forward to look at the body of the maid. She was middle-aged, gray hair dyed blond, face blue-black, the garrote still embedded in her neck—she had been dead before he ever knocked, before I fired—

"Mark! That package!"

I turned and saw that, beside the unconscious man, there was a small cardboard box that could be a shirt, or some pastry, or—

There was a great flash and roar, and the world got very dark and quiet.

I woke up very slowly. As I did, I began to take stock . . . my nightmares begin with the idea of being captured by the Closers and waking up in one of their hospitals. They wouldn't save my life because they liked me or out of any humanitarian purpose, and I know too well what advanced technology can do to the nervous system. If I was waking up slowly, and in Closer hands, it just might be possible I wasn't in restraints, and in that case I could kill one or more of them—or kill myself before they got to work on me. The kind of torture they can do, no one stands up to for even a moment; it's not so much pain that you can't bear, but the fact that they just strip-mine your mind till there's nothing left, and you can feel the whole process. Your consent doesn't really matter.

Nightmare number two is waking up in a modern twentieth-century hospital. They mean well, but the buildings themselves are nests of germs, most of the available drugs are poisons—and, most of all, our doctors can't really *heal*, that is, they can't make things grow back good as new. And it could be a long time before I got a replacement eye or leg, and if I lost a limb and had to maintain a cover, I'd have to live without the arm or leg until the cover wasn't needed anymore . . . bad news, too, but not as bad as being captured by the Closers.

I couldn't feel sheets or anything around me, but I could feel considerable pain. So I wasn't under a twenty-ninth-century pain block, which meant I wasn't back in the hospital at Hyper Athens. Bad news . . . that left the more nightmarish possibilities . . .

I opened my eyes slowly and blinked twice. It made no difference. I was either blind or in total darkness. I tried to grope toward my face, and my right arm wouldn't move. Broken? It didn't feel like it. Pinned against my side somehow.

My left arm would move but only in a small space next to my body. I was getting the pain localized to the middle of my back, the back of my legs, and a little bit on my head. I was also trying to figure out whether I had been out at all . . . I could smell cordite, and some other explosive.

My right hand groped again and found the butt of the .45 under me, dragged it around, confirmed the barrel was warm. If I'd been unconscious, it had been for less than a minute. I knew the worst, anyway. I was buried in rubble.

I tried shouting, then, and heard nothing right away, but of course all that means is the pile was thick. Besides, from the way my ears felt, I had probably been deafened by the blast.

When you're buried in rubble, the big danger is that you'll make it collapse around your air-space, or make it shift and bend some part of yourself in a direction it shouldn't go. I shouted for help a couple more times, and then decided I'd work on getting out, in between shouting.

A lot of slow, careful groping determined that I was in a narrow space with something heavy and soft digging into my back. I was in pain from what felt like bad bruises, but I wasn't burned anywhere except a bit on my face, and I didn't seem to be leaking blood.

"Help! Help! I'm in here!" I yelled again, waited for an answer, and went back to groping around me.

It didn't take much more to determine that my head was in the biggest space I had available. It was hard work feeling around behind me, but what was pushing down on me directly seemed to be a mass of cloth, hair, and wires. I tried raising my head and bumped it on the hard surface above me; a flat stick was pressing across my shoulders, not painfully, but annoying me all the same.

I yelled again, and heard nothing again. For good measure I yelled for Chrys a couple of times. The bomb blast had had a much straighter shot at her than at me, but she'd been aware it was a bomb sooner . . . and she'd been by a window. Maybe she was able to duck and cover and then get out?

At least I hadn't smelled smoke, and there was air in here, so probably the building was not burning over my head.

I yelled again, and no one answered. I decided, very, very tentatively, to try to push the "roof" upward on my little safety space. Maybe I wasn't buried by much, and even if I was, maybe I could get to a better space. And why hadn't I heard any of the search parties?

The little space I was in wasn't much bigger than a coffin, and it took a while just to get my hands under my shoulders to try this extradifficult push-up. By the time I did, I could feel sweat pouring down my back. There seemed to be air but not much.

I pushed hard, and something gave above me. Dirty, dusty, but open air hit my lungs at exactly the same instant that I realized that there was light, and I could *see*.

Forgetting the possible danger, I pushed hard and suddenly everything broke loose, but in eerie silence. I sat up to see Chrys, still clutching her NIF, standing in the wrecked hotel room. Her mouth moved, but no sound came out, and then I reached up, touched my ears, and found blood running out.

I staggered to my feet. I had been under an armoire which had fallen, open, over me while I lay beside the maid's body; the "wires, hair, and cloth" had been hangers, coats, and clothes, the "stick" in my back the clothes rod. The great pile of weight had been the shattered plaster wall that lay on top of the armoire.

And Chrysamen was up and moving. "I can't hear," I cried. "My eardrums are ruptured."

She nodded and appeared to motion to me, but before I could read any of her signals, she stepped back and gestured.

A gate was opening in front of us, the gray void forming there. The two couriers who had passed through the airliner bathroom to ATN before—the woman, this time, tanned darker, and with her hair done like Chrysamen's—stepped out and gestured for us to get in. We did, and it became deep gray, then there was nothing at all, and after a while it all came swimming back in a way not too different from some old television sets—a glow, a sound, black-and-white, color.

We were on a small receiving dock at ATN's Hyper Athens spaceport—the overhead view is unmistakable once you've been there a few times—and a couple of doctors were converging on us. In a minute they'd sprayed something in my ears to make them stop hurting, gotten us both on stretchers, and loaded us into one of the little electric airplanes they use inside the station (when a space station is tens of miles across, and in low gravity it's easy to fly, air travel makes a lot of sense). My last thought before I passed out on the stretcher was that I wasn't going to get to hear Porter's concert after all, and that I had really been looking forward to it.

The next morning I was ravenously hungry—the "nanos," the microscopic machines they inject into your bloodstream to repair the damage, live on your blood sugar just as you do, and they eat up a lot of it doing repairs. I now had two good eardrums again, and in the places where I should have had bruises, the nanos had reabsorbed the blood and rebuilt the tissue, so I was fit and healthy, if terribly hungry.

It turned out that Chrys had been badly shaken, cracked a couple of ribs, and broken one tooth, so all that had to be repaired on her.

As we sat and gobbled down the local equivalent of pancakes with the local equivalent of jelly, Ariadne Lao filled us in on the situation.

"As far as we can determine," she said, "the attack was coordinated with a couple of people who were going to set up to take down Porter Brunreich's helicopter. They wanted you out of the way so that they could get a clear shot. We've captured one of them alive, and we're trying to find out who he was working for—not ultimately, of course, since we all know it has to be the Closers, but what organization in your timeline, how he's being controlled. We may have to resort to mind-stripping, which I'm not crazy about, but . . ." She sighed and shrugged. "This is important, and we can't trust him to tell the truth. And we can certainly tell that he is lying to us."

"Go ahead, if it's up to me," Chrys said. She can be kind of vengeful, but then she really hates getting hurt.

"I'll weigh your vote in," Ariadne Lao said, with a faint smile. "At any rate, as soon as we know, we'll be dropping you back in to finish the mission—about three minutes after your stand-ins get there. Oh, and we've surgically altered that corpse so that it won't be too obvious that she was shot, Mr. Strang. That way you won't be doing jail time while the authorities back in your own timeline figure it out."

"Great with me," I said. "I don't relish the idea of a German jail."

She looked a little baffled. "In our timeline, the Germans have an image of being rather sweet, gentle, and ineffectual," she said. "There's a comedian who does a routine about German jailers who are constantly worrying that the prisoners aren't happy."

"Not exactly the image I grew up with," I said.

A few minutes later we were once again headed back to my home timeline—and though we had spent the better part of a day healing back at Hyper Athens, we were only gone from our own timeline for about thirty seconds, just the time needed for safety. We had just traded places with our stand-ins, and the gate had just closed, when we heard screams and running. I holstered my .45.

A moment later, there were fifty hotel employees standing around, and the hotel detective was making officious noises. I showed him a huge sheaf of official paper, and while he was puzzling and harrumphing his way through that, the regular cops showed up, and right on their heels the antiterror unit out of Dresden, which had taken advantage of a *Bundeswehr* chopper that was available at that moment.

We all had a very good time exchanging stories, and fortunately although the Germans are the people who lead the world in bureaucracy (Bismarck invented it and Weber named it), that does mean that they've had a lot of practice and are pretty good at doing bureaucratic things quickly. Also, even though there was a lot to do, the computers were doing most of it, and they move pretty fast—in very little time it had been established that we were both licensed bodyguards, married, legally armed, and here to guard someone's body.

A few more checks turned up the important information that we were there to meet Porter Brunreich, and identified both my personal connection to her and the fact that she had already been attacked in Norway. All of a sudden we had crack German antiterror forces surrounding the helicopter landing area, and some serious VIP treatment for Porter.

In the middle of all the crashing, bustling arrangements, someone tapped my shoulder, and I turned around to see—"*Paula!*"

She hugged me, and it was a good thing I wasn't still sore from the bomb blast, because Paula, besides being built like a bear, seems to be about as strong as one. And a lot meaner, for that matter, when she needs to be.

"Boss, I'd ask what you're doing here, but life is full of surprises enough already. I got out here to meet Porter's chopper, and I found you'd shown up with the German Army."

I grinned back at her. It's always great to have trusted people around, and though I knew the German forces were a lot more capable than anything my agency could have put on the ground, it felt good to have Paula there as another backup.

That also reminded me that it had only been a day in that timeline since the first attack on Porter, a day since Chrysamen and I had stopped that bank robbery in New York. Time certainly flew when you were having fun.

We were set up on a parking lot, not at a regular helipad, with an eye to better security. The German troops, silent and fierce-looking, were scattered around, some visible as a deterrent, some undercover to supply backup. The whole area could be brought under interlocking fields of fire at any instant.

The major in charge of the AT troopers, a quiet guy named Kurtz, who didn't smile much and seemed a little bemused by the whole job of landing a child-prodigy pianist safely, came over to talk to me. "Herr Strang?"

"Yes, Major Kurtz?" The chip behind my ear let me speak and understand German without an accent.

"As far as I can tell, we have everything secure. I am making sure there is nothing I have overlooked. At the moment, radio contact informs me that the helicopter carrying Fraulein Brunreich is a few kilometers away. They will come in low, hopping and jigging near ground level on an indirect route, hoping to avoid the danger of a shoulder-fired missile."

"That seems smart," I said. "And your men understand that if it looks bizarre, it's probably the enemy?"

"Yes, sir. Though next to what has already happened I can't imagine what it would take to look bizarre."

I nodded. "I can understand. Nonetheless, I have good reason to think it *can* get more bizarre."

"That suggests that you know more than you have told us."

"I don't know more, but I suspect more. Don't forget, you're dealing with an organization—not just an individual but a group of them—who are interested in killing a child because she plays the piano beautifully. If that doesn't make you suspect more bizarreness may be in waiting—"

"I take your point." Kurtz sighed. "Not like the old days, when it was just some liberation army for people you had never heard of. That was comparatively simple."

His cellular phone pinged, and he brought it to his ear. "Yes? Good. All right, we're ready. Thank you. Good-bye." He turned back to me, and said, "Well, our 'delivery' is under way. The helicopter should arrive at any moment."

I looked across the broad parking lot; they had knocked down a dozen light poles and hauled them away to make a clear landing space. There were concrete wedges of "New Jerseys"—the traffic barriers you see on highways all the time—set up in zigzag rows, with troopers crouching behind them, on two sides of the lot. The big department store across the way was empty, commandeered for the time being, and behind its dozens of windows there were crack snipers.

I didn't bother to turn and look, but I knew that in the highway ditch behind, there were another thirty ATs, all ready for action.

I also knew that if Chrys and I were to jump in here with our SHAKKs and NIFs going, we could wipe out every one of them before they had half a chance to shoot back. And I knew that if the Closers had it together enough to jump in here—and knew exactly where and what they were aiming for—they could put anything on top of us, up to and including enough nukes to cut Europe in half from the Baltic to the Med.

I didn't like knowing that. I prefer operations somewhere way the hell away from people who aren't in the war—or at least don't know they're in it. I guess if you look at it from a certain point of view, all of the possible histories the world has had are in the war. But nonetheless, I think most of the time you can tell a soldier from a civilian, and most of the time you can tell a soldier with a stake in your war from a soldier on other business, and if it were up to me, we'd be fighting the Closers in the middle of the Sahara in some timeline where life never moved out of the oceans. I don't *like* the idea of innocent bystanders getting hurt, and even though these guys were armed to the teeth, and sent to guard Porter, in another sense they truly were innocent bystanders. That is, they didn't know what the hell was going on or who they might be up against.

So I looked over the array of armaments and just didn't feel as secure as I was probably supposed to.

After a few long breaths, I heard the beat of the rotor and saw the flash of the chopper rising over the trees. The pilot was pretty good in a flashy kind of way; he bounced down, then up, coming in over the department store, and made a rapid descent to the parking lot, stopping the rotor almost as soon as he touched down. The door opened and Porter ran out toward us.

She was most of the way to us when I saw a gray shimmer forming behind the helicopter, and, without stopping to think, I shouted, "Down, Porter, down!"

I always give my ward a lot of credit for alertness and common sense, and once again she was on top of matters—she hit the dirt right away. There was a roar as something shot out of the emerging gate and hit the chopper. The fuel tank blew, enveloping the helicopter in dense orange flames and black smoke. The pilot staggered out, his clothes on fire, and was shot in the back.

From behind the New Jerseys around the edge of the lot, the ATs opened up on whatever was coming through the now-open gate. I tore my coat down the back drawing the SHAKK from between my shoulder blades, and to my right Chrysamen yanked hers out; we each took three quick sidesteps and hit the ground.

The burning remains of the helicopter flew into pieces as another explosive round hit. Blazing wreckage and chunks of iron rained down on the lot. I could hear the steady rattle of automatic-weapons fire from the ditch, the New Jerseys, and the store windows.

But I could see it wouldn't be enough. The first Closers to charge through the gate had fallen, but there was already a ring of them surrounding their gate, setting up bulletproof barriers, getting return fire aimed back at us. I'd seen no superweapons yet, but it wasn't atypical of the Closers to push sacrificial lambs through first.

I ripped a SHAKK burst across the barriers; they fell over and shattered, and several of the bodies twitched and fell. The rest, exposed to the fire of the German commandos, were hit almost immediately. Chrysamen's burst into the gate would have slowed them further—if there had been troops in there.

Instead, what was crawling out of the gate was a silver dome floating just off the ground. I had seen those before, and I knew what this one was. Under the gleaming surface there were a dozen hypersonic homing-projectile guns, each delivering enough force to take down a house on every shot.

It was the Closer equivalent of a tank, rolling out into an ordinary department-store parking lot in our century. It must have cost them more electric power than the USA produces in a year to get that thing back here.

Chrys's rounds rang off its surface repeatedly, bouncing and then turning around to try again until they were out of energy. She might as well have been firing puffed rice. I fired, too, but more from a need to do something than from any belief that it would succeed.

The Closer "tanks" never appear to pivot; either their surfaces are so smooth we can't see them turn, or they can fire from any point on their surfaces. There was a deep, rumbling roar, and the row of New Jerseys on one end of the parking lot flew into gravel—mixed with flesh, blood, and bone—that sprayed across the empty field behind.

Chrys hurled a PRAMIAC through the Closer gate, and a moment later the red glow was followed by the gate switching off. But she had been able to set the PRAMIAC all the way up to ten megatons because the explosion would happen on the other side of the gate—in our timeline, it didn't actually "exist" at all.

The Closer tank was already here, and anything that would take it out would take out half of Weimar with it.

·5·

When there's no hope you do what you can think of. I emptied the SHAKK at the thing. We knew they never appeared to be harmed, but maybe I was giving everyone inside a terrible headache, maybe I was blinding the defense system, and just possibly there was actually a vulnerable spot, and one of the rounds would find it by accident.

None of the above happened. They screamed off it as uselessly as the much slower, unguided bullets from the AT forces, and just as Chrys's rounds had, they rattled against it repeatedly with no discernible effect. The tank drifted outward, as if looking around.

Porter, staying low to the ground, crawled slowly toward us.

At least the tank no longer had its infantry cover. They're supposed to be vulnerable when that happens, but of course that's one of our tanks, from our timeline. If this thing was vulnerable, it wasn't vulnerable to anything much we had on hand.

Chrys rolled a PRAMIAC toward it, along the ground; it ran over the tennis ball–sized object.

There was a sudden red glow over the surface of the tank; just for good measure, I sprayed it some more with the SHAKK.

The red glow faded, and the tank continued to roll across the pavement as before. Shots were still pinging off it, but there was no effect.

Meanwhile, Porter was still crawling steadily on her belly toward me. I wriggled forward toward her, still firing at the tank.

Again it blasted away, this time at the other set of New Jerseys. Whatever it fired, it was hypersonic and came in a broad band rather than as individual shots. The surfaces of the New Jerseys pitted, broke up, and crumbled like a wall of sugar hit by a hot spray of water. The roar of the concrete being ground to bits was deafening.

The tops of the New Jerseys crumbled, and they began to break into large pieces. The spray of invisible hypersonic particles was hitting with such force that the remaining pieces—the size of grapefruits and softballs—flew backward like cannonballs, killing the men behind them.

An instant later, the deadly wash of hypersonic particles had sanded the rest from existence; what was left of the men was a reddish tinge in the smear that stretched into the shattered forest beyond.

The tank advanced slowly toward us.

Porter was squirming forward for all she was worth now, the black sweatshirt and jeans she usually wore getting smeared with mud and gravel, her blond hair shining in the autumn sun. (Abstractly I hoped the Closers wouldn't be able to use that to spot her; at least we were in a country with a lot of blond people.) I saw that she had managed to get the .38 I'd given her out, but she wasn't trying to get it into play—another sign of her common sense, for at that range she couldn't have hit a thing, and if the SHAKK wasn't denting that monster, and a PRAMIAC was barely warming it up, they'd never even notice .38 snakeshot.

I crawled forward toward her, not because I could do anything effective, but just to be with her. We were nearly touching when the tank suddenly zagged toward us.

Chrys fed it another PRAMIAC, and this time it glowed a much brighter red—she must have notched the power setting on the PRAMIAC up a little—and actually sat still for a moment before it again began to move toward us. Probably she'd made everyone inside feel like they'd gotten a bad sunburn. Certainly she couldn't have safely gone any higher on the PRAMIAC setting, as it was a hard gust of wind that blew out from under the tank and I felt tremendous heat on my face.

The Closer tank drew nearer; Porter was now so close that I reached out and squeezed her free hand in front of me.

"Doesn't look good at all, kid," I said.

"I'm glad you're here," she replied.

The tank was looming large as it bore down on us; I was practically out of SHAKK ammunition anyway, and it seemed futile to try firing any more.

The light shifted and changed somehow, a flickering grayish glow on the other side of us from the tank. I looked over, and then up, to see a circle of colorless gray appear in the blue autumn sky; I couldn't tell how far away as there were no reference points.

It was another gate, but was it ours or theirs?

The question was answered in a flash—literally. A straight black line emerged from the center of the gate, and touched the Closer tank. The tank changed color, first from silver to gold, and then from gold to dull red.

Then it flew into pieces—big, hot glowing pieces that blew over our heads and crashed to the ground all around us. That settled the question as far as I was concerned—whoever it was on the other side of that gate were the good guys.

But as I was raising my head cautiously, I saw something that both startled me and explained a lot. We knew that Closer tanks were hard to knock out and that they seemed to fight as if in perfect condition right up till the moment when they were knocked out. They also never seemed to run out of fuel or ammo.

Now I saw why. Where the tank had stood, there was now a naked, gray gate.

The tanks had never been anything more than tough, mirrored armor over a gate; the power sources, ammunition, even parts of the weapons and crew themselves had been on the other side.

And now that the gate was exposed, they were still not giving up. Before I had time to react, twenty of them had raced through the gate. I gave them a quick blast with the SHAKK, and several fell dead, in that characteristic collapsing-bag way. Beside me, Porter's .38 barked, and then I heard the whiz of Chrysamen's NIF. We were back to an old-fashioned firefight around the mouth of a gate.

Except that the Closer tank had managed to wipe out most of our allies. I heard Paula's 9 mm also, and saw that the Closer troopers were now down flat. You could hardly ask for a more dangerous situation—there were superweapons around, and everyone could see everyone else.

Four of them convulsed and died from the fléchettes of Chrys's NIF, but they were working on getting an angle on us—

A curtain of fire ripped over our heads, sounding like outsize SHAKK rounds. All of the people facing us twitched once, a bouncing motion that might have been the last gasp of the nervous system, or might only have been the physical shock from the momentum of the projectiles.

Once again, the straight black line stabbed out, this time into the gate itself, which abruptly glowed deep red, and then white— and then went out, a lot faster than any candle ever had.

We all took a long breath, and then I slowly rose to my feet. There were fewer than a dozen German commandos still alive, and none of them was an officer. Paula, Chrys, Porter, and I were all still fine.

There was an immense number of dead Closers around where the two gates had been; most of the bodies had been hit multiple times.

I had a feeling that this was not going to be easy to explain to the German authorities.

A dark shadow fell across the parking lot, and I turned to see that the gate had widened till it took up a big part of the sky immediately above us—and through it, there emerged the great, dark bulk of a dirigible.

The airship slid neatly out of the gate, which closed in a blink behind it, and descended slowly to the pavement; long, spidery legs telescoped out of it.

Though it flew and maneuvered like a dirigible, it didn't land like one; it came down quickly and precisely, like a helicopter, and it didn't bounce in the breeze.

A ramp descended, and out came a circus ringmaster, flanked by two extras from *Ben-Hur*. At least that was *my* first thought. The top hat and the tux were sort of flashy and bright-colored, and something about the centurion outfits (which really did look a lot like the Roman Meal Bread version) suggested that they weren't well cared for.

But a closer look revealed that the reason the Roman armor, helmet, and leggings looked so casually treated was because those guys were wearing them like clothes; I suddenly realized that, just possibly, this was what they always wore. Moreover, though they had scabbards with short swords, they were holding big, blocky objects that looked a lot like flattened overhead projectors—but were probably weapons, and I would guess of neither the neural-induction nor the hypersonic-projectile types that we and the Closers had been fighting with for so long.

Something about those objects told me that the SHAKK in my hand was about as up-to-date, as of that moment, as a Pilgrim musket.

The guy in the top hat and tails, on the other hand, did not look the least bit comfortable. The outfit's basic color seemed to be mauve, though it was fighting it out with enough reds and purples in the pattern to not be the clear winner. The shirt had too much lace and too many ruffles for a production of *The Three Musketeers*, and the cummerbund clashed with everything else in a way that I'd never quite seen colors do before.

He wore a waxed mustache and an enormous white tie that added to the ringmaster effect—though now that I thought about it, he might also have passed for a stage magician, or possibly for the groom at the tackiest formal wedding you ever attended.

He glanced from side to side, looked at each of us in turn, and then walked slowly in my direction. The two guys in the Roman outfits moved a little to the side and followed; that easy, practiced motion told me that I shared an occupation with them. They were his bodyguards.

I was already carefully slipping my SHAKK back into its sheath between my shoulders, under my ripped coat. I knew in my bones these guys were friendly, and, anyway, if they hadn't been, I might as well have had a kid's popgun or a fistful of soggy noodles to throw at them.

Beside me, Porter was returning her .38 to its shoulder holster, and everyone else seemed to have reached the same conclusion I had, and decided that there was no point in being ready for a fight we would be sure to lose, even if these guys didn't show every sign of being our friends.

The ringmaster was very tall and slim, and I realized now that either his blond hair or his black mustache must be a dye job. He had approached close enough to touch me, and as he did, Porter and Chrys closed in around me.

"Do I have the honor of addressing Mr. Mark Strang?" he asked, in perfect English.

"I'm Mark Strang," I said. "And you are . . . ?"

The whole thing was seeming much too real for a hallucination, and besides, I've been knocked out, beaten senseless, drugged in various ways, and hit with all kinds of neural induction, and I've never had the kind of hallucination they depict in the movies. Not to mention that if you work for ATN, you get used to seeing all sorts of things; I was in a timeline once where the King of Scotland routinely dressed like Carmen Miranda, but that's another story.

The man appeared to be disconcerted by the question of who he was, for just a moment; then he swallowed hard and said, "I'm just a minor functionary, sir. My only job here is to bring the ship to you, to Ms. Brunreich, and to Ms. ja N'wook so that we can take you to a meeting with our leaders."

I nodded. "Nonetheless, I would prefer to know your name."

"My name is Caius Xin Schwarz," he said. "Now, may I request again, sir, that we be allowed to take you to our timeline for a conversation with people who can actually answer your questions?"

I checked the weapons, without turning my head. We sure as hell couldn't draw on them. And god knew what might be trained on us from the airship. They'd done nothing hostile; they were just a little rude, and "rude" is a culturally relative term—this might be the way they all talk to each other. In plenty of nations on Earth, people answer the phone with "Who is this?" and for that matter in California the car-rental people call everyone by first name . . . possibly he came from an even ruder timeline than our own.

So there was nothing much to be done, and it might turn out all right. I let my eyes stray sideways to Chrys, and her hand flickered in a "balancing" gesture with the thumb crossed—"better do what he says but I'll back you if you want to try something else," at least that's how I read it. Such codes have to be subtle and all but invisible, so it's never possible to be sure it isn't just a case of an itchy thumb.

"All right," I said, "we'll come along, as long as we're permitted to stick together and to retain our weapons."

He nodded. "Of course. Please come with us—er, just the three people named, please."

I decided to see how much weight I swung, and said, "Paula is very much a valued assistant, she speaks no German, and I don't want to leave her here to take the heat for all these corpses."

Again he nodded. "We may be gone for a long time, and I cannot assure her safe return."

"Nonetheless, if she chooses to go, I want her with me."

Caius Xin Schwarz nodded, and said, "All right, then. Are there any other people you wish to add to the party?"

"Not at present." I looked around at the dazed, baffled German AT troopers, pointed to one of the ones with some stripes on his shoulder, and said, in German, "You."

"Sir?" He seemed relieved to have some idea what to do; answering questions must be a lot better than standing there wondering which parts of your world had fallen away into chaos . . .

"Please inform the authorities that I will return to this spot within twenty-four hours to offer a full explanation. Don't worry about further attacks; with myself, my wife, and Fräulein Brunreich removed, there will be no cause for them, and this site will not be attacked again. Please repeat back what you will tell your superiors."

"You will return here within twenty-four hours to explain, and there is no reason to fear any further attack."

"Good." I turned to Caius Xin Schwarz, and said, "We are ready to go."

The gadget that extended down from the side of the airship, which I had thought was a simple ramp, turned out to be a moving sidewalk of sorts, though I couldn't see anything actually moving. When we stepped on it, we were carried by something that moved our feet rapidly up the ramp, and we found ourselves standing inside a large lounge or saloon within the airship.

I suppose waiting rooms are one of the things that are most alike from timeline to timeline and civilization to civilization. What you want the person waiting to do is to sit there and not do anything until he or she is wanted. And the way you achieve that is to make the environment very soothing, supply just enough distractions to keep them from revolting out of sheer boredom, and above all else make remaining seated the easiest possible thing to do. These folks were past masters at it, clearly; Caius Xin Schwarz gestured for us to sit, and we found we were all in the sort of chair that is just low enough and just squashy enough so that there is a little extra effort required to get up.

They also brought out cups of a steaming milk, coffee, and cocoa mix that was surprisingly tasty; I realized, too, that a little coconut milk must be in there, probably as a sweetener. Since all of us had just been terrified out of our minds, the combination of comfortable chairs and hot milk promptly made us all drowsy.

Porter, now that Chrys and I were there, probably felt perfectly safe. Even at eighteen, even with the terrible things that had happened in her past (she had seen her mother murdered by Closer agents), she still figured she was perfectly safe with two of her three big heroes there. (Chrys and Paula—I qualify as "good old Mark," mainly in charge of spoiling her rotten. The third hero is Robbie.) For the rest of us it just made staying awake that much harder.

But Paula is about as good a bodyguard as there is, and Chrys and I had been trained pretty well, so we didn't nod off. Instead, we looked around and watched things.

The furniture was in reds and blues; was that a clan color, national color, something the culture valued, or pure coincidence? It vaguely matched the clothing on the few people we had seen, but were they in uniform or did they just like those colors for their own clothing?

There was space in here to seat twenty, which argued that this space was not particularly for us; ergo this airship had other missions at other times. ATN, for a special mission, might have built such a ship, but it would have built it for that one special purpose, and it would have been much too expensive to operate as a regular thing. So if these people were operating it regularly, they were somewhere far in advance of ATN—or say a thousand years beyond what we had in my timeline.

We had seen nothing that resembled a flag, but besides the Roman look to the guards' outfits, there were a lot of eagles around, and since the Romans hadn't used flags and had had a major eagle fetish, I was pretty secure in identifying them as Roman. However, I hadn't noticed any "SPQR" ("senatus populusque Romanus"—meaning "this was done by the Senate and the people of Rome"), which in our timeline the Romans put on everything from roads and bridges to monuments and outhouses.

That could either mean they never got in the habit of using it, or that maybe the Senate was abolished. Or maybe their timeline was only partly descended from Rome. I could hear conversation in the distance, but not clearly enough to be sure of the language, and of course even that wouldn't tell you much about their time-line.

While I had been trying to hear, the airship had lifted off. The movement was fairly swift, but there was little sense of acceleration; one moment we were looking out at the land around us from an effective height of maybe twenty feet, the next we were rising into the sky. We turned to face the wind, and still there was no audible motor, propeller, turbine, or jet in the process; the ship just did what it did, no fuss or noise about it.

Through the windows, we saw the sky ahead of us darken. A moment later it got gray, then dark, then sounds went away, and then any sense of being there; after an eternal while, light, then sound, then definition, and finally color came back. We had crossed over into another timeline. "Some budget they have here," Chrys observed. "Rather than walk through a gate to us, they send a whole ship through and back? Either they have more energy than they need, or they don't mind burning it, or both."

I nodded. The major reason that nobody has wiped out all the other timelines is that travel is very expensive, and the more you send through, the higher the cost goes. It was just about inconceivable that anyone would send anything this big through on what seemed to be purely a diplomatic mission—but there you had it, here we were.

Which meant they were economically *far* in advance of ATN, and to judge from the way this airship performed, they were probably way out in front technologically as well.

"How do you suppose this thing is working?" I asked Chrys. "It's pretty clearly lighter than air whenever they want it to be, so it doesn't work by filling a gasbag, like our blimps, and it doesn't work by using vacuum gels like the ATN ones. How can they add or remove so much weight without making any sound?"

"We rotate it into the collapsed dimensions," Caius Xin Schwarz said, entering. "The ship is made of cells within cells; any cell can make the matter inside itself vanish, and restore it later, by causing it to rotate into one of the dimensions that didn't expand when the universe was formed. We can get right up to the edge of the stratosphere using that technique."

I had once read something about the collapsed dimensions, I vaguely recalled, in an issue of *Discover*. Chrys is from a timeline some centuries in advance of mine, and she looked as blank as I did. Oh, well, we have a saying in the Crux Ops that once you're fifty years in advance of your own time, everything is magic.

"Can you tell us where, exactly, you're taking us?" I asked.

"To Rome, of course. You'll be addressing the tribunes and the Senate."

"What about?" I knew enough Roman history from my years as an art historian to ask, "And I assume the consuls as well?"

"Of course, all the ceremonial offices. And then there will be a festival, and—" He stopped and stared at me. "What on Earth do you mean, 'what about'?"

"I have no idea why anyone in this timeline would want me to speak to them," I said. "I figured you'd be telling me what it was all about sooner or later."

He scratched his head. "You *are* Mark Strang? Native of Pittsburgh, Pennsylvania, United States of America?"

"Yep. And where I came from the North won the Civil War, World War I ended in November 1918, Elvis never entered politics, McGovern lost in 1972, and the Soviet Union broke up after a crisis in 1991." Since he was obviously familiar with our family of timelines, giving him the major breakpoints would at least let him decide whether he had a guy from the wrong timeline.

He shook his head—obviously that gesture went back a long way. "You're the right one, but I will have to talk to my superiors before I can tell you anything else. And probably they will insist that I bring you to them before explaining anything. Something is seriously wrong here." He got up and headed for the door.

"Thanks for zapping the Closers anyway," I said.

He stopped and nodded. "We were surprised to find them there, but we thought it was a last-minute counterattack. But now that you mention it, it may be a clue to the whole problem."

He shot through the door like a rocket; I guess he was a bit nervous. "Well," Paula said, "since it looks like we will have some time on our hands, I don't suppose anyone here would mind telling me absolutely everything that's going on, and then maybe following up by explaining why three people I thought I had known for years have this secret life I've never heard of that apparently involves flying saucers and armies from nowhere?"

We were both grateful to have something to do other than worry; we started at the beginning, explaining about the war between ATN and the Closers, about how I had accidentally fallen into the middle of it in my home timeline, that the three years when I was supposedly working "undercover," a few years before, had actually been the time when I had stowed away and entered a Closer timeline and conducted my own private war there. We told her about the dozens of cases, and she was even sharp enough to ask why we didn't seem to have aged much. Finally she asked, "And you've never seen these guys before? They don't look like anybody else?"

"Well, they're clearly Roman-descended," I said, "and like most of the timelines based on Greece or Rome, they've pretty well intermarried everybody, at least if our friend Caius is any indicator. Roman first name, Chinese or Korean second, and something Germanic for the third . . . the ancient civilizations didn't worry much about intermarriage. But as to which of the many Romes they hail from, we don't know. We've only explored a bit over a million timelines, and there's maybe a million in Closer territory we can't get to—by 'we' I mean ATN, because Chrys and I have only been to about a dozen each, not counting short visits and some training camps and things. But the best guess is that there are a few octillion timelines. Figure in any civilization that makes it all the way to modern industrial technology and so forth, there are going to be at least twenty or so turning points in their history. Figure most turning points could have gone several ways. It adds up in a hurry, once there are time travelers going back there to change things."

Paula shook her head, and said, "I will never, never say again that people don't appreciate how many alternatives there are."

I laughed; if her sense of humor was intact, we hadn't freaked her out too much. "Anyway, for some reason I'm apparently important to these people, and so are Chrys and Porter. And it looks like we were supposed to know what we did. I sure don't, and if Chrys did, she'd have spoken up. And Porter knows about ATN, but this is the first time she's been crosstime, so I don't think she'll have any idea either. No, we just have to wait and—"

Once again, the door opened abruptly, and our unhostly host came in. "We've determined that a mistake was made, and that it wasn't the fault of anyone on board this airship."

"Well, that's a load off my mind," I said.

He ignored the sarcasm, and said, "Unfortunately, as I had guessed, the mistake is serious enough so that we are going to have to have you meet with the Chief Tribune first, and he will explain matters to you. So I'm afraid I will have to leave you still puzzled for a while; can I at least offer you refreshments or answer any other questions?"

"Hmmm," Chrysamen said, "I don't suppose you've thought of this yet, but practically any question we can think of probably leads straight to things you aren't allowed to talk about. If there's time for us to have a meal, why don't we do that? Afterward maybe we'll have thought of something."

Another dead giveaway that you've stumbled into a Rome-derived timeline is the enormous variety of chopped, pickled fish that turns up on the table. They brought in about ten kinds, and a lot of flat hard bread, and we spent a while chewing and at least making sure that whatever happened next, we wouldn't be hungry. I noticed, too, that all of us were practiced enough at the way things can get fraught so that we were all careful to visit the toilet before the ship landed.

Then, finally, we were coming in over Rome. The first thing I noticed was that several of the landmarks I'd associated with the Romans weren't there, but then if "consul" was a purely ceremonial job, there had never been an Empire—it sounded as if the Roman Republic might still be a going concern. We landed on a wide terrace on the side of a gigantic building, stepped onto the moving-sidewalk-that-moved-you-but-not-itself, and stepped off onto the middle of the terrace on a fine, warm afternoon.

Caius Xin Schwarz walked out onto the terrace with us, saluted by sticking his arm straight out, and without a word went back inside. The ramp folded in behind him, and the ship rose into the sky.

The man who came out to greet us was wearing a toga of a deep reddish purple; probably it didn't mean he was emperor, but surely it meant he held considerable power. "Mr. Strang, I'm honored and a bit amazed to meet you," he said. His English was just as flawless as Caius Xin Schwarz's had been. "I am Marcus Annaeus Scipio, and I'm the Chief Tribune here. I believe we've found the nature of our error, and it's really quite embarrassingly simple. We'd never made such an enormous crosstime leap before, and it had not occurred to us that you would be in the same place in the same small city, so far from where you live, on two occasions exactly twenty-four hours apart. We gave poor Schwarz orders to pick you up twenty-four hours earlier than he should have."

" 'So far crosstime,' " I echoed. "What year are we in?"

"Oh, it was almost purely a crosstime trip. You would count it as somewhere just before your own year 2000, and we would count it as 2750 A.U.C." So they were still measuring dates from the founding of Rome . . . yes, it looked like this was a world where the Roman Republic had managed to overrun the Earth without ever having had an emperor. He smiled gently. "Believe it or not we thought we were just throwing a party for you, so we sent Captain Schwarz and his gunboat to bring you along."

"Uh, he's not the most party-hearty type I've ever met." To judge from the way the Chief Tribune snorted with laughter, it looked like the translation chips were doing everybody proud. "But what was the party *about*?"

"The idea was an historical commemoration—to have one of the most important, perhaps from our viewpoint the most important, crosstime traveler of all time come and visit us on what is both a significant year since the founding of Rome, and a significant anniversary in time travel. We first developed our own crosstime equipment just fifteen hundred years ago—tomorrow is the anniversary of our first test."

Somehow or other they had managed to be two hundred years ahead of my timeline's 1990s . . . and they had done it in the 400s A.D. They were seventeen hundred years in advance of my home timeline. No wonder I didn't understand them at all.

And he had said . . . just what had he said?

"Er," I asked. "This will sound very stupid, but I don't think I've done whatever it was, that I did, that was so important to you people. I mean, I probably did it, or rather I will do it . . ." Time travel can be so confusing. "But I haven't done it yet, in my chain of experience."

"So I gathered. Well, that's easy enough to fix; we can send you back to do it, and indeed we shall. What we're celebrating is the glorious day on which you saved the Roman Republic, Mr. Strang, by assassinating Gaius Julius Caesar."

· 6 ·

I don't suppose my jaw could have dropped any farther, but while I was still thinking about it, Chief Tribune Scipio looked up over his head and said, "Yes?"

He appeared to hear something from nowhere, and then said, "Yes, of course, that's exactly what I wanted you to do. Show him in at once."

A door opened at the far end of the room, and General Malecela strode in. For a guy who had probably just been snagged as bizarrely as we had, he seemed pretty self-possessed.

I even had the impression he managed to wink at us as he walked up to join our group.

"I assume," he said, "that I'm in the presence of President Brunreich and Chief Tribune Scipio, and you must be Mr. Strang's personal associate—?"

"Paula Renatsky. Who are you?" Paula was not going to let herself be thrown by the unexpected addition of another person, no matter how impressive and dignified-looking.

He grinned. "Just so. I'm General Malecela, and within Crux Operations, I'm the boss, for Mister Strang and Friend-mother ja N'wook." He turned to Scipio, and said, "Your Captain Schwarz is quite possibly the rudest officer I've ever encountered in my life."

Scipio nodded. "I would be surprised if you had found a ruder one. At any rate, were you given an adequate briefing on the matter?"

"Believe me, I would not have stepped onto your airship if I had *not* had an adequate briefing." It might have been a bit of humor if Malecela had bothered to smile, but he didn't.

"Well, then I suppose the time has come to settle on what ought to be done—and perhaps to demystify our companions, here."

"Fine by me," Porter said. Paula quietly stepped on her foot.

The biggest problem with time travel is also its greatest virtue; once you can move around in time, you often have all the time you want to get something done.

When they thought they had grabbed me for a victory celebration, they had slipped only slightly; everything would work out fine, apparently, if they just made sure they returned me to Weimar, in my own timeline, twenty-four hours after I had left.

That is, fine with everyone else. The "approaching group of timelines" that Citizen-teacher Zouck had been so excited about (and Thebenides so afraid of) seemed to be descended from this one right here. Time travel had grown so inexpensive with them, and remote sensing of timelines so accurate, that they were able to do what was only theoretically possible for the Closers and ATN—whenever a major decision came along, they were able to try out all the possible consequences, creating a new timeline for each one, keeping them all in touch with each other, and then, if it had turned out badly for any of the timelines, correcting those so that no one had to live in a failed one.

Moreover, they had been able to institute regular and reliable communications to reshape their own past; this meant that when they knew they would be taking on the Closers and showing up to aid ATN, they had relayed the information back thousands of years so that their ancestors could put some effort into getting ready, and take advantage of a longer technical lead time.

This had given them such a tremendous boost over everyone else that even General Malecela simply shook his head and said he had spent his brief visit to their twenty-ninth-century (or by their figuring, thirty-sixth-century) entirely in awe of their technology; when he tried, later, to explain to us how amazing it was, we realized you had to be from a highly advanced civilization like ATN just to understand that this Roman timeline was doing things that ought to be impossible.

They had been willing to share, too—apparently their first contacts had been with the timelines in which Porter had been president of the United States (hey, I always knew my ward had a lot of potential) just at the time when those timelines came under Closer attack. The Romans had sized up the situation, figured out who the bad guys were in zip time (small wonder, since they were already looking for the Closers), and beaten the living daylights out of the Closers, tracking them from timeline to timeline too fast for them to even warn each other of what was happening until it was too late.

According to General Malecela, the Romans appeared to be generous with technical assistance, material goods, and everything else, and seemed to have very little urge to meddle in anyone's affairs except for a strong desire for an open trade door. This didn't surprise me—the Roman Empire, in my timeline, was noted for always starting out with as generous a policy as possible, usually by making nations into honored allies and friends.

Of course if the honored ally and friend were ever so stupid as to try to give up the benefits of Roman alliance, then they stomped them flat.

Chrys and I, not knowing what might be bugged, managed to communicate our concern about those issues to each other (her timeline diverged from mine shortly after the death of Mohammed, so we shared the same Roman Empire in our past) without coming up with anything we could do about it.

Besides, I was much too bothered about the rest of it.

They didn't want to spill any more details than they already had, but it was clear that when the Romans found ATN, they were really just coming home; this timeline had been founded by an ATN Special Agent, and it was one of the "lost" timelines, one of the cases where a timeline got started and then communication was lost so thoroughly that it wasn't possible to find it again, to pick it out from all the myriad streams of events that made up time across all the parallel histories. So whatever had happened to the Special Agent, a fellow named Walks-in-His-Shadow Caldwell, no Crux Op had been dispatched to find him.

Or rather, that was what ATN thought. Caldwell had been dispatched about twenty years before General Malecela's time, in a failed ATN project where they spent an enormous amount of energy to move a gate through a gate—in this case, moving it to Diego Garcia in the early 1200s A.D. Thus there was nobody there to be interfered with, and it was possible to erect a huge power plant to drive the gate, and to send a dozen Special Agents farther back in time than anyone had ever gone before.

Unfortunately, every one of those timelines had promptly gone off the map; the farther back you go, the more widely things can diverge, and in these cases they had diverged so far and so fast that no one had been able to track them.

Until now, when this one had shown up, won the war, and made everybody happy.

Well, everybody except certain diehards like Thebenides, who were worried about the independence of all the ATN timelines and about whether the people liberated from the Closers would ever have any free choice.

And me, of course. Because it seemed to be universally agreed that I was going to kill Julius Caesar and that this was a good thing. And now it was clear that as a Crux Op, what I should do is go back to the lost timeline in 49 B.C.—or 704 A.U.C., as the Romans counted time—and get things back on track, apparently by murdering Caesar. Indeed, they weren't sure of all the details, but it didn't look like Mark Antony or Pompey was supposed to make it through the year either. Cicero, on the other hand, was supposed to live another thirty years, till he was almost ninety, retiring to write more books, instead of being murdered by Mark Antony's agents.

"So, just to begin with," I said, "every Latin student in thousands of timelines is going to hate me." I was pacing the floor in the gigantic bedroom they had given us.

"Be serious," Chrysamen said. "It's all right to tell me what you're upset about. I'm your wife, remember?"

I sighed and flopped down backward on the bed. "Well, look, the first thing to say is that I don't really see a way out of this, and even though they haven't exactly asked, I'm certainly going to go back there and see what I can do. And you know, I've shot a historical figure or two in my time, and been there when people who should have lived to ripe old ages died, and so forth. But the fact is, Chrys, you know they always send us back in a state of complete ignorance. We know a timeline is out of whack, and we're just supposed to bring it back into line, that's all.

"This is totally different. What if, in my judgment, old Julius—"

"Gaius."

"What?"

"Gaius. His first name is Gaius. If you're trying to make fun of him by being informal, that's what you call him. Julius is the family name and Caesar is the branch of cousins he belongs to." Her eyes had a slight twinkle to them, and her mouth had a funny turn; she seemed to be enjoying needling me. I wasn't sure why she didn't see it as being as serious as I did, and wasn't sure I wanted to know, either.

"Okay, anyway, what if this guy Gaius looks to me like the good guy in the picture? It could happen, you know. The Roman Civil War is pretty complicated, there's never fewer than three sides in the game, and what happens if I look around and say to myself that the best thing is for our boy Gaius to win?"

She shook her head sadly. "Mark, you're making too big a deal out of this. What if you had jumped back into the first timeline you ever fought in and decided that Hitler was the good guy? What if you jumped back into some other one and decided Mao or Stalin was? It isn't going to happen with cases like that. And Caesar was not a good guy. He was a good administrator, but he destroyed Roman self-government for all time, he got his famous victories in Gaul mostly by breaking the laws of war of his time, and in short he's just about the model of a power-mad dictator. If you have to see that for yourself first, go right ahead. Then shoot him. And then we'll go back home, to your timeline, and live a pleasant retired life with tons of money. You can chair the Brunreich for President Committee for Allegheny County, and I'll have another six babies or so. What's the problem?"

"Well . . . jeez, Chrysamen, I wish I could explain it to you better. It just doesn't seem like a Crux Op job. We're supposed to have some kind of judgment in all of this, you know . . . we've always jumped in as the only good guys in the timeline—and what I'm supposed to be doing this time feels more like a mob hit. And I really don't like the short list of people who 'died in mysterious circumstances' in that same year, either. It sounds like I'm supposed to be a serial killer."

"So do them in parallel."

"Chrys!"

"Mark, I'm sorry," she said. "I can understand how upset you must be about the idea of just going back into a timeline to kill somebody. That's a natural enough reaction. But in fact that isn't the whole reason you're going, or even the major part of the mission. You're supposed to find out what happened to Walks-in-His-Shadow Caldwell, first of all, and secondly to do whatever you think best. It just happens to be known in advance that what you think best is going to involve shooting Gaius Julius Caesar, that's all. You could just look on it as having more information than usual going in."

I groaned. If I couldn't explain what was bothering me to Chrys, I probably couldn't explain it to anyone.

"Look," she said, "I know it's not the usual job. But it's the job that wins the war. And you seem to be bothered just because it's crossing up your ideas about free will or something. Well, all right, so it's not quite as free as some of your other jobs have been. On your first one you didn't even know that you were ever going home. And here you end up knowing in advance what you're going to decide. I can understand how that feels, but it's not the worst thing that could happen. Not by a long shot. A few days ago subjectively, we were thinking we would grow old and die with the war still going on—if one of us didn't have to see the other one blown to pieces. Now it's all different. Now there's going to be real peace and a real chance to lead a more or less comfortable, more or less normal life. And it's all going to come to us through your efforts! You're a hero for all time, Mark . . . and so I'm having a little trouble seeing why you're complaining about having to follow that particular script."

I shrugged, and said, "Well, as I said, I'm certainly not going to turn the assignment down. There's no way I could walk away from it in the circumstances. But I just don't like it. I really just don't like it."

And it didn't seem practical—partly because the room might be bugged, but also because she seemed to have no sympathy with the viewpoint—to say that I was beginning to think old Thebenides might have a point. The citizen-senator might have rubbed me the wrong way, but it did seem to me that putting ATN in the position of being a client state to a vastly superior civilization was not exactly in line with what we got into the war to do. We were the Allied Timelines for Nondeterminism—meaning all the timelines that did not want to go down the Closer road to become giant, hierarchical slave states—and it seemed to me that our Roman "friends" were bound to do a lot of determining.

It didn't seem like a change of masters was all that we should be accomplishing after all the fighting.

I got another unpleasant surprise the next day when it turned out that according to the Roman historical records, Chrys and Porter had been along on the expedition, too. Apparently we had all returned safely, or else everyone was keeping up a brave front about it.

There was no mention of Paula in the list, but if Porter was going, she wanted to go. After all, she'd been guarding the kid for years, and if Porter was going to jump into danger, Paula wanted to be there. I took advantage of that to see how much clout I had. Malecela seemed very displeased, but Scipio was actually pretty reasonable about it; he agreed that if Paula wanted to go, she could, noting only that since there was no evidence for her in the historical record, it didn't look good. "But on the other hand, our attitudes about women weren't terribly enlightened at the time," the Chief Tribune added. "We know about unusual things that Friendmother ja N'wook and Ms. Brunreich did. We don't know about Ms. Renatsky. That may only mean she didn't do anything that a historian or chronicler of the time found interesting. Or it may mean something went very wrong, very early in the mission. We have no way of knowing. But if she is willing to assume the risk, we're certainly willing to have her assume it."

At least it ticked off Malecela, which meant I could sound him out on how he felt about our new ally.

One reason that the idea of Paula going didn't sit very well with Malecela, of course, was that this was supposed to be an ATN operation. As far as he was concerned, all we were doing was borrowing these high-tech Romans' gear to get a Crux Op back to a crux for a normal search-and-rescue operation. And Malecela didn't want to send untrained (by him) and inexperienced operatives back to a crux. He had bowed grudgingly about Porter (and I wished he hadn't!) because it was clear from the records that she had gone, but Paula, as far as he could see, ought to be sent home and told sternly not to talk about what she had seen. And having anything else happen—against his wishes—meant that ATN wasn't in charge of the operation.

That seemed like a sympathetic enough view. We were sitting out on a terrace, drinking coffee while he tried to persuade me to ask Scipio to send Paula home instead of with me, and I decided to see how he felt about the whole problem of connecting ourselves to a larger and more powerful civilization, up at the other end of time.

It didn't do me any good. He'd seen the wonders of what they could do nine centuries ahead of this, and he'd heard them declare a complete "open labs" policy, so it looked as if they really intended to share everything they knew. The mopping-up operation against the Closers was going so fast that the Romans were already opening up a lot of timelines to tourism. He himself was actually thinking about retirement and about what he might enjoy doing—horse-breeding seemed to be his choice, and with all the grasslands of all of history to pick from, he was really more interested in talking about the perfect place for a ranch.

In short, just like Chrys, he could taste the victory so thoroughly that the "free will" issue seemed like mere abstract philosophizing to him. Of course it wasn't *his* free will that was being tampered with . . .

So there seemed to be nothing more to do than get our gear together and get ready to go. Malecela had thoughtfully brought along SHAKK- and NIF-reload materials (the weapons make their own ammo, but it helps to be able to put the right mix of chemical elements into the hopper) and a fresh set of PRAMIACs; Paula got the equivalent of a SHAKK from the Romans, as did Porter. We were probably well enough armed to take on a small infantry division back home.

The step through the gate went about as it always did; over a period of time that you could perceive but not measure, the world around us went away, and then came back. We stepped out onto a bleak, freezing cold Roman road, north and east of Rome, not far from modern Bologna, in January of 49 B.C.

"Not a real prepossessing place, is it?" Chrys commented.

The road wound around a large mountain on one side of us, and crossed an arched bridge over a stream before going straight over a hill on the other side. The day was gray and a bit foggy, with an unpleasant spitting mist that seemed to blow right through the heavy, hooded cloaks we had been fitted with. As my cloak flapped open and the wind blew in and around my short fighting tunic, I had a sudden, acute appreciation of why so many women complained about miniskirts.

The land around us was a patchwork of green and brown, green on the hills where it was pasturage, brown down lower where it was tilled fields. There were some low, not yet fully grown windbreaks of trees in the distance—that hadn't been a Roman practice, so I figured it was some evidence that Special Agent Caldwell had passed this way.

In the hollows and on the north sides of trees and rocks, there were little patches of grainy, soggy snow. At least we all had new boots.

"Well," I said, "the orders were to try heading north from here. We should reach Fanum Fortunae by dusk, if they managed to put us where they were supposed to—but not if we just stand here."

We started walking. The Roman roads were rightly famous; despite the wet weather, and even this close to the coast, this one had no puddles or standing water, and it was easy enough to walk along. Of course, in the rotten weather, it was still anything but pleasant, but at least it wasn't storming, and we were probably no more than a two-hour walk from the Fanum Fortunae city gates.

We rounded one wide turn and saw the sea off to our right, the broad Adriatic; today it was gray-green and looked terribly cold. I had been along this coast several times in my own timeline. I had worked a dig here a long time ago, and we weren't far from Pesaro, where Chrysamen had dragged me a few times on pilgrimage—it was Rossini's hometown, and there's a festival of his operas there that's pretty terrific. January was just not the best time of year for this coast.

Back home in my timeline, Fano is a little fishing port and light-industrial city, just a spot on the coast road between Ancona and Pesaro—but in Roman times, Fanum Fortunae was a vitally important city, in many ways the key to Italy, because that was where the Via Amelia, the coastal highway between Ancona and Ariminum (or Rimini if you're looking at a modern map) met the great Via Flaminia, the major highway leading to Rome. If you were invading Italy from the north or the west, the Via Flaminia was your best, straightest shot toward Rome itself.

Not to mention that in time of peace a huge amount of trade flowed through it. It was one of those places that was important because it was on the way to so many other places—sort of the Sioux Falls, or the Columbus, Ohio, of its day.

Right now we were walking into the city from the southeast, as if we were coming in from Ancona. The day before, Julius Caesar had defied the Roman Senate and consuls, just as he had in our timeline. They had ordered him to keep himself and his army within Cisalpine Gaul, the province he was supposed to be governor of (which he had enlarged by overrunning everything else up to Scotland—clearly a difference since in our timeline he had been turned back by the Britons). The southern border of Cisalpine Gaul, on this western side of Italy, was a little river only fifteen miles long, the Rubicon, and our boy Gaius had taken his troops across it—which meant they had told the general "no," and he had said, "yes." The Civil War was on.

He would have to take Fanum Fortunae within a short time, and so we needed to be in the city, undercover, waiting for him. Our best guess was that he would be there in three to five days, at the pace at which legions could march comfortably, assuming, too, that he was keeping his army close together. Thus we were walking north toward him; he was marching south toward us; and though he didn't know it, we had a date in Fanum Fortunae.

"Boss," Paula said, "I just want you to know I'm having trouble believing all this."

"That's pretty much the way everyone reacts on their first trip in time," Chrysamen said, sympathetically.

"No, not being in ancient Rome and all that," she said. "I mean that there's a guy on a bicycle coming up behind us."

·7·

We turned and looked. She was absolutely right.

Half a mile behind us, just coasting down the hill, was a man in the full regalia of a legate—that is, what we'd call a junior officer—riding a bicycle. We moved out of his way as he came over the hill, but he didn't bother to look at us.

The bicycle had wooden spoked wheels, but the tires were pretty obviously rubber. The "chain" was a knotted rope, which ran through large wooden pin gears, and it didn't look like they'd developed the coaster brake yet, which may have explained why the helmet was in the shape of a modern bicycle helmet and had a number of prominent dents.

Of more interest to me was the fact that he had what looked like a crude shotgun slung over his shoulder, and a brace of seventeenth-century horse pistols across his chest.

Still, apparently nothing had yet made the Romans wear pants; he was wearing a short tunic, and the bicycle was what I'd have called a girl's model, though not to this guy's face, if he was half as tough as he looked. The bicycle had pannier baskets, which seemed to be carrying dispatches, over its rear tire.

He rolled on by and vanished up the road. I noted that on the back of his tunic was the phrase "Necesse litterae transeat."

It is essential that correspondence pass, if you were being formal and trying to pass Latin class. But *The mail must go through* was close enough.

I distinctly sensed that Walks-in-His-Shadow Caldwell had been here, and I kind of liked his sense of humor.

About an hour of unpleasant, cold wet walking brought us to the city of Fanum Fortunae. Porter hadn't said much on the way; "surprisingly quiet" is the only kind of quiet that kid ever has been, at least once she got into an environment where she could play and could behave more or less normally, so I had been keeping an eye on her. Paula seemed to have crossed the timeline boundary with about as much aplomb as she crossed into Germany—maybe more, because the chips implanted in our heads allowed us all to speak Latin without an accent, and Paula spoke no German.

Chrysamen was treating it like I did, or like anyone with practice would—it was gray, dingy, wet, and cold, and she wanted to get inside. This just wasn't a big part of the job.

After a while, as Paula took her turn at tail and Chrys at point, I found myself walking beside Porter. "I don't suppose you'd be interested in telling me what's on your mind?" I asked.

"Aw, Mark, you'll pick on me for it."

"Vicious accusation, unless what's on your mind is some worthless guy who wants to date you, or some lunatic notion you have like getting another hole punched in your nose." We'd had a few go-rounds about nasal jewelry, which, in absolutely typical fashion for me, I'd lost. Probably because ultimately it was her nose; one way that I'll never make parent material, I suppose, is that I tend to see too much value in such arguments.

"No, it's not a guy, and it's not piercing," she said. There was a long pause while we walked along, the fine grit of the road crunching under the heavy leather of our boots. Finally, after a very long while, she asked, "Are you going to say, 'So, what is it, then?' "

"I was trying to be quietly supportive."

"I think you're easier to deal with when you're repressing me. Okay, here's what it is, Mark, and you can go right ahead and tell me how silly you think I am. Uh—is this a timeline where they could have us bugged?"

"It's not very likely that there would be any listening devices around here," I said, "and even less likely that anyone is going to have a station to pick up something planted on our clothes. I don't think you have to worry about any outfit that does time travel. And to judge from the looks of the bicycle that went by, I'd say you don't have to worry at all about the locals."

"Okay, then." She took a deep breath. "When you hear this, please don't tell me to grow up, or anything like that."

"Wouldn't dream of it. Really. What's the matter, Porter?"

"Well, it's that . . . a couple of people slipped, and I don't think they were supposed to do it, but they addressed me as President Brunreich. And I know that I'm supposed to be very important in history and all that, so I just kind of put it all together. I'm going to be, uh, president of the United States, I guess?"

"It sounds that way," I said, noncommittally.

"Well, what if I don't want to be?" It came out kind of choked and strangled in sound, and when I looked closer I saw that she was crying. "I mean, I *like* music. I *like* playing the piano and organ, and I really want to get more composing done. All right, so maybe I'm famous, but nobody's ever even asked my opinion about anything—though if they did, I could certainly tell them that things aren't being run very well—but that doesn't mean I want to run them myself. . . ." She was actually blubbering now, and wiping her face with the back of her hand, though a slight spitting rain was picking up so much that her face was hardly getting any dryer for the process.

"Aww, Porter," I said, because I couldn't think of anything better to say, and threw an arm around her.

She hung on to me for a second, and seemed to be sobbing. "And another thing," she added. "If that's all the way it is . . . if the Closers always knew that the timelines where I was president were ones they wanted to prevent . . . then that's why they tried to kill me, isn't it? And they ended up killing *my m-m-mother!*"

That made my mind flash back to when I had been working for ATN for less than three days—when Harry Skena and I had managed an impromptu rescue from a hostage situation. Ostensibly the Blade of the Most Merciful had been a Mideastern terrorist group noted for being erratic to the point of psychotic. Really, they had been a Closer front whose whole purpose was to eliminate the two biggest threats to them in our timeline: me and Porter.

Porter had been alive when we arrived only because her mother had switched IDs with her; at the age of ten she'd seen her mother shot to death in front of her.

For that matter, it had only been a few years before that I'd seen about half of my family die at the hands of the same outfit.

There's a bond Porter and I share that's a little hard to explain to other people . . . and now, of course, poor old Harry Skena had been dead for years, and so were a lot of old friends and comrades, just to get us to this point.

"Porter," I said, "the way you are feeling is the most natural thing in the world. Really. You're suddenly finding out that the whole world had big plans that turned around you, and you never got to have any say in them. You were just sort of dropped into the middle. It's no wonder that you feel upset. And of course you're wondering how much of your actions are really your own, and it doesn't seem fair at all—plenty of people get through life without anything like this happening. Even geniuses and important people. You never asked for anything like this to happen, and there are better things you could be doing with your time. Am I right?"

She snuffled. "Good guesses all around." She smeared her face with her hand, still trying to get the tears and snot under control. She'd really been bearing up pretty well in a completely confusing situation; though I had never kept my work for ATN secret from her, or from my father or sister, it still must have been bewildering.

"Well, it's pretty much how I've been feeling lately."

She looked sideways at me. "Really?"

"Yeah, really. It is not normal for them to tell us what we do back in the past timelines. In fact usually they don't know. Usually the job is, go back and fix things so that they come out right. How is up to you. This time the job is more like a mob hit; go shoot old Gaius in the back so that a civilization can come into being. Not even a suggestion that I ought to help decide whether Caesar needs shooting. And the worst part is not just being given the order—it's knowing that I'm going to carry it out, whether I decide I want to or not. They've got it down in their history books that I shot Julius Caesar. No getting away from that one—I'm going to do it. Just like you're going to end up as President Brunreich, and apparently to hell with whatever time you need to practice."

She sighed. "I just figured they must always know how it was going to come out."

"No—they only know in a general way that it did come out okay, sometimes. The details have always been up to us. But this is one hell of a detail to have them take control of. And I just think you probably feel exactly the same way about having to be president."

"Yeah." She sighed and snuffled once again; I was getting to hate that hopeless little sound. "Mark, do you suppose I'll be the first woman president?"

"I don't know. I suppose it's possible. Why do you ask?"

"Well, 'cause—well, I'm only eighteen right now. Do you realize how long that means we'll have to wait for a woman president? And what a mess things are likely to be in by the time I get the job?"

I laughed and gave her a quick hug; it was hard to believe this little wisp of a young woman was ever going to command anything more imposing than a piano keyboard, but then how could one know? Abe Lincoln must've looked like the class geek, or would have if he'd been able to get to school, and I always kind of suspected that they used to take Teddy Roosevelt's glasses and make him bob for them in the boys' room toilets.

"You'll be fine at the job," I said, "if that's any consolation. Hell, considering who ran the last few times, I'd be perfectly happy to vote for you next time."

She shrugged. "Yeah, but that's not the issue. Thanks for listening, though, Mark. I do feel better."

That left me alone with my own thoughts until we had a change of positions, and the thoughts were not the kind to be alone with. The overwhelming thing that kept coming back to me was that where at least Porter only knew that she would have a job and be important in the job, I knew something I was going to do. I was going to take a person of extraordinary energy and ability, one of the great complex figures of history, and turn him into a heap of meat.

We had just changed over, so that I was on point (despite her protestations, we kept Porter in the middle for the whole journey), when the gate of Fanum Fortunae came into sight.

It was a pretty typical Roman walled town—apparently the new military hardware had not yet strongly modified architecture, or maybe Fanum Fortunae just hadn't been forced to adapt yet. The wall was high enough so that you would need a ladder to climb it, and wide enough for soldiers to be walking around on top of it. There were three big stone arches set in the wall, a large one over the road for carts and carriages, flanked by two small ones for pedestrian traffic.

On this cold and generally rotten day, the city was sending up a substantial plume of brown smoke from its many chimneys—and that, I realized, was the most un-Roman thing about it, and another sign of Caldwell's influence—the chimney was a late-medieval innovation in our timeline. Before that they had used various kinds of open hearths and smoke holes.

But here was Roman Fanum Fortunae with belching chimneys. Moreover, as we drew nearer, I saw that the guards and watchmen on the city wall were wearing rubberized-fabric ponchos. Not elegant, but a sight more comfortable than what we had on.

This guy Caldwell clearly valued comfort and had clearly exerted quite some influence. I was beginning to look forward to finding a place for the night.

That turned out to be remarkably simple. As we entered the city, we saw the typical layout of a Roman town—stepping-stones over the major thoroughfares because streets doubled as sewers, and streets laid out in straight lines, with everything of military importance kept near the walls. We were coming in through the main gate, so the military parade ground was the first thing we walked past.

But as we topped a slight rise at the end of the parade ground, I saw a beautiful sight: a billboard.

The face on the billboard was rather startlingly piggish in aspect, with a kind of cunning expression that didn't breed trust. All the same, he was smiling, and below, in Latin, was the announcement that we need only continue for eight hundred paces to reach the "Crassus Inn Fanum Fortunae"—"low rates and available throughout the Roman world."

I found myself wondering at once . . . a fast review of history was in order—

"Hey," Chrysamen said, "remember the data we memorized? Does this mean Crassus is still alive? In our timeline he was killed with his troops in Parthia, six years ago. If he's still around, that really changes the balance of power."

"Sure does," I said, "but I see more of the handiwork of Caldwell than I do Crassus here. The chain of hotels exists, anyway—and not a minute too soon because there weren't any in the ancient world of our timeline. But just because Crassus's name is on it doesn't mean he'll be at the front desk. Colonel Sanders is dead, but that doesn't stop KFC."

"Well, then I guess we walk up there and find out," Chrysamen said. "Which I do believe was the original plan."

The organization of the Crassus Inn was so much like a modern hotel that I suspect you could have checked in without knowing Latin—they must have had plenty of foreign travelers. In short order we were being shown into a large room, which they assured us was the cleanest and most modern in the place.

I handed over the sesterces from the pouch on my belt, and they were gone at once. Only then did Porter say, "I see a problem here."

The problem was that the room was furnished with one bed—large and circular—and one tub—ditto.

Modesty was going to be a bit tricky to serve, at least if I stuck around. "Well," I said, "looks like Porter and Paula bathe first, while we go reconnoiter for what's to eat. Then we take a turn. Then we all sleep dressed tonight."

Paula nodded. "Uh, boss, I didn't stay awake in Latin class, but I just thought of something funny." She had a slight crooked grin.

"Yes?" I asked.

"I think the desk clerk, if that's what the guy was, figured that all three of us are your harem. He's going to be mighty surprised when two of us depart."

"Well, it'll broaden his horizons. All right, we'll see you in about an hour."

As we were walking out into the street, Chrys commented, "You know, there are people back in your home timeline who would be freaked by what you just did."

"What did I do?"

"Well, um, you know that Paula—well, of course you know that she and Robbie are—"

"Of course," I said.

"And you left her alone with a teenage girl, to take a bath together."

"In case it hasn't occurred to you," I said, "I'm attracted to women myself, and I certainly wouldn't attack Porter. And Paula's devoted to her. You've been listening to too much talk radio, and it's given you a dirty mind." I was really annoyed.

"Mark?"

"Yeah?"

"I love you. Don't change."

I swear, it is not possible for a married guy to understand his wife even when they come from the same history. So I don't know why I expected the present situation to make any more sense.

Anyway, we found that though Fanum Fortunae was pretty much battened down against the bad weather, there were plenty of shops open, even if you did have to knock for admittance. One of the shopkeepers finally explained to us that on days like this, any ship out in the Adriatic was running for harbor early (when they could, Roman ships put in to port every night), and so you never knew how many seamen might turn up in the afternoon; the shops that were open would get all the business.

A little exploration revealed that Caldwell had introduced a lot of other things. There were printed posters, for one thing, which meant he'd brought the press, movable type, and paper here (along with the secret of postering glue, as well, to judge from the dates on some of the posters, which had clearly been on those walls for years). There were a few very expensive horse cabs in the streets, with double-bowed axles and horse collars, the kind of thing that in our timeline wasn't developed until centuries or millennia after Rome fell. There were mailboxes everywhere, so apparently among the other benefits of modernism, Caldwell had given them the post office. It made me wonder just how benign his intentions really were.

The other thing we found was that employment seemed to be running pretty high. The background from my own time had suggested that this was an age of the urban mob, fueled by unemployment, when lots of people without jobs wandered around with nothing to do other than join riots and political campaigns. (Of course a riot and a political campaign were pretty much the same thing at the time.) This had no such aspect to it; everyone we saw was busy, and the harbor was a wild confusion of longshoremen and sailors getting things on and off the ships, merchants looking at the wares, captains announcing bargains. Fanum Fortunae looked like a city that had a lot to do.

"Caldwell is one hell of a Special Agent," I muttered to Chrys. "Can you believe the work he's done?"

"It's remarkable," Chrys agreed. "And if all the timelines really do open up for tourism, we're coming back here. Have you noticed the silverwork on display?"

We found a place that sold sausages in rolls, something not a lot different from the modern hot dog, and stopped to eat there; by then we were fairly damp and cold and figured that it was about time to head back to the room, get a hot bath ourselves, and see how the other two were doing.

Just as we started to stroll back to the Crassus Inn, there was a great uproar that seemed to come from everywhere at once. We looked around and saw that the guards were running back and forth on the walls like madmen; a moment later we heard the crashing sound of the big city gates being dropped, and we began to hurry toward the inn. "What do you suppose—"

"Caesar might not be sticking to schedule," I said. "That would be just like him, from everything we know about his history. And if he's got enough bicycles for his legions, he moves a *lot* faster than we estimated."

We had to flatten ourselves against a building the next minute, and were splashed with the nasty mix of slush and sewage that ran between the stepping-stones, as fifty soldiers on bicycles shot by, moving fast and not looking much where they were going. "They're in a hurry, and they looked scared," I said. "This is bad, whatever it is."

I took Chrysamen's hand and we ran through the streets together, trying to find a way to the inn that wasn't hopelessly blocked with people. We had no luck—everywhere, people were rushing into the street to grab children or bring in a mule or horse. Shutters were slamming closed all around and everywhere there was the sound of hammering as shopkeepers and property owners boarded up their belongings.

From a quiet city on a slow winter day, a few minutes ago, Fanum Fortunae had whipped into a panic; these people were on the brink of fleeing.

All around us we could hear the word being shouted again and again—it sounded like "Kye Sarr," in Latin, and it was the way they pronounced Caesar. Apparently his legendary ability to move an army fast—probably plus the technical boost of the bicycle—meant that he had gotten south much faster than we had thought he would.

Caesar was not a nice guy; aside from the testimony of generations of Latin students, let me just mention his habit of accepting the surrender of cities and then abrogating the terms he had promised. Lying under a flag of truce is treacherous and needlessly im-

CAESAR'S BICYCLE 545

perils the lives of soldiers, but it does have the advantage of utterly crushing a helpless enemy. And his carefully constructed reputation for utterly crushing his enemies was helping him now—the city was ready to surrender.

Or parts of it were. With a crash and jingle, a group of men armed with pistols strode into the square we were struggling across. The crowd parted around them, and the leader of the group began to read, very loudly and not at all well, a proclamation that the "Citizens for Caesar" were going to assume command of the town for everyone's safety and that as long as they were permitted to surrender it "in good order" no harm would come to anyone.

He was just beginning to announce the proscriptions—which citizens he was putting a price on the head of—when a shot boomed out from the crowd and he fell dead. An instant later another shot hit one of his followers in the back, and then the mob closed around them. I didn't look; I've seen before what mobs do to people they don't like, and even though I felt no sympathy at all for the men (whose groans and screams I could hear), it's a hideous way to die.

The shift in the crowd freed up Chrys and me; we turned and ran, though she wasted one step to take a snap kick at an older man with a cane. The man flew over backward, his face spraying blood from his broken teeth and nose.

"What—?" I asked Chrys as we raced down another street, fighting fleeing civilians the whole way.

"Old bastard groped me in the crowd. Taking advantage of the situation, I guess you'd call it. I hope he learned some manners."

We kept running. It was just a short way now.

High above us something that sounded like a freight train rumbled; an instant later, there was a low, thudding boom. Caesar's cannon were within reach of the city.

We put on an extra burst of speed, but it gained us less than fifty yards before we were hopelessly pinned. The Latins of Fanum Fortunae had never heard cannon fired before—they were far enough from the frontier so that they had not seen battle up close in a couple of generations. Moreover, cannon themselves were only about twenty years old in this timeline.

But they had been reading Caesar's *Commentaries on the Gaulish War* and his *Commentary on the Conquest of Britain*. They had read his vivid—maybe a better term would have been "lip-smacking, gloating, joyful"—descriptions of what artillery fire did to cities. He had spread more than enough terror of the cannon ahead of him; these people fell apart at the thought. When you've dreaded something long enough, imagined it hard enough, you don't stand up and fight when you encounter it.

I found out later that most of the garrison of the city wasn't even able to get to the walls through the mob of panicking civilians. The cannonballs booming into the city were solid stone shot, not incendiary shells, but they might as well have been filled with napalm, because there were thousands of cooking fires and fires on hearths everywhere, and where one of the massive stones fell, it overturned braziers, threw stoves into thatch, made people run away in a panic from the fires they had tended. Before Chrys and I could even struggle off the wall that our backs had been pinned to by the howling mob, there was a distinct scent of smoke.

And as the cry of "Fire!" spread among them, people began to pour away in every direction. There was no hope of getting bucket brigades formed to fight the fire; most people standing next to burning buildings couldn't even get away thanks to all the pushing, shoving, and snarled traffic.

From the walls came the sounds of fusillades of musket fire. The gadget Caldwell had introduced had been about as good as you could do with Roman iron—basically a length of drilled-out iron pipe (because any seam would be sure to split) with a rammed-paper cartridge, a separate percussion cap, and a lead bullet that was based on the same principle as the Minié ball—designed to expand against the walls of the barrel on its way out, so that it would form a better seal and pick up some velocity. Necessarily that had to be limited in its effectiveness, because Roman iron wouldn't take the pressures that a really effective seal would have made.

Still, you could get just as dead standing in front of one as you could get from a twenty-ninth-century SHAKK.

The percussion cap, cartridge, and Minié-ball design had leap-frogged firearms far past what would have been their "natural" pace of development if the Romans had merely been given gunpowder and some introduction to the principle. They loaded a lot faster than any gun in my own timeline had until close to the American Civil War, and though not accurate at any great distance, they required little training to learn to operate and were more than deadly enough for their purpose.

The first volleys were sweeping the guards from the walls; moments later we heard a huge, booming crash, which we only realized later had been a particular innovation of Caesar's for taking walled cities—a battering ram driven by gunpowder.

The smell of smoke and the screaming were everywhere. The crowd hesitated and then began to pour away from the gate where the crash had happened, knowing full well that the first hour or so as soldiers invaded the city would be much the worst; if they could avoid coming to the attention of Caesar's troops for one or two hours, they stood a chance of surviving with their property and without severe injury.

Unfortunately, the crowd was flowing exactly opposite the direction we wanted to go. There seemed to be no way to get through them.

"NIF?" Chrys asked. "We could stun a few hundred."

"And they'd be burned, trampled, or raped by Caesar's troops," I shouted back into her ear. The wailing, shrieking crowd, the rumble of cart wheels, and the crashes of musketry were so loud it was hard to hear each other without shouting directly into the ear. "Plus the ones we didn't get would be screaming that we were wizards or in league with spirits or something, and they'd stone us."

She nodded, clearly not liking it. The smoke was growing thicker, and I realized with a grim, sinking feeling that it was thickest in the direction of the Crassus Inn. Caesar must have circled the city before attacking from the unexpected direction—another favorite tactic of his.

With a terrible thunder, the wall opposite us came down. I don't know if it was the mob pressing up against a weak structure, an internal fire, or perhaps a cannon shot that landed inside, but the whole thing fell outward like a house of cards, and the three-story-high masonry wall slammed into the crowd below, crushing many, wounding others with sharp pieces of rock. The building stood for one instant in cross section, as if it had been cut away—I saw people in the uppermost story, mouths wide with horror, and a mother with her baby on the second floor turn to run for a staircase that was already falling out of reach—and then with a twisting, grinding sound, it all came down in a heap, forming a steep pile that then slid and broke out into the crowd around.

Immediately, smoke curled up from the pile; the gods alone knew how many braziers and stoves had spilled into the mess.

There was a great wail from the crowd; hundreds rushed onto the pile, seeking to rescue those inside (or to rob them); hundreds more fled as if the bad luck might well be contagious. The ones in the back pushed forward, the ones in front pushed back, and brawling erupted everywhere. Meanwhile the smoke grew thicker, more musketry and cannon fire crashed in the distance, there was a rumbling of horses' hooves, and then, with a great, thudding *whump*, the center of the pile of rubble went up in flames.

The toga, tunic, and chiton were never designed for situations like this. Dozens of men, women, and children went up in flames and staggered into the crowd, desperately trying to peel their burning garments off themselves. A woman in front of us tore her blazing garments from her body, only to be pulled down by two strong men who pinned her to the ground and forced her legs apart—

Before they both fell over dead, as empty bags of bloody skin. Chrys, beside me, held her SHAKK level and ready. In the volume of noise, I had not even heard her fire.

I drew my own SHAKK from between my shoulder blades and looked around. The naked woman had fled; we would never know what became of her. The crowd had not noticed our weapons; they were still milling and groaning.

Then there was an astonishing sound. All the voices seemed to stop at once.

There came the tramping of horses' hooves on cobblestones, and people pulled away from the middle. As if by magic, room began to appear.

There were about thirty of them, a troop of Caesar's auxiliaries, and they rode into the middle of that panicked mob as if they were out to give their horses a little light exercise on a spring day. When they reached the center of the crowd, the legate heading the group looked around and bellowed, "Citizens of Fanum Fortunae. It is hereby ordered that you are to cease resistance at once. Your city is on fire. Go immediately to your stations for fire fighting. No one who is fighting fires will be harmed. As soon as resistance in the city ends, Caesar's troops will also help you put out the fires. Now, if you wish to save your city, *hurry!*"

It was like magic, and magic of the strangest sort. There had been a rioting mob there, in a panic, ready to trample the helpless and filled with people whose only motive, besides stark terror, was to take advantage of the ones around them—and at the word of the legate, with the command of Caesar behind it, they were suddenly tough, disciplined Romans, getting the job done. In moments the square had more than half-cleared as people ran to pump water or to join the bucket brigades. As others milled around, not having definite fire-fighting stations, the legate would point, and bellow, "All of you, there, over to that pile of rubble, and pick it apart carefully to see if anyone is alive inside" or "You people there— start pulling rubbish out of that well, see if we can get some water."

Before he looked our way, Chrys and I holstered our SHAKKs and slipped off into the winding alleys between the buildings. Roman cities were laid out in a geometric grid for the major streets, but what happened inside the blocks was pretty much improvised on a catch-as-catch-can basis, so there were a lot of narrow passageways and winding alleys to move through.

It took us another ten minutes to reach the Crassus Inn, because there were so many patrols and work parties on the street. One hour before, Fanum Fortunae had been slumbering through a cold winter day; half an hour before it had been enveloped in flames, rage, and terror; now it was rebuilding itself in an orderly way. Caesar sure knew how to make an entrance.

When we finally popped out of an alley facing the Crassus Inn, I had steeled myself, but still, what I saw made me gasp. The building was falling apart in flames; a firebreak had been cleared around it, but they were letting it burn itself out. From the yardarm where the sign with the picture of Crassus had been, the body of the desk clerk hung, his face black, clothes smoldering; someone had fired a shot into him after he was dead, to judge from the mess of his belly.

There was absolutely no sign of Porter or Paula, and that was the best news there could have been at that point. "God, of all the places to be when Caesar attacked," I said, softly. "Next to Pompey, Crassus has to be the man he hates most on Earth. The mob probably did this just trying to appease Caesar."

"As a matter of fact, that *is* what happened," a voice said behind us. We turned to find ourselves facing a young legate, with several tough legionaries behind him. He had a horse pistol leveled on us.

"You look very much like the people Caesar told me to look for," he said. "So I shall take you to him to find out if you're the right ones. If you are worried about friends inside, I would not be. I believe only that wretched slave died in this, and several of the guests were taken as personal prisoners by Caesar. Chances are your friends are alive and well, though they are no longer free. And this is after all a circumstance you are very likely to share with them soon."

It took me a moment to remember what that all meant, as we marched along, the legate's pistol at our backs, toward our meeting with the man I was supposed to kill. In the ancient world, prisoners taken in war—especially including civilians—were sold as slaves. All four of us were going to be auctioned off, and as far as the Romans were concerned (even ones who might prove friendly to us) once that had happened, we were slaves until we bought our freedom or our masters freed us.

The boots I was wearing were new, and I tried to savor their crunch on the pavement; they would go to some poorer supporter of Caesar, along with the good clothes I was wearing. Slaves did not dress this well.

·8·

Caesar had set up his headquarters in Fanum Fortunae's Praetorium. The Praetorium originally meant where the praetor, a high-ranking government official, stayed, but the term had come to mean first the place where he stayed when he was in town (so that every town had a praetorium) and later simply the center of government. This town was large enough to have an impressive one, about the size of a modern basketball gym, with many benches and tables for the public business inside, and a second floor on which there was a courtroom.

That was the room Gaius Julius Caesar had appointed his own. When we arrived, there was a long parade of prisoners ahead of us, but it appeared we were something special, because they marched us straight to the head of the line.

The man sitting next to Caesar was not wearing a toga, like a Roman, or a chiton, like a Greek, or even pants like a barbarian. He wore a simple one-piece coverall that looked like practical work clothing anywhere—in my timeline or in any advanced industrial one.

It was not any ATN uniform I recognized, and then, as we drew closer, I saw the symbol on his breast—a black-on-white image of two hands, crossed at the wrists, one forming a fist and the other held up like a cop stopping traffic.

This was a Closer agent.

His hair was very dark, his skin a coffee color not unlike Chrys's. His nose was small but hooked, making him look a little like a parakeet, but his expression was sharp and intelligent. He looked very much like a man who knew what he was doing.

And he was on the other side.

The SHAKK between my shoulders could not have been farther away if it had been on Mars; the NIF in my boot was equally far. So far I had not been searched, but they would find both with any kind of a pat-down—ATN's superweapons may be very high-tech, but they are also large, solid lumps on the human body where it normally doesn't have them.

There was also my old, reliable Model 1911A1, the military-make Colt .45 that sat in my shoulder holster. My best guess was that I could draw that before anyone realized, and I might get off one shot.

Now here was an interesting dilemma. I could accomplish the mission—as far as I knew it—with that one shot, assuming fate didn't decide to intervene. Caesar was right there, and I could just put a round through him and trust to the fact that we were somehow alive back in the future.

But for my money the most dangerous man in the room had to be that Closer agent. He alone had the potential to turn the whole timeline permanently against us; he was the source, I had no doubt, of much of Caesar's advanced weaponry. (I was just realizing that one reason Caldwell had done so well was probably that an arms race had gotten started, and that always accelerates technology.)

I had a few seconds before they searched me; all I had to do was decide whether to get the designated target and hope to have time for the vital second shot, or get the one I thought most dangerous and hope to have time to get Caesar as well.

I've never had any trouble gunning down a Closer bastard; I owe them more deaths than I'm likely to repay, as far as I'm concerned, and knowing what their idea of fun is (they teach their children to kill favorite slaves in order to harden their hearts, and thirteen-year-old Closer boys often kill or mutilate the slave girls they have just lost their virginity to), it didn't seem like such a bad idea to get both of us killed abruptly and immediately. On the other hand, I was still having a major set of butterflies in the stomach about assassinating Caesar. Maybe I'd seen Shakespeare's play once too often or something.

So I walked forward, calmly drew the Colt and leveled it on the Closer in one smooth movement, and squeezed the trigger.

There was a roar from the muzzle, but the Closer had been alert, and while it must have scared hell out of him, he had sidestepped just as I fired; the round sprayed gravel chips from the wall behind him, but that was all. I squeezed the trigger again and nothing happened; I looked down to see the open top of the spent casing sticking up out of the .45.

Smokestack jam. I had barely brought my left hand to the pistol, still working to clear the jam, when the butt of a spear knocked the gun from my hand, and a solid fist swung in under my jaw and put me on the floor. Then there were hands all over me, and I could feel the rest of the armament being stripped off.

Over to one side there was another flurry of struggle, by which I knew Chrys was being disarmed in about the same way.

The world was still spinning from the force of the blow to my jaw, and anyway there were just too many bodies holding just too many parts of me down. I made myself relax and stop struggling— sometimes that will help somebody let their guard down—and waited.

After a lot of rough poking around, including being turned over for a cavity search, they all agreed that I was harmless, or at least unarmed, and braced me up facing Caesar. I was naked now, which didn't exactly help my self-confidence.

Beside me, Chrys was braced up in exactly the same way, hands locked behind the back in a double hammerlock, feet wide apart, three men holding on to her in a very businesslike way. I had the sudden, sad thought that my wife was very beautiful and that if I had been granted a last request just before execution, one more look at her might very well have been it.

They pressed me forward so that I was now facing Caesar, who sat on the raised dais, where the judge would have sat in a Roman court, with an expression of alert amusement. The Closer agent beside him seemed to be tense and ready to spring, though whether at the prospect of working over two ATN agents or with anger at my attempt to kill him, I couldn't say.

"And so then," Caesar said, very conversationally, as if we were just guests in his living room, "I suppose that you are yet another person sent to dispose of me. I believe I am in the presence of Marcus Ajax Fortius, if the registry of that inn is to be believed. You really might have had better taste than to stay at Crassus's place, you know; if you had gone to one of my Barrel Tile Roof franchises, I might still be looking for you."

"My mistake," I admitted. "I'm new here."

"You will be happy to hear, I'm sure, that both of your female companions—in addition to this lovely one here—are quite well and safe; in fact if I permitted you to look all the way behind you, you could see them both. I'm afraid their proclivities are a bit like yours; Hasmonea here made some not quite tasteful remark, and the larger and stronger of the women struck with remarkable force. I don't suppose you've actually found the land of the Amazons? You certainly seem to be surrounded by women who are proficient in a fight."

"They're just well trained," I said. Anything that kept us talking was likely to be better than anything that would happen when the talking stopped.

"Now," Caesar said, leaning forward, "I could understand that it was entirely possible that Hasmonea's insulting behavior and lack of decent breeding"—the Closer beside him stirred a little at that, but not enough to take his eyes off me or Chrys—"might have provoked your female guard to doing what she did. On the other hand, I note with some interest that you looked at both of us and chose him as target with almost no hesitation. At the time that happened you probably believed you were also a dead man.

"It so happens I am not noted for my modesty. I find myself wondering what about this advisor is of such value and interest that you prefer to kill him rather than to kill Caesar. I know, of course, that there is a deadly war between your kind and his, and that to some extent you have made the Triumvirate and the Senate into mere pieces on the board for your purposes. Thus I can suppose that your reaction was without thought.

"But this I do not believe. And while Hasmonea has been of immense value to me, I find myself thinking that should anything happen to him, those who sent him will most likely send another. I think this in particular because the most likely reason you are here—or so Hasmonea told me—is to find out what happened to that barbarian fellow Caldwell.

"Thus if you had killed Hasmonea, I have no doubt his people would have sent someone after him, perhaps someone whose fighting skills and knowledge were as superior to Hasmonea's as yours are to this Caldwell's.

"So it could not have been for a mere momentary advantage that you decided to pass up your opportunity to kill me, and instead decided to kill this agent of the 'Masters,' as they style themselves. You had some other reason behind that decision." Caesar now leaned forward, letting his elbows rest on his knees in a not-at-all-patrician way, and peered intently at my face. "Now, I suggest you explain yourself to me. Think for a long time about how matters are apt to go with you, and decide to tell me the truth."

I looked back into his eyes. At the time, Gaius Julius Caesar was just past fifty years old, a vigorous and strong man in the prime of life. He had spent ten years fighting in Gaul and Britain, and though he had certainly had it easier in this timeline than in my own, it was still remarkable that so much warfare had taken so little toll.

His cheekbones were heavy and relatively low, his brow unusually wide, giving most of his face a flat look, but his nose was thin and sharp, his lips a mere slash in his face, and the intelligence that stared out of his wide-set eyes was terrifying. He was mostly bald and did nothing much to hide it; his face had exactly the kind of "lean and hungry look" that Shakespeare's Julius Caesar claims to find frightening. This was a man who had made a life out of devouring everything in his path, and he liked that about himself.

He would be difficult to lie to, not for moral reasons but because he was so sharp, and because he had no sentimental expectations that anyone would ever tell him the truth.

I let his stare rest on me for a long moment, then watched as his eyes roamed speculatively over Chrys's naked body. I knew he was doing it to provoke me, to see if he could get my thinking to muddle, and I held myself in check, much as I wanted to grab him by his wisps of remaining hair and batter his face on the table in front of him. I let him have his long pause to challenge me in that way, so that he could see that we were equal in that sense—we didn't scare each other.

It occurred to me then that if I did go ahead with killing him, later, that it would be a good idea to get him from behind, when he wasn't watching out. And that it might be a very long time before he wasn't watching out.

Finally I spoke, and I kept my voice soft and reasonable but firm. "Let me tell you of these ones who call themselves 'Masters,' but who we call 'Closers.' Did Caesar ever speak to my comrade Walks-in-His-Shadow Caldwell about this?"

"I have not spoken to him in several years; as you well know, he has taken the part of Crassus in these matters. I first met Hasmonea while I was in the field, in Gaul, and he has proved an invaluable advisor on weapons and tactics, though I'm afraid he has a bit of a weak stomach for the real necessities of warfare."

So Caesar apparently made the Closer uncomfortable . . . I wondered if this was a matter of his treatment of prisoners and civilians (which seemed unlikely) or probably just a matter of anyone from a more advanced civilization being used to killing at a distance rather than by shoving a sharpened slab of iron into a human body. I took a long extra moment to consider, and then Caesar said, "So tell me what you know of them."

"You know well that they are descendants of Carthage," I began, "and one might well ask what one of the oldest families of Rome is doing in consorting with a Carthaginian."

There was a low stir in the room; a lot of Caesar's soldiers had heard that, and it sounded like it was news to them. But Caesar himself nodded, and said, "We have suspected this though he has not told us; his native tongue is a bit like Punic. Tell me, then, why it is that you oppose these people."

"For the same reason Rome opposed Carthage," I said, milking it for all it was worth. "Because they are the sworn foes of everyone's freedom."

"Great Caesar—" Hasmonea began.

"You will remain silent until Caesar has need for you to speak," Caesar said, without taking his eyes off me. "Now tell me everything, Marcus Ajax Fortius. Tell me why they are called 'Closers' and what they are after."

For the next half hour I did myself proud at speechmaking. It wasn't the easiest thing in the world, but at least I had a lot of material. I talked about the Closer view that divides all the timelines, everywhere, into Closers and prey. I talked about the deliberate hardening of their hearts, the systematic extermination of sympathy among them. I talked about the pleasures they took in cruelty and in being obeyed.

I admitted to my personal biases and told them a little of Closer crimes I had encountered, that my first wife, my mother, and my brother had died at their hands, that my sister Carrie had lost both legs and an arm at the same time. I went out of my way to detail their barbarities in a dozen worlds where I had known them, and laid it on fairly thick that they were still worshiping Moloch.

That seemed to be getting the kind of attention I wanted; Moloch was a concept that horrified the Romans nearly as much as it would us. He was the cruelest of any gods, an enormous metal idol, hollowed inside to form a furnace, into which Carthaginians threw children to be burned alive in his belly. Once, in a very distant timeline, I had burst into a temple of Moloch and had the pleasure of slaughtering the priesthood there. It would never trouble my conscience one iota.

The reaction around the room was fairly satisfying, but Caesar continued to stare. Finally, he said, "You make your case well. Cato himself could hardly have made a better one."

At that name, Hasmonea stirred uncomfortably—in the Closer timelines, Cato had been the last great opponent of the Carthaginians. His stirring did not go unnoticed—I could hear people muttering and pointing—and I realized that the Closer agent had probably not made himself popular with the common footsloggers in this timeline. Closers think it's degrading to treat inferiors well; I've seen Closers stick knives in their bosses' backs, literally, because the boss treated them too leniently and thus lost their respect.

"Now," Caesar said, "tell me of your own cause."

I drew my breath and began with the phrase they always hammer into us. "It is our desire only that each history should find its own way into the future. We would have no quarrel with the Closers had they left every other timeline alone. It is only in their seeking to make everyone else conform to their ways, in their attempt to reduce all of history to a set of identical timelines, that we oppose them." I went on to sketch out, briefly, as much of ATN's history as I thought was germane. It took a while, and my first sign that things were going well was that servants arrived with clothing for Chrys and me, plus some warmed wine that Caesar extended with the comment that he had forced me to spend a great deal of time talking without adequate shelter from the cold.

I would come to realize that that was like him. Caesar could be brutal, perhaps even could enjoy being brutal, but he never did it without cause, and, most especially, he also knew that kindness extended to an opponent could be a powerful weapon as well.

After the pause for refreshment, Caesar asked some more questions. I knew the Romans admired all things Greek, so I stressed ATN's connection to the Athenian civilization and to Perikles; I knew they admired courage and soldierly virtues, so I made sure they heard much of ATN's long-running war, and of our heroes. I kept that notion that Closers were followers of Moloch firmly in front of them, and since it had been only about a hundred years since Rome decided to solve the Carthaginian problem once and for all by leveling the city, this worked pretty well.

I had anticipated that it would. There are hatreds in the modern world, of course, but few like the one between Rome and Carthage. The wars between them were wars to the death from the outset, and if the Romans had made something of a hero out of Hannibal and his brother Hasdrubal, they had done so only once both men were safely dead. Hannibal's army had come "within the third milestone"—that is, so far along the road to Rome that they passed mile marker three before being turned back. They had succeeded in turning substantial numbers of Rome's allies in Italy against her, and this was a thing that stirred Roman paranoia as nothing else did; the Romans believed in being generous to their opponents, in making the enemy from this war the ally for the next one, but necessarily this bred the nervous feeling that their "friends" were not entirely friendly. Anything that involved turning the sympathies of Rome's allies tended to get Romans at least as freaked out as anything that involves race does the average American.

All in all, I thought I gave a damned fine performance.

The question, however, was what Caesar would think of it. He sat there, listening carefully, studying me and my face, occasionally raising an eyebrow to make me nervous or seeing if a glance at Chrys could rile me. (Not at all, now that she was dressed. I thought any hetero guy who didn't stare at her was blind or crazy.) He was sizing me up at least as much as he was concerned with the case I was making, and we both knew that. There would be a decision of one kind or another, but he wasn't going to make it till he knew what he thought.

Then he would probably make it without any regret or remorse in either direction.

When I finished, he sat back and thought for a long time. "Hasmonea," he said, "do you deny the essential correctness of Marcus Fortius's charges? Or do you merely propose to offer me more advantages than Fortius is able to offer?"

The Carthaginian licked his lips and seemed to take a long time to think. That was probably a mistake—it made you wonder what he was going to say, rather than what he actually thought. Finally, he said, "It is true, Caesar, that I worship Moloch, and you yourself have long known this. And it is true that we of the Masters are destined by our gods to rule all times and places. But we can be generous to those who accept the will of our gods, and in any case the end is not yet—it would be many centuries before direct rule was imposed here."

"And thus," Caesar said, his eyes narrowing, "you tell me that Caesar will not be enslaved, but only his grandchildren, and thus Caesar ought to welcome you?"

Hasmonea looked a little pale.

"Moreover," Caesar said, "I deny absolutely that I had any knowledge of your vile worship. This is a lie made to separate Caesar from his army, and it is a very clumsy lie."

Hasmonea seemed to stagger; I realized later that it was only that he had seen that expression on Caesar before, a certain narrowing of the eyes and tightening of the mouth that meant that something unpleasant needed to be done, that Gaius Julius Caesar was just the man to do it, and that he was going to make people pay for forcing him to do it.

Then the general sat back, stared into space, and said, "It seems to me we have an insoluble problem here. We are told that Hasmonea is from a civilization which is in all ways repugnant to us and threatens to enslave ourselves and our posterity. We are also told that this ATN has supplied a military advisor and engineer to Crassus, our onetime friend and bitter foe." He appeared to hesitate over the options, and then finally said, "Let us settle this matter by putting it in the hands of the gods. We will prepare the arena here in Fanum Fortunae, and tomorrow, using only their own skills and with no weapons, these strangers from other times will fight each other to the death. Venus, who guards my family, and Mars, whose servant I have ever been, and mighty Jupiter himself, will send victory to he who is deserving."

The way Hasmonea turned green told me two things—first of

all, that he probably wasn't trained much at hand-to-hand, and secondly, that he had figured out the same thing I had. I was supposed to win the fight tomorrow.

I also realized just how he had sealed his doom, and that he had not had any choice in the matter. By telling the truth he effectively sentenced himself to death—that was clear. Caesar's army were Romans, and patriotic Romans, and the notion of yoking themselves or their grandchildren to Carthage was impossible to accept. Add to that Hasmonea's worship of Moloch, and you had an open-and-shut case against him; the army would gladly see him executed.

Moreover, he had accused Caesar of knowing about the Moloch worship. That particular stain had to be scrubbed off right now; Caesar couldn't afford the kind of evil reputation that would give him in Roman politics.

But if Hasmonea had lied, it would have gone worse. It would not have *forced* Caesar to act, as doing this in public had, but it would have shown Caesar at once that he could not trust Hasmonea, and that would have been a different sort of death sentence.

Could Caesar somehow be aware how the timeline wars were going? Was he trying to get in with the side that seemed to be winning? Did he genuinely prefer us?

It was impossible to say, and, anyway, tomorrow I apparently had to kill a man with my bare hands. I was glad it was at least a Closer.

"Let both men be watched, but restore them to their companions for the evening, and let the legates see that they are comfortable and well fed," Caesar said. "That is Caesar's decision. Let the combat happen at the second hour after sunrise. Let these men be escorted away and let them be kept away from each other and from their weapons."

The "let"s were a minor defect in the translating software, I figured; Latin tended to use the subjunctive to give an order, particularly when who carried it out or how it got carried out was being left up to the discretion of subordinates, and there's no real subjunctive in English, so instead it kept saying, "Let." But the message was clear enough; we would be treated well tonight and then tomorrow one of us would kill the other.

Not the most heartwarming thought I've ever heard, but at

least it was clear. That night, the bed was comfortable, the food was good, and we got caught up on what had happened to Porter and Paula. Apparently the inn had been hit by one of the very first cannon rounds, and Caesar's cavalry had been there by the time the two of them had managed to get out the front door. The desk clerk was already hanging from the yardarm at that point; they had both been scared silly, and both were deeply annoyed by the cavity search, but "It wasn't that big a deal, boss, these soldiers are disciplined as all get out. They told us what they were going to do— poke a finger up and see if we had anything hidden—they put oil on the finger first, and they were at least as embarrassed as we were. I think 'cavity searches' are probably one of Hasmonea's innovations—there's not any really significant weapon in the local technology you could hide there."

Paula seemed so anxious to reassure me that I turned immediately to Porter, and said, "So are you all right? Were you scared or hurt?"

Porter shrugged and kept looking at the floor.

"Porter," I said. "It's me. You can tell me."

"Well, it made me feel gross. I wanted to throw up, having an old man feeling around like that. He tried to be polite and all that, but it was still gross."

"Yeah," I said, "it must have been." I sat down next to her without quite touching her.

"But I feel like a big baby," she said. "All you guys just shrug it off—"

Chrys sat on the other side and took Porter in her arms. "Sweetheart," she said, "we're all professional killers. We get strip-searched and messed around with a lot, all the time. Sometimes by people a lot ruder than that. We're used to it. We all felt terrible the first time it happened. And it's still not a good thing to do to a person. The fact that it doesn't bother us is something wrong with us, really."

Porter started to cry, quietly, and Chrysamen held her for a long time. I sat and stared like a fool; you can spend an eternity of time and a fortune in cash on keeping bad things away from your family, and they find a way to you anyway. I realized, too, that bad as things had been for Porter, she had probably felt safe after she started living with me and my family and employees—something about the presence of so many people who love you (and who are armed to the teeth and good with what they carry) must breed the feeling that the bad things are all in the past.

A lot worse could happen, of course, and easily might, but this was the first time she was really aware that it could.

As usual, I felt like an idiot in the situation, and wondered what I would do without Chrysamen.

After a while Porter stopped crying, dried her eyes, and tried to apologize for upsetting everyone. We all told her not to worry about it, and by then we figured we were all tired enough to sleep.

Caesar's courtesy even extended far enough to supply us with three beds, smaller ones for Porter and Paula and a big one for Chrys and me. The room was warm and comfortable—one of those Roman inventions that should never have gone out of use was central heating—and pitch-dark with the blinds pulled. Paula snores now and then, and Porter occasionally mumbles in her sleep; after a few minutes there was enough snoring and mumbling so that I figured they were both out.

Chrysamen is hard to tell about; she's so silent and wastes so little energy in her movement, like the superb natural athlete she is, that when there's nothing that needs doing she simply doesn't move. Thus in the dark you can't really tell if she's asleep or lying awake.

I certainly knew that I was lying awake. I couldn't quite figure it out. I had shot Closers, pushed them from high places, set buildings on fire and shot them as they ran out, exposed them to the naked fury of nuclear reactions. In all this I felt about the same way I did about killing copperheads or rats—i.e., it was a job, and it badly needed doing.

But somehow this thing with Hasmonea was different. Maybe because I would have an audience—it was quite clear from hints dropped by the servants that most of the staff were looking forward to this in exactly the way they looked forward to gladiatorial combats. The Romans were a people of war, whatever they thought of themselves, and they were always interested in seeing how strangers fought. Having people applaud and cheer while I was killing a Closer seemed too much like having a cheering section while I cleared a poisonous snake from a trail.

Or then again, maybe I was just afraid; I'm a great believer in using whatever advantage you have, and I've never in all the fights I've been in worried about "sportsmanship." When only one of you gets to walk away afterward, it's pretty stupid to worry about whether it's with honor. Violence is dirty and ugly, and you can't beautify it by treating it like a sporting event.

Not that there would be a referee here, but it was going to be an absolutely fair fight, and I had always preferred having it rigged in my favor, and doing the rigging myself.

Or then again maybe it was that I knew a little too much. I knew that Hasmonea was his name, and I knew what he looked like, and that he was easily rattled and sometimes said things that weren't wise. I knew he was frightened by something about me and didn't carry himself in the well-balanced way of an athlete or a fighting man. And he didn't have either my reach or my muscle development.

Chances were good, in short, that I was going to win, and much as I despised what he was, it's one thing to hate a set of ideas and a culture, like the Closers, and quite another thing to take away the life of a single human individual, especially when you have a pretty good idea of what he must be feeling and experiencing while you do it.

So there were a lot of good reasons not to be able to sleep. The only good reason for falling asleep, actually, was so that I could win tomorrow. *If* I won. Which got me back on the same train of thought, and around the track we went again . . .

Chrys's hand gently stroked down the side of my body, running over the hard muscles of my chest, finding my stomach. Her soft lips brushed my ear. "Mark?"

"I'm awake."

"Tell me about it. You're wound up like a spring. What's the matter?"

"Everything, I suppose."

"Yeah, I guessed as much." She snuggled against me; her breasts were still high and firm after our years of marriage, and her skin was still soft and smooth. Her hands worked at my chest muscles. "Jeez, how can a guy clench his chest?"

"It's easier than it sounds."

"Shh. Don't talk. Let me fix a few things. Roll over."

So I did and she started working on my back. It was great, but I noticed that the lower back was getting all the attention, and then my buttocks. After a while her hands moved around to the front.

"Do you want to do this?" I asked.

"I want to because you need it, husband. And if I didn't usually want to do it with you, I'd never have married you."

"Okay."

"And if you give me any crap about it slowing you down or spoiling your eye tomorrow, I'll tie your dick in a knot."

I couldn't help it; I giggled a little at that, and then she licked my neck, which always seems to hit a magic switch. When I rolled over and pressed her thighs apart, she was already warm and ready for me. We had to keep the noise down so as not to wake the others, but occasionally that's an amusing challenge in its own right.

Afterward, as we lay together, I kissed her very tenderly; she pressed my head back and returned the kiss—and that's the last thing I remembered till morning.

When I woke up, there were pancakes and honey for breakfast, together with a little goat cheese. It was a decent enough way to start the day, but I ate just enough to keep hunger pangs at bay. It's undignified to throw up on your opponent, even if you go on to kill him.

The guards arrived promptly, one set to take the women to the arena—they were being "honored" by being allowed to sit in Caesar's box—and another set to take me to a different door.

It was cold and clear today; everyone was bundled tight, but the sun was shining brightly, and it made the great plumes of everyone's breath shine white and silver in the narrow, dim street they led me up. The last couple of blocks, several young women turned up to throw roses at me. I wasn't at all sure what that symbolized, and I was even less sure I wanted to know.

·9·

What they put us in looked more like holding pens for animals than anything else; it was a stone cell with a barred door and window looking out on a hallway on one side, and a barred door into the arena on the other. I made the mistake of getting too close to that door just once, and suddenly the crowd was going crazy, whooping and cheering.

They had stripped me to fight; I was wearing a leather jock, a pair of boots, padded fingerless leather gloves, and that was all. They gave me a blanket to keep me warm as well.

When I backed away from the window, a voice said, "They did the same thing for me, but more of them whistled."

Whistling was a sign of disapproval, the chip in my ear informed me. I looked around and saw that Hasmonea was in the cell across the hallway. "I was trying to sleep," he said.

He looked about as scared and miserable as a human being can; I decided then and there that since there wasn't any getting around killing him, I would make it quick. I knew if he had the chance, being a Closer, he would naturally kill me without compunction, and quite possibly torture me first, and I knew how dangerous his kind was—but I saw no reason to inflict any more pain than I had to.

Hasmonea hung on to the bars and looked at me a little hungrily. "The woman you were with is your wife? The girl is your daughter?"

"My ward, actually."

He sighed. "That's the tough part of all this. I know what the odds are, which is not going to help my chances any. But I wish I had some way of saying good-bye to my family. Not that they would want me to—that's a disgrace and so forth. But I've noticed, after a lot of missions, that other cultures manage to say good-bye, and mourn for their dead, and it doesn't seem to hurt their fighting ability."

"How many timelines have you been to?" I asked, to keep the conversation going. I didn't want to be alone with my thoughts, and I doubted he wanted to be alone with his.

"Just over thirty. Thirty, uh, three, I think. You lose count after a while."

"Yeah, I've only been to a dozen."

"You're a Crux Op, aren't you?"

"Unhunh."

He half groaned. "I knew I shouldn't ask, and I did anyway. This doesn't look good for me at all. I'm not even a soldier—I'm just a Slave Searcher."

Slave Searchers were the equivalent of our Time Scouts. When a new timeline was identified, there was only so much you could accomplish with hidden cameras, listening devices, and so forth. Sooner or later somebody had to walk through a gate and go see what it was really like over there.

After that the equivalency ended. Sometimes our Time Scouts were sent into known timelines, to start new branch points that could eventually grow into timelines that might join ATN. Other times a Time Scout just jumped through the gate into a timeline that needed investigating—usually not knowing whether the Closers were active there (and had perhaps started the timeline), whether some independent time-traveling civilization had started it, or whether (perhaps—there were arguments about whether or not this ever happened) it had just occurred naturally.

In every case the mission was the same. Make contact. Decide whether the civilization was advanced enough and psychologically stable enough to open full relations crosstime. If no, then help them move toward maturity as fast as they safely could (and hope the Closers don't show up before you do). If yes, then open up relations and see if they'd like to join ATN. Even if they didn't want to join on, at least they would know where to call for help if Closers invaded, and they could be on their guard.

The Closer approach was much simpler. Find the most militarily formidable civilization in the timeline. Assist it in conquering the Earth. Find the most ruthless potential dictator and assist him in taking power. When the whole Earth was under the rule of one man or at most a few families, kill the top people and move in to run the show yourselves, turning the whole Earth into one big plantation.

It had never occurred to me before that there might be any other resemblances between the jobs, but life can surprise you; obviously their Slave Searchers had to know something about the cultures with which they interacted, and perhaps even study them and learn to see things from their point of view. Know thy enemy, and all that, especially if you can know him thoroughly before he knows you're his enemy.

Morbid curiosity caused me to ask the next question. "So have you liked this timeline?"

He shrugged. "At least slaves are cheap, and there's a wide variety of them. The wine isn't bad, and the baths are pleasant. But it's really much too far north, and there are really too many people in the middle class. Most of them would benefit from being owned, even if only by other people like themselves."

"Benefit?" I asked.

"Of course. How many people are really fit to run their own lives? And let's be honest here . . . how many servants are any good if they can change masters? They only learn to please when they have no choice. That's why we always say that an ugly girl you own is better than a whore you rent, and both are better than a wife. They have some reason to be."

There might be things worse than being alone with your thoughts, after all. But I asked, "And yet you say you miss your family?"

He shrugged. "It's an emotional weakness. Like most of my weaknesses. They couldn't do anything with me, and I was too high-ranking to sell or kill, so they put me into the Slave Searchers because I was medically unfit for the Army. Every so often I write home to them, and I've occasionally gone and visited my sister and her children. They find me very embarrassing—Moloch's jaws, *I* find me very embarrassing—but duty is duty, and they let me hang around. Which comforts me a great deal, weak though it is."

"Have you liked being a, uh, Slave Searcher?"

"Oh, actually, a lot. I like observing other cultures. You can learn a lot from them."

For an instant there, I thought I might have to kill a Closer I liked, but then he went on, "For example, the Romans make such effective use of crucifixion in keeping slaves in line. It takes the slave a long time to die, and it's right out in public, so it gets the message through to every single slave without wasting much of the stock. And, of course, it's fascinating to see how easy or difficult it is to domesticate the various cultures. The Romans are tough and independent and so forth, but they will make better slaves exactly because they are used to seeing the world in terms of masters and slaves. Where some very gentle, even servile populations are hard as Moloch's teeth to enslave because they don't understand what it means when we tell them that they are property and they exist only for us." He sighed. "At any rate, it hasn't been a bad life, really, and I have few regrets. I wish I had spent more time at home with my mother—I liked that a lot—and I wish I had pleased my father more. It will please him to know I died as a Slave Searcher, heavily decorated, and thus kept up the family honor, but that will never wipe out his memories of how weak I really am."

By Closer standards, I realized, this was a sentimental and rather sweet poet-type. Any more sensitive (or any less politically connected), and they'd have fed him to Moloch. But the real reason he was still alive was probably that fundamentally he agreed with them; his impulses toward sensitivity, his interest in other cultures, his preference for real affection—he and his culture both agreed that this was an illness, something that regrettably had not been cured yet.

"But you're fond of them?"

"All babies are," he said. "Some of us just have more trouble growing up. I've even gotten fond of my wife, even though she's a low-status type and has just as big an affection-craving problem as I do."

Whatever he had actually said, "affection-craving problem" was probably as close to the meaning as the translator could get, taking it from his language into Latin and then from Latin into English.

But there was something in his tone that made it sound like it was a disease, and a shameful one.

"And you wish you could kiss her good-bye, hold hands, maybe even hold each other a little or have spent a night sleeping next to each other?"

He gave me the strangest look I've ever seen from anyone, and his voice choked. "Is this a tactic?"

"If it is, it's backward," I said, and suddenly realized just how tired I felt. "Look, it might surprise you, but what you're feeling is what I think it's healthy for human beings to feel. That's all. I probably feel a little less like killing you because of it."

He sat there on the cold floor, wrapped in his blanket, and very quietly said, "You know, if anyone had talked to me that way when I was ten, so that I had grown up with maybe a slight idea that it was all right to be the way I am . . . I'd have ended up fed to Moloch by the time I was twelve."

I couldn't help it—I laughed, and so did he. "Make it quick," he said, "if you win. I'll do the same for you. Caesar likes to see people play with each other, but there's not any reason to do that. As long as Crassus still has the one from your timeline, Caesar will have to keep at least one of us alive. As soon as one of us is dead . . . well, there you go. Perfect security for the other one."

"You've got it," I said.

Unfortunately, there were two acts ahead of us. One was a couple of Gauls, big crude types who were handed short axes, had their knees tied together, and who simply whaled away at each other until one of them fell over. They came out and cut them apart, carried off the bodies—I wasn't sure either of them was alive—and then a big cart came out, a lot like the Zamboni at a hockey game, and slaves threw sand all over the arena.

Caesar hadn't shown up yet. I guess when you head an army of tens of thousands who all think you're god, you can be as late as you like, and just enjoy your breakfast.

The next little crowd-warmer was four naked girls, not much out of puberty, armed with spears, against a very large and not happy bear. It took a long time, and I just kind of sat in the corner away from the front grating, not watching it, hoping Porter and the others had sense enough not to watch. As it ended, Hasmonea said, "It's over, and, if you want to know, it looks like two of the girls will live."

"Were you rooting for the bear?"

"Moloch's jaws, no. These Romans are much, much too crude. I tried to enliven their gladiatorial games a little by suggesting that perhaps they could move away from professional killers and explore what happened with amateurs and with animals. After all, in the timelines where there's a Court of Nero, there are some wonderful shows. Unfortunately I underestimated their crudity."

"One thing I can't stand, it's *crude* barbarity," I said.

Hasmonea chuckled. "I think we have again reached the edge of the cultural divide."

"Pretty clearly. Has the big cheese shown up yet?"

"I think so. I think that was all the crowd noise in the middle of the act. Nothing much was happening at the time in the arena. If you want to look again, they've carried off the bear, the dead girl, and the one who I think is going to bleed to death. The other two walked off some time ago."

"I'll wait till they get the sand down, thanks."

I had the grim and slightly sad realization that if Hasmonea and I had ended up in the same prison together for years instead of hours, we might well have worked out a way to stand each other, and even begun to like each other. Even though I knew, for example, that as a high-ranking Closer he had probably tossed his first child into Moloch . . . it's funny what loneliness and stress will make you overlook.

There was more wild cheering from the arena, and a couple of priests came out to bless all the fresh sand that had been thrown down. Then a bunch of standard-bearers carrying the eagles of Caesar's various legions came out, and paraded them around while the crowd cheered loudly. There was one voice that sounded like it was coming through a megaphone, and I figured it was probably someone rattling off everything each legion had done.

That took a while, because the crowd had to cheer loudly each time an announcement was finished, and also because since there were four main banks of seats in the arena, each eagle was also collecting a cheer as it was presented to each bank. So that added up to five cheers per eagle, and that took some time.

"Are there any more curtain-raisers before us?" I asked.

"Couldn't say; they didn't give me a program," Hasmonea said. "If you win, make it *quick*, remember."

"It's a deal. I'd like you to know I won't enjoy killing you," I said.

"And I'd like you to know I'd rather kill somebody else than you," Hasmonea said.

Hell, by Closer standards that probably made us *compañeros*, blood brothers, and best buddies forever.

There was another delay or two while they got everything blessed, but now there were plenty of criers standing out there making all sorts of announcements about the two of us, building us up into a couple of exciting supermen versed in every art of death-dealing there was.

At least we were getting star billing.

I didn't speak to Hasmonea again, nor he to me; there was nothing really left to say, and we shared nothing except the arena, when you came down to it. Still, there have been times since—late at night, say, when I wake from dark dreams that I can't recall—when I see his face in my memory, and hear his voice, and strangely enough the thing I really regret is not having asked him what his wife's name was or if they had any kids.

It doesn't happen often.

Anyway, by now it was close to noon, and the sand outside was bright enough to stab at my eyes a little. The various criers were spewing steam with each announcement, and it sparkled in the sun.

The moment came. The grates rumbled up. The guard behind me said, "Leave the blanket." I felt a lot more like killing him than Hasmonea.

We entered the arena, and the guard who was waiting inside said, "Turn left and walk all the way around the arena. When you get back to me I'll tell you what to do."

So I did, and the crowd applauded wildly. Hasmonea had turned the other way and gone around the other side; I could hear him getting whistled at and people yelling various terms that the gadget in my ear kept translating as "Carthaginian. Carthaginian. Punic. Poenian. Carthaginian. Worshiper of Moloch."

I suspected the terms were a lot more pejorative than that.

We passed each other just in front of Caesar's reviewing stand. I saw that Caesar was lounging comfortably, obviously enjoying a warm bowl of wine. Paula, Chrys, and Porter were dressed in better clothes than they had brought, and they all looked unbearably tense. I wondered—if I lost, what might Caesar do to them? Put them into the arena? I'd pit Chrys and Paula against anybody . . . give them to Hasmonea as a reward? I hoped his gentle impulses might win out . . . so that Chrysamen would get a chance to kill him.

It was fruitless to worry about it. The thing to do was to not lose.

Walking around the arena had at least given me some idea of how the boots fit—pretty well, actually, so I wasn't expecting any trouble from that quarter. The fresh sand didn't seem to be too slick, and, with the sun reflecting off the sand, it was quite a bit warmer than I would have expected it to be out there.

I had also been flexing my hands like mad, trying to get them loose and relaxed enough to be effective. And I had noted that the leather jock wasn't too terribly uncomfortable, though in a long fight it would probably chafe my thighs. Probably they had a lot of experience with fitting these things.

That gave me another thought, so I tripped and fell; people laughed, and while they were laughing I got a nice big wad of damp sand in my left hand. Years ago, when I was stuck in an airport waiting and had nothing to read but a cheap adventure book, I ran across the phrase, "The first rule of unarmed combat is to not stay unarmed." It works for me, anyway.

I passed the last part of the crowd and was almost back to my guard—second? trainer? handler? I didn't really know what his function was in all this.

He led me out to the middle; Hasmonea's guard led him out to face me. We stood facing each other, about ten feet apart. A little guy with a megaphone came out and announced that we would be fighting to the death, unless it was voted to spare one of us, and that this was to be no-holds-barred, any-which-way-you-can fighting. Then he told us to face Caesar, and to extend our right arms and repeat after him, loudly.

It was the phrase you've heard in a thousand movies—"*Salute, imperator,* we who are about to die, salute you." The Latin "Salute" means something a bit like "Hail" and a bit like "Viva." "Imperator" later meant "emperor," in our timeline, but at this time it meant "guy with real good mojo." The Romans had the idea that an army whose leader had *imperium*—which you might as well translate as "the Force was with him"—was invincible, so it was a heavy-duty compliment. Calling him by name would have been a bit more normal and a lot more modest. But as I was to learn, old Gaius could never really get enough of praise of himself. Even from people who he'd decided ought to fight to the death with each other for his amusement.

Then we turned to face each other, the crowd started whooping, and they signaled for us to start.

For a guy with a tenth of my training at fighting—and maybe one one-hundredth of my experience—Hasmonea put up a hell of a fight; he didn't really hurt me, but he forced me to worry about it.

We closed with each other right away—after all we had said we'd be quick—and I shot what looked like a left jab at his face. He blocked, but of course the fistful of sand I had picked up went into his eyes, blinding him. I sidestepped and snap-kicked as hard as I could; my boot flung his elbow upward and connected hard with his rib cage. He made an "oof" noise, but it hadn't felt like I'd cracked any ribs. I closed in.

I don't know if he was lucky or had already gotten one eye cleared of sand, but he managed to swing an arm around my head, forcing it down, and got in a respectable knee to my nose, not hard enough to break it because he didn't really know what he was doing, but certainly hard enough to hurt. He followed through, too slowly, with a solid punch to the side of my jaw. (If he had known what he was doing he should have hit me, two or three times, in the temple or the throat, or driven a thumb into my eye.)

It hurt like hell for a short instant, but as my jaw went numb, I scooped his supporting leg with my free hand and shoulder-rolled out, planting my shoulder in his ribs as I went.

I spun before I hit and lunged forward for a grip at his throat, but he was too fast and had already gotten turned—my hands clawed at sand, and then his were on my face, groping for my eyes. He was beginning to learn, and that was bad news.

I pulled my head back and trapped one of his hands, turning it against the little finger, taking up the slack skin around the wrist, and finally levering it against my opposite arm. He screamed then, as his elbow joint went, and I flung sand into his open mouth, making him choke and gasp. I rolled to my feet and circled toward his left arm, which now hung at a funny angle, the palm facing uselessly out from his body.

He was half-blind and choking, but when I tried a driving kick into his ribs on that side, his leg rose to block and turn mine, and in as neat a little motion as you've ever seen in dojo, his leg extended hard. He was shorter than I was, and a fraction too far away—otherwise, he'd have nailed my scrotum to my backbone with his boot toe. But since he missed, and didn't hit my thigh with enough force to make a difference, I continued the motion, planted the kicking foot, and whipped a roundhouse at his head. It connected, badly, but enough to throw him off-balance—which is serious when your arm is out of joint at the elbow.

He staggered in a little spiral and barely righted himself. I took two giant steps and felt my blood go cold as ice; now I would kill him.

I had finally slipped behind him. Most of the good places for killing a human being quickly, if you've only got your hands to work with, are behind him.

I kicked hard again, and caught one of his kidneys. From the way he grunted I had hurt Hasmonea badly at least, and if I was lucky, I might actually have ruptured the kidney and started the hemorrhage that would finish him in a minute or so.

He tried to turn to face me. His face was now a mask of hideous pain, with one eye swollen shut from the sand, and his mouth hanging open to breathe. I skipped sideways and used the leather on my left palm to smash his septum, sending a spray of blood from his nose. The odds of driving the bone into the brain that way are practically nil (though it does happen), but the pain is blinding and incapacitating, and that was all I needed.

He fell forward to his knees, and then sat back as if trying to rise. I turned and kicked his other kidney, harder than I had the first. With a moan of pure agony and despair, he went forward onto his hands and knees, his left side buckling at once as his broken arm would not bear the weight.

From here on it was by the book. I slapped a half nelson around his neck, using his good right arm as a brace (and thereby taking his working arm out of the contest). From the way his hand was beginning to twitch, I think he may have been passing out by that point.

I surely hope so. I had promised him that I would be quick, and I was being as quick as I could. But still, he was bound to suffer horribly before it was all over. If both people know it's a fight, and both are fighting, it is not within the power of bare human hands to be painless.

With his head locked, I wrapped my other arm around so that it would brace against my own arm and against his carotid. I twisted my two arms like a rope knotting, shutting off the blood flow to his brain, and then used my own arms as a fulcrum to somersault over his body, stretching him out and further crushing his neck. My legs whipped around to brace his thighs apart, my hips lifted his buttocks, and the move was complete; nothing shielded the arteries of his neck from the crushing force of my arms. I counted thirty seconds, slowly, to myself, while keeping his limp body torqued as hard as it would go; when I released my grip, I wanted to be sure he was dead.

At twenty seconds into my count, on the front of my leather jock, I felt something warm and wet; a moment later the stench told me that he had voided his bowels. I kept the lock on and kept counting. Hasmonea was a clever man and it could be a last-instant fake.

Could have been, might have been, but whether it was or not, I kept the lock on long enough. When I finally released his limp body, he was thoroughly dead. I flung him off me like an old towel and stood up; Hasmonea's body lay crumpled and still, and a legion doctor ran out to check him. It didn't take much of a look, apparently, because he announced at once that the man was dead.

The place went up in wild cheering, then into rhythmic clapping like you hear at the Olympics. Caesar stood up, nodded at me, and then turned to the crowd, raising his arms. The crowd went so crazy you'd have thought Caesar had been doing the work.

It was a strange moment. The sun beat down through the icy air, reflecting off the sand onto me, and I realized I was getting a little bit of a sunburn. The glare was blinding, the roar of the crowd deafening.

Behind Caesar, I could see Porter looking pale and sick with what she had seen. Paula was impassive, Chrys clearly just relieved, but all of them had managed to sit as far away on the bench from Caesar as was practical.

I looked down at my arms and saw that the sweat was not only drying but freezing on me, and that it was mixed with blood, though whether mine or Hasmonea's I had no idea. I began to shiver all over, and I wanted desperately to heave up breakfast.

It was then that I found myself wishing I had asked that poor sad crumpled heap of broken bones leaking blood into the sand what his wife's name was, what he loved about her, how many children they had, and so forth. It would have been far better than what I had heard him talk about, and it would have comforted him to talk about it.

I looked back up into Caesar's eyes. That slash of a mouth was drawn in a tight smile, the kind that some people put on when they think they must appear pleased and don't feel it, but Caesar's pleasure seemed real enough; his eyes had that strange, farseeing look to them again, like a thousand-yard stare but with every intention of coming back in just one more moment. He thought a little farther ahead than most people, lived in a slightly wider mental space and time, and it showed through now and then.

He turned to the guard next to him, and an order was given. I couldn't hear it over the noise at the distance, but the crowd began to quiet at once.

Behind me there was a squeaking sound. I turned to see a twin-drive pedicab—I don't know how else you could describe it—pulling up behind me.

It was built like the bicycles we had seen the other day, or rather like two of them stuck on the front of a chariot. The men peddling it seemed to be slaves, probably Gauls or Britons to judge by their blazing red hair. A legate rode on the back.

He stepped off, and they stuck out their feet to stop. Then he walked up to me, threw a heavy robe around my shoulders, and put a wreath of some kind onto my head. "Get into the chariot," he said. "We will circle the arena once. You will wave to the crowd. You will lead them in cheers of 'Caesar! Caesar!'"

The horse pistol he held under his cloak seemed very persuasive.

I always had a hard time understanding how anyone could be a cheerleader—my brother, my sister, and I were always participants and bouncing around and looking pert didn't enter into our idea of how to spend our time—but let me tell you, there's no skill easier to acquire when, first of all, you've got a man with a gun making you learn, and, secondly, you've got a crowd that has been terrorized into cheering as if their lives depended upon it. Which, in a certain very real sense, they did.

We ended up circling the arena three times, and when we were done, my throat was good and hoarse from shouting "Caesar! Caesar!" to them. They cheered back wildly, and then finally, after it was all done, I got to go back to the room where we had slept the night before, and they had a hot bath waiting for me. They also had a slave girl that I would have guessed was about thirteen, who I gently sent on her way, pleading that I had vowed to my gods to have sex only with Chrysamen. In a little while they brought all three of my companions back to join me, but I sure wasn't in the mood. Mostly I just wanted to sit in the hot water and let the feelings of the day soak away.

I hated killing Closers who had names, and it occurred to me that probably all of them did—I just usually didn't know them. There were a lot of things I didn't like about this mission, but if it really meant an end to this war, I was all for it.

"One thing you can say for the Romans," Chrysamen said, "they don't do things quickly unless they have to. The games were the big event of the day. Caesar has gone back to his quarters to think about things and isn't expected to come out till tomorrow morning. We have sort of a lunch date with him, I guess, in which he'll finally explain what he is going to do with all of us. Meanwhile, we're here, we're warm and well fed, and you don't have to kill anybody tomorrow morning, at least not that we know about."

"What's been going on out in the city?"

"Well, Caesar's supporters posted a long list of proscriptions, but Caesar ordered that taken down and commuted the sentence of anyone who will formally surrender and swear an oath of allegiance. So there haven't been many executions so far—everyone who could had already fled, and everyone who couldn't swore the oath. So I'd say the city is thoroughly in his hands."

"What's he going to do now?" I asked.

She shrugged. "We were thrown in with slave women for a while, and all of them had picked up gossip. Everyone agrees he's going to take Rome. The only real question is whether he'll cut over to one of the coasts and then head south, or take the direct route south. But the last word from bicycle post is that the direct road, down the Via Flaminia, is open. And with bicycles, if he goes that way, he's only a two-day forced march from Rome. All that's between him and the capital is whatever Pompey has scared up— assuming Pompey hasn't just cut and run like he did in our timeline."

"Where's Crassus? I thought everyone figured *he* was Caesar's main opponent. And from what Hasmonea told me, if our boy Caldwell is still alive anywhere, it's with Crassus."

Paula made a face. "Well, then don't bet on the cavalry turning up soon. Word is that Crassus made his winter encampment in Egypt. I'm afraid we're stuck with Caesar for quite a while."

·10·

At least he was slow about getting around to things the next morning as well, so there was a lot of time to just hang out. It might have been tough on the nerves, but on the other hand we didn't have too much to fear just then, so we played some silly word games, talked about nothing, and generally enjoyed being bored in comfort. Or at least Paula, Chrys, and I did. People in violent occupations learn to enjoy boredom.

Porter was sulking. Teenagers, even when they know there's violence around, don't appreciate boredom enough.

We had played "Categories" about one time too many, and we were actually starting to wonder if we should ask the guards for a midday meal when the summons came, and when we got there we discovered we were all supposed to stretch out at the table for Roman-style dining.

There was the expectable vast load of pickled fish and the heavy flat bread; the soup was good, the wine was plentiful, and Caesar seemed mainly interested in talking about the political structure of ATN, and about the people who headed it, and why exactly they might object to one person or support another.

This was making me slightly more uncomfortable than before, but I think I did a decent job of hiding it. It would have been one thing if he had given me the creeps, but although I had certainly seen that he could be cruel and arbitrary, nothing about him was really bothering or repelling me. Which was what the problem was—thus far Caesar had done nothing that would even remotely make me think of shooting him.

Of course he was a first-class jerk, but if I went around shooting all of those, I'd never have to leave my own timeline, and I'd still never get finished. And then again orders were orders . . . but they hadn't told me where or when to shoot him. In fact Chief Tribune Scipio had told me that there was a certain amount of historical confusion about the whole thing and thus they figured it would be better not to tell me, because I could easily end up staking out a place where it didn't happen.

When he had told me that, my judgment had been that he was lying. But he had told me in front of General Malecela, and when I tried to talk to Malecela about it later, Malecela had strongly discouraged the question.

Now I wondered why, and more than that, I wished I had extorted everything they knew from Scipio and Malecela—because I was sure that was much more than they had told me.

And just when had I started distrusting Malecela? It had been a relief to have him show up in the timeline to which we had been carried off, but by a few days later when our party left to come here, I had already begun to wonder what was up. Whatever it was, Malecela was in on it, and something smelled really bad when an agent with a record as long and as good as mine—I had known him back when he was a captain—couldn't be trusted with whatever the secret was.

I tried to remind myself to cool down, *after all, it may be something that mustn't fall into enemy hands, and if you don't know it, they can't get it out of you.* For that matter there could easily be a good reason I hadn't thought of, or maybe there was a reason why they couldn't tell me why they couldn't tell me . . . my thoughts were beginning to go in circles.

Naturally I was trying to have that argument with myself while I also listened to Caesar and attempted not to drop all of the food onto my chest, eating lying down. It's not as easy as it looks, at least not if you don't want to end up shaking dinner out of your toga for the next three days.

The real trouble was that I knew Malecela well enough to figure that in any normal circumstances he'd at least have told me that there was something he couldn't tell me. That would have been enough.

But just to try to hide it from me entirely . . . that didn't sit well. It made me think that what he was up to was something I wouldn't have liked, and he knew it.

I did my best to distract myself by paying attention to the conversation. After a while I noticed that Caesar was paying a lot of attention to Porter, which might have worried me for a second—technically we were all spoils of war and she, like all of us, was his slave—except it was mostly her music that interested him. She, in turn, had never seen a lyre; he had one brought in, along with a Roman version of a flute, and she spent the rest of the time softly noodling around over in the corner, getting the feel for the instruments. I guess when your setting is totally unfamiliar, the most comforting thing possible is a familiar task, one you find easy—and for Porter nothing was easier than learning a new instrument.

At last the wine came in, and the conversation turned serious. Caesar was a blunt man by nature, but capable of subtlety when he needed it; this time bluntness suited him. "So this timeline in which I live is to be a very important one," he said. "The Republic will flourish, the tribunes will gain power, and the Senate and consuls lose power, and eventually Rome will rule the entire Earth, even the two whole continents across the sea, that Caldwell led us to sail to, where the colony of Terra Elastica was planted. And in a few thousand years we will be the most advanced timeline of all.

"This interests me. It has always seemed to me that my destiny and Rome's are intertwined to our mutual benefit. You say that in your timeline, I became dictator after taking Rome—"

"And emperor for all practical purposes, until you were assassinated in 709 A.U.C.," I said. "March 15. I would suggest that on that day, you don't go to the Senate house, and listen to the soothsayers." What the hell, it was five years in the future; by that time either I'd have done it, or things would be drastically changed.

Caesar nodded. "Though of course all things have been changed by your intervention, and the Closers'."

"Things that have been changed have a way of turning out the same," I said. I was thinking of the fact that twice I had seen John Glenn be the first American to orbit the Earth.

"I see. Well, then, 709 A.U.C. And the conspirators—"

"Mostly are your allies nowadays," I said. "They turned against you when you became dictator."

He nodded. "I see more and more advantage in working behind the scenes. And young Marcus Antonius is a fine tribune; through him I can exert more than enough control. I think I will avoid the step of becoming dictator. Yes, once we are off to a good start here, I think much can be done." The general sat up a bit more and poured himself some wine. "And there is something wonderful about it, you know. That silly old Pompey has a tendency to think he is Alexander reincarnated, merely because he has some flair for tactics and logistics, but then what Roman general doesn't dream of just extending conquest till we have the whole Earth sworn to alliance? And then, of course, we realize that if we were to accomplish that, men like Pompey and I would be nothing again . . . and much like Alexander, we would be left weeping because there would be no more worlds to conquer.

"But what you describe is wonderful. Not just more worlds to conquer, but an unlimited number of worlds with an unlimited number of challenges. Room for the biggest heart, spirit, and intellect. A man with the right *genius* could go farther than most men could imagine." It took me a moment to realize that he had said "genius," because the word came out with a hard *g*, like GENN ee oose, and the translator in my ear just let it through because there's no such word in English. Your *genius*, if you're a Roman, is the god you're assigned at birth, who looks after you and your interests as long as you're careful to say the right prayers and do the right rituals. Which means if you've got a real hotshot *genius*, and you take care of him, you're going places.

Caesar seemed to just sit and watch quietly while I thought. I don't think he realized that I had had to take a moment to figure out what he had said. When my expression cleared, and I stopped looking confused, he smiled and explained further that, "It was just the thought—the question really . . . well, if it should happen that the world is unified during my lifetime, or that there is no longer an urgent need for me here . . . do you suppose your ATN might want a general or an administrator of some kind?"

I was startled, and Chrys looked like she'd choke. "We do sometimes recruit from other timelines," I said. "The founding leader of my nation—which only exists in some timelines—became an ATN agent in one timeline where there was nothing much for him to do. So it is not impossible. But we do know that contact was lost for a very long time, so the odds of your being able to cross over are small."

Caesar shrugged. "It was a thought, only. I've got at least twenty vigorous years left, if I can contrive not to be shot or stabbed, and chances are that the possibilities of this world will not be exhausted at all by that time. But I hate limits of any kind, you know. The Senate was very foolish to draw a line and tell me not to cross it—I can't imagine anything that would make me want to defy them more." He sighed and stretched. "I'm looking forward, one of these days, to having a villa on the Bay of Naples, and sitting there warm and comfortable, with no bigger question in mind than what book to read that day. All in the sun. The Gaulish winters are horrible, and the British winters make them seem bearable by comparison.

"Meanwhile, however, there's a delicate question that I've refrained from asking for some time. When this Caldwell person set himself up as a business partner with Crassus, it seemed of very minor interest to me. He had come in with his strange 'rubber,' showing off how many uses it had like any vulgar tradesman, and only a complete boor like Crassus would have been taken with him. We all thought it was the end of Caldwell when he set sail in his ten ships with all those free craftsmen and skilled slaves—we figured Crassus had truly thrown the money down a rathole—and yet just three years later, back he came with a load of rubber and requests for more colonists. Even then, we just thought, 'Well, no matter, a plebeian is growing wealthy. They have grown wealthy before.' Even when he introduced his firearms and his bicycles, and suddenly all of us had to relearn the art of war, we thought only, 'Now that Rome has these things, we are truly invincible.' But now I see how much he has changed us, and how much Hasmonea has changed us as well."

"Did you know him well?" I asked.

"Too well. He disgusted me; his worship of Moloch was the least of it. He was a coward when he could get away with it, soft in the worst ways to be soft, and hard-hearted where any real man ought to have some compassion."

"Then why did you have him—"

Caesar made an irritated chopping gesture with his hand. I'm not easily intimidated but I stopped, right then, with my mouth open. "Because," the general said, "I knew that eventually I would have to contend with Crassus for leadership of Rome, and that might well mean fighting. And Crassus has your Walks-in-His-Shadow Caldwell advising him, or did until recently, anyway—my spies tell me he has disappeared, and Crassus seems to be frantic with worry. At any rate, having seen what one man could bring with him, I *had* to have an advisor of my own. It took me no time at all to realize this was a real Carthaginian, a truly unrepentant child-sacrificer, and all the rest, but I had absolutely no other choice, as a practical matter. As soon as I had another option, I took it; I had no doubt at all that you would win, and thus Caesar disposed of an unpopular person in favor of one who could do him more good."

I had another moment to think, and what I thought was that his reasoning was cold, logical, and exactly the kind of thing Thebenides might have said.

On the other hand I wasn't supposed to shoot Thebenides.

"What are you hoping, exactly, to arrange with us?" I asked Caesar. "And you should be aware that Chrysamen is fully my partner; if you're going to deal with ATN, you should learn that we practice equality of the sexes."

"Mostly," Chrys said.

Caesar appeared slightly amused, though whether at Chrys's comment or at the notion of "equality of the sexes" I couldn't tell. "Very well, then. Let me make a suggestion as to our course of action. Clearly ATN wishes this timeline to succeed, and will want to deal with whoever is in charge of it. It so happens that both Crassus and I also want this timeline to succeed—I doubt his competence but not his patriotism. So in a real sense it is a matter of indifference to you which of us eventually emerges on top. Thus my suggestion is only that you and your wife act as advisors to me in exactly the same way that this Caldwell acts as advisor to Crassus." I started to speak, but he held up a finger. "I understand fully that you cannot be expected to assist in injuring the agent you came here to rescue. Thus I offer this—if you take my offer, I shall do my utmost to see that Caldwell goes unharmed, even at peril to my personal safety, and even at some peril to my potential victory. If I know he is present on the battlefield, my orders will be that he is to be captured unharmed, and permitted to escape if there is the slightest potential he may be harmed.

"Thus ATN will secure the relations it wants with this timeline,

I will secure an even footing against Crassus—and believe me, no one knows Crassus better than I, and with an even footing I cannot lose. ATN will have Caesar as its ally, and surely you know—from what you know of my many timelines—that this is no bad thing?"

As a matter of fact, I knew Caesar's record was so mixed that nobody in his right mind would try to sum the man up. He accepted surrenders on easy terms, then turned around and plundered the cities and enslaved their inhabitants. But he also systematically forgave and forgot once he took power. He used his admitted military brilliance to smash the armies of his own nation on his way to power—but then he treated the veterans of both sides of the conflict with tremendous generosity and fairness. He was known to be ruthless, but he could be very kind; known to care passionately what people thought of him, but able to completely ignore public opinion when it disapproved of something he wanted to do.

In short, he was utterly his own man. If he was inconsistent, it was because he chose to be; he didn't live his life with an eye to the history books, the way that a lot of recent presidents had. That was about all you could say. And compared to a lot of my own timeline's pussyfooting, PR, spindoctoring, and other forms of lying, it was sort of refreshing to run into a guy whose two interests were 1) ruling the world, and 2) ruling it better than anyone else possibly could.

"And what if I don't take the offer?" I said. "Let me say first of all I find it attractive, but I also want to know every option you are offering us."

"If you don't take the offer," Caesar said, taking a sip of his wine and staring off into space, "then what I would say is that after all, whatever ATN's rules might be, you are among Romans now, and among Romans you will live by Caesar's rules. And under those rules, my dear Marcus, all four of you are slaves. That would mean you will do what I say or you will suffer punishment—and I remind you that in our law, I may kill my slaves at any time I wish. But you did say you found the offer attractive? Surely I don't need to speak of such terribly unpleasant things?"

The strangest part, I realized, was that he was sincere; he really wanted to have our loyalty and service because it was what we thought best, and he really didn't want to have to talk about what he would do if we didn't offer it to him. It was part of that strange inconsistency that ran through his character like hot lava pouring through a forest; on either side it was familiar, and in the center of it all, it looked like the dark side of the moon.

I had never been quite so afraid on a mission before—but I also felt oddly comfortable. "We'll take the deal, then," I said.

Gaius Julius Caesar's face broke into a real, honest-to-all-the-gods grin of pleasure; I'm sure he had not forgotten his threat, and neither had we, but the business was settled, and that was all he cared about.

We went back to our quarters soon after; he told us that he would make arrangements for us to travel with him, and as the merest afterthought, presented Porter with the lyre and flute, suggesting that she continue to practice.

At least I wouldn't have to amuse a teenager along with all the other things we needed to do.

The next morning, we found out what the difference was between a day Caesar spent in camp and a day Caesar spent on campaign. Servants came and woke us two hours before the cold winter dawn, gave us five minutes to wash with the pitchers of warm water they had brought, fed us bowls of warm gruel with beef chips, and stuffed us, our clothing, and our baggage out the door and into a spitting predawn rain, all within seemingly no time at all.

By the time we were out there, Caesar had been up for two hours, and the legions, allies, and auxiliaries were all there in full array, on their bicycles. While we waited for it to be light enough to start, the centurions and legates roamed back and forth, shouting at men and getting the units together.

"How do you tell what rank everybody is, and why aren't there any uniforms?" Porter asked, shivering beside me.

"They have a pretty flexible notion of rank," I said. "A legion is sixty centuries, and a century is one hundred men. A century is commanded by a centurion—see, it's easier to remember than you thought, right?"

"Wise-ass," Paula muttered, but I noticed that she, too, was leaning in to hear. I suppose nobody wants to go to a battle without a scorecard.

"The centurions have a mixture of power and authority that sort of ranges from what in a modern army would be a sergeant, all the way up to what might be a captain. A legate is any guy who can speak for the commander. He sort of assigns them any way that makes sense to him—kind of like a free-floating officer corps. So a very respected and experienced legate might command a legion, but a very young and inexperienced one might be assigned to run alongside an experienced centurion until he got some idea of what was going on."

"Then there aren't any real tight rules about that?" Porter asked.

"There are Caesar's rules. You can't get any tighter than that," Chrysamen said.

Paula nodded. "I understand that. Okay, boss, that's legions. Who are the other guys?"

"Well, the auxiliaries are cavalry, or sometimes other specialty troops like archers, slingers, and that kind of thing. It looks like Caesar's guys are equipped with stirrups, which weren't invented for a few more centuries in our home timeline. So they're probably a lot more effective than Caesar is used to."

"Because they have stirrups?"

I nodded. "Think about a knight jousting. If he has no stirrups, what happens when his lance hits something?"

"He lands flat on his ass. Got you, boss. And I suppose that applies to almost anything else he could use; the stirrups would give him firmer footing for using a pistol or a bow, too."

Another troop of auxiliaries rumbled by, and I turned and then stared.

"What is it, Mark?" Porter asked.

Chrysamen sighed, then spoke before I could. "It's a field gun. I don't think they were supposed to have anything more than big siege guns at this point in their accelerated development. The idea was supposed to be to get the world politically unified, technologically progressive, and sympathetic to ATN, as far back in history as they could go. The weapons that were introduced here were bound to accelerate the killing, too, but we were trying to hold that in check. Unfortunately I bet Hasmonea wasn't . . . so he gave Caesar the neat idea for how to kill a whole bunch of people at once. Those field guns are going to send the death rate sky-high."

"What's the difference?" Porter asked. "Doesn't any cannon kill a lot of people?"

"Siege guns like the ones that were supposed to be introduced here are mainly aimed at walls and towers," I said. "They take so much effort to move and re-aim that you can't use them very much against troops in the field. So what they're good for is taking a city, where you have a wall or a fortified part to batter apart. And naturally people don't just stand there and die while the battering happens, so the casualty rate isn't necessarily very high.

"But a field gun is intended to be wheeled onto a battlefield and pointed and fired wherever it's needed. That's why those things have wheeled carriages and limbers—the things the mules are pulling them by. So a field gun is fired against troops in the open field—and it kills a lot of them."

"I wonder if that hole in the shield and the musket rest is Caldwell's trick, or Caesar's?" Chrysamen said, as another legion went by. "And will the armor stand up to the shot, anyway?"

"If they're far enough away," I said. "But I have a feeling we'll know way too much about it before this is over."

"It was my invention, by the way," Caesar said, behind us. He was smiling again, that tight-lipped look that I was coming to realize meant he felt very alive and full of energy. "It took me quite a while to figure out how men could fire muskets from behind a shield wall—and I had to modify a lot of things to make this practical."

He was perched on a bicycle of his own, and now he slapped the seat, and said, "My other great invention is the idea of springs under the seat. My men can ride a lot farther than anyone else's."

I didn't have the heart to tell him, and besides, why shouldn't he be proud? He had indeed thought of it himself.

"I assume you all can ride these, since the device came from an ATN timeline," he went on, oblivious to us. "I'm having four of them brought to you; naturally, most of your things will be in the baggage wagons." Then he jumped on his cycle and pedaled away; I noted how straight and stiff he sat as he rode, and figured the springs were getting some extra workout. I also was surprised at just how dignified he seemed to be.

A dozen young legates formed a squadron dashing along behind him on their cycles, and then, in the dim predawn gray light, he faded into the huge crowd of armed men, all in process of assembly.

Half an hour later, we were sitting on our bicycles—all "girls' models" since everyone in this timeline wore a skirt—with a whole party of miscellaneous slaves of Caesar's. They were a lively bunch, and educational in their way; they all seemed to be competing for the position of Caesar's favorite bed partner, and I didn't notice that the men were any less competitive than the women. There was a vast array of skills among them—cooks, musicians, poets, painters, a couple of very attractive young redheads of each gender whose skills were probably not displayed in public much—bodyguards, dancers, actors, everything you could think of that went into making life comfortable. There were half a dozen strong young men whose major duty was putting up the several large tents that served as field quarters for Caesar's party.

And whose minor duty, as far as I could tell, was to look great in a jockstrap and a coat of oil.

I'm not a prude, per se; Caesar was a powerful man in a culture that kept slaves, and I wasn't terribly shocked that he liked to be comfortable, or that he tended to mess around in his own household. What was bothering me was that Porter was getting ears full of all this. Girls a lot younger than she were vying with each other over who "dearest Gaius" had dragged into bed how often. If it had been just Chrysamen and Paula, the three of us might have found it all amusing, but I was dying of embarrassment on Porter's behalf.

I guess it showed, because Porter suddenly whispered to me, in English, "Oh, grow up, Mark, these are Romans; of course they have sex all the time."

"You're confusing the late Empire with the late Republic," I stammered. "Caesar is a bit unusual for his day, and a lot of people thought this was all made up by his political enemies."

People were beginning to stare at us because we were speaking a language they couldn't understand, so we clammed up at that point. But I figured as long as Porter wanted to pretend she could be sophisticated and cool about it, it wasn't my place to get bent out of shape on her behalf.

I even began to find some of the razzing the cooks were getting amusing.

At last the command came to mount up, and the whole vast column of bicycles that had been painstakingly assembled on the Via Flaminia got into motion. Because the knotted rope as chain, and the wooden pin gears, did not permit a derailleur or a hub shift, the cranks had to be a little outsize, so against the just-turning-light skyline in front of us, the legions seemed to bob up and down in great waves, their round cycle helmets and the shoulder pieces of their gear giving them a strangely uniform look in silhouette, like a vast horde of beetles doing the Wave. The weather was improving a tiny bit—the rain wasn't freezing, and there was less of it—and we got off smoothly.

An hour later I was beginning to admire the hell out of Roman training. My bottom was promising to be sore soon, if it wasn't already, and my thighs were killing me. Chrys, beside me, seemed a bit more comfortable, but I think her cycle fit her better. Porter looked like she'd die rather than complain, and like the choice was coming up pretty quickly.

Paula was chugging along strongly, apparently enjoying the ride; she was more athlete than any of us, actually, and back home she was the sort of person who enters marathons at the last minute because she's not doing anything that weekend.

It was a pretty long ride. Forum Sempronii, the next big town, was about fifteen miles away by road, almost all of it uphill—a day's march for the legions in the old days, but now just a three-hour ride, with a break of about five minutes every hour.

The second break was prolonged quite a bit for most of us; we saw a group of cyclists leading strings of horses start out in advance of us.

"What's that?" Porter asked.

About all I know about horses is that you put oats in one end and the feet move, and that the maintenance is a lot more complicated than it is for a motorcycle, which is saying something. They made us learn to ride and to care for horses (and camels, llamas, mules, donkeys, water buffalo, and several things you don't find in our timeline) at the ATN training camp, and I spent just as little time on it as I could get away with.

But Chrys and Paula both loved riding, even though they'd never gotten Porter very interested in it, and so it was Chrys who answered, "Human beings are actually some of the most efficient distance-running animals there are. The reason people ride horses is because the horse does all the work, not because the horse does it better. And the bicycle drastically improves human performance. I was noticing before that they keep switching off horses on the baggage wagons—they pretty much have to—and that most of the time most of the horses are completely unloaded. So my guess is that we're getting ready for battle, and the horses—oh, and look, there's a string of mules—have to be sent on ahead, or given a head start if you want to call it that, and then the cavalrymen will ride up on bicycles to join them."

"There's something strange in the balance of power," I said, "when people are working that hard for horses."

"Human chauvinist," Paula said.

"Species traitor," I retorted. "Yeah, that makes sense. And it's sort of in keeping with the Caesar we know; systematic and thorough. This way he arrives with a whole army ready to fight."

"Is there going to be a battle, do you think?" Porter asked.

"Forum Sempronii is a lot smaller than Fanum Fortunae," I said. "It's really just a garrison town and a way stop for traffic. If they have any sense, they won't fight at all; the garrison might even have been pulled back toward Rome. I'm surprised they haven't just sent a message out to surrender; surely they've known Caesar was coming."

An hour later, as we rolled into Forum Sempronii, the mystery became clearer. The city government had taken one look at the situation, and being all pro-Senate, had fled toward Rome, taking the whole garrison and the militia as well, leaving no one in charge to surrender or even to keep law and order. Caesar's scouts had found a certain amount of petty looting and rioting going on, which they had suppressed (the bodies of several looters were still dangling in the town's forum), and a large crowd of people in the forum looking for something to do, which they had taken charge of. The citizens of Forum Sempronii, who had been frightened out of their wits, were given the basic course in Caesar's approach: be cool and nobody gets hurt. Within hours he had appointed a new city government, distributed the property of those who had deserted to Rome, and made most of the people still there into passionate Caesar fans. It was a hell of a performance; watching him, I thought that if there were an election, I might have voted for him myself.

·11·

There wasn't room enough in Forum Sempronii to put everyone up for the night, but luckily we were either privileged advisors or pet slaves, depending on how you looked at it, so we got a small room in a confiscated villa. The scuttlebutt was that the next day would be much the longest ride, and considering the way my thighs and ass felt, I was dreading it. We all traded around back rubs, put warm ointment where we thought it would count, and worked out ways to put some additional padding on the seats, though, as Paula pointed out, that meant being a little more wobbly and what we saved in butt bruises would be paid back in harder work on our thighs.

Porter was tireder than the rest of us—she'd never much liked athletics of any kind and was in crummy shape—but she had the resilience of youth and bounced back a lot faster. As the rest of us were getting ready for bed, she sat and picked at the lyre.

"Hoping to revive the instrument in our timeline?" I asked.

"Just maybe, Mark, just maybe. It's got some interesting possibilities. With this alternate tuning, check out this bit from Praetorius." She played a little baroque passage, picking it carefully. "Just happened to be a piano piece I knew well. You see what I mean? Interesting sound, but the instrument is technically demanding." She set it aside. "Now try this one—it's the flute part for a Handel sonata, the part I never get to play when I play harpsichord with that nice old French guy. I think with the softer, rounder tone, it sounds pretty neat on this thing."

I had to admit that it was beautiful, but Porter is a world-class musician, and I pretty much have to admit that everything she plays is beautiful.

"You're still going to wish you'd taken some extra sleep in the morning," Chrysamen grumbled—which wasn't like her, but I think she was tiredest of all of us.

"Sure," Porter said, putting her instruments away and heading for bed. She was so pleasant and cooperative, especially compared to the way she had been a couple of years ago, that I wondered if she were feeling well.

Sure enough, the next day's ride was truly a ride from hell, or maybe *to* hell.

The problem was this. The Apennine Range runs down the spine of Italy like the plates on a dinosaur, and there are large parts of it, even today, that are a hassle to go over on the ground. Back in World War II, when the Allies and the Germans were slugging it out on the peninsula, both sides left a fifty-mile gap in their lines between east and west, just to accommodate the Apennines, and neither side could find a way through the other's fifty-mile gap. And that was with jeeps, bulldozers, and trucks available.

So you had to go through one of the few passes. Since Caesar had been at Ariminum, after he crossed the Rubicon he could either go directly down the Via Flaminia to Rome, or he could backtrack a long way north into Cisalpine Gaul on the Via Aemilia, all the way to Bononia (which was where Bologna is on the modern map), and then come back down through Clusium on the Via Cassia. And off of the *viae*—the paved military roads—travel was just plain impossible in the Apennines in the winter.

Thus Caesar had picked the shorter way; the moment he had struck down to Fanum Fortunae was clear. Dispatch riders on cycles would be reaching Rome soon, if they hadn't already, with the news (which would come as no surprise—it would not have been like Caesar to leave his own territory exposed and take the long way around, just for a surprise that was sure to collapse soon afterward).

Now, the problem with all that is that it's tough to march or attack uphill; the old thing about getting the high ground. So it was vital that Caesar reach and cross the divide—the high pass between the eastern and western watersheds of Italy—before Pompey did.

Unfortunately, at least for our little group, that divide was right around the city of Spoletium—just under a hundred miles away by the Via Flaminia. And since we were riding with the legions, somehow or other we were going to have to manage to ride these silly contraptions a hundred miles the next day. So early bed after a big meal seemed very much in order.

The ride wasn't quite as bad as I had feared. Even though the Via Flaminia had been built for marching troops rather than bicycles, it was well banked and had plenty of switchbacks; parts of it are used for highways even today, because it takes the easiest route through that part of the mountains. Moreover, though we were up just as early, we'd all slept well, and though it was just as cold, it was a bright, sunny day. And with the exercise, we didn't feel cold for long.

Still, by midafternoon we were only halfway there, and I for one would have said it had already been a long day. We did the last ten miles with soldiers leading each contingent using candle-lamps mounted on their bicycles.

Spoletium was another military-base city, which had been built there to guard the road and provide services to the soldiers who did the guarding, and then had grown because the road was the logical way for freight to travel, and the people who moved the freight needed somewhere to stop for a meal or for the night. We ate because they ordered us to, and then fell into our beds.

I also let myself feel a certain amount of awe at the legions. The pass was actually a few miles east of Spoletium, and two of the legions riding out front had actually managed to get there during daylight, dig entrenchments by lamplight, and then settle in to guard Caesar against a surprise attack coming up from Rome.

But the next morning we could all sleep in; with forces up at the pass, and with entrenchments dug there, Caesar was as secure as he could be. According to scuttlebutt, the spies in Rome said Pompey's army there would not be moving against us for at least another day, and we now occupied a strong position. Thus a couple of days could be spent gathering and resting our forces.

So we spent most of that day groaning and stretching out from time to time. Caesar was busy and didn't pay much attention to us, which was fine by me; late that evening he invited us to dine with him, and Porter played some Praetorius, as well as some Bach, Handel, and Haydn. He seemed to like it a lot, and made a point of congratulating us all around.

While we were sitting over wine, he was quizzing us both very heavily over all the histories of all the timelines we knew. Another thing I got to admire and respect about Caesar—he had one of those minds that picks up theory and detail, fitting them together seamlessly, and absorbing it very rapidly. I knew of six different important battles, in six different timelines, that had been fought at Dien Bien Phu, and eight at Gettysburg (I had been to one at each place), and he not only wanted to know what the ground was like and how each battle had gone, but he seemed to have no trouble, after hearing it once, keeping all the different cases straight in his head and comparing them. Indeed, he rapidly developed convincing opinions about the style and methods of different generals, and could at the least persuade me that he had a good take on why the Patton–Rommel tank duel at Gettysburg, in one timeline, was so much more difficult for Patton than the equivalent battle had been for Meade in 1863 of my timeline. I began to think that if he was sincere in his interest in working for ATN, perhaps we ought to consider carrying him off.

Then again he was also a crafty, sneaky, devious, master politician, and we seemed to have more than enough of those already.

A messenger came in just as we were saying good night; Caesar took the dispatch, looked at it for one long second, and said, "Well, then, it begins. Plan for a long ride tomorrow, but it will be downhill. Pompey is moving, and I know where he thinks he's going. We're going to hand him a surprise."

The next morning, well before it was light, we got up and walked up the hill with Caesar's slaves, who were giggling about Caesar having abruptly helped himself, after we left, to one of his female food servers, a Gaulish girl who didn't look like she'd hit puberty yet and spoke Latin very badly. They were laughing; she seemed to be in tears, which they all found made it much funnier; whatever her name had been, all of them were now referring to her as "Face Down," which was apparently as much as Caesar had talked to her. I was beginning to see why freeborn Romans despised slaves, and why many people especially seemed to dislike Caesar's slaves.

Considering our position, maybe I should say Caesar's *other* slaves, but Caesar was being fairly careful not to rub it in that officially he owned us; he wanted real partnership, and he was prepared to act like it.

Dawn found us just saddling our bicycles on top of the divide; behind us, to the west, water flowed to the Chienti; in front of us, it flowed into the Tiber—which is to say, down to Rome.

Nobody knew exactly how far we were riding that day, but it stood to reason that if Caesar was going to be fighting a hostile army, he wasn't going to have us ride all day long. On the other hand, he had said a "long ride."

The mystery got solved fairly quickly, but by the time it did I wasn't much worried. It was downhill most of the way from the pass, and so for a large part of the trip everyone was coasting, which the bicycles did pretty well. Every half hour we had to pull over and let the bearings cool—no ball bearings meant that moving, as we were, at twenty miles per hour would eventually overheat the axles, most especially with only bacon grease as a lubricant. Every so often one of the bicycles would begin to smoke at the hub, and once the younger slave riding one was so negligent that by the time he pulled over the hub and two spokes were actually on fire, and with no water handy in that dry part of the mountains, the whole bike ended up going up in flames. They sent him back several miles, to walk with the prisoners.

That was about the peak excitement for the day. It was bright and sunny, and a bit warmer, and we made excellent time. When the time came for the noon meal, we were told to eat a couple handfuls of hardtack and about a half cup of chipped dried beef, and then get back on the road; it wouldn't be long till we were there.

When the valley opened out in front of us, it was really very beautiful, even in January. The dark green grass showed through the thin snow in many places, the little farmsteads were decorated with thin drifts of snow, and the bare trees stood out with every twig in sharp detail against the bright blue of the early-afternoon sun.

Far down below us, as the road ran straight down the gentle slope, the Tiber wound its way through the valley; the land rose a bit afterward, and just where low hills lay on the horizon we could see a town.

"That's Falerii," said one of the slaves riding with us. "I hear that's where we'll be stopping."

I had come to have a great respect for scuttlebutt, at least in this timeline; when communication is not terribly fast, nobody is very careful about security, and things leak pretty fast. Besides, I could see about half the army stretched out in front of us on the road, with occasional glimpses of parties of riders on the road beyond the Tiber, also headed for Falerii.

It made sense, too—it was the first big town after the pass, so it would have to be Pompey's staging area if he were going to attack uphill. Moreover, because it sat on the other side of the Tiber, which was covered in large places around the bank with thin ice, and infested everywhere with blocks of floating ice, Caesar could approach only over the bridge, which Pompey could easily hold.

Or he could have if he had gotten there first. Now I saw Caesar's plan, and like so much of his best strategy, it was a very simple idea executed well. Pompey's army was going to have to ride uphill to get here; clearly he had planned to do it in a single forced march and dig in, so that at least there would be a stalemate—Caesar couldn't get to Rome at an acceptable cost, and would have to squat at the Tiber, with nowhere to go except backward (or try to break out and face terrible losses).

But now the plan had been turned against Pompey. Caesar's men were good at entrenchments, and the city fortifications themselves would help. Pompey's army would arrive, having worn itself out with a long uphill ride, late today, and would either have to fight while exhausted and cold with night falling, or (more likely) build a field fortification far into the night, and then get up for a dawn attack (or face one). All Pompey's options were bad.

If you're looking at a map, Falerii was a little west of where Civita Castellana is now, and on a low rise; in addition to everything else, Pompey would be forced to attack uphill, whether he fought on the offense or defense, and whether he gave battle that night or the next morning. Reports were that his army was a full four legions smaller than ours, and had many fewer cavalry—plus, I had learned, the horse pistols I had seen so many of had been an introduction of Hasmonea's—the Gaulish cavalry with Caesar had them. Pompey's Roman cavalry (which was less skilled than Gaulish cavalry anyway) would have only lances.

In short, this had all the makings of a massacre.

I rolled down the long hill and over the Tiber bridge, lost in my own thoughts. There seemed to be trouble if Chrys and I spoke in English, particularly if other slaves finked on us, so we weren't discussing it, but I learned later that she had figured it about the same way I had.

The Tiber bridge was one of those things the Romans built to last forever, or maybe longer; their system of paying for public works was that the contractor got half on completion, and half after forty years, *if* the structure was still standing. It was a bit rough on contractors, but everywhere in Europe you can see what it did for buildings.

That night I slept uneasily; Pompey's army had not come all the way up to Falerii, but that only meant that he had found out his situation. I didn't like what tomorrow was promising.

Well before dawn, I heard footsteps running and orders being shouted. Leaving Porter back in the room, and Paula to guard her, Chrys and I ran to the battlements to see if we could find out what was going on.

There was almost no one up there except townspeople sight-seeing, but as dawn rose we saw the two armies opposing each other. Caesar's forces had their backs to us; Pompey's faced the city.

"Did you manage to smuggle anything when they strip-searched us?" I asked Chrys.

"Distance glasses, holy-shit switch, transponder tracker, that's all," she said. "I don't see any of the gendarmerie around if you want to try the distance glasses."

"Hmm. I saved the distance glasses and the thumbnail atlas. Please don't pick on me, but I didn't manage to hang on to the holy-shit switch."

"Mark . . ." She sighed. "Are they ever going to teach you that it's okay to push that thing now and then?"

I shrugged; it's a bigger issue with her than with me. The "holy-shit switch" is actually the call for help communicator; it contacts an Earth satellite that's been placed in the same timeline with you and triggers a crosstime signal to let them know you're in trouble. I had only pushed it a couple of times in my career, a lot less than most senior Crux Ops. Maybe it was because my first mission had been an improvised affair, without even a SHAKK for most of it. I had just sort of lost the tendency to call for help, even when it would have made sense.

So there was probably a little truth in what she was implying; I hadn't kept my holy-shit switch because I hadn't thought it was that important. And considering how much trouble we were already in, that was a pretty hard thing to justify.

Years of marriage had taught me that whenever you realize your partner is right, you should agree, and then change the subject. So I said, "Well, you're right, of course, but at least you kept yours, so no harm done so far. Anyway, I don't see anyone who looks enough like a cop to ask nosy questions about the distance glasses." In fact the wall was rapidly getting deserted except for the few soldiers standing at the towers and firing positions; civilians were too nervous to stick around.

We put on our distance glasses, and since they only require one finger to control, we held hands.

"Weird to be on the sidelines for a battle," I said. "Especially without a weapon."

The two lines advanced slowly toward each other; I had a few minutes to see what the differences were.

The classic Roman way of fighting is sort of a zone defense; you keep your *gladius*, a short sword that's about the size and weight of a machete, in your right hand, and your *scutum*, a small shield, in your left. You are in charge of staying in your position relative to the other legionaries, and whacking anything in a rectangle that extends about three feet in front of you and a bit under three feet to each side of your right foot. If you're in an interior rank, your zone is bordered on all sides by other legionaries' zones.

It worked because the Romans had nearly perfect discipline. They would die in their tracks before allowing a hole to open in the ranks; if someone fell dead or wounded, his buddies would step over him, close up the hole, and keep going. Furthermore, after a few years of training, they were effectively martial-arts masters with those *gladii*; they had the same kind of perfect concentration and ability to strike hard and accurately without having to think first.

The classical way of attacking was that each man carried two *pila*, or javelins, and as they closed with the enemy, on command the soldiers flung two volleys of javelins, then closed in for sword-to-sword fighting.

But I could see there had been modifications. Pompey's men still carried *pila*, but mixed in with each century there were ten musketeers, armed only with the musket, forming a back rank. Caesar's men had no *pila*, and every man carried a musket; from behind we could see there was something different on the shield, too, but we couldn't see what exactly.

"Pompey is treating muskets as auxiliaries," I said. "Caesar's made them the primary weapon. Bet on Caesar, if you weren't already."

The lines drew closer, and as they did I let my eyes wander farther out on the plain. The first thing that caught my eye was a strange shape—like a forest of pipes—

"Don't look now," I said, "but I think Pompey has invented the Stalin organ. We just might be in deep shit."

We clicked in on it, taking things up to highest magnification, and it was clear as a bell. The round objects lying next to the sets of tubes were pretty clearly rockets; Pompey had found out about rockets one way or another.

"I'm surprised he doesn't just build big cannon," Chrys said.

"Roman iron won't take the pressure very well," I said. "For a long-range weapon, if you can't hold much breech pressure, rockets are better. Even if they're just fueled with black powder like old-fashioned skyrockets."

The first volley of shots rang out from Pompey's lines; at the extreme range for the muskets, they did no damage, for with breech pressures so low, velocity fell off rapidly, and a hundred yards away they weren't hitting hard enough to pierce the shields of Caesar's men.

Immediately on firing the volley, Pompey's legionaries had broken into a trot, obviously intending to close the distance and create a shield wall behind which the musketeers could reload.

But as Pompey's men formed their shield wall, something strange happened. Caesar's front rank knelt; with distance glasses now I saw that a little shelf had been attached to the bottom of each *scutum*. They put their knees down on those shelves, so that the *scuta* stood up like a garden rake with a man standing on the tines, and withdrew their left arms. The muskets slid neatly through the small holes; a moment later, they fired.

The second rank advanced past them, and repeated that procedure; then the third. Meanwhile the first rank reloaded, then picked up their shields and advanced again.

"They're firing about six volleys to Pompey's one," Chrysamen said. "It looks like this is it."

Pompey's forces took the first couple of volleys on the shield wall, with only a couple of men falling, either by stray rounds that had enough energy to penetrate the shields, or more likely shots that had found their way through niches between. But as Caesar's force worked its way inexorably forward, shots began to break through, and the wall wavered. The next time Pompey's front centurions turned their shields for their own musketeers to fire a volley, two of the musketeers and several of the legionaries fell; before they could reorganize, another volley tore into them.

Centurions bellowed commands, and Pompey's legion broke its shield wall and trotted forward. A half dozen men in each century fell over dead as another of Caesar's musket volleys struck, but they kept coming, like the real Romans they were, maintaining their positions.

The centurions barked almost in unison, and a flight of *pila* sailed toward Caesar's forces; unable to raise their shields quickly, many men were killed and wounded. The second flight of *pila* found them better prepared, but still many hit home. Moreover, the two flights of javelins had disrupted Caesar's volleys, which were now coming more raggedly along the line.

If Pompey's men had somehow been carrying two more *pila* each, for a total of four, they might have carried right through. But with that much weight, they couldn't have moved.

And when the javelins stopped falling, most of Caesar's legionaries were still alive and well. As I watched from the wall, distance glasses set for a fairly wide view, the second rank of Caesar's troops moved forward and knelt beside the first, forming a tighter line. All of them slung their shields to their backs, but stayed kneeling.

The third and fourth ranks closed up into a single line, and now there were just two lines. The troops in the rear line also slung their *scuta,* and stood up.

"*Street Firing!*" I said.

"What?" Chrys asked.

"Street Firing! I recognize it from my trips to Revolutionary America. It's the system for getting the highest rate of fire out of a unit of muzzle loaders—"

The first rank fired; a great cloud of black-powder smoke

belched forth, and the field was obscured as it blew back. I clicked
to infrared, and saw the soldiers stand, as the second rank stepped
through to kneel behind them. Even as they stood, their hands
stayed busy—"Of course! Caldwell gave them percussion caps! It
takes a lot less time to load than a flintlock—they just ram down a
paper cartridge whole, set a cap on the nipple, cock the hammer,
and shoot. No tearing the cartridge open, no firing pan or priming
powder to deal with. Right now those troops could—"

The new first rank, now kneeling, fired, but this time when
they stood they stepped back. "Now that Pompey's men are trying
to close up," I said, "they're backing up to prevent them from
closing, and make them take more volleys before it gets down to
cold steel. I wonder if Caesar invented all of this? It would be like
him—"

There was another huge boom as a volley ripped into Pompey's
troops. Through the smoke, using infrared, I could see what was
happening—Pompey's men were struggling through the thick,
choking clouds, trying to keep their positions, their lines being
raked by the volleys coming at them. Meanwhile, Caesar's centuries
were leapfrogging backward, firing at what had to be six rounds
per minute—twice as fast as the best British troops had done in
1800. It was turning into a slaughter.

The Romans had a verb, "*superare,*" for what Caesar's legions
were doing to Pompey's—usually it's translated as "overcame" or
"defeated," but it means more than that. It means "they threw
their swords and shields down and ran like bunnies." Which is
exactly what happened at that moment.

I saw Caesar's men stand up, form ranks, draw their *gladii* and
bring their *scuta* back to guard position, and advance on the
double. Now it would be naked butchery.

Something moved in my peripheral vision, and I scanned the
back of the battlefield. No question they were loading the "Stalin
organs," which I had expected, but—

There was a big, dark mass there, and it was splitting in half
like an amoeba. I stared . . . I considered . . .

"Shit," Chrys said. "This is all a setup for Hannibal's double
bow."

"I think you're right."

It was just about the most famous battle plan of ancient history.
You advance in a long curved line with the center contacting the

enemy first. The center fights hard, then turns and runs away. Since there are no radios on the ancient battlefield, no general can tell his men to "hang back." The enemy pursue into the center, as your big curving line turns inside out.

Then your center meets up with your reserves, your flanks close in, and the enemy is caught in a crossfire and surrounded.

The giveaway to all that is when troops in the reserve body at the rear start to flow toward the flanks, instead of up to the middle where the fighting is.

And Chrys had just spotted that.

I scanned the field. Sure enough, Pompey's flanks were moving in fast. Moreover, the legions on the flanks were, all of them, equipped with muskets, and the cavalry had long heavy lances like a medieval knight's. "They're going to crash in any second now," I said, and even as I spoke, the legions went to double time, and the auxiliaries broke into a trot.

Gaulish cavalry from both of Caesar's flanks charged to meet the threat.

"Looks like we're going to see whether the pistol or the lance is superior," I said.

And then we heard a familiar sound—a deep, bass buzz that is made by only one thing in the universe—

—*a SHAKK firing on full auto.*

It took me a moment to find where the sound was coming from, and then I saw—Caesar himself stood on a small wooden tower, holding the SHAKK, spraying one of Pompey's flanks.

He didn't really have to aim and he didn't bother. The S in SHAKK stands for "Seeking"—each individual round was finding a target. There are two thousand rounds in the magazine of an ATN-issued SHAKK, and Caesar had two of those; he sprayed down Pompey's left flank with one of them, picked up the other, and sprayed Pompey's right flank with the other. Then he calmly pulled out the SHAKK-equivalents that Porter and Paula had been given—they had smaller magazines because they had smarter ammo, rounds that communicated with each other in flight and picked targets based on maximum coverage and evaluated threat. He emptied five hundred rounds from each of those, again spraying each side equally.

I was finding myself thinking of a lot of Latin today. Our word "decimate" comes from the Latin for "ten"—if you killed ten men out of a century, the century was usually too disrupted to fight effectively.

That was approximately what Caesar, single-handedly, had just done. Everywhere out there, men or horses were converted into bags of red jam and collapsed. It was terrifying and inexplicable, and the scent of so much blood maddened the horses. Furthermore, the more-advanced SHAKKs from the Roman future apparently had some way of spotting officers, for every centurion and legate on the field seemed to fall victim to them.

By the time the Gauls got to the front ranks, neither Pompey's legions nor his cavalry had any effective command at all. They collapsed in a screaming mess, some trying to fight, many to run away, some just to hide and stay alive. The Gauls didn't make any fine distinctions—they used their horse pistols on everything that wasn't Caesar's.

Even the ones who were trying to surrender.

Sickened, I looked away, and scanned to the back. Pompey's center didn't know that when the trap had sprung, its jaws had broken. Thus they moved forward confidently, not knowing the battle was lost. At the range I couldn't see exactly, but I knew more or less what happened from the clouds of smoke and the glimpses I was able to catch.

Caesar's forces advanced until the last of Pompey's old, false center fled into the reserves ahead. By now Pompey must have known something was wrong, but not quite what it was, by the fact that so few of his front line had returned. They were supposed to *fake* losing, not get clobbered.

Then the legions of Caesar stopped as one man, formed up for Street Firing, and waited for the surge out of Pompey's reserves. They didn't have to wait long.

As Pompey's legions attacked, this time all carrying muskets and *pila*, Caesar's troops opened up at long range. Pompey's men formed the shield wall, turned the shields to fire from behind it, and continued.

"Not as dumb as we thought he was," Chrysamen commented.

"Well, historically he had a good rep," I said. "But look how tricky Caesar is here—his troops are backing up in Street Firing, and between lugging a firearm *and* javelins, Pompey's troops are weighed down. Caesar's men can fire and retreat faster than Pompey can advance, and Caesar's giving them several rounds for every one of theirs. They may not know it yet, but they're going to lose."

A moment later we saw exactly how they would lose. Caesar's mule-drawn field artillery had finally gotten into place on the flanks of his legions, now that Pompey's flanks were eliminated. It became quite evident that Hasmonea had given him grape and canister shot—the trick of loading a cannon with musket balls, to make it work like a giant shotgun, or of putting the musket balls in a paper canister that would then burn away in flight, leaving them in a tighter pattern.

And the reason it became evident was that Pompey's troops went over like bowling pins. They were packed in close, and the field artillery simply tore huge holes in their lines, slaughtering dozens and hundreds at a shot. Within two minutes, as the guns continued to boom on both flanks, Pompey's center collapsed really, and for good.

It was an utter, smashing victory for Caesar, and though I couldn't say yet what difference it would make, I knew that all of history had just been altered; Caesar would not have to pursue Pompey to Spain to beat him, at least—

There was a white-hot flash on my distance glasses. I had set them for infrared; now what had they picked up? I was all but dazzled—

"Shit!" Chrys said. "*Down!*"

I trusted her reflexes too much to ask; I was on my belly before I had really figured out what she had said. I drew a long deep breath, and heard a high-pitched scream—

There were a dozen powerful explosions nearby. I turned, and looked to see flames leaping up from several places in the city. I heard a distant rumble and realized—"Those Stalin organs!" I set my glasses back to normal vision so as not to be blinded, and peered over the wall.

A dozen bright flashes in less than a minute meant that perhaps two hundred rockets were on their way, and behind me I heard the first few land in the city. A preindustrial city has no pumped running water, and its alleys are full of hovels that burn like matchwood. The city was going to die in flames; nothing and no one could stop it now. Curtains of flame were leaping into the air, and sobbing and screaming resounded in all directions.

I looked back the way we had come to the wall, to the villa six blocks away with Paula and Porter in it. It was already on fire.

Grimly, Chrys and I vaulted down the ladders and raced up the street, hoping to reach the burning villa before the hysterical mob, just beginning to form, could block our way.

·12·

Within two blocks I started to doubt that we would make it. I found out later that Pompey's rockets were his own invention—he wasn't a stupid man, in fact he was one of the best generals the world has ever seen, but his reputation has always suffered a bit because he was up against Julius Caesar.

In this timeline his luck was even worse than it was in mine. When the Senate realized how fast Caesar could move, they still didn't act like people with an emergency on—they acted like rich people who needed to save their financial assets in a hurry. This was perhaps not so surprising, since the Roman Senate was not elected—it was made up of retired high-level civil servants, almost all from the hereditary nobility, plus a few who had bought their way in. Thus they decided they needed a few days to get their more important possessions onto ships and out of Caesar's reach, and this mattered much more than the lives of Pompey's men, so to get those few days, they told Pompey that either he could give up his army (and let them send it to its death under some political hack) or he could go fight Caesar right now.

Pompey wasn't nearly the shrewd politician that Caesar, or even Crassus, was. He had actually disbanded his army when he was supposed to, once, when he was younger, and been horribly shocked and disappointed when the Senate promptly kicked his veterans in the teeth and undid all the arrangements he had made for them. Still, he knew he was being had—but there was a simple problem. The Senate was the real soul of the Roman state, and everyone knew it. If you didn't have the Senate, you weren't really the leader, and whatever you did was never quite legitimate.

On the other hand, if the Senate made you consul, or dictator—even if they did it with your army's bayonets at their throats—you were in. You were legit. Anyone else was a usurper.

Pompey didn't have an army the size of either Caesar's or Crassus's. He didn't have Crassus's vast empire in the East or tremendous wealth, and he didn't have Caesar's new possessions in Britain and Gaul, let alone the more advanced tech both of them had. All he had was a good record, the admiration of many citizens, the respect of his soldiers—and a claim to legitimacy, via the Senate, that the other two did not.

When the Triumvirate had been organized among the three men, to divide up power, Pompey had thought he was the senior partner—he was higher ranking and had a more distinguished record than Caesar, and he certainly had more prestige than Crassus. But in a three-way contest between glory, brains, and money, don't bet on glory.

So it was not a surprise to discover that he had been tinkering with some of the toys that Hasmonea and Walks-in-His-Shadow Caldwell had brought, and made some improvements of his own. I later learned that what Pompey had come up with amounted to a crude kind of napalm—Hasmonea had introduced distilling, and Pompey had played around with distilling petroleum—in little "bomblets" with percussion-cap tips, all tied together at their tails with a gunpowder-filled knot. When the rocket burned out, it lit the gunpowder knot and set the cardboard nose cone on fire; long before the bomblets hit, they were all tumbling freely, and came down widely scattered.

There were ten bomblets to a rocket, and each bomblet was about five pounds of napalm, to be blown apart with half a pound of black powder. That meant that, when Pompey fired his two hundred rockets into the city of Falerii, he set somewhere just under two thousand fires.

Preindustrial cities burn very easily. That's why in all the cities in all the timelines that haven't advanced far enough to have piped water and regular fire companies, there is always an unwritten but important rule—no matter what else is happening, if fire breaks out, everyone fights it, because any fire could lose the whole city for you.

Unless, of course, the city is already lost—and if that's the case, then the rule is, run and save yourself.

Three big fires, or five, would have been a struggle for Falerii to fight in normal times. It wasn't a large city. And ten separate fires would probably have been too much to hold against.

Many hundreds meant there was no hope, and everyone knew it.

I never did find out whether Pompey's rockets were fired as a sort of last "spite hit" to stop Caesar from pursuing his army and let the remnants escape, or if perhaps the rocketeers had their orders and carried them out because that was when the launch was supposed to happen and no one told them not to.

But whatever the reason, when Chrys and I tried to fight our way up that street, there was little hope. Dozens of buildings were on fire, and the air was thick with the stench of burning thatch, rich and heavy like a compost heap on fire. Underneath it, already, there was the more acrid smell of wood burning and plaster roasting, the wet ammonia smell of blazing stables, the occasional scent of charred meat where some luckless soul was trapped.

You've probably never heard a whole city scream at once. My suggestion is that you avoid ever hearing it if you can help it. Horses, men, cows, women, chickens, cats, sheep, dogs, children, everything that had a voice was roaring its terror into the street.

As the crowd packed thick around us, Chrys and I found it harder and harder to push and shove our way through. We were trying to figure out what we could do; you can use martial arts to get through a mob only if none of them are armed and there's somewhere for all of them to go. We were bare-handed, and no one could hear us or would have much cared that we wanted to go the opposite way. There was no likely way to get through, and the side streets were already turning into seas of fire as the little lean-tos the poor built there went up in blazes. As I was pinned for a moment against a wall by an alley, I saw a woman in rags rooting through a collapsed, blazing lean-to; a moment later she pulled out a bundle, and I realized it was her baby.

The child must have been dead, for the woman screamed, and as her head cloth fell back I saw she was a lot younger than Porter.

Then I saw that her clothing was burning, smoke pouring off the hem of her skirt, about to go up in flame.

It's senseless but true—in the middle of a burning city, surrounded by a mob, you can be as ruthless as anyone, but when you see one single isolated crisis, you can suddenly find yourself forgetting even an urgent errand or self-preservation, because even though we all have plenty of the beast in us, we also all have plenty of civilized training. Neither one wins all the time.

I darted into the alley, tackled her, tore off the biggest burning piece, stamped out the rest, and yanked her to her feet. Her legs were horribly red, and I expected that the blisters of second-degree burns would start at any moment, but I shoved her hard to get her running before she collapsed, toward the city gate. I never saw her again. I have no idea what became of her.

I looked around. Chrys had not followed me. The alley was filling with smoke and getting unbearably hot as stone walls reflected the burning junk and hovels; I did not try to run back to the street I had been on, but instead ran around the corner to see if the side street there was as yet unburned.

It was. That meant I had a clear passage, and I managed to run a long way toward the villa before, very suddenly, a huge load of roof tiles from one of the buildings plunged into the alley in front of me. I leaped back, choking from the hot dust and smoke that came with it, and looked up to see evil orange flame licking the sky from the three-story building that had burned to a shell; I dove sideways to the left, down another alley, and then was flung flat by the gust of blazing wind as the wall came down behind me with a grinding, ripping crash.

Jumping to my feet, I hurled myself down the alley—the jet of flame that had passed over my back while I lay prone had ignited dozens of flammable surfaces, and I had to get out of there in the seconds before the alley became a furnace.

I made it with not much time to spare; there was a sort of "whump" sound behind me as the fresh fires grabbed a lot of the oxygen and pushed out a harsh wave of heat.

I was back in the main street. The building across the way was blazing, the one beside it had fires inside—and the next one was the villa where we had left Porter and Paula asleep that morning. I ran toward it; its roof was being licked by flames from under the eaves, but perhaps—

I rushed toward the building, and was just approaching the main doorbell when something knocked me flat. A moment later I was being held down on the ground, and, inexplicably, somebody was slapping at me and pounding me with hands—I placed my hands to roll suddenly and get at them—

"Boss-don't-it's-me-and-you're-on-fire!"

It was Paula, and what she had been doing was beating out the blaze on the back of my tunic, which must have gotten set on fire while I was getting out of the alley. She let me up and I rolled over. The air was unbelievably hot and dry, the smoke terribly thick, and I was gasping, not least because even when she's doing it to help, if Paula slaps you, you have been *slapped*.

Porter was standing beside her, looking very worried. "Chrysamen—" I gasped out.

"She's not with you?"

"We got separated." I sat up, wheezed, and gagged. Here, in the open street, it was blazing hot in January, and dark with smoke despite the sunlight, but we were far enough away from any individual burning building to take stock for a moment. "I last saw her about two hundred yards back—" When I pointed, I looked. "Shit."

There was one vast sheet of flame across the street; one whole side of the Praetorium had come down into the street, and the rugs, furniture, tapestries, and all were burning there.

"Well, it's for sure she didn't come that way, and she won't," Paula said. "Do you think she followed you?"

"I'm pretty sure she didn't," I said. "And if she did, the way got cut off in front of her. I'm going to try not to panic about this. She can certainly handle herself, but, on the other hand, *anything* can happen out there. Anybody could have bad luck. We didn't have time to set up a rendezvous point—we were trying to get back to you guys."

Paula nodded. "Well, it's for sure she won't stay in the city. And neither should we. What happened in the battle? Caesar must have gotten clobbered."

I shook my head. "Caesar won. This was sort of Pompey's last gasp. I don't know how much baggage train they lost, but his legions still have all their fighting gear and their bicycles, and with Pompey's army in a shambles, this force can be in Rome tomorrow.

It's down to Crassus versus Caesar. And from what I've seen, I'd
bet on Caesar."

"Me too," Porter said. "Why are you so down on him? Is it
because you're looking for an excuse to . . . you know?"

"Could be. Could also be that I notice how many other people
suffer and die for his great achievements. To paraphrase a great
poem, 'Caesar conquered Gaul / Did he take no one with him? /
Not even a cook?' Meaning he does great things—for Caesar. And
what I just saw out there was an ingeniously orchestrated murder
of a whole army—of his fellow Romans, mind you. There are probably twenty thousand dead, or more, out there, for Caesar's ambi-
tion. I don't exactly call that patriotic, no matter what he does for
the country afterward." I peered at her intently. "Are you being
pulled in by his charm? Do you want them calling *you* 'Face Down'
sometime soon?"

Porter sighed. "No, not really. I mean, no, I'm not falling for
him or anything. All I meant was . . . well, he's fascinating. And of
course he likes my music, and there's something about flattery from
a famous genius . . ."

"I understand," I said, thinking of how it felt when I got to
meet and become friends with Wernher von Braun, Dr. Samuel
Johnson, Daniel Webster, Leonardo da Vinci, and George Washington, among many others. For that matter I certainly hadn't
taken them up on it, but I'd kind of enjoyed the attention from
Oscar Wilde and Michelangelo. So I knew some of what Porter was
feeling.

The trouble was that Caesar was still a spectacularly dangerous
man, in every sense of the word.

"Anyway," I said, "chances are good that Chrysamen will find
us." Inspiration hit, and I said, "And she probably still has her
transponder-tracker. She can find me with that, for sure. So she
will."

"Transponder-tracker?" Paula asked. "Are you wearing a transponder?"

"Yep, inside one of the bones in my pelvic girdle. Approximately the same place Chrys wears hers. Unfortunately I'm not
quite the wizard smuggler that Chrys is—she managed to hang on
to her tracker. But if I'm within about two miles, she can find me."

"And if you're not?"

"Then she'll keep looking until I turn up at the right distance.

She's as good at this as I am, you know. Let's get going." The very last thing I wanted to do was to worry about Chrysamen any more than I already was—and I was already feeling sick with worry. True, the Romans from the future of this timeline had acted like they expected her back when they showed up to take me to the victory parade . . . but, on the other hand, they'd gotten some things wrong. And there was something or other they didn't want to tell me about the whole assassination of Caesar bit, as well.

So the range of things I had to worry about was so large that if I had had the time, I could have sat down and spent the next several hours doing nothing else but worry about them. And that would get nothing accomplished toward alleviating the problem.

So I needed to shake off the fears and worries, remind myself that Chrysamen was not just a big girl but one of the toughest people in a million timelines, and focus on the problem at hand.

"Probably if we move fast, we can escape from Caesar," I said, "but it's an interesting question whether we want to. He has most of our gear and all kinds of valuable resources, and I have no doubt he'd help us look for Chrys. And his offer of a temporary alliance seemed perfectly legit to me. We could just link backup with him and take advantage of what he has to offer—not to mention build quite a bit of trust in him."

"And if we escape?" Porter said.

"Well, then we have no money, no tools worth speaking of, zip for weapons other than bare hands—"

"And this," Paula said, producing a .38 snubnose from somewhere or other, "and I've got a nice little switchblade, but it would take me a second to fish it out, boss."

"You've got a lot of talent," I said, "and I hope ATN processes your job application a long time before they process Caesar's."

"Might take you up on that." The pistol vanished, and this time I was watching. It didn't help.

"Well, then, we'd be lightly armed. Otherwise out in the cold. Hard to say how we'd solve the problem," I said.

Porter nodded. "You've worked that way before."

"Yeah, by myself or with Chrys. Paula, I think, has had some relevant practice. But I'm afraid we don't know whether you have any talent for all this, Porter. How'd you feel about the guys you shot after Robbie got hit?"

"I threw up a lot, and I was pretty upset."

"And you know you have the same habit any musician does, worrying about hurting your hands. Could you forget about your hands for the duration, and just figure ATN would fix them afterward? They have the medical tech to do anything up to and including growing you new ones."

"Looking out for my hands is kind of a habit by now." She sighed. "I'm a little scared of Caesar, but I guess the advantages are all that way. And besides, I'm sorry, but I have a pretty good memory for what sleeping rough was like—and it's not a good memory."

I nodded. I wasn't comfortable myself with those months she had spent on the street at age thirteen. "All right, mixed bag on that side, leaning toward going with Caesar. Paula?"

"Caesar makes me nervous, too, but if we leave him, the first thing we will have to come up with is some way to keep track of him," Paula said. "And we have no idea which side is the most desirable; no reason to think Crassus is any better, except maybe that he's old and fat and couldn't rape kids if he wanted to. So we might as well stay put; right now nobody is mad at us, and Caesar would be a bad person to have mad at us."

"Then it's unanimous," I said. "Let's cut through this alley to the next major street, head out the gate, and see what we can find; for all we know, Chrys is standing around waiting for us to be smart enough to leave a burning city."

The big square we were in was a lot safer than most other places—Falerii was neither large enough nor built high enough to have a firestorm like a modern city might—and the real problem was figuring out the safest way to get from it to a gate. We finally settled on walking through an alley that was already burned out to the next large street over; that turned out to be unblocked, so we walked up it toward the city gate.

There were a few bodies in the street; most of them were probably disguised crime, people bashing a rich guy to get the jewels or gold he was carrying. In the age before plastic, credit cards, or banks, disasters were the best possible time for robbery.

We emerged from the gate. There was no trace of Chrys, so we walked toward the side of the city on which the battle had been fought. We might as well have been all alone on the planet.

Now that we were out of the burning town, it was very suddenly clear just how cold the day really was, and that evening was coming on. The sun was just barely above the dark blue of the western hills, the sky had turned a deep blue smudged with a little black, and the cold air was finding its way through the holes in my clothes. I shivered; this would be a bad night to spend in the open, with as little gear as we had. We might end up going back into the city just to find a fire to sleep next to.

I glanced back behind us. Falerii's walls still stood; no shot or ram had touched them. But from behind them, there were columns of whirling sparks, streams of ink black smoke, and occasional still-rising flames. The city's gates were thrown open, and through them there was only the flickering light of fire; the arched gates in the white walls of the city looked like the eyeholes of a skull, and the fire was like the delusion of a madman, capering and dancing visibly in that empty city, through those empty eyes.

I shivered, and we continued on around, aiming to join the Via Flaminia as it ran toward Rome, for surely Caesar would be on it or near it.

"You!" a voice shouted.

I turned. A legate was riding up on a bicycle. "Are you speaking to us?" I asked.

He stood very straight and erect. "I am ordered by Caesar himself to bring you to Caesar; he has need to confer with you. I am ordered not to harm you, but to use force if necessary."

"It won't be necessary," I said, "but I'd like to know how you would have used it without harming us, if it had been."

There was a faint twitch in the legate's stiff upper lip, which he contained, and then he said, "Best, then, that we don't try. I am not sure what I would do either, sir. But I was instructed to find four of you; where is the fourth?"

"Gods, I wish we knew," I said.

·13·

"So she has simply vanished," Caesar said, that evening. We had only a few minutes to meet with him, for the victory celebration was extensive, and he was expected to put in an appearance at many different parts of it. He had dropped by the tent where they quartered us; little more than a pup tent, it was originally intended for two people at most, but the army's supply of shelter had been severely stressed by the need to get the town in out of the weather.

"That's about it," I agreed. "If she were nearby, she'd have contacted me by now."

Caesar nodded. "I've given orders that any body looking at all like hers is not to be buried; we'll let you check for her among the dead. But from what you say, it seems terribly unlikely that she was killed."

There was something deeply reassuring in the way he said that; it made me feel, at once, that he believed it, too. I don't know if that was just his amazing political sense, or if it was just Caesar facing facts as he always did. Either way I was comforted.

And that kindness he had just shown made the next thing I had to do all the more difficult. "You realize," I said, "that since it is ineffective to upbraid you, I won't, but I'm quite annoyed by your appropriation of our weapons to your cause this morning."

Caesar nodded. "I can understand that you might be. I ask only that you understand that I am a general; men's lives depend on what I do. It is my job to keep my men alive, and to make sure that the dying is done by the enemy. I could not and would not do things any differently. I can also imagine that you will be in some trouble over having allowed those weapons to fall into my hands. You have my sympathy, but I think an apology unwarranted."

"I understand," I said. And strangely enough, I no longer seemed to be angry. I even thanked him. He asked if Porter had been able to save her flute or lyre, and when it turned out she hadn't, he told her he'd have new ones sent around in the morning. Then he smiled, said that this stop was more interesting than most of the others, and was out the door. I heard later that he visited everywhere that night, from enlisted men drinking around a bonfire to officers throwing orgies with slaves, and at every one he was friendly, polite, a little distant, and warmly appreciative of what the legion, century, cohort, or tribe of Gauls or Britons had done that day.

I suppose you can never really explain how someone has that kind of effect. You can only note that they do, and marvel at it.

Meanwhile, Chrysamen was still missing, possibly staying loose but nearby, possibly off on some promising tangent of her own, and possibly in real trouble. The bed was pretty lonely that night; you can remind yourself a lot of times how professional someone is, and how many bad spots she's been in, but at three in the morning the thought that she could be dead in a ditch tends to keep coming back anyway.

Even though it was terribly cold, I was glad to see the sun come up the next morning—and I rolled out of the too-big bed at the first sign of light through the fabric of the tent. At last I could stop pretending that I could sleep, get up, get moving, and see what I could do about the problem.

The attendant, a little British kid who spoke some Latin, went to grab me some breakfast from a legion mess, as I hastily dressed. He came back with a heavy, brownish glop that was made by boiling wheat and rye flour, a small pitcher of scalding-hot milk, two hard-boiled eggs, and a fistful of prunes. I wolfed most of it down in just a few minutes, and gave the rest to the kid, who was just hitting that age when you can't possibly get too many calories.

"Are they feeding you?" I asked, wondering how the remnants had vanished so quickly.

"Oh, yes, they are, I'm just hungry all the time, master," the boy said. "Is the lady going to come back? Is she all right?"

"I'm working on that," I said.

"She's very kind," he said.

This didn't surprise me; Chrys wants to keep every stray kitten that finds its way to our doorstep back home in Pittsburgh.

"She is," I agreed. "I'm doing what I can for her. When the others rise, tell them I'll be back for the midday meal, unless something comes up."

"Yes, sir."

Soldiers get up early for a lot of reasons, and in wintertime anyone who works outdoors gets up early because there's only so much time that the lights are on and you don't want to waste it. So the camp was already bustling and busy, with legion messes going full blast, legates drafting orders for the day, centurions checking on the readiness of their centuries, farmers driving in livestock that they hoped to sell to Caesar. Even as worried as I was, it's pretty hard not to crack a grin when a guy in a big straw hat, which looks sort of like a sombrero with a pointy top, cuts across your path herding a dozen squalling geese.

I hadn't gone far when the little British attendant came running up behind me, gasping, "Word from Caesar, sir. He says he's heard something about the lady, and he will see you in his tent as soon as you can get there."

I tipped him five times what you're supposed to and got to Caesar's tent at a dead run.

Caesar wasn't a guy who lived cheap, or who roughed it on purpose. That tent was a lot more comfortable than most of my student apartments, or than Marie's and my first apartment. They had spread ground cloths and put heavy carpets over them; there was a second, inner tent to hold the warmth, and slaves brought in heated rocks from the fire outside to keep the place warm—indeed they ran in and out constantly, always careful to pull flaps closed behind them so that hot air didn't escape.

The rocks were great big thirty-pounders, so hot that you could see that most of the slaves had a lot of little burns from wherever the cloth in which the rocks were wrapped had slipped; they ran frantically, and I knew they were probably scared to death of what might happen if they screwed the job up.

It might be a hell of a place to be a slave, but it was pretty comfortable to be Caesar. He was naked when I got there, just stepping into his tub, which was steaming hot and perfumed with dried rose petals. (I could just imagine Generals Patton, Washington, Gordon, Giap, Crazy Horse, Sherman, or Marlborough—all of whom I had known fairly well in one timeline or another—having "rose petals," "perfumed soap," and, for that matter, a "large bathtub" in the baggage train. It was a bad century to be a grunt, and a pretty good one to be a general—but then most centuries are that way.)

Over in the corner, I saw a couple of slave women tending to the little girl that seemed to be Caesar's current favorite victim; she was crying, but all they were doing was first aid. I thought seriously, then, about a way the world would be better if I pulled the trigger on Gaius Julius Caesar, and that might have been a great moment to do it, but if there was news of Chrys . . .

"Thank you for your promptness," Caesar said, lowering himself into the tub. I noted abstractly that, at least in the light of the little oil lamps, he looked pretty good for his age; his body was still hard and lean, with little extra flesh, and though he was almost entirely bald now and his skin was lined and wrinkled from all the time he spent outside, still the muscles underneath would have looked good on a man twenty years younger than he was. It was the kind of body that fascinates a modernist sculptor, not classically beautiful or perfectly proportioned, but worn and shaped by its work and habits until the body becomes a perfect expression of the character, until if you can capture what he really looks like, you've captured the man's soul.

I thought about what it would be like to pull out Paula's .38, jam it behind that lean jaw just by the ear so that the round would cut the carotid on its way in, and pull the trigger. The little girl in the corner started to sob, and one of the slave women slapped her silent.

It would feel pretty good to shoot Caesar, on the whole. Just as soon as I found out about Chrys.

"We received a message earlier today," Caesar said, "from Pompey. I have never been very fond of Cnaeus Pompeius 'Magnus.' " The way he said "magnus," which means "the great" and was a name awarded to Pompey by the Senate, was loaded with such vicious bitterness that you'd have thought Caesar was spitting out rat turds. "And I think you and I may share this opinion." A slave brought up a small silver salver, on which was a written note and something else. He held it out to me, and Caesar said, "Read."

I lifted the message and read:

> *To Gaius Julius Caesar from Cnaeus Pompeius Magnus, greetings.*
>
> *I have something here, the evidence of which I enclose, which will be of great interest to one who travels with you. I shall await you in Rome, and there I will treat with you for whatever terms you care to offer me for the safe return of this thing.*
>
> *That is, if Great Caesar is still his own master, and not the lackey of the one he travels with. I offer the thing I have to either of you, indifferently; I wish terms, and honorable terms, and will hold this thing only so long as is needed. While I hold it, however, you will neither enter Rome, nor fire upon the city, nor surround it or blockade it, upon pain of losing this much-valued thing forever.*
>
> *I await your reply.*

The "Great Caesar" was a calculated insult; Caesar had not been granted such a title as Pompey had. The message seemed alarmingly clear, and when I looked back at the salver, it confirmed my worst fears—there was a hank of Chrysamen's dark, curly hair. I looked closely, but, speaking as her husband, friend, and lover of many years, I was quite certain it was hers.

Then I looked again, peered closely, and hissed with fury.

"Yes," Caesar agreed, "it looks very much as if it has been pulled out by the roots."

"I don't know how he could have—"

"Quite. But I am told that when his damned rockets flew yesterday, he was quite near the point of launch, and when my men closed in to overthrow the launchers, Pompey escaped on his bicycle, back through my lines, into the confusion between my army and the city. We would guess he hid among the refugees after dark—"

"But he's one of the most widely known faces in Roman territory!" I protested.

"Just so and part of that boldness of his," Caesar said. "I've never faulted his manhood or his guts. He is, after all, Rome's second-best general. At any rate, one of my agents thought he saw

Pompey in the city, shortly after the rockets fell and the fires began, but unfortunately failed to take steps because it seemed too impossible to him. It's the sort of disaster that happens whenever a slave attempts to think.

"At any rate, I have learned a few things from this. One is that, as I should have anticipated, Pompey's intelligence is first-rate, and he already knew the significance of you and your party, including knowing enough to be able to recognize all of you. Probably he struck within minutes of your being separated."

"He'd have to be hell on wheels at hand-to-hand," I said. "In a fight to the death between Chrys and me, you'd have to bet it fifty-five me forty-five Chrys, but that's just based on difference in body size. She's a bit faster and a little more skilled than I am."

Caesar scratched his head. "It doesn't entirely make sense, I admit; I had thought of that myself. But his evidence does look like evidence—and we hardly want him to produce anything more convincing, after all."

I shuddered. "Right. So we at least have to assume he's captured her and is taking her to Rome with him. I'd call that more than enough bad news. Now what can be done about it?"

Caesar smiled grimly. "Exactly the question to be discussed. It seems to me that you are used to operating by yourself, that you have a notable ability to improvise, and so forth. That's my first reason for sending you after her."

"You have others?"

"I doubt you'll be any use to me until she is rescued."

I had to admit, silently, that he had a point.

"Therefore," he went on, "I am deputizing you to go rescue Chrysamen, and you are authorized to do whatever you think fit for the purpose. If by some accident a few of Caesar's enemies should die—" Caesar said, grinning, "—do remember that I am currently the most popular author of histories, and, moreover, that most of Rome's better-known prosecutors, notably that prissy prude Cicero, are on the other side and will have no authority. So little harm will come to you from such circumstances."

"I understand," I said.

"Now, there's the matter of armament," he said. "If you would like to reload one of the weapons I used yesterday, and take it with you, then—"

I had been thinking ahead of him, and I said, "I'm sorry, but there's no way to reload them in this timeline. We don't normally use them on full auto, so the number of shots in the magazine is far in excess of what we can be expected to need—but now that it's drained, it's drained. It would have to go home for a refill."

I was lying to him. If he knew that, he would probably kill me right now. If not, then he wouldn't be able to use the SHAKKs again, and his plan of world conquest would take a big step backward. It seemed worth the gamble.

The fact is that the "ammo powder" we feed into SHAKKs is merely a carefully balanced mixture of the chemical elements needed, so that the elemental separator won't have to spend any time or power pulling out the excess of things it doesn't need to make ammunition. But in fact you can load them with anything that will go into the hopper—sand, rocks, bugs, scrap metal, seawater (sea salt, rusty nails, and sawdust works pretty well), hot fudge sundaes. It really doesn't care as long as it gets enough of each element.

If Caesar merely stuffed some miscellaneous junk into the reload slot of each SHAKK, in very little time they'd be as deadly as ever, with thousands of fresh shots in each magazine. This was the last thing I wanted him to know.

It was always possible that he knew already, and this was a trap, in which case I would be executed in about five minutes, tops. I was betting he didn't.

I won my bet. He shrugged. "Well, that's the way of it then. I shall retain the other devices I confiscated, though I don't expect that you or your companions will explain them unless I torture one of you, which would be the end of voluntary cooperation. Since your voluntary cooperation is valuable, and I can probably conquer the whole world without the use of the superweapons, clearly it is best for me to refrain from such methods . . . though if either of those circumstances should change, well, then that decision would have to be reevaluated, wouldn't it?

"Still, it seems that I ought to provide you with a better weapon, and I note that you do have along one very simple-seeming gadget, something that bears a great similarity to our muskets." He gestured to a slave, who handed me my .45 Colt automatic, plus all the clips of ammunition I had been carrying. "We assumed it was a gun and treated it like one, so it has been kept from moisture, extreme heat, and extreme cold. I hope we have not damaged it."

"They're hard to damage," I said, "and it should be fine. I'll strip and clean it before I go."

"Excellent. Am I right in my surmise that the percussion cap is somehow included in the cartridge, and that the device is set up to cock itself and chamber another round after each shot?"

"That's the basics," I said.

"I shall have my armorers think about these things at some length," Caesar said. "And why are the casings brass, instead of paper, which burns away?"

Sometimes the best way to slow somebody down is to make him conscious of the difficulty of what he's trying to do, so I explained, as casually and accurately as I could manage, "Oh, because if you load at the breech, you need to seal the breech against gas leaks, and that's what the brass does that the paper couldn't do. You have to use a special kind of brass, I don't know exactly how that's made, so that it will expand to seal but still eject easily. Also, to get the very high muzzle velocities these things have—this weapon isn't very accurate but its slugs are deadly at four times the distance your muskets can achieve—you have to seal everything tightly, and right now you aren't making iron good enough for the job." I figured that I didn't really want to tell him about steel, either.

Caesar nodded, turned to a slave who had been standing quietly by, and said, "Repeat that, please." The slave recited exactly what I had said, pauses and all.

I congratulated him on his accuracy, and Caesar said, "It's his accuracy that makes Memorex valuable."

I gaped for a second, and then asked, "How did he get his name?"

"Oddly enough, he was named by your agent, Walks-in-His-Shadow Caldwell. He said it was an honored name in your time-line."

"It certainly is," I hastened to say. No reason to hurt poor Memorex's feelings. I was beginning to really look forward to meeting Walks-in-His-Shadow Caldwell, however; the guy's sense of humor appealed to me, every time I ran into an example of it. "I was just surprised to hear the word here. If I may, then, I'll draw a pack of supplies from one of your quartermasters, take the bicycle I've been using, and be on my way within the hour."

"Excellent," Caesar said. "Oh—an afterthought. It occurs to me that the safest place possible for your two remaining female friends to be is here with my army. That is, it's the safest place for them if you and I truly are the friends I hope we are. If on the other hand, you have any *other* notions about it, from my standpoint, it is also the safest possible place for your two friends to be. So naturally they will be staying here."

That was not an afterthought, as he had said it was. That was the thought he wanted me to leave with. "I expected as much," I said, and smiled in the friendliest way I could manage.

He smiled back at me, and said, "Gods and fates aid your genius, Marcus Fortius."

"Be strong, Caesar," I said. And with that, a slave showed me to the door.

By the time I got back, the others were just getting up. I sent the little British slave to fetch me a packed field kit from the quartermaster, at Caesar's instruction if they asked. That got at least one set of ears out of the tent, and then I sat down and fieldstripped and cleaned the .45 (though in fact they'd done a perfectly fine job of maintaining it), working the slide hard or thumping something on key words so that anyone listening outside the tent would have a hard time hearing.

A few short sentences were enough to explain the basic situation and what I intended to do about it. None of us was happy about leaving Porter here with only one trained person for protection, but none of us had any other ideas; we knew that if Chrys were alive, free, and in the neighborhood, she'd have contacted us by now, and that meant that she was either still captive or a long way away. Probably she was still Pompey's captive, or if she had escaped (which you could never rule out with Chrysamen—she was smart and fast and improvised well), then she was either making her way back here or heading on to Rome, depending on what looked like it would get the mission accomplished fastest.

That other possibility was one I had decided not to think about.

"Basic thing," I said, "Ifway ouyay etgay away ancechay, eakbray ailjay andway eadhay orfay omeray. Damn, my translator is malfunctioning! Brillig and the slithy toves—mimsey were the borogroves and the mome raths outgrabe."

"I think something is wrong with gamboling on the gumbo with me gambits all a-gear," Paula said.

"Mairzy doats and doazy doats and little lamsy divy," Porter agreed.

"Ixnay, Daddio," I said, and then slid the clip in. My old Model 1911A1 was as good as ever; it felt good in the shoulder holster. "Whoops, that's the problem, when you pull out the hemulator on the gun it jams the fratistat on the translator and we can't understand each other."

Five minutes later, after I'd checked through the pack that the kid had brought me, I was throwing my leg over my bicycle and setting off down the Via Flaminia. It was mostly downhill from here, but not terribly steep; I had only about thirty miles of that downhill to cover, and *I* did not have to go more slowly so that horses could keep up.

The biggest problem with these bikes, which required a little concentration, was that they didn't have any kind of coaster arrangement; the pedals always turned with the wheels. Thus, for control, it was really better to pedal constantly, or on steep downgrades to resist the pedals a little with your feet. That was very tricky compared with the bicycles of my timeline, and it raised my admiration for those adaptable Romans another couple of notches—if they could learn to balance and ride on a bicycle with never-quite-straight wheels, as well as control the bicycle without real brakes, they were pretty amazing guys.

The Via Flaminia was one of those famous cases of all roads leading to Rome, and as I neared the city, the traffic of local merchants and farmers, from the villages and small towns around, got thicker and thicker. I had not overtaken Pompey, but then it was possible that I had passed him—he might have pitched camp somewhere off the road behind me, though in the gently rolling hills it seemed improbable that I wouldn't have seen an army.

Then again, how much army could he have left after yesterday? They could probably all hide in a phone booth, if there were any phone booths.

That was actually a pretty good thought, because while even somebody with Chrys's talent for sneaking around and barehanded mayhem might have trouble sneaking out of a large Roman army encampment, getting away from twenty guys would only demand somebody's attention wandering for a second or two—the way it might tend to do if the guy had just been on the losing end of a huge battle and run for miles to get away from it.

Then again . . .

I did my best to force the speculations out of my mind. It was a nice, bright, winter day, and since I was bicycling, I was pretty warm and comfortable. After a while I realized that by just blending into the traffic flow and taking my time, I was overhearing a lot of conversation; there were no windows or windshields in the way, and no running engines to fill the air with noise. The loudest thing I passed on the road was one wagonload of ducks and geese. It was enough to give you some doubts about that word "progress."

The road got more and more crowded as I neared Rome, and now I was hearing a lot, but of course people don't talk much about current events, or when they do they assume the other person understands the reference. The one thing I gathered clearly was that there were a lot of live animals and produce going to Rome right now "while the selling is good" and that everyone wanted to get there, sell what they had for gold only—a couple of them said, "Nothing in trade today," very emphatically, as if repeating a slogan—and get back to the farm in a hurry.

Nobody was interested in selling jewelry, but some of them were talking about how much of it they expected to acquire.

Finally I overheard one farmer talking to another, and he said, "So do you believe Pompey is really going to make that last stand he's talking about, on the Palatine Hill, with the special blessing of the gods?"

"I think it sounds good to the Senate, and he wants a few of them to stay there as bait for Caesar," the other said. "And I don't think it will work on any of the smart ones. I just hope there are enough left who will need provisions today, because I'd say it's two days at most till Caesar comes in, and I'd wager he'll be here tomorrow morning."

"I reckon you're right," the other said. "But while he's claiming to make preparations, and working his big magic up on the Palatine, at least a lot of the Senate will stay in the Curia, trying to make up their minds, and there we'll be, right next door in the Forum, with all the things they'll need to run away with right there—for a price."

"Reckon so. I'm thinking besides the jewels and the gold, I might just want to pick up some slaves in trade."

"Bah. Houseworkers from the city. I don't need none of them. They're soft, and if you put 'em to honest work, they'll die."

"Oh, but Quintus, you're a married man. I'm a bachelor.

Thought I'd get myself some patrician's bedwarmer and find out what the aristocracy gets—"

"It's all the same, theirs is just better washed."

I passed that wagon, finally, when there was an opening in the traffic stream going the other way. Well, that seemed to answer the mystery. The translator in my head gave me a quick map of Rome; I would be coming in from due north, past Pompey's temple and the main military parade ground (the Campus Martius in those days) and directly into the Forum, so there was no sense taking any of the ring roads around to enter by any other gate; they would all be just as jammed, and I was on a direct route.

It was late afternoon, and I was fairly hot and sweaty, even in the crisp cold of January, by the time I rolled over the Milvian Bridge, a heavy, arched bridge across the Tiber north of the city, and then down through the gate in the Aurelian Wall, the outermost wall of the city.

Rome had grown a lot in the centuries just before, and they had only recently annexed a lot of the "suburbs" by building a city wall that enclosed them; the Aurelian Wall had been a state-of-the-art defensive system when it was built, but now it would be only an hour's work for Caesar's field guns to breach it wherever they wanted.

It was a couple of miles to the old inner wall of the city, the Servian Wall, and the Forum was on the other side of that from where I was. To my right the Campus Martius stretched out, but there was no cutting across—the troops milling about there, survivors of Pompey's legions and raw recruits from the city being formed hastily into centuries, might very well decide I looked like a recruit. On the road I was safe enough, because I looked like a military courier, but let anyone who was able-bodied get too close to the Campus Martius, and he was going to be marching back and forth with a *gladius* and *scutum* in no time.

I really hoped that pathetic excuse for a legion—all that seemed to be assembling there was one scrawny legion—would not be forced to go out and fight Caesar; there was no reason for them to be massacred, except that the patricians who ran the Senate were simply not prepared to face reality in any form.

That last two miles took almost as long as riding into town had, and it was almost fully dark by the time I made my way through the gate in the Servian Wall, now pushing the bike because it was easier than trying to keep my balance in the press of people.

As I passed through the great arched gateway in Rome's inner wall, into the old part of the city, I saw the Forum was lit by torch-light and lanterns at hundreds of stalls, and everywhere, there were long lines of people bargaining for food and for plebeian clothing. As I watched, a couple of stagecoaches rumbled up, lights blazing, and I saw that one of them had Crassus's image on it, clearly sten-ciled on. Below that it said "Fontes Ultra Ire."

Half a minute later I slapped my forehead; it was another one of Caldwell's pranks. You could translate that as "Wells Far Go."

People were still getting onto the stages in an orderly way, but the line was getting longer and longer. I'd been in a city or two that was about to be attacked or brought under siege, and I knew how fast the lines formed at the train station. I was just glad I wouldn't need to be leaving in a hurry.

As I passed the Forum and the Curia (the building where the Senate met), I looked to my right; there wasn't much light, but I saw something enormous, tall as an eight-story building, up on the Palatine Hill, where the farmers had talked about Pompey making a stand. There had been no building that big there in my time-line—hell, there had been no building that big in Rome—and the shape was odd, too round and too large.

Whatever Pompey was up to, if he had Chrys, he would have her with him up there, and that tall building—lit occasionally by a roaring fire beneath it—would be the first and most logical place to look. Probably the fire that occasionally flared there was for the sacrifices; if Pompey was organizing a sacred band for a last stand, he would be sacrificing a lot of animals.

That made a certain amount of sense, except that I doubted that Pompey was any more superstitious than Caesar was, and if the situation were reversed, Caesar would be headed for Crassus like a bat out of hell, trying to get some kind of deal. Compared to Pom-pey and Caesar, Crassus was no general, and even Crassus knew it. A talented guy like Pompey—especially since he had a reputation for being good-looking, smooth, and a natural diplomat—would logically be on a stagecoach headed south, or leaving on a ship this minute.

Which meant he was up to something, and that something was

probably a technological trick, maybe even something more impressive than the rocket launchers.

Most likely something connected with Chrys.

I took the turn onto Vicus Tuscus, a large street that ran through a patrician neighborhood at the base of the Palatine Hill, and headed that way. When I saw a gate with enough darkness, I ditched the bicycle and most of the pack there; I took a deep draft of water and forced in the last of my hardtack, made sure I had all the money, my distance glasses, and the dagger. I left the *gladius* behind, though it was a good one, because the last time I had practiced with one had been at Crux Ops training camp, more than a decade before subjectively, and if I pulled a *gladius* out here, practically every free adult male would know more about how to use it on me than I would about how to use it on him. Besides, I had the .45 and half a dozen clips of ammo, and I'd take that up against a *gladius* anytime I could get six feet of clear space.

I ran one last check. I had the works, everything I was likely to need for whatever came up; was there anything I could forget? I found the thumbnail atlas under my fingers and jammed it into my personal pouch of stuff. Partly that was habit—we weren't supposed to leave bits of high tech lying around for the natives—and mostly that was because you never know.

Then I realized what was missing.

I spent two long, stupid minutes groping around in the pack before my fingers closed on my wedding ring. I had taken it off because it seemed like an invitation to bandits on the road, and whenever armies start moving around, there are bandits. I slipped it back on.

It seemed like an omen of some kind; I decided to believe it was a good one. Of course, the real omen was that after being around the superstitious Romans for so long, I was starting to think about omens.

With a shrug, I bent my concentration to the job at hand; I slipped into the depths of the shadows and made my way up the Palatine. On the way I passed a couple of pickpockets, three sentries, and a lady of the evening. None of them ever knew.

I was in my element—it was dark, and there was a mystery ahead, one that would require some violence before it was over.

·14·

The Palatine Hill was supposedly the first part of Rome ever to be settled, and nowadays it was mostly public buildings—temples and government things—on top, but the patrician families still clung to its sides in huge, well-guarded old houses.

The patricians were the people who claimed to be descended from the gods; considering the behavior of Roman gods (plus the ones the Romans plagiarized from the Greeks), I don't know how that was supposed to be to anyone's credit, but they didn't consult me. For generations, the Roman Republic had been dominated by these people, much more thoroughly than the United States had ever been dominated by its First Families of Virginia, Nob Hill Aristocracy, or Boston Brahmins, even more thoroughly than Britain had been dominated by the old peerage. These people ran the show, were used to running the show, and had no concept that anyone else might have a stake in it.

A century of that arrogance had left them with no power base on which to stand. One of their own, Caesar, had won the hearts of the people, even though—or perhaps because—he was ruthless and determined to rule as dictator. Pompey, the most talented man on their side, had been hamstrung and pulled down, in part, by his own allies' paranoia and need to throw their weight around; no general could have tried harder or done better, having to carry the Senate on his back. Crassus and the other "new men"—people who had no patrician ancestry and were merely very capable, people who got rich by talent and hard work—no longer had any faith in a system that had nothing for them. In their desire to preserve their power and privileges, the patricians had made it pay to be their enemies; they had made it cost to be their friends; and now they were reaping the consequences of that decision.

The houses on this dark hill might have symbolized it all, that night. Many of them blazed with candlelight and lamplight, for the patrician families who lived there were preparing to run for their lives—but they were planning to run with strongboxes of gold, trunkfuls of fine clothing, everything that might turn into loot. They couldn't possibly pack their own possessions, let alone carry them, and so, though Caesar and his legions might be there early in the morning, though there was no one left to hold the walls of Rome, though the stagecoaches in which they would travel could be easily overtaken by the legions' bicycles—they were still packing, screaming at each other and the servants like cages full of parrots.

Surrounding each shrieking pool of light was a ring of frantically working, terrified slaves, desperately trying to get everything in order for their now-refugee masters, responding to the hysterical orders as best they could. In the outer rooms and dark corners of each villa, there were other slaves, no longer following orders, hiding where they could and stealing what they could; and finally, out in the streets, where I was, there were hundreds of slaves escaping with bits of their masters' property, running away in the hope that with a bit of luck and the jewelry or money they had grabbed, they might win some kind of freedom somewhere.

That made the job a little trickier; I had to swing wide around many houses because so much light was spilling out, and when I crept through the shadows I was constantly coming upon huddled slaves trying to hide, and other slaves moving more or less quietly and carefully. For a while I thought there were a few slaves who were almost as good as I was at creeping through the dark—I was moving along behind one of them and sort of admiring his technique, the way he placed his feet and avoided backlighting.

Then he came up from behind on a small figure, barely perceptible in the dark but revealed by candle-glare reflected off a wall, if you were on the shadow side of him. The one I was following closed in on the other figure, who was carrying a large sack—I guessed it was probably the master's silver service, from the way the figure hefted it.

There was just one flash of the blade, and then the man who had had the sack lay still, and the man with the blade had the sack—and was gone.

I crept forward and confirmed that the slave—an old man, physically weak, with no signs of ever having done any real work—was dead. His face was slack—when you suddenly have your throat opened with one blow, there's no time to form any lasting expression, and whatever he might have looked like in the brief instant he was killed had now disappeared. He looked like he had gone to sleep there in the street—if you could ignore the immense extra mouth leaking blood from under his jaw.

Probably he had been a tutor, or perhaps a butler or head chef. In this neighborhood almost all the pricey slaves would be Greek. Probably he had dreamed about getting back to his home city with a little bit of money from the stolen silver.

Probably he had gotten about three hundred yards.

I slipped on into the night, my dagger already drawn, keeping that additional thought in mind—probably every footpad and low-life possible was prowling the Palatine tonight, looking for runaway slaves.

I rounded another corner and crept forward. Suddenly light spilled out of the main doorway of a house, and I slipped into a dark alley, low and sideways, to wait out whatever was happening.

I almost laughed out loud. It was somebody fleeing in a litter—four slaves bearing the heavy load down the hill, two others carrying torches in front of it, and a scattering of armed guards around the litter. The litter itself, like most patrician ones, was an object of considerable value, a piece of fine furnituremaking inlaid with gold and silver and decorated with gems.

All it would take, really, would be enough of an attack to convince the slaves that their interests lay elsewhere—and that wouldn't be much—and that expensive litter would spill its expensive and helpless owner into the street like a toy poodle thrown into a kennel of Dobermans.

Undoubtedly the owner thought he or she was "fleeing for my life with just the few things I could carry" and, if by some miracle he or she reached the stagecoach station or the river wharves, would complain bitterly at the crowded and inferior service available.

I reminded myself that though I wasn't much concerned about these voluntarily helpless, spoiled patricians, who had brought it all on themselves, that Rome could easily be burned and looted by Caesar's troops, if something put Caesar into the mood to do it, and it would not be these people, but the ordinary citizens—merchants, artisans, and laborers—who would lose everything they had.

Something moved beside me, and I slipped a bit farther into the shadow. The next moment, something was swinging in at my face—I felt it more than saw it—and I snapped an arm block up, caught the wrist on the little-finger side, drew the arm, and slid my dagger once into an exposed belly, striking upward at the heart and lungs, and then slashed the throat as she screamed.

I knelt and felt the bloody corpse in front of me. Female, as I had thought from the scream, and quite young—her still-warm breasts were small and firm, her hips not yet much widened. Next to her there was a bag of loot, probably not what she had stolen from her own household—probably what she had gotten by knifing people here in this dark corner.

More feeling around revealed three more bodies in the alley— an old woman and two fairly young males. The girl had been pretty talented, but an amateur, and her unwillingness to let go of the bag of loot before attacking me with her knife had made killing her fairly easy.

The litter had passed now, and no one had come in response to the girl's scream. I wiped as much blood as I could off myself, using the bag she had been carrying her loot in, and left the corpses and loot for some other lucky escaped slave. I slipped quietly out of the alley and continued upward.

The distance I had to cover was only eight or nine city blocks, but in pitch-darkness, trying to move undetected, with the streets full of escaping slaves, muggers, and the occasional litter or patrician family with their torchbearers, it took me the better part of the night to get anywhere near where I had judged the giant building to be.

At least for the last two blocks I was able to go a great deal faster—houses were emptying out all over the Palatine, and everyone was fleeing downhill; thus by the time I reached the uppermost

blocks, the bulk of escaping slaves and fleeing patricians was already down the hill, most of the houses were already deserted, and
with so little prey around, the two-legged predators too were gone.

Finally, though, I got near enough to the building I was trying
to reach to get occasional glimpses of it through the narrow streets,
and I was able to see the flickers of light on its sides, and the big
yellow letters SPQR on its red surface. I crept closer, until finally I
found that I was peering across a torchlit street at a small group of
soldiers—real professionals, not just slave bodyguards, to judge by
the way they held their *gladii* and the muskets slung over their
shoulders.

With a group of professionals on the alert and the light against
me, there was no going through by the direct route here; I would
have to circle and probe. Depending on how determined you are,
and how big the risk you can run is, there's usually a way in.

It didn't take long to establish that these guys were *really* pros.
Half an hour of dedicated sneaking and skulking in the perimeter
showed me that every post was visible from every other, there were
three guards to a post, and they had managed to get enough
torches into enough places so that there was no really good band of
darkness to crawl through.

Well, that meant taking on a bigger risk, I figured. I could fire
a couple of shots somewhere to make a diversion—but here in the
dark my muzzle flashes would draw more attention than whatever
the shots hit. The opposing roofs were too high to throw a rock
onto. Besides, these guys did not seem dumb or naive enough to
fall for such a trick. I could wait around and hope, but there were
probably just a couple of hours of darkness left, and I had no idea
what Pompey was up to in there.

Something startled me, and I looked again, then saw what it
was. A ripple had run down the bright red side of the "giant building." Abruptly my brain adjusted to the data, and I knew what I
had been looking at, realized I would have recognized it if I had
only allowed myself to think without first deciding what it couldn't
be. I guess you're never too trained or too experienced to stop
making dumb mistakes.

It was a hot-air balloon, a very large one, and undoubtedly the
way in which Pompey was planning to escape. Naturally without
propane or any other really hot fuel, it was taking a while to get it
hot enough, and that was what the big fires burning under it were

about. The SPQR on its side probably meant it had originally been a military project funded by the Senate, but I saw now what Pompey was up to; the wind blows west to east, and flying out of Rome, if he kept it aloft long enough, he was bound to come down either in unclaimed territory or at least somewhere Crassus controlled.

It was sort of like a punt in football, except that Pompey was both the punter and the football. Almost anywhere and any situation had to be better than the one he was in; and if he fled on foot, horse, or bicycle, Caesar or his agents had the means to catch him.

It occurred to me that I was one of Caesar's agents, and I was working on the means to catch Pompey. And I didn't have a lot of time left.

I crept forward again and moved around to the place I had picked as the weak spot. There, an alley between two temples opened out toward me, and both guard posts, though able to cover the street, had to move forward to see each other, or the alley between them, because of the way the temples protruded. If Pompey or his legates had had a few extra men, they could have stationed them at the alley mouth and closed the gap completely. The fact that they had not done so meant that their resources were strained, and that reassured me a lot—probably they had few or no patrols inside the perimeter.

The basic problem in coming up with a good diversion is that what you want to do is to pull them off where you're going, ideally without giving them any more idea than they had in the first place that there is anything big to worry about. You don't want them poked up and looking for trouble. That wasn't going to be easy.

The perfect trick would be to land something between one of the guard posts and its neighbor, on the side away from the alley I wanted to get into, so that the alley I was interested in would be unwatched for an instant, and I could slip across. At the time that seemed a bit like saying the perfect way to win a marathon would be to run at twenty miles an hour for one hour and eighteen minutes; the theory was easy, but it neglected the facts.

So I sat down, watched, and hoped for a break. The guard might change, rioting might break out, anything could happen.

But it didn't. The part of my brain that counts breaths hit six hundred, which meant I had been there two hours. I stretched silently, in place, and was about to start thinking more seriously about taking action, when finally something happened.

A musket volley cut down the farthest guard post I could see, bringing all three men to the ground, and something or someone, bent low, barely illuminated by the lights of the city behind it, ran across into the area Pompey's men had cordoned off. There were blazing flashes as other guard posts fired their muskets, but whoever had just shot his way in was moving too fast for anyone to have time to fire—the figure was gone into the shadows just as the muskets fired—and besides, the things were so inaccurate that with only three muskets in each of the volleys, probably nothing could have found a mark if the intruder had stood still with a fluorescent bull's-eye on his chest.

My Model 1911A1 was in my hand before I even began to think, and my feet were slamming into the pavement. Sure enough, the guard post to my right pulled over to cover the situation, and I ran behind them into the alley; an instant later the guard post to my left had rounded the temple and was racing past the alley entrance. I was in Pompey's compound, at last. I knew nothing of its layout, it sounded as if there were troops running everywhere firing at shadows, and there was at least one trigger-happy force of some kind or other (quite possibly hostile to me as well as to Pompey) present in the compound—but I was inside, and that was a lot farther than I had been seconds before.

I dove into the shadow nearest the exit of the alley. Nothing seemed to be happening in my view, but I heard running feet and gunshots, so I stayed put.

In a few seconds a group of soldiers came into view. "Anything?" barked the centurion in the group.

"Nothing, sir!" they all said.

"Our men are firing at shadows out there, sir," one added. "We've got to get organized, or there's going to be someone shooting a friend."

"Don't I know it," the centurion said, and started bellowing orders.

They assembled in the small square there, beside the big building that I later learned was the Temple of the Great Mother. I had nowhere to go but back—which would get me nothing—or forward, which would get me shot, so I stayed put. The false dawn wasn't far away, and from the sight of the stars overhead, I judged there was going to be a lot of light pretty soon. It didn't look particularly great.

The group of soldiers were doing a fast roll call, and they didn't like what they were finding; mumbles were running through the crowd. Three men dead at the guard post, eight men missing. Some of those were probably guys who had taken a chance to desert and would be making their way to Caesar to sell whatever they knew—but eight was a lot.

A moment later there was a shout—one of the eight coming out of another alley. There was horror in his cry.

The centurion barked, "Rufus! Humilis! Sine-colle! Get over there and help him! All others, load muskets, form a circle, wait for my command!"

Three men sprinted out of the group and the rest rapidly formed their circle. Moments later, there were two more groans in two more voices, and then one of them shouted, "Sir, it's Quintus and Decius. They've both been knifed in the back. Titiculus here just about fell over them."

"Come back *real* slow," the centurion said. "Everyone make sure you know what you're looking at before you pull the trigger!"

"Leave the bodies, sir?"

"We'll have to. They won't care, and you need to get back here. Now *move.*"

A few moments later four figures—one of them moving strangely, probably Titiculus—emerged into the dim light of the square and rejoined the group. They formed up quickly, and the centurion said, "Decurion Alba, take your men and reinforce the guard at the platform. Tell the *imperator* that we cannot hold for long, that we are already breached, and he must act quickly if he is to act at all. The rest of you, we're going to sweep the compound and see if we can turn up this mystery enemy. We'll start to the west."

Dead away from me. I all but sighed aloud with relief.

Sure enough, in just seconds, the century was moving away from me, and one little knot of men—a decurion was supposed to command ten men, but in fact the numbers varied between units the size of one of our squads and one of our platoons—moved to the right, then forward.

I nerved myself and dashed to the next shadow, following Decurion Alba and his men. I really did not like this; you shouldn't know too much about your enemy. It occurred to me that this last century, of all of Pompey's legions, was being literally loyal to the death. I revised my estimate that any of the missing men had deserted; probably they were all dead or mortally wounded, somewhere in the cold dark alleys. Whatever was loose in the compound, it was like walking death.

And there had been no collapse of discipline or morale. These men were trained to die in their tracks, and they were doing it as necessary, for the sake of their commander. It wasn't as if their commander were a better man than their enemy; really there wasn't much to choose between any of these guys, so far as I could see.

I came slowly and quietly around the corner to find that Alba and his men had reached their goal; there was the platform, with great roaring fires leading into bent chimneys that then passed into the balloon through the opening at its bottom. The slight smell of roasting rubber told me that the balloon was made of rubberized linen, the same thing the legion ponchos were made of; under it hung—it took me a moment to realize—a stagecoach body, minus the wheels and axles, mounted on a small boat. Clearly landings were something they weren't terribly sure about just yet.

The balloon was tied down by a cable that looped from eyebolts driven into the pavement around it up to the large band that ran horizontally around the circumference of the balloon, through a grommet there, and then back down to another eyebolt, until finally both ends of it were tied together between two eyebolts on the platform. It would take just one stroke of a sharp ax to send the balloon on its way.

Below the boat, hanging from short improvised davits that protruded all over it, were dozens of big sandbags.

On top of the stagecoach was a pile of wood, not yet lit. I realized at once that there was no easy means of controlling that fire in flight, and since it would be the one thing keeping Pompey aloft, he wouldn't light it until he was in the air, or just before; once it burned out, he would be on his way down to the ground.

It was a big payload, which was why the balloon had to be so large and why it was taking so long to get hot enough for takeoff, but it looked very much like Pompey could probably leave now if he had to.

Over the rumble of the fires burning in the three furnaces heating the balloon, there was a distant boom, and Alba looked around instantly. "Cannon, sir," he called to someone inside the stagecoach body. "From the north, I think; perhaps they're already at the Aurelian Wall, though I can't imagine why anyone would be stupid enough to try to stop them now."

Whatever Pompey said back was lost on me, but all the men laughed, the kind of warm laugh that breaks the tension. I had a sense of just why these men would follow him everywhere.

My problem was that at the current range, with the .45, I could probably take all the men guarding the balloon before anyone could get a shot into me; they'd have to close with cold steel, and I could turn and run if need be, since I was not weighted down by armor as they were. So purely in theory, I should have started shooting, probably Alba first, then a lot of them. The rest might turn and run, and then I could leap up the ladder into the balloon, put a pistol to Pompey's head, and demand to know what he had done with Chrys.

Possibly, I thought, *she's even in there—she'd be valuable enough for him to hold prisoner, surely. He had suffered a great deal because he didn't have an ATN or Closer advisor, as Caesar and Crassus had. He might very well be willing to have even one he had to keep at knifepoint.*

So the plan was pretty simple. Four or six shots—and four or six men dead—would get me into the balloon, and I could work from there.

The only problem was that I had been watching these guys in their very difficult circumstances for the last hour, and I just didn't want to. Alba and his men were a bunch of fine fighters with exceptional loyalty; the centurion was a guy any fighting man would have followed to hell and back. It didn't seem like they had to die for having picked the wrong side.

You see how it is. I like my enemies either deeply personal, like certain Closer bastards or like the one time I fought myself from another timeline, a timeline where I had actually gone to work for them; or if not that, I like them to be completely impersonal—just figures that pop up and shoot at me, and then I shoot back at them, and that's that.

Either way, that's fine. I sleep okay after that. But when you know just enough for them to be human, and all they are is in the wrong place at the wrong time—well, back before I met Chrys, back when I was still an embittered ash of a human soul with no desire other than revenge, I didn't much care. Being in the wrong place at the wrong time was a perfectly valid reason for someone, even someone likable, to die.

Life had changed a lot. Now it wasn't. I kicked myself mentally for a sentimental fool, but I didn't feel like gunning down several good, decent soldiers just doing their jobs, and I couldn't seem to make my hand reach for the automatic. I had not turned pacifist, or anything—if a Closer had popped up, I'd have been firing before thinking—but I had started to think a little too much and feel a bit too much empathy to be the same guy I had been before.

Why is it that changes of spirit never come when it's convenient?

The cannon in the distance were pounding now, and we heard bugles. Caesar's forces were entering the city, an hour before dawn, in a surprise attack that would carry everything before it. Later I learned that they caught practically the whole patrician class at the riverboat docks and the stage stations.

I stood there with that invading army coming in, with Pompey's balloon ready to go at any moment, and unable to move forward because there were a couple of ordinary guys I couldn't quite kill in cold blood. The first gray streaks of light from the false dawn were reaching across the sky, and in a moment or two I would be visible.

The night was suddenly alive with musket fire, volley meeting volley, and light flashed through the alleys in a bewildering pattern, casting long macabre shadows across the courtyard toward the platform, like dark demons leaping toward the balloon. Alba stepped down and looked around for an instant, clearly unsure what to do; then Pompey leaned out and shouted something, and Alba picked up the ax to cut the lines.

It tipped the balance; if Pompey took off without my getting hold of him, I would lose any chance of finding out where Chrys was. The .45 in my hand barked, and Alba fell dead; I fired double-handed, in the approved police style, and took down two other men.

They shot back, but that ragged volley from men scattered that widely could have hit something only by chance, and they were firing into the dark.

There was another roar of musketry. Clearly an advance guard of Caesar's had arrived and was trying to fight its way to the balloon. Inexperienced as they all were with the effects of musketry at close range, probably what was happening was that two centuries were slaughtering each other, leaving no one able to do anything more than keep firing.

The men who had just fired at me hesitated, moving back and forth as they reloaded. I shot another, and that decided about half of them—they ran to join the others. The rest pointed their muskets, half-blinded probably by their own muzzle flashes before, not able to see where I was.

A voice shouted from the stagecoach, and they turned and ran to join the rest of their century. The stagecoach door popped open as I ran toward it, and a horse pistol pointed out—I fired a shot, but an upward shot at such a small target, especially while I was running, was hopeless. Still, the hand jerked in for an instant, and that gave me time enough to reach the ladder and scale it, leaping up it several rungs at a time, .45 gripped in my teeth.

The pistol boomed above me, a great spray of red, and nothing happened—he was shooting out into space as far as I could tell, not down the ladder. Then another pistol boomed, and I heard the long hiss of the cable running through its eyebolts and grommets— Pompey had managed to sever the cable, and if you broke it in any one place, it released the balloon.

The ladder, propped against the side of the boat, began to go over, and I flung myself forward off it. I was fifteen feet above the ground, and even as I did it I thought I might well hit the pavement or the hot side of one of the furnaces, but my hands found the knot at the top of a sandbag.

My body swung forward and smashed into the bag, and the pistol in my teeth slammed further in, but I managed to keep my grip. We lurched up into the air, me hanging on to the sandbag by wrapping my legs all the way around it and keeping my hands locked on the knot.

We rose rapidly, the sandbags clearing the top of the three-story-high Temple of the Great Mother by about fifteen feet. If I had let go about then, I might have had a fifty-fifty chance of survival—but that wasn't what I was after.

There was a roar down below; they were trying to bring us down with musket fire, but even at our altitude of less than a hundred feet, the muskets didn't have the *oomph* to get anything up here at any dangerous velocity. For one instant, a lead ball hung in the air, a bit below me and ten feet out in front; then it fell back to earth.

We drifted out over the city; the light was getting brighter by the moment, a pale pink spreading across the deep blue behind us as we drifted westward over the city. I could see the alleys of the city filling with marching troops and bicycles—Caesar had indeed arrived in force. Probably even as I floated upward then, Cicero was hiding under the docks, and Cato Uticensis was being beaten to death by Caesar's legionaries in front of his family, but I knew none of that at the time—all that I saw were the great columns of troops pouring into the city.

There was a little flicking of gunfire from the Servian Wall— probably some of those hastily organized volunteers hadn't quite had the sense to desert. A field gun roared in the dark Via Nomentana ahead and to my left, sending a streak of red fire against the wall. Two more bellowed, and then there was flame and smoke from the Porta Collina; the inner city had fallen already, but Caesar's forces were destroying resistance wherever they found it, rather than bypassing it to give a chance for surrender.

It was thorough and brutal—he was making sure that anyone with the means and the courage to resist did so now, and was killed or captured doing it, so that there would be no nucleus around which to form an opposition. The whole thing was perfectly Caesar—it solved all his political problems efficiently, and in its willingness to slaughter a lot of untrained draftees, it was cruel enough to frighten his enemies into quiescence.

As I had been watching the invasion roll in, we had passed on from the top of the Palatine Hill, and since it's steep, this meant we were now a few hundred feet in the air.

I was still hanging on to that huge sandbag, my legs wrapped around it, my hands on the knot, the pistol in my jaws. I cautiously let loose with one hand, took the .45 in hand, and carefully tucked it into the shoulder holster, fastening it closed. At least I didn't have to worry about breaking my teeth.

One of the hardest things to get used to about ballooning is how silent it all is, and how still, especially in a balloon like this, with no burner going. Thus when I heard the general's boots on the boat over my head, they boomed distinctly in the morning air, and I breathed very slowly and cautiously, hoping not to be detected.

There was a scraping noise—it sounded like he was climbing

around on the lines—and then the *whump!* of a fire starting. He had ignited the additional burner; we would be going up and staying up a lot longer. The balloon rocked gently at the pressure on the various lines as he clambered back down into the boat body.

I was still working on a way to get over the gunwale and into the main body without being detected. The davit stuck out from the side of the boat about two feet over my head; the sandbag between my legs was about the size and shape of a boxer's heavy bag, and not at all easy to climb.

Cautiously, I humped upward once, hard, and got my hands a few inches from the davit. The clump of Pompey's boots was over on the other end of the boat, as best I could tell, and I reached up to grip the line well above the knot.

I tried not to look down at all, or to think about just how far down it was or how long I could fall before I hit.

I pulled myself up on the rope, cautiously unwrapping and rewrapping my legs, getting ready for the hard push up to the davit, still six feet overhead. Another hard pull should bring me to the point where my feet rested on the bag—

With a sickening lurch, the balloon shot upward, rocking hard. I hung on as long as I could, and despite my own advice to myself, I looked down.

A sandbag, like the one on which my feet rested, was tumbling away in the bright morning sun, no doubt to terrify everyone wherever it might crash into the city. Pompey was dropping ballast; now that I listened, I could hear his knife sawing another line; I dared not let go of my grip, for when that line parted—

There was a noise a bit like a pistol shot as the line went. Another sandbag plunged down through the cold morning air. Another line dangled empty from another davit. I realized, suddenly, that given the way this balloon worked, and that he was trying for the maximum possible distance, he had every good reason to get rid of most of the sandbags as soon as possible.

I heard him sawing again, and I threw myself up the line, getting my feet on the sandbag this time and taking a hard grip. Once again the balloon lurched upward as another bag went, and my feet swung off the swinging bag below; I hung by my hands fifteen hundred feet above the ground.

Pompey's footsteps were now coming toward the stern of the

boat, where my sandbag hung; probably he was about to balance the load. Even as I thought that, I heard the sawing, closer than ever, and saw the sandbag directly across from mine begin to vibrate. Mine would be next.

·15·

Climbing up hand over hand, not using your feet, is one of those things you do so endlessly in ATN Training School that it's second nature, and I was climbing as hard as I could before I even had put my situation into words. Still, I had never done it when it was quite so far to the ground, nor when at any moment there might be another hard yank.

Just as I reached for the davit, the jerk came, another sandbag plunging away. I was ready for it, but it did make me swing backward and forward alarmingly before I got a hand on the davit.

A shadow fell across me, and before I could think—and a good thing, too, thinking is way too slow at a time like that—I had kept my grip on the davit, let go of the line, and yanked the .45 out, pointing it upward into Pompey's surprised face as he was about to slash my hand, which would have severed the tendons and sent me plunging.

"Don't even think it," I said.

He leaped back out of sight, and I started to work on swinging up onto the davit, using just one hand. I couldn't holster the gun without the risk that he would be back to cut my hand, and I had only one hand to hang on with, so I was trying to get my legs up and around the davit, which was taking a lot of swinging.

It didn't get easier when, with a bang, he used one of his horse pistols to cut another sandbag free, and yet another. The jerks made my swinging wilder and uncontrolled, and for one god-awful second all the pressure of my weight was on my wrist, torqued as far as it would go, with all the city of Rome and the land around it spread out far below me, and my body swung far out away from the hull of the boat, feet pointing into empty sky.

But that gave me the momentum I needed, and he was reloading, so I whipped forward, kipped up, and got my legs around that davit. My thighs locked, and now at least I would be harder to get rid of.

Two more bangs dropped two more sandbags—now only the one below me was left—but I no longer cared much, securely locked on as I was; I sat up hard, caught the gunwale with my left hand, levered myself into position, and came up pointing the Model 1911A1. Pompey crouched in the bow, his horse pistol braced and leveled, about fifteen feet from me.

"You've got about a 50 percent chance of hitting me, maybe, if you're really good with that thing," I said, "and I suspect you know that."

"Granted," Pompey said.

"Watch this," I said, and fired two rounds out to the side. "I've got three left. If we start shooting, figure the odds are overwhelming you're dead."

"Very obviously true," he said, and sat down, keeping the horse pistol level at me. "Depending on just what you intend to do to me, however, it might be better to take your chances. I assume I am in the presence of Marcus Fortius, the ATN agent?"

"You are. And I believe you sent me a note implying that you were holding Chrysamen ja N'wook prisoner. Do you have her with you?"

What he did next I could never have anticipated.

He burst out laughing. There was a strange quality to it, because he seemed not quite able to stop, and he kept right on laughing till tears ran down his face, and he got quite red in the face.

He had been a handsome man in his youth, with curly hair, a firm chin, flashing eyes, and high cheekbones—he could have been a film star in my timeline, kind of a squared-off Kirk Douglas. Now, he was close to sixty and running to flesh, a baggy second chin hanging in and his jowls a little too prominent. The laughter brought so much color to his face that I could see a few little broken veins in his nose, probably not so much from drinking as from having been out in the weather too much.

It was the kind of laugh that makes you think of every really sick joke you know, the kind that you laugh at because they are so nakedly horrible in their implications that it's the only way the mind can defend itself. And at the same time, there was something brave in it—a little touch of courage, like the kid who whistles when he goes by the cemetery, but goes by it anyway.

At last he stopped, and said, "Thank you for not shooting me for a madman, sir. Well. The gods have often had their way with me. The Judeans claim that this is because I invaded their Holy of Holies and saw their Ark of the Covenant, which they say contains the tablets on which their god wrote down some wholesome advice for them. Perhaps they are right, for ever since I returned from the East, there has been one catastrophe after another, whether I tried to act nobly for the common good or merely to look after my own interests. And so often it has been just this sort of bizarre prank of the gods. It is said my *genius* is somehow bound up with Mercury, who is the god of transformations and changes, and moreover is reputed to have a dreadful sense of humor."

"Our *genii* probably know each other," I said. "Suppose you tell me the joke, so we can both laugh."

He sighed. "It was a bluff, you see. I had almost caught her, but she turned out to have some unexpected skills, and, well, she escaped from several of my best men, leaving a couple of them dead, if that's of interest, even while I was drafting the message. Suddenly all I had of her was a few curls from her head. So I enclosed those in the letter, and I calculated that if she got back to you soon enough, the only harm done was that Caesar would know I was willing to lie to him—which he surely knew already. But in a war zone, many things can happen, and besides, ATN has a program of its own that might send her in another direction. If she didn't make her way back to Caesar, I might get him and you to expend valuable effort in finding her. So now I find that all that I did was very nearly ruin my escape . . . or perhaps it's already ruined. Well, you may keep me at gunpoint as much as you choose, and you can trust me or not, but I know that ATN has no preferences about who wins this struggle, so I shall put this thing away"—he tucked the horse pistol back into its scabbard—"and now, if you're willing, we can wait out the journey. There's more than enough food and water on board for two."

I thought for a long while. "You have no idea what direction she escaped in?"

Pompey sighed. "Alas, no information I can trade with. She escaped from us near the Via Flaminia, when we stopped to eat and rest, about ten miles outside the city. That is all I can tell you. Whether she went forward toward Rome or back toward Caesar, I couldn't say."

I figured Chrys must have gone forward toward the city, because if she'd headed back toward Caesar, I'd have met her on the road early that morning, or she'd have even arrived in camp. Which meant I'd probably been pretty close before, and I was getting farther away all the time.

On the other hand, now that I knew she was alive and free, in the city, able to go to Caesar if she needed to, I was a lot less worried.

"Sure," I said. "Why don't we get something to eat, and then see if there's anything to talk about? If you don't mind, though, I'm going to keep this thing trained on you."

"Understood, as I said before. I suppose we should retain that last sandbag in case we need it for landing—or do you perhaps have a sentimental attachment to it?" His mouth curled puckishly.

"Oh, there was a time when I couldn't have parted with it, but I feel different now," I said.

There was clearly no hope of talking him into landing soon—that would amount to a death sentence for him—and for that matter it would have been pretty tough to bring the balloon down even if we had been trying. And now that I suspected Chrys was probably okay, the major worry was Paula and Porter, for whom I could do little even if I were right there in Caesar's camp.

There are times when there's nothing to do but drift and enjoy the scenery. The biggest problem was with staying awake; I had been up all night, but I had a feeling that if I fell asleep and left Pompey on guard, I would be apt to wake up without the .45 and tied up—unless he had decided that I was just a complete liability, in which case I would probably wake up somewhere in the sky, with the ground spread out far below me, coming up faster and faster until a last instant of oblivion.

Pompey undoubtedly had a similar feeling about me. The trouble was that neither of us *knew* about any good reason the other might have for killing him or tying him up; but we also didn't know of any good reason the other might have *not* to, and we also had no way to evaluate how many other deals the other person might have going. Clearly we were on our way to join Crassus, where either of us might expect a warm welcome—or not.

So instead we sat and ate; one advantage of the abundance of slaves (as long as you got to be a master) was that a lot of things were first-rate. He had a bunch of hampers packed with all kinds of goodies, and we ate one of the two hot ones first while it was still hot. Italy rolled by underneath us—we seemed to be being pushed along by a front line from an incoming winter storm, moving steadily to the southwest.

Italy itself runs to the southwest, so we were very slowly drifting down the spine of the Apennines, passing mostly over uninhabited country, edging slowly over to the western side of the peninsula. I got out my thumbnail atlas, which could call up a navigation unit that ATN had implanted on the moon when we first got here, and we determined that we would probably head to the west of the Gulf of Tarentum (or Taranto, in the modern spelling) and pass out over the bootheel someplace. It at least gave us a fighting chance to come down in Macedonia or Greece—Roman territory where the garrisons would still be sympathetic to Pompey.

It occurred to me that the situation now was that each member of the Triumvirate had an advisor from ATN, assuming that Walks-in-His-Shadow Caldwell was still with Crassus, and that his "disappearance" there had been temporary.

"I would assume so," Pompey said. "He does tend to take off for long periods of time. He might have been needed at that western colony, Terra Elastica, or possibly down in Africa Australis, the new colony that he had launched far down Africa. Of course in these days anyone can have bad luck with a knife or a cup of poison, you know, but he had very few real enemies, despite having a very odd sense of humor."

"You've noted that, too?" I asked.

"Do you know him?"

"Haven't met him yet. He's done a fine job here, by the way," I said, "though I'm sure it doesn't seem that way to you. Most timelines that we try to advance don't move nearly this fast or well.

Partly it's a matter of this historical period and place being such a good one for it, but it's also Caldwell's effort."

"He's a tall, thin man," Pompey said. "His skin's a sort of brownish shade, roughly the same color, I'm told, as the inhabitants of Terra Elastica. Likes to talk and laugh. Sort of a deep spirit of fun about him. I'm afraid Crassus was the most natural one of the Triumvirate for him to end up with—both men seem to have *genii* that love the mundane and the small details. I have some knack that way myself, as you might have noticed with my use of the rockets—all we Romans do—but Crassus could never look at a thing without thinking of three ways to make it better and six ways to sell it. Not a general at all, poor fool, and of course hopelessly without grace or breeding, but his practical gifts are remarkable, and that seemed to mesh naturally with your man Caldwell."

I nodded. There was no particular reason to try to persuade Pompey that it was his attitude, and those of the other patricians, that had blinded him to why people like Crassus were bound to take power, eventually must take power.

We passed a pleasant enough afternoon, watching Italy roll slowly and all but silently by beneath us. Pompey was an educated, cultured man, in many ways like Caesar but with much more personal charm, a livelier sense of humor, and a keen feeling for irony that his last few years of disappointments had given him.

We talked about books and poets, Greek literature mainly since it was the same for both of us (though of course much more of it still existed in his timeline). We discussed the battles that had been fought at dozens of places we passed over, for it had taken the city of Rome centuries just to conquer the peninsula, Italy itself had been invaded a number of times, and more than once the parts of Italy that were supposed to be Roman allies had risen to throw off the yoke, causing yet more wars to blaze back and forth. Pompey seemed a little sad at all that, finally commenting only that although muskets demanded courage and presence of mind, they would never require the ability to "look a man in the eye, shove a bar of iron into his guts, and wrench it around as he dies before you—and it's that spirit that makes our fighting men invincible, at least in even numbers on level ground."

We even managed to talk a little politics; he was fascinated with the setup of the United States, though I'm afraid he perceived all the checks and balances of the Constitution as a way for rich people to keep their money, and things like the space program, the interstates, and the national parks as ways to buy off the populace to avoid revolt, those being the only purposes of government he could really comprehend.

We were a lot lower than most airplanes commonly go, and the wind was moving us along at not more than about thirty miles per hour, so it was almost sundown when we first sighted the sea ahead of us. It would still be at least an hour until we crossed the coastline, and it was beginning to get cold in the boat, so we decided to dine inside for our next meal, the second hot hamper (or as hot as the straw it was packed in could keep it, anyway).

"This is a very civilized way to travel," Pompey said as he finished the last of his meal, "as long as you don't have much concern about where you're going or when you get there." It was now fully dark outside.

"One of my favorite books when I was a child made that point," I said, polishing off something that could easily have passed for baklava at any deli in New York. Then a thought struck me. "I think we're in trouble."

Pompey was instantly alert. "Explain," he said; it was as if the mask of command had simply dropped across his face.

"It's a cold clear January day out there, and we're at probably ten thousand feet. We should have been freezing our asses off. In fact it was freezing cold when I was first working my way aboard, right?"

"True—*Jupiter!*"

"Yep," I said. "The metal bottom of the burner has been acting as a space heater outside, which is why it was so pleasant and warm all day—and that burner is what was keeping us up. It must have burned out much faster than you had planned on."

We burst out the door; it was dark, and we saw at once that we really were in just that kind of trouble; the underside of the balloon reflected only the faint red glare of a few coals. The fire would surely be out within the hour.

We were just passing over the coast. "That's Barium below," Pompey said, pointing to the faint grid made by the white-stone streets in the dim moonlight. "I recognize it by the plan. Well, we have at least seventy miles to go, a hundred if we're swept farther south. How fast are we going down and how fast are we moving?"

I got out the thumbnail atlas and called in a request; the atlas included a clock, so I then waited five minutes and called in again. Then I worked the calculator; saw the result, worked through it again. "Uh-oh," I said. "We were at 11,604 feet five minutes ago. Now we're at 11,501. And in that time we've covered 1.9 miles. If you project that out, unless the wind picks up, we're going into the drink 50 miles from here. Not far enough."

"Well, first measures first," Pompey said. "Let's see what we've got around that will burn—we need to lose weight, and we need to warm the air."

There wasn't much to start with. The picnic hampers were the biggest single item; we decided we'd want to hang on to a couple of blankets, the rope, the oars, and the maps (Pompey insisted on that last—he clearly had a healthy distrust of technology). It took a little climbing, and there is something about being up in the rigging of a balloon, even in fairly calm air, at night that is tough on the nerves, but we managed to get them thrown into the hopper, where after a minute or two they blazed up.

"What next?" I said. "We don't need the sandbag davits, and that's a few substantial sticks of wood."

We broke them off, and I started to climb up to pitch them in, except for the one that still held our sandbag—we wanted some control on landing if we could manage it—and one other davit, after Pompey suddenly said, authoritatively, "Save that one out."

I set it down in the bottom of the boat, put the tied-together davits into a pack on my back, and worked my way up the lines again until I was over the brazier. The hampers, straw, and spare blankets had mostly burned out already, but when I tossed the davits in among them there was a brief flare-up. I just hoped it was hot enough to get the davits going.

When I got back down, Pompey handed me a large piece of wood, and said, "If you don't mind climbing, I'll be happy to keep handing you wood. I'd like to get that fire built up before it has a chance to go out completely—I don't relish the thought of climbing into the brazier with flint and steel."

"My thoughts exactly," I said, and climbed back up. There was a hole in the chunk of wood, so I put my arm through that, and it was fairly easy climbing.

The problem was that the lines had to run away from the brazier to avoid getting burned, and the most natural and easy way to climb on a rope that goes up at an angle is with your body underneath it. That meant by the time you were even with the brazier, you were too far away from it to throw anything in; you then had to climb back along the lines that ran to the bottom hole of the balloon. Thus you were at least twenty feet up from the boat, and ten feet above the metal brazier, before you could drop a load in.

At least it was easy this time. I dropped in the chunk of wood, right on top of where a few of the davits had begun to burn, and climbed back down. There were several boards tied together waiting for me; Pompey shouted that he thought he had gotten all the nails, but I should be careful. I slung it up, climbed up again, saw that the first piece of wood had caught, and tossed in the bundle. There was a great crash, and sparks flew up into the balloon; I hoped that whatever fireproofing there was continued to work.

When I climbed back down, there was still more wood, including a piece like the first one. It finally occurred to me to ask, "Where are you getting this?"

"I'm taking the stagecoach cabin apart, of course," Pompey said. "The balloon is secured to the boat, not to the cabin, and I'd rather be cold and land in Macedonia than settle comfortably onto the sea."

"Agreed," I said, and set off back up the lines. This was turning into a lot of exercise, so it was warming me up considerably, and the wood in the brazier was beginning to catch as well, so it was getting warmer still. Moreover, as the fire got bigger there, it wasn't quite so necessary to climb all the way out over the brazier in order to hit the fire exactly with each addition of fuel, so the job went faster. After perhaps forty minutes of dedicated work, we had put the whole cabin into the brazier, and it was blazing brightly. The balloon over our heads glowed yellow and red with reflected light, and the bottom of the brazier was hot enough to warm the boat pleasantly.

We helped ourselves to some wine from the supplies, and assisted the balloon further by pitching the empty bottles over the side. Then I got out the thumbnail atlas, and said, "All right, now let's see what effect we're having."

We were back up at twelve thousand feet, and holding steady, now moving at just over two miles in five minutes. "If that fire lasts another hour," I said, "we should make it easily. And with probably only a couple of hours of being unpleasantly out in the weather."

Pompey made a grunt of satisfaction. "After it burns out, you'll see why we saved the entrenching tool. I plan to climb up there and shovel out the dead ashes as well. That should amount to at least half as much as the sandbag."

Another hour went by; on the course that the wind was taking us, we should be coming down in Macedonia in just about three and a half hours—if the fire kept burning long enough.

It actually went a little longer. We had no objections. "We'll actually get there before midnight," I said. "Depending on where we come down, we may not even have to camp out."

We had another bottle of wine—there would be nothing that required us to be sober for at least two hours, and it seemed like a pleasant way to pass the time. Pompey taught me a couple of the basic dirty songs of the legions, and I gave him a couple from ATN training camp. We were delighted to discover a couple that seemed to overlap between the two sets; apparently people who do violence for a living have very similar tastes down through the centuries.

Even through the mild buzz of alcohol, I was still forming my basic assessment, and it was this: Pompey was a brilliant man, and much the more likable guy as opposed to Caesar. You could trust Pompey in a way that you could never trust Caesar.

But Caesar had more brains and more imagination. I hated noticing that, because of what it foreboded, but there you had it; in any kind of contest between the two of them, I would bet on Pompey to put up a brave, honorable, and intelligent fight, and then to lose.

For the hell of it, I asked Pompey how he felt about Caesar's proclivity for raping younger slaves.

"Oh, hell, yes," Pompey said. "Want another glass?"

"Sure," I said. "No point pouring it over the side without straining it through us first."

"By Castor, that's true," Pompey said. He seemed pretty fond of the bottle, I noted, and he was drinking about two to my one. Well, people said he looked a lot like Alexander the Great, who also had a booze problem; and in Pompey's case, given his generally successful career, I wasn't sure it was really a problem. A man can adore getting drunk and still not be an alcoholic.

The thought brought a need to both our consciousnesses, so we both lurched to our feet, grabbed a line, raised our tunics, and lightened the balloon some more. "Hope there are no fishermen down there," I said, joking.

"Ah, fuck 'em. That's what plebeians are for," Pompey said, laughing.

As we sat down, it occurred to me that though we both found that funny, Pompey meant it. But I kept the thought to myself.

As we settled back, Pompey handed me my glass, and said, "Now, where were we? Oh, yeah, Gaius and raping slaves. Well, god knows we've all done that, when we were teenagers; something about the way a slave boy or girl will scream and cry, because of course they're afraid to strike us or really stop us, you know, gets the blood pumping. But most of us find out very quickly that a hurt slave is a bad slave, and that it's far better to treat them with kindness and gentleness so that they'll want to be in your bed, they'll be jealous of whoever else is, and determined to please, and so forth.

"But for Gaius it's just . . . well, he loves power. He's also about as sex-mad as any man I've ever known—even his best pal and favorite catamite, Marcus Antonius, says that Gaius is 'a woman to every man and a man to every woman.' There are those of us who think that that shows, well, a lack of control at the least.

"And then, finally, there's the matter of . . . now this is talking out of school, you know, but the truth is, Marce, I've gotten to like you. You're a good man for an emergency like this, and I'd rather trust you than not, so if you're plotting to kill me, be quick and give me no warning."

"I'm not," I said, and shuddered, for it echoed what Hasmonea had said a little too closely for my liking.

"I didn't think you were, since you so easily could have," Pompey said. "Anyway, as I said, it's not utterly unknown, there are rumors, but as you probably know, Caesar was my father-in-law for a long time."

I remembered that detail; Caesar was a few years younger than Pompey, and his daughter would have been a whole generation younger, but it was not uncommon for political marriages to have big age gaps in those days. Hell, if you looked at some wives of senators and governors, it wasn't all that uncommon where I came from. "Yes, I remember—her name was—"

"Julia, of course. The family name becomes the praenomen when a woman marries. Well, not to make the story too long, apparently most of the dark rumors are true, and even his daughters knew about it when they were quite young; some of them had slave playmates who were badly hurt by Caesar on his little forays. Now don't misunderstand me—it's a master's right to do whatever he likes with his slaves—but still and all, a man who can't control himself and puts his household into that kind of uproar—well, I think Julia was very happy to be with me, because I certainly run a quieter and kinder house than that. Indeed it was one of the better political marriages I've ever seen, if I do say so myself. And at least this way there's an heir out there descended from both Caesar and me. That might help, someday, in patching all this back together."

We drifted on; I stopped drinking soon enough to be sure of sobering up. As it began to get cold again, I checked our position and rate of descent; if the wind held, we would make Macedonia with twenty miles to spare, so we decided it wouldn't be necessary for the two of us—just a bit alcohol-impaired if the truth be known—to make the dangerous climb up into the brazier and shovel out ashes. We pulled blankets over ourselves and sat idly chatting and eating some hardtack and fish paste; if I was short on sleep, at least I was well fed.

An hour later we had descended to an altitude of only about a mile, and I put on the distance goggles and set them for infrared. Sure enough, there was a swath of coast to the east; though the moon had set and it was too dark to see, especially through the winter fogbanks, the distance glasses showed it thoroughly.

"Piece of cake," I said.

Pompey seemed a bit baffled, and explaining it didn't help much, but really explaining it was just a way to pass the time while we waited out the last hour before landfall in Macedonia. Unless he had a balloon himself, it would take Caesar weeks to get this far; we were perfectly safe. I just hoped that the same was true for Chrysamen, and for Paula and Porter.

After half an hour I got impatient and decided to check again, so I put on the distance glasses and looked.

The coastline was gone; there was nothing but water as far as I could see.

I grabbed the thumbnail atlas, and the way I did must have tipped Pompey that something was wrong; he was instantly wide-awake and cold sober, and he said, "Are we off course?"

"It looks like—"

Then the image flashed up on the map, showing our course for the last hour and a half. We had come within three miles of the Macedonian coast.

And then we had made a neat little buttonhook, and headed back out to sea. You can't feel a change of direction in a balloon; since you move with the air, there's no wind to go by, and the accelerations are usually very gentle. Thus there had been nothing to alert us to the reversal of our course. Not that we could have done much if there had been; we had no means of spilling warm air from the balloon.

We were now only a thousand feet above the waves, and we were about fifteen miles out to sea, moving farther away from land every minute. "We forgot about the land breeze," I said, suddenly realizing. "At low altitudes, the wind blows strongly away from land during the first few hours of the night."

"*You* forgot," Pompey said cheerfully. "I never knew. Well, I'm glad we saved the oars, and I'm glad you still have your wonderful little navigation gadget. I predict we will have no trouble at all keeping warm tonight."

·16·

Fortunately for us the sea was reasonably calm, which doesn't happen often in those waters, and most especially not in January. The balloon settled gracefully, and the one sandbag still dangling turned out to be invaluable, for when it hit the water it took on seawater and sank, pulling us down instead of leaving us bouncing. We rose and fell ever so slightly on the sea, the balloon still holding its lines taut above us.

We waited five minutes, to let the balloon cool further, and then cut the sandbag free, sending it to the bottom. The boat stopped listing and righted itself; we began to saw through the lines on the bag of the balloon itself. We didn't want to run the risk of capsizing, so we cut them in pairs, diagonally, one of us on each side of the boat, until finally we severed the last pair of lines and the gasbag rose slowly and majestically above us, drifting off downwind at a few miles per hour.

We turned from watching it go to getting out the oars; the thumbnail atlas could be used to hold us on a course, so we plotted the shortest one to the coast—it was all stony beaches along there anyway, and it wouldn't much matter where we came in, we'd be walking for quite a while—and started pulling away. I was in pretty good shape, though tired, and Pompey seemed to be up to the job as well despite his overweight. Though the wind was against us, it was close to low tide now, and in another hour would be running in our favor; unfortunately, tides in the Med don't amount to much, but we'd take anything we could get.

Rowing is not a real efficient way to get anywhere; that's part of why it's such good exercise. After a long hour and a half, we took a break for some cold food, and to work a little congealed bacon grease into our hands. By now we were in fairly thick fog, and all the more grateful for the thumbnail atlas. We seemed to be drifting a little toward the coast at this point, probably on some local current, and I figured we might as well take advantage of it.

We had just finished the meal—and it was occurring to me that I had been up for almost thirty straight hours and that getting us navigated to the coast was about as much as I could do before I would have to sleep, whether I really trusted Pompey or not— when we heard a strange sound; a splashing that sounded like a big rock with water running against it, or maybe—

The prow of the ship reared out of the fog like a dark avenging god. There was no time to do anything before it was upon us; we weren't hit right on the prow, but slapped hard to the side, hard enough to capsize the boat and hurl us both into the water.

The black waters of the Adriatic closed over me and instantly I was chilled to the bone, colder than I had ever been before. I came up for air with the lookout's cry ringing in my ears, and something splashed next to me; instinctively I grabbed it and felt it drag me forward in the water. Stupid, half-frozen, and still exhausted by my lack of sleep, I took long seconds to realize they had thrown me a log with a rope tied to it, and were dragging me in.

Minutes later I was alongside, bumping the side of the ship, and they were shouting for me to hold on tight. A few quick heaves brought me out of the water and sprawling on the deck. I looked to my left and saw Pompey, gasping and blowing like a fish.

There were shouts and cries all over the sea, I realized, many of them from the ship we had been brought into. We were not merely in a passing freighter, but in some kind of a fleet.

They rolled us unceremoniously onto stretchers and carried us downstairs. I felt sailors' hands searching around on my body but couldn't seem to move my arms to stop them, not even when they began to pull my clothes off; then I heard some exclamations.

Suddenly there was a blinding glare; I blinked indignantly, as I had been almost asleep, and then saw two men bending over us. "Well, we know who this one is," the older man was saying, looking down at Pompey. He was a small, plump older man who could easily have played a corrupt city councilman, a rude uncle, or perhaps an unsuccessful car salesman in any Hollywood picture, wearing a lumpy-looking not-quite-straight toga under his cloak. "Though how he got here or what he's doing here is a complete mystery."

The other fellow was tall and thin, and when he looked more closely at me, he said, "Oh, I know who this one is, too."

My blurry eyes focused, and I said, "Caldwell?" He looked just slightly familiar, and I couldn't think why.

"Yep. Looks like somebody decided I needed rescuing, back at ATN's Central Command. And might be they're right."

"How—did—you—know—me?" I said. Plainly the older guy must be Crassus, and we had found what we were looking for; so there couldn't be anything so important that it couldn't wait until I got some sleep.

I was just drifting out when he said, "A few times they had me doubling for you, though god knows we don't look alike. I sure hope you're not mad about the little joke on the airliner, years ago—"

"Small universe," I muttered, and fell asleep.

When I awoke, twelve hours later, Pompey was already up and about. My clothes had been wrung out and mostly dried and were sitting at the foot of the bed. I figured I wasn't a prisoner, since my thumbnail atlas, spare clips for the .45, and distance glasses were on top of the pile, along with the .45 itself, still in its shoulder holster. I got up and went up on deck, to find it was another warm, sunny day. I borrowed some olive oil from the cook (it's not gun oil by any means, but it beats the hell out of saltwater), went and found the others, and sat stripping, cleaning, wiping, and reassembling my weapon while I got caught up on what was going on.

Once I heard it, it all fell into place. Walks-in-His-Shadow Caldwell (he was a Mandan, from a timeline where they had been much more successful in dealing with the white man and had a state of their own in the High Plains) had been over in Persia and India, getting his innovations introduced among the Bactrian Greeks that Alexander had scattered through that area two hundred years before, and creating a new trade network, one of many, for Crassus's banks and trading companies to control. "Give it a hundred years," Caldwell said, "and I think we'll have Roman roads from Lisbon to

Saigon, carrying trade in quantity both ways. And probably rail-roads as well, if I can ever get us off the jam point with making good quality iron, which is turning out tougher than I expected.

"But anyway, when I got back and heard that Caesar hadn't been kept in line with Crassus's cash, like we were hoping he could, then it was obvious the Civil War was going to break out after all, and right on schedule. That's an obvious catastrophe—I mean, look at what happened even in the unaltered timeline, the Romans lost two whole generations of young men and had huge numbers of foreigners to demob from the legions and settle into Roman society. This could be a lot worse—what you saw at the Battle of Falerii was an example. Neither side really understands in the gut just how much muskets, horse pistols, field artillery, and for that matter plain old stirrups will add to the slaughter."

"Oh, I'm getting an idea of it," Pompey said, a little impa-tiently. "Yes, I realize neither Caesar nor I had ever fought against an army equipped with firearms, and we had no idea how much damage could be done to our own forces. The butchery was dread-ful, and there isn't really time to retrain, either, so I imagine the next battle will be just as bad."

Crassus nodded; he was swaddled up in six blankets and looked like he should be playing some role written for Rodney Dangerfield as he sat there, sipping spiced wine from a cup. "For that reason, Cnaeus, I was delighted to pass my *imperium* to you. I'm not so stupid as to have any trouble telling who the real general is here. Do you see no way of minimizing the slaughter?"

Pompey spread his hands. "I don't, and I doubt that Caesar does. If only we could trust him—but his *genius* is so influenced by Mercury, you know, and by Venus. He *might* decide to offer honor-able terms and then abide by them. Now that he has wiped out the Senate, for every practical purpose, there is no longer a Roman Republic—there is only Rome and its territories. There's no reason why the Triumvirate could not be put back together, perhaps some kind of new Senate created, and our offspring intermarried enough to create a workable ruling house and line of succession, as long as we avoid that explosive word 'king.' I have a son who is Caesar's grandson, you know, and if you have a suitable grand-daughter, Marce—"

"This is all in anticipation," Crassus said firmly. "Even if he makes us a decent offer, it will be hard to know whether or not he will keep his word. He has generally been an honorable man—but there's his treatment of the Gauls to be considered, and I find that I feel that if a man keeps his word only when it's not too inconvenient, you might as well just say he doesn't keep his word, and have done with it. I think if he beats us, he will want to consolidate his power, and therefore will be generous—perhaps astonishingly generous—in peace, hoping to make allies of us. By the same token, if we win, and we are generous . . . well, Caesar was always a man who was either at your throat or at your feet. I am afraid we cannot treat him in the way he would treat us."

By the time we finished our conversation, we were coming into the harbor at Barium, which Pompey and I had passed over the night before. The night's fog was gone, and I could see that there were hundreds of ships following Crassus's lead vessel; they had made an unprecedented night crossing, taking advantage of the sea breeze at night in Greece and the land breeze in the morning off Italy, because Caldwell also had a thumbnail atlas.

Nobody would have expected them anytime so soon, and with luck they would be one full day's travel on their way to Rome before Caesar's agents alerted him.

Moreover, Caldwell had come up with a secret weapon—the rubber-coated horseshoe. Apparently in his timeline the horse had lasted a little longer in competition with the automobile, and it was discovered that horses' feet, like anyone else's, preferred "sneakers" for walking on hard pavement. The Romans didn't even shoe their horses, so what Caldwell's newest innovation meant was that Crassus and Pompey could bring a much larger force of cavalry onto the field. Further, he had duplicated Caesar's field artillery, though he didn't have quite so much of it, and the armorers even now were looking at Pompey's multiple-rocket launcher.

Of course, Caesar might have a trick or two of his own.

Pompey had stolen the horse pistols, hoping to have them duplicated for the next time he commanded cavalry, but oddly enough it didn't matter that they had gone to the bottom of the Adriatic. Crassus had brought something better than the pistol; he had Parthian cavalry.

The Parthians were a tough bunch of nomads who had been running Persia and most of Mesopotamia before Crassus turned up with muskets. (In my timeline, or for that matter in Caldwell's or Chrys's, Crassus and a Roman army had been wiped out by the

Parthian cavalry at Carrhae in 53 B.C. I thought it wouldn't be discreet to mention that.) The secret of their success was a short, powerful bow and ages and ages of practice at firing it from horseback.

Caldwell had given them stirrups, for a more stable platform, and the compound recurve bow—which meant that they had three or four times the rate of fire, accurately and at longer range, than Caesar's Gauls did. Plus, if we met somewhere in the middle of Italy, as was expected, Caesar's cavalry would have many more horses unfit for service, due to fast marches on winter roads, than Pompey, whose Parthian archers would have shod horses.

We had superiority in cavalry. He had superiority in field artillery—Caldwell had only been able to make a few pieces, and his crews had nothing like the experience of Caesar's legions. And naturally infantry would be what would settle it anyway, and that was about even. So at the moment it looked like a toss-up.

They were planning to stay one day at Barium, and Pompey was already trying to figure out how to get kneelers and musket holes on every *scutum,* plus have enough drill time to get everyone acquainted with Street Firing. I told him about the hollow square technique that was used in the eighteenth century of my timeline for a defense against cavalry, and he groaned. "Oh, Jupiter, Marce, not *another* thing for them to learn. These forces are good—no, they're magnificent—but so much to learn in one day, and then to march the next and quite possibly fight within days of then! And if you've got a defense against the kind of cavalry attack that threw my flanks back at Falerii, I *have* to make time to teach it to my men. I can't let them die from being underprepared." He sighed again, turned back to work, and then sent a legate after me to take down notes on everything I remembered about the hollow square, which wasn't nearly enough.

The reason that we had sailed into Barium, instead of other ports like Brundisium or Tarentum, was that it offered the maximum surprise; if we had sailed farther up the coast, the next road suitable for moving legions was at Hadria, hundreds of miles to the north, and we'd have been detected; if we had come in any farther south, we would have had to travel farther by road, giving Caesar more lead time. Barium, located right where the heel joins the Italian boot, was perfect, with a road connection from the Via Minucia to the Via Appia, and thence to Rome. It meant a long hard march for Caesar, no way of sneaking around to get at our backs, and therefore—we hoped!—victory.

Always assuming Caesar didn't think of something even more clever.

Even in winter, the southern parts of Italy are mild, and it was a bright, sunny day in Barium. I enjoyed a day of loafing, went to bed early, and found myself on a bicycle, riding with Caldwell and the generals, very early the next morning. At least this mission was getting my thighs in shape.

We took our time, keeping the army and the horses in peak condition and also giving us more time to drill. We camped that afternoon just twenty miles from Barium and spent several more hours working through everything—Street Firing, hollow squares, firing from behind the *scutum*. The next town of any size was Canusium, a bit over twenty miles away, and we rode there the next day and repeated the process. It was deliberately kept pleasant and simple, but discipline was kept tight.

"What I hope," Pompey explained to me, "is that Caesar will note, for example, that Canusium threw open its gates for me. With a bit of luck we can make it appear that the whole south is solidly for us, and our slow, steady progress will help put political pressure on him to beat us before too many territories ally themselves to our cause. Already we've got a dozen garrisons in the south going over to our side.

"And if he's forced to act quickly, then it is all to our advantage to keep our marches short. He's going to have to come to us for his battle, and I want him to have to come a long way in a hurry."

Before dawn, I was dozing uneasily in the room that had been found for Caldwell and me in Canusium when suddenly there was a crash of horns and the sound of many feet running. I jumped up and was dressed just an instant before a messenger boy arrived to tell us that we were needed in Pompey's quarters.

When we got there, the noise and confusion were overwhelming, but Pompey looked as if he always rose at this hour and had just gotten out of his morning bath. "Well," he said, "I have to admire the old bastard. Caesar not only got here, he found a way to get behind us, and one that few Romans could resist. He's at Cannae—the battlefield where Hannibal won his biggest victory."

I looked at the map spread out before us. Cannae was almost on the coast, less than ten miles from Canusium in the valley of the Ofanto. "How did he—"

"A forced night march down an old unpaved military road in the valley, after a forced day march of more than forty miles. His scouts stalked mine, and his whole army slipped in between patrols! Magnificent! I can only hope his men are as tired as they should be from all that."

Outside, centuries were forming up, and soon the creak and thud of thousands of wooden bicycles filled the air. The finest army Rome had ever seen was rolling out.

The old road down the river valley was not a good one, but it was adequate for the purpose, and the way it was rutted told us clearly that Caesar had indeed passed this way. The dawn found us forming up on the broad plain of Cannae, where Hannibal had thrashed a Roman army 150 years before, using the same double-bow tactic that Pompey had tried unsuccessfully against Caesar.

Caesar's forces, seen through distance glasses, were unprepossessing; he seemed to have left most of his cavalry and even a great deal of his field artillery behind. If he had hoped to take us from the rear, entirely by surprise, he must have been counting excessively on the power of that surprise, for "I'm not sure there would be enough forces there just to watch us all, even if we were all unarmed prisoners," Pompey said. "I suppose it could be the madness that is supposed to come with power. Or he has a huge reserve somewhere, but my Parthian scouts have not been able to find that, and two of them have circled his whole force looking for some hidden line of communication. It's as if he's daring us to attack. And why no attempt at a last-minute parlay? With the new weapons, even if this is as one-sided as it looks, there will be tens of thousands unnecessarily dead . . . well, gods hear me, on his head be whatever comes."

Strangely, too, Caesar sat there waiting for us. His position was good, and well entrenched—we couldn't take him by surprise with a sudden assault—but he did no probing, did not seem even to be interested in what our scouts were doing around his forces.

"Gods, gods, gods," Pompey muttered. "It's so utterly unnecessary if he's going to do it like this. He didn't bring forces adequate to win, but he brought more than enough to bring the death toll to the highest Rome has ever seen in battle. What can that madman be thinking? And as the weaker party, I would have expected him to take advantage of the first attack, but no—he sits and waits." Pompey pushed the map away and straightened. "We can find no trap. If he wants to kill himself in such a novel way, I suppose we shall have to let him."

The forces had been in position for some hours now; the mus-ket-armed legions mainly in the center, with wings of Parthian cav-alry and Greek and Judean archers on the near flanks, and the field artillery to the rear of the flanks, ready either to execute an "end run" and catch Caesar's army in the cross fire, or to move in and provide cover for the center.

Normally the battle would have been joined within an hour of dawn, but Caesar had not cared to attack, and Pompey had pre-ferred to use the time for thorough preparation, trying to hold the death toll, at least on his own side, down. As I looked out over the broad plain, from where I stood on the hastily erected observation tower with Walks-in-His-Shadow Caldwell, I finally said, "Pompey is right, you know, Walks. This whole thing makes no sense at all."

"I don't understand it either," the Time Scout answered. "And I don't trust anything I don't understand. Not when Caesar is in-volved. There's something up his sleeve for sure."

The signal was given, and the standard-bearers advanced; slowly, deliberately, the legions in the center of Pompey's line be-gan to advance. Just as slowly, those from Caesar's line—only about two-thirds as many—advanced toward us. I put on my distance glasses and looked; I could see that some of them were exhausted and stumbling already, and my heart ached a little for the fact that they had poured their hearts into getting here for the battle, and now they were not the least bit fit for it. It appeared Pompey was to preside over a massacre, whether he wanted to or not.

Now the Parthians were in motion, swinging wide, getting ready to shower Caesar's legions with a cross fire of their deadly arrows. The tower under us vibrated so that we could feel it through our feet, and the distant thunder of their hooves put us in awe. In the bright winter sunlight, it was like a scene out of some great epic, the slow-advancing lines in the center led by their eagle standards, and the great sweeps of horsemen on either side.

From the middle of Caesar's forces came a thin, black stream of something into the air—something almost invisible that seemed to scatter. "Walks," I said, "what do you think that is?"

"What do I think *what*—Holy shit."

The Parthians went first, horses slowing to a walk and then stopping, their bewildered riders perhaps kicking them once before falling off them. Then the legions began to fall over, and I realized that "I think he has—"

Suddenly my knees became very warm, soft, and weak, and I sank to the floor of the observation tower. It got really dark, darker than it ever does at night, and I had the most wonderful, happy dreams.

When I woke up, three hours later, I was quite hungry, and there was the pleasant odor of hot beef soup. I opened my eyes to find I was sitting upright, with my feet in leg irons, inside a large tent. Crassus and Pompey sat facing me, and Walks was to my left, and all of them were locked up, too. All of us were just coming awake, Pompey next after me, then Walks, and finally Crassus, who had a joyous, beaming smile on his face until he began to wake.

With all of us awake, none of us could think of anything to say, so we remained silent. I kind of wished I could fall back into my dreams.

The smell of soup got stronger, and the tent flap opened, and in came Gaius Julius Caesar himself, followed by slaves with the hot soup. "Now, gentlemen," he said, "you are supposed to be hungry, so first you will eat and then we will talk."

I was about to say something when a bowl of soup was put in one of my hands, and a spoon in the other; then I was eagerly gobbling it, as was everyone else there. When we had all finished, I said, "You figured out how to use the NIFs. And you must have figured out how to reload them as well, because they don't carry enough rounds to knock out the whole army. You took us all prisoner—"

"Almost all," Caesar said. "I'm afraid there were at least eight broken necks from people who fell unconscious at bad times—snipers dropping out of trees, men whose horses hadn't been knocked out first, that sort of thing. It's odd, but I find I'm made more sad by those deaths than by all the ones my legions ever suffered—perhaps because I know all their names, and saw all their bodies, and I am now writing letters back to their families."

Pompey sighed. "So now you have us utterly in your power. What do you intend to do with us?"

Caesar smiled. "Would you concede that I have the power of the *imperium*? I mean, in all truth, Cnaeus. Does it seem to you that my *genius* has given me that?"

"I suppose I must concede it—I would have to be stupid not to. And I must say that I don't feel very confident that I have any such power anymore."

"Nonsense," Caesar said. "It is only that mine is superior to yours. Is that clear to you?"

"Painfully so."

"And you, Marce," he said to Crassus. (Crassus's name was also Marcus, like mine. The Romans only had fourteen first names, so it was hardly surprising that there were a lot of us.) "Would you, too, bow to my *imperium* —if it were understood that you had an *imperium* of some worth yourself, inferior only to mine, coequal with Pompey's?"

Crassus seemed uncomfortable. "Gaius," he said, "the gods alone can bestow *imperium* or take it away from us; we claim that we have it, but it is up to them to make that true or not. I would not want to tempt divine authority, but, nonetheless, I would say that it is clear your *imperium* supersedes mine, and I bow to your better judgment for the rest."

"One might even argue," Caesar said, "that a better judgment in such matters is very nearly a matter of divinity. But this would be for later."

"You would dare that?" Pompey said. There was no horror in his voice, the way a modern Christian might feel about a man declaring himself to be god; there was only admiration at the audacity, I realized.

"I would," Caesar affirmed. "Though not just immediately. But how is a man to know what he can grasp unless he reaches, eh? Well, then, you see what I offer."

"You would like," Crassus said slowly, "to merge our armies, to re-create the Triumvirate, and then, I should guess, to reconstitute the Republic with your family as the most important, and with ours heavily married into it. You will make great men of us so that you can be the greatest man in history, without rivals."

"Just so."

"I accept," Pompey said at once. "I have battled your *genius* too long, Caesar, and mine is not up to yours."

"And I accept as well," said Crassus. "So far as I am concerned, you are the one true *imperator*."

Imperator, I thought to myself. One who has the power of the *imperium*. In my timeline, that title came down to English as *emperor*.

The Republic had died here, too—five to twenty years early, depending on what you counted as its end—and here, too, the Empire had been born. Brutus and Cassius, along with most of the Senate, were already dead. Julius Caesar was the true first emperor—

"And as for you of ATN," Caesar said. "Hear me. I shall move my timeline forward as fast as I can, and I acknowledge that your enemies, the Closers, are equally my enemies—*any* Roman's enemies in that they are Punics and Moloch-worshipers. I will gratefully accept any assistance you offer. I trust that this is satisfactory?"

Walks-in-His-Shadow glanced at me, and said, "You're the senior ATN officer in this timeline."

"Then it's fine with me," I said. "More than fine. I am delighted that matters have come out in this way."

Inside me there was a sigh of relief; mad as Caesar might be in some ways, and repellent at the personal level, we knew also that he was brilliant, and that in his drive to make Rome great, he would build us a powerful ally. Something somewhere had gone wrong, clearly; perhaps Hasmonea had managed to divert the timeline a little bit. But still, we had given them a huge technical boost, and Walks-in-His-Shadow would have decades more here to move them along. With the Triumvirate intact again, there was also little to fear in the way of a civil war; the battles of Falerii and of Second Cannae would be the whole history of the war.

The new Empire would still have the military genius of Pompey and of Caesar himself, and the business acumen of Crassus, working together in a world that was much larger and much less damaged. Their future, in short, was as bright as it could be, and if Caesar was not a paragon of virtue, he would rule efficiently, intelligently, and humanely, and that's what matters in a ruler.

Then Caesar knelt and unfastened the leg irons on all of us; more than that, he handed me my .45 in its shoulder holster. Clearly he believed that when you trust a man, you should trust him all the way.

I fastened on the holster, knowing now that whatever I had been told, it was wrong. I would never assassinate Caesar; my mission here was accomplished, and no such thing had been necessary. If this was a screwup, I was damned proud of it.

"For the rest," Caesar said, "I regret to say that we haven't found any trace of your wife yet, though I do still have people working on that. We'll provide you every assistance once we get back to Rome, where you can draw on whatever resources you need in your search."

I nodded. "Thank you, *imperator*." The term seemed to come very naturally to the tongue already.

"And also," Caesar said, "there are some people who would like to see you."

Five minutes later I was being hugged as hard as Porter and Paula could manage. I wanted Chrysamen to turn up, and I was worried, but there was a good chance that she had just been lying low in Rome until it became clear which way the wind was blowing. If so, she would probably come out to meet the army as we moved up to Rome. Somehow I felt very sure that I would see her again.

That evening, there was another special event; Porter had been practicing for many hours on the lyre and the Roman flute, having nothing better to do with her time, and she gave a private concert for the Triumvirate and a small circle of invited guests. I sat next to Paula, who said, "I worry a little about her and Caesar."

"Is she, uh, encouraging—"

"God, no, but she still glows with pleasure at the attention from him, and *that* encourages him even though she doesn't mean it to. And besides, she really is fascinated with the Roman instruments, and he really does have a great ear for music."

The music was just beautiful and everyone applauded madly; Porter seemed delighted, and I don't think I've ever heard her play better. During the party afterward, everyone crowded around her to praise her playing, and I could see the kind of glow that Paula was talking about. It did look really good on her.

The celebration of the New Triumvirate and of Caesar's investment as *imperator* was made all the more uproarious by the fact that so many thousands of men who had expected to die, or to see their friends die, were alive and unhurt. The release from the terror of the new weapons seemed to come out in a sort of joyful silliness that veered between an orgy and a really good kids' birthday party.

It was a long party, and it got pretty wild after a while; I noticed Porter had gotten drunk, and in my guardianly role, I had Paula drag her off to bed, not complaining much. Paula had had about two beers, I think (Roman beer was heady stuff but they served it in small cups), and they hadn't affected her at all. I figured Paula was probably glad to go—she must be missing Robbie, the Romans were extremely uptight about the kind of things Paula enjoyed, and besides, some of the men had been leering and making suggestions to her.

They were starting to bring in the slave girls, and being the married kind of stodgy guy I was, I wasn't interested. That reminded me that I still didn't know where Chrys was, let alone know for certain if she was okay, and at that point it became a little too depressing to stay at the party. I made my excuses and staggered back to the small tent I had, next to Caesar's, between his tent and the one Porter and Paula shared.

Where the hell was Chrys? It profits a man nothing if he saves the whole universe and loses his reason to live there . . .

Tired as I was, and even having consumed as much alcohol as I had, I was really having trouble sleeping. I thought I might get up and take a walk through the camp, but then on the other hand, getting dressed seemed like too much work. I let my mind drift to happier times, but all the happier times brought my thoughts back to Chrysamen.

There was a scream; I sat straight up in bed. It was Porter's voice. I had thrown my tunic on over my head before I knew what I was doing, yanked my boots onto my feet, and was racing around to Porter and Paula's tent. The tent suddenly glowed as someone unshuttered the night lantern inside it. Porter screamed again. I rushed harder, for I could see motion that looked like a struggle.

Then I heard Caesar's voice say, "Don't, don't, please"—and then I heard a flat barking shot: Paula's .38 had fired once.

There was a long, frozen silence, before the camp had time to react to the shot. In that dull silence, knowing what I would find, I walked to the lit tent, parted the flap, and silently stepped inside.

·17·

Porter lay on her bed, yanking her nightclothes back down—Caesar had apparently pulled them all the way up, just taking what he wanted, as he always did. Paula still held the .38 snubnose in her hand, her face a mask of flat, bitter hatred.

I reached and took the gun from her. "You don't want to see what kind of justice they have for women here," I said. I felt curiously numb and dead; it was as if I could see the future.

The future arrived in the form of a muscular centurion who seized the gun and knocked me flat with one blow of his fist. I had an untreated concussion from that and didn't wake up for two days, but that posed no problem to Roman justice; it wasn't at all necessary to have the defendant present at his own trial. If he made it to his punishment, that was plenty.

Paula and Porter weren't called on to testify either. There was this minor problem that I had been a prisoner of Caesar's, and he had never formally manumitted me; I was therefore his slave. And when a slave killed a master, no matter what the provocation, there was exactly one possible penalty. Walks-in-His-Shadow couldn't even get in to talk to Pompey or Crassus about it (they were as adamant as any other Romans), and the deliberation lasted a couple of minutes.

It was a good thing my head was still spinning, and I was still dizzy; I had only about enough concentration to wonder why it was in movies and books that if you got knocked hard on the head, you got up in three hours without even a headache. I had been knocked out once playing football and a few times in martial-arts practice, plus I'd had such concussions here and there as bodyguards and Crux Ops will tend to have.

And never once had I felt just fine afterward. Rather, it usually required days to get over it, and I often wasn't quite myself again for two weeks.

Roman justice was not the kind that waited two weeks. As soon as I was coherent enough, and a squint-eyed legion surgeon who smelled heavily of wine attested that he thought my pupils were the same size, they scheduled the execution for the next day at noon.

At least it was winter; that would make it quick. I found out later that Walks-in-His-Shadow had lost his holy-shit switch somewhere in India, in one of those stupid things that can happen to anyone, and that was why a dozen Crux Ops hadn't shown up to whisk us all away, but it was so foreign to my nature to think about calling for help that I never even wondered why he hadn't. Indeed, that was part of why his had gotten lost, the same reason mine had so often—he didn't think about it much either.

You could call it an exaggerated form of not wanting to stop and ask for directions.

The day came, and I finally got to see Porter and Paula, though I was still too dizzy to sit up, so they had to kind of hug me on the pallet where I was lying. Paula was in worse shape than Porter, but both of them were crying. "Boss, I'm so sorry—even now I could—"

I shook my head emphatically, and whispered back, "Are you crazy? Do you know what impalement involves? Just think about having a stake forced into you till it comes out your mouth, if you get tempted to confess. The only reason you shot the bastard, instead of me, was because you got there with a gun first, that's all. We'd have had to kill him. He'd never have left Porter alone, and he'd never have stopped threatening us, if we had just tried to scare him off with the pistols. So I'm just as guilty as you are, and I get a lighter sentence."

"Crucifixion is a lighter sentence?" Paula demanded, still whispering.

"Comparatively, comparatively. I'm a scholar by trade, you

know, we make these fine distinctions." I started to giggle; concussions do strange things to you.

After that little performance, Paula and Porter tried to persuade a couple of surgeons to take a look at me—the universal reaction seemed to be that if I was conscious, I was fit to be crucified. After all, it wasn't as if I were going to be doing any of the work.

At least they didn't put me on the upright cross; that would have been a little tough on a boy who was raised as a good Episcopalian. They used the X-shaped cross that is sometimes called the Cross of St. John or the Cross of St. Andrew; it occurred to me as they were dragging me off the litter that it was probably an honor, among the saints, to get a cross named after you, even if you had to share honors with some other saints, but that what you had to do to get your own cross was pretty tough.

It looked like I might be asking them about it myself in a bit. I wondered in that dizzy kind of way, unable to focus, just how the problem of so many alternate souls was handled in heaven. I mean, what do you do with four thousand Mother Teresas, sixty-seven hundred Francises of Assisi, and so forth? It made me giggle again, which got me slapped hard enough to take out a front tooth. My face was exploding with pain, but I was a little too disconnected to be able to concentrate even on how much my face hurt.

My limbs were limp and heavy after the slap—probably he'd started the bleeding in my brain again—so there was no putting up a fight as they held me down on the rough, X-shaped wood. Since one beam lapped over the other, it meant the whole thing pushed a big, heavy beam directly into the small of my back, with my left arm and right leg jammed a bit back behind me. I could tell that in normal circumstances my back would be getting all my attention, but I was still running my tongue over the broken place where my left front tooth had been, and wondering if what I felt on my upper lip was blood from an abrasion there, or if maybe the guy had ruptured a sinus.

The nails hurt, but they hurt most for the second while they go through. They don't put them in your palms, no matter what the religious paintings have told you, or through your wrists either. Your palms are too frail to carry your weight and would tear through; and a nail among the wrist bones would probably bend, and very likely cut an artery and allow you to expire much too quickly.

They put them into the forearm, well up toward the hand, with your thumb turned slightly back to open the space between the radius and ulna, and they put a couple of them in just to be on the safe side. They do the same number with the tibia and fibula on the lower leg.

It hurts like hell, but flesh is soft and the Roman carpenters were practiced at this—each nail went in in just two or three quick strokes, the first one going all the way through the flesh into the wood, the next usually burying the special broad head into the flesh and taking the nail the rest of the way into the crosspiece.

The first jolt of each nail going through was pretty bad, even through the fog of my brain injuries, and the second and third, as the nail moved through my flesh, wasn't so great either. It sort of gave me perspective on my other injuries and the pain where my back was pinned backward.

Then they set the cross up, and my arms and legs had to take the load. The nails tore the flesh a bit before settling into their new positions, and that hurt quite a lot; I apparently screamed and lost consciousness.

I woke up as they threw a bucket of vinegar over me; the strong smell in my cracked sinuses actually hurt a lot worse than the nails. I hung there, sputtering and gasping, while Pompey and Crassus made speeches that I didn't quite catch the gist of, except that they dwelt at great length on what a bad fellow I was, what a swell guy Caesar had been, and just how much I deserved this.

Already I was beginning to feel a little warmer; I was being crucified naked, and I had been kind of counting on hypothermia to give me some anesthesia.

There was quite a crowd, I realized, and I seemed to be the center of attention. I was vaguely bothered by the fact that I couldn't do anything to cover up. I looked around the crowd for a familiar face, but just the effort of doing that made them swirl and whirl like people had when my brother Jerry, my sister Carrie, and I had ridden the "Tempest" at the county fair, as kids. Jeez, with such a big event, I wished they could be here to give me a little support, they'd never missed my football games—

Holding my head steady gradually stabilized the view, and I began to think a bit more coherently. Very slowly I looked around, noting that my arms and legs already felt dead but very warm. Then I saw a face under a hood and felt my heart leap up for a second with happiness, because on a big day like this, with so many people here, I really wanted—

Something made me rear against the nails, sending agony through my arms as I convulsed savagely several times. I felt myself foaming and my tongue coming out of my mouth; I was vaguely aware of the cries of disgust from the soldiers standing guard around my cross, as I lost bowel and bladder control. I could smell the effect even through the vinegar still burning in my wounded sinuses.

It got really dark, and this time there were nightmares.

"Mark? Are you awake?"

I stretched and found that I could move my arms and legs; this seemed like a good sign. I sighed, let my eyes open, and looked up to see the most beautiful sight in the world—Chrysamen ja N'wook bending over my bed. "Am I at—"

"Hyper Athens, of course. You've been under for a week. The nanos are asking for overtime pay, hubby. When the Romans decide to mess a guy up, they're awfully thorough."

I drew a deep breath. "Porter and Paula—"

"Waiting to go back with us. Porter's getting treated like royalty—apparently some of her later recordings in this timeline are definitive pieces of music for them. Though they're being very careful not to let her hear them—I mean, imagine what could have happened if the young Beethoven had gotten to hear the Ninth Symphony. So she's just playing her early compositions, and some Roman music, and of course some of her piano show-off stuff. Oh, and she's doing a great job of putting off meeting with Thebenides, who's frantic to lobby her for something or other."

"Any girl who can say no to Julius Caesar shouldn't have any trouble fending off a two-bit politician," I said. "How long till they let me get up?"

"About one more day. Meanwhile, at least, they're letting me feed you. Will it be hospital soup, hospital noodles, or hospital hot cereal first?"

It's amazing that a civilization that advanced can't come up with hospital food that tastes any better than ours. I didn't mind, all the same. The company was good.

For some reason it's a big deal to Mark that everything gets recorded. I don't know why he writes these books about our adventures since they can't possibly be published, and Porter and his father and sister all hear the story directly from his own lips anyway. Probably all historians are crazy. But since he asked, and since I have most of today while he's resting, I'm writing this while my memory is fresh.

When Mark ducked into the alley in Falerii, I was going after him until all of a sudden a hand twined in my hair (the damned curls are a little too perfect for being grabbed by). The next thing I knew, I was being pinned by Pompey and two of his centurions—they had gone into the burning city looking for a hostage or for anything that might make them valuable to Crassus, with the army lost. It was the kind of bold maneuver Pompey did without worrying much about the risk, the sort of thing that meant he was never more dangerous than when almost defeated, and this time it paid off.

In the process of getting me tied up, one of them lost an eye, the other one got a broken arm, and I lost a couple of hanks of hair. If Pompey hadn't been there, insisting he wanted me alive and unhurt, I suspect they'd just have stomped me to death there in the alley.

The whole thing took just a few minutes; then they faded into the refugee train that poured out of the city, commandeered a cart, tossed me into it under a load of straw, and carried me off to where Pompey's army was regrouping.

No matter what the incentive, the Romans of that day just could not get it through their heads that a woman might be dangerous, particularly an unarmed woman. And the fact that I was out in public, and not an aristocrat, made them think I must be some kind of camp follower, which is the polite word in the history books for "soldiers' whore." So, sure enough, I got a guard to untie me by promising to show him something he'd never seen before, and then showed him the road to Hades with a quick maneuver that snapped his neck, just when he thought we were about to get to the good part.

I saw Mark ride by on the Via Flaminia, but I was staying off the road for safety's sake. I figured I'd meet up with him in Rome.

After a while I joined a refugee column, stole myself some rags to make a generic "beggar" disguise, and got into the city that way. I had lost all my gear except the holy-shit switch, so I had no way of locating Mark, but clearly Pompey's balloon was the biggest thing going on at the time, so I figured I needed to penetrate the compound on top of the Palatine Hill. There were so many more muskets than there were men to use them that it was no trouble to steal eight of them from the Campus Martius, and since I figured they were pretty useless singly, with their short range and miserable accuracy, I did a little tinkering, saving only the barrels and lashing those together with the fireholes all facing inward to a single percussion cap, to make sort of a giant shotgun.

Then I mounted it in a window facing a guard post, set a fuse to make it go off, and figured it could serve as my diversion. It worked like a charm—that was the "volley of musket fire" that Mark heard that night.

They were looking for at least ten guys, of course, so a single woman slipping through the shadows could get pretty much what she wanted. The trouble was, it turned out all the action was at the balloon, which was still under heavy guard, and I had no way of fighting my way aboard that. So I kept skulking, and a few times I ran into soldiers in dark alleys. When that happened, I hit hard and silently, generally before they knew they were attacked, and they died right there.

It might not have been sporting, but this was hardly a game. If I were Mark, I guess I'd give you the details of each knifing, but it's the sort of shoptalk that doesn't interest me. Sure, everyone is different on some level, but basically the experience of cutting a man's throat so suddenly that he can't cry out, or of smothering his cry for the critical second while you open his femoral artery and kidneys to knock him unconscious, is alike every time. And, to use a great word I learned from Porter, it's mega-icky.

Anyway, I heard the roar of Mark's .45 and got back to the platform just in time to see him departing, hanging on to the sandbag on Pompey's balloon. I really thought he would try the drop onto the roof of the Temple of the Great Mother—it was a lot better bet than trying to fight his way aboard—but what can I say, we're all individuals. He does things his way, I do them mine.

It seemed to me there was now a good chance that Mark would start working some deal with Pompey, or maybe with Crassus, and since we already had an "in" with Caesar, and were about to have one with the other army, it was probably best to stay loose and see what else I could manage. You never know when the ability to act independently can come in handy.

Naturally I followed Caesar's army south—and that was quite a ride, the worst part of the whole job really, especially since I had to pull over to avoid his rear scouts now and then, and then make up the distance after they'd gone on. I got to Cannae just in time for the aborted battle, and figured I would walk in and say "hi" to Mark the next day, once it was clear that the deal was firm.

Well, as they say, things get in the way. I didn't get a clear shot at helping Mark out of that jam until they actually had him nailed up, so I used my idle days to burgle Caesar's effects and retrieve a bunch of ATN hardware, including the NIFs, which I did some field-programming on so that I could have an effect that looked like "having a major seizure from neural damage and then dying on the cross" and would leave him in a pretty cold coma for a day or so. It worked fine; I gave Mark one shot of that, let them return his body to Porter and Paula, then slipped into their tent and at last hit the holy-shit switch. ATN grabbed all four of us, neat as you please, and that was the end of that mission.

I suppose Mark will complain that I didn't dwell on things enough, but really, though it was scary at times, it was a pretty standard ATN mission. And don't get me wrong—for all his tendency to overdramatize, my husband is the guy I'd most prefer to have on my side in a fight, anything from a barroom brawl to a duel with atom bombs, anywhere and anytime.

Well, Chrys absolutely refuses to expand that part at all, and since I wasn't there, I can't revise it into anything more interesting. You'll just have to take my word for it that she's terrific and much too modest.

A couple of days later, subjective, we stepped back onto the pavement in a parking lot in Weimar, Germany, in our own time-line, where a battle had just finished the day before. The place was crawling with media—when an internationally renowned child-prodigy pianist disappears in a UFO, and then pops back into existence twenty-four hours later just as was promised, I suppose you have to expect that.

You've all seen the speech she made, and nowadays every grade-school kid sees it, so it's probably time to admit, at least in this book, even if it can never see publication for centuries, that Porter had had weeks to think about what she wanted to say. But the words were her own, and they weren't lies. If you look at the story she told, it wasn't *that* far from the truth. There *are* forces out there greater than we are, and they *do* want us to live at peace with each other—and they *have* left it up to us to find a way to do so.

It helped too that she had never played better than she did that night in the National Theater. There were a lot of ghosts in Weimar that night, I think, and most of them would have been very proud to be present at the first of Porter's dozen Concerts for Peace.

I think that Chrys and I were actually the only people who made it to all of them, even the one in Ulster that was almost canceled because of the threats. It's a pretty strange world when you're sitting there, bursting with pride, because the kid you've tended, worried about, loved as your own for so many years, is working so hard to put you and your wife out of work.

Pretty strange, but you can get to like it.

▪ AFTERWORD ▪

Every so often I take it into my head to rush in where angels fear to tread, and usually the way I do that is to set one of these adventures in a period that's familiar. Hardly any historical period of Western history has received, over the last few centuries, the attention that the collapse of the Roman Republic in the last century before Christ has received. The cast of characters alone is wonderful; the heights of courage and depths of depravity are all there.

As may also be obvious, I am not in sympathy with what has been the most common reading of the period; it seems to me that this was not the time when Roman freedom was lost, but merely an inevitable change of jailers. The Senate had stymied every possible measure to empower the poor and to alleviate their sufferings. It was no surprise, then, that ambitious men made the just demands of the poor into the ladder on which they climbed to power. The tragedy was not that the "Old Romans" fell from power, but that they had ever held it in the first place—and that the ones who toppled them were truly little better, indeed, were men of the same kind.

For those who like a history full of noble Brutuses and wise Ciceros, I remind you only that at that time the Latin word *libertas*, the root of our word "liberty," had nothing to do with what we would think of as civil liberties—and everything to do with preserving the privileges of the few, though it brought the world crashing down around their ears.

But I am forgetting myself; at the end of these, I always remind you that these are works of fiction, and that after all they have nothing to do with our present-day lives, or indeed even with our own real pasts.

And also, I always thank that wonderful gang of picky people, the best players of the game of alternate history I know, the group of writers and historians that meets in the Alternate History category of the Science Fiction Round Table (SFRT1) on the GEnie on-line service. I could have done it without them, I guess, but what fun would that have been?

This time around, though, I guess I should remind you strongly that the ideas here are mine; credit the folks below for anything that's accurate, and for being inspiring people to bounce ideas off of, and throw the errors or the parts you don't like at my door. I'd like to thank: Tony Zbaraschuk, Bill "Sapper" Gross, Tom Holsinger, Robert Brown, Kathy Agel, Steve Stirling, Todd "The Mule" Huff, David Burkhead, Timothy "Squire" O'Brien, Al Nofi, Susan Shwartz, Daniel Dvorkin, William Harris, and Dana Carson.